MAP SCALE

| 0 | 200 | 400 | 600 | (statute miles) |

| 0 | 200 | 400 | 600 | 800 | (kilometers) |

EA

KINAWA

PINES

J A P A N

CHINA

HONG KONG

Hainan

MAP SCALE

| | | | (statute miles) |
| 0 | 200 | 400 | 600 |

| 0 | 200 | 400 | 600 | 800 |
| | | | | (kilometers) |

*South China
Sea*

PHILIPPINES

VIETNAM

Mindoro

•Camranh Bay

Palawan

Spratly Islands

*Sulu
Sea*

*Celebes
Sea*

MALAYSIA

SKY MASTERS

SKY MASTERS

Dale Brown

DONALD I. FINE, INC./G. P. PUTNAM'S SONS
New York

G. P. Putnam's Sons
Publishers Since 1838
200 Madison Avenue
New York, NY 10016

Endpaper maps and maps on pages 267 and 370 by Lisa Amoroso.

Library of Congress Cataloging-in-Publication Data

Brown, Dale, date
Sky masters / Dale Brown.
p.   cm.
ISBN 0-399-13705-X (Putnam)
I. Title.
PS3552.R68543S58   1991   90-56053 CIP
813'.54—dc20

Printed in the United States of America
1   2   3   4   5   6   7   8   9   10

This book is printed on acid-free paper.
∞

Sky Masters is dedicated to General Curtis E. LeMay, the "Iron Eagle" and the "Father of Strategic Air Power," a man who envisioned much of what *Sky Masters* is all about.

Sky Masters is also dedicated to the men and women who served as part of Operation DESERT SHIELD and DESERT STORM. I wish to especially dedicate this story to my brother, Second Lieutenant James D. Brown, 3–35 ARMOR, First Armored Division, United States Army, and his wife, Leah, and all of our military forces serving ashore, afloat, and aloft for all the sacrifices they made in their personal and professional lives.

ACKNOWLEDGMENTS

To my friend Lieutenant Colonel George Peck (who was instrumental in the research for *Day of the Cheetah* and who, like Loki's eternal fate in Norse mythology, seems destined to be forever bothered by my insistent questions and requests); TSgt Alan Dockery, Captain Harry G. Edwards, and the other helpful and professional persons in the Office of Public Affairs, Headquarters, Strategic Air Command (SAC), Offutt AFB, Nebraska, for their assistance in gathering information on SAC conventional and maritime operations and the Strategic Warfare Center, and for their help in reviewing the manuscript;

To all the men and women of the Strategic Air Command and Pacific Air Forces whom I met during GIANT WARRIOR '90, a multinational, multiservice combat strike and deployment exercise conducted by SAC's Fifteenth Air Force in August of 1990 at Andersen Air Force Base on Guam. I wish to especially thank Lieutenant General Robert D. Beckel, Fifteenth Air Force commander, for allowing me the privilege of observing his super exercise; Brigadier General David J. Pederson, Third Air Division commander, and Colonel Alan Cirino, Third Air Division deputy commander, and their staff for their hospitality and helpfulness in explaining the intricacies of Pacific theater combat operations; and to Colonel Arne Weinman, Ninety-second Bomb Wing commander and joint air forces commander of GIANT WARRIOR '90;

Special thanks to Captain Cynthia Colin, Fifteenth Air Force Public Affairs, and the other professionals at Fifteenth Air Force Public Affairs, March AFB, California; MSgt Ron Pack, Ninety-second Bomb Wing public affairs; MSgt Al Dostal, Ninety-sixth Bomb Wing Public Affairs; Second Lieutenant Darian "Slick" Benson, Fifty-seventh Air Division Public Af-

8 ACKNOWLEDGMENTS

fairs; the feared terrorist-group-turned-media-pool known throughout the Pacific as the Dream Team; and everyone who helped make my visit to Guam and GIANT WARRIOR '90 a pleasure and a success;

To Brigadier General Larry Dilda, DCS/Communications and Computer Operations, HQ SAC, for conducting a very special tour of SAC Headquarters, where I learned much about the "new" Strategic Air Command and its people and its new arsenal of weapons; and to Ron Silverstein, B-2 Project Senior Engineer and Chief Spokesman, and the others at Northrop Corporation, Air Force Plant 42, Palmdale, California, for an amazing tour of the B-2 bomber assembly facilities;

To Colonel Thomas A. Hornung, Chief of Public Affairs, Air Force Public Affairs–Western Region in Los Angeles, for his invaluable assistance throughout the making of *Sky Masters* and for arranging a spectacular tour of SAC headquarters; and to Major Ron Fuchs, former Deputy and Chief of Media Relations in Los Angeles, for his time in reviewing the manuscript and offering some valuable comments;

To CDR Bruce R. Linder, commanding officer of the guided missile frigate FFG-55 USS *Elrod,* who was extremely helpful in providing details pertaining to naval operations in the South China Sea, Palawan Passage, and the Philippines;

To Richard Herman, famous author of *Warbirds* and *Force of Eagles,* for his technical knowledge on aerial combat in the F-4E and other facets of fighter combat;

To Rockwell International for information on the B-1 bomber; also to Orbital Sciences Corporation for information on the Pegasus air-launched space booster;

To my executive assistant, Dennis Hall, for his hard work and support.

GLOSSARY

*All items are real-world terms except
where designated with "F."*

AAA—Anti Aircraft Artillery

Advanced Missile Warning System—next generation of satellites that detect enemy missile launches

Aegis—advanced naval air defense radar system

AGM-84E SLAM—modified Harpoon long-range cruise missile with TV and satellite navigation system guidance

AGM-130 Striker—rocket-boosted two-thousand-pound glide bomb; range ten to fifteen miles

AIM-7—Sparrow radar-guided medium-range air-to-air missile

AIM-9—Sidewinder infrared (heat) guided short-range air-to-air missile

AIM-54—Phoenix radar-guided long-range air-to-air missile

AIM-120—Scorpion radar-guided medium-range air-to-air missile

ALARM—(F) Air Launched Alert Response Missile; aircraft-launched space booster

AMRAAM—AIM-120 Advanced Medium Range Air-to-Air Missile; next generation of "launch-and-leave" guided missiles

AMWS—Advanced Missile Warning System, next-generation radar/ laser system to warn pilots of incoming antiaircraft missiles

ASEAN—Association of South East Asian Nations, cooperative council of nations, generally aligned to counter growing influence of China: Philippines, Singapore, Malaysia, Brunei, Thailand, Vietnam, Indonesia

ASIS—(F) Attack Systems Integration Station, the mission commander's area (right seat) of a B-2 stealth bomber, responsible for navigation and attack

ASROC—nuclear-tipped antisubmarine rocket torpedoes, launched by Navy ships

ASTAB—automated status board monitors, part of AEGIS radar system

AWACS—Airborne Warning and Control System, the E-3 radar plane that can detect, track, identify, and control air targets at long range

AWG-9—long-range, high-powered attack radar on Navy F-14 Tomcat fighters

BGAAWC—Battle Group Anti-Aircraft Warfare Center, the control center for all antiaircraft warfare in a Navy battle group

Bhangmeters—nuclear detonation detection system on satellites; detects and measures the flash of a nuclear detonation and estimates the strength of the warhead

BLU-96—fuel-air explosive bomb, a weapon that disperses a fuel oil into the air; many times more powerful than a conventional bomb of similar size because it does not carry its own chemical oxidizers

BMEWS—Ballistic Missile Early Warning System, a radar system used to detect launch of submarine-launched ballistic missiles

BNS—Bombing and Navigation System

BUFF—Big Ugly Fat Fellow, nickname for the B-52 bomber

C101—long-range ship- or land-launched antiship missile built by China; Silkworm

C601—long-range air-launched antiship missile built by China

C801—medium-range Chinese antiship missile

CAP—Combat Air Patrol, layers of fighters set up in an area to search for enemy attackers

CIC—Combat Information Center, the central communications and control area on board naval vessels

CINCSAC—Commander in Chief, Strategic Air Command, the four-star Air Force officer responsible for strategic bombers, land-based strategic ballistic missiles, and long-range communications and reconnaissance aircraft

CINCSPACECOM—Commander in Chief, Space Command; the four-star Air Force officer responsible for all North American space activity including space surveillance, satellites, and rocket launches

COBRA DANE—long-range radar system designed to provide technical information on Soviet and Chinese ballistic missiles, especially impact points of warheads

COMSUBFLT—Commander, Submarine Fleet, the four-star Navy officer responsible for all American submarines

DARPA—Defense Advanced Research Projects Agency, an office of the Department of Defense responsible for new weapon and aircraft research

DC-10—wide-body cargo and passenger carrier made by McDonnell-Douglas Aircraft Co.

DCI—Director of Central Intelligence, responsible for all intelligence-gathering activities in the U.S.

DEFCON—Defense Condition; ranges from 5 (peace, no advanced readiness) to 1 (all-out war); denotes worldwide readiness of U.S. military forces

Defense Satellite Program (DSP)—name of agency that operates all military reconnaissance and intelligence-gathering satellites

DF—direction-finder, a radio beacon that allows other DF-equipped units to locate it.

DR—dead reckoning; estimating position by best-known heading and speed information

Dreamland—unclassified nickname for military research area in south-central Nevada

DSCS—Defense Satellite Communications System, a network of voice and data satellites to connect military and civilian defense agencies all over the world

Durandal—French-made runway-cratering bomb that uses a rocket engine to burrow deep under a runway surface before detonating its high-explosive warhead

E-2 Hawkeye—naval carrier–based airborne radar plane used to monitor friendly aircraft and search for enemy aircraft and vessels

E-3—Sentry airborne radar plane (see AWACS)

E-4B NEACP—(pronounced "kneecap"); National Emergency Airborne Command Post, a heavily modified Boeing 747 airliner used as a communications plane for the President of the United States and other high-ranking government officials in wartime

EB-52—(F) modified B-52 bomber with air defense and defense suppression weapons and equipment

EC-18—next-generation electronic intelligence aircraft operated by the Strategic Air Command

EC-135C strategic communications aircraft—current-generation communications relay and electronic intelligence aircraft, operated by Strategic Air Command

ECM—electronic countermeasures

ELT—emergency locator transmitter, a radio that transmits a beacon signal on special search and rescue frequencies to facilitate rescue operations

EMP—electromagnetic pulse, the high burst of energy from a nuclear explosion that can disrupt communications and electronic circuitry for long distances and for long periods of time

ETA—estimated time of arrival

ETE—estimated time en route

F-4E Phantom—current two-seat fighter-bomber built by McDonnell-Douglas

F-16 ADF Fighting Falcon—lightweight fighter built by General Dynamics; ADF (air defense fighter) model specially modified to intercept unidentified bomber aircraft at long range

F-23 Wildcat—(fictional, but X-23 is actual) next-generation fighter built by Northrop and McDonnell-Douglas

Fei Lung-7—Chinese ship-launched medium-range antiship missile

Fei Lung-9—(F) Chinese ship-launched long-range antiship missile with nuclear warhead

FIE—fighter-intercept exercise, where fighters practice finding, identifying, intercepting, and attacking bombers

FOREST GREEN—Defense Department program developed to detect and measure nuclear explosions on Earth or in the atmosphere

Form 781—standard aircraft maintenance log

Fox Three—in an air intercept, a code meaning the aircraft's machine gun or cannon is being employed

GCI—Ground Controlled Intercept, ground radar station that controls fighters to intercept unidentified aircraft

Global Positioning System (GPS)—constellation of satellites in Earth orbit that provide very precise time, position, and groundspeed information to aircraft and vessels

GUARD—121.5 or 243.0 megahertz, the international emergency radio frequencies

HADES—(F) BLU-96 fuel-air explosive bomb

Harpoon—U.S.-made AGM-84 long-range antiship missile

HAVE NAP—AGM-142 Israeli-made long-range air-launched attack missile

HAVE QUICK—secure antieavesdrop air-to-air radio used by friendly fighters

HAWC—(F) High Technology Aerospace Weapons Center, a secret U.S. Air Force research facility in Dreamland that conducts flight-test experiments on new and modified aircraft and new weapon systems

HDTV—high-definition television

Hong Qian-61—short-range antiaircraft missile system deployed on medium-size Chinese warships

Hong Qian-91—medium-range antiaircraft missile system deployed on large Chinese naval vessels

Hornet—F/A-18 carrier-based fighter-bomber built by McDonnell-Douglas

HUD—heads-up display, a system that projects flight and weapons information in front of a pilot's field of view to allow him to read important flight information without looking back down inside the cockpit at his instrument panel during critical phases of flight, such as air combat

ICBM—intercontinental ballistic missile, very long-range nuclear-tipped attack missiles

IFF—Identification Friend or Foe, a radio system that broadcasts coded identification information to other aircraft or radar systems

IN—instructor navigator

IRSTS—infrared search and track system, an electronic weapon system for fighters that detects heat energy and can transmit azimuth (bearing to the target) data to the fighter's fire-control weapon system

ISAR—Inverse Synthetic Aperture Radar, a radar system that uses the motion of the object being tracked to sharpen and define the radar image; commonly used to identify ships by naval reconnaissance aircraft

J-2—part of the Joint Chiefs of Staff joint staff, J-2 is the JCS directorate of intelligence

JCS—Joint Chiefs of Staff, the commanders of the five main branches of the American military that serve as the interface between the National Command Authority (President and Secretary of Defense) and the military forces. The Chairman of the Joint Chiefs of Staff is the NCA's primary uniformed military adviser.

KA-6—aerial refueling tanker version of the A-6 Intruder carrier-based attack aircraft

KC-10—aerial refueling tanker version of the McDonnell-Douglas DC-10 airliner

KC-135—aerial refueling tanker version of the C-135 transport plane

KH—Keyhole series of photographic reconnaissance, surveillance, and intelligence-gathering satellites; produces very high-resolution photographs; the code name KEYHOLE refers to overhead photographic imaging systems, including aircraft and satellites

LACROSSE—new generation of high-resolution radar imaging satellites; transmits intelligence data to Earth by data link

LSD—large-screen display; main processed radar data display of the Aegis naval battle group air defense system; also Landing Ship, Dock, an amphibious assault ship that carries large floating dock pieces to offload supply ships during beach assaults

M61A1—standard 20-millimeter cannon of many American fighter aircraft

MAC—Military Airlift Command, the Air Force organization responsible for most American military transport duties

MAJCOM—Major Command, the main organizations directed by the Joint Chiefs of Staff and the National Command Authority; divided into specified (single-service) or unified (joint-service) commands

Megafortress—(F) unclassified nickname of the EB-52 strategic "battleship" escort aircraft

MEU—Marine Expeditionary Unit, the smallest and most responsive of the U.S. Marine Corps' air-ground task forces; usually made up of two thousand Marines and Navy personnel and usually deployed with Navy fleets

MFD—multi-function display, an instrument screen in a modern aircraft cockpit that displays different data and performs different functions, depending on the selected mode

Mk 82—standard five-hundred-pound general-purpose high-explosive bomb

MNP—Moro National Party, the pro-Islamic political organization active in the southern Philippines

MOA—Military Operating Area, a piece of airspace set aside for high-performance fighter activity; the military is responsible for aircraft separation

Murène NTL-90—French-made air-launched torpedo

MUTES—Multiple Target Emitter Site, a mobile electronic threat complex used in training missions by the Strategic Air Command; simulates many different types of enemy radar-guided air-defense weapons

MV-22A—Marine Corps amphibious assault version of the V-22 Osprey tilt-rotor aircraft

Nansha Dao—Chinese name for the Spratly Islands

National Security Advisor—coordinates activities of the National Security Council and reports directly to the President

National Security Council—principal advisory group to the President on defense matters; composed of the Vice President, Secretaries of State, Treasury, and Defense, the Chairman of the Joint Chiefs of Staff, and the Director of Central Intelligence

NAVSTAR—unclassified nickname of the Global Positioning System of navigation satellites

NCA—National Command Authority, composed of the President of the United States and the Secretary of Defense, who command all combat forces through the operational chain of command

New People's Army—the Communist guerrilla forces of the National Democratic Front, a major antigovernment force in the Philippines

New Philippine Army—the name of the reorganized Philippine defense forces

NIRTSat—(F) Need It Right This Second satellites, a series of lightweight communications, intelligence, and reconnaissance satellites launched by small, quick-response space boosters such as ALARM.

NMCC—National Military Command Center, the main command-control-communications facility for senior Pentagon commanders

NORAD—North American Aerospace Defense Command, the joint multi-service U.S. and Canadian organization responsible for surveillance and air-defense operations of North America; located within Cheyenne Mountain, Colorado

NSA—National Security Agency, the agency responsible for interpreting and disseminating intelligence information

NSC—National Security Council

OPLAN—Operations Plan, generally referring to the pre-planned series of military responses drawn for various parts of the world

OSO—Offensive Systems Officer, the navigator-bombardier on a B-1 strategic bomber

PACAF—Pacific Air Forces, the major Air Force command responsible for all air operations from the U.S. West Coast to Africa

PACER SKY—(F) a satellite-based reconnaissance system that transmits real-time infrared, visual, and radar satellite data to a ground or airborne terminal to provide aircrews or commanders with up-to-the-minute information on enemy troop positions

Palawan—the westernmost island province of the Philippines; very sparsely settled and remote

PCS—permanent change of station; generally any military assignment lasting more than 180 days

Phalanx CIWS—CIWS, or Close-In Weapon System; Phalanx is a radar-guided 30-millimeter Gatling gun used by many classes of naval vessels for last-ditch defense against antiship missiles

Powder River—a MOA (Military Operating Area) covering parts of Montana, Wyoming, and South Dakota, part of the Strategic Training Range Complex of the Strategic Air Command; used as a fighter-intercept area and bombing range

PRC—People's Republic of China

PRF—pulse repetition frequency, the rate at which a radar system transmits electronic signals; faster PRF rates usually denote very high-precision radar tracking, as for gun or missile control

PT—physical training

Puerto Princesa—the main city and capital of the island province of Palawan in the Philippines

RC-135X—a version of the Strategic Air Command's series of strategic reconnaissance aircraft, specifically designed to locate, classify, and target enemy surface-to-air missile sites

RCS—radar cross-section, the apparent size of a target on a radar, referring to the ability of a radar to detect a target at a given range; mostly a function of the size and structural composition of the target

RED FLAG—a large-scale tactical air war game exercise held several times a year at Nellis Air Force Base in southern Nevada, involving hundreds of aircraft from all over the world

RHAWS—Radar Heading and Warning System, a display in many modern fighter aircraft that warns of the presence, direction, and type of enemy radars

RIO—Radar Intercept Officer, the "backseater" in an F-14 Tomcat carrier-based fighter responsible for locating enemy targets

RK-55—standard twenty-kiloton tactical nuclear warhead designed in the Soviet Union and used extensively by many Soviet client countries

ROE—Rules of Engagement, the set of orders briefed to military personnel (usually fighter pilots) on when they may attack enemy forces; designed so that commanders may have strict control of a situation at all times, but also to provide maximum protection for crew members on the scene

RON—Remain Overnight; usually referring to an unplanned diversion

RPG—rocket-propelled grenade, usually an antitank weapon carried by infantry

RTB—Return To Base

SA-2—Soviet long-range surface-to-air missile system; older system, capable only against high-altitude targets

SA-11—Soviet medium-range, high-performance surface-to-air missile system

SAC—Strategic Air Command, primary long-range air offensive military organization in the United States, responsible for land-based strategic bombers, long-range land-based nuclear missiles, aerial refueling tankers, and long-range strategic reconnaissance and communications aircraft

SATCOM—Satellite Communications System, the U.S. Air Force's primary satellite communications system

SCARAB—(F), Self Contained Air Relocatable Alert Booster, a highly transportable small space booster system designed to quickly launch lightweight satellites into Earth orbit from any location

Sea Ray—small, inexpensive air-launched antiship missile, usually carried by helicopters based on naval vessels

SECDEF—Secretary of Defense, a member of the President's Cabinet who makes the day-to-day decisions in all defense matters

Shuihong-5—principal Chinese amphibious patrol and attack aircraft

SIOP—Single Integrated Operations Plan, the multi-service attack plan for all American military forces for the conduct of a strategic nuclear war

SITREP—Situation Report; usually refers to a request for a quick summary of a battle or the status of forces involved in a battle

SLAM—Standoff Land Attack Missile, the TV-guided version of the AGM-84 Harpoon missile

SM-2—Standard Missile, the primary surface-to-air missile on large Navy warships

SMFD—Super Multi Function Display, a large aircraft instrument computer display that presents flight information in a pictorial icon-based format instead of alphanumerics

SPACECOM—Space Command, the Air Force major command responsible for all military space activities

SPO—Senior Project Officer, the director of a particular weapon-development project

Spratly Islands—a chain of small islands, atolls, and coral reefs in the South China Sea between the Philippines and Vietnam, long contested by several nations because of its strategic position and because of its natural resources

SPY-1—primary three-dimensional radar system of the Aegis battle group air-defense system

SR-71—"Blackbird" strategic reconnaissance aircraft, the fastest air-breathing manned aircraft ever built; retired in 1989 from the Strategic Air Command

SRAM—Short Range Attack Missile, a nuclear-armed inertially guided attack missile carried by B-52, B-1, FB-111A, and B-2 bombers

SS-25—Primary Soviet-made nuclear-armed mobile intercontinental ballistic missile

START—Strategic Arms Reduction Treaty, a proposed treaty between the U.S. and the USSR to limit the number of long-range strategic nuclear weapons by both sides

STRATFOR—Strategic Forces group, a team of Strategic Air Command commanders deployed ahead of a combat group to establish a headquarters team and set up support operations for combat aircraft

STRC—Strategic Training Range Complex, an extensive series of low-level navigation corridors, radar bomb-scoring sites, live bombing ranges, and fighter-intercept exercise areas in the north-central United States, operated by the Strategic Air Command for bomber aircrew training

STS—Shuttle Transportation System, the official name of the Space Shuttle program

sugar pills—doughnuts, rolls, and other such snacks

TACIT RAINBOW—AGM-136 antiradar cruise missile designed by Northrop Ventura Corporation; seeks out and destroys enemy radar sites from as far as fifty miles; if the enemy radar shuts off, it can orbit the area until the radar is reactivated, at which time it will home in and destroy it.

Tank—nickname for the main Joint Chiefs of Staff conference room; also called the "Gold Room"

TCS—Telescopic Camera System, the long-range optical sight used on F-14 Tomcat fighters to identify enemy aircraft from beyond unaided visual range

TDRS—Tracking and Data Relay System, a series of satellites used to relay information from spacecraft to ground-control facilities without using other Earth stations; provides continuous and rapid data exchange for spacecraft

TDY—temporary duty, usually referring to military assignments lasting less than 180 days

Tomahawk—long-range, very accurate attack cruise missile; can be launched by submarines or naval vessels, and can carry a variety of warheads including nuclear, antiship, land attack, antirunway, or antipersonnel mines

Type EF5 guided missile destroyer—new class of primary Chinese heavy warships

UHF—ultra-high-frequency; primary line-of-sight radio frequency band

UNIDO—United Nationalist Democratic Organization, the principal political party in the Philippines organized to oppose the Marcos regime; placed in power in 1986

VFR—Visual Flight Rules; good-weather flight rules

VLS—Vertical Launch System, the current standard Navy missile-launch system, which uses a large box of missile cells instead of rotary missile storage magazines and which fires its missiles straight up instead of on rails

VPVO, VIPVO—*Voyska Protivovozdushnoy Oborony,* the Troops of Air Defense of the Soviet Union; here referring to the complex of fixed and mobile simulated enemy radar threat sites in the Strategic Training Range Complex operated by the Strategic Air Command to train bomber crews

WSO—Weapon Systems Officer, the navigator-bombardier on most tactical bomber aircraft such as the F-4, A-6, F-111, etc.

ZSU-23-4—mobile air-defense gun unit built in the Soviet Union and used all over the world, consisting of four rapid-firing radar-guided 23-millimeter cannons; deadly to all aircraft which come within range

Zuni—standard unguided attack rocket carried by tactical fighter attack aircraft

ACTUAL NEWS EXCERPTS

Date: 5/21/90

PENTAGON DECLARES PHILIPPINES
"IMMINENT DANGER" AREA

WASHINGTON (MAY 18) UPI—The Defense Department designated the Philippines Friday as an area of imminent danger for special pay purposes, which means US military and civilian employees will be getting slightly larger paychecks.

The Pentagon said it took the action because of the "current unstable conditions" in the Philippines, where three American servicemen have been killed in politically motivated attacks this month alone.

Imminent danger pay is an additional 15 percent of basic salary for American citizens who are department employees and $110 per month for all US military personnel.

• • •

Date: 5/22/90

"Well, first in my mind, the communist dream in the Philippines will always be there. The communist dream of taking over and dominating the country will always be there because you can't kill an ideology."

General Renato S. de Villa, Chief of Staff, Armed Forces of the Philippines, from *Asia-Pacific Defense Forum,* U.S. Pacific Command, Winter 1989–1990

• • •

Date: 11/2/90

". . . Turmoil in China . . . combined with speculation about U.S. forces departures from the Philippines, have merged to cause a new appreciation for U.S. regional security presence. . . . I believe there is a growing realization in the Pacific that U.S. presence cannot be taken for granted. If the U.S. presence is substantially reduced, many Pacific nations perceive the danger of other nations moving into the vacuum created by our departure, with a potential result of conflict and instability."

Admiral Huntington Hardisty, U.S. Navy, Commander in Chief, U.S. Pacific Command, from *Asia-Pacific Defense Forum,* U.S. Pacific Command, winter 1989–1990

• • •

Date: 11/6/90

MELEE MARS INAUGURATION OF AUTONOMY IN SOUTHERN PHILIPPINES

COTABATO (NOV 6) REUTER—Police punched and clubbed 17 Moslem students before dragging them off by their hair on Tuesday after they disrupted President Corazon Aquino's inauguration of an autonomous government in the southern Philippines, witnesses said.

The students, members of an organization supporting Moslem rebels demanding a separate state on Mindanao island, chanted slogans against the autonomous government about 20 meters from where Aquino was speaking.

Manila has set up the autonomous government, dominated by Moslems, as a way to end separatist violence on Mindanao, the second-largest island in the Philippines.

The government, headed by former Moslem rebel commander Zacaria Candao, can pass its own laws, collect taxes and license fees, and set up a regional police force in the four predominantly Moslem provinces on Mindanao island it controls.

Manila would retain control of defense and foreign policy. —from U.S. Naval Institute Military Database *Defense News.*

• • •

Date: 14 January 1991

AIR FORCE TO CREATE TWO NEW COMPOSITE AIR WINGS BY 1993

WASHINGTON—The U.S. Air Force will develop by 1993 two composite tactical air wings that combine different types of aircraft in the same unit. The new wings will serve as prototypes for the possible reorganization of the service's tactical force structure along more mission-oriented lines. . . . [The composite air wings] would include aircraft that could perform attack, defensive, standoff jamming, and precision-strike missions. —from *Aviation Week and Space Technology* magazine, p.26

PROLOGUE

"T minus two minutes and counting . . . mark."
Lieutenant Colonel Patrick McLanahan glanced up
at his mission data display just as the time-to-go clock clicked
over to 00:01:59. Dead on time. He clicked open the command
radio channel with the switch near his left foot. "Vapor Two-
One copies," he reported. "CROWBAR, Vapor Two-One requesting final range clearance."

"Stand by, Two-One."

Stand by, he thought to himself—not likely. McLanahan and
his partner, Major Henry Cobb, were flying in an FB-111B
"Super Aardvark" bomber, skimming two hundred feet above
the hot deserts of southern Nevada at the speed of sound—
every five seconds they waited put them a mile closer to the
target. The FB-111B was the "stretched" version of the vener-
able F-111 supersonic swing-wing bomber, an experimental
model that was the proposed interim supersonic bomber when
the B-1 Excalibur bomber program was canceled back in the
late 1970s. Only a few remained, and the High Technology
Aerospace Weapons Center (HAWC)—the Defense Department's secret test complex for weapons and aircraft, hidden in
the restricted desert ranges north of Las Vegas—had them.

Most F-111 aircraft were seeing their last few years of service, and more and more were popping up in Reserve units or sitting in museums or base airparks—but HAWC always made use of their airframes until they fell apart or crashed.

But the "Super Vark" was not the subject of today's sortie. Although an FB-111B could carry a twenty-five-thousand-pound payload, McLanahan and Cobb were carrying only one twenty-six-hundred-pound bomb that morning—but what a bomb it was.

Officially the bomb was called the BLU-96, but its nickname was HADES—and for its size it was the most powerful non-nuclear weapon in existence. HADES was filled with two hundred gallons of a thin, gasoline-like liquid that was dispersed over a target, then ignited by remote control. Because the weapon does not need to carry its own oxidizer but uses oxygen in the atmosphere to ignite the fuel, the resulting explosion had all the characteristics of a nuclear explosion—it created a mushroom cloud several hundred feet high, a fireball nearly a mile in diameter, and a shock wave that could knock down buildings and trees within two miles. Oddly enough, the BLU-96 had not been used since the Vietnam War, so HAWC was conducting experiments on the feasibility of using the awesome weapon again for some future conflict.

HADES had been designed as a weapon to quickly clear very large minefields, but against troops it would be utterly devastating. That fact, of course, would go into HAWC's report to the Department of Defense.

"Vapor, this is CROWBAR, you are cleared to enter R-4808N and R-4806W routes and altitudes, remain this frequency. Acknowledge."

McLanahan checked his watch. "Vapor acknowledges, cleared to enter Romeo 4808 north and Romeo 4806 west routes and altitudes at zero-six, 1514 Zulu, remain with CROWBAR. Out." He turned to Cobb, checking engine instruments and the fuel totalizer as his eyes swept across the center instrument panel. "We're cleared in, Henry." Cobb clicked the mike twice in response. Cobb never said much during missions—his job was to fly the plane, which he always did in stony silence.

Romeo 4808N—that was its official name, although its unclassified nickname was "Dreamland"—was a piece of airspace
in south-central Nevada designated by the Federal Aviation
Administration and the Department of Defense as a "restricted" area, which meant all aircraft—civilian, commercial,
other military flights, even diplomatic—were prohibited to fly
over it at any altitude without permission from HAWC. Even
FAA Air Traffic Control could not clear aircraft to enter that
airspace unless in extreme emergency, and even then the violating aircraft could expect to get intercepted by Air Force
fighters and the air-traffic controller responsible could expect
a long and serious scrutiny of his actions. R-4808N was surrounded by four other restricted areas that were meant to act
as a buffer zone to give pilots ample warning time to change
course if they were—accidentally or purposely—straying toward R-4808N.

If one entered R-4808N without permission, military aircrew members would at best lose their wings, and commercial
and civilian pilots would lose their licenses—and both would
be in for an intense multiday "debriefing" conducted by teams
of military and CIA interrogators, who would discard most
articles of the Bill of Rights to find out why someone was stupid
enough to stray into Dreamland. At worst, one would come
face-to-face with McLanahan and Cobb's FB-111B racing
across the desert floor at the speed of heat—or nose-to-nose
with a BLU-96 fuel-air explosive bomb or some other strange
and certainly far deadlier weapon.

Several thousand workers, military and civilian, were shuttled from Las Vegas, Nellis Air Force Base, Beatty, Mercury,
Pahrump, and Tonopah every day to the various research centers there. Most civilian workers reported to the Department
of Energy facilities near Yucca Flats, where nuclear weapon
research was conducted; most military members traveled forty
miles farther northeast to the uncharted aircraft and weapons
facilities northeast of Yucca Flats called Groom Lake. A series
of electronic and human observation posts was set up just south
of Groom Lake in Emigrant Valley, where they could observe
the BLU-96 HADES bomb's destructive power.

At the northern tip of Pintwater Ridge, the navigation computer commanded a full 60-degree turn toward the west. McLanahan clicked on the command channel: "CROWBAR, Vapor Two-One, IP inbound, unlocking now at T minus sixty seconds. Out." It took only seconds to configure the switches for weapon release, and finding the target on radar was a snap—it was a six-story concrete tower, resembling a fire-department training tower, surrounded by trucks, a few surplus tanks and armored personnel carriers, and surrounded by about a hundred mannequins dressed in various combat outfits, from lightweight fatigues to bulky chemical suits. Obviously, HAWC was not concerned about evaluating the effects of a HADES bomb on minefields—they had "softer" targets in mind for the BLU-96. Surrounding ground zero were several thirty-foot-high wooden blast fences erected every one thousand feet, which would be used to gauge the effect of the HADES bomb's shock wave.

McLanahan could shack this bomb with one eye—it was hardly a test of either his or Cobb's skill. This was going to be a "toss" release, where the bombing computer displayed a CCIP, or continuously computed impact point, steering cue on Cobb's heads-up display; the steering cue was a line that ran from the target at the bottom of the heads-up display to a release cue cross at the top, with the release pipper in the middle. Cobb would offset the bomber to one side of the release cue line; then, at the right moment, would turn and climb so as to "walk" the pipper up the release cue line and eventually place the release cue cross directly in the center of the aiming pipper. When the cross split the pipper, the bomb would release—the hard turn would add "whipcrack" momentum to the bomb, allowing it to fly farther than a conventional level release.

It was all a very computer-controlled and rather basic bombing procedure—hardly a difficult task for a fifteen-year Air Force veteran bombardier. But sortie rates were down and flying hours were being cut, and McLanahan and his fellow flight test crew dogs were sniveling every flight they could. Except for a few high-value projects—Dreamstar, ANTARES, the Megafortress Plus, the A-12 bomber, the X-35 and X-37 superfighters, and a few other aircraft that were too weird for words and probably would never see daylight for another decade—research activity at Dreamland had almost ground to a halt. Peace was breaking out all over the world—despite the efforts of nut-cases like Saddam Hussein, Moammar Quaddafi, and a few renegade Russian generals to disrupt things—and the military would be the first to pay for the "peace dividend" that most Americans had been waiting for at least the past five years.

"T minus thirty seconds, final release configuration check," McLanahan announced. He quickly ran through the final seven steps of the "Weapon Release—Conventional" checklist, then had Cobb read aloud his heads-up display's configuration readouts. Everything was normal. McLanahan checked the crosshair placement on target, made a slight adjustment, then told Cobb, "Final aiming . . . ready. My dark visor's down." McLanahan told Cobb his dark visor was down because Cobb seemed never to check around the cockpit, although McLanahan knew he did. "Tone on." McLanahan activated the bomb scoring tone so the ground trackers would know exactly when the release pulse from the bombing computers was generated.

"Copy," Cobb said. "Mine too. Autopilot off, TF's off. Coming up on break . . . ready . . . ready . . . now." He said it as calmly, as serenely as if he were describing a china teacup being filled with afternoon tea—but his actions were certainly not dainty. Cobb slammed the FB-111 in a tight 60-degree bank turn to the left and hauled back on the control stick. McLanahan felt a few roll flutters as Cobb made minute corrections to the break, but otherwise the break was clean and straight—the more constant the G-forces Cobb could keep on the BLU-96, the more accurate the toss delivery would be. Through the steady four Gs straining on every square inch of their bodies, Cobb grunted, "Coming up on release . . . ready . . . ready . . . now. Release button . . . ready . . . now." McLanahan saw the flash of the release pulse on his weapon control panel, but he jabbed the manual release "pickle" button just in case the bomb did not separate cleanly.

"This is CROWBAR, good toss, good toss," McLanahan heard on the command channel. "All stations, stand by . . ."

Cobb had just completed a 180-degree turn and had managed to click on the autopilot again when both crew members could see an impossibly bright flash of light illuminate the cockpit, drowning out every shadow before them. Both men instinctively tightened their grips on handholds or flight controls just as a tremendous *smack* thundered against the FB-111B's canopy. The bomber's tail was thrust violently to the left in a wide-sweeping skid, but Cobb was waiting for it and carefully brought the tail back in line without causing a roll couple.

"Henry—you okay?" McLanahan shouted. He could see a few stars in his eyes from the flash, but he felt no pain. He had to raise his dark visor to be able to see the instrument panels.

Cobb raised his own visor as well. "Yeah, Patrick, I'm fine." After returning his left hand to his throttle quadrant, he made one quick scan of his controls and instruments, then resumed his usual position—eyes continually scanning, head caged straight ahead, hands on stick and throttles.

"CROWBAR, this is Vapor Two-One, condition green," McLanahan reported to the ground controllers. "Request clearance for a flyby of ground zero."

"Stand by, Vapor." The wait was not as long this time. "Vapor Two-One, request approved, remain at six thousand MSL over the target."

Cobb executed another hard 90-degree left bank-turn and moved the FB-111B's wings forward to the 54-degree setting to help slow the bomber down from supersonic speed. They could see the results as soon as they completed their turn back to the target. There was a ragged splotch of black around what was left of the concrete target tower, resembling a smoldering campfire thousands of feet in diameter. The tanks and armored personnel carriers had been blackened and tossed several hundred feet away from ground zero, and the regular trucks were burned and melted down to unrecognizable hunks. Wooden blast targets up to two miles away had been singed or knocked down, and of course all the mannequins, regardless of what they had been outfitted with, were gone.

"My God . . ." McLanahan muttered. He had never seen an atomic ground zero before except in old photos of Hiroshima or Nagasaki, but guessed he was looking at a tiny bit of what such devastation would be like.

"Cool," was all Cobb said—and for him, that was akin to a long string of epithets and exclamations.

McLanahan turned his attention away from the ugly burn mark and the holocaust below: "CROWBAR, this is Two-One, flyover complete, request approach clearance."

"Vapor, this is CROWBAR, climb and maintain eight thousand, turn left heading three-zero-zero, clear to exit R-4806W and re-enter R-4808N to PALACE intersection for approach and landing. Thanks for your help."

"Eight thousand, three-zero-zero, PALACE intersection, Vapor copies all. Good day. Out."

McLanahan set up the navigation radios to help Cobb find the initial approach fix, but couldn't shake the powerful impression HADES had left on him. It was a devastating weapon and would represent a serious threat and escalation to any conflict. No, it wasn't a nuclear device, but the fact that one aircraft could drop one bomb and kill all forms of life within a one-to-two-mile radius was pretty sobering. Just one B-52 bomber loaded with thirty to forty such weapons could destroy a small city.

Thankfully, though, there wasn't a threat on the horizon that could possibly justify using HADES. Things were pretty quiet in the world. A lot of the countries that had regularly resorted to aggression before were now opting for peaceful, negotiated settlements. Flare-ups and regional disputes were still present, but no nation wanted war with another, because the possibility for massive destruction with fewer military forces was a demonstrated reality.

And for McLanahan that was just as well. Better to put weapons like HADES back in storage or destroy them than to use them.

What Patrick McLanahan did not know, however, was that half a world away, a conflict was brewing that could once again force him and his fellow flyers to use such awesome weapons.

ONE

Just as fifty-seven-year-old Fleet Admiral Yin Po L'un, commander of the Spratly Island flotilla, South China Sea Fleet, People's Liberation Army Navy of China, reached for his mug of tea from the young steward, his ship heeled sharply to port and the tray with his tea went flying across the bridge of his flotilla's flagship. Well, evening tea would be delayed *another* fifteen minutes. Sometimes, he thought, his lot in life was as if the gods had sent a fire-breathing dragon to destroy a single lamb—and the dragon finishes drowning in the sea along the way.

The skipper of Yin's flagship, Captain Lubu Vin Li, chewed the young steward up one side and down the other for his clumsiness. Yin looked at the poor messboy, a thin, beady-eyed kid obviously with some Tibetan stock in him. "Captain, just let him bring the damned tea, please," Yin said. Lubu bowed in acknowledgment and dismissed the steward with a slap on the chest and a stern growl.

"I apologize for that accident, sir," Lubu said as he returned to stand beside Yin's seat on the bridge of the *Hong Lung*, Admiral Yin's flagship. "As you know, we have been in typhoon-warning-condition three for several days; I expect all the crew to be able to stand on their own two feet by now."

"Your time would be better spent speaking with Engineering and determining the reason for that last roll, Captain," Yin said without looking at his young destroyer skipper. "The *Hong Lung* has the world's best stabilizer system, and we are not in a full gale yet—the stabilizers should have been able to dampen the ship's motion. See to it." Lubu's face went blank, then pained as he realized his mistake, then resolute as he bowed and turned to the ship's intercom to order the chief engineer to the bridge. The most sophisticated vessel in the People's Liberation Navy should not be wallowing around in only force-three winds, Yin thought—it only made the rest of his unit so unsightly.

Admiral Yin turned to glance at the large, thick plastic panel on which the location and condition of the other vessels in his flotilla were plotted with a grease pencil. Radar and sonar data from his ships were constantly fed to the crewman in charge of the bridge plot, who kept it updated by alternately wiping and redrawing the symbols as fast as he could. His ships were roughly arranged in a wide protective diamond around the flagship. The formation was now headed southwest, pointing into the winds which were tossing around even his big flagship.

Admiral Yin Po L'un's tiny Spratly Island flotilla currently consisted of fourteen small combatants, averaging around fifteen years of age, with young, inexperienced crews on them. Four to six of those ships were detached into a second task force, which cruised within the Chinese zone when the other ships were near the neutral zone.

On the outer perimeter of the flotilla, Admiral Yin Po L'un deployed three Huangfen-class fast-attack missile boats, capable against heavy surface targets, and four Hegu-class fast-attack missile boats with antisubmarine and antiaircraft weapons. He had an old Lienyun-class minesweeper on the point, a precautionary tactic born of the conflict with the Vietnamese Navy only six years earlier. He also had two big Hainan-class fast patrol boats with antiair, antiship, and antisubmarine weapons operating as "roamers," moving between the inner and outer perimeters. All were direct copies of old World War II Soviet designs, and these boats had no business being out in the open ocean, even as forgiving and generally tame as the South China Sea was. The ships in Yin's flotilla rotated out every few weeks with other ships in the six-hundred-ship South China Sea Fleet, based at Zhanjiang Naval Base on the Leizhou Peninsula near the Gulf of Tonkin.

Yin's flagship, the *Hong Lung,* or Red Dragon, was a beauty, a true oceangoing craft for the world's largest navy. It was a Type EF5 guided-missile destroyer that had a Combination Diesel or Gas Turbine propulsion system that propelled the 132-meter, five-thousand-ton vessel to a top speed of over thirty-five nautical miles per hour. The *Hong Lung* had a heli-copter hangar and launch platform, and it carried a modern, French-built Dauphin II patrol, rescue, antimine, and antisub-marine warfare helicopter. Yin's destroyer also carried six su-personic Fei Lung-7 antiship missiles, the superior Chinese version of the French Exocet antiship missile; two Fei Lung-9 long-range supersonic antiship missiles, experimental copies of the French-built ANS antiship missile; two Hong Qian-91 sin-gle antiair missile launchers, fore and aft, with thirty-missile manually loaded magazines each; a Creusoit-Loire dual-pur-pose 100-millimeter gun; and four single-barreled and two double-barreled 37-millimeter antiaircraft guns. It also had a single Phalanx CIWS, or Close-In Weapon System gun. Devel-oped in the United States of America, Phalanx was a radar-guided Vulcan multibarrel 20-millimeter gun that could destroy incoming sea-skimming antiship missiles; from its mount on the forecastle perch behind and below the con, it could cover both sides and the stern out to a range of two kilometers. The *Hong Lung* also carried sonar (but no torpedoes or depth charges) and sophisticated targeting radars for her entire arsenal.

The *Hong Lung* was specifically designed to patrol the off-shore islands belonging to China, such as the Spratly and the Paracel Islands, and to engage the navies of the various coun-tries that claimed these islands—so the *Hong Lung* carried no antisubmarine-warfare weaponry like the older Type EF4 Luda-class destroyers of the North Fleet. The *Hong Lung* could defeat any surface combatant in the South China Sea and could protect itself against almost any air threat. The *Hong*

Lung's escort ships—the minesweepers and ASW vessels—could take on any threat that the destroyer wasn't specifically equipped to deal with.

"Position, navigator," Admiral Yin called out.

The navigator behind and to the Admiral's right called out in reply, "Sir!", bent to work at his plastic-covered chart table as a series of coordinates were read to him from the LORAN navigation computers, then replied, "Sir, position is ten nautical miles northwest of West Reef, twenty-three miles north of Spratly Island air base."

"Depth under the keel?"

"Showing twenty meters under the keel, sir," Captain Lubu Vin Li replied. "No danger of running aground if we stay on this course, sir."

Yin grunted his acknowledgment. That was exactly what he was worried about. While his escorts could traverse the shallow waters of the Spratly Island chain easily, the *Hong Lung* was an oceangoing vessel with a four-meter draft. At low tide, the big destroyer could find itself run aground at any time while within the Spratly Islands.

Although the Spratlys were in neutral territory, China controlled the valuable islands informally by sheer presence of force if not by agreement or treaty.

Yin's normal patrol route took the flotilla through the southern edge of the "neutral zone" area of the island chain, scanning for Philippine vessels and generally staying on watch. Although the Philippine Navy patrolled the Spratlys and had a lot of firepower there, Admiral Yin's smaller, faster escort ships could mount a credible force against them. And since the Philippine ships had no medium or long-range antiship missiles or antiair missiles in the area, the *Hong Lung* easily outgunned every warship within two thousand miles.

They were currently on an eastward heading, cruising well north of the ninth parallel—and as far as Yin was concerned, the "neutral zone" meant that he might *consider* issuing a warning to trespassers before opening fire on them. The shoal water was also south of their position, near Pearson Reef, and he wanted to stay clear of those dangerous waters.

"CIC to bridge," the interphone crackled. "*Wenshan* reports surface contact, bearing three-four-zero, range eighteen miles. Stationary target."

Captain Lubu keyed his microphone and grunted a curt, "Understood," then checked the radar plot. The *Wenshan* was one of the Hainan-class patrol boats roaming north and east of the *Hong Lung;* it had a much better surface-search radar than the small Huangfen-class boat, the *Xingyi,* in the vicinity; although the *Xingyi* was equipped with Fei Lung-7 surface attack missiles, often other ships had to seek out targets for it.

Lubu turned to Admiral Yin. "Sir, the surface contact is near Phu Qui Island, in the neutral zone about twenty miles north of Pearson Reef. No recent reports of any vessels or structures in the area. We have *Wenshan* and *Xingyi* in position to investigate the contact."

Yin nodded that he understood. Phu Qui Island, he knew, was a former Chinese oil-drilling site in the Spratly Islands; the well had been capped and abandoned years ago. Although Phu Qui Island disappeared underwater at high tide, it was a very large rock and coral formation and could easily be expanded and fortified—it would be an even larger island than Spratly Island itself. If Yin was tasked to pick an island to occupy and fortify, he would pick Phu Qui.

So might someone else. . . .

"Send *Wenshan* and *Xingyi* to investigate the contact," Yin ordered. "Rotate *Manning* north to take *Wenshan*'s position." *Manning* was the other Hainan-class patrol boat acting as "rover" in Yin's patrol group.

Captain Lubu acknowledged the order and relayed the instructions to his officer of the deck for transmission to the *Wenshan.*

Yin, who had been in the People's Liberation Army Navy practically all of his life, was proud of the instincts he'd honed during his loyal career. He trusted them. And now, somewhere deep down in his gut, those instincts told him this was going to be trouble.

Granted, Phu Qui Island, and even the Spratlys themselves, seemed the most unlikely place to expect trouble. The Spratlys—called *Nansha Dao,* the Lonely Islands, in Chinese—were a collection of reefs, atolls, and semisubmerged islands in the middle of the South China Sea, halfway between Vietnam and the Philippines and several hundred kilometers south of China. The fifty-five major surface formations of the Spratlys were dotted with shipwrecks, attesting to the high degree of danger involved when navigating in the area. Normally, such a deathtrap as the Spratlys would be given a wide berth.

Centuries ago Chinese explorers had discovered that the Nansha Dao was a treasure trove of minerals—gold, iron, copper, plus traces or indications of dozens of other metals—as well as gems and other rarities.

Since the islands were right on the sea lanes between the South China Sea and the Indian Ocean, the "round-eyes" eventually found them, and the English named them the Spratlys after the commander of a British warship who "discovered" them in the eighteenth century. It was the British who discovered oil in the Spratlys and began tapping it. Unfortunately, the British had not yet developed the technology to successfully and economically drill for oil in the weather-beaten islands, so the islands were abandoned for safer and more lucrative drilling sites in Indonesia and Malaysia.

As time progressed, several nations—Indonesia, Malaysia, and the Philippines—all tried to develop the islands as a major stopover port for sea traffic. But it was following World War II that the Chinese considered the Spratlys as well as everything else in the South China Sea as their territory.

As oil-drilling platforms, fishing grounds, and mining operations began to proliferate, the Chinese, aided by the North Vietnamese, who acted as a surrogate army for their Red friends, began vigorously patrolling the area. During the Vietnam War radar sites and radio listening posts on Spratly Island allowed the Vietcong and China to detect and monitor every vessel and aircraft heading from the Philippines to Saigon, including American B-52 bombers on strike missions into North Vietnam.

But the most powerful navy in the postwar world, the United States Navy, exerted the greatest tangible influence over the Spratly Islands. Through its sponsorship, the government of the Philippines began patrolling the islands, eradicating the Vietnamese espionage units and using the islands as a base of operations for controlling access to the western half of the South China Sea. The Chinese had been effectively chased away from the Spratlys, ending five hundred years of dominance there.

That became a very sore point for the Chinese.

After the Vietnam War, the American presence weakened substantially, which allowed first the Vietnamese Navy, and then the Chinese Navy, to return to the Spratly Islands. But the Philippines still maintained their substantial American-funded military presence there, although they had ceded most of the southern islands to China and Vietnam.

The lines had been drawn.

The Philippines claimed the thirty atolls north of the nine degrees, thirty minutes north latitude, and the territory in between was a sort of neutral zone. Things were relatively quiet for about ten years following the Vietnam War. But in the late 1980s conflict erupted again. During the war, Vietnam had accepted substantial assistance from the Soviet Union in exchange for Russian use of the massive Cam Rahn naval base and airbase, which caused a break in relations between China and Vietnam. Vietnam, now trained and heavily armed by the Soviet Union, was excluding Chinese vessels from the oil and mineral mining operations in the Spratlys. Several low-scale battles broke out. It was discovered that the Soviet Union was not interested in starting a war with China to help Vietnam hold the Spratlys, so China moved in and regained the control they had lost forty years earlier. Faced with utter destruction, the Vietnamese Navy withdrew, content to send an occasional reconnaissance flight over the region.

That was when Admiral Yin Po L'un had been assigned his Spratly Island flotilla. To his way of thinking, these were not the Spratlys, or the Quan-Dao Mueng Bang as the Vietnamese called them—these were the Nansha Dao, *property of the People's Republic of China.* China had built a hard-surfaced runway on Spratly Island and had reinforced some stronger reefs and atolls around it enough to create naval support facilities. Their claim was stronger than any other nation. Several other nations had protested the militarization of Spratly Island, but no one had done anything more than talk. To Admiral Yin, it was only a matter of time before all of the Nansha Dao returned to Chinese control.

But the Filipino Navy, such as it was, still held very tight control over their unofficially designated territory. Yin's job was to patrol the region, map out all sea traffic, and report on any new construction or attempts to move oil-drilling platforms, fish-processing vessels, or mining operations in the neutral zone or in the Philippine sector. He was also to report on any movements of the Philippine Navy's major vessels in the area and to constantly position his forces to confront and defeat the Filipino pretenders should hostilities erupt.

Not that the Filipino Navy was a substantial threat to the Chinese Navy—far from it. The strongest of the Filipino ships patrolling the Spratly Islands were forty-year-old frigates, corvettes, radar picket ships, and subchasers, held together by coats of paint and prayers.

Still, a threat to Yin's territory—no matter whom it was from—was a threat, in his mind, to all of China.

Thirty minutes later, Yin's task force had closed to within nine miles of the contact while *Wenshan* and *Xingyi* had closed to within one mile; Yin positioned his ships so that he could maintain direct, scrambled communications with his two patrol boats but stay out of sight of the contact.

"Dragon, this is Seven," the skipper aboard *Wenshan,* Captain Han, radioed back to Admiral Yin. "I have visual contact. The target is an oil derrick. It appears to be mounted or anchored atop Phu Qui Island. It is surrounded by several supply barges with pipes on board, and two tugboats are nearby. There may be armed crewmen on deck. They are flying no national flags, but there does appear to be a company flag flying. We are moving closer to investigate. Request permission to raise the derrick on radio."

So his instincts had been right. . . . "An oil derrick in the neutral zone? How dare they place an oil derrick on Chinese property." Yin turned to Lubu. "I want the transmissions relayed to us. Permission granted to hail the derrick. Tell Captain Han to warn the crew that they will be attacked if they do not remove that derrick from the neutral zone *immediately.*"

A few moments later, Yin heard Han's warning: "Attention, attention the oil derrick on Phu Qui Island. This is the People's Republic of China frigate *Wenshan* on international hailing channel nine. Respond immediately. Over." Captain Han on *Wenshan* was speaking in excellent English, the universal sailors' language even in this part of the world, and Yin had to struggle to keep up with the conversation. He made a mental note to congratulate Han on his resourcefulness—the *Wenshan* was not a frigate, but if the crew of the oil derrick believed that it was, they might be less inclined to resist and more inclined to follow orders.

"Frigate *Wenshan,* this is the National Oil Company Barge Nineteen on channel nine. We read you loud and clear. Over."

Admiral Yin seethed. The National Oil Company. That was a Philippine company run by a relative of the new Philippine president, Arturo Mikaso, and headquartered in Manila. Worse, it was financed by and operated mostly by rich Texas oil drillers. American capitalists who obviously thought they could, in their typically imperialistic way, just set up an oil derrick anywhere they pleased.

The audacity.

To even attempt to build a derrick in a neutral zone . . .

And Yin knew it wasn't really neutral at all. It was Chinese territory. And the Americans and the Filipinos were trying to rape it.

"National Oil Barge Nineteen," Han continued, "you are violating international agreements that prohibit any private or commercial mineral exploration or facilities in this area. You are ordered to remove all equipment immediately and vacate the area. You will receive no further warnings. Comply immediately. Over."

"Vessel *Wenshan,* we are involved in search and salvage operations at this time," a new voice on the radio, young and at ease, replied. "Salvage operations are permitted in international waters. We are not aware of any international agreements involving these waters. You may contact the Philippine or American governments for clarification."

"National Oil Barge Nineteen, commercial operations in these waters are a direct threat to the national security and business interests of the People's Republic of China," Captain Han replied. He knew that Admiral Yin would not approve of his debating like this over the radio—he was a soldier, Yin would tell him, not a scum-sucking politician—but he wasn't going to move a meter closer to the Philippine oil derrick unless everyone on board understood why. "You are ordered to discontinue all operations immediately or I will take action."

There was no further reply from the barge crew.

"HF radio traffic from the barge, sir," Lubu said, relaying a report from his Radio section. "They may be contacting headquarters."

Contacting headquarters? There was no reason for the people on the drilling platform to do anything other than *dismantle*. And to do it immediately. Yin shook his head in disbelief. And anger. China had been forced to cede an island chain that was rightly theirs, forced to set up a neutral zone and allow free navigation in the area, only to have it thrown back in their faces. The arrogance!

"This is unacceptable!" Yin spat. "Any idiot knows this is Chinese territory, whether this is called neutral territory or not. How dare they . . . !"

"We can relay a message to Headquarters and report the violation, sir . . ."

Yin bristled. "This is not a mere violation, Lubu. This is an act of aggression! They know full well that the neutral zone is off-limits to all commercial activity, and that *includes* salvage operations—if indeed that is what they are *really* doing. This task force will not sit idly by while these bastards ignore international law and challenge my authority."

Lubu had not seen his Admiral this angry in a very long time. "Sir, if we are seriously considering an armed response, perhaps Headquarters . . ."

Admiral Yin cut him off. "These people aren't worth the aggravation of an explanation. Have you forgotten that I'm in charge of this area? It is my responsibility to protect our territory." Yin shook his head angrily. "The brazenness of this is what's so astounding to me. Don't they remember history? Hasn't there been enough of their blood shed over these islands? Have they gone senile? Well, let's remind them of the

full power of this force." Yin turned to Lubu. "Captain, relay
to Captain Han on *Wenshan:* 'You are ordered to move within
one thousand meters of the platform so as to provide sufficient
lighting and covering fire from your deck guns, then dispatch
a boarding crew to take the captain, officers, and other personnel on board the derrick into custody. After the crew is
removed from the barge, *you will destroy the entire facility
with heavy gunfire.'* To *Xingyi:* have them move closer and be
ready to assist. To the rest of this task group: 'go to general
quarters.' Relay the messages and execute."

"Number-one launch is manned and ready, sir," the officer
of the deck reported. "The chief reports davits for launch
number three are fouled; he recommends switching to launch
four."

"So ordered. I want that launch freed up as soon as possible.
Have other launches checked and report status to me immediately." Han wasn't going to say why—he was afraid they might
need the damned launches for *themselves.* A few minutes
later, with the *Wenshan* barely maintaining a close and comfortable position away from Phu Qui Island, the motor launches were lowered overboard. Each wooden launch, forty feet
long and eight feet wide, carried a crew of three and eight
sailors armed with AK-47 look-alike Type 56 rifles and sidearms.

The launches were only a few dozen meters away from the
Wenshan when the world seemed to explode for Admiral Yin,
Captain Han, Captain Lubu, and the rest of the task force.

The engines on the *Wenshan* had been racing back and
forth in response to the helmsman's attempts to hold the ship's
position steady. Han had been watching the number-four
motor launch moving away from the ship and did not hear his
crewman's warning: "Shoal water! Depth three meters . . .
depth two meters . . . depth under the keel decreasing."

From the barges on Phu Qui Island, bullets began pelting
the starboard side of the *Wenshan* as the crewman aboard the
oil-derrick barges fired on the approaching launches and at the
Wenshan itself.

Captain Han had not heard the shoal-water warning. He ran

back into the bridge. "Radio to *Hong Lung,* we are under fire from the oil barges . . ."

"Captain, depth under the keel . . . !"

Suddenly the *Wenshan* was pushed laterally toward the island and struck a coral outcropping surrounding Phu Qui Island. The patrol boat heeled sharply to starboard, the sudden, crunching stop flinging every crewman on the bridge off his feet. The gusting winds only served to push the *Wenshan* harder against the coral, and although the brittle calcium formations gave way immediately under the four-hundred-ton ship, the sound of straining steel combined with the howling winds and the cries of the surprised crewmen made it seem like the end of the world was at hand.

The officer of the deck had raised his headset microphone to his lips and shouted, "Comm, bridge, relay to *Hong Lung,* we are under fire, we are under fire . . ." Then amid the tearing and crunching sounds: "We have hit the reef, we have hit the reef." But the message transmitted to the rest of the task force group by the startled and terrified radioman was, *"Wenshan* to *Hong Lung,* we are under fire . . . we have been hit."

ABOARD THE FLAGSHIP *HONG LUNG*

When the warning from the *Wenshan* pierced the air in the bridge of the *Hong Lung,* Admiral Yin spun on his heels to Captain Lubu and shouted, "Order *Wenshan* and *Xingyi* to open fire, full missile and gun salvo."

Lubu wasn't going to question this order—he had been fearing just such an occurrence. He quickly relayed the command to his officer of the deck.

Seconds later the stormy night sky erupted with flashes of light and streaks of fire off in the distance. Using their sophisticated Round Ball fire-control radar, the fast attack craft *Xingyi* had maintained a continuous attack solution on the barges with their Fei Lung-7 surface-to-surface missiles. As soon as the warning cry had been issued by Captain Han on *Wenshan,* Captain Miliyan on *Xingyi* had ordered all missiles and guns made ready for action. When he received the message from Admiral Yin, the Fei Lung guided missiles were in the air.

The Flying Dragon missiles received initial course guidance from the Round Ball targeting radar, and a small booster engine ignited that punched the twenty-two-hundred-pound missile out of its storage canister. After flying a hundred yards away from the ship, the big second-stage sustainer motor kicked on, accelerating the missile to Mach one. A radar altimeter kept the missile precisely at one hundred feet above the choppy waters until it hit the easternmost barge and exploded six seconds after launch.

The pointed titanium armor-piercing warhead section thruster cap of the Fei Lung missile allowed the missile to drive through the thin steel hull of the outermost barge before detonating the warhead. The four-hundred-pound high-explosive warhead created a massive firestorm all across the Philippine oil platform, spraying red-hot chunks of metal and propellant for hundreds of yards in every direction. A wall of fire caused by a wave of burning petroleum washed across Phu Qui Island, swirling into an inverted tornado that defied the late summer rains and stabbed skyward.

Captain Han watched the spectacular firestorm that was once a Philippine oil derrick for several moments until he realized that the *Wenshan* had returned to an even keel and that the forward 76-millimeter gun had opened fire on the platform, pounding the mountain of flames with twenty kilogram radar-guided shells. "Cease fire!" Han shouted at his officer of the deck, who was staring in rapt fascination out the forward windshield at the maelstrom. "Cease fire!" he repeated before the forward 76 was silent. "Helm! Move us out to two kilometers from the island. Signal the motor launches and the *Hong Lung* that we are maneuvering out of shoal water."

As *Wenshan* eased away from the huge fires still raging on the Philippine oil barges, *Xingyi* launched two more missiles at the barge until Admiral Yin on the *Hong Lung* ordered him to stop. One Fei Lung missile was quite enough to suppress any hostile fire from the small oil facility, and two missiles would have completely destroyed it—four missiles, half the *Xingyi*'s load, could devastate an aircraft carrier.

Admiral Yin's intent was clear—he wanted no one alive on that platform.

"Seven, this is the Dragon," the radio message began. "Recover your boarding parties and rejoin the group. Over."

Captain Han picked up the radio microphone himself. "I copy, Dragon," Han replied. "I recommend that one of my motor launches search for survivors. Over."

"Request denied, Seven," came the reply. "Dragon Leader orders all Dragon units to withdraw."

One hour later, all traces of the Philippine oil derrick and barges were swept away in the rising tide of the windswept South China Sea currents. Except for a few pieces of pipe and half-burned bodies, the oil platform had ceased to exist.

MALACANANG PALACE, MANILA, THE PHILIPPINES
THURSDAY, 9 JUNE 1994, 0602 HOURS LOCAL

Since the Marcos years, the official residence of the Philippine President, Malacanang Palace, had undergone a major transformation. Concerned for his security, Marcos had transformed the graceful eighteenth-century Spanish colonial mansion into an ugly fortress—he had blocked most of the windows and replaced stained glass and crystal with steel or reinforced bulletproof glass. Wishing to distance her government from the dictatorial excesses of the Marcos regime, Corazon Aquino had chosen to live in the less pretentious Guest House and had turned the palace into a museum of shame, where citizens and tourists could gape in wonder at Marcos' underground bunker—some called it his "torture chambers"—and Imelda's cavernous bedroom, stratospheric canopy bed; her infamous shoe closets and her bulletproof brassiere.

The new President of the Philippines, seventy-year-old Arturo Mikaso, changed the Malacanang Palace back into a historical landmark that his people could be proud of, as well as a livable residence for himself and a workable office complex for his Cabinet. The style and grace of the pre-colonial Philippines were restored, the heavy security barriers were removed, and, like the American White House, large portions of Malacanang Palace were now open for tours when they were not in use by the President. In time the palace again became a symbol for the city of Manila itself.

But now, in the growing summer dawn, the palace was the scene of a hastily arranged meeting of the President's Cabinet. In Mikaso's residential office, where the President could see the Pasig River that wound through northern Manila, President Mikaso sipped a cup of tea. Mikaso was the elder statesman, a white-haired man who was taller and more powerful-looking than most Filipinos, a wealthy landowner and ex-senator who was immensely popular with most of his people. Mikaso had been elected as President of the nation when Corazon Aquino's second four-year term came to an end. He won the election only after forming an alliance with the National Democratic Front, the main political organ of the Communist Party of the Philippines; and the Moro National Liberation Front, a pro-Islamic political group that represented the thousands of citizens of the Islamic faith in the south Philippines.

"How many were killed, General?" Mikaso asked.

"Thirty men, all civilians," the Chief of Staff of the New Philippine Army, General Roberto La Loma Santos, replied somberly. "Their barge came under full attack by a Red Chinese patrol. No orders to surrender, no quarter given, no attempts to offer assistance or rescue the attack. The bastards attacked, then slinked away like cowardly dogs."

A tall, dark-haired man, standing alone near the great stone fireplace, turned toward General Santos. "You have still not explained to us, General," Second Vice President José Trujillo Samar said in a deep voice, "what that barge was doing in the neutral zone, anchored to Pagasa Island . . ."

"And what are you implying, Samar?" First Vice President Daniel Teguina, who was seated near the President's desk, challenged. Teguina was politically an ally of Samar but ideologically a complete opposite. Part of the coalition formed during the 1994 elections was the appointment of forty-one-year-old Daniel Teguina. Much younger than Mikaso, Teguina was not only a vice president, but also the leader of the Philippine House of Representatives, an ex-military officer, newspaper publisher, and leader of the National Democratic Front, a leftist political organization. With General José Trujillo Samar—who besides being the second vice president was also governor of the newly formed Commonwealth of Mindanao, which had won the right to form its own autonomous commonwealth in 1990—these three men formed a fiery coalition that, although successful in continuing the important post-Marcos rebuilding process in the Philippines, was stormy and divisive.

"Those were innocent Filipino workers on the barge . . ." said Teguina.

Samar nodded and said, "Who were illegally drilling for oil in the neutral zone. Did they think the Chinese were going to just sit back and watch them work?"

"They were not *drilling* for oil, just taking soundings," said Teguina.

"Well, they had no business there," Samar insisted. "The Chinese Navy's actions were outrageous, but those workers were in clear violation of the law."

"You're a cold bastard," Teguina cut in. "Blaming the dead for an act of aggression . . ."

"Enough, enough," the elderly Mikaso said wearily, gesturing for the men to stop. "I did not call you here to argue."

Teguina glared at both men. "Well, we can't just sit back and do nothing. The Chinese just launched a major act of aggression. We must do something. We must—"

"Enough," Mikaso interrupted. "We must begin an investigation and find out exactly why that barge was operating in those waters, then . . ."

"Sir, I recommend that we also step up patrols in the Spratly Island area," General Santos said. "This may be a prelude to a full-scale invasion of the Spratlys by the Chinese."

"Risky," Samar concluded. "A naval response would be seen as provocative, and we have no way of winning any conflict with the People's Liberation Navy. We would gain nothing . . ."

"Always the general, eh, Samar?" Teguina asked derisively.

He turned away from him to the President. "I agree with General Santos. We have a navy, however small—I say to send them to protect our interests in the Spratlys. We have an obligation to our people to do nothing short of that."

Arturo Mikaso looked at each of his advisers in turn and nodded in agreement. Little did he realize the extraordinary chain of events he was about to set into motion with that slight nod of his head.

TWO

With his boyish face, long, gangly arms and legs, his base-ball cap, and his thirty-two-ounce squeeze bottle of Pepsi-Cola—he drank five such bottles a day yet was still as skinny as a rail—Jonathan Colin Masters resembled a kid at a Saturday afternoon ball game. He had bright-green eyes and short brown hair—luckily, the baseball cap hid Masters' hair, or else his stubborn cowlicks would have made him appear even younger, almost adolescent, to the range officers and technicians standing nearby.

Masters, his assistants and technicians, and a handful of Air Force and Defense Advanced Research and Projects Agency (DARPA) officials were on board a converted DC-10 airliner, forty-five thousand feet over the White Sands Missile Test Range in south-central New Mexico. Unlike the military and Pentagon officials, who were poring over checklists, notes, and schematics, Masters had his feet up on a raised track in the cargo section of the massive airliner, sipping his cola and smil-ing like a kid who was at the circus for the first time.

"The winds are kicking up again, Doctor Masters," U.S. Air Force Colonel Ralph Foch said to Masters, his voice one of concern.

Masters wordlessly tipped his soda bottle at the Air Force range safety officer and reached to his control console, punched in instructions to the computer, and studied the screen. "Carrier aircraft has compensated for the winds, and ALARM has acknowledged the change," Masters reported. "We got it covered, Ralph."

Colonel Ralph Foch wasn't mollified, and being called "Ralph" by a man—no, a kid—twenty years his junior didn't help. "The one-hundred-millibar wind patterns are approaching the second-stage 'Q' limits, *Doctor,*" Foch said irritably. "That's the third increase over the forecast we've seen in the past two hours. We should consider aborting the flight."

Masters glanced over his shoulder at Foch and smiled a dimpled, toothy smile. "ALARM compensated OK, Ralph," Masters repeated. "No need to abort."

"But we're on the edge of the envelope as it is," Colonel Foch reminded him.

"The edge of *your* envelope, Ralph," Masters said. He got to his feet, walked a few steps aft, and patted the nose of a huge, torpedo-shaped object sitting on its launch rail. "You established your flight parameters based on data I provided, and you naturally made your parameters more restrictive. ALARM here knows its limits and it still says go. So we go."

"Doctor Masters, as the range safety officer I'm here to insure a safe launch for both the ground and the air crews. My parameters are established to—"

"Colonel Foch, if you want to abort the mission, say the word," Masters said calmly, barely suppressing a casual burp. "The Navy doesn't get their relay hookup satellites on the air until tomorrow, you can spend the night at the Blytheville, Arkansas, Holiday Inn again, and I can bill DARPA another one hundred thousand dollars for gas. It's your decision."

"I'm merely expressing my concern about the winds at altitude, Doctor Masters . . ."

"And I replied to your concerns," Masters said with a smile. "My little baby here says it's a go. Unless we fly somewhere else to launch, away from the jet stream . . ."

"DARPA is very specific about the launch area, Doctor. These satellites are important to the Navy. They want to monitor the booster's progress throughout the flight. The launch must be over the White Sands range."

"Fine. Then we continue to monitor the winds and let the computers do their jobs. If they can't properly compensate without going outside the range, we turn around on the race-track and try again. If we go outside the launch window, we abort. Fair enough?"

Foch could do nothing but nod in agreement. This launch was important to both the Navy and Air Force, and he wasn't prepared to issue a launch abort unilaterally.

The object called ALARM that Masters so lovingly regarded was the Air Launched Alert Response Missile; there were two of the huge missiles on board the DC-10 that morning. ALARM was a four-stage space booster designed to place up to three-quarter-ton payloads in low-to-medium Earth orbit by launching the booster from the cargo hold of an aircraft—in effect, the DC-10 was the ALARM booster's first stage, with the other three stages provided by powerful solid-fuel rockets on the missile itself.

The ALARM missile had a long, slender, one-piece wing that swiveled out from its stowed position along the missile's fuselage after launch. The wing would supply lift and increase the effectiveness of the solid rocket motors while the booster was in the atmosphere, which greatly increased the power and payload capability of the booster. An ALARM booster could carry as much as fifteen hundred pounds in its ten-foot-long, forty-inch-diameter payload bay.

On today's mission, each of Masters' ALARM boosters carried four small two-hundred-pound communications satellites, which Jon Masters, in his own inimitable way, called NIRT-Sats—"Need It Right This Second" satellites. Unlike more conventional satellites, which weighed hundreds or even thousands of pounds, were placed in high geosynchronous orbits almost twenty-three thousand miles above the Equator, and could carry dozens of communications channels, NIRTSats were small, lightweight satellites which carried only a few communications channels and were placed in low, one-hundred-to-one-thousand-mile orbits. Unlike geosynchronous satellites, which orbited the Earth once per day and therefore appeared to be stationary over the Equator, NIRTSats orbited the Earth once every ninety to three hundred minutes, which meant that usually more than one satellite had to be launched to cover a particular area.

But a NIRTSat cost less than one-fiftieth the price of a full-sized satellite, and it cost less to insure and launch as well. Even with a constellation of four NIRTSats, a customer with a need for satellite communications could get it for less than one-third the price of buying "air time" on an existing satellite. A single ALARM booster launch, which cost only ten million dollars from start to finish, could give a customer instant global communications capability from anywhere in the world—and it took only a few days to get the system in place, instead of the months or even years it took for conventional launches. NIRT-Sats could be repositioned anywhere in orbit if requirements changed, and Masters had even devised a way to recover a NIRTSat intact and reuse it, which saved the customer even more money.

Masters' customer this day was, as it usually was, the Department of Defense, which was why all the military observers were on hand. Masters was to place four NIRTSats in a four-hundred-mile-high polar orbit over the western Pacific to provide the Navy and Air Force with specialized, dedicated voice, data, air-traffic control, and video communications between ships, aircraft, and land-based controllers. With the NIRTSat constellation in place, the Navy's Seventh Fleet headquarters and the Air Force's Pacific Air Force headquarters could instantly talk with and find the precise locations of every ship and aircraft on the network. Coupled with the military's Global Positioning System satellite navigation system, NIRT-Sats would continually transmit flight or sailing data on each aircraft or vessel to their respective headquarters, although the vessels might be far outside radio range. The second ALARM booster carried another four NIRTSat satellites and was aboard as a backup if the first launch failed.

Jon Masters' cocky attitude toward this important launch made Colonel Foch very uncomfortable. But, he thought, the little snot had every reason to feel cocky—in two years of testing and over two dozen launches, not one ALARM booster had ever failed to do its thing, and not one NIRTSat had ever failed to function. It was, Foch had to admit, quite a testament to the genius of Jonathan Colin Masters. Worse, the bastard was so young. Boy genius was an understatement.

When Jon Masters was barely in grade school in Manchester, New Hampshire, his first-grade teachers showed Jon's parents a one-hundred-page treatise on the feasibility of a manned lunar landing, written by a youngster who had only learned to write a few months earlier. When asked about the essay, Jon sat his parents down and explained all the problems inherent in launching a rocket to the moon and returning it safely back to Earth—and the Apollo space program had just gotten under way, with the first lunar landing still three years away.

It didn't take Jon's parents a blink of an eye to figure out what to do next: he was enrolled in a private high school, which he completed three years later at age ten. He enrolled at Dartmouth College and received a bachelor of science degree in aeronautical engineering at age thirteen. After receiving a master's degree in mathematics from Dartmouth, he enrolled at the Massachusetts Institute of Technology and after a tumultuous five years finally earned a doctorate in engineering at the age of twenty.

The first love of Masters' life was and always had been NASA, the National Aeronautics and Space Administration, and in 1981 he went to work for the space agency immediately after leaving MIT. The Shuttle Transportation System, or STS, program was just heating up by then, and Jon Masters was an integral part of the development of special applications that could take advantage of this new flying workhorse. Almost every satellite and delivery subsystem developed for the shuttle between 1982 and 1985 was at least partially designed by Jonathan Masters.

But, even as the shuttle transportation system was gearing up for more launches per year and more ambitious projects, including the space station, Jon Masters saw a weakness. It was an obvious problem that was creeping into the successful STS program—the spacecraft were accumulating a lot of miles, with even more miles slated for them each year, and no more orbiters were being built. When the success of the shuttle program became obvious, Masters thought, NASA should have had one new orbiter per year rolling off the assembly lines, plus upgraded solid-rocket boosters and avionics. But they had none.

Jon Masters took an active interest in the numerous small companies that built small space boosters for private and commercial applications. In 1984, at age twenty-four, he resigned from NASA and accepted a seat on the board of directors of Sky Sciences, Inc., a small Tennessee-based commercial space booster company that sometimes subcontracted work for the fledgling Strategic Defense Intiative Organization, the federal research and development team tasked with devising an intercontinental ballistic missile defense system. Soon afterward he became vice president in charge of research for the small company. Masters' presence on the board gave the company a shot of optimism—and a new line of credit—that allowed it to stay fiscally afloat.

With the NASA shuttles grounded indefinitely following the *Challenger* disaster in 1986, expendable boosters were quickly back in vogue. While NASA was refurbishing old Titan ICBM rockets for satellite booster duty and bringing back the Delta line of heavy boosters, in 1988 Jon Masters, now the twenty-eight-year-old chairman of the board and new president of Sky Sciences, soon renamed Sky Masters, Inc., announced that he had developed a new low-cost space booster that was small and easy to transport and operate. Called SCARAB (Small Containerized Air Relocatable Alert Booster), it was a ground-launched rocket that could be hauled aboard a Boeing 747 or military cargo plane, set up, and launched from almost anywhere in a matter of days or even hours. SCARAB restored NASA and the military's ability to launch satellites into Earth orbit on short notice.

His next project was a booster system similar to SCARAB but even more flexible and responsive. Although SCARAB could place a two-thousand-pound payload into low Earth orbit from almost anywhere on Earth, it still needed a runway for the two cargo aircraft that carried the rocket and the ground-launch equipment, an extensive ground-support contingent, and at least fifteen hours' worth of work to erect the launch structures and get the rocket ready to fly. In several practice tests, Masters needed no more than thirty hours from initial notification and delivery of the payload to T minus zero. But he wanted to do better.

That was when ALARM was born. ALARM was merely a SCARAB booster downsized to fit in a transport plane and fitted with wings. It used the launch aircraft as its first-stage booster, and it used lift from its scissor-action wings to help increase the efficiency of the smaller first- and second-stage boosters. Two ALARM boosters could be standing by on board the carrier aircraft; they would only need to bring the payloads on board and take off. With aerial refueling, the ALARM carrier aircraft could stay aloft for days, traversing the country or even partly around the world, ready to launch the boosters.

Masters had developed several different payloads for his small air-launched boosters. Along with the communications satellites, he had developed a small satellite that could take composite radar, infrared, and telescopic visual "photos" of the Earth, and the resulting image was dozens of times more detailed than standard visual photos. The images could be digitized and transmitted to terminals all over the world via his small communications satellites, giving commanders real-time reconnaissance and intelligence information. Combined with powerful computers, users from the Pentagon or White House to individual aircrew members on board strike aircraft could conduct their own sophisticated photo intelligence, plan and replan missions, and assess bomb damage almost instantaneously.

With several different payloads on board, the flexibility of the ALARM system was unparalleled. A communications-satellite launch could immediately change to a satellite-retrieval mission or a reconnaissance-satellite mission, or even a strike mission. A single ALARM carrier aircraft could become as important a national asset as Cape Canaveral.

"Fifteen minutes to launch window one," Masters' launch control officer, Helen Kaddiri, announced. Kaddiri was the chief of Masters' operations staff and the senior launch-control officer, in charge of monitoring all flight systems throughout each mission. In her early forties, exotically attractive, she'd

been born and raised in Calcutta. She and her parents immi-
grated to the United States when she was twelve and she
changed her name from Helenika to Helen. She was a completely career-minded scientist who sometimes found it very
frustrating working for someone like Jon Masters.

She regarded Masters warily with her dark, beautiful, al-
mond-shaped eyes as he studied the command console. Masters was so relaxed and laid-back that all the uptight
techno-types he worked with, especially those developing new
space technologies, got really rankled—herself included.
Maybe it was because Masters seemed to treat everyone and
everything the same . . . like work was one big beach party.

The government officials they dealt with almost always shud-
dered when working with Masters. Even socializing with him
was a strain. Kaddiri thought that every time they got a new
government contract was a matter of luck. If it weren't for his
genius . . .

"Fourteen minutes to launch window one," she said.

"Thanks, Helen," Jon replied. He pushed his baseball cap up
higher on his forehead, which made him look even younger—
like "Beaver" Cleaver. "Let's get Roosevelt-One in position
and ready."

Kaddiri grimaced at another of Masters' quirks—he named
his boosters, not just numbered them. He usually named them
after American presidents or Hollywood actors or actresses.
Helen thought that if Jon had a dog, he would probably number *it* instead.

Jon swung his headset microphone to his lips: "Crew, Roose-
velt-1 is moving stage center. Stand by."

The interior of Masters' converted DC-10 was arranged
much like the firing mechanism of a rifle. Like a cartridge
magazine, the two boosters were stored side by side in the
forward section of the one-hundred-twenty-feet-long, thirty-
foot-wide cargo bay, which afforded plenty of room to move
around the fifty-feet-long, four-foot-diameter rockets and their
stabilizers. Forward of the storage area was the control center,
with all of the booster monitoring and control systems, and
forward of the control room was a pressure hatch which led to
the flight deck—for safety's sake, the flight deck was sealed

from the cargo section so any pressurization malfunctions in the cargo end would not prevent the flight crew from safely recovering the plane.

The back fifty feet of the cargo hold was occupied by a large cylindrical chamber resembling the breech end of a shotgun, composed of heavy steel and aluminum with numerous thick Plexiglas viewports all around it. The boosters would roll down a track in the center of the cargo hold into the chamber, and the chamber would be sealed from the rest of the aircraft. Just prior to launch, the chamber would be depressurized before opening the "bomb-bay" doors. With this system, the entire cargo section of the aircraft did not have to be depressurized before launch. Floodlights and high-speed video cameras inside the launch chamber and outside the DC-10 launch plane were ready to photograph the entire launch sequence.

With two of Kaddiri's assistants with flashlights watching on either side, the first forty-three-thousand-pound space booster began rolling on its tracks toward the center of the cabin. The crew, especially the cockpit crew of two pilots and engineer, had to be notified whenever one of these behemoth rockets was being moved. Whenever they moved a rocket, the flight engineer had to begin transferring fuel to the side where the booster was moved to keep the launch aircraft stable. The booster moved about ten feet per minute, which was the same speed that a similar weight in jet fuel could be transferred from body tanks to the corresponding wing tanks.

In two minutes the booster was in position in the center of the launch cabin, and it began its slow journey aft into the launch chamber. This time, to ensure longitudinal stability as the twenty-one-ton rocket moved aft, a large steel drum filled with eight thousand gallons of jet fuel in the belowdeck cargo section would slowly move forward as the booster moved aft, which would help to keep the aircraft stable; after the booster was launched, the drum would quickly move aft to balance the plane.

It took much longer for the booster to make its way aft, but it was finally wheeled into position in the chamber and the heavy steel hatch closed. Once in place, retractable clamps held the booster in place over the bomb-bay doors. "Roosevelt-

One in position," Kaddiri called out as she peered through the observation ports in the chamber. "Flight deck, confirm lateral and longitudinal trim."

"Aircraft trim nominal," the flight engineer reported a few seconds later. "Standing by."

"Roger. Confirm hatch closed and locked."

Masters checked the console readouts. "Launch-chamber hatch closed, locked, green lights on."

"Engineer cross-check good, green lights on," the flight engineer reported after checking his readouts from the flight deck.

Kaddiri reached into a green canvas bag slung over her shoulder into a portable oxygen pack and withdrew an oxygen mask, checked the hose and regulator, and then clicked the mask's built-in wireless microphone on. Her assistants in the aft end of the DC-10 did the same; Masters and Foch had already donned their masks. "Oxygen On and Normal," she said. She got thumbs-up from her assistants after they checked their masks, then said, "Ready to depressurize launch chamber."

Masters got a thumbs-up from Foch, then replied, "Oxygen On and Normal at the control console." He called up the cargo-section pressurization readout and displayed it in big numerals on a monitor screen so both he and Foch could read them easily—two sets of eyes were always better than one. "Launch chamber depressurizing—now."

For all that cross-checking and preparation, it was quite unspectacular. In two minutes the launch chamber was depressurized and the cargo-bay pressure was stable. After monitoring it for another minute to check for slow leaks, Masters removed his mask and radioed, "Cargo-section pressure checks good, launch chamber fully depressurized, no leaks." The computer would continue to monitor the cabin pressure and warn the crew of any changes. Masters and everyone else kept their masks dangling from their necks . . . just in case.

"Data-link check." Masters checked to be sure that the booster was still exchanging information with the launch computers. The check was all automatic, but it still took several long moments. Finally: "Data connection nominal. Two minutes to launch window." Masters turned to Colonel Foch. "We need final range clearance, Colonel."

Foch was staring intently at one of the screens on the console, which was displaying atmospheric data relayed from the White Sands Missile Range headquarters through their extensive sensor network. "I show the winds at the maximum Q limits, Doctor Masters," he said. "We should abort."

"Roosevelt says he's a go," Masters replied, ignoring the warning and checking the readouts again. "Let's proceed." Jon looked at Kaddiri as he hit the intercom button. "Helen?"

She removed her oxygen mask as she walked back to the command console. "It's pretty risky, Jon."

"Helen, 'pretty risky' is not a 'no.' Unless I hear a definite no, I'd say we proceed."

Foch cleared his throat. "Doctor, it seems to me you're taking a big chance here." He glanced at Kaddiri, expecting a bit more support from someone who obviously wasn't sure of what Masters was doing, but he got nothing but a blank, noncommittal expression. "You're wasting one of your boosters just to prove something. This isn't a wartime scenario . . ."

"Colonel, this might not be a war we're fighting, but to me it's nothing less than an all-out battle," Masters said. "I have to prove to my customers, my stockholders, my board of directors, and to the rest of the country that the ALARM system can deliver its payload on time, on target." He turned to Foch, and Kaddiri could see a very uncharacteristic hardness in Masters' young face. "I programmed these boosters with reliability in mind—reliability to deliver as promised, and reliability to do the mission in conditions such as this."

Foch leaned forward and spoke directly at Masters in a low voice. "You don't have to tell me all this, Doctor. I know what you want. You get paid if this thing gets launched. My flight parameters insure both safety for ground personnel and reliability of the launch itself. Yours only covers the launch. My question is, do you really care what happens after that? I think you care more about your business than the results of this mission."

Masters glared at him. He whipped off his baseball cap and stabbed at Foch, punctuating each sentence: "Listen, Ralph, that's my name on that booster, my name on those satellites, my name all over this project. If it doesn't launch, I take the heat. If it doesn't fly, I take the heat. If it doesn't deliver four healthy satellites in their proper orbits, I take the heat.

"Now you might think you know my contracts, Ralph. You're right—I do get paid if Roosevelt-One is launched. I get paid if we bring it back without launching it, too. I've already gotten deposits for the next six launches, and I've already received progress payments for the next ten boosters. But you don't know shit about my business, buddy. I've got a dozen ways to fail, and each one can put me out of business faster than you can take a pee. I *do* care about that. And still I say, we launch. Now if you have any objections, say it and we'll abort. Otherwise issue range clearance, sit back, and watch the fireworks."

Helen Kaddiri was surprised. She'd never seen Jon so wound up. He was right about the pressure on him and the company—there were more than a dozen ways to fail. Friendly and unfriendly suitors were waiting to snap up the company. The aerospace sector had fared very poorly in the recent U.S. economic mini-recession, and it was worsened by the declining outlook on all defense-industry stocks with the advent of *glasnost, perestroika,* the opening of Eastern Europe, the unification of Germany. Sky Masters, Inc., had to indeed prove itself on each flight.

But Jon Masters had always let the pressure roll off his back. He paid lip service to the concerns of his board of directors and partners, and treated military experts like Foch and scientists like Kaddiri as part of his road show. He listened only to those who agreed with him. Sometimes he seemed too busy having a good time to see the danger in what he was doing.

Colonel Ralph Foch clearly was not having a good time. He turned away from Masters and checked the data readouts being transmitted to Masters' launch aircraft from the White Sands Missile Test Range; the data was a collection of sensor readings, meteorological-balloon measurements, and satellite observations about conditions both in the atmosphere and in the region of space that the four NIRTSats would travel. Foch checked several screens of data with a checklist and binders of computer models devised for this launch, then compared the information with corrective actions being reported by Masters' launch aircraft as well as the data from the ALARM booster itself. Since the launch was, in effect, the ALARM booster's first stage, the rocket was already "flying" the mission—issuing corrections to the jet's flight crew, updating its position, and continually plotting its new route of flight—while still within the cargo bay of the converted DC-10.

"You're right on the borderline, Doctor Masters," Foch finally said. "But you're still within the safety margin. Pending final clearance from White Sands, you're cleared to launch." Foch swung his headset microphone in place and made the radio call to the missile-range headquarters, recommending clearance to launch. With airborne clearance received, the ground range safety headquarters made a last-minute sweep of the range, alerted Albuquerque Air Route Traffic Control Center to assist in keeping aircraft out of the area, then issued final range clearance.

Masters grinned at Helen. "You've got the con, Helen." He liked to use nautical terms like "con" although Masters had never been near a naval vessel. "Initiate launch sequence."

"Crew stand by for launch sequence," Kaddiri sighed over interphone as Masters made his way aft with the two launch technicians. Kaddiri began to read off the fifty-one-item checklist steps, most of which were simply verifying that the computer was reporting the proper readings and was progressing smoothly, with no fault reports. The automatic countdown stopped on step 45, "Final Launch Clearance, Crew Notified," at T minus sixty seconds, where the computer initiated an automatic countdown hold and transferred control back to Kaddiri. "T minus sixty second hold," she announced. "Flight controls visually inspected and checked in manual mode."

Jon Masters liked to accomplish this last check himself instead of sitting up on the launch-control console—it was his last look at each missile before sending it out into the world, like a parent dressing the child before sending him off for the first time to kindergarten.

Both launch officers and Masters checked the long, slender scissor wings and vertical and horizontal stabilizers on the tailplane. When they reported OK, Kaddiri activated the flight-control self-test system. The scissor wings swiveled out two feet until several inches of the wingtips were visible, and the rudder and stabilators on the tailplane jumped back and forth in a pre-programmed test sequence.

"Self-test in progress," Masters called out. "X-wing to fifteen-degree position, left wingtip right . . . rudder right . . . rudder center . . . rudder left . . . left stab up . . . center . . . down . . . center . . . right stab up . . . center . . . down . . . center."

The test lasted only ten seconds. Kaddiri canceled the self-test, then manually set the booster to launch configuration. The wings swiveled back to lie along the top of the booster's fuselage. "Verifying flight-control settings for launch," Masters called out. "X-wing centered. Rudder centered. Stabilators set to trailing-edge down position." With the horizontal stabilizers in the trailing-edge down position, the nose of the ALARM booster would dive down and away from the DC-10 after launch, minimizing the risk of collision.

"T minus sixty countdown hold checklist complete," Kaddiri reported. She checked the navigational readouts. "On course as directed by Roosevelt-One, time remaining in launch window one, six minutes fourteen seconds." By then Jon Masters had walked up beside her and had taken his seat again, taking a big swig from a squeeze bottle.

"Resume the countdown," Masters said, watching the TV monitors on the console. As he spoke, the pressure-secure bay doors on the lower fuselage snapped open, revealing a light-gray cloud deck a few thousand feet below. Other cameras mounted on the DC-10's belly, tail, and wingtips showed the gaping forty-foot hatch wide open, with the ALARM booster suspended in the center of the dark rectangle. "Doors open. Thirty seconds to go . . ."

Those thirty seconds seemed to take hours to pass. Masters was about to call to Helen to ask if there was a problem when she started counting: "Stand by for launch . . . five . . . four . . . three . . . two . . . one . . . release!"

It was a strange sensation, a strange sight. The ALARM booster just seemed to shrink in size as it fell out of the launch chamber—it continued to fly directly underneath the open doors as if it were frozen in place. The doors stayed open long enough so that Jon could see the X-wing begin to move slightly to provide a bit of stability as it cruised along. The DC-10's tail heeled upward as the twenty-one-ton rocket dropped away— it would take a minute for the movable counterweight tank to rebalance the plane. The crew members in the cargo section held on firmly to handholds in the ceiling or bulkheads as their bodies were pressed to the floor.

"Rocket away, rocket away," Helen called out. Immediately, the DC-10 began a 30-degree bank turn to the left, and Roosevelt-1 was lost from the bomb-bay camera. Helen switched to a wingtip camera to monitor the motor firing.

"We're clear from booster's flight path," Kaddiri called out. "Coming up on first-stage ignition . . . ready, ready . . . now."

Like a giant stick of chalk drawing a fat white-yellow line across the sky, the first-stage motor of the ALARM booster ignited, and the rocket leaped ahead of the DC-10 in a blur of motion. When the rocket was about a mile away, the X-wing scissored out until the wing was almost perpendicular to the rocket's fuselage, and the ALARM booster reared its nose upward and began to climb. Nineteen seconds after launch, the booster was traveling almost twice the speed of sound and had recrossed its launch altitude as the wing generated lift. Seconds later, the rocket was lost from view, traveling too fast for the high-speed cameras to follow.

"T plus thirty seconds, Roosevelt-One on course, all systems normal, passing one-twenty-K altitude, velocity passing Mach three," Kaddiri reported.

"Launch-chamber doors closed, chamber repressurized," one of the techs reported. "Ready to reload." They were in no hurry to load Roosevelt-Two into position on this mission, but Masters liked to practice rapid-fire procedures to demonstrate that a multiple ALARM launch within a single launch window was possible.

"T plus sixty seconds, fifteen seconds to first-stage burnout," Kaddiri reported. "Altitude one-eighty K, passing Mach six, pitch angle thirty degrees. All systems nominal."

Using the scissor wings to augment the motor's thrust with

lift, the booster climbed quickly through the atmosphere. As the air started to thin and less lift was being generated by the wings, they scissored back closer and closer to the booster's fuselage until, just before first-stage motor burnout, the wings were fully retracted back along the body of the rocket. Seventy-six seconds after ignition, the first-stage motor burned out and the rear half of the fifty-feet-long booster, carrying the rear tailplane and the scissor wings, separated from the rest of the booster. The rocket was at the very edge of space, nearly 250,000 feet above Earth. Nine seconds later, the second-stage motor ignited, sending the booster streaking into space.

The first-stage section began its controlled tumble to Earth, and four recovery parachutes opened at sixty thousand feet above ground. A specially equipped Air Force C-130 cargo plane would snag the parachute in midair and reel the first-stage booster in somewhere over the northern section of the White Sands Missile Test Range. This recovery procedure would allow them to use the ALARM booster system anywhere in the world without hazard to people on the ground, even near heavily populated areas. The second- and third-stage motor sections would re-enter the atmosphere from space and burn up.

"Good second-stage ignition," Kaddiri reported. "Altitude passing three hundred forty K, velocity passing Mach eleven, on course." She turned to Foch with a look of concern, then at Masters. "Second-stage nozzle reports a gimbal-limit fault, Jon. It might have overcorrected for winds at altitude and sustained some damage."

Masters had a stopwatch counting down to the second-stage burnout. "Forty seconds to second-stage burnout," he muttered. "Is it still hitting a stop? Is it correcting its course?"

"Continuous faults on the nozzle," Kaddiri replied. "It's maintaining course, but it might slip out of stage-three tolerance limits." The third-stage section of the booster was much smaller than the first two stages, designed only to increase the booster's velocity to Mach 25 for orbital insertion; it could not perform large course corrections. If the second-stage motor could not hold the booster within a gradually narrowing trajectory corridor, the booster could slip into a useless and possibly dangerous orbit. Numerous "safe" orbits were computed where the NIRTSat satellites would not interfere with other spacecraft and where they could be "stored" until it was possible to retrieve them, but it was usually very difficult to place a malfunctioning booster into a precomputed "safe" orbit. If it could not be placed in a position where it was not a hazard to other satellites, it could damage or destroy dozens of other payloads and re-enter the atmosphere over a populated area. Before that could be allowed to happen, they would destroy it.

That was exactly what Foch had in mind as he opened the plastic-guarded safety cover on the command destruct panel. Foch, Kaddiri, Masters, and the ground safety officers at the White Sands range could command the ALARM booster to self-destruct at any time; now that the booster was flying, Masters had very little authority over its disposition—he could not override a "Destruct" command. "I told you this might happen, Doctor Masters," Foch said. "The booster was obviously shaken off course by the strong, high-altitude winds, and it sustained some damage and can't correct its course enough."

But Masters sat back and, to everyone's surprise, put his feet up on the control console. "Ten seconds to second-stage burnout," he said, sipping his soda. "Sit back, relax. It'll stay in the groove long enough."

"The decision doesn't rest with you this time, Masters," Foch fumed. "The command'll come from White Sands or the Air Force Space Tracking Center. White Sands will initiate the destruct sequence. If their command doesn't work, I initiate mine."

"Well, well . . ." Masters laughed, pointing to the computer monitor. Foch turned to look. "Second-stage burnout, and Roosevelt-One is still on course." They studied the readouts for a few more moments. The booster, headed into a polar orbit over Canada, was picked up by Alaskan radar sites as it continued its climb to its orbit altitude. Soon its orbital insertion would be picked up by space-tracking radars at San Miguel Air Force Station in the Philippines, and the NIRTSats would begin their work.

After a while, Masters turned to Foch with a smug expression. "Minor course corrections being made, but it's right on course. Expect third-stage ignition in four minutes." He took another big sip of soda, then punctuated his victory with a loud burp. "I'd get your finger away from that destruct button if I were you, Colonel. The Navy wouldn't appreciate you blowing up a perfectly good booster."

CLARK AIR BASE, ANGELES, PAMPANGA PROVINCE
REPUBLIC OF THE PHILIPPINES
PHILIPPINES INDEPENDENCE DAY
SUNDAY, 12 JUNE 1994, 1147 HOURS LOCAL

One of the first major uses of Masters' new NIRTSat constellation of real-time position and communications reporting capability for Air Force aircraft was a few days later—and it was the most inauspicious. It was the day the last of the United States Air Force's aircraft departed the Philippines as the Americans turned over their military bases to full Filipino control. The satellites would control the last of the American fighters and tankers as they withdrew from the Philippines to bases in Japan and Guam.

Headquarters of the U.S. Air Force's Thirteenth Air Force at Clark Air Base, sixty-five miles north of Manila, was in a magnificent white six-story stucco building, at the end of a long grassy mall between the NCO and officers' family-housing areas. Both sides of the mall along the Weston and Wirt Davis avenues had once been lined with flags of the numerous military units of several nations that had liberated the Philippines from Japan during World War II, standing as a monument to those who had died defending this island nation against the Axis. Now the sixty poles were vacant except for the three flagpoles at the head of the mall opposite the headquarters building—the flags of the Philippines, the United States, and the U.S. Air Force.

From his vantage point on the review stand in front of the headquarters building, Major General Richard Stone noticed that someone had lowered the American flag down several feet from the top of its staff—it almost appeared to be at half staff. Perhaps it should be so.

Stone's aide, Colonel Michael Krieg, stepped over to his boss and handed him a Teletype report. "Latest on that skirmish near the Spratlys, sir," Krieg said. "The Chinese are still claiming they were attacked by heavy antiship weapons. Twenty-seven Filipinos dead, six Americans, and five missing."

"Christ," Stone sighed. He had watched the repercussions build over the last week since the skirmish. "Do the Chinese expect anyone to believe that? Why the hell would an oil company have any antiship missiles on an oil-exploration platform?"

"They did have machine guns, sir. Twenty-millimeter. World War Two vintage American Mk 4. Pretty good operating condition, too—before the Chinese melted it with a Fei Lung-7."

"Idiots," Stone muttered. "Opening up on a warship like that. So what are the Chinese doing now?"

"Laying low," Krieg replied. "Only occasional incursions in the Spratly Island neutral zone. President Mikaso's government is being very understanding about it so far. Vice President Samar issued a statement calling for reparations from the Chinese."

"Lots of luck."

"Vice President Teguina called for an investigation—not of the Chinese, but of Mikaso's government," Krieg added.

"Of *Mikaso's* government? Not the Chinese? 'Course—that's typical," Stone said. "Whatever it takes to distance himself from Mikaso . . . just as he's always done. Anything for a headline."

"The little bastard's got balls, that's for sure."

Major General Stone grunted. "You can say that again—Teguina loves to stir things up. Now, what do we have out there keeping an eye on things?"

Krieg looked at his boss with a look of pure concern. "In two hours—nothing."

"What?"

"Message from CINCPAC." CINCPAC was the acronym for Commander in Chief Pacific Command, the U.S. military organization responsible for all military activities from the West Coast of the United States to Africa. "He wants no combat aircraft or vessels near the area until they can get a reading from the Chinese. Strictly hands off."

"Well, what *did* we have out there?" Stone grumbled, irritated at CINCPAC's order.

"A couple F-16s from here checking it out, maybe a P-3 subchaser diverted to Zamboanga Airport or Bangoy Airport near Davao—er, sorry, they call it Samar International Airport now—to take some pictures. Apparently the Chinese feel our presence is threatening. CINCPAC agreed. No more flights within fifty miles."

"A fitting end to a perfectly lousy day," Stone said, straightening his uniform and heading toward the reviewing stand for the ceremony.

Major General Richard "Rat" Stone was the commander of the now disbanded Thirteenth Air Force—the principal American air defense, air support, and logistics support organization in the Republic of the Philippines. General Stone—whose nickname was short for "Rat Killer" after a strafing run in his F-4 along the Ho Chi Minh Trail in Vietnam had killed dozens of rats with 20-millimeter cannon fire—commanded the twenty different organizations from five major operating commands at Clark Air Base.

Principal of all the organizations on his base was the Third Tactical Fighter Wing, composed of F-16 fighter-bombers and F-4G "Advanced Wild Weasel" electronic warfare and defense suppression fighters; and the 6200th Tactical Fighter Training Group, who operated the various tactical training ranges and fighter weapons schools in the Philippines and who ran the seven annual "Cope Thunder" combat exercises to train American and allied pilots from all over the Pacific. The Third Tactical Fighter Wing, whose planes had the distinctive "PN" letters on the tail plus either the black "Peugeots" of the Third Tactical Fighter Squadron or the "Pair-O-Dice" of the Nineti-eth Tactical Fighter Squadron, flew air-to-air and air-to-ground strike missions in support of American interests from Australia to Japan and from India to Hawaii.

Clark Air Base had also been home to a very large Military Airlift Command contingent of C-130 Hercules transports, C-9 Nightingale flying hospitals, C-12 Huron light transport shuttles, and HH-53 Super Jolly and HH-3 Jolly Green Giant rescue and special-operations helicopters. The 374th Tactical Airlift Wing shuttled supplies and personnel all across the South Pacific and would, in wartime, deliver troops and supplies behind enemy lines. The Ninth Aeromedical Evacuation Squadron, the Twentieth Aeromedical Airlift Squadron, and the Thirty-first Aerospace Rescue and Recovery Squadron all provided medical airlift support and would fly rescue missions over land or water to recover downed aircrews—these were the organizations that first welcomed the American prisoners of war from Vietnam in 1972. Clark also housed the 353rd Special Operations Wing, whose MC-130E Combat Talon aircrews trained to fly psychological warfare, covert resupply, and other "black" missions all across the Pacific.

The base also supported the other American and Filipino military installations, including Subic Bay Naval Station, Sangley Point Naval Station, Point San Miguel Air Force Station, Camp O'Donnell, Camp John Hay, Wallace Air Station, Mount Cabuyo, Mactan Airfield, and dozens of Philippine Coast Guard and National Guard bases.

In essence, Clark Air Base had been a vital link to the Pacific and a major forward base for the United States and its allies since it opened in 1903. Now it was all being handed back to the Philippines—handed back to them during some of the most volatile and dangerous times in the country's history.

Stone's gaze moved from his country's flag to the throngs of noisy protesters outside the perimeter fence less than a kilometer away. At least ten thousand protesters pressed against the barbed wire–topped fences, shouting anti-American slogans and tossing garbage over the brick wall; Stone had arranged armored personnel carriers every one hundred yards along the wall surrounding the base to counter just such a demonstration. The Americans inside those carriers were armed only with sidearms and tear-gas-grenade launchers, and the Filipino troops and riot police outside the gates had nothing more lethal than fat rubber bullets. They were being pelted by rocks and bottles so badly that the carrier's crews dared not poke their heads out or even open one of the thin eye-portals. The throngs could easily overrun them all if they were stirred up. Occasionally a shot could be heard ringing out over the din of the crowd. Stone realized that, after weeks of these protests, he no longer jumped when he heard the gun-fire.

The Thirteenth Air Force commander had aged far beyond his fifty years in just the last few months. Of no more than medium height, with close-cropped silver hair, piercing blue eyes, broad shoulders narrowing quickly to a trim waist, and thin racehorse ankles, Stone was a soft-spoken yet energetic fighter pilot who had risen through the ranks from a "ninety-day-wonder" Officer Training School pilot candidate during the Vietnam War to a two-star general and commander of a major military installation defending a principal democratic ally and guarding America's western flank. In the past year, however, he had found himself supervising a degrading, igno-ble withdrawal from the base and the country he had learned to love so well. It was deeply depressing.

From a contingent of nearly eleven thousand men and women only twelve months earlier, Stone had assembled the last remaining two hundred American military personnel on the mall in front of the reviewing stand, to march one last time in parade. Although there were supposed to be ten persons from each of the twenty resident and tenant organizations on the base, Stone knew that most of the two hundred men and women who marched before him were security policemen, who had been hand-picked to ensure the safety of General Stone and the other Americans from Clark AB as they de-parted that day.

Part of the reason for the huge demonstration outside the perimeter fence was the presence of the two Filipino men on the reviewing stand with Stone: Philippine President Arturo Mikaso, and First Vice President Daniel Teguina. Teguina had carried the cry for the Philippines to cut all ties with the West and to not renew the leases on American military bases. Unlike the refined and elderly Mikaso, Daniel Teguina liked to be in the public eye, and he carefully polished his image to reflect the young radical students and peasants that he believed he represented. He dressed in more colorful, contemporary clothes, dyed his hair to hide the gray, and liked to appear in nightclubs and at soccer matches.

The National Democratic Front, despite reputed ties to the New People's Army, the organization that controlled the Communist-led Huk insurgents in the outlying provinces, flourished under the Mikaso-Teguina coalition government. Under Mikaso's strong popular leadership, the military threat to the government from the extremist Communist forces subsided, but the new, more radical voices in the government were harder to ignore. It didn't take long for a national referendum to be called after the 1994 elections, which forbade the President to extend the leases for American bases any further. The referendum passed by a narrow margin, and the United States was ordered to withdraw all permanent military forces from the Philippines and turn control of the installations to the Philippine government within six months.

Second Vice President General José Trujillo Samar, who was not present at the ceremonies, shared the majority of Filipinos' distaste for American hegemony, and he fought hard for removal of the bases.

Leaving, Rat Stone was out of a job.

Over the slowly rising screaming and yelling from the protesters, the American airmen marched in front of the reviewing stand, formed into four groups of fifty, and were ordered to parade rest by Colonel Krieg, acting as the parade adjutant general. Surrounding the grassy mall were two sets of bleachers, where guests of the government and a few American family members and embassy personnel watched with long faces the lowering of the colors for the last time over Clark Air Base. Banks of photographers, television cameras, and reporters were clustered all around the reviewing stand to capture the ceremonies. While several network news companies were on hand, no live broadcast of the ceremony was permitted. General Stone had felt, and the Air Force concurred, that a live broadcast might cause widespread demonstrations all across the country. That was also the reason no high-level American politicians were on hand. The official transfer had been made in the safety of Washington, D.C., weeks ago.

President Mikaso stepped forward to the podium as a taped trumpet call was played. The crowd began to cheer, and an appreciative ripple of applause issued from the bleachers. When the music stopped, Mikaso spoke in flawless English: "My friends and fellow Filipinos, we are here to mark a historic end, and a historic beginning, in the relations between the Republic of the Philippines and the United States of America. On this day of freedom and independence, we also mark a significant milestone in the future of the Philippines.

"For over ninety years, we have relied on the courage, the generosity, and the strength of the people of the United States for our security. Such an arrangement has greatly benefited our country and all its people. For this, we will be eternally grateful.

"But we have learned much over these long years. We have studied the sacred values of democracy and justice, and we have strived to become not just a dependency of our good friends in the United States, but a strong, trusted ally. We are here today to celebrate an important final stage of that education, as the people of the Philippines take the reins of authority of our national security responsibilities. We are thankful for the help from our American friends, and we gratefully recognize the sacrifices you have made to our security and prosperity. With your guidance and with God's help, we take the first great step toward being a genuine world power. . . ."

Mikaso spoke eloquently for several more minutes, and when he was done, appreciative applause made its way from the bleachers all the way out beyond the wall, over the crowds.

The people clearly loved their President.

But Teguina listened to the speech and Mikaso's praise for the United States with growing impatience and disgust. He loathed the Americans and had always resented their presence. As for Mikaso, he owed him nothing. He'd agreed to this hybrid coalition only after he'd realized he didn't have enough votes to win the presidency himself.

As taped music was played over the PA system, Mikaso, Stone, and, reluctantly, Teguina, positioned themselves in front of a special set of three flagpoles behind the reviewing stands.

An honor guard stepped onto the stand and positioned themselves around the flagpoles. As Mikaso placed a hand over his heart in tribute, the Philippine flag was lowered a few feet in respect. Then, as "Retreat" was played, the American flag was raised to the top of the staff, then slowly lowered.

"Why is our flag lowered?" Teguina whispered, as if to himself. When no one paid him any attention, he raised his voice: "I ask, why is the Philippine flag lowered first? I do not understand . . ."

"Silence, Mr. Teguina," Mikaso whispered.

"Raise the Philippine flag back to the top of the staff," he said, his voice now carrying clearly over the music. "It is disrespectful for any national flag to be lowered in such a way."

"We are paying honor to the Americans—"

"Bah!" Teguina spat. "They are foreigners returning home, nothing more." But he fell silent as the American flag was lowered and the honor guard began folding it into the distinctive triangle. When the flag was folded, the honor guard passed it to General Stone, who stepped to Arturo Mikaso, saluted, and presented it to him.

"With thanks from a grateful nation, Mr. President," Stone said.

Mikaso smiled. "It will be kept in a place of honor in the capital, General Stone, as a symbol of our friendship and fidelity."

"Thank you, sir."

At that, the two men looked skyward as a gentle roar of jet engines began to be heard.

Flying over the base and directly down the mall over the reviewing stand were four flights of four F-4 Phantom fighters, followed by a flight of three B-52 bombers, all no more than two thousand feet above ground—and everyone could clearly see the twelve Harpoon antiship missiles hanging off the wings of each B-52. The audience in the bleachers applauded and cheered; the crowd outside the gate was restlessly cheering and shouting at the impressive display.

But Daniel Teguina decided he had had enough.

This . . . this American *love feast* was too much for a native Filipino. He pushed past Stone and Mikaso and quickly lowered the Philippine flag from its pole, unclipped it, and reattached it to the empty center pole where the American flag had just been removed.

"What in God's name are you doing, Teguina?" Mikaso shouted over the roar of the planes.

Teguina ordered one of his bodyguards to raise the Philippine flag. He turned, glaring at Stone, and said, "We are not going to defer to Americans any longer. This is our land, our skies, our country—and our flag!"

As the flag traveled up the pole, Stone heard one of the most chilling sounds he'd ever experienced—the screams of fury, anger and, ultimately, jubilation coming from the thousands outside the gates. As the Philippine flag reached the top of the pole, the screams reached a deafening, roaring crescendo.

Teguina and Stone stared long and hard at each other, while President Mikaso began babbling apologies for his First Vice President's behavior.

Thus ended the American presence in the Philippines.

After the ceremonies quickly ended, Rat Stone made his way to the air terminal to supervise the final departure—he still preferred not to call it an evacuation—of American military personnel from Clark Air Base. He couldn't shake the feeling deep in his gut that this cessation of mutual defense arrangements had happened too quickly, too abruptly. The skirmish just last week in the Spratly Islands was still fresh in his mind. And so was the look in Daniel Teguina's eyes . . . it chilled him to the bone.

No, Rat Stone decided, this would not be the last time he would see the Philippines. . . .

The question was when.

HIGH TECHNOLOGY AEROSPACE WEAPONS CENTER (HAWC), NEVADA
MONDAY, 13 JUNE 1994, 0715 HOURS LOCAL

"Tell me this is a joke, sir," Lieutenant Colonel Patrick McLanahan said to Brigadier General John Ormack, "and—with all due respect, of course—I'll beat your face in."

John Ormack, the deputy commander of the High Technology Aerospace Weapons Center—nicknamed HAWC, the Air Force's secret flight-test research center that was a part of the Dreamland complex—didn't have to look at the wide grin on McLanahan's face to know that he wasn't seriously threatening bodily harm to anyone. He could tell by McLanahan's voice, wavering with pure excitement, that the thirty-nine-year-old radar navigator and flight-test project officer was genuinely thrilled. They were standing in front of the newest, most high-tech aircraft in the world, the B-2 stealth bomber. And best of all, for the next several months, this B-2—nicknamed the "Black Knight"—belonged to him.

"No joke, Patrick," Ormack said, putting an arm around McLanahan's broad shoulders. "Don't ask me how he did it, but General Elliott got one of the first B-2A test articles assigned to Dreamland. That's one nice thing about being director of HAWC—Elliott gets to pull strings. This one has been stripped down quite a bit, but it's a fully operational model—this was the bomber that launched the first SRAM-II attack missile a few months back."

"But they just made the B-2 operational," McLanahan pointed out. "They don't have that many B-2s out there—just one squadron, the 393rd, right?"

Ormack nodded.

"What are *we* doing with one?" McLanahan asked.

"Knowing Elliott, he put the squeeze on Systems Command to begin more advanced weapons tests on the B-2, in case they begin full-scale deployment. Air Force stopped deployment, as you know, because of budget cutbacks—but, as we both know, General Elliott's projects aren't under public scrutiny."

Ormack went on. "He was pushing the shift from nuclear to conventional warfighting strategy to Congress, just as Air Force did. It was hard for the Air Force to sell the B-2 as a conventional weapons platform—that is, until Elliott spoke up. He wants to turn this B-2 into another Megafortress—a flying battleship. The man managed to convince the powers-that-be to let him use one for advanced testing.

"Of course we need a senior project officer with bomber experience, experience on EB-series strategic-escort concepts, and someone with a warped imagination and a real bulldog-type attitude. Naturally, we thought of you."

McLanahan was speechless, which made Ormack smile even more. Ormack was an Air Force Academy graduate, medium height, rapidly graying brown hair, lean and wiry, and although he was a command pilot with several thousand hours' flying time in dozens of different aircraft, he was more at home in a laboratory, flight simulator, or in front of a computer console. All of the young men he worked with were either quiet, studious engineers—everyone called them "geeks" or "computer weenies"—or they were flashy, cocky, swaggering test pilots full of attitude because they had been chosen above 99.99 percent of the rest of the free world's aviators to work at HAWC.

McLanahan was neither.

He wasn't an Academy grad, not an engineer, not a test pilot. What McLanahan was was a six-foot blond with an air of understated strength and power; a hardworking, intelligent, well-organized, efficient aviator. The eldest son of Irish immigrants, McLanahan had been born in New York but raised in Sacramento where he attended Air Force ROTC at Cal State and received his commission in 1973. After navigator training at Mather AFB in Sacramento he was assigned to the B-52s of the 320th Bomb Wing there. After uprating to radar navigator, he was again assigned to Mather Air Force Base.

Along the way, McLanahan became the best radar bombardier in the United States, a fact demonstrated by long lines of trophies he'd received in annual navigation and bombing exercises in his six years as a B-52 crew member. His prowess with the forty-year-old bomber, lovingly nicknamed the BUFF (for Big Ugly Fat Fucker) or StratoPig, had attracted the attention of HAWC's commanding officer, Air Force Lieutenant General Brad Elliott, who had brought him to the desert test ranges of Nevada to develop a "Megafortress," a highly modified B-52 used to flight-test high-tech weapons and stealth hardware. Through an unlikely but terrifying chain of events, McLanahan had taken the Megafortress, idiomatically nicknamed the Old Dog, and its ragtag engineer crew into the

Soviet Union to destroy a renegade ground-based antisatellite laser site.

Rather than risk discovery of the highly classified and politically explosive mission, McLanahan had been strongly encouraged to remain at HAWC and, in effect, accept an American high-tech version of the Gulag Archipelago. The upside was that it was a chance to work with the newest aircraft and weapons in the world. McLanahan had happily accepted the position even though it was obvious to all that he had little choice. The Old Dog mission, one of the more deadly events that ultimately drove the Soviet Union to *glasnost,* had to be buried forever—one way or another.

Many successful, career-minded men might have resented the isolation, lack of recognition, and de facto imprisonment. Not Patrick McLanahan. Because he was not an engineer and had very little technical training, his job description for his first years at HAWC consisted mainly of answering phones, acting as aide and secretary for General Elliott and General Ormack, and rewriting tech orders and checklists. But he educated himself in the hard sciences, visited the labs and test centers to talk with engineers, begged and pleaded for every minute of flying time he could, and, more important, performed each given assignment as if it were the free world's most vital research project. Whether it was programming checklists into a cockpit computer terminal or managing the unit's coffee fund and snack bar, Patrick McLanahan did his work efficiently and professionally.

Things began to change very quickly. The Air Force promoted him to Major two years below the zone. He was given an executive officer, then a clerk, than an assistant, a staff, and finally his own office complex, complete with flight-test crews and dedicated maintenance shops. The projects began to change. Instead of being in charge of documentation and records, he was heading more concept teams, then more contractor-MAJCOM liaison jobs, then more subsystem projects, and finally full-weapon systems. Before the ink was dry on his promotion papers to Major, he was promoted to Lieutenant Colonel.

His "exile" was occasionally broken, and the young "fast-burner" was frequently "loaned" with assignments with other research, development, and government agencies, including Border Security Force, Special Operations, and the Aerospace Defense Command. Very soon, McLanahan had become a fixture in any new project dealing with aviation or aerospace. He was now one of the most highly respected program managers in the Department of Defense.

The mission of the High Technology Aerospace Weapons Center had changed as well. With budget cutbacks and greater downsizing in all strategic bombardment units, some place had to be designated to keep all these inactive aircraft until they might be needed again. Although most were sent to the "boneyard," the Air Force Aerospace Maintenance and Restoration Center at Davis-Monthan Air Force Base near Tucson, Arizona, to be stored for spare parts or for scrap, a few were secretly sent to Dreamland, in the desert of central Nevada, for research and special missions.

The place was the Strategic Air Reserve Group, commanded by General Elliott. SARG took the work of the High Technology Aerospace Weapons Center one step further—it created an operational unit out of exotic research experiments. Whereas the Old Dog became an operational mission completely by accident, now other "Old Dogs" were being created and held in reserve until needed. The new Old Dogs collected over the years now included six B-52 bombers; two B-1 bombers—both original A-models; six F-111G fighter-bombers, which were formerly SAC FB-111A strategic bombers; and the newest arrival, McLanahan's B-2 Black Knight bomber.

"The other task you've got is ASIS," Ormack continued. "Air Force is finally considering putting a pilot-trained navigator-bombardier on board the B-2 instead of the current navigator-trained 'mission commander' layout. The cockpit is designed for two pilots; you have to redesign it for a weapons system officer and defensive systems operator, but retain the dual pilot control capability. You've got a few months, no more than four, to get ASIS ready for full-scale production and retrofit, including engineering blueprints and work plan."

He smiled mischievously and added, "The B-2 pilot 'union'

is not too happy about this, as you might expect. They think ASIS is a bunch of crap, that the B-2 is automated enough to not need a navigator, and the B-2 should keep its two pilots. I think our experience with the Old Dog proved otherwise."

McLanahan laughed. "That's an understatement. Now, what's ASIS stand for?"

"Depends on who you ask," Ormack said dryly. "Officially Attack Systems Integration Station. The flight test pilots and B-2 cadre call it something else—in honor of all navigators, of course."

"What's that?"

"*Additional shit inside.*"

McLanahan laughed again. "Figures." Slamming navigators was common fare in this fighter pilot's Mecca in southern Nevada. Still awestruck, he walked toward the huge bat-winged bomber sitting inside the brilliantly lit hangar.

The Black Knight was designed specifically to attack multiple, heavily defended, and mobile targets around the world with high probability of damage and high probability of survival. To fly nearly five thousand miles unrefueled, the B-2 had to be huge—it had the same wingspan as a B-52 and almost the same fuel capacity, able to carry more than its own weight in jet fuel.

In the past, building a bomber of that size meant it was a sitting duck for enemy defenses—a quarter-to-half-million pounds of steel flying around made a very easy target for enemy acquisition and weapons-guidance radars. The B-52, first designed in the 1940s when it was designed to fly at extremely high altitudes, eventually had to rely on flying at tree-top level, electronic jammers and decoys, and plain old circumnavigation of enemy threats to evade attack. The B-58 Hustler bomber relied on flat-out supersonic speed. The FB-111 and B-1 strategic bombers utilized speed, a cleaner "stealthier" design, advanced electronic countermeasures, and terrain-following radar to help themselves penetrate stiff defenses. But, with rapid advances in fighter technology, surface-to-air missiles, and early warning and tracking radars, even the sleek, deadly B-1 would soon be vulnerable to attack.

The black monster before Patrick McLanahan was the latest

answer. The B-2 was still a quarter-million-pound bomber, but most of its larger structural surfaces were made of nonmetallic composites that reduced or reflected enemy radar energy; reflected energy is dispersed in specific narrow beam paths, or lobes, which greatly decreases the strength of the reflected energy. It had no vertical flight-control surfaces that could act as a radar reflector—viewed on edge, it appeared to be nothing more than a dark sliver, like a slender tadpole. Each wing was made of two huge pieces of composite material, joined like a plastic model—that meant there were no structural ribs to break, no rivets attaching the skin to a skeleton, producing an aircraft that was as strong at the wingtips as it was at the fuselage.

Its four turbofan engines were buried within V-shaped wings, which eliminated telltale heat emissions, and engine components were cooled with jet fuel itself to further reduce heat emissions. Its state-of-the-art navigation systems, attack radars, and sensors were so advanced that the B-2 could strike targets several miles before the bomber could be detected by enemy acquisition radars.

The cost of the Black Knight bomber program was staggering—a half billion dollars per plane and nearly eighty billion dollars for an entire fleet, including research, development, and basing. A planned total purchase of one hundred and thirty-two B-2s in five years quickly went away, replaced with an extended procurement deal that would bring only seventy-five bombers on-line over ten years. Even that reduced production rate had been compromised—by April of 1992 there were only twelve fully operational B-2 in the inventory, including the initial three airframes used for testing and evaluation and nine more that had been purchased in 1991. The 1992 and 1993 budgets had carried only "life-support" funding for the B-2—just enough money to keep the program alive while retaining the ability to quickly gear up production if the need arose. Because there would only be seventy-five B-2s active by the turn of the century, the B-52—slated for replacement by the Black Knight—would still be in the active strategic nuclear penetrator arsenal well into the twenty-first century.

But the B-2, despite charges of being a "billion-dollar boondoggle" and obsolete before becoming operational, was now a reality and had proven itself ready to go to war in extensive flight testing. The first Black Knight bomber squadron—the 393rd Bomb Squadron "Tigers"—the same unit that had dropped the atomic bomb on Hiroshima during World War II—had been activated at Whiteman Air Force Base in Missouri a few months earlier, and when that happened, it had rendered billions of dollars' worth of the enemy's military air-defense hardware instantly obsolete.

"Got time for a walkaround, sir?" McLanahan asked.

"You bet," the young Air Force General replied. Ormack let Patrick drink in the sight of the magnificent black bomber before him as Patrick stepped toward it for a walkaround "get-acquainted" inspection.

The B-2 had no fuselage as on more conventional airplanes; it was as if someone had sawed off the wings of a B-52, stuck them together, and put wheels on it. For someone like McLanahan, who was accustomed to seeing the huge, drooping wings of the mighty B-52, it was amazing to notice that the B-2s, which were just as long and easily twice as wide, did not droop one inch—the composite structures were pound-for-pound stronger than steel. The skin was perfectly smooth, with none of the stress wrinkles of the B-52, and it had no antennae attached to the hull that might act as a radar reflector. The plane's "flying wing" design had no vertical flight control surfaces that would create a radar reflector; instead, it achieved stability by a series of split flaps/ailerons on the wing's trailing edges, called "flaperons," which would deflect in pairs or singularly in response to a triple-redundant laser optic flight computer's commands. The unique flaperon flight-control system, plus a thrust ejector system that directed engine exhaust across the flaperons to increase responsiveness, gave the huge bomber the roll response of a small fighter. To prevent any radar image "blooming" when the flaperons were deflected in flight—even the small flaperon deflection caused by a 5-degree turn would increase the radar image size several times—the trailing edge of the B-2's wings were staggered in a zigzag pattern, which prevented any reflected energy from returning directly back to the enemy's radar receiver.

Patrick ducked under the pointed nose on his way back to the double side-by-side bomb bays, the natural part of such an aircraft that would attract any SAC bombardier. The lower part of the nose section on either side of the nose gear had large rectangular windows protected by thick pads. "Are these the laser and IR windows?" Patrick asked Ormack.

"You got it, Patrick," Ormack replied. "Miniature laser spotters/target designators and infrared detectors, slaved to the navigation system. The emitter windows and the cockpit windows are coated with an ultrathin material that allows radar energy to pass through the windows but not reflect back outwards, much like a one-way mirror. This reduces the radar reflectivity caused by energy bouncing off the crew members or equipment inside the plane itself. If allowed to reflect back, the radar return from the pilots' helmets alone can effectively double the B-2's radar signature."

"Where's the navigation radar? Is there one on the B-2?"

"You bet. The Black Knight has an AN/APQ-181 multi-mode radar mounted along the wing leading edges, with ground-mapping, terrain-following, targeting, surveillance, and rendezvous modes—we can even add air-to-air capability to the system . . ."

"Air-to-air on a B-2 bomber?" McLanahan whistled. "You're kidding, right?"

"Not after what we did on the B-52 Old Dog," Ormack replied. "After our work in Dreamland putting antiair missiles on a B-52, I don't think there'll ever be another combat aircraft that can't do a dozen different jobs, and that includes heavy bombers carrying air-to-air weapons. It makes sense—if you can take sixteen to twenty weapons of *any* kind into battle with you, you have the advantage. Besides, the B-2 is no slouch of a hot jet any way you look at it—the B-2 bomber has one–one hundredth the radar cross-section of an F-15 Eagle Fighter, one-twentieth the RCS of an F-23 Wildcat fighter—which means it could engage targets before the other guy even *knows* the B-2 is out there—and at high altitude it has the same roll rate and can pull as many Gs as an F-4 Phantom."

The underside of the B-2 was like a huge dark thundercloud—it seemed to stretch out forever, sucking up every particle of light. Patrick was surprised by what he found—two cavernous weapon bays. "It's a hell a lot bigger than I thought, General," he said.

"Each bomb bay carries one Common Strategic Rotary Launcher filled with eight SRAM short-range attack missiles," Ormack replied. "Sixteen SRAM missiles—it packs quite a wallop. Putting B61 or B83 gravity nuclear bombs on board is still possible as well, although using standoff-type weapons instead of gravity bombs makes the B-2 a much greater threat. The Black Knight can only carry four cruise missiles, so there are no plans to include AGM-129A cruise missiles although we modified the weapon-delivery software to do so."

"It'll make a great battleship escort," McLanahan said. "I think the boss is right—it's a waste to have these babies sitting on the sidelines with nukes on board while we're getting hammered in some non-nuclear dogfight. Air Force talks about 'global reach, global power,' but they don't talk much about how long-range bombers can defend themselves in a hostile environment without an initial nuclear laydown. They talk about sending B-52s from Guam, Diego Garcia, or Loring to anywhere else in the world in twelve hours, but they don't explain how the bomber is supposed to survive its attack. With the Black Knight configured as a counterradar escort, it can do it. It has the range to fly just as deep as the strike bombers, and it carries as much firepower as a B-52. We'll put that new PACER SKY satellite data stuff on it, maybe an ISAR radar, smart bombs . . ."

"We've tested every possible weapon on a B-2," Ormack acknowledged, "from AGM-130 Striker glide-bombs—your personal favorite, I know—Harpoon antiship missiles, sea mines, MK 82 iron bombs, AMRAAM missiles, Sidewinder missiles, the TACIT RAINBOW antiradar cruise missiles, Durandal runaway-cratering bombs, AGM-84 SLAM TV-guided missiles, hell, even photoreconnaissance pods. At half a billion dollars a pop, Congress didn't want to buy a nuclear-only plane, so we're going to demonstrate that the B-2 could be flexible enough for any mission." Ormack shrugged, then

added, "I'm not convinced myself that the B-2 can make a
good defensive escort plane. If a fighter or ground missile site
gets a visual on this thing, you're dead."

"I don't know about that," Patrick said. "I think it'd be tough
to kill in a tactical battle."

"Yeah? Most of the Air Force would disagree," Ormack replied. "Look at these wings—this thing is huge, even when
seen from several thousand feet up. It's subsonic, which makes
it a more inviting target and less elusive. No, I think the Air
Force would forgo risking B-2 on a conventional raid." He
looked at McLanahan for feedback and was surprised when
the young navigator gave him an unsure shrug in reply. "You
still disagree?"

"I haven't flown fighters as long as you, sir," McLanahan
said, "but I have a tough time finding an airport from five
thousand feet in the air, much less a single plane. At five thousand feet, a pilot is looking at almost four hundred square miles
of ground. If he's flying, say, eight miles per minute on a low
combat-air patrol, forty square miles zip under his wings every
ten seconds—twenty on each side of his cockpit. If he can't use
a radar to at least get himself in the vicinity, his detection
problem is pretty complicated."

"If a combat air patrol always had that wide an area to
search, I might agree with you," Ormack said. "But the field
of battle narrows down rapidly. One lucky sighting, one
squeak of a radar detector or one blip on a radar screen, and
suddenly the whole pack's on top of you."

"But I might have my missiles in the air by then," Patrick
said. "If not, I sure as heck will not stay high over a target area.
I've got an infrared camera that can see the ground, and the
pilots have windows—those boys better be flying in the dirt
with fighters on my tail. Even the F-23 advanced tactical
fighter can't fight close to the ground—they have to rely on
taking 'look-down' shots from higher altitudes. That's where a
stealthy plane has the advantage."

Ormack didn't have a reply right away—he was thinking
hard about McLanahan's arguments. "You bring up a few good
points, Patrick," Ormack admitted. "You know what this calls
for, don't you?"

"RED FLAG," McLanahan replied. "No—better yet, the Strategic Warfare Center. General Jarrel's little playland up in South Dakota."

"You got it," Ormack said. "We'll have to put an EB-2 up against a few fighters on Jarrel's range and see what happens. Maybe even have them fly along with other aircraft on the range to see if our escorts can be effective with other strike aircraft." He smiled at McLanahan and added, "I think that can be arranged. We can send you out to the Strategic Warfare Center for some operational test flights when the 393rd Bomb Squadron goes to the SWC in a few months. I'll bring it up to General Elliott, but I think he'll go for it. You might have just found yourself a new job, Patrick—developing penetration and attack techniques for Black Knight stealth escort crews."

"Throw me in the briar patch," McLanahan said as they moved forward to the entry hatch.

McLanahan's new bird was AF SAC 90-007, the seventh B-2 bomber built. He found the plane's nickname, "License to Kill," stenciled on the entry hatch as he and Ormack walked to it and opened it up to climb inside—it was a perfect nickname. Patrick checked that the "Alert Start" switch was off and safed—the B-2 had a button in the entry hatch that would start the bomber's internal power unit and turn on power and air before the pilots reached the cockpit. With this system, the B-2 could have engine started, the inertial navigation system aligned, and the plane taxiing for takeoff in less than three minutes, without any external power carts or crew chiefs standing by. Ormack did activate the "Int Power" switch in the entryway, which activated internal power on the plane.

Unlike the B-1 bomber, whose offensive and defensive stations seemed to have been put in reluctantly, almost haphazardly, the B-2's cockpit was massive. There was almost enough room for McLanahan to stand up straight as he slid into the right seat and began to strap in.

Ormack looked at the young navigator with amusement as he set his seat and even put on a pair of flying gloves. "Going somewhere?"

"You want a redesigned cockpit, sir, then you gotta do it with the crew dog strapped into position," McLanahan replied. "The reach is much different. If I had a helmet, I'd put it on." Ormack nodded his agreement and smiled—as usual, McLanahan was getting right down to business.

The bomber's left instrument panel was like a television director's console. Four color MFDs, or multi-function displays, dominated the instrument panel; each MFD was encircled with buttons that would change the screen's function, allowing hundreds of different displays on each screen. The bomber used small sidestick controllers, like a fighter plane, with throttle quadrants to the left of each seat and the button-festooned control stick to the right. Each seat also had a wide, oval-shaped heads-up display, or HUD, that would project flight and attack information on the windscreen.

"Where're all the instruments?" McLanahan exclaimed with obvious surprise. "There's hardly anything installed in here. Did they give us a stripped-down test article or what?"

"This *is* a fully functional production model, Patrick," Ormack replied. "Everything is done on the MFDs or using switches on the throttles and control stick. The screens show menu choices for selecting options for each piece of equipment, and you just push a button to select it or use the set button on the stick."

"But I don't see any flight-control system switches," McLanahan persisted. "What about a flap lever? Gear handle? How do you raise the landing gear—haul it up with a rope?"

"This is almost the twenty-first century, my friend," Ormack replied. "We don't move levers—we tell the plane what to do and it takes care of it." He pointed to the right-hand MFD at each station, which showed a simple five-line menu: BATT POWER, APU POWER, ALERT START, NORMAL START, and EMER START. Each item was located next to a corresponding button on the screen.

"To start engines, you simply press the button and advance the throttles to idle," Ormack explained. "The computer takes care of everything else. Start engines, and up comes a different menu of items. Select TAKEOFF. The computer configures the plane for takeoff and continues to configure the plane during the climbout and all the way to level off—it'll raise the gear and flaps, monitor the power settings, everything. Once at cruise altitude, you select CRUISE and it'll fly the plane, manage the fuel, and report any errors. It has several different modes, including LANDING, LOW LEVEL, GUST for bad weather conditions, GO AROUND, and ATTACK modes."

"Computerized flying, huh?" McLanahan muttered. "Pretty slick. You almost think they could do away with the pilot and nav."

"It's advance hardware, but not totally foolproof," Ormack said. "The pilot in the loop is still important."

"And the nav in the loop as well," McLanahan said with a smile, examining the right-hand seat. "Or should I say, 'mission commander'? I like the sound of that."

The right-hand instrument panel had boles and slots for the same size and number of color MFDs as the pilot's side, but technicians had already removed the monitors themselves. "This looks like a duplicate of the pilot's side," McLanahan observed.

"I think it is," Ormack said. "The original idea was to have two pilots, remember. They decided it—" As Ormack watched, Patrick suddenly reached down to an awkwardly mounted keyboard on the right bulkhead and pulled it out of its slot. "Hey—!"

"Sir, having these nice color MFDs on the right side for the nav would be fine," McLanahan said, "but it would also be a huge waste. Small MFDs are nice, but they're old technology . . ."

"Old technology? These MFDs are the latest thing—high-resolution, high-speed, one twenty-eight K RAM per pixel, the whole nine yards . . ."

"Compare it with pilot's side," McLanahan said. "Look here. The pilot can sit back, set up a scan, and fly his plane with complete ease and confidence. What does the nav have? The nav has got to focus on one screen at a time to do his job. His eyes lock on one screen—they *have* to, because you got one screen that displays only one set of information. What happens then? He loses track of what's going on around him. He loses situational awareness. Something important might be happening on one of the other screens, but he doesn't know that because he's got to stare at this screen for several seconds. The setup forces him to divert his attention in several different directions at once, and by doing so you make him *less* effective, not more."

"These are the best MFDs available," Ormack said wryly. "You can swap displays around on each screen, split the screens and have two displays on one screen, even have the computer shift displays for you—sort of an autoscan. What's wrong with all that?"

"They're great, but they're outdated," McLanahan repeated. "We can get something better." He shook the keyboard at Ormack, then tossed it over his shoulder. "And no important keyboards on the side instrument panels. If the nav has to take his eyes off the scope on the bomb run, it's no good and it shouldn't be in the plane. That's what gets crews killed."

"We can rig up a swivel arm for the keyboard . . ." Ormack began, but McLanahan was clearly unimpressed. "I don't know exactly what you have in mind, Patrick, but I don't think you can just decide to replace the *entire* avionics suite . . ."

"You want my recommendations, you'll get them," McLanahan said. "You didn't mention any restrictions or specifications, so I'll build you the best cockpit I can think of." He paused for a moment, then said, "And we'll start with the Armstrong Aerospace Medical Research Laboratory at Wright-Pat."

"Armstrong? What . . . ?" And then he realized what Patrick was getting at: "The Super Cockpit program? You want to put one of those big six-square-foot screens in the B-2?"

"Sir, it's tailor-made for the Black Knight," McLanahan said excitedly. "The screen would fit perfectly in this big cockpit, and they can rewrite the software in a matter of months. We can bring it in within a few weeks and have a demo flight within four months, I guarantee it." He paused for a moment, then added, "And once we get Super Cockpit installed, we can install that Sky Masters PACER SKY system General Elliott is working on—real-time satellite target reconnaissance. That'd be awesome. A satellite sending you real-time pictures of a target area, a computer drawing your route of flight, and having it displayed on a huge mother Super Multi-Function Display? Oh, man, this is gonna be great!"

John Ormack thought about the idea for several long moments. He knew McLanahan was nothing if not a walking idea machine, but he never expected him to devise two such radical ideas in so short a time. It was an interesting combination: Super Cockpit was a 1980s technology demonstration program that had never been implemented in any tactical aircraft, and PACER SKY was a brand-new idea that was just now being operationally tested.

Ormack knew Sky Masters' NIRTSats could make combined synthetic radar, infrared, and visual photographs of a geographic area in one pass, uplink it to a satellite, then download it. But uplinking it to a TDRS satellite (Tactical Information Distribution System used by the Army and Air Force) then downloading it to a targeting computer on a strike aircraft was brilliant. The computer would be able to classify each return with known or suspected targets, measure the precise target coordinates, and load them into the crew's bombing computers. The crews could then call up each target, evaluate the information and direct a strike against the targets in virtually real-time.

It would be the first time crews would have access to virtual real-time imagery during a conflict.

Leave it to McLanahan, Ormack thought proudly.

"Jesus, Patrick," Ormack said, "you've already come up with six months' worth of work and you haven't been in the seat five minutes—and you've probably busted the bank as well."

"Well, we can eliminate a lot of this stuff, then," McLanahan said, gesturing to a small shelf under the glare shield. "We can ditch this attempt at a work desk—with the Super Cockpit installed, we won't need charts and books out cluttering the cockpit—but we'll need coffee-cup holders, of course . . ."

"Coffee-cup holders!" Ormack cried. McLanahan's extraordinary capacity for coffee was well known throughout Dreamland. "On a B-2? Get outta here!"

"You think I'm kidding, sir?" McLanahan replied. "I'll bet you lunch for a week that there's not only coffee-cup holders for the pilot over there, but a pencil-holder and maybe even an approach-plate holder. How about it?"

"You're on, buddy," Ormack said. "Coffee-cup holders on multimillion-dollar warplanes went out with khaki uniforms and nose art. Besides, everything on this plane is computerized—why would the pilots need pencils and approach plates when everything's on the multi-function displays in living color?"

Ormack searched the aircraft commander's station for a moment as McLanahan confidently sat back in his seat and waited. A few moments later he heard a muttered, "Well, I'll be damned . . ."

"Find something, General?"

"I don't believe it!" Ormack shouted. "Chart holders, pencil holders, coffee-cup holders—no ashtray, hotshot . . . unbelievable."

"Let me guess," McLanahan teased, "there's a space up there for an inflight lunch box?"

"Box lunches and even a stopwatch holder. I just don't believe it. There are twenty systems on this plane that'll give you a countdown. The plane practically flies itself, for God's sake! If you want, a female electronic voice'll even give you a countdown over interphone. But they went ahead and put in a black rubber stopwatch holder anyway."

"The Air Force probably paid a thousand dollars for it, too," McLanahan added dryly. "The more things change, the more they stay the same. We'll have developed a hypersonic bomber that can circumnavigate the globe in one hour, and someone'll still put a stopwatch holder in the cockpit."

Ormack tried to ignore McLanahan's smug smile. "Well, you've got your work cut out for you over here, that's for sure, but you've made a terrific start. When can you get to work?"

"Right away, General," McLanahan replied. "The F-15F Cheetah project is off the flight line for a few months, so this'll work out perfectly. I've got a staff meeting with J. C. Powell and McDonnell-Douglas in about an hour, and I'll clear the desk and schedule an afternoon staff meeting on this project. We'll be back out here taking measurements"—he paused, then gave Ormack a sly smile—"right after we get back from lunch. Your treat, I believe?"

THREE

"Good morning, sir," Navy Captain Rebecca Rodgers, senior staff officer, Pacific, of J-2, the Joint Chiefs of Staff Intelligence Directorate, began. "Captain Rodgers with this morning's intelligence report. The briefing is classified top secret, sensitive sources and methods involved, not releasable to foreign nationals; the room is secure." She paused to double-check that the thick mahogany double doors to the Pentagon's Joint Chiefs of Staff Conference Center, referred to as the "Tank" or the "Gold Room," were closed and locked and that the red "Top Secret" lights were on. Rebecca "Becky" Rodgers could feel the tension of the men and women in the Tank that morning, and her news was not going to help to cheer them up one bit.

Captain Rodgers was at the briefer's podium at the base of the Tank's large, triangle-shaped conference table where everyone could see her and the screen clearly. It was a most imposing and decidedly uncomfortable spot—seven of the most senior, most powerful military men on the planet watching her, waiting for her, no doubt evaluating her performance every moment. The first few sessions in this room had been devastating for her. But that was a half-dozen crises ago, and it seemed like old hat now. She didn't need the old trick of trying to imagine the Joint Chiefs naked to get through her nervousness—the fact that she knew something that these powerful men and women did *not* know was comfort enough.

Present for the briefing was JCS Chairman General Wilbur Curtis; the Vice Chairman, Marine Corps General Mario Lanuza; the Chief of Naval Operations Admiral Randolph Cunningham; Commandant of the Marine Corps General Robert Peterson; Air Force Chief of Staff General William Falmouth; and Army Chief of Staff General John Bonneville, plus their aides and representatives from the other J-staff directorates. Curtis insisted on attendance by all Joint Staff members and directorates for these daily briefings—it was probably the only opportunity for the staff to get together as a team during their busy week.

The Chairman sat at the blunted apex of the triangle, with seats available beside him at the head of the table for the Secretary of Defense and the President of the United States if they chose to attend, although in his two years of office, the President had never set foot in this place. The four-star Joint Staff members and their aides and staffers sat on the Chairman's left, the J-staff directorate representatives on the right, and guests and briefers at the base of the triangle near the back. Each seat had a small communications console and computer/TV monitor embedded in the table, which was fed from the giant Global Military Communications, Command, Control, and Intelligence Network operations center on another level of the Pentagon. The back wall of the Tank was a large rear-projection screen. Arranged above it was a series of red LED digital clocks with various times, and several members of the staff, by force of habit after long years aloft or at sea, gave themselves a time hack from those ultra-precise clocks every morning.

"The number-one topic I have for you today is the Philippines and South China Sea incidents," Rodgers said after concluding her routine force status briefings. "In response to the attack on an oil-exploration barge a few months ago in the neutral zone in the Spratly Island chain, both the Philippines and China have stepped up naval activity in the area.

"Specifically, the Chinese have not added any new forces except for a few smaller shallow patrol boats. They have a very strong contingent there, including the destroyer *Hong Lung*, which carries the Hong Qian-91 surface-to-air missile system, the Fei Lung-7 and Fei Lung-9 antiship missile systems, and a good complement of dual-purpose guns. Additionally, they have two frigates, four patrol boats, some minesweepers, and other support vessels. They usually detach into three smaller patrol groups, with a missile craft leading two groups and *Hong Lung* and its escorts comprising the third. Vessels from the South Sea fleet, headquartered at Jhanjiang, rotate with the ships about once per month; however, *Hong Lung* rotates very seldom. Their base on Spratly Island is very small, but they can land medium-size cargo aircraft there to resupply their vessels.

"The Filipinos have substantially increased their presence in the Spratly Islands following the attack on the oil barge. They have sent two of their three frigates into the disputed area and are now patrolling their section vigorously with both sea and air assets.

"But despite the naval buildup, the Philippine naval fleet is practically nonexistent," Rodgers concluded. "All of their major combatants are old, slow, and unreliable. The crews are generally not well trained and rarely operate more than a day's cruise away from their home ports."

"So without the United States forces to back them up, they're sitting ducks for the Chinese," Admiral Cunningham said.

"Sir, the Chinese fleet is not that much more advanced than the Philippine fleet, at least the vessels that operate near the Spratly Islands," Rodgers said. "Most are small, lightly armed patrol boats. The exception, of course, is the flagship, *Hong Lung*. It is without question the most capable warship in the entire South China Sea, comparable in performance to U.S. Kidd-class destroyers but faster and lighter. The frigates are heavily armed as well; most have HQ-61 SAM missiles, which would be very effective against the Filipino helicopters and may even be capable against the Sea Ray antiship missile. All are comparable in performance to U.S. Oliver Hazard Perry–class frigates, except without helicopter decks or the sophisticated electronics.

"The main Chinese offensive thrust would obviously be their overwhelming ground forces—they could land several hundred thousand troops in the Philippines in very short order," Rodgers concluded. "Although we generally classify the Chinese Navy as smaller and less capable than ours, their naval forces are very capable of supporting and protecting their ground troops. An amphibious assault on the Philippines by the Chinese would be concluded very quickly, and it would push the necessary threshold of an American counterstrike to very high levels—very much along the lines of our DESERT SHIELD deployment, although without the advantage of forward basing."

"So if the Chinese want to take the Spratly Islands, there's not much we could do about it," General Falmouth summarized.

"Sir, at the current force levels in the area, if the Chinese wanted to take the Philippines, there would be little we could do about it . . ."

There was a very animated murmur of voices at that comment. Curtis was the first to raise his voice above the others: "Wait one, Captain. Is this a J-2 assessment or an opinion?"

"It is not a directorate finding, sir, but it is nevertheless a statement of fact," Rodgers replied. "If they so decided, it would take the People's Liberation Army Navy less than a week . . ."

"Ridiculous . . ."

"They wouldn't dare . . ."

"Absurd . . ."

"According to the directorate's preliminary report, sir," Rodgers explained, getting their attention, "if the Chinese captured five strategic military bases—the naval facilities at Subic Bay and Zamboanga, the Air Force bases at Cavite and Cebu, and the Army base at Cagayan de Oro—and if they defeated Second Vice President Samar's militia at Davao, they could secure the entire country." She paused, then looked directly at them. "Gentlemen, the New Philippine Army is nothing more than a well-equipped police force, not a defense force. They have relied on the United States for its national defense—and obviously would have to again, if the need arose. General Samar's Commonwealth Defense Force is a well-trained and well-organized guerrilla-fighting force, but they cannot stand up against a massive invasion. The Chinese have a thirty-to-one advantage in all areas."

General Wilbur Curtis surveyed his Chiefs of Staff with a look of concern—the information Captain Rodgers had just conveyed had silenced them all. He had heard a lot of bad news during the past six years that he'd chaired the Joint Chiefs. He had learned to quickly decipher between isolated incidents and incidents that had a broader, far more serious impact if left untended. He knew the implications of what Rodgers was saying could be far more serious than any of them had previously thought.

"I think we all wanted to believe this was just another skirmish. But with the United States out of the Philippines, there is a large power vacuum in the area. We knew there'd be that danger. Still, I don't think anyone believed the Chinese would consider moving so soon—if they really are." Curtis turned to Captain Rodgers again and asked, "Are the Chinese likely to attempt an invasion?"

"Sir, if the Joint Chiefs would like a detailed briefing, I should get Central Intelligence involved," Rodgers said. "I had been concentrating on the military aspects and hadn't prepared a full briefing on the political situation. But J-2 does feel that the Philippines are ripe for the picking."

Curtis waited for additional thoughts from the Joint Chiefs; when there appeared to be no concrete suggestions, he said, "I'd like to review the current OPLANS for dealing with a possible Chinese action in the Philippines, then. I need to know what plans we have built already, and if they need to be updated. Captain Rodgers, I'd like Central Intelligence to get involved, and I'd like Current Operations to draft a response plan that I can present to the Secretary of Defense for his review. Include a Philippines update in the daily briefings, including satellite passes and a rundown on naval activity in the Spratlys and in the Chinese South China Sea fleet. Let's get on top of this thing and have a plan of action *before* it threatens to blow up in our faces."

HIGH TECHNOLOGY AEROSPACE WEAPONS CENTER (HAWC)
DREAMLAND, NEVADA
WEDNESDAY, 17 AUGUST 1994, 0905 HOURS LOCAL

The phone line crackled. "Brad! How the hell are you?"

Lieutenant General Brad Elliott leaned back in his chair and smiled broadly as he recognized the caller. "I was expecting you to send young Andy Wyatt out here to harass me again, sir, but I'm glad to hear from you."

"Can the 'sir' stuff with me, you old warhorse," Chairman of the Joint Chiefs of Staff Wilbur Curtis said over the snaps and crackles in the scrambled phone line. "You know better. Besides, it's been a long time since we've spoken. When are we going to get together?"

"I have a feeling it'll be soon, my friend. I've been getting calls from half the J-staff, a bunch of calls from Space Command—you *had* to be the next caller. Let me guess—you want some air time on some satellites of mine."

"Now how the hell did you know that?"

"Every time I build a new toy, you want it, that's how I know it."

"That's why you're out there, you stupid bastard. You're supposed to be developing toys for us to play with, not polishing your three stars. Stop whining."

"I'm not, believe me." Elliott chuckled. "I assume you want to use the new Masters NIRTSats, the ones that can downlink radar, infrared, and visual imagery all in one pass in real-time both to the ground stations and aircraft. Right?"

"You're not telepathic are you?" Curtis joked. "They tell me you can receive satellite images on your B-2 bomber as well as your B-52 Megafortress?"

"We flight-test PACER SKY at the Strategic Warfare Center in a couple weeks," Elliott said, "but ground tests have gone really well. Let me guess some more: you want pictures of a certain area, but don't want to use DSP or LACROSSE satellites because you don't want certain superpower countries to know you're interested. Am I close?"

"Frightfully close," Curtis said. "We're watching a Chinese naval buildup in the South China Sea. We think they might be getting ready to plug away at either the Spratlys or the Philippines. If we send a DSP or KH-series bird over the area, we risk discovery."

"The Philippines? You mean the Chinese might try an invasion?"

"Well, let's hope not," Curtis said. "The President is a big fan of President Mikaso's. We've been expecting something like this for years, ever since we realized there was a good possibility we were going to get kicked out of the Philippines—now it might actually happen. We've got our pants pretty much down around the ankles as far as Southeast Asia goes right now. What with the buildup in the Persian Gulf and the closing of a bunch of bases overseas, we've got zilch out there . . ."

"Well, if you need the pictures, you got 'em," Elliott said, running his hand across the top of his hair. "We can transmit the digitized data to J-2, or Jon Masters can set up one of his terminals right on your desk there—providing you don't keep stretching your secretary out over it all the time."

"My secretary is a fifty-year-old Marine Corps gunnery sergeant that could grind us both down into little nubs, you old lech." Curtis laughed. "No, transmit it to J-2 and J-3 out here at the Pentagon soonest. They'll give you a call and tell you exactly what they want . . ."

"I know what you want, sir," Elliott said.

"Hey, don't be so sure, big shot," Curtis said. "Man, some guys—they get on the fast track, tool around the White House for a few months, and it goes right to their heads. And stop calling me sir. You'd have four stars, too, if you'd climb up out of that black hole you've built for yourself out there and join the real world again."

"What? Leave Dreamland and miss the opportunity for some first-class, four-star abuse? No way." Elliott gave his old friend a loud laugh and hung up.

U.S. AIR FORCE STRATEGIC WARFARE CENTER
ELLSWORTH AFB, SOUTH DAKOTA

"Room, ten-HUT!"

Two hundred men and women in olive drab flight suits moved smartly to their feet as Air Force Brigadier General Calvin Jarrel and his staff entered the auditorium briefing room. The scene could have been right out of *Patton* except for the ten-foot-square electronic liquid-crystal screen onstage with the Strategic Air Command emblem in full color, showing an armored fist clutching an olive branch and three lightning bolts. Otherwise it looked like the setting for countless other combat-mission briefings from years past—except these men and women, all SAC warriors, weren't going to war . . . at least not yet.

It was easy to mistake General Cal Jarrel for just another one of the four hundred or so crew dogs at the Air Force Strategic Warfare Center, and that was just fine with him. Jarrel was an unimposing five foot eleven, one-hundred-sixty-pound man, with boyish brown hair and brown eyes hidden behind standard-issue aluminum-framed aviator's spectacles. Many of those close to the General thought that he was uncomfortable with the trappings of a general officer, and everyone on the base agreed that at the very least he was the most visible one-star anyone had ever known. On the flight line or on the indoor track in the base gym, he could be seen jogging early each morning with a crowd of several dozen staffers and visitors, which was how he kept his slight frame lean and trim despite an ever-increasing amount of time flying a desk instead of a B-52 Stratofortress, B-1B Excalibur, or F-111G Super 'Vark bomber. He was married to an environmental-law attorney from Georgia and was the harried father of two teenage boys.

Like many of the men and women in the Strategic Air Command of the mid-1990s, Jarrel appeared studious, introspective, unobtrusive, and soft-spoken—unlike their hotshot fighter-pilot colleagues, it was as if they understood that the awesome responsibility of carrying two-thirds of the nation's nuclear deterrent force was something that was not to be advertised or bragged about.

Certainly, the critics thought, SAC's twenty thousand aircrew members had little to boast about and nothing to look forward to for the next century—the fifty B-2s and one hundred rail-garrisoned Peacekeeper ICBMs planned to be operational by then might very well be the only nuclear-armed weapons in SAC's inventory. Virtually all of the B-52s, B-1B bombers, cruise missiles, and reconnaissance aircraft were rumored to be headed for conventionally armed tactical-support roles, in the inactive reserves—or, worse, in the boneyard.

It was a winding-down period for SAC, which created questions about readiness, training, and motivation. That's where Jarrel's Strategic Warfare Center School, and the Air Battle Force, came in.

"Seats," General Cal Jarrel said in a loud voice as he made his way to the stage. The aircrew members in the room took their seats and restlessly murmured comments among themselves as Jarrel stepped up to the podium. He was there to give the welcoming speech to a new crop of aircrew members that were to begin an intensive three-week course on strategic air combat—SAC's "graduate school" on how to fly and fight. As was the case for the past year since becoming director of the Strategic Warfare Center, he had to convince each and every one of these men and women of the importance of what they were about to learn—and, in a very real sense, to convince the rest of the country and perhaps himself as well.

Lieutenant Colonel McLanahan listened to General Jarrel's comments, sitting on the edge of his auditorium seat. All around him were stealth bomber crews, who, like him, were there to attend the Strategic Warfare Center school.

When General Jarrel acknowledged the B-2 crews in his opening remarks, a ripple of applause—and a few Bronx cheers—passed over the crowd for the B-2 crews.

This is where I belong, McLanahan thought: in a flight suit, getting briefed with these other crew dogs. He had, he realized, been isolated at Dreamland far too long. Sure, he was one of the most dedicated and successful aircrew members and weapon-systems project managers in the entire military. But where had that gotten him? Flying a battle-scarred B-52 fully renovated with modern hardware deep into Soviet airspace to knock out Russia's state-of-the-art armaments? It should have been the most rewarding mission in his career. Instead it had landed him at HAWC, where he'd been ever since. But flying was in his blood. McLanahan knew the score—because of the highly classified nature of his work he'd probably never get beyond 0-6 (Colonel), or if he was lucky, 0-7 (Brigadier-General). But at least they were letting him fly a dream plane. The only problem was he couldn't tell anyone about it. His cover story was that he was "observing" the school for the Pentagon. Still . . . he was here. And the real excitement was coming. . . .

General Jarrel was well into his talk.

"SAC is being tasked with much more than delivering nuclear weapons—we are being tasked with providing many different elements of support for a wide variety of conflict scenarios," Jarrel went on, speaking without a script and from his heart as well as from the numerous times he'd given this speech.

"The way we do it is through the Air Battle Force," Jarrel continued. "From this moment on, you are not members of any bomb squadron, or fighter squadron, or airlift group—you are members of the First Air Battle Wing. You will learn to fly and fight as a team. Each of you will have knowledge of not only his or her own capabilities, but those of your colleagues. The Air Battle Force marks the beginning of the first truly integrated strike force—several different weapon systems, several different tactical missions, training, deploying, and fighting together as one.

"Because the Air Battle Force concept is new and not yet fully operational, we have to disband each task force class and return you to your home units. When you leave this Center, you will still belong to the Air Battle Force, and you are expected to continue your studies and perfect your combat skills from within your own units. If a crisis should develop, you can be brought back here to be placed back within the Air Battle Force system, ready to form the Second or Third Air Battle

Wings. Eventually, Air Battle Wings will be formed on a full-time basis for extended tours."

Jarrel talked for several more minutes, giving the history of the Strategic Warfare Center's mission, which since 1989 had conducted strategic combat training exercises through sorties that were spread over three thousand miles of low- and high-altitude military training routes over nine Midwestern states.

When he had finished, he said, "All right, ladies and gentlemen, get out there and show us how a strategic battle can be fought by America's best and brightest!"

The auditorium erupted in cheers, and somewhere in the middle of the crowd, Patrick McLanahan was cheering the loudest.

Late one night a couple of days after General Jarrel's Strategic Warfare Training Program was under way, Brigadier General John Ormack, who had come with Cobb, McLanahan, the EB-52 and B-2 bombers, and the rest of the support crew from HAWC, found Patrick McLanahan sitting in the cockpit of his Black Knight. External power and air had been hooked up, and McLanahan was reclining in the mission commander's seat with a computer-generated chart of the Strategic Training Range Complex on the three-by-two-foot Super Multi Function Display before him. Patrick had a headset on and was issuing commands to the B-2's sophisticated voice-recognition computer; he was so engrossed in his work—or so deep in daydream, Ormack couldn't quite tell which—that the HAWC vice commander was able to spend a few moments watching his junior chief officer from just behind the pilot's seat.

The guy had always been like this, Ormack remembered—a little spacy, quiet, introverted, always preferring to work alone even though it was a genuine pleasure being around him and he seemed to enjoy working with others. He had the ability to tune out all sound and activity around him and to focus all his attention and brainpower on the matter at hand, whether that was a mission-planning chart, a bomb run at Mach one and a hundred feet off the ground, or a Voltron cartoon on television. But ever since arriving here at Ellsworth, McLanahan had become even more hardworking, even more focused, even more tuned out—to everything else but the task at hand, which was completing the curriculum at the Strategic Warfare Center and the Air Battle Force with the highest possible grade. Even though McLanahan himself was not being "graded" because the HAWC crews were not official participants, he was slamming away at the session as if he were a young captain getting ready to meet a promotion board. It was hard to tell if Patrick was working this hard because he enjoyed it or because he was trying to prove to himself and others that he could still do the job. . . .

But that was Patrick McLanahan.

Ormack stepped over the center console and into the left-side pilot's seat. McLanahan noticed him, straightened himself up in his seat, and slid the headsets off. "Hey, sir," McLanahan greeted him. "What brings you here this evening?"

"Looking for you," Ormack said. He motioned to the SMFD. "Route study?"

"A little mission planning with the PACER SKY processor," McLanahan said. "I fed the STRC attack route through the system to see what it might come up with, and it turns out if we attack this target here from the west instead of from the northeast, the MUTES in Powder River MOA site won't see us for an extra twenty-one seconds. We've got to gain sixty seconds after the Baker bomb site to get the extra time to get around to the west, so we'll lose a few points on timing, but if this works we'll gain even more points on bomber defense." He shook his head as he flipped through the computer-generated graphics on the big screen. "The rest of the crews in the Air Battle Force would kill me if they knew I had something like PACER SKY doing my mission planning."

"That reminds me," Ormack said. "General Elliott got a tasking for NIRTSat time for a Joint Chiefs surveillance operation. Something to do with what's going on in the Philippines. You might get tapped to show your stuff for the J-staff."

"Fine. I'll water their eyes."

"The guard said you've been up here for three hours working on this," Ormack said. "You spent three hours just to save
twenty seconds on one bomb run?"

"Twenty seconds—and maybe I take down a target without
getting 'shot' at." He motioned to the SMFD and issued a
command, which caused the scene to go into motion. A B-2
symbol on the bottom of the screen began reading along an
undulating ribbon over low hills and dry valleys. Dead ahead
was a small pyramid symbol of a target complex—small "signposts" on the ribbon marked off seconds and miles to go to
weapon release. Off to the right of the screen, a yellow dome
suddenly appeared. "There's the threat site at one o'clock, but
this hillock blocks me out from the west—whoever surveyed
the site for positioning this MUTES site obviously didn't think
crews would deviate this far west."

The computerized mission "preview" continued as the yellow dome began to grow, eventually engulfing the B-2 bomber
icon and turning red. McLanahan pointed to a countdown
readout. "Bingo—I release weapons ten seconds after I come
under lethal range of the MUTES site. If I carry antiradar
missiles, I can pick him off right now, or I just turn westbound
around the hillock to escape."

Ormack nodded in fascination at the presentation, but he
was more interested in studying McLanahan than watching
the computer. "There's quite a party at the O-Club, Patrick,"
he said. "This is your last night of partying before the weekend,
and a lot of your old cronies from Ford Air Force Base asked
about you. Why don't you knock off and join us?"

McLanahan shrugged and began reconfiguring the SMFD
for another replay. "Crew rest starts in about an hour . . ."

"One beer won't hurt. I'll buy."

McLanahan hesitated, then glanced at Ormack and shook
his head. "I don't think so, sir . . ."

"Something wrong, Patrick? Something you're not telling
me?"

"No . . . nothing's wrong." Patrick hesitated, then issued
voice commands to the computer to shut down the system. "I
just . . . I don't really feel part of them, you know?"

"No, I don't."

"These guys are the real crew dogs, the real aviators," Patrick said. "They're young, they're talented, they're so cocky they think they can take on the whole world."

"Just like you were when I first met you," Ormack said with a laugh. "We used to think you had an attitude, but that was before we knew how good you really were." He looked at McLanahan with a hint of concern. "You were pretty excited about coming to the Strategic Warfare Center, about getting back to the 'real world' . . ."

"But I'm not back," Patrick said. "I'm farther from them than I ever thought I'd be. I feel like I've abandoned them. I feel like I should be out there pulling a crew or running a bomb-nav shop, but instead I'm . . ." He shrugged again, then concluded, "Like I'm playing around with gadgets that probably won't have anything to do with the 'real world' . . ."

"That's not what you're down about," Ormack said. "I know you better than that. You're down because you somehow don't think you deserve what you've got. I see you around your buddies out there: they're old captains or majors, and you're a lieutenant colonel; they're still on line crews, flying dawn patrols and red eyes and pulling alert, doing the same thing they did ten years ago, while you're flying starships that most of those guys will never see in their careers, let alone *fly*—they're talking about their last bomb-competition mission or their last Operational Readiness Inspection, while your job is so classified that you can't talk about it at all. You're down because you can't share what you have with them, so you hole yourself up in here thinking that maybe you don't really have what it takes to be a good crew dog.

"Patrick, you're where you are because you're the best. You did more than be chosen for a job: you excelled, you never gave up, you survived, and you saved others. Then when we stuck you in Dreamland to keep you quiet, you didn't just vegetate until completing your twenty years—you excelled again and made yourself invaluable to the organization.

"You deserve what you have. You earned it. You should go out and enjoy it. And you should also buy your boss a beer before he drags your ass out of this cockpit. Now move it, Colonel."

NEAR PHU QUI ISLAND, IN THE SPRATLY ISLAND CHAIN
SOUTH CHINA SEA
THURSDAY, 22 SEPTEMBER 1994, 2344 HOURS LOCAL

The number-two task force of Admiral Yin Po L'un's Spratly Island flotilla was again cruising within radar range of Phu Qui Island, the large rock and coral formation in the disputed neutral zone between the Philippine-occupied islands to the north and the Chinese-held islands to the south. Unlike the more powerful ten-ship task force that surrounded Admiral Yin's flagship, this one had only four ships—two Hainan-class patrol boats, a Lienyun-class minesweeper, and a Huangfen-class fast attack missile craft, the *Chagda,* which acted as the command vessel for this faster, shallow-draft patrol group.

Commander Chow Ti U, skipper of the *Chagda,* felt uneasy with his latest series of orders. It had been over three months since the attack on the Philippine oil-drilling barge, and the tension in the region had been escalating on a weekly basis. Now it was so thick one could cut it with a knife—and much of the heightened tensions could be directly attributed to the way Admiral Yin had handled the entire affair.

Despite what was originally and officially reported, Yin had departed the area after attacking the oil barges; his contention that the seas were too rough to begin rescue operations did not sit well with anyone. When the weather cleared, it was found that Yin had steamed back to the Chinese side of the neutral zone, well away from Phu Qui Island—again, his contention that he was concerned about retaliatory attacks from Philippine warships did not explain why he did not offer to assist in rescue operations.

Chow would never say so to anyone, but Yin's actions could be characterized as unprofessional, exhibiting a total disregard for the rules of naval warfare, international law, and common decency between sailors. Chow felt that the Admiral had every right to confront the illegally placed oil-drilling rig, and he was well within his responsibilities when he returned fire—even such devastating return fire as he used. But to simply slink away from the area without offering any help or without radioing for help was very suspicious.

Since then, while there'd been no skirmishes, there had been a few close calls. Everyone was on edge, looking, waiting, wondering. . . . Chow and his fellow Chinese crewmen privately felt it was only a matter of time before something else happened, and after witnessing the way Admiral Yin had handled the first skirmish, everyone was skittish about how he would proceed in an escalated conflict.

"Range to Phu Qui Island, navigator," Chow called out.

His crewmen were obviously keeping very close track themselves, for the answer was almost instantaneous: "Sir . . . we are presently twenty-five kilometers southwest of Phu Qui Island. We will be in radar range within minutes."

"Very well," Chow grunted. Twenty-five kilometers—they were right on the edge of the neutral zone—perhaps inside it by no more than a kilometer. Unlike Admiral Yin, Chow had no intention of tempting fate by openly cruising the neutral zone. Pearson Reef was indisputably the property of the People's Republic of China, so he would stay close to it. His radar could survey enough of the neutral zone to check for any other intruders.

Still . . . he was uneasy. Perhaps because Admiral Yin chose not to continue operating his larger, more powerful task force along the border as before—but had instead chosen to operate farther south, well in undisputed Chinese waters. The first explanation was, of course, that Yin had been ordered to keep away from the neutral zone, but as weeks went by, the rumor was that Yin simply did not want to risk the wrath of the Philippine Navy and put his precious flagship *Hong Lung* in harm's way. Instead, he had ordered Chow's smaller, less powerful, less capable task force to patrol the area. Admiral Yin's task force was seventy-two kilometers to the southwest, fairly close to Nansha Dao Island itself, which meant Yin was in very real danger of running aground in the shallow waters. Commander Chow's force was better suited for those interreef patrols—but if that was where the Admiral preferred to stay . . .

"Surface contact, sir," an officer in the Combat section of the bridge crew blurted out. "Bearing, zero-five-zero degrees, range twenty kilometers. Speed zero." Chow turned to the plotting board as another crewman penciled in the contact on the clear Plexiglas board.

Phu Qui Island.

"Confirm that contact," Chow ordered. "Make sure you're not painting the island itself." But he knew it was not possible for his radar to paint the shallow, half-submerged outline of a coral "island" at this extreme range. Someone was on or near the disputed island. The Filipino salvage crews, along with the inevitable warships, had long since departed—there had been no large vessels near the island now for several weeks. Since Yin's attack, ships transiting the neutral zone, including Chow's small task force, had been careful to report their movements to the governments of each country that had claims on the islands—Chow had a list of every ship that planned on plying these waters in the next several days.

There had been no reports of any vessels that sought to anchor on Phu Qui Island.

"Radar confirms contact as a vessel," the Combat officer replied a few moments later. "Definite cultural return. Unable to get an ISAR reading on the contact, but it is not terrain or sea shadows." ISAR, or Inverse Synthetic Aperture Radar, was a new feature of the "Square Tie" surface-search radar that could combine vertical and horizontal radar scans with Doppler-frequency shift information to get a two-dimensional "picture" of a surface return; ISAR could usually identify a vessel at ten to fifteen miles, well beyond visual range.

Commander Chow hesitated—he couldn't believe the Filipinos would actually attempt to set up their oil-drilling rigs on the island again. It was tantamount to a declaration of war. He was also reluctant to cruise farther into the neutral zone without specific orders from Admiral Yin. Let *him* take the responsibility for another attack.

"Send a FLASH emergency message to Dragon," he finally ordered his officer of the deck. He could feel the first prickles of tension-heated sweat forming on the back of his neck, and it wasn't from the humidity. "Inform him of our radar contact. We will stand by for instructions." He paused momentarily, then added, "Send the minesweeper *Guangzou* from present position northwest and secure the north and northeast axis. If we have to move toward Phu Qui, I want the lane clear. I give specific orders for *Guangzou* to enter the neutral zone on my authority; record the order in the log." The minesweeper, although based on a Shanghai-class patrol boat, had no offensive armament except small-caliber machine guns and could not be considered a warship; therefore sending a minesweeper alone into the neutral zone could not be considered a hostile act.

The officer of the deck issued the orders; then: "Sir, I suggest we request the helicopter on *Hong Lung* be sent to investigate the contact ahead of the task force. It would be much less threatening to whoever is on Phu Qui Island."

"We will be ordered to move closer to Phu Qui Island whether we see what is out there or not," Chow predicted. "But it's a good suggestion. Get it in the air."

They did not have to wait long for the order: "Message from Dragon, sir," the officer of the deck reported. " 'Task force two is hereby ordered to cross into the neutral zone immediately. Investigate contact on Phu Qui Island with all possible speed, identify all intruders, detain all persons. Peacetime rules of engagement in effect—do not fire unless fired upon, but repel assaults with all available resources. Helicopter will be dispatched immediately to assist. Dragon task force en route to your location. ETA two-point-three hours.' Message ends."

"Very well," Chow replied, nodding confidently and pumping his voice up with as much enthusiasm as he could muster. "Sound silent general quarters, repeat, silent general quarters. Relay to all vessels, go to silent general quarters."

It was a fairly calm night, and the noise of alarm bells and sirens going off might very well be heard twenty kilometers away. This was the first time that Commander Chow had ever faced a real confrontation between two powerful, hostile navies, and so far his thin, forty-six-kilogram body was not taking the excitement too well. His stomach was making fluid, nervous rumblings.

"Have *Guangzou* complete a zigzag pattern along the zero-five-degree bearing from us, then begin a search pattern direct to Phu Qui Island. Transition *Yaan* and *Baoji* into trail and forward-scan each flank for signs of intruders." He was glad when his officer of the deck and the rest of the bridge crew went about their duties—he was feeling worse by the minute. He had never experienced seasickness in his sixteen years in the People's Revolutionary Army Navy, but this time, at the worst possible moment, he just might. . . .

He tried to ignore his stomach and ordered his ships in the best formation in which to approach a hostile island. The mine-sweeper would execute a zigzag pattern in front of *Chagda* perhaps a kilometer wide, clearing the path of any hidden mines while maintaining good forward speed toward the target. With his two Hainan-class patrol boats in trail position, one behind the other and spaced about a kilometer apart, whoever was on that island might not detect the two trailing vessels until the shooting started. The two patrol boats, each one configured for both antiaircraft and antisubmarine warfare, would be scanning the skies and seas ahead and to each side of the formation, searching for hostile aircraft, ships or submarines.

"All ships are at general quarters," the officer of the deck reported with a bow. Chow was just donning his life jacket and baseball cap, in lieu of a combat helmet. "All ship's weapons manned and report ready."

"Very well. I want range to Phu Qui Island every kilometer," Chow ordered. "Have the vessels maintain ten knots until—"

"Sir! Acquisition radar detected, bearing zero-five-zero," Combat reported.

"Well, what in blazes is it? Analysis! Quickly!"

There was another interminable delay; then: "C-band acquisition, sir . . . probably Sea Giraffe 50, OPS-37, SPS-10 or -21 surface-search system . . . slow scan rate . . . Calling it an SPS-10 now, sir . . ." Chow scowled at the reports from his Combat section; they were rattling off Swedish and Japanese radar systems when they knew that the only C-band radar in the Spratlys had to be Filipino.

"Nineteen kilometers to Phu Qui Island and closing," came the range report from the navigation officer. "Speed ten knots."

"Negros Oriental class," the officer of the deck announced. "Latest intelligence reports had the *Nueva Viscaya* putting out to sea. It may have arrived here in the Spratlys." Chow nodded his agreement. The *Nueva Viscaya* was one of two active ex-U.S. anti-submarine-warfare vessels operated by the Philippine Navy as coastal patrol boats, another fifty-year-old rust bucket rescued from the scrap heaps. It was small, slow, and lightly armed. They used old American C-band SPS-10 or French Triton II surface search and acquisition radars as well as older-model ULQ-6 jammers. Fortunately, its heaviest weapon was a 76-millimeter cannon, as well as 40- and 20-millimeter antiaircraft and antimissile guns that might be a danger to the *Hong Lung*'s helicopter as far as six kilometers away.

"Relay to *Hong Lung* that we suspect the Philippine vessel PS80 to be in the vicinity of Phu Qui Island," Chow ordered. "Inform them we have detected acquisition C-band radar emissions and that—"

"Message from *Baoji,* sir!" the radio technician yelled. "Radar contact aircraft, bearing one-niner-zero, fifteen kilometers!"

"Air-defense alert to all vessels," Chow shouted. "Order five-kilometers free-fire to all vessels. Broadcast on emergency frequencies for all aircraft to stay out of visual range of Chinese warships." He dashed over to the radar display on the center bridge pedestal. The composite radar images showed nothing but Pearson Reef and Cornwallis West Reef, two very large coral formations on the southeastern edge of the Spratly Islands—and it was then obvious what had happened. The single blast of radar energy from whatever vessels were near Phu Qui was enough to divert all attention to the northeast, while aircraft managed to sneak around behind Chow's task force, hide in the radar clutter created by the coral reefs, and slip in close.

"Radar now showing three aircraft, altitude less than ten meters, speed sixty knots," Combat reported. "Suspect rotary-wing aircraft. Range now thirteen-point-five kilometers and closing . . ." The radar display suddenly showed several bright white spikes radiating out from center. The spikes seemed to spin around the scope, dim, disappear, and reappear seconds later with even greater intensity. "Jamming on all systems."

"All ships, defensive maneuvering," Commander Chow ordered. "Active ECM and decoys. Signal Dragon in the clear, report possible air attack from the southeast—"

"Missile in the air!" someone screamed. Directly ahead, right on the dark horizon, a bright flash of light could be seen, followed by an arc of light that flared quickly, then disappeared. Another flash of light followed, the trail of the missile straight this time—headed right for *Chagda*.

"Hard starboard!" Chow shouted. "Flank speed! Chaff rockets! Release batteries on all guns! All guns, antimissile barrage!" The portside 30-millimeter antiaircraft guns, twin-barrel automatic guns housed in two-meter domes, began pounding into the sky, guided by the Round Ball fire-control radar. The furious hammering, so close to the bridge, turned Chow's guts inside out. At the same time, small rockets fired off the fantail into the night sky—this was the ERC-1 decoy system, which consisted of racks of small cylindrical mortars that fired parachute-equipped shells several hundred meters away and about a hundred meters high. Some of the rockets streamed pieces of tinsel that would act as bright radar-reflectors, while others would spew globes of burning phosphorus that would decoy an infrared-guided missile. His ship also carried floating radar reflectors, buoy polelike devices, like tall punching bags, that were weighted to pop upright when tossed overboard; they were laughably inadequate devices, but someone always found the time to heave a few over the side in the slim hope that a missile might find it more appealing than a two-hundred-ton patrol boat.

Every member of the bridge crew was staring out toward Phu Qui Island when suddenly a terrific burst of light split the air, and for several seconds the low profile of the minesweeper *Guangzou* was highlighted in a huge ball of fire. Several secondary eruptions quickly followed—the shock wave and sound of the explosion that hit the *Chagda* several seconds later was like a three-second hurricane and thunderstorm rolled into one. Commander Chow had never seen such a horrifying sight. *"Guangzou* . . . the minesweeper's been hit . . ."

"Look!" someone shouted. Chow turned in time to see a streak of light pass not more than a hundred meters astern of *Chagda,* a blur of a missile-looking object, just before another huge explosion rocked the patrol boat. The second missile fired from near Phu Qui had miraculously missed the patrol boat and homed in on the chaff cloud and formerly comical-looking radar reflectors, detonating after hitting the floating decoy. The blast was so tremendous that Chow thought his eardrums had ruptured. Except for a loud ringing in his ears and a few crewmen knocked off their feet by the concussion, the small patrol boat was unharmed.

The attack continued. Even though *Yaan* and *Baoji* were larger and better equipped than *Chagda,* neither of them carried any decoy rockets, and their electronic countermeasures emitters were small; they relied on their antiaircraft guns, two twin 57-millimeter and two twin 25-millimeter rapid-firing cannons, to defend themselves. Both ships' guns were lighting up the sky as the helicopters closed in from the southeast.

"Sir! *Baoji* reports the helicopters are launching missiles!" Commander Chow swung his seat over to search the horizon, but could see nothing through the darkness except for the thin bursts of light from his escort's antiaircraft guns.

But the fast attack boat *Baoji* lost its battle seconds later. The Filipino helicopters carried two Sea Ray missiles each, small, short-range laser-guided antiship missiles with one-hundred-and-fifty-pound fragmentation warheads; one helicopter was paired with one patrol boat, and they drop-launched their missiles when within four miles of their targets. The patrol boat *Yaan* destroyed its helicopter with a burst of 40-millimeter gunfire, which caused the Sea Ray missiles in flight toward her to break lock and fall harmlessly into the ocean. But the helicopter tracking *Baoji* managed to swerve and dodge around long enough to keep the laser beam on target. Both Sea Ray missiles guided directly on the forecastle of the *Baoji,* and although the warheads were small and probably would not have done much damage if they had hit the hull or decks, the missiles plowed into the bridge and combat control center, killing the captain, twelve senior crewmen, and decimating its fighting capability.

Chow did not see the explosion aboard *Baoji* several kilometers astern; he was frantically trying to sort out the jumble of targets that had suddenly seemed to surround his tiny task force. The jamming was so heavy now that *Chagda* was virtually blind, the surface-search radar a jumble of spikes and false targets, the electronic countermeasures ineffective. "Come to heading three-zero-zero, flank speed," Chow ordered. "Designate radar return on Phu Qui Island as target one and launch a two-missile C801 salvo."

He felt *Chagda* begin its sharp turn left, but the Combat officer shouted the response Chow had been fearing: "Sir, radar target track information unreliable . . . switching to manual target track . . . sir, I can't get a track with all this jamming . . ."

"Helm, come to heading three-five-zero," Chow ordered. "Nav, get us headed direct to Phu Qui Island. Fire missiles in inflight acquisition mode as soon as we get headed back toward the island." The C801 missile normally needed "pre-flight" radar-derived information—target range and bearing, own-ship speed, heading, and vertical reference, etc.—to point itself toward the target, where its onboard terminal radar would guide the missile to impact. But in heavy ECM environments, the missile could be launched with manually input pre-flight data and with the terminal radar on, where it would fly straight ahead and lock onto the first significant radar return it could find. Chow hoped the Filipino frigates were still hiding near Phu Qui—the C801's radar was sophisticated enough and powerful enough to burn through heavy ECM, separate out sea clutter, and find its quarry. . . .

Chagda made a slight turn to the right, and seconds later two C801 missiles leaped into the sky from their canisters. The first missile's fiery exhaust trail continued straight ahead, while the second missile's exhaust seemed more erratic, weaving into the night sky. Hopefully it had locked onto the damned Filipinos who had the audacity to attack a Chinese task force!

But as Chow and his bridge crew stared out the forward

windscreens, they saw a tremendous barrage of gunfire erupt from out near the horizon. It lasted only a few seconds, punctuated by a brilliant flash of light and a cylindrical spinning object that landed in the water and burned for several seconds before winking out. It was one of *Chagda*'s C801 missiles, hit by a furious barrage of gunfire that definitely wasn't from anything like a Negros Oriental-class patrol vessel. The other C801 never turned in the direction of the gunfire and had probably self-destructed.

"What was *that?*" Chow shouted to his Combat bridge crew. "That wasn't a patrol vessel out there."

"Unknown, sir," his officer of the deck replied. "Analyzing radar signals at this time, but nothing definite."

"Where did those helicopters come from?" Chow shouted, puzzled and more than a bit afraid. "How did they get out here so fast without being detected? We're over five hundred kilometers from a Philippine base."

"They either staged their attack helicopters on barges or oil platforms, or—"

"Or there's a ship out there large enough to land a helicopter on board," Chow interjected. "The Philippines have only one vessel large enough to land a helicopter and load antiship weapons on board—Rizal-class corvette. But that still doesn't explain that gunfire we saw on the horizon. What other—"

And it was then that Commander Chow realized what it was—the largest, most powerful vessel in the Philippine inventory, the PF-class destroyer escort frigate. The ex–U.S. Navy Cannon-class frigate, another World War II relic, had no fewer than twenty large-caliber radar-guided guns on board, along with two 76-millimeter guns and a four-shot Mk-141 Harpoon antiship missile launcher. That was no oil-drilling rig on Phu Qui Island—it was a major Philippine combat fleet, with at least three of its largest class of warships lying in wait.

"Signal Dragon that we believe there is at least one PS-class corvette and one, possibly two PF-class frigates in the area of Phu Qui Island," Chow ordered. "Direct *Yaan* to assist *Baoji,* and I want the task force to turn south away from Phu Qui Island. I need Admiral Yin to signal."

"Missile launch detected!" the Combat officer cried out. "Ku-band radar! Harpoon missile in the air!"

That was the last coherent sentence Commander Chow Ti U was to hear. He ordered electronic countermeasures, expendables, and his guns to open fire on the attacking missiles, but the electronic jamming was too strong; the *Chagda* did not pick up the missile until the Philippine ships ceased jamming, which was moments before the Harpoon's active radar seeker would be programmed to activate and search for its target, about twenty seconds from impact. By that time the Harpoon missile had begun a series of random jinks, punctuated by a high, looping terminal "pop-up" maneuver, a feint that was all but impossible for the *Chagda*'s defensive guns to follow.

The missile slammed into the Chinese patrol craft traveling close to the speed of sound, pierced the main superstructure, and drove down several decks before its four-hundred-and-eighty-pound warhead detonated.

A second Harpoon missile followed seconds later, adding to the swift destruction of *Chagda* by exploding in the engine room, creating a blossom of fire so huge that it created shadows on the water for five miles in all directions.

ABOARD THE SPRATLY ISLAND FLOTILLA FLAGSHIP *HONG LUNG*

"Lost contact with *Chagda*, sir," the Combat Information Center officer reported to Admiral Yin. "Last report was of a PF-class frigate and a PS-class corvette near Phu Qui Island. No other details."

"Attack helicopters, jammers, now a possible Philippine strike fleet," Admiral Yin muttered. He had been in his command chair in the center of the *Hong Lung*'s small Combat Information Center, trying to piece together the situation as bits of radio messages were slowly merged with long-range radar data.

Were the Filipinos out of their minds? Yin wondered. To attack the Chinese naval forces after the events of just a few months ago wasn't merely outrageous, it was, in Yin's mind,

idiotic. Certainly they didn't think they had a chance at defeat-
ing a force the strength of his . . .

Or did they?

What did they know that he didn't? He mulled this over for
the briefest minute. He would have to play this very, very
carefully.

"Bridge to Admiral Yin," Captain Lubu's voice reported
over a loudspeaker. "We are overtaking *Wenshan.*"

The *Hong Lung* was at flank speed, which was at least six to
ten knots faster than any of his flotilla's other vessels except for
two of his small Hegu-class fast attack missile craft, *Fuzhou* and
Chukou. That would mean that *Hong Lung* would have no
antimine or antimissile protection other than its own 37-milli-
meter guns and its phalanx Gatling-gun system. "Shall we pass
to port or join up?"

After giving the facts—and his own fears—careful consideration, Yin radioed back: "Pull ahead of *Wenshan,* reduce speed
to twenty until *Xingyi* catches up, then resume thirty knots
until within radar range of *Chagda*'s last known position."
Xingyi was his Huangfen-class fast attack missile boat, which
also carried the supersonic Fei Lung-7 antiship missile as did
Hong Lung. "Have the rest of the task force extend and follow.
Have *Fuzhou* and *Chukou* continue at flank speed towards
Chagda's last-known position."

Yin wasn't about to storm into a hostile region alone, with
only a few lightly armed twenty-seven-meter boats as protection—he was going to send the two small boats to "beat the
bushes" and find the Filipino bastards who were doing the
shooting.

"Yes, sir," Lubu replied crisply. "Expect *Xingyi* to rendezvous in thirty minutes."

"Message from patrol craft *Yaan,*" the CIC officer reported.
"*Chagda* in sight and on fire. Reports from crewmen say they
were hit by sea-skimming missiles. Patrol craft *Baoji* heavily
damaged but under way, moving southwest at five knots. No
contact with minesweeper *Guangzou. Yaan* requests permission to assist *Chagda.*"

"Permission granted," Admiral Yin replied crisply. "I want

a report on the Philippine vessels. Direction, speed—I want it right *now.*"

"Yes, sir," the CIC acknowledged.

Other crewmen in the Combat Information Center were turning to look at Yin, to see the anger and frustration spilling out. Many of them had angry questioning looks on their faces when Yin ordered the reduction in speed—shouldn't they get over there as fast as possible to help their comrades?

"Report from *Yaan,* sir," the CIC officer said a few minutes later. "Commander Ko reports three, possibly four vessels moving away from Phu Qui Island, heading east at twenty knots. Surface-search radars only. Acquisition radars not detected. Helicopters appear to be rendezvousing with the vessels."

Inwardly, Yin breathed a sigh of relief. At least this wasn't more complicated than he'd first feared.

Apparently the Filipinos had no stomach for a real fight. And obviously they weren't seeking to consolidate their gains, refortify Phu Qui Island, or take any other islands in the neutral zone. It was a simple retaliatory battle—swift, decisive, and over with. Cut and run. They probably could have stayed and continued to bombard *Yaan* and *Baoji,* board *Chagda,* take prisoners—that was what Yin would have done—or set up an ambush for *Hong Lung,* using the crippled ships, but they were doing nothing more than escaping. It put the onus right back on the Chinese—escalate the conflict or end it. Yin had no desire to drive his beautiful ship right into an ambush or into a battle-ready Filipino fleet of unknown size, but neither did he want any appearance of backing away from a fight.

And so he became a picture of triumph. He turned to his men, who had turned to look at him with querying expressions. "They're idiots. You see how they run? They steal out of the night, attack us like frightened children throwing rocks, then run in the face of something far more powerful. I loathe such spinelessness."

He clicked open the microphone and said in a loud voice, so everyone in CIC could hear him: "Captain Lubu, open a satellite channel to Dongdao Airfield immediately." Dongdao was the new Chinese Air Force airfield in the Paracel Islands; it was almost seven hundred kilometers north of their present location, but it was the closest Chinese airfield with any sort of strike capability. Although there was an Air Force general on the island in charge of the base, most of the air-strike assets at Dongdao belonged to the Chinese Army Navy, and to Yin. "I want a Shuihong-5 patrol craft fully armed for surface combat to rendezvous on this flagship immediately, and another standing by to relieve the first. The patrol had better be airborne in thirty minutes or else . . ." That got the CIC operator's attention—they all concentrated hard on their consoles, praying their Admiral would not turn on them.

Yin considered radioing the South China Sea Fleet Headquarters at Zhanjiang directly, but so far Admiral Yin had not really done anything noteworthy except get one-sixth of his flotilla destroyed or damaged; he needed to show some initiative, some decisive action, before informing his headquarters of the disaster and awaiting instructions. The Shuihong-5 was a large turboprop flying boat used primarily for antisubmarine warfare and maritime patrol, but the ten aircraft assigned full-time to his Nansha Island flotilla were fitted for antiship duties, with French-made Heracles II sea surveillance and targeting radar, two C-101 supersonic antiship missiles hung under the wings, and six French-made Murène NTL-90 dual-purpose lightweight torpedoes, also on wing pylons. The Shuihong-5 was a significant threat to any ship that did not possess antiaircraft missiles, and to Yin's knowledge no Filipino warship carried antiaircraft missiles except perhaps short-range Stinger shoulder-fired weapons.

It was enough to bomb the hell out of whatever Philippine forces were out there. Then, when his commander, the notoriously mercurial High General Chin Po Zihong, called him on the carpet for the destroyed *Chagda,* he'd have a large, ample helping of dead Filipinos to serve up. And *that* would certainly make High General Chin happy.

FOUR

It was an absolutely spectacular day for flying. The skies were clear, with only a few stray wisps of clouds to break up the blue all around. The winds were relatively calm and turbulence-free, which was rather unusual at forty thousand feet.

Things were not quite as calm, however, inside the special, heavily modified Sky Masters, Inc., DC-10 aircraft orbiting off the California coast.

There was only one booster in the cargo section of the special DC-10 that morning, which presumably would have made Jon Masters half as anxious as when he was carrying two. Instead, Masters was agitated and irritable, much to the chagrin of the rest of the crew. The source of his irritation was Sky Masters' newest air-launched space booster, Jackson-1, a dark, sleek, bullet-nosed object whose very looks promised powerful results. But the booster, named for the seventh President of the United States, wasn't going anywhere. And that was the problem.

"What's going on?" Masters demanded over interphone, drumming his fingers on the launch-control console.

Helen Kaddiri sighed. "We're still tracking down the problem, Jon. We're having trouble on the Ku-band downlink from Homer-Seven."

"You've got five minutes," Masters reminded her. "If we can't talk to that satellite, we'll have to abort."

Kaddiri sighed again. As if she didn't know. An assistant handed her yet another self-test readout. She rolled her eyes and crumbled the paper up in her hands. She took a deep breath and keyed the interphone mike: "There's still a fault in the bird, Jon, and it's not at our ground station. We're going to have to abort. There's no choice. Air Force is saying the same as well."

That was not what Masters wanted to hear. "Homer-Seven was working fine just seventy minutes ago." Homer-Seven was one of the constellation of eight TDRS, or Tracking and Data Relay Satellites, launched in the late 1980s and early 1990s to provide uninterrupted tracking, data, and communications coverage for the space shuttle and other military satellites, including spy satellites. They replaced several slow, outmoded ground communications stations once located in remote areas of the world such as the Australian outback and the African Congo.

"Now the Air Force wants to abort? After they've been screaming at me to get these fuckers in orbit so they can eyeball the Philippines? That's typical. Tell 'em to keep their nose out of my business and find out where the problem is in *their* satellite."

Even as the words came out of his mouth, though, Masters knew that wasn't what the Air Force was going to want to hear. Besides, the TDRS system had proved generally reliable in the past, and all of Jon Masters' NIRTSats relied on TDRS to beam status and tracking information to his Blytheville, Arkansas, headquarters as well as to the military and government agencies using the satellite.

So the problem had to be on the plane. . . .

"Get another system check at Blytheville and another here," he ordered. "Right now. Get on it."

Kaddiri had quickly grown tired of being ordered around. "We've checked our systems. They're fine and ready to receive. The problem's in the TDRS satellite, not with our gear."

Masters muttered something under his breath, threw off his headset, and got up out of his seat. The senior launch-control technician, Albert "Red" Philips, immediately asked, "Jon, what about the countdown?"

"Continue the countdown, Red," Jon snapped. "No—hold. I'll be back in one minute." He then hurried forward to the flight deck.

Despite the roominess of the launch-control cabin and booster section in the rear cargo hold of the DC-10, the flight deck up front was cramped and relatively uncomfortable. Along with the two pilots, there was the flight engineer's station behind the copilot, with his complex system of fuel, electrical, hydraulic, and pneumatic controls and monitors; he also controlled the aircraft's weight and balance system, which was designed to compensate for each ALARM booster launch by rapidly distributing fuel and ballast as the boosters were moved or launched.

Behind the pilot's station, back-to-back with the flight engineer, was the alternate launch-control console and the primary launch-communications center. The system handled the communications interface between satellites and ground stations and the ALARM booster until a few seconds before launch, when the booster's onboard computer received its last position and velocity update from the launch aircraft and was sent on its way. The ALARM booster's onboard flight computers continuously navigated for itself and provided steering signals to the launch aircraft to position itself for orbital insertion, but it needed information sent to it through the launch aircraft's communication system, and right now the system was not picking up data from the tracking satellites. Helen Kaddiri, who was in charge of the console for this launch, had been trying to restore communications, but with no luck.

She rolled her eyes in exasperation as Masters rushed through the pressurized cabin door. "Jon, if you don't mind, I can handle this . . ."

Masters immediately checked the status screen for the launch aircraft's communication system—everything was still reporting normal. "I asked you to run a self-test of our system, Helen."

Kaddiri sighed as Masters peered over her left shoulder to watch the test process on the screen. . . .

"There!" Masters announced. "Umbilical fiber optic hardware continuity. Why did you bypass that test?"

"C'mon, Jon, get real," Kaddiri protested. "That's not an electronics check, that's a visual check—"

"Bullshit," said Masters, dashing out of the cockpit and back into the cargo section.

The ALARM booster, its gray bulk huge and ominous in the bright inspection lights of the cargo section, had been wheeled out of the airlock and back into the cargo section so technicians could look it over again.

"Push her back in and check the umbilical connections," Masters said. "We might have a bad plug."

"But we need a safe connectivity readout before we can push her into position," Red Philips said. He checked the status board on the launch-control panel. "I'm still showing no tracking data from—"

"Bypass the safety locks, Red," Masters said. "Get the booster into position to launch."

"We lose all our safety margins if we bypass the safety locks, Jon—" But Philips could see that Masters didn't care. He punched in instructions in the launch-control console to bypass the safety interlocks, which usually prevented an armed but malfunctioning booster to be wheeled into position for release. The interlocks prevented an accident on board the plane and the inadvertent dropping of a live booster out the launch bay— now there were no safety backups.

The bypass showed up immediately on Helen Kaddiri's alternate launch-control board. "Jon, I've got an 'Unsafe Warning' light on. Is the booster locked down? I show the interlocks off."

"I turned them off, Helen," Jon said on interphone. He stood with a flashlight at the mouth of the launch-bay airlock as the huge ALARM booster was motored back into launch position. "We're checking the umbilical plug."

"You can't do that, Jon," Helen warned. "If it's more than just a plug problem, the booster might proceed to a final launch countdown before you can open the bay doors or before we can inhibit the ignition sequence. You're cleaning a loaded gun with your finger on the trigger and the hammer pulled back."

Masters glanced up at the cylindrical launch-bay airlock, which actually did resemble the chamber of a gun; inside, he could see the nosecap of the Air-Launched Alert Response Missile, which certainly resembled a bullet, as it motored into position. His head was right in the muzzle. "Good analogy, Helen," he said wryly.

The booster slid into position. "Try the umbilical self-test," Masters said to the launch-bay technician.

A moment later, Philips gave him his answer: "That's it, Jon!" he said with a shout. "There's a break in the umbilical connector—we had proper voltage but no signal. Come out of there and we'll have it fixed in no time."

"Forget it. No time. I'll do it myself." Before anyone could say anything else, Masters had scrambled inside the launch airlock and began crawling down along the ALARM booster.

"Jon, are you nuts?" the technician said. "Helen, this is Red. Jon just crawled down into the airlock. Put the interlocks back on."

"No!" Masters radioed from inside the launch airlock. "Continue the countdown."

"This is Kaddiri. I'm setting the interlocks, operator-initiated countdown hold. Crewman in the launch airlock. Interlocks on."

Just then the self-test on the booster's umbilical ended with a satisfactory reading. "Continuity restored . . . you got it, Jon, you got it," Philips said. "But we've passed the launch window."

"Start the countdown at T minus sixty," Masters said. "The booster has the endurance to make the corrections, and we built a little leeway into the launch window. Continue the countdown . . ."

"I am not going to reactivate the system until you are out of there," Kaddiri said testily.

"I'm out, I'm out," Masters said as his sneakers appeared from the muzzle of the airlock. "Let's do it." Masters closed the airlock doors the second he was out of the chamber. Philips gave him his portable oxygen bottle, and he was just putting it on and strapping himself into his seat when the airlock was depressurized. Less than sixty seconds later the booster was on its way.

"Good separation, good first-stage ignition," Helen reported as the forty-three-thousand-pound missile accelerated ahead of the DC-10 and roared skyward. "Clear connectivity in all channels . . . wings responding, swiveling on schedule . . . twenty seconds to first-stage burnout . . ."

Masters waited a few more moments as Kaddiri continued to monitor the launch, then said with a faint smile, "Well, that was close. You know what happened? The plug was off by a fraction of an inch. It was in close enough to report a closed and safe reading, but there wasn't any data transfer. Worse, that would have only shown up when the booster was in launch position and the interlocks were removed. On the dock, it was hooked into a different data bus and reported okay. No wonder we thought it was TDRS' fault."

Kaddiri continued to read off the booster's primary performance more for the benefit of the mission voice recorder than anything else. The recorder served as a backup to the computerized data-retrieval system. She didn't say a word to Masters. Wouldn't even look at him.

Masters noticed the silence and fidgeted a bit. Every launch flight lately seemed to bring out the worst in her. Where was her sense of adventure? Forget it, he decided, she didn't have one. Still, she was part of his team and he wanted to keep things on an even keel.

"Good thing I caught it, huh?" he asked almost sheepishly.

"No," Kaddiri said evenly, not looking at him. She didn't want to go into it with him. Not now. They were, after all, being recorded. Still, he had removed all the safety interlocks, leaving them totally unprotected in case there'd been an ignition-circuit malfunction or a guidance-computer malfunction. That booster could have easily gone off in the cabin and killed them all. Worse he'd reconnected a malfunctioning plug on a live booster. Who knows, she wondered, what *that* would have done?

Masters knew she was reviewing the past few minutes and said, "Helen . . . it was on countdown hold."

"Because *I* put it there, Jon." And, she thought, if we'd done it your way and continued the countdown, Masters might be splashing down in the Pacific right now, right behind our twenty-million-dollar booster—if the thing didn't cook off first.

"Well," Masters said expansively, "it's dead on course, dead on speed, dead on altitude. It'll be in orbit in eight minutes and the friggin' Air Force can get a look at all that shit going on in the Philippines."

"Whatever you say, Jon . . ."

"Helen, come on . . ."

"Drop it."

And he did.

PALAWAN PASSAGE, NEAR ULUGAN BAY
PALAWAN PROVINCE, THE PHILIPPINES
THURSDAY, 22 SEPTEMBER 1994, 0417 HOURS LOCAL

The *Hong Lung* task force had driven to within twenty kilometers of the fleeing Filipino fleet when the first Shuihong-5 antiship flying boat arrived on the scene. The Chinese flotilla was picking its way through a series of reefs and shoals along the Palawan Passage on the west side of the island of Palawan, the westernmost province of the Philippines. Most of the island was remote and sparsely settled, but Ulugan Bay, the Filipino fleet's obvious destination, had the best-outfitted port facilities at Nanan. It was also only forty-five kilometers north of Puerto Princesa, a former United States Air Force base on Palawan that was now a Philippine Air Force base; that base was the largest airport on Palawan and the center of the isolated island's meager population.

"Talon Eight-One, this is Dragon," Admiral Yin Po L'un radioed to the pilot of the flying boat. "Reconnoiter the Filipino attack fleet to the east. Report on any hostile activity. Authorized to return fire if fired upon. Warning, Chinese vessels have already been attacked and destroyed by this combat group. Proceed with caution." It was a moot warning for the

Shuihong-5 crew—if they followed their previous pattern, the Philippine vessels would fire on the flying boat. The Shuihong crew would then return fire with their murderous cargo and destroy most of the Filipino warships.

But it did not happen. Several minutes later, the pilot of the Shuihong-5 antiship aircraft reported, "Sir, Talon Eight-One reporting. We are in contact with four surface vessels, repeat, four vessels. The larger vessels identified as PF-class frigates, repeat, two PF-class frigates. Two smaller, probably PS- or LF-class patrol vessels. Over."

"Commander Chow had reported possibly two PS patrol boats out there," Captain Lubu said. "He mentioned a corvette . . ."

"But there are two frigates instead of two patrol boats," Yin said. "Chow can't identify ships very accurately at night at distances over five kilometers, even with ISAR radar."

Lubu nodded, not quite convinced but accepting the explanation for now. "The PS patrol boat is probably the Rizal identified as the helicopter platform," he added. "We should be on the lookout for another missile attack from the helicopters."

"They're running," Yin said confidently. "The fight has gone out of the cowardly bastards. What is the status of the enemy ships now? Why haven't they opened fire on the patrol plane?" A large patrol plane like the Shuihong-5 was a major threat to any ships such as those of the Filipinos', which had no antiaircraft missiles. "What is his range?"

"Nine kilometers," Lubu reported, relaying the information from the Combat section. "They detect search and navigation radar only—no target-acquisition radars detected. He is awaiting instructions."

Incredible, Yin thought—how could the frigate captain stay so cool in the face of an airborne hostile contact? Surely he must realize that the Chinese Air Force had such strike aircraft in the region? And then he realized that the Philippine vessels probably had no antiair weapons other than their guns, which had a maximum range no farther than four to five kilometers; the *Hong Lung*'s Hong Qian-9 surface-to-air missile had a range of about seventy kilometers, and Yin would not hesitate to use them against any unidentified aircraft that flew within range of his ship.

"Close to five kilometers, maintain contact, report any change in hostile status," Yin ordered the patrol plane. "I want positive identification of all vessels in that formation."

The Shuihong-5 pilot hesitated for a few long moments—he realized that his commanding officer had just ordered him to fly within gun range of the Filipino vessels. The pilot responded hesitantly, "Yes . . . sir. Talon Eight-One copies."

There were a few warning messages broadcast in English on international emergency channels, but Yin ignored them all. The plane drove only a few kilometers closer before the slow-scan P-band air-search radar switched to a high-PRF X-band fire-control radar, and soon, at precisely five kilometers range between the largest ship in the Filipino battle group, Admiral Yin heard the satisfyingly terrified voice of the pilot screaming in the radio that he was under fire from heavy antiaircraft artillery.

"Return fire," Admiral Yin ordered angrily. "Clear to launch air-to-surface missiles. Stay out of gun range and at high altitude; Dragon task force will be attacking as well." Yin turned to Captain Lubu. "Are we receiving target telemetry from the patrol plane?"

"Yes, sir," Lubu responded, double-checking with his Combat Information officers. The Shuihong-5 patrol plane could transmit radar data from its Heracles II surface-search radar to other ships capable of accepting the information; the *Hong Lung* could use this information to target the Fei Lung-7 anti-ship missile as if it were picking up the radar data from its own transmitters.

"Very well," Yin said smugly. "Begin our attack. Launch two Fei Lung missiles from long range, get a strike report from the plane, and re-attack with two more. I want this battle concluded as quickly as possible, Lubu."

PUERTO PRINCESA AIRFIELD, PALAWAN, THE PHILIPPINES

The naked young girl lying on Colonel Renaldo Tamalko's chest was so thin and lithe that he inadvertently tossed her onto the floor as he reached for the incessantly ringing phone. He grunted an apology to the girl as he picked up the receiver. "What?"

"Command Post, Sergeant Komos, sir," the voice of the NCO in charge of the tiny Philippine Air Force base at Puerto Princesa, Palawan, replied. "We've received an urgent message from a naval task force group west of Palawan, requesting immediate assistance."

"Wait a second." Tamalko flicked on the light and rubbed his eyes sleepily. All that registered to the Philippine Air Force squadron commander was that his command post senior controller was excited, and that usually meant bad news.

The old window-mounted air conditioner was on full force, but the room was still hot and steamy. He motioned toward a glass of clear liquid on the table in the center of the room, silently ordering the girl to bring it to him and hoping that it wasn't more booze. He watched the young maid's gentle curves and tight butt as she brought the glass over to him—she didn't look any older than fourteen or fifteen, but her sexual skills were certainly well developed, he thought. He grabbed her wrist, pulled her back over to him, and guided her hand back to his crotch. The glass had a bit of whiskey mixed with several melted ice cubes, so he contented himself with pouring the liquid over his face to help wake himself up. "Say again, Sergeant?"

"A Navy captain Banio of the Thirty-first Patrol Group from Zamboanga has issued a tactical emergency warning message to all military units," the NCO said. "He states that a Chinese naval force is in pursuit and is approaching Palawan, about forty miles west of Ulugan Bay. He requests immediate air support."

"A Chinese naval force? In pursuit? Of who? Pursuing *him?* What kind of air support does he need? What the hell is going on out there?"

"We're trying to raise him again, sir," Komos said. "There was a brief radio message about an attack in progress, but no more details are available."

"Shit," Tamalko swore. Fucking Chinese. To Komos he said,

"This had better not be some kind of joke, Sergeant. Did you receive any kind of verification? Was the message authenticated?"

"No, sir," the controller replied. "Contact has not been reestablished."

Tamalko swore to himself. This could be some kind of drill or exercise—it was similar to the kind of stuff the Americans liked to pull, when the Americans used to be here. But since the Americans had been kicked out of the Philippines, things had been very, very quiet . . .

Too quiet, as matter of fact.

The Communist guerrillas, who were numerous and strong on Palawan and the other outlying provinces, had stepped up their recruitment drives and had certainly become much more active, but incidents of violence were not as common— he hadn't had one of his officers shot or beaten up downtown in weeks. Before the Americans departed, it seemed to happen every weekend. As much as almost everyone in the military hated having a Communist like Daniel Teguina as First Vice President, it was obvious that his election had a stabilizing effect. Tamalko would probably have shot the bastard if he met up with him in a dark alley, but if, because Teguina was in office, the peasants liked him and quit shooting up the villages, so much the better.

So what was this shit with a Chinese invasion? It had to be bogus, an exercise cooked up by some know-nothing staffer in Manila. He had been involved with many such scenarios with the American Navy and with other military units in ASEAN, the Association of South East Asian Nations, whose member nations frequently ran joint exercises with the newly independent Philippine military. But bogus or not, Tamalko knew he had to act decisively. He had to do everything he could to make sure that his cushy job here at Puerto Princesa, one of the most beautiful seacoast towns in all the world, was protected. Puerto Princesa was a diamond surrounded by jungle and mountains, far enough from Manila to retain a very relaxed atmosphere. He was in charge of a small squadron of F-4E fighter-bombers and F-5R day fighters purchased from the United States, and he also maintained the base for other miscellaneous military and civilian air operations. There was no job on Earth better than his, and he guarded it jealously.

The girl was halfheartedly trying to arouse Tamalko with a rather distracted pumping action, obviously hoping he would leave soon so she could get some sleep. He pushed her head into his crotch, watched her begin her work, which she did as if completely bored, then turned back to his phone: "Sergeant, start a squadron recall immediately. Tell Captain Libona in Maintenance to get two F-4s fueled and ready to fly in twenty minutes; I will take one, and I'll take the first sober crew that shows up with me."

The girl between his legs nipped at him, and the sudden pain sent a bolt of dazzling blue energy radiating from his penis through the rest of his body. "I want a full combat generation begun immediately—no simulated weapons or procedures—until I give the word," Tamalko continued. "Major Esperanza will command the battle staff until I return. Inform the flight leaders that I will have Security arrest any crew members they find that do not respond to the recall.

"After you start the recall, call headquarters at Cavite and advise them that we are generating combat sorties in response to an all-units emergency message, and give them the details. Then call Zamboanga Naval Yard and get a confirmation on this Captain Banio. That is all."

Tamalko let the receiver drop back into its hook. Well, a squadron recall was the most active thing he could have ordered, he thought. He had no alert fighters, no aircraft configured for combat on a day-to-day basis. Launching two fighters, even if unarmed, would be a positive action as well. As long as the first follow-on fighters were armed, fueled, and manned within the next sixty minutes, he would have done everything possible to respond to this "exercise."

Finally relaxed, knowing that he had done the right thing, Tamalko turned his attention to the young girl's oral ministrations, and he was quite pleased to find that his nearly fifty-year-old body still responded quickly to the task at hand.

CHINESE REVOLUTIONARY NAVY DESTROYER *HONG LUNG*
THIRTY MINUTES LATER

"Talon Eight-One reports one vessel afire, the PS-class patrol craft," came the report from Admiral Yin's combat section. "One vessel believed to be an LF-class fire-support landing craft has moved alongside to assist. The PF-class frigates have split up north and south of the stricken vessel and appear to be in position to provide fire support."

Admiral Yin pushed himself away from his seat on the bridge of the destroyer *Hong Lung* and cursed everyone he could think of, especially the manufacturers of the once-vaunted Fei Lung long-range antiship missile. The sonofabitches responsible for the missiles should be shot. The Shuihong-5 attack plane had fired both its C101 antiship missiles and had hit the patrol boat with one, but *four* Fei Lung-7 missiles launched from *Hong Lung* had either missed or been destroyed.

In Yin's long experience with the missile, this was by far its most miserable performance, and coming at the worst possible time. His destroyer had only two Fei Lung-7s remaining.

With those two missiles he would have to defend himself against two of the Philippines' largest warships.

He cursed angrily at the gods while pacing the bridge, feeling more boxed in by the moment, seeing his glorious career destroyed by the tiny, insignificant Philippine nation. That would not happen. Could not happen. It would be a dishonor to himself, to his commanding officer, to his Premier, to all Chinese.

He calculated his options. The *Hong Lung* did carry two more long-range missiles, the Fei Lung-9 supersonic missiles. Unlike the Fei Lung-7s, the 9s were designed for extreme long-range naval attack, as far as one hundred and eighty kilometers, and the missile could travel as fast as Mach 2.5 during the high-altitude portion of its deadly flight. The Fei Lung-9 was an unlicensed copy of the French-German ANS missile, which had been intended as a high-performance replacement for the Exocet missile (of which the C801 was a copy—the

Chinese were never shy about stealing other weapon designs).
Fei Lung-9 was similar in size to Fei Lung-7 and was launched
by four solid rocket boosters and sustained by a boron-hydride
ramjet engine . . .

And they had nuclear warheads.

Each Fei Lung-9 carried a single twenty-kiloton-yield RK-55
thermonuclear warhead, a copy of the Soviet RK-55 warhead
carried on sub-launched cruise missiles and nuclear-tipped
torpedoes. All deployed Chinese flagships carried nuclear
weapons, and Admiral Yin's Spratly Island flotilla was no different—even though the RK-55 warhead was the smallest and
"dirtiest" warhead in China's arsenal. Roughly equal in yield to
the weapon that destroyed Hiroshima in World War II, it could
easily sink the largest aircraft carriers or devastate a port city.

Admiral Yin had never considered the use of these missiles,
and still did not consider it—as distasteful as it was to him, he
would withdraw from the fight and run for the safety of the
Spratly Islands or the Paracels before employing them. The
nuclear warhead could be removed, however, and a conventional 513-kilogram shaped-charge warhead installed. The Fei
Lung-9 was a superior weapon, much more accurate, much
faster, and was much more difficult to shoot down.

But Yin did not order the RK-55 warheads removed from
the Fei Lung-9 missiles.

He still had two Fei Lung-7 missiles and the firepower of the
rest of his task force to use, and besides it was somewhat dangerous for the crew to download a missile from its launch
canister and change high-explosive warheads at night during
a combat situation—never mind that two of those warheads
would be nuclear.

"Status of Talon Eight-One," Yin ordered.

"Combat-ready, sir," Captain Lubu replied after relaying
the request to Combat. "Armed with six NTL-90 torpedoes.
Data link is still active in all modes. Loiter time . . . estimated
at one more hour for min fuel return to the Paracels, one point
five hours for an emergency landing on Spratly Island. They're
still transmitting targeting data and awaiting orders to re-
attack."

Yin nodded. The Murène NTL-90 dual-purpose torpedoes,

capable against both surface vessels and submarines down to depths as great as five hundred meters, were substantial weapons of their own. Their maximum range was slightly greater than the eight kilometers—which was greater than the range of the guns on Philippine warships, although it was much less accurate against surface targets and, for greatest accuracy, the Shuihong-5 patrol aircraft would have to move in to four or five kilometers to drop the torpedo. Yin hesitated sending the Shuihong-5 back in within gun range, because if the patrol aircraft was struck down, he would have no choice but to move his precious *Hong Lung* in closer to the enemy to target his remaining antiship missiles, but he knew he had little choice.

"Order Talon Eight-One to attack with torpedoes," Yin told Captain Lubu. "Order them to specifically target the northern frigate. I want targeting information for the southern frigate and a second Fei Lung-7 salvo launched against it immediately."

"The waters in the Palawan Passage may be too shallow for torpedoes, sir," Lubu reminded Admiral Yin. "The torpedoes dive as far as fifteen meters before beginning their climb to the surface—there may not be enough depth in the area to accommodate that."

"Then order Talon Eight-One to attack at slower speeds," Yin ordered, "but I want the northern frigate prosecuted immediately. If the Filipino fleet is allowed to cross the Passage toward Palawan, we will have to withdraw before shore forces can react. I do not want these people to escape, Lubu, do you understand me? I will teach these Filipino cowards a lesson— the People's Republic of China will defend its territory and its borders with all the power at its command. We will destroy ten ships for every one of ours that is attacked. Now carry out my orders, Captain."

HIGH TECHNOLOGY AEROSPACE WEAPONS CENTER (HAWC),
NEVADA
SAME TIME

If there was a room in all the huge expanse of desert known as HAWC in the restricted area known as Dreamland that was more classified or more restricted than any other, it was Building Twelve, otherwise known as Hassle Hall. It was so named because every occupant undergoes a scrupulous security check before entering the building, and each and every room in the complex conducts it own security check for every individual, arriving and departing.

On the second-floor offices of the project known as PACER SKY, a huge high-definition TV monitor had been set up against one wall. A bank of computers and control equipment fed satellite data from the expansive Earth station mounted atop Skull Mountain within the Dreamland complex, and the digitized satellite data was unpacked from its microburst transmission format, decoded, processed, reassembled, and displayed on the huge monitor.

The four occupants of that super-secret room could scarcely believe what they were seeing—a real-time image of a Chinese warship over eleven thousand miles away, taken from a satellite about the size of a welder's acetylene tank traveling five hundred miles overhead at seventeen thousand miles per hour. The image was so clear that they could count the different antennae on the vessel.

"My God, that's incredible," Air Force Colonel Andrew Wyatt, one of the Joint Chiefs of Staff's senior project officers, exclaimed. "And that photo was taken at night? It's amazing."

"We can do everything but read the name on the stern, sir," Major Kelvin Carter said proudly. Carter was one of the heads of the EB-52 Megafortress strategic escort "battleship" bomber project, a command pilot, and the special project officer in charge of interfacing the PACER SKY satellite system with the Megafortress fleet. "It's not an actual photo—it's a composite image, combining radar, infrared, and low-light visual-spectrum data. We can do this with every ship that's out there. We've spotted whales, dolphins, schools of fish, and even people on some of the smaller inhabited islands. But keep in mind, this is not the usable display."

Carter motioned to the console operators, who switched the display to a larger-scale map of the area. The screen was filled with icons representing different vessels, along with data blocks near each icon. "Here's the plan view of the area around the vessels out there. The computer issues identification icons to each and computes its track, speed, and plots past and probable courses. In attack mode, the computer will plot routes around the different threats displayed, select weapons to strike each target, and prioritize targets according to parameters entered by the commander." Carter turned to a young Air Force officer beside him. "Ken?"

Air Force Captain Kenneth F. James, assisting Carter with his presentation to the Joint Chiefs of Staff representative, motioned to a smaller monitor on another console. "As you know, Colonel McLanahan is out flight-testing his modified B-2 Black Knight at SWC. Here's what he's watching in the bomber, sir," James explained. "It's an instant intelligence and operations display. With this, a bomber doesn't need to launch with a completed flight plan, decode targeting messages, or even stay in touch with his headquarters or task force commander. He can launch and drive right to the target, knowing that he'll have the best and most current intelligence and flight plan available."

Wyatt shook his head with amazement. "Incredible. Really incredible. Do you see that display in your plane someday, Captain? I understand you're involved in a very futuristic fighter program."

James glanced at Carter, momentarily unsure how to respond. "Captain James is a stickler for security, sir," Carter explained. James smiled, apparently relieved that Carter had stepped in to intercede for him. "He's understandably hesitant to talk about his DreamStar project, even to you."

"I understand," Wyatt said. "You guys live with security measures that really infuriate the Joint Chiefs. I don't think there could be a bad guy within five miles of this place, right, Captain James?"

The young test pilot looked a bit startled at the question directed at him, but gave Curtis' aide a weak smile and replied, "Security becomes a way of life around here, sir. You get very close-lipped after a while."

"I'll bet you do."

"I think we can safely say that DreamStar is light-years ahead of even PACER SKY, sir. In my Megafortress strategic escort project, which I know you are well familiar with, PACER SKY would be ideal. One EB-52 acting as escort to a flight of bombers on a long-range strike mission will use PACER SKY to plan and update strike routes, pre-plan defenses, and optimize weapons usage."

"All this . . . from a satellite that weighs only four hundred pounds," Wyatt said. "Amazing."

"It looks like Colonel McLanahan is getting ready to enter the low-level route, sir," James pointed out. "When he switches between his Super Multi Function Display modes, we'll be able to watch his entire run on this screen."

POWDER RIVER MOA, NEAR BELLE CREEK, MONTANA
SAME TIME

They called it Powder River. It was a pleasant-enough sounding name, almost relaxing—completely out of place for a high-tech bombing, navigation, and gunnery range.

The Powder River weapons complex encompassed the southeast corner of Montana, a bit of the northeast corner of Wyoming, and an even smaller part of northwestern South Dakota. It was almost perfectly flat, with only a few windswept rolling hills and gulleys to break up the awful monotony of the terrain. In nearly eight thousand square miles of territory, there were only six towns of any size, mostly along route 212 that ran between Belle Fourche, South Dakota, and Crow Agency, Montana. The northern edge of Powder River A contained parts of Custer National Forest, while the very southern tip of Powder River B claimed an even greater landmark— Devil's Tower, the unusual cylindrical rock spire made famous in the movie *Close Encounters of the Third Kind.* Other than Devil's Tower, however, there was almost nothing of interest—this was truly the "badlands," as depicted by writers of the Old West.

It was truly the badlands this day. Sixteen men had already been "killed" in Powder River in one day.

Men were "dying" because the Happy Hooligans from Fargo, North Dakota, were having an exceptionally good day. The 119th Fighter Interceptor Group was out in force, with four F-16 ADF Fighting Falcon air-defense fighters and two F-23 Wildcat advanced tactical fighters rotating shifts, plus two KC-10 aerial refueling tankers, and they were running rampant through the wide-open expanse of sky under Powder River MOA (Military Operating Areas) A and B.

The training sorties, which they had been running for the past several weeks, were all a part of General Calvin Jarrel's Strategic Warfare Center program designed to train the aircrews that made up the newly integrated First Air Battle Wing.

Late on this particular afternoon, two F-23 Wildcat fighters were patrolling the Powder River MOA. In the lead was Colonel Joseph Mirisch, the deputy commander of operations of the 119th Fighter Interceptor Squadron from Fargo; his wingman was a relatively low-time Wildcat fighter named Ed Milo. After checking his wingman in, Mirisch took him over to the tactical intercept frequency and keyed his mike: "TOPPER, this is raider Two-Zero flight of two, bogey-dope."

No reply.

"TOPPER, how copy?" Still no response. They were within range—what was going on here?

On interplane frequency, Mirisch said, "I've got negative contact with the GCI controllers. Looks like we might be on our own."

"Two," was Milo's response.

Mirisch tried a few more times to raise TOPPER, the call sign of their ground radar intercept team in the Strategic Range Training Complex, at the same time steering the formation toward the entry point of the military operating area. When they were at the right spot, Mirisch called out on an interplane, "Raider flight, still negative contact with GCI. Go to CAP orbit . . . now."

"Two," Milo said. On Mirisch's order, Milo made a hard left bank and executed a full 180-degree turn until he was heading southeast toward the center of the MOA, while Mirisch continued heading toward the entry point of the MOA. They would continue to orbit the area in counter-rotating ovals, offset about twenty miles apart, so that their radars would scan a greater section of sky at one time. When radar or visual contact was made, the other plane would rendezvous and press the attack.

There was only one more training sortie scheduled that day, call-sign Whisper One-Seven, that was not identified by type of aircraft. That didn't matter, of course—it was a "bad guy," it was invading the territory of the Happy Hooligans, and it was going to go down in flames.

That is, as soon as they could find it.

For some reason, both the VIPVO GCI radar sites at Lemmon and Belle Fourche had failed to report the position of any attackers—and now the sites were off the air, which in General Calvin Jarrel's make-believe world on the Strategic Training Complex meant that the sites had been "destroyed." But someone was out there, and the Happy Hooligans were going to find them. . . .

ABOARD WHISPER ONE-SEVEN

"Twenty minutes to first launch point, Henry," Patrick McLanahan announced. "Awaiting final range clearance."

The B-2 Black Knight stealth bomber pilot, Major Henry Cobb, replied with a simple "Rog" on the interphone.

Patrick McLanahan looked over at his pilot. Cobb was not young—he had spent nearly seventeen years in the Air Force, most of it as a B-52 or B-1 aircraft commander—and had been with the HAWC at Dreamland for only a year, specifically to fly HAWC's B-2 bomber test article. Cobb was a most talented but, to McLanahan's way of thinking, unusual pilot. Except to push a mode button on the main multi-function display, Cobb sat silently, unmoving, with one hand on the side-stick controller and the other on the throttles, from takeoff to landing. He flew the B-2 as if he, the human, were just another "black box," as integral a part of the massive four-engine bomber as the wings. If he hadn't been in a military aircraft with the threat of an "enemy" attack so imminent, Cobb seemed so calm and relaxed that it would have looked natural for him to cross his legs or recline in his seat and put his feet up.

In contrast to Cobb, Patrick McLanahan's hands and body seemed in an almost constant state of motion, due mostly to the high-tech cockpit layout in the right-seat mission commander's area. Dominating the entire right instrument panel was a single four-color multi-function display, called an SMFD, or Super Multi Function Display, measuring three feet across and eighteen inches wide, surrounded by function switchlights. The massive monitor had adjustable shades that could block out most of the light in the cockpit and reduce glare, but the big screen was so bright and had such sharp high-resolution images that glare shields were generally unnecessary—McLanahan kept them retracted so Cobb could easily see the big screen. The right-side cockpit had several metal bars around the SMFD that acted as handholds or arm-steadying devices so the screen could still be accurately manipulated even during radical flight maneuvers.

The main display on the huge SMFD was a three-dimensional view of the terrain surrounding the Black Knight, along with an undulating ribbon that depicted the bomber's planned course. The B-2 was depicted riding the flight-path ribbon like a car on a roller coaster. The ribbon had "walls" on it, depicting the minimum and maximum suggested altitudes they should fly to avoid terrain or enemy threats—as long as they stayed within the confines of the computer-generated track, they could be on course, safe from all known or radar-detected obstructions and avoiding all known threats. Messages flashed on the screen in various places, several timers were running in a couple of corners of the screen, and "signposts" along the undulating flight-plan route ribbon flashed to warn McLanahan of upcoming events. The "landscape" in the God's-eye view display was checkered with colored boxes, each depicting one square nautical mile, and small diamonds occasionally flashed on the screen to highlight radar aimpoints or visual navigation checkpoints.

To General John Ormack, the deputy commander of the High Technology Aerospace Weapons Center, seated in the instructor pilot's seat between the two cockpit crew members, it seemed like a completely incomprehensible jumble of information flitting across the big screen. Ormack was along to observe this very important test of the Sky Masters NIRTSat reconnaissance system interface on an Air Battle Force bombing exercise, but for most of this incredible mission he had been hard-pressed to keep up with the flurry of data. Patrick McLanahan, the B-2's mission commander, seemed to drink it all in with ease.

McLanahan was using three different methods to change the display or call up information. The two primary methods were eye-pointing and voice-recognition commands. Tiny sensors in McLanahan's helmet tracked his eye movements and could tell a computer exactly where his eyes were focused. When his eyes were on the SMFD, McLanahan could call up information simply by looking at something and speaking a command—the computer would correlate the position of his eyes, the image on the screen, a set of commands associated with that image, then compare the digitized spoken command with the preprogrammed set of allowable commands and execute the proper one. All this would occur in less than a second. McLanahan could also point to the SMFD and touch a symbol or image to get more information or move the image where he wanted it.

It was actually funny for Ormack to watch and listen to McLanahan as he worked—his interphone sounded like a series of unintelligible grunts and incomplete sentences. Ormack would see a cursor zip across the big screen, and he would hear a guttural "Pick." A submenu would appear, and Patrick would read the information, then utter a quick "Close" to erase the display and return it to the main God's-eye display. Every second was like that. McLanahan would be manipulating several different windows on the SMFD at once, zooming around each window, calling up streams of data that would be visible for only seconds at a time, and all while letting fly with a stream of seemingly random words: "Radar . . . pick . . . close . . . zoom . . . zoom . . . close . . . one . . . five . . . close . . . pick . . . pick one . . . close . . . track . . . one . . . left . . . close . . ."

Weapon-status information was arranged along the bottom

of the display so both crew members could check their weapon status instantly. McLanahan could resize any display, move displays around the SMFD, and even program certain displays to appear or disappear when a timer expired or when he switched in or out of certain modes. He was getting very adept at using his left index finger to move or change displays while his right hand worked a keyboard or hit the voice-command button mounted on the control stick on the side instrument panel.

To Ormack, it was like watching a kid play six different video games at once. McLanahan was flashing the different screens around the SMFD at an astounding rate. He was calling up radar images, scanning for fighters, setting up his bombing systems, talking on the radio, monitoring terrain, and sending messages on SATCOM, all with incredible speed and without missing one bit of information. "Wait a minute, Patrick, wait a minute," Ormack said over the interphone in absolute frustration. "You had the radar screen up for just a few seconds and then you took it down. Why?"

McLanahan put the radar image back on the left side of the SMFD so Ormack could see it clearly and explained, "Because all I need to check on that screen is whether or not the crosshairs fell close to the offset aimpoint—here . . ." He pointed to the screen.

"I don't see anything."

McLanahan touched the circular crosshairs on the radar display and a menu appeared. He slid his finger down to a legend that read, 1/10 MRES. The screen instantly changed to show a tiny white dot near a cluster of buildings. A circular cursor was superimposed over the dot, with a set of thin crosshairs lying right on it. "Here's the offset, a grain storage bin." He motioned to a set of numbers in a corner of the enlarged display. "Crosshairs are within a hundred feet of the offset, so I know the system is good. I also check for terrain, but since we're VFR and heads out of the cockpit, and it's so flat around here anyway, I don't have to spend too much time worrying about the terrain—the nearest high terrain is Devil's Tower, over fifty miles away."

"I get it," Ormack said. "You also don't want to be transmitting that long either, right? The fighters can pick up your radar emissions . . ."

"I was transmitting for about three seconds," McLanahan explained. "I was in 'Radiate' on the radar long enough to get this image, then shut down. But the bombing computer digitizes the radar image and stores it in screen memory until I release it. I can complete the rest of the bomb run with a radar image that's over two minutes old, and aim on it right up to release. When we get closer to the target I'll start fine-aiming on the release offsets, which are much more precise, but right now I'm trying to find those fighters."

"How does that compare with the satellite data you received?"

"There is no comparison," McLanahan said with true enthusiasm in his voice. "The NIRTSat stuff is incredible—and I thought, sitting here in the most incredible machine I've ever seen, that I'd seen it all. I can't wait to see the data from the Philippines that we're supposed to be collecting as well."

He punched instructions into a keyboard, and the graphic display of the terrain and symbols on the SMFD changed—it was as if he had switched from a fuzzy turn-of-the-century snapshot to a high-resolution color laser photo. The image was slightly different from the main SMFD display, but it still showed the ribbon "highway" of the pre-planned route, the timing and mileage icons, and target markers throughout the area. "The strike computer has already redrawn the route to real-time data—our route of flight goes farther west, and the launch point for the SLAM missile is earlier than before."

McLanahan zoomed in on the target area and switched from a bird's-eye view to a God's-eye view, which showed the target area from directly above but enhanced to show objects in three dimensions. "There's a whole row of simulated mobile-missile launchers out here . . . ?" McLanahan touched the screen and zoomed in closer to rows of cylinders on flatbed trailers. "They all look the same, but I think we can break out the real ones on the next NIRTSat pass. We should be receiving the new data in a few minutes.

"Watch this, John—with the NIRTSat data, I've already seen what the bomb run and missile launch will look like." McLanahan changed the screen again to show a photograph-quality view of the same cylinders. "Here's what the computer thinks the SLAM missile will see a few seconds before impact—the computer doesn't know which one is the real one, so it's aiming for the middle one in the group." He changed screens again, this time to a more conventional-looking green and white high-res radar image. "Here's the computer's predictions for the target-area radar-release offsets, based on the NIRTSat data. Here's the mountain peak and grain-storage bins I was just using . . . here are the two release offsets. I can start aiming on these offsets and not touch anything until release."

"Amazing," Ormack said. "Friggin' amazing. The NIRTSat system does away with shadow graphs, year-old intelligence data, hand-drawn predictions, even charts—you have everything you need to do a bomb run right here . . ."

"And I received it only thirty minutes ago," McLanahan added. "You can launch NIRTSat-equipped bombers on a mission with no pre-planned targets whatsoever. You no longer need to build a sortie package, brief crews, schedule simulator missions, or get intelligence briefings. You just load up a bomber with gas and bombs and send it off. One NIRTSat pass later, the crew gets all its charts, all its intelligence, all its weapon-release aimpoints, all its terrain data, and all its threat data in one instant—and the computer will plot out a strike route based on the new data, build a flight plan, then fly the flight plan with the autopilot plugged into the strike computers. The crew can replay the satellite data from the point of view of the flight plan and can even dry-run the bomb run hours before the real bomb run begins."

McLanahan then switched the SMFD screen back to the original tactical display, but this time with NIRTSat data inserted into it. "Unfortunately, you can't search for fighters with the NIRTSat data," he said, "and it takes a few seconds of radar time to update the screen . . ."

Suddenly several symbols popped onto the right side of the big screen, resembling bat's wings, far to the west of the B-2's position. Each bat-wing symbol had a small column of numerals near it, along with a two-colored wedge-shaped symbol on the front. The wider edge of the outer yellow-colored portion of the wedge seemed to be aimed right for the symbol of the B-2 in the center of the SMFD, while the red inner portion of the wedge seemed to be undulating in and out as if trying to decide whether to touch the B-2 icon.

"And there they are," McLanahan announced. "Fighters at two o'clock. Two F-23s. Doppler frequency shift processing estimates they're twenty miles out and above us. Signal strength is increasing—their search radar might pick us up any second. I don't think they got a radar lock on us yet, Henry . . . their flight path is taking them behind us, but that could be a feint."

Cobb seemed not to have heard McLanahan—he remained as motionless as ever, as if frozen in place with his hands on the throttles and control stick and his eyes riveted forward—but he asked, "Got jammers set up?"

"Not yet," McLanahan said, double-checking the SMFD display of the fighter's radar signal. The colored portions of the fighter's radar wedges, which represented the sweep area, detection range, and estimated kill range of the fighters, was still not solidly covering the B-2's icon, which meant that the stealth characteristics of the B-2 were allowing it to continue toward the target without using active transmitting jammers. He selected the ECM display and put it on the right side of the SMFD, ready to activate the electronic jammers at the proper time. "PRF is still in search range, and power level is too weak. If we buzz them too early, they can get a bearing on us."

"If you buzz them too late, they'll get a visual on us."

"Maybe, maybe not," McLanahan said. "In any case, they're too late." He brought the communications screen forward and activated a pre-programmed SATCOM message, then transmitted it. "Sending range-clearance request in now," he said. Sent by SATCOM and coded like normal SAC message traffic, the message or its response would not alert the fighters searching for them.

The reply came thirty seconds later: "Range clearance received, all targets clear," McLanahan reported. "Less than fifteen minutes to first launch point."

He enlarged the weapons screen and brought it higher up on the large SMFD screen so Cobb could check it as well. The

B-2 carried one AGM-84E SLAM conventional standoff missile in the left bomb bay and a three-thousand-pound concrete shape, which simulated a second SLAM missile but was not intended to be released. With its turbojet engine, the AGM-84E SLAM, the acronym for the Standoff Land Attack Missile, could carry a one-thousand-pound warhead over sixty miles. It had an imaging infrared camera in the nose that transmitted pictures back to its carrier aircraft, and it could be flown and locked on target with pinpoint precision. It was designed to give SAC's bombers a precision, high-powered, long-range conventional bombing capability without exposing the bomber to stiff target-area defenses. The right bomb bay carried two AGM-130 Striker rocket-powered glide bombs, which had a range of only fifteen miles but carried a two-thousand-pound bomb with the same precision as the SLAM. Striker worked in conjunction with SLAM to destroy area defenses and strike hardened targets with one bomber—and with the B-2 stealth bomber, which could penetrate closer to heavily defended targets than any other bomber in the world, it was a lethal combination.

McLanahan glanced at the weapons arranged along the SMFD, then spoke, "Unsafe . . . ready," to ready all weapons. Each weapon icon changed from red to green, indicating all were ready for release. "Weapon status verified, full connectivity."

Cobb turned to look, then nodded his agreement. "Checks."

McLanahan relocked all weapons, then unlocked the SLAM rocket bomb only. "Left bay SLAM selected," he told Cobb.

Another quick glance from Cobb, then he resumed his seemingly petrified position. "Checks. Left bay weapon unlocked. All others locked." McLanahan thought Cobb looked a little like the Lincoln Memorial, sitting erect and unmoving in his seat, hands on either side of him, staring straight ahead.

McLanahan selected a special symbol in the upper-right corner of the SMFD with his head-pointing system. He spoke "Active" and it began to blink, indicating that it was active and preparing to send data. "I'm calling up satellite-targeting data from the latest NIRTSat surveillance scan," he told Ormack. "In a few minutes I should have an updated radar image of the target area, and with the composite infrared and visual data, I should be able to program the SLAM missile for a direct hit. We got this bomb run wired."

ABOARD THE F-23 WILDCAT FIGHTERS

The F-23 pilots, Lieutenant Colonel Mirisch and Captain Ed Milo, felt as if they were chasing a ghost ship—there was an attacker out there, but he barely registered on any of their sensors. If they didn't find him within the next five minutes or less, they would lose max points for any intercepts done outside the MOA.

Well, Mirisch thought, this mystery plane couldn't escape the Mark One attack sensor system—their eyeballs. Jarrel's Air Force Battle had B-1 and B-2 bombers in it now, so just maybe this attacker was one of those stealthy beasts. Mirisch noted the direction of the shadows on the ground and began to search not for the airplanes themselves, but for big, dark shadows—a bomber's shadow was always many times larger than the plane itself, and there was no camouflaging a shadow . . .

Got it!

"Tally ho!" Mirisch shouted. He was so excited that he forgot his radio discipline: "Jesus Christ, I got a B-2 bomber, one o'clock low! It's a fucking B-2 bomber!" That's why their attack radars wouldn't lock on or the infrared scanners wouldn't work—the B-2 was supposed to have the radar cross-section of a bird, and birds don't paint too well on radar. Mirisch was expecting a black aircraft, but this bat-winged monstrosity was painted tan and green camouflage, blending in perfectly with the surrounding terrain. It was flying very low, but the late afternoon's shadows were long and it was a dead giveaway. At night, Mirisch thought, it would be next to impossible to find this bastard. "Raider flight, this is Raider Two-Zero flight, we got a Bravo Two bomber, repeat, Bravo Two, at low altitude. Closing to . . ."

Suddenly there was the worst squealing and chirping on the UHF radio frequency that Mirisch had ever heard. It completely blotted out not only the UHF channel, but the scrambled FM HAVE QUICK channel as well. Except for the Godawful screeching, the jamming was no big deal—they had a visual on the bomber, and no B-2 was going to outrun, outmaneuver, or outgun an F-23. This guy is toast. The newcomer, whoever he was, was too far out to matter now. He would deal with the B-2, then go back and take care of the newcomer with the big jammer.

Mirisch had a solid visual on the B-2, so he took the lead back from Milo and began his run. The B-2 had begun a series of S-turns, flying lower and lower until his shadow really *did* seem to disappear, trying to break Mirisch's visual contact. In fact it did take a lot of concentration to stay focused on the bomber as it slid around low hills and gullys, but the closer the F-23 got, the easier it was to stay on him. Now, with the B-2 noticeably closer, the attack radar finally locked on at four miles. The heavy jamming from the bomber occasionally managed to break the range gate lock and spoil his firing solution, but the F-23's attack radar was frequency-agile enough to escape the jamming long enough for the lead-computing sight to operate. No sweat . . .

ABOARD WHISPER ONE-SEVEN

The throttles were at full military thrust, and Cobb had the three-hundred-thousand-pound bomber right at three hundred feet above the ground, and occasionally he cheated and nudged it even lower. He knew the wild S-turns ate up speed and allowed the fighters to move closer, but one advantage of the water-based custom camouflage job on the B-2 that had been applied specifically for this mission was that it degraded the one attack option that no B-2 bomber could defend against—a visual gun attack.

With the fighter's attack radars in standby or in intermittent use, the B-2's most powerful sensor was the ALQ-158 digital tail-warning radar, a pulse-Doppler radar that scanned the skies behind the bomber and presented a picture of the positions of the fighters as they prosecuted their attack. Each time the fighters began to maneuver close enough for a gun shot,

McLanahan called out a warning and Cobb jinked away, never in a predictable pattern, always mixing sudden altitude changes in with subtle speed changes. Without their attack radar, the F-23 pilots had to rely on visual cues to decide when to open fire. If nothing else, they were losing points or wasting ammunition—at best, the B-2 might escape out of the MOA before the fighters closed within lethal range.

Plus, they had one more ace in the hole, but they were running out of time. "Guardian must be around here close to be blotting out the radios like this," McLanahan told Cobb and Ormack, "but I have no way of knowing where he is. He might be only a few minutes away. . . ."

ABOARD THE F-23 WILDCAT FIGHTERS

"Fox three, Fox three, Raider Two-Zero, guns firing," Mirisch cried out on the primary radio. The B-2 had finally remained steady for the first time in this entire chase, long enough for Milo to safely join on his wing and for Mirisch to get his first clean "shots" off at the big bomber's tail. The B-2 had accelerated, *really* accelerated—it was traveling close to six hundred nautical miles per hour, much faster than he ever expected such a huge plane to travel.

Suddenly the threat scope lit up like a gaudy Christmas wreath. There was a powerful fighter radar somewhere up ahead, *dead* ahead, not a search radar, but a solid missile lock-on. A "Missile Launch" warning soon followed. It wasn't coming from Milo—there was another fighter out there, and it was attacking *them!* His RHAWS was indicating several different threats in several different directions—surface-to-air missiles, fighters, search radars, at least a dozen of them. It was as if six VPVO sites and six "enemy" fighters had appeared all at once.

Mirisch had no choice. He couldn't see his attackers, he had no radio contact or data link with GCI to tell him what was out there, he was less than two thousand feet above ground, and the loud, incessant noise of the jamming on all channels, bleeding through the radios into the interphone, was beginning to cause disorientation. He checked to be sure where Milo was—

the kid had managed to stay in formation with him, thank God, and had not yet moved into the lead position—then called out on the emergency Guard channel, "Powder River players, this is a Raider flight, knock it off, knock it off, knock it off!"

Whoever was jamming him obviously heard the call, because the noise jamming stopped immediately. Mirisch leveled off at two thousand feet, waited until Milo was back safely in position on his wing, then scanned the skies for the unknown attacker.

He spotted it that instant. He couldn't believe his eyes.

It was a damned B-52 bomber. But it was like no B-52 he had ever seen before.

As it banked right, toward the center of the Powder River MOA, Mirisch saw a long pointed nose, a rounded, swept-back V-tail, eight huge turbofan engines, and twin fuel tanks on each wingtip. But the strange bomber also sported a long wedge-shaped fairing on its upper fuselage resembling a specialized radar compartment, and . . . he saw pylons between the fuselage and the inboard engine nacelles, with what looked like AIM-120 air-to-air missiles installed!

"Lead, I've got a tally on an aircraft at our eleven o'clock high, five miles . . ."

"I see it, Two, I see it," Mirisch replied. Dammit, Mirisch cursed to himself, why didn't you pick that sucker up two minutes ago? But it was too late to blame anyone else. Whatever that plane was out there, it had "killed" them both. "I don't know *what* the hell it is, but I see it."

ABOARD WHISPER ONE-SEVEN, OVER POWDER RIVER MOA, MONTANA

General Ormack strained against his shoulder harness to look out the B-2 bomber's cockpit windscreens just in time to see the huge EB-52 Megafortress do a "wing wag" and then bank away to the north. "Jesus, what a beautiful plane. We could use a hundred of those."

McLanahan laughed. "Well, it just sent those F-23s running, didn't it? That thing is tailor-made for the Air Battle Force.

You give every heavy bomber going in a Megafortress to provide jamming and air-defense support, you've got an awesome
force."

McLanahan and the other participants at the Strategic Warfare Center had been hearing about the EB-52 for weeks.
Nobody had expected it to show up during the exercises. But
it had, and McLanahan was right, it was awesome. It had a
radome on its spine that had been taken off an NC-135 "Big
Crow." The radome could probably shut down all communications in and out of Rapid City. It certainly jammed everything
the F-23s who'd been on McLanahan's tail had on them. The
plane also had capability of carrying twenty-two AMRAAMS—
twelve on the wings, up to ten internally on a rotary launcher,
including rear-fighting capability. Plus HARM missiles, TACIT
RAINBOW antiradar missiles, rear-firing Stingers, Harpoon
antiship missiles, conventional cruise missiles, SLAM and Mav-
erick TV–guided missiles, Striker and Hammer glide-bombs,
Durandal antirunway bombs . . .

General Brad Elliott had six such planes. One was under
repair and two more were authorized.

They would revolutionize SAC and SWC.

PUERTO PRINCESA AIRFIELD, PALAWAN, THE PHILIPPINES
SAME TIME

The first instructor pilot to show up on Colonel Renaldo Tamalko's orders that evening was twenty-three-year-old Lieutenant José Borillo, one of the newest and most energetic
young flight instructors at Puerto Princesa; it was no surprise
that an enthusiastic hotshot such as he reported immediately
when the squadron recall was issued. The "old heads" usually
answered the phone call right away—Sergeant Komos had all
the phone numbers of the pilots' mistresses and girlfriends as
well as their home numbers—but took their time getting back
to base. Colonel Tamalko paired Borillo up with Captain
Fuentes, an experienced and competent but unmotivated
weapon systems officer (WSO), and he took a relatively new
WSO named Pilas with him as his backseater.

The maintenance squadron commander, Captain Libona, was also wide-eyed and enthusiastic as Colonel Tamalko made his way out to the flight line to inspect his jet and brief Borillo.

After the inspection and briefing, Tamalko asked Libona, "Did we get a confirmation that this wasn't a drill?"

"No, sir. Sergeant Komos, who called you, hasn't been able to get any confirmation at all. We're assuming it is real."

"Don't be so sure. What about a confirmation on that Captain Banio, the Navy guy who alerted us? Anyone authenticate his identity?"

Libona shook his head. "No one's been able to, sir . . ."

Tamalko let out a string of four-lettered words. This was either a really well-executed drill . . . or it wasn't a drill at all. He sure as hell didn't know. More than likely, it was a drill, but he still had to respond as if it wasn't. After all, what with all the tension in the Spratlys. . . .

Tamalko turned to Borillo. "Once we're airborne, you leave your fucking finger off the trigger, hotshot, or so help me I'll shoot you down myself. Stay on my wing, keep your mouth shut and your eyes open. If the Navy files a bad report because of you, you'll be flying a garbage scow on Mindanao five minutes after you land. Now mount up and let's see what the hell is going on out there." Tamalko stomped off to do a fast walk-around, leaving Borillo and Libona in his wake.

Five minutes later the two fighters were airborne and heading north across Honda Bay toward Ulugan Bay.

"Bear flight, two-three-seven point zero," Tamalko radioed to Borillo, directing him to dial in the assigned Navy fleet common frequency.

There was a pause; then: "Say again, lead?"

Oh, Christ! Tamalko thought, and hissed: "One-three-seven point one-five." Borillo should have known enough to ask his WSO for the frequency if he missed it—asking the flight leader to repeat a new frequency was a mortal sin during night formation flight.

"Two," Borillo finally replied.

Tamalko switched frequencies himself and was about to call to order Borillo to report up on frequency, but the channel was a mass of confused voices in several different languages.

And then . . .

"Mayday, Mayday . . . I'm hit, I'm hit . . . get over here, someone, help me . . . missile in the air! Missile in the air . . . ! Hard to port . . . Watch it . . . !"

"Bear flight, check!" Tamalko yelled. He heard a faint "Two" over the radio, and he hoped that was Borillo. "Cowboy, Cowboy, this is Bear Zero-one flight on fleet common. Over." "Cowboy" was the call sign Sergeant Komos had given him for Captain Banio's ship, but Tamalko couldn't tell who was on freq or what was going on. There was so much chatter on the channel that he wasn't sure if anyone heard him. "Cowboy, come in!"

"Bear flight . . . Bear flight, this is Cowboy." The voice was frantic. "What is your position? Say your position!"

"I need authentication before I can report, Cowboy . . ."

"We are under attack, Bear flight, we are under attack," the voice—now firmly racked with terror—replied. "Smoke . . . fire in all sections . . . we need you over here right now, Bear flight, we need you down here right *now!*"

"Mode two, three, and four squawk is set, Cowboy," Tamalko reported, informing the ship that his radar identification system was set and operating. The ship's radar should be able to identify his coded signals and give him steering commands, if it was indeed Cowboy he was talking to. Part of an exercise would be to check if Tamalko would fly off following directions from an unverified radio voice, and Tamalko was going to play this one by the book—as much as possible. "Give me a vector, Cowboy."

"Can't . . . Combat section evacuated . . . ship on fire, Bear flight. Please, *help* us . . . !"

And then Tamalko saw it, off the nose at about forty miles into the inky night sky—two blobs of light in the ocean, shimmering dots of red and yellow fire. The dot off his nose was dimmer than the northern one, which looked like a huge magnesium flare, as bright as watching an arc-welding flame. Just then he saw several bursts of light issue from some other nearby spots in the dark ocean farther to the south, with tracers speeding out farther to the west. "Cowboy, I see fires and tracers. Who is shooting?"

"Bear flight, this is Cowboy," a different voice came on the radio. "Bear flight, this is Lieutenant Sapao, engineering officer aboard the frigate *Rajah Humabon*. We are under attack by Chinese naval warships. We have been hit by missile fire. Patrol boat *Nueva Viscaya* also hit by missile fire . . ." The slightly calmer report was interrupted by shouts and cries, and the newcomer Sapao issued a few orders of his own before returning to the radio: "Chinese warships estimated thirty miles west of Ulugan bay, estimated ten vessels including one destroyer. Also Chinese attack aircraft in vicinity, a naval-warfare craft launching antiship missiles and torpedoes. Frigate *Rajah Lakandula* is operating south of our position, and patrol boat *Camarines Sur* is assisting the *Nueva Viscaya*. Can you assist, Bear flight?"

As Tamalko got closer, he could see more and more details— there were indeed two ships burning in the Palawan Passage just outside Ulugan Bay. Sheets of gunfire continued to erupt from the southernmost ship, which was darting back and forth, firing in all directions. "Cowboy, can you give us the position of the aircraft?"

"Negative, negative, Bear flight," Sapao's tortured voice responded. The transmission began to break up. "Portable radio running out of power . . . negative, our combat systems are out and we are beginning evacuation procedures. If *Rajah Lakandula* comes up on frequency, he can assist—"

The transmission went dead.

Tamalko started to feel uneasy. The possibility that this wasn't an exercise hadn't been fully realized until now. Naturally, he assumed . . .

Of course, it could still be an exercise, he reasoned, although a very elaborate one. He knew he shouldn't commit any aircraft unless he received some sort of authentication, and yet . . .

. . . what he was seeing, hearing, looked very real indeed. Horrific, in fact.

"Bear flight, coming left," Tamalko radioed on interplane frequency. "Take spacing, line abreast. Wide area search. Find the damned aircraft."

Moments later, Borillo had moved alongside Tamalko,

spaced far enough apart to search a greater section of the sky but not far enough to lose visual contact. Tamalko's weapons system officer began a procedural radar sweep of the skies. "Search plus one to plus ten degrees," he told his inexperienced WSO just in case, like Borillo, he was getting too caught up in the action to think straight. "Fuentes will search zero to minus ten degrees."

The search took only a few moments: "Lead, radar contact, one o'clock, twenty miles, altitude one thousand feet, airspeed three hundred knots," Fuentes reported. "Looks like it's heading south toward the frigate."

"Can you find it?" Tamalko called out to his backseater.

"Not yet, sir . . ."

"Two, take the lead," Tamalko radioed to Borillo. "Center up and let's go see who it is. I'm in fighting wing position. Go!" Cautiously, Borillo moved forward until he was ahead of Tamalko's plane. Tamalko swung out a few more yards to let Borillo pull ahead, then eased behind and above him so he could see all around his new leader. "You've got the lead, Two," he radioed to Borillo.

"I've got the lead," Borillo replied hesitantly. "Bear flight coming right."

"Don't *tell* me, Two, just *do it.* I'm on your wing," Tamalko said. He followed Borillo easily as the young pilot made a ridiculously slow 15-degree bank turn to the right—apparently he was overly concerned with how his squadron commander was doing. They began a slow descent to six hundred feet, which allowed the radar beam to angle up at the target and away from the radar clutter caused by shallow waters of the Palawan Passage.

Meanwhile Fuentes had locked the radar target on his attack radar, which gave Borillo steering commands to an intercept position. Borillo eased his F-4E farther right, keeping the radar image on the left part of his radar screen—this kept his fighter's nose aimed ahead of the target, along the target's flight path and not directly on the target itself. "Bear lead judy," Fuentes radioed, advising the formation that he had radar contact on the air target.

Just then they heard on the naval fleet common channel: "This is PF4 *Rajah Lakandula* to all units, we are under attack by Chinese aircraft! Bear flight, Bear flight, this is Cowboy! Can you help us? Can you find the aircraft!" All attempts at radio discipline were gone now—whoever was on that radio now was crying out for the life of himself, his crew, and his ship.

This, Tamalko knew, was no fucking drill. "Cowboy, this is Bear flight. We do not have visual contact. We are at five miles and closing. Stand by."

"Bear flight, don't wait for visual contact! That plane is on a torpedo-attack profile! You've got to destroy that plane!"

"I don't have proper identification, Goddammit!" Tamalko screamed. "I can't open fire on an aircraft without identification and authorization!"

"This is an emergency, Bear flight!" the radio operator—it was a different person again, which only intensified Tamalko's doubts—yelled on the radio. "If you are locked on to him, attack! If he gets within five miles of the ship, he'll drop torpedoes! Attack!"

"*I need authorization!*" Tamalko screamed back. This was a setup, Tamalko told himself over and over, it was a tremendous setup. Someone wanted his job at Puerto Princesa, he decided. Someone wanted him to screw up so he could be replaced and sent to some other Godforsaken base. Well, he was going to play this one by the book, dammit.

By the book all the way . . .

And that's when Borillo opened fire on the airplane.

In a blinding streak of light, Borillo pumped out all eight of his five-inch unguided Zuni rockets at the Chinese patrol plane, at a range of about three miles. It was doubtful that Borillo had ever fired a Zuni before; the F-4E's attack radar had no ballistics or mil settings for a Zuni; there was no way the rocket could guide on its intended target or glide into a kill like most air-to-air missiles. Trying to hit the plane with a Zuni rocket was like trying to shoot down a bullet with another bullet.

"*Cease fire!*" Tamalko shouted. "Cease fire, you fucking idiot . . ."

But somehow one of the big rockets found its target. A huge cloud of fire erupted off into the distance, and a trail of flames peeled off to the right and spiraled down into the darkness.

"What the hell did you do?" Tamalko screamed on the interplane frequency. *"What did you do?"*

"They were calling for help, sir," Borillo replied, trying to force a bit of righteous authority in his voice. "They were under attack . . . we . . . I had to do something . . ."

"Start a left turn, see if you can find where the plane went down," Tamalko ordered. "Jesus Christ, Borillo, that could have been one of *our* planes, don't you understand that? Unless we are under specific, positive direction from ground controllers or we have positive ID on an intruder, we are not authorized to open fire on *anyone.* God, I don't believe it . . ." He gained a few hundred feet to stay away from the ocean—he knew he was less than a thousand feet above the water—then banked gently to the left and stared hard out his canopy to try to get a visual check on the target. He saw nothing but empty darkness. "Pilas, did you see what it was?" Tamalko cried out to his WSO.

"No," Pilas replied. "I saw a couple hits and a flash of fire, but no identification." His backseater's voice was high and cracking, and when his interphone mike opened he could almost feel the tortured breath of his terrified crewman—until Tamalko realized that he was listening to his *own* breathing.

I'm a dead man, he said to himself as Borillo began a gentle turn. I am a dead man. . . .

ABOARD THE CHINESE DESTROYER *HONG LUNG*

"Lost contact with Talon Eight-One, sir." Captain Lubu Vin Li reported solemnly. "The pilot reported that he was ditching. Crew reported under attack by enemy aircraft."

Admiral Yin Po L'un rested a hand under his chin, resisting the urge to swear aloud on his combat bridge as he did when he learned the results of the first Fei Lung-7 missile attack. The downing of the Shuihong-5 patrol plane was a serious loss, almost as serious for Admiral Yin's fleet as the loss of the patrol boat would be to the Philippine Navy. This battle was beginning to unravel right before his eyes, like a magician's magic knot—it seemed strong and unbreakable, yet was pulled apart by the slightest touch. . . .

"The Shuihong-5 might survive the landing," Yin muttered. "Send *Wenshan* and *Xingyi* to investigate. Be sure they maintain data link with us at all times." *Wenshan* had an excellent surface and air search capability, along with the ability to transmit radar data to *Hong Lung;* it would act as radar warning vessel until Yin decided what to do. *Xingyi* carried six C801 antiship missiles that could be targeted by *Wenshan*'s fire-control system. He had a decision to make.

He had two choices left. His first option: run and regroup. Yin doubted that the Philippine vessels would follow him back to the Spratly Islands—they had only one PF-class frigate and a small LF-class patrol boat nearby, with two other major ships damaged or destroyed. Even though they were only fifty kilometers from shore and there were already Philippine aircraft in the area, he believed that the fight was over. Both sides had taken their tolls, got in a few good hits, and now they were disengaged.

The second option: stay and fight. Yin could press the attack by moving closer to get within radar range of the Philippine vessels and launch another missile or gun attack. He had finally scored a big hit on the Philippine frigate *Rajah Humabon* with the last of his Fei Lung-7 missiles, so he was out of antiship missiles except for the Fei Lung-9 missiles. Again, unbidden, the thought of using those weapons entered his mind, and he immediately quashed the idea. But he still had a sizable force in position: two Huangfen-class fast attack missile boats, four Hegu-class patrol boats, two Hainan-class patrol boats, and a minesweeper. His Huangfen-class ships carried a full complement of Fei Lung-7 and C801 antiship missiles, and all of his ships had dual-purpose guns to use if he moved into knife-fighting range. His flotilla still had a lot of fight left in it.

But Yin's battle group had been hit hard by the upstart Philippine raiders—one minesweeper, one attack boat, the fast attack missile boat *Chagda,* and the Shuihong-5 patrol plane. In exchange they got one frigate and a patrol boat. A

very poor performance for the world's largest navy versus a
virtually nonexistent navy. . . .

"What are your orders, Admiral?" Captain Lubu asked him.
"Once *Wenshan* and *Xingyi* get into position to assist the
Shuihong-5 crew and reconnoiter the area, what will we do?"

Yin looked at Lubu, then at the other crew members on
Hong Lung's bridge. He did not see much fight in their faces.
What he saw was fear—plain old fear. Should he take these
youngsters into combat again? Should he decimate the Philippine Navy with guns and missiles, risking the safety of his
already hard-hit fleet for a hollow victory?

"Withdraw," Yin heard himself say in a low, tired voice.
"Twenty knots, then twenty-five as soon as the fleet is re-
formed. Maintain contact with *Wenshan* and *Xingyi*, but plot
a course out of this shallow water and prepare—"

"Radar contact aircraft!" Lubu suddenly shouted, relaying
reports via headset from *Hong Lung*'s Combat Information
Center. "Bearing zero-three-zero, turning toward us, range
fifteen kilometers and closing! Radar now reports two aircraft
in formation, altitude one thousand meters, airspeed four-
eight-zero. Combat estimates aircraft on missile-launch profile!"

He was quickly running out of options now. A severely damaged fleet, a dangerous depletion of long-range antiship weapons, shoal waters all around them, and now armed Philippine
aircraft nearby with the threat of more just over the horizon.
They could withdraw, back to the relative safety of the Spratly
Islands, but they would have to fight their way out.

"Signal to all ships: release all antiair batteries," Yin ordered.
"Protect yourselves at all cost."

ABOARD BEAR ONE-ZERO

"Close it up, Two, close it up," Tamalko shouted to Borillo on
interplane frequency as he watched the second F-4E slowly
drift in and out off his right wing. "Don't get sloppy on me
now."

Tamalko was maneuvering back to the lead position. They
had climbed back to a safe altitude of three thousand feet,

executing circles over the area where the unidentified plane appeared to have gone down. Borillo was so erratic that Tamalko's backseater frequently lost sight of him. It was some of the worst formation flying he had ever seen. The short air battle had really rattled the kid.

Tamalko was ready to send the kid home, or perhaps even put him in the lead and tell him where to go, but he needed the word from Headquarters first before anything else. In between yelling at Borillo to stay in close to avoid going lost wingman, Tamalko was on the UHF radio to Puerto Princesa, trying to set up a relay from Palawan to the Philippine Air Force headquarters at Cavite, near Manila. It was not going well.

Meanwhile, aboard Bear Zero-Two, Lieutenant Borillo's weapons system officer, Captain Fuentes, was dividing his time between coaching Borillo on night-formation flight and checking his radar, searching for other aircraft that might be in the vicinity. By depressing the antenna angle on his attack radar, the WSO could paint several ships ahead of them at twelve miles. His RHAWS indicator, the screen that showed the direction, intensity, and type of enemy radar threats in the vicinity, showed several search radars all across the horizon to the west. The threat-intensity diamond shifted between "S" designations on the scope as the system tried to decide which was the greatest threat. "Lead, looks like several ships at eleven o'-clock, twelve miles," Fuentes radioed to Tamalko. "Search radars only."

"Copy . . . Two, close it back in, will you?" Tamalko said irritably. "If you go lost wingman it'll take a damned hour to rejoin back up again."

"Suggest a turn back to the east," Fuentes said. "I don't want to get any closer to those ships."

"Stand by, Two," Tamalko snapped. "I'm trying to talk with the command post."

Fuentes looked up from his radarscope just in time to see his plane's wingtip drift ever so slowly toward Tamalko's right wing. "How you doing up there, Lieutenant?" he asked Borillo.

"Fine . . . fine," Borillo answered hesitantly. "I'm moving in closer." Judging by how the control stick and throttle quadrant in the backseat were wobbling around, Borillo wasn't fine. But he was closing in nicely, so Fuentes took another look in the radar.

"Surface ships still at eleven o'clock, now ten miles, lead," he radioed to Tamalko. "We can't stay on this heading, sir."

"Just stand by," Tamalko radioed back angrily. "Just stay in route formation and—"

Just then several of the "S" symbols on the RHAWS scope changed to blinking "6" and "8" symbols, and a slow wavering tone could be heard on the interphone; red "Missile Warning" lights were flashing on the threat-indicator panel. "Acquisition radar, eleven and one o'clock positions," Fuentes radioed to Borillo. "Naval SA-6 and -8 systems. We need to get out of this area . . ."

The tone suddenly shifted to a fast buzzer, and "Missile Launch" lights illuminated in both front and rear cockpits. "Missile launch!" Fuentes screamed. "Descend and accelerate! Now!" Fuentes searched the sky ahead of them, and he felt his face flush as he saw two bright yellow dots streaking toward them—antiair missiles. Thank God it was so easy to see them at night. "I see them! Right off the nose, just below the horizon! Aim right for them and get ready to break!"

But Borillo panicked. With a missile launch off the front quarter, the best defense was to point the fighter's nose at the missiles, presenting the smallest possible radar cross-section, then jink away from them at the last possible moment. Young Borillo did exactly the wrong thing—he heard the word "Break" and started a hard right turn away from the oncoming missiles at 90 degrees of bank. With the full outline of the big F-4E presented belly-out toward the missile and its tracking radar, it was an easy target. Fuentes tried to wrestle the control stick back over to the left, but he was far too late—one of the *Hong Lung*'s HQ-91 missiles, a copy of the Soviet Union's advanced SA-11 antiaircraft missile, hit Borillo's fighter and instantly turned it into a huge fireball.

Tamalko never got a verbal warning from his backseater— young Pilas was too scared or had the volume turned down on his threat-warning receiver, Tamalko didn't know—but when the "Missile Launch" warning sounded he promptly forgot about trying to contact Cavite and looked up to see the second HQ-91 missile streak past him, less than a hundred feet behind. He banked right, toward the threat indications, just in time to see the first missile destroy his wingman.

Pilas was screaming in the backseat as the shock wave from the explosion crashed over them. Tamalko tried to ignore the screaming as he pushed his fighter down in a six-thousand-foot-per-minute descent, yanking it level as he passed three hundred feet. "Shut up, Pilas—*shut up!*" Tamalko roared. The screaming finally ceased.

"Borillo got hit! Christ, they're *shooting* at us!" Pilas shouted. "I thought this was an *exercise!*"

"Well, it's not a fucking exercise. Those *are* Chinese ships out there, and they're attacking." And then Tamalko realized that Borillo really *did* shoot down an attacking Chinese patrol plane—it was he who probably saved hundreds of lives on *Rajah Lakandula.* And since Pilas never warned him of the threat until after missile launch, Borillo also saved Tamalko by banking away from the missiles. Even though he screwed up most of the flight, the young pilot was a damned hero.

"Give me a heading to that ship," Tamalko told Pilas. "We're attacking."

"Attacking? With *guns?* All we have are guns, sir . . ."

"I know, I know," Tamalko said. He readjusted his heads-up display for air-to-ground strafing, resetting the depression angle on the HUD to 37 mils. "Where are the damned ships?"

There was a slight pause, and Tamalko thought that Pilas was either not going to answer or was suffering a nervous breakdown. Then: "Radar contact, one o'clock, ten miles. Come right ten degrees. Target heading two-six-zero." Tamalko made the turn and began pushing up the throttles in military power, saving afterburner thrust for the final few miles of his pass. . . .

ABOARD THE CHINESE FLAGSHIP *HONG LUNG*

"High-speed aircraft approaching *Wenshan,* sir," Captain Lubu reported. "Range sixteen kilometers. No contact on second aircraft. *Wenshan* maneuvering to put his aft 57-millimeter guns on the target."

"He'd better stop turning and start shooting," Admiral Yin said half-aloud. "If those planes are carrying Harpoon antiship missiles, he's run out of time already."

"Emergency message from *Wenshan!*" a radio operator called out. "They've run aground!"

"What?" Yin shouted. For the second time, the deep-draft patrol boat *Wenshan* had fallen victim to the shoal waters of the South China Sea—and the second time it had done so at a critical moment, while under attack from hostile Philippine forces. The image of the dragon drowning in the ocean rushed upon the Chinese Admiral once again—the battle, it seemed, always came to *him.* . . .

"*Wenshan* is taking water," the radio operator reported. "They are requesting fire support and assistance. Casualties reported."

"Range to that fighter?"

"Range to *Wenshan,* eight kilometers," the Combat technician reported. "Fighter still headed inbound. Passing eleven hundred kilometers per hour."

"Sir, radar reports the second frigate has appeared over the horizon to the east," Captain Lubu reported. "Range thirty-two kilometers, closing slowly."

The Philippine ships were pressing the attack, Yin thought. So close to utter destruction, and now the mouse is turning to bite the nose of the tiger. "Order *Fuzhou* to intercept—"

"Sir, radar reports another contact off to the south," Lubu interrupted. "Range thirty-seven kilometers, approaching at medium speed. They appear to be helicopters, sir. Three helicopters approaching."

"Missile-launch detection!" Combat reported. "Frigate to the east launching missiles, sir!"

The battle was on in earnest.

The reports were flooding past Admiral Yin almost faster than he could assimilate them. Faces glanced at him, some doubtful, others accusingly, most of them fearful. Voices were bombarding him, rising in intensity and volume—the racket was getting loud, almost deafening . . .

"Fighter closing to within five kilometers, sir," another report cut in. *"Wenshan* listing to starboard. Captain Han reports his stern is resting on the bottom and is unable to move . . ."

"Vessel to the south identified as PS-class corvette," Lubu reported. "There *was* a fifth ship out here, Admiral. The helicopter landing platform . . . it must have separated from the rest of the Philippine task force and maneuvered to our right flank . . ."

"Missile-launch detection! Corvette to the south launching missiles . . ."

"Radar contact, third vessel, identified as LF-class fire-support craft . . ."

"Shoal water dead ahead, three meters under the keel. Suggest hard starboard twenty degrees . . . !"

"Execute turn . . . !"

"Missile-launch detection! Helicopters launching missiles, sir!"

"Chukou reports missile strike on the waterline, sir!" another report came. "No damage report . . . lost contact with *Chukou* . . ."

"Lost data link with *Xingyi,* sir. No reports yet . . ."

"LF-class fire-support vessel on suspected torpedo run, sir," Lubu shouted. "Range down to eighteen kilometers, speed thirty knots . . ."

"Radar contact aircraft, range fifty-two kilometers, heading west at high speed," another report came. "Fighter aircraft from Puerto Princesa. ETA, five minutes."

"Sir," Captain Lubu said, stopping and standing as close to Yin as he dared, "we are running out of maneuvering room, one patrol boat is grounded, and the other ships are scattering and disoriented—they are unable to defend themselves or defend the flagship. Recommend we reduce speed and provide fire-support coverage for our escorts. Once we are reorganized, we can steam out of the passage . . ."

Yin appeared not to have heard him. Not four inches from Captain Lubu's face, Yin was breathing heavily through his nose. Perspiration was running down the sides of his temples. His face was flushed, his brow furrowed, his mouth a tight line.

It was as if he were not there, but instead somewhere else far, far away, thinking . . .

. . . about how there was no way out.

. . . about his duty to protect his men, his ship.

. . . about saving face at all costs.

Finally, after what seemed like an eternity, but was really less than fifteen seconds, Yin unbuttoned the top button of his tunic, reached inside, and withdrew a large silver key.

Lubu's mouth dropped open in surprise. His eyes grew wide as he realized what it was. "Sir . . . Admiral, you can*not* . . . *!*"

"We cannot be razed like this, Captain," Yin said calmly. "I will not suffer defeat at the hands of these people." He inserted the key into a lock on a flat panel on the instrument console in front of his seat, waited as the door popped open. Inside the compartment was a red-colored telephone handset with communications cords and several unmarked buttons. Yin pressed the yellow button. A buzzer sounded around the entire ship. With Lubu looking on in absolute horror, men throughout the ship scrambled to prepare for an order that had never before been executed. . . .

Admiral Yin picked up the red-handled phone within the unlocked compartment before him on the instrument console. "This is Admiral Yin," he said. "Command is Battle Cry. Battle Cry. Over."

"Initial code verified," a voice on the other end of the line asked. "Targets, sir?"

"Target the southern corvette, turn, and target the eastern frigate," he said in a low voice. "Execute in three minutes, system automatic. Authentication is Red Moon. Repeat, Red Moon. Over."

"Understood, sir. Authentication verified. Full connectivity check . . . received. Execution in three minutes . . . mark. System automatic engaged. Countdown hold in two minutes. Combat out." Yin replaced the red phone in its cradle.

A crewman dashed up to the two senior officers, carrying heavy gloves, a heavy black smock that resembled a thick poncho, and a heavy helmet with large gold protective eye goggles and a plastic face shield with respirator. Lubu accepted his but did not don it. "Admiral, I ask you to reconsider.

We should receive authority from headquarters before attempting this . . ."

Yin allowed the crewman to help him on with the lead-impregnated smock, placed the helmet on his head, connected the interphone cords and breathing apparatus, and rolled down his sleeves. Inside the helmet, he could hear the reports coming in to Lubu as each desk and each station reported its Red Moon status.

"Admiral, you must stop this . . ." Lubu persisted.

"Two minutes to Red Moon execution," the loudspeaker blared. "Two minutes to Red Moon execution . . . mark. All decks report ready."

"My fleet is surrounded, we are under attack, we are in danger of losing the Spratly Islands and indeed most of the South China Sea to the Filipinos," Yin said through the respirator. His flashblindness goggles and oxygen mask made him look sinister, even deranged, like a sea monster from a horror movie. "I have the power to stop them. My only other choice is to surrender to them, and that I will never do."

"But this will create a disaster of international proportions," Lubu argued. "We are too close to the Philippine shoreline. The water is too shallow—we will do irreparable harm to the coral reefs and the sea bottom in these shallow waters. You must cancel the order."

"Put on your protective gear and prepare for Red Moon execution, Captain," Yin said through the mask and respirator. "That is an *order*."

"You cannot do this. We will be in a state of war, with the Filipinos, the Americans, the entire *world*."

"Range to the south target?" Yin radioed to Combat.

"Thirty kilometers and closing," came the reply. "Helicopters at seven kilometers, ETA three minutes . . . sensor warning missiles on intercept course, ETA forty seconds, AA batteries and close-in systems manned and ready . . ."

"Admiral, *please* . . ." Captain Lubu shouted, his hands on the armrest of Yin's chair. "At least . . . at least broadcast a warning message, sir." Yin shook his head, a slow, ghastly gesture that made it look like the Death's Head itself refusing the pleas of the ones condemned to die.

"You old *fool,* you can't do this!" Lubu shouted. He turned to the officer of the deck, who was fully outfitted in his nuclear-chemical-biological–warfare gear. "Cancel Red Moon execution on my order, Commander. Broadcast on emergency frequency that this fleet is disengaging and departing Filipino waters immediately."

"Sir, I must have the cancellation code," the officer of the deck shouted through his mask. The officer of the deck was trained to respond to orders from the ship's captain, not the Admiral on board; therefore there was no question that he would obey lawful orders from Lubu. But procedures still had to be followed, especially in combat conditions and with the flotilla commander on deck in active command.

Lubu looked at the dark visage of Yin behind his mask. The Fleet Admiral made no movement, spoke nothing. Lubu said angrily, "On my authority, Commander. The codes are in a safe in my cabin. You know I have them. Until I retrieve the codes, I order you to cancel the execution order immediately."

The officer of the deck turned to look at both Yin and Lubu. Most of the rest of the bridge crew was watching the exchange as well. Then the officer of the deck said, "I'm sorry, sir, but the Admiral is still on the bridge and he has command. I cannot supersede his orders."

"Sixty seconds to Red Moon execution. All decks report ready . . . fifty seconds . . ."

"Cancel the order, Admiral," Lubu warned him.

"Don your protective gear and stand by, Captain," Yin said evenly.

Lubu's eyes telegraphed his next move—he lunged forward for the silver key in the lock of the Fei Lung-9 command-control panel. Removing the key would disable the direct line to Combat, which would prevent the final execution order from being given from the bridge. The launch officer would hold the final launch countdown at twenty seconds if the final order was not given either by the direct phone or in person.

Just as Lubu touched the key, a shot rang out. Lubu was thrown away from Yin's chair and onto the floor, a dark red stain spreading across his belly.

"You are a coward and a dishonorable man, Lubu Vin Li,"

Yin said half-aloud, placing the smoking 7.62-millimeter Type 54 automatic pistol on the instrument console in front of him. "You cannot change my destiny. You have disgraced yourself trying." Yin then picked up the red phone, lifted his mask and helmet, and spoke: "Combat, this is Admiral Yin."

"Combat. Entering Red Moon countdown hold."

"Execution order is Dragon Sword. Dragon Sword." And he dropped the phone once more and lowered his respirator into position. As he closed the elastic seals on his gloves and neck of the protective smock, he spoke into the helmet's interphone system: "Seal the bridge. Order all antennae and receivers into standby and—"

But just then Yin heard the collision-warning horn sound on the bridge loudspeaker and the loud, angry buzz of the Phalanx Close-In Weapon System. The radar-guided Gatling gun automatically tracked inbound targets and opened fire with a murderous hail of 30-millimeter bullets when it computed the object within range—Yin knew it was a last-resort weapon, and that its chances of stopping an incoming missile were slim.

Yin heard another warning horn blare—it was the T minus ten-second Fei Lung-9 launch-warning horn—just as a huge explosion erupted outside the port observation windows. The incoming Harpoon missile had been hit by the Phalanx cannon and detonated as it began its terminal pop-up maneuver, creating a huge overpressure in Yin's ears seconds before the big, thick observation windows bowed inwards, then outwards, and exploded like a balloon. The overpressure seemed to suck the air out of Yin's lungs, and the very air he was breathing seemed as if it were on fire. . . .

ABOARD BEAR ZERO-ONE

Tamalko saw the patrol boat at about three miles' distance, and opened fire just inside one-half mile. The Chinese warship opened fire immediately with what appeared to be a solid wall of tracers, and for a moment he thought he would have to break off his run and try a different attack axis; but just then, a half-second later, the firing abruptly stopped. Tamalko walked his 20-millimeter shells up to the ship's stern, using short bursts from the four-thousand-rounds-per-minute M61A1 cannon, then, banking hard left and controlling his fighter's swaying action with rudder pressure, managed to stitch a line of bullets right down the centerline. He was rewarded with a few secondary explosions, and it even appeared that the ship was listing to one side, although he doubted seriously that single gun pass had anything to do with it.

"Radar contact on another vessel, now one o'clock, three miles," Pilas called out. "Locked on, steering is good."

"Roger," Tamalko replied.

Just as he rolled out on his new heading toward the second Chinese vessel, he saw a huge cloud of fire burst directly abeam the radar cursor in his HUD. The ship was clearly illuminated for a second or two, and Tamalko could not believe the *size* of the ship—it was as big as an aircraft carrier, he thought, and as tall as a skyscraper. It was easily the biggest ship he had ever seen so close to Palawan. Only a search radar still emanating from this one—it seemed unaware of his presence.

Well, perhaps not.

Just as Tamalko considered the lack of threat signals from the big vessel, he saw a streak of fire arch skyward from the rear of the Chinese ship. It trailed a line of fiery exhaust that could be seen for dozens of miles, and it flew fairly slowly, picking up speed only several seconds after launch.

The big missile continued south and made no attempt to turn east toward him. That was odd, Tamalko thought.

"Coming within two miles," Pilas said. "Two miles . . . now." Just then, the heads-up display circular firing cue began its clockwise sweep, like a racing timer—when the sweep circle passed the three o'clock position on the HUD, he could open fire. Tamalko checked his switches visually instead of by feel, double-checked his gun status—still not jammed after 340 rounds fired off, which was above-average for the M61A1 cannon—and by the time he faced forward to line up on target, he was within a mile and a half. Pipper in the center of the radar diamond, a good ARM 260 indication—and Tamalko let loose, maintaining short trigger pulls, feeling the reassuring buzz of the gun when it fired, keeping the pipper lined up on the radar target diamond. There was no return fire from the big Chinese ship.

The cannon jammed with thirty rounds remaining, but every one of the others had been placed neatly into the ship's midsection. Tamalko clicked the gun to "Safe" and banked up on his left wing, keeping a low, thin profile to the ship as he passed overhead. He caught glimpses of flickering lights on deck as he screamed over the ship at Mach one, but whether they were secondary explosions or reflections of light, he couldn't tell.

Tamalko banked left, heading south, keeping his engines out of afterburner to avoid attracting any heat-seeking missiles or optically guided guns. The threat radars from the big destroyer were gone. Maybe he *did* hit something vital!

And then it happened.

For a millisecond Tamalko's eyes registered the brightest flash of light he'd ever seen. It was just on the horizon, almost directly off the nose. And just as quickly the light enveloped and blinded him. His eyes became two red-hot spheres of excruciating pain, burned, it seemed, by molten lava.

Behind him, Pilas was screaming and Tamalko realized he, too, was screaming.

The roar of the F-4E's big engines was gone, which meant they had been hit by something big enough to cause a double flameout—a big missile must have exploded right in front of them, blinding them and shelling out the engines. The control stick was beginning to tighten up as hydraulic power bled away—soon it would freeze up completely.

He hauled back on the stick to try to start a zoom maneuver and trade some of their Mach one speed for altitude—if they ejected at Mach one, the windblast would tear them apart. He couldn't tell if they were gaining altitude . . . there wasn't time to think. "Eject! Eject!" Tamalko screamed, then crossed his wrists in front of him, grasped the ejection ring between his legs, and pulled.

The canopy ripped off in the slipstream before the crewmen's heads crashed through it, and both he and Pilas were rocketed free and clear of the stricken plane.

Tamalko's body was flying forward at almost seven hundred feet per second.

The wall of compressed, superheated air rushing toward him from the explosion of the single RK-55 nuclear warhead of the Fei Lung-9 missile was traveling at two thousand feet per second. When the two met, Tamalko, Pilas, and the crippled F-4E Phantom II fighter were mercilessly crushed into powder, then vaporized by the five-thousand-degree heat of the fringes of the fireball that had already destroyed the Philippine corvette *Quezon* and its three antiship helicopters.

FIRST AIR WING COMMAND AND CONTROL OPERATIONS CENTER
CHEYENNE MOUNTAIN AFB, COLORADO
SAME TIME

A young Air Force staff sergeant, Amy Hector, was on the FOREST GREEN console at the U.S. Air Force Space Command's Command and Control Operations Center, deep within the Cheyenne Mountain NORAD complex, when her detection board went crazy.

"Red Collar, Red Collar," Staff Sergeant Hector called on the center-wide intercom, pressing the "Call" button on her console so that her warning message would override all the other transmissions in the Operations Center. The words "Red Collar" would also ensure immediate attention by all—the effect those simple code-words had was akin to her screaming at the top of her lungs:

"FOREST GREEN with an event-detection warning, all stations stand by . . ." Hector waited a few more heartbeats, then quickly began reading her detection figures aloud, knowing that the senior controller and the various section chiefs were scrambling to their seats and checking their own readouts. "FOREST GREEN shows three units with amplitude pulse threshold readings. System reports confirmation of readouts, repeat, system reports readout confirmation, event confidence is high." Technicians at Cheyenne Mountain seldom used words like "nuclear detonation" or "explosion"—these were collectively called "events" and "readouts." There was an odd emotional detachment prevalent inside the Mountain, as if they could somehow block the horrors they saw by naming them something harmless.

It was a relatively low-tech device that issued a warning on that Wednesday afternoon, a device that had gone all but unused for years. In an effort to increase the number of nuclear detection devices in orbit without increasing the actual number of satellites, in the late 1970s and early 1980s a secret program code-named FOREST GREEN was implemented. NAVSTAR Global Positioning System navigation satellites were fitted with electromagnetic pulse sensors and devices called (quite appropriately for nuclear detonation detection) Bhangmeters, which were sensitive optical flash detectors that could determine the explosive yield of a nuclear explosion by the brightness of the flash. Unlike AMWS, which were used only on specific (albeit very wide) areas of the Earth, FOREST GREEN had global coverage because the eighteen-satellite NAVSTAR constellation had at least three satellites looking at every piece of the Earth at every moment.

A nuclear explosion has a definite pattern of two pulses—the first less intense than the second—caused first by the detonation of the triggering device, followed exactly one-third of a second later by the main explosion; this was the reason Bhangmeters were mounted in pairs, with one more sensitive than the other. The EMP detectors on the three FOREST GREEN satellites also registered the disruption of the ionosphere before communication between the satellites and their receivers on Earth were abruptly cut off.

The senior controller in the Operations Center, an Air Force colonel named Randolph, immediately put the staff sergeant's console display up on the "big board," a rectangle of six 2-by-3-foot screens in the front of the Operations Center. The display was relatively uninformative at this point—three lines out of eighteen on the display were flashing, with a string of numbers showing the system readings and the threshold levels preprogrammed into the system.

"All stations, this is Randolph. I confirm a FOREST GREEN event detection and classification, I need a status check and report in thirty seconds, all stations stand by."

The problem with the FOREST GREEN sensors was that they were not highly directional—the sensors could accurately record a nuclear detonation but not precisely pinpoint the explosion's location; when the Bhangmeters were installed on older Vela nuclear-detection satellites, the device's telescopic eye could pinpoint the location of the detonation, but on NAV-STAR satellites the sensors were relegated to area reports only. In a few moments Amy Hector had replaced the cryptic lines of data with a graphic pictorial of the information: a chart of the Earth that was within line-of-sight reach of the three NAV-STAR satellites that had suddenly gone off the air. Somewhere within the three overlapping shaded spheres, the first above-ground nuclear device in thirty years had detonated.

Unfortunately, the display showed the explosion could have occurred anywhere from Hawaii to Thailand and from Japan to Australia. "I need better information than that," Colonel Randolph said. "Find out why no DSP systems issued an alert."

DSP was a constellation of satellites so sensitive that they could detect brush fires, structure fires, or even high-performance aircraft using afterburners—all from twenty-two thousand miles in space.

"Sir, this is Staff Sergeant Hector on FOREST GREEN," Hector interjected. "I think I can come up with a rough triangulation."

"Let's have it, Sergeant."

"I've got the exact time when all three of the NAVSTAR satellites shut down," Hector explained, "and I've got the time down to one-one-hundredth of a second. I can—"

Randolph looked at her. "I get the picture, Sergeant Hector. Speed of gamma particle versus time. Are the off-air times that different?"

"Stand by, sir." There was a slight pause, then Hector replied: "Two times are the same; the other is different. I can poll the sensor threshold-release circuits and get a more exact time; I can also try a laser orbital velocity measurement to see if the event changed the orbits—"

"Just do it, Amy." This was the first time he had ever recalled calling Hector by her first name, but it seemed oddly appropriate now. "But first, I need an acknowledgment of a suspected

FOREST GREEN event from CINCSPACECOM right away—
also get SAC and JCS on the line."

"Yes, sir."

"NORAD hasn't issued an alert yet," Randolph muttered
half-aloud. "Why the hell haven't they said anything? Something big enough to knock out three satellites is not good
news. . . ."

ABOARD SKY MASTERS' DC-10, OVER CALIFORNIA
SAME TIME

Jon Masters had his feet up on the bulkhead, was on his third
plastic squeeze bottle of Pepsi and halfway through a bologna
and cheese sandwich when the toneless, emotionless voice of
the Air Force mission control tracking officer on the radio said,
"Masters One, College, contact lost with Jackson One."

Masters sat upright, put down the Pepsi, and quickly
checked his readouts. "College, this is Masters One, I—" He
did a double-take. Seconds ago he'd been getting a stream of
position and velocity readouts from the NIRTSat in its orbit.

Now the readouts were zero.

Masters sighed. "Confirmed on this end. Stand by. I'll try to
re-establish communications." On the interphone to his crew,
he said, "Give me a turn westbound and a climb to best altitude. We've got a problem with the satellite."

Helen Kaddiri entered the flight deck. "What is it, Jon?"

"We lost contact with the satellite."

She looked at him as if to say, I'm not surprised. Instead, she
said, "Same problem we had before?"

"That was a loose plug, Helen, this"—he scratched his head
in an uncharacteristic moment of confusion—"has got to be
something else. But what, I don't know."

ABOARD WHISPER ONE-SEVEN, OVER POWDER RIVER MOA,
MONTANA
SAME TIME

McLanahan began programming the final launch instructions
on his Super Multi Function Display so they could take out the

last few sortie targets in General Jarrel's setup and then head home.

The display shimmered and abruptly changed.

"What the—" McLanahan muttered.

Instead of the gently rolling hills and dry gullies of southeastern Montana, the SMFD showed a confusing pattern of light spots in a blank, featureless background. It did have one very prominent terrain feature—a mountain nearly twenty thousand feet high and sixty miles wide. It was as if Mount Everest had just been transplanted into the middle of the Great Plains.

"I don't believe this . . ." McLanahan said, staring at the SMFD.

"What is it?" Ormack asked. "That doesn't look like the target area."

"The computer must be decoding the signal wrong," McLanahan guessed.

Amazingly, the computer began plotting a recommended course on the erroneous computer display, with sharp changes in heading away from the larger moving spots but fairly close to the smaller, non-moving ones. The computer even made weapon selections, although with only two weapons on board the choice was relatively simple—the longer-range SLAM missile for the large moving spots that were to be circumnavigated, and the STRIKER glide-bomb for the smaller, stationary ones.

The strike computer began the arming and countdown procedures to attack these "targets," and that's when McLanahan got tired of this. "There's some glitch in the system and it's not clearing. I'll reset the system and go manually until I get a usable display back." But he did not simply reset the computers—he used the on-board computer memory to save the last few seconds of images first before clearing the bogus display.

"What do you think is the problem?" Ormack asked.

"I don't know," McLanahan replied. "I'll check switches— the system will report on any switches out of position in the post-mission computer dump. Maybe there was a glitch in the satellite. Who knows?" He bent toward the screen and began identifying radar aimpoints, getting ready for the "bomb" releases. "Probably something minor . . ."

But that new satellite image did not look like something minor, McLanahan thought uneasily. It was more than a glitch. The computer was processing the data it received from NIRT-Sat as if it were real, uncorrupted data, and he knew enough about the NIRTSat system to know that the computer would reject false data.

No, whatever that twenty-thousand-foot-high "mountain" was, McLanahan thought, it was real. Something very serious had just happened somewhere in the world.

HIGH TECHNOLOGY AEROSPACE WEAPONS CENTER

"What the *hell* happened?" Colonel Wyatt exclaimed. They were looking in stunned amazement at the high-definition TV monitor, and at the monstrosity that the computer was showing them: a mountain thousands and thousands of feet high and dozens of miles wide, engulfing ships in its path with devastating power.

"Must be a sensor glitch . . . a solar flare or a power spike," Major Kelvin Carter tried. He spoke with the technicians, but none of those present could understand the display. "Whatever it is, it killed the satellite," Carter said. "This is the last image received; the satellite is off the air."

"Too bad," Wyatt said. "McLanahan's run was looking real good, too."

Captain Ken James' attention was riveted on the display frozen on the screen. "It's a weird picture, but the computer is displaying valid data on it," he said. "Look: height, width, speed, density, course—the thing is moving and growing all at once."

"But it's showing it as terrain, Ken," Carter said. "That can't be right. We were looking at the Philippines first, then at Montana. There's no mountain in either place."

Wyatt shrugged, then began packing up his notebook. "It was still a spectacular display, gents," he said, "but I—"

"Sir, phone call for you," one of the technicians said. "Urgent from NMCC."

As Wyatt trotted to the phone, James turned to Carter and asked, "Nimic? What's that?"

"National Military Command Center," Carter replied. "The War Room at the Pentagon."

James nodded, making a mental note.

FIVE

General Larry T. Tyler, commander in chief of the Strategic Air Command, was getting ready to make his first serve of the tennis match between members of the headquarters staff when the beeper on his portable radio went off. But, like a baseball pitcher halfway into his windup, he completed the serve and managed to hit his Reserve Forces Advisor, Colonel Hartmann, in the left leg. Hartmann was distracted and didn't expect his boss to finish his serve.

"Cheap shot, General," Hartmann shouted.

Tyler raised his racket to offer an apology to Hartmann, who politely waved it off, then trotted over to the bench, where his radio was sitting. Tyler's driver, a young buck sergeant named Meers, heard the beeper and immediately started up the General's staff car, which was waiting just a few dozen yards away. In Tyler's footsteps was his doubles partner, the former commander of Pacific Air Force's Philippine-based Thirteenth Air Force, Major General Richard "Rat Killer" Stone, who was to become Tyler's Deputy Chief of Staff of Pacific Operations in a few weeks.

It had been said that CINCSAC—the Commander in Chief

of the Strategic Air Command—was a prisoner of his job, and
to a certain extent it was true—the radio, the car, and the
driver were his constant companions. But the fifty-six-year-old
ex–Notre Dame football quarterback was determined not to
let the awesome responsibility of his position disrupt his life—
and that responsibility was truly awesome.

Tyler was in charge of the United States' smaller but still
potent nuclear combat force of ninety B-1B Excalibur bombers, two hundred B-52G and H-model Stratofortress bombers,
ten B-2A Black Knight stealth bombers, six hundred Minuteman III intercontinental ballistic missiles, one hundred rail-
garrison Peacekeeper ICMBs, fifty MGM-134A Mustang
road-mobile ICBMs, eight hundred AGM-129A advanced
cruise missiles, and one thousand AGM-131A Short-Range Attack Missiles.

In addition he commanded several hundred aerial refueling
tankers, strategic reconnaissance aircraft, airborne command
posts, and communications aircraft, and a total of about eighty
thousand men and women, civilians as well as military, all
around the globe—and his job was to stay within moments-
notice contact with each and every one of his sixty active and
reserve units at all times.

Although he was at the very pinnacle of his Air Force career,
he was determined not to get jabbed in the ass by its sharp
point.

As Tyler made his way to the bench where his radio sat, he
noticed the amber rotating lights at the street intersection
nearby—the SAC command post was recalling the alert crews,
and the amber warning lights told other drivers to be aware
of alert crews heading toward the flight line. Offutt Air Force
Base had an alert force of four KC-135 aerial refueling tankers
that would prepare for takeoff to support airborne command
post aircraft at Offutt, as well as other strike and communications aircraft.

The alert crews were tested regularly to make sure their
response time was always within limits. But Tyler knew the
schedule of all alert crew exercises, especially for the E-4 and
EC-135 aircraft—if enemy warheads were inbound, Tyler
himself would transfer his flag of command and take an EC-

135 airborne—and this wasn't a scheduled exercise. His pace quickened as he grabbed for the radio; his tennis partners sensed his sudden anxiety, saw the rotating lights, and immediately made their way to their staff cars as well.

With Stone standing a discreet distance away—he had a Top Secret security clearance but was not yet recertified for the SIOP, or Strategic Integrated Operations Plan, after losing his command in the Philippines—Tyler keyed the mike to turn off the beeper and spoke: "Alpha, go ahead."

"Colonel Dunigan, Command Center, sir," came the voice of his command center's duty senior controller, Colonel Audrey Dunigan. Dunigan was the first woman senior controller, rising through the ranks from KC-135 tanker pilot all the way to a Headquarters senior-controller slot. Dunigan was now the senior controller of the busiest shift in the Command Center, in direct communication with the Pentagon and all the SAC's military forces around the globe, and she seemed to take charge of the place like no one else before her. "Zero-Tango in ten minutes. Command Center out."

"Alpha copies. Out," Tyler replied. Turning to Stone, he said, "Let's go, Rat Killer. In my car. We'll have a little impromptu on-the-job training." He dropped his racket on the bench and loped toward his waiting sedan, not even bothering to make apologies to his staff—whom he knew would be right behind him anyway. Stone piled into the front seat beside Tyler's driver and they roared off.

"We got a Zero-Tango notification," Tyler told Stone. "You should be familiar with that: notification by NCA or Space Command directly, teleconference of the NCA, JCS, specified and unified commanders, all that stuff."

"I've only been in one," Stone replied, "and I was the one who called it. Just before the Philippine elections last year, Manila was a war zone. I thought Clark was going to be overrun. I had to kick General Collier at PACAF in the butt to do something. I raised a ruckus that obviously went right to CINCPAC, but he finally made the call and we got the support we needed."

"I remember that," Tyler said. "From what I read in the messages, Rat, Clark could have looked like the American embassy in Tehran in '79. Landing that Marine Expeditionary Unit on Luzon may have seemed like overkill to most of the Pentagon and the press, but it defused the situation perfectly."

"Sure it did," Stone added dryly. "And I got shit-canned for even suggesting it."

"Best thing that could have happened to you was getting bumped out of Pacific Air Forces and coming to work at SAC, Rat," Tyler said. "You know as well as I do that everyone will remember the last commander of Clark Air Force Base. Wherever you went in PACAF, that stigma would have followed you. It would have hurt your chances for promotion—I know it sounds shitty, but shit happens. Here at SAC, I get a topnotch expert in the Pacific Theater and maritime warfare, and you get a fair shot at your third star."

A coded message was being read over the radio, and Tyler squelched it out. Stone said, "You're not going to monitor the alert network?"

"The messages are for the crews, not for me," Tyler replied. "When I try to second-guess those messages, I give myself ulcers. Now I try to relax, think about what I need to do, and think about what I should be hearing when I get to the Battle Staff area."

"And the whole staff gets notified and called in?"

"Yep," Tyler replied, hanging on to the seat back as Meers negotiated a tight turn, switching on the siren to clear some traffic out of an intersection. "At this time of day it's no problem. When we get one at two in the morning, it can get real hairy."

"How often do you get these notifications?"

"Not very often lately," Tyler admitted. "A lot of the notifications can be expected—the riots in Lithuania just before their independence, the SCUD missile attacks during DESERT STORM, the assassination in Iraq, shit like that. You can read the evening paper and pretty much anticipate that a Zero-Tango was going to be called. But things just aren't all that critical in the real world these days."

They were approaching SAC Headquarters, a low, generally unimpressive building in the center of the base. The building was unimpressive because only three stories were above

ground—there were five more stories underneath. Stone could
see the Minuteman I missile out in front of the building, a lone
dedication to the thousands of SAC crew members who spent
as much as a third of their careers on twenty-four-hour alert,
sitting near their planes, in underground missile-launch com-
plexes, or in windowless command posts, ready to respond in
case deterrence failed—in case they were called on to fight
World War III.

He also saw the weeping willow on the lawn in front of the
headquarters building, and the sight struck Richard Stone as
oddly ironic. Fifty feet under that lone weeping willow, men
and women were ready, at the direction of the President of the
United States, the Secretary of Defense, and the man in the car
with him, to unleash thousands of megatons of explosive power
all across the planet with uncanny precision. The location of
the willow, Stone realized, was even a little absurd—several
nations probably had their thermonuclear weapons aimed at
that precise spot, ready to knock out the two-thirds of America's nuclear forces controlled from this one location.

No wonder Tyler turned off his radio, Stone thought. Even
in these days of relative stability and peace, the thought of
being flattened and vaporized by the first incoming warheads
was enough to drive a guy crazy.

"In ten, Sergeant Meers," Tyler told his driver.

"Got it, sir."

"Keep your badge in sight and follow me in, Rat," Tyler told
Stone. "We might have to put you in the 'press box,' but you're
certainly cleared inside the Command Post. It should be fun,
whatever we got going here."

Stone blinked at the four-star general. "General, you mean
you don't know what's happening?"

A grim-faced expression from Tyler gave Stone his answer.

At the outer gate to the parking lot/security perimeter
around SAC Headquarters, a security guard had his M-16 rifle
in one hand, and with the other hand he held up four fingers.
Meers flashed the guard five fingers, then one finger, and the
guard let him through. If Meers had added wrong and flashed
the wrong number—he had to add the right amount of fingers
to the guard's fingers to equal ten, the security number that

Dunigan had relayed to Tyler in the notification message and the one that she would have relayed to the gate guards—they would probably have had their tires shot out by two or three well-trained guards, and their noses would be pinned to the pavement a few seconds later. They had to pass through a second gate before reaching the building, and this time the guard was kind enough to flash eight fingers so Meers had to raise only two fingers in response.

Meers stopped the car just outside an enclosed doorway, guarded by a single security policeman. Tyler and Stone ran past him, not bothering to return his salute, and Tyler punched in the code to the Cypher-Lock beside the steel door. The door buzzed, and Tyler yanked the heavy steel door open, ran inside, flashed his security access badge to a guard in a bulletproof booth, and trotted to the private elevator that would take him four floors down, directly to the underground Command Center. The guards, Tyler noticed, all wore subdued smiles as he dashed by—it must be fun for them, he thought, to see a two- and four-star general in warmup suits running around the place. One more guard in a bulletproof booth checking ID badges, through a metal-detector device, another guard, two blast doors, past the Command Center weather station, and they were in the SAC Command Center itself.

The Command Center consisted of three areas, separated by thick soundproof glass and remote-controlled privacy shutters—the Battle Staff area on the main auditorium floor area, the Essential Elements area behind the main auditorium, and the Support Staff area in a balcony over the auditorium. All three areas could see the "big board," the eight 5-by-6-foot computer screens in the front of the Command Center, but depending on the security classification of the activity and the occupants, the senior controller could seal off either area to prevent eavesdropping—an unclassified briefing could be going on in the Support Staff area while a Top Secret briefing could be given in the Battle Staff area, with complete security.

Tyler glanced up at the Command Post status board just inside the entrance and found red lights flashing near the signs that read "Battle Staff" and "Essential Elements"—the rooms were both classified Top Secret. Tyler pointed to a doorway to their right. "Take those stairs up to the Support Staff room, Rat," he said. "They'll direct you from there." Stone did not argue or hesitate, but went through the door, which locked behind him. A set of stairs took him up to the glassed-in observation area overlooking the Battle Staff area, where a technician had him put on a pair of headphones as he sat down to watch. The shutters remained open, which meant he could watch the big board but not hear any of the conversation going on below.

The Battle Staff area below him resembled a small theater, with forty seats of three semicircular levels facing the big board in the front of the Command Center. Tyler took his seat in front row center, behind a director's computer console with two phones, a keyboard, and four 19-inch color monitors. The seat beside him was already occupied by the Vice Commander in Chief of the Strategic Air Command, Lieutenant General Michael Stanczek. Around them were arranged the various deputy chiefs of staff of the Command, most of whom were already in place by the time Tyler had arrived from the tennis court. Each staff position had two flip-up color computer monitors, a small keyboard, a telephone, and a microphone.

The first thing Tyler did after taking his seat in the Command Center was check the rows of digital clocks above the computer monitors. The first row of clocks had times in various places in the world—Washington, Omaha, Honolulu, Guam, Tokyo, Moscow, and London. London was labeled "Zulu," the time along the zero-degree-longitude Greenwich meridian used by SAC as a common time-reference point. Below that were three event timers, and one was already activated—it read 00:15:23. The third row of timers and clocks were thankfully still reading zero—those were the clocks that set reference times used by American strategic nuclear forces to execute their nuclear strike missions. Two of those timers, the L-hour and A-hour, were set by Tyler himself, but the other one, the ERT, or Emergency Reference Time, could be set by the National Command Authority if the President himself ordered a nuclear strike.

Tyler hit the mike button on his console: "Alpha in position. Log me in, please, and let's get started."

A voice on the auditorium's loudspeaker immediately chimed in: "Major Hallerton, with an Event One situation briefing." Hallerton was the shift's ADI, or Assistant Chief of Intelligence. "Approximately fifteen minutes ago, Space Command was alerted by a FOREST GREEN nuclear-detonation-warning sensor on three different NAVSTAR satellites. The event remained unclassified by NORAD and DIA for several minutes until verification could be made by DSP resources, and they have not made a conclusive evaluation yet. However, by authority of CINCSPACECOM, an Event One warning was issued to us and to JCS and Zero-Tango conference initiated. SPACECOM is currently reporting a high probability of a small-yield nuclear explosion in the South China Seas region near the Philippines."

Tyler felt his jaw drop. "Ho-ly *shit.*" Stanczek just sat there, a blank expression on his face. Tyler asked, "Just one explosion?"

"Yes, sir," Hallerton replied. "No other large-scale weapon detonations detected might suggest counterattacks. However, SPACECOM advises that the three NAVSTAR satellites have gone off the air and no other DSP or AMWS resources are on station to confirm any reports."

"Estimate on yield?"

"No official reading yet, sir."

"Well, anyone got an *estimate?*" Tyler grumbled. The sheer magnitude of the thing was bad enough, but being in the dark about even the smallest detail was worse. "Anyone got an educated *guess?*"

"Sir, the only other indications we have are that COBRA DANE or BMEWS have not detected missile tracks from land- or submarine-launched missiles," Hallerton said uneasily. The long-range over-the-horizon radars would have picked up the tracks of international missiles long ago. "All other stations are quiet, and intelligence reports no buildup of strategic forces or mobilization. This incident cannot be part of any massive attack against the CONUS."

Tyler couldn't believe it. A real nuclear detonation. But not a prelude to general war—or was it?

"When was the Pentagon notified and what did they say?"

"NCA was notified five minutes ago by Space Command, sir," Hallerton replied. "They requested follow-up notification from Teal Ruby satellite data on incoming missile tracks and received a negative reply. They are assembling the commands for a teleconference."

Tyler looked surprised. "That's it? A teleconference?" He turned to Stanczek. "What's *our* status?"

"The notification message from Space Command didn't direct any particular posture or DEFCON," Stanczek said. "There's a breakdown in communications somewhere. Anyway, since I didn't have a checklist to work off, I went right to the posture-four checklist and ran it. I heard the word 'nuclear' and thought the crews should be heading to the ramp."

Tyler nodded agreement. Most of SAC's forces were positioned at the discretion of the National Command Authority, either directly or through the Joint Chiefs of Staff acting as military advisers to the White House. Although Tyler could position his forces in almost any way he felt prudent, most of his decisions came from guidance or direct orders from the President or the Secretary of Defense, in the form of DEFCON, or Defense Configuration, orders. But in any case, especially when communications had broken down or the President wasn't in the position to make decisions like this, Tyler had the responsibility to see his men and machines were ready to fight. He did this by setting postures for SAC alert forces. "Good decision," Tyler told Stanczek. "I wonder what the hell the Pentagon is waiting on?" Sounds like nobody was doing anything, Tyler thought—they didn't see any incoming missiles, so everyone hesitated, waiting for someone else to act. Well, now was the time.

"Colonel Dunigan, place the force officially at posture four," Tyler ordered. "Then get the Pentagon on the line and inform them that I upgraded the SAC alert force posture and I'm recommending a full DEFCON change."

"Yes, sir," Dunigan replied. Part of the awesome responsibility of CINCSAC was his control over SAC's nuclear strike forces. It was his responsibility to keep the bombers and land-based ICBM forces safe and viable. Tyler had a long list of options, all designed to put the nuclear strike forces in the best possible position to survive an attack against the United States but to avoid unnecessarily moving too many nuclear weapons around or causing undue alarm to either the enemy or to American citizens.

Launching the bombers, either to dispersal airfields, airborne alert orbits or to their fail-safe positive control orbits, probably wasn't warranted yet. What was warranted, however, was stepping up everyone's overall readiness a couple of notches until the White House and the Pentagon figured out what was going on. That should have been automatic as soon as they discovered that it was in fact a nuclear explosion, but at least now it was getting done.

In the Essential Elements section of the Command Center, two positive-control technicians quickly prepared the radio message for the SAC alert force crews. Using a computer, they devised a forty-character message, triple-checked it manually for accuracy, using the same code books that the crews in the field would use, then broadcast the message via telephone, radio, and satellite communications channels to all SAC units in the United States, England, Germany, and Japan. The message directed all SAC units to stand by for further emergency action messages; it placed SAC's two hundred B-52 and ninety B-1 bombers, and thirty Minuteman ICBM launch-control centers, into higher readiness states, which would make their reaction times much shorter should they be directed to execute their SIOP war plans.

It would also direct twenty-two rail-garrisoned Peacekeeper missile convoys out from their shelters onto the nation's rail system and put twenty MGM-134A Mustang missile crews on full-deployment alert.

After receipt of the message, each SAC unit would verify and authenticate the coded message, rebroadcast the message to their forces, then compose and send a coded acknowledgment message back to SAC Headquarters. The entire process took approximately two minutes. Tyler watched one of the big digital screens before him as a list of all the SAC units was displayed, with red dots indicating connectivity with each unit; as the acknowledgment messages came in, the red dots disappeared.

"All units acknowledge, sir," Colonel Dunigan reported. "Expect status report from the field in about five minutes."

"What's the latest status on the units?" Tyler asked.

In reply, Dunigan put up a computerized listing of the latest status reports of all the SAC bases in the world, beginning with the SAC bomber units, and read off how quickly—or not so quickly—the units could move.

"What's the status of the Air Battle Force?"

"The current session reports ninety percent manned, due to some elements being recalled by their parent units before the session completed," Dunigan answered. "The new session that began training last month has the first B-2 bomber elements"—she paused as she referred to her notes, then said—"plus some GENESIS elements."

"GENESIS?" Tyler exclaimed. He had forgotten all about *that*—but it was easy to forget about Lieutenant General Brad Elliott's research group, lost from view in the middle of Nevada. Tyler had remembered granting approval for Elliott's weird hybrid planes to participate, but had not bothered to check up on their status during their course. "Jesus, I completely forgot about that. Refresh my memory, Colonel—what's he got at Ellsworth now?"

"He's got four modified B-52 bombers, six stretched F-111G bombers, and a B-2 bomber involved in the Air Battle Force session," Dunigan reported. "The -111's and the B-2 are garrisoned at Ellsworth; the B-52s—I should say, the EB-52Cs—are stationed at HAWC but still participate in Air Battle Force activities." She paused, then said, "I can get General Elliott and General Jarrel on the line and—"

"We don't have time," Tyler said. What a time to have Elliott's mutant planes out flying around in the Air Force Battle, Tyler thought. Christ, it was like Elliott *knew* there was going to be trouble. "It'll have to wait for the Air Battle Force status report. Move along."

Up in the Support Staff area, General Stone could not hear most of the interphone exchange between Tyler and his staff—but he was familiar enough with the items up on the big board to know that something serious was going on.

He saw lists of all the SAC bases in the world on the big

board, saw the status indicators change as he received the
message sent by Tyler, and saw weather maps, charts, and
checklist pages being put up on the board so everyone knew
where the staff was in the Zero-Tango response procedures.
But the left-center screen had something more interesting—
satellite photographs.

Stone turned to the technician seated beside him. "Is that
real-time imagery?"

"Not real-time, but very recent, sir," the tech replied. He
checked a computer screen and replied, "It's about ten to
thirty minutes old. DSP Control Center will automatically
upload the latest satellite imagery of a subject area. I don't
exactly know what the source of this imagery is, though—it's
not from Colorado Springs . . ."

"Any ideas when we can get the real-time pictures of the
area?"

"I'm sure the request is being made right now, sir," the tech
replied. "The request will probably come through whatever
command is placed in charge of the current emergency, or
direct from JCS or the National Security Council."

Stone's ears buzzed when he heard the words "current
emergency," but he didn't bother to ask what was going on—
he was busy scrutinizing the satellite photos being flashed on
the board.

"Ulugan Bay," Stone observed. He turned to a technician
seated a few chairs beside him. "I recognize that harbor. Ulugan Bay, Palawan. The Philippines. But that big ship . . . I don't
recognize it. What's going on?" The technician seemed to ignore him, but he had depressed his mike switch and had sent
a message down to the Battle Staff area.

Then, as the satellite imagery of the warship zoomed in
closer, maintaining remarkably high resolution even in ultra-
closeups, Stone realized that what he was watching was not a
Filipino ship. *"Hong Lung,"* Stone declared. "It's the Chinese
destroyer *Hong Lung.* What's it doing so close to Ulugan Bay?"

Just then Stone's headset clicked to life. "Rat—Tyler here,"
the Commander in Chief of SAC said. "Sergeant Rowe says you
seemed to recognize that harbor and that ship. What is it?"

The technician pointed to a button near the base of the

microphone on the desk in front of him, and Stone depressed the button and replied, "Yes, sir, Ulugan Bay on Palawan in the Philippines. Palawan is a large island about two hundred miles southwest of Manila. That ship looks like the Chinese destroyer *Hong Lung*. It's one of the two EF5-class destroyers in China's fleet. It's the flagship of the Spratly Island flotilla."

There was a long pause; then: "Well, you're right about the Philippines," Tyler said. "But what's the Spratly Islands? I never heard of them."

"It's a small island chain between Vietnam and Palawan in the South China Sea," Stone replied. "China claims them but legally occupies the lower one-third; the Philippines, Vietnam, Indonesia, and Malaysia occupy the northern third, with the middle third a neutral zone. Those five countries have been fighting over the islands for decades."

"Well, the fighting has just reached a new level, Rat," Tyler said dryly, "because someone set off a nuke right near the Philippines just a few minutes ago."

Richard Stone was so surprised that he forgot to press the mike button. "A *nuke?*" He paused, then managed to find the button. "Someone set off a nuke . . . ? General Tyler, that destroyer, the *Hong Lung*—it carries nuclear-tipped missiles."

Tyler and half-a-dozen other staff members in the Battle Staff area looked up in the Support Staff area. The near–real-time satellite photo of the Chinese ship had changed several times by the time a shocked Tyler asked, "That Chinese warship carries nuclear missiles? I never heard that before, Rat." He shook his head, stared hard at the charts of the South China Sea region, then rubbed dried sweat from his eyes in exasperation. "Jesus Christ, what's a Chinese ship doing cruising around the Philippines with nukes aboard?" He turned to Stone again and asked, "Can you verify that, Rat? What kind of nuclear missiles? How many . . . ?"

"It's never been verified as far as I know, sir," Stone replied, "just like we never verify that American warships carry nukes. But it's a well-known fact that EF5-class destroyers carry at least two Fei Lung-9 antiship cruise missiles with RK-55 warheads—twenty-kiloton yield. I can't believe the Chinese would actually cook one off, though."

"Do the Filipinos have nuclear weapons?" Stanczek asked.

"Not to my knowledge, sir," Stone replied. "We had some nuclear weapons stockpiled at Clark for a few years, but they were removed years ago."

"Could they have built a weapon of their own? Are they advanced enough to do that?"

"I'm surprised there was a Philippine Navy out there for a nuke to destroy," Stone said. "Everything they have is at least twenty to fifty years old, and most of it is World War Two vintage. As far as weaponry, they have Sea Lance and Harpoon missiles, but nothing more potent than that. No, they couldn't have built a nuclear device."

Stone could see Tyler shaking his head in amazement at the news, and it was then that he began to get a real feeling for the pressure that was on Tyler and his staff right now. In a few minutes the President of the United States was going to get on the line with Tyler and ask him how he should respond to the incident.

That call came a few moments later, but not from the President.

After a ten-second warning tone on the microwave telephone hookup, a voice began, "All stations, all stations, this is RENEGADE on Zero-Tango action teleconference network. Security classification is Top Secret. All stations stand by. Network poll in progress. National Command Authority, White House . . ."

While the lengthy teleconference poll continued, Tyler got on the intercom to Stone. "Rat, tell me more about the Chinese and the Philippines. Are the Chinese a threat to the Philippines or is their involvement limited only to the Spratly Islands? I mean, could they have been victims here, caught in the explosion?"

"Hard to say, sir," Stone replied. "The Communist movement in the Philippines has very close ties to the mainland Chinese, but as far as I know, the link is only ideological. Until the current regime got into power, there wasn't any direct contact between the Philippine Communists and the Chinese. But I've never heard of the Chinese ships operating so close to Palawan before, especially not a destroyer—and especially not the EF5 class. It's their newest, most modern and well-equipped model, and they're risking a lot driving that big boy around in those shallow waters around Palawan."

"What do you mean, the current regime?"

"Teguina, the First Vice President," Stone replied. "He's the leader of the pro-Communist National Democratic Front. Some say he's the leader of the main Communist armed opposition, called the New People's Army, that's been operating in the outlying provinces for the past several years. Teguina has been active in strengthening economic and cultural ties with China over the past few years; China has become a big trading partner with the Philippines and the United States. But it has been suggested that Teguina is working not only to strengthen economic ties to China, but military and political ties as well."

"China and the Philippines?" Tyler remarked. "Is that really possible?"

"Very possible, sir," Stone confirmed. "The Philippines have a large population of ethnic Chinese, and mainland Chinese own several large businesses and banks there. But more importantly, China sees itself as the protector of world Communism these days. With the Soviet Union becoming more democratic and capitalist every year, China is the last and perhaps the greatest exporter of Communism in the world. I'd say the Philippines are very fertile ground for them."

He went on. "I doubt Teguina's had anything to do with this Chinese fleet off Palawan or the nuclear explosion, but because of his presence in the Philippine government and his relations with the PRC, this could turn out to be a lot more complex than it is right now."

"What do you mean?"

"My guess is we probably won't see a total condemnation of the Chinese from the Philippine government," Stone said. "I don't know any details, of course, but when it comes time to point the finger, you won't see all the fingers pointing at China—you'll see a few pointed at President Mikaso."

"Mikaso? Why?"

"Mikaso is popular, but perceived as weak," Stone said. "Teguina is considered a strong leader. Mikaso was also too friendly with the United States. Although Mikaso is much more

of a nationalist than Teguina, Teguina's call for eliminating all
U.S. presence in the Philippines was a strong stand that most
Filipinos liked to hear." Stone decided against injecting his
own reservations about Teguina into the discussion, but remembered all too well the look in Teguina's eye that last day
at Clark.

"I still don't get it," Tyler said with rising exasperation.
"Why would Mikaso suffer by having the Chinese explode a
nuke near Palawan?"

Just as Stone was about to answer, the poll was completed
and the situation briefing began. Five minutes later, the briefing concluded with no mention of the Chinese destroyer or its
weaponry. Space Command or the Defense Intelligence
Agency refused to comment on the origin of the explosion.

Fine—Tyler would tell them himself. "General—Tyler at
SAC," Tyler said, interrupting the Space Command briefer.
"My staff expert here has possibly determined the origin of
that nuclear detonation."

There was a bit of a pause, then: "Go ahead, SAC."

"China. Satellite imagery confirmed their presence in the
area, and my expert reports that the Chinese ships seen in the
satellite imagery carry nuclear weapons—"

"Defense Intelligence here," a voice chimed in. "We have
no information of any Chinese vessels carrying nuclear weapons in the South China Sea. In fact the idea is ludicrous."

Tyler clicked on the intercom to Stone. "You sure of your
data, Rat Killer?"

"Positive, General," Stone said. "My intelligence may be a
few weeks old, but it's reliable."

The intercom clicked off, then on, and this time Stone could
hear the entire conversation on the network. "My expert
maintains that the Chinese vessel in the satellite imagery
we've just received carries nuclear-tipped antiship missiles.
The vessel is a Chinese destroyer, the *Hong Lung,* which is the
flagship of a large patrol fleet that operates in the Spratly
Islands."

"JCS copies, SAC," came the reply after a few moments: the
reply came from the chairman himself, General Curtis, and he

seemed curiously unsurprised at the revelation. "What is the current status of your units at this time, General Tyler?"

"Sir, I'm showing one hundred percent of the force fully mission ready," Tyler said, checking the connectivity readout of all his SAC units on the big board. The force is currently under posture four, under my authority. However, please be aware that the current SIOP OPLAN has no contingencies for operations against China or in the east Asian region. We hold no Chinese targets at risk."

"Understood," Curtis replied. "It may be premature to declare an A-hour, however. We will defer that decision for the NCA when we call the Charlie conference."

"Discharge of nuclear weapons automatically invokes at least a DEFCON Three level," Tyler said. "I recommend we proceed with that. Undoubtedly the Russians and the Chinese will respond by increasing their readiness levels as well; we should take the first step and then re-evaluate the situation."

"We'd have time for a discussion about contingency planning at a later time," General Curtis said. "Right now I want recommendations for the NCA as to the status of our deterrent forces."

"SAC recommends DEFCON Three, posture four," Tyler said.

"Forces concurs," General Jackson, commander of the Army Forces Command, said. As the largest single military command, the Army needed the most time to generate its units to go on a wartime footing and therefore had an equal say in whether a higher readiness state should be declared.

"COMSUBFLT concurs," Admiral Towland, commander of strategic nuclear submarines, added.

There was a slight pause, followed by a cryptic "Stand by" from General Curtis. Tyler found his palms moist and clammy. He rubbed them on his warmup-suit pants to dry them.

The Chairman of the JCS came back on: "All units, this is RENEGADE. Implement DEFCON Three. Posture will be no higher than that implemented by DEFCON Three. Stand by."

A few moments later, a warbling tone was heard over Tyler's headset and through the interphone system. The DEFCON lights above the big board changed from "4" to "3" and all of the Command Center status lights changed to red Top Secret indications. The Joint Chiefs of Staff communications center had assembled a coded message and broadcast it to all of the major commands. When received in the Essential Elements section, the message was decoded, checked, and the checklist for that order run immediately. "What do we got, Audrey?" Tyler asked.

"DEFCON Three, posture three," the SAC senior controller replied. "No A-hour specified. Time-control clock start in five . . . four . . . three . . . two . . . one . . . now." Just then, the second event-timer above the big board started counting. "Message acknowledged to JCS, checked and verified, standing by for retransmit."

"Retransmit," Tyler ordered. The message ordering an increased state of readiness would now be sent to all SAC alert units in the United States. The DEFCON change would also affect nuclear-capable Tactical Air Command units in Europe and Asia, all of the Navy's ballistic missile submarines, and the Sixth and Eighth Armies in Europe and Korea, which were some of the few Army units with deployed nuclear weapons.

After acknowledgment messages were received from all the major military commands, General Curtis said to the poll participators: "I will convene a Charlie conference as soon as possible. Have a breakdown of the pre-planned options for this contingency, along with your further recommendations. RENEGADE out."

The connection was then terminated.

"So what do we do now?" Stone asked.

"Run the checklists," Tyler said. "It's not unlike flying a fighter—we follow the checklist and it generally keeps us out of trouble."

A yellow light flashed on the telephone beside Tyler. "Well, here we go." He sighed. Before he picked up the phone, he turned and requested that iced tea be brought for him and Stone. "This is going to take awhile," he predicted. "We do it a little bass-ackwards, but it usually works.

"Curtis does a Charlie conference to direct each service branch to review the pre-planned contingency OPLANS, and the JCS decides which one to run. Then Curtis'll go to the President and SECDEF face-to-face and make his pitch. The President usually signs off on the plan just to get the ball rolling—then, when his Cabinet, the Congress, and the press find out, shit hits the fan. But that's not our concern."

"Where do you need me?" Stone asked.

"Right with me, Rat Killer," Tyler replied. "You're my resident Philippine expert. We built a new Philippine contingency plan when Clark closed, but I'll need you to look it over, tell me if it's still valid in the face of what the Chinese have out there."

"I'm ready," Stone said. "Is there any time to get out of these sweats, though? I'm not sure the staff will be able to work closely with me if I stink like an old pair of sneakers."

"Don't worry about it," Tyler said, a grim smile on his face. "Before long, everyone here will be just as nervous and sweaty as you are—except it won't be from exercise, it'll be from good ol' fear."

THE MALACANANG PRESIDENTIAL PALACE
MANILA, THE PHILIPPINES
SAME TIME

Philippine First Vice President Daniel Teguina paced restlessly as he, the Second Vice President Samar, and the Cabinet awaited the arrival of President Mikaso in the presidential conference chamber. Everyone was tense and worried. A few were terrified. All had rushed to the presidential palace immediately after being advised of the disaster in Palawan.

Finally, President Arturo Mikaso entered the conference chamber. Unlike the others gathered, who were dressed casually, Mikaso was in a dark-gray business suit, polished shoes, and a tie. His appearance was so crisp that a few wondered silently if he hadn't just dressed.

"Gentlemen . . ." Mikaso said, his old body moving as quickly as it could into the room. "Please take your seats." The elder statesman stiffly took his at the center of the oblong maple conference table and the other Cabinet members immediately sat down.

"As you know, a terrible tragedy has occurred," Mikaso began. "Less than thirty minutes ago, a patrol task force from this country was attacked by a large Chinese naval patrol off the coast of Palawan."

The Cabinet members exchanged looks of complete shock. They'd been advised of a major sea disaster, but given no details. Murmurs went around the room.

Teguina immediately spoke up. "A Chinese naval patrol? Judging by the state of our naval force, I assume we were beaten badly?"

Mikaso nodded sadly. "We were indeed. We've suffered serious losses—"

"Naturally," Teguina interrupted. "What do we have to fight with? Outdated, expensive, useless American equipment that we were suckered into buying."

Mikaso glared at Teguina. "Daniel, now is hardly the time for editorializing. There are far more serious considerations at hand." Mikaso looked at the men gathered in the room and said, "Gentlemen, the worst part of this confrontation, which involved two of our F-4E fighters, was that the Chinese launched a nuclear missile against our force."

Gasps went around the table, followed by immediate cries of outrage which echoed off the walls of the conference room. Everyone was talking at once until Mikaso rapped his knuckles on the table. "This has not been confirmed by us yet," Mikaso said, "but the detonation was detected by American and Japanese monitoring stations."

Again everyone started talking at once, their voices reaching a crescendo of questions of concern: What about the fallout? The food and water supplies? How could the Chinese have justified a nuclear-tipped missile? Did it mean this was a prelude to a full-scale invasion? Question piled upon question.

Mikaso tried to calm them down.

"We have no definite reports of an invasion," Mikaso said, "although the Chinese warships are in Ulugan Bay on Palawan, being guarded by our Army."

"But how did this happen?" demanded Second Vice President José Samar. "Civilized nations don't just set off nukes!"

Mikaso nodded in agreement. "One would think. However,

this was a battle between our forces and theirs. They ventured into the neutral zone, were going to attack a drilling platform, and we opened fire."

"What was a drilling platform doing there anyway?" Teguina asked, even though he knew. "Those islands are not for exploration or drilling. The Chinese have long considered that their territory, even though we don't. Why were we provoking the Chinese?"

"We weren't," Mikaso said pointedly. "Exploration is allowed within ten miles of the boundaries of the zone, Daniel. Learn your treaties. If you did, you'd know that the Spratly Island agreement not only allows that, but also prohibits a deadly force to patrol the zone. Armed warships must stay on their own side. We've seen how the Chinese violated that in the past—the previous incident was just a few months ago. I authorized our forces to protect themselves if the Chinese prepared to attack again, and that's what they did."

Teguina shook his head. "Why don't you tell them who we were really protecting? Unless I'm mistaken, it was an *American*-financed company who erected the oil platforms in the zone to begin with." He looked directly at Mikaso: "A company, I believe, Mr. President, run by one of your relatives?"

More murmurs went around the room.

"That is beside the point. It's a Philippine company and they had every right to explore the island and the resources on it."

The two men stared at each other.

"What about fallout?" another Cabinet member demanded.

Mikaso nodded. "That is our first priority. Daniel, you will immediately dispatch National Guard forces to Palawan to assist in the recovery efforts. In fact, I think the people of Palawan would appreciate seeing you there to help in the effort. Use all available transport assets and—"

Teguina pushed back his chair and stood up, something he usually did in Cabinet meetings to stress a point. He leaned over the table, looking at the others seated. "I will be honored to help our fellow Filipinos in Palawan, but there's one point we've dismissed too easily: who really launched that missile?"

Rumbling went around the table, and Mikaso pointed his finger at Teguina: "Daniel, I don't know what you're up to, but it's not going to work. I resent the dissension you're trying to create in the middle of a crisis. It—"

"Yes, sit down!" Second Vice President Samar said.

Teguina ignored them. "You say that the Chinese are at fault, but what you really meant to say is that it's not known who's to blame for the attack. That nuclear explosion could have just as easily been caused by an American nuclear device, either delivered by covert American forces or by Filipino airmen under orders by the American military or Central Intelligence Agency—"

"What are you talking about, Teguina?" Mikaso snapped angrily, his hands and lips trembling as much from confusion and exhaustion as from fury. "Are you that paranoid? There aren't *any* nuclear weapons on Filipino soil, no American airmen, and we did not launch any sort of nuclear attack. It was a *Filipino* vessel that was destroyed, for God's sake!"

"Do you deny that there are still American Intelligence agents here in the Philippines?" Teguina asked, his eyes darting between Mikaso and Samar.

Mikaso hesitated—only for a moment, but the pause was the answer.

The Cabinet officers looked at each other, then at Mikaso with undisguised shock. "Then it is true?" one of the Cabinet officers gasped.

"The American consulate is still open," Mikaso explained, trying hard to ignore the accusing glances, "and yes, I gave permission for several CIA officials to be stationed here."

"No, Mr. President . . ."

"This is outrageous . . ." Samar said.

Teguina couldn't believe it—he had stumbled onto something that at least for the moment overshadowed even the nuclear explosion in Palawan. The American CIA had long been blamed for the Philippines' internal turmoil, and Mikaso's admission could, even after all American military personnel had left the country, eventually bring down Mikaso's government. A common fear among the newly "liberated" Philippine government was that America would leave "moles" in place who would report to Washington and who could easily take over the Filipino government and realign with Washington in a coup. The Americans had left easily when ordered out—too easily, many thought. . . .

"You did this in direct violation of the law, without consulting your Cabinet or Congress?" the Minister of the Interior asked incredulously.

"Why weren't we informed?" another Minister demanded angrily.

As the chorus of other voices rose up in angry protest, Daniel Teguina sat back down in his chair, listening and inwardly smiling. Even in the middle of a crisis there was more than one way to skin a cat. . . .

ELLSWORTH AIR FORCE BASE, SOUTH DAKOTA
SAME TIME

Generals Calvin Jarrel and Brad Elliott had been waiting on the tarmac for the F-23 fighter pilots returning from their Powder Run sortie. Elliott especially was looking forward to giving the pilots some good-natured ribbing about the surprise they encountered with the EB-52 Megafortress that he'd gotten Jarrel to put in the air. Elliott was willing to bet that McLanahan had gotten a big kick out of seeing the F-23 pilots turn and run.

Just then a dark-blue staff car pulled up a few parking spaces from where Jarrel and Elliott were standing. Out of the car came Major Harold Briggs, General Elliott's aide and chief of security. Plugging his ears with his index fingers, he strode toward Elliott clutching a sheet of paper. He handed it to him.

Elliott read the note, and Briggs saw the expression on his boss's face change. "I'll take you back in my car, General," Briggs said loudly over the whine of the nearby jet engines.

"Problem?" Jarrel asked. Elliott showed Jarrel the note, keeping the sheet of paper tight in his fingertips—it was stamped Top Secret on both the top and bottom.

"Christ," was all Jarrel could say.

"I'll give you a ride back to your command post," Elliott said. They hopped in the sedan the second Briggs braked to a stop beside them.

In the car, Briggs passed out two red-colored vinyl folders, one to each of them. "Full text of the classified FLASH message for you, sir," he indicated to Jarrel. "Message from Colonel McLanahan from the Black Knight bomber sortie." Elliott frowned at the folder he was given and was about to set it unopened on his lap, but Briggs added, "I think you should read it, sir. I think it might have a connection with the DEFCON Three message."

There was silence in the sedan for several moments. Then, as though they were thinking the exact same thing, they handed their folders over to each other.

"Holy shit," Jarrel finally exclaimed. "This NIRTSat thing—your SPO actually thinks this satellite got pictures of a Chinese nuclear attack against a Philippine patrol?"

"Well, God knows it was possible," Elliott said. "If they had the NIRTSat up there, and it was over the Philippines at the time, it's more than possible. That might also explain why the satellite went off the air for McLanahan. Except it didn't go completely off . . . the thing was alive long enough to download the last of its photos to McLanahan in the B-2 during his bomb run here."

"But McLanahan says here the data wasn't transmitted to SPACECOM . . ."

"Space Command wasn't one of the users," Elliott said. "They provided launch and orbiting monitoring and had backup-performance telemetry but weren't scheduled to receive the imagery." Elliott paused for a moment, then said, "You know, Cal, if you're in DEFCON Three . . ."

"Yeah?"

Elliott knew that if Jarrel was going to be in a conventional contingency operation, which was very possible, he would be deploying, as priority one, the Air Battle Force. "Well, I think we've got the ultimate mission-planning tool in the world available for you if you want it. All we need to do is hook you up with Jon Masters and his NIRTSat boosters, and you can build mission packages for the STRATFOR so detailed that you'd think someone already flew the mission."

"Maybe not," Jarrel said, motioning to the message from

McLanahan. "Your SPO says that SPACECOM will deorbit the NIRTSat. SPACECOM didn't know about the nuke—they thought it had malfunctioned."

"Hal, step on it," Elliott told Briggs. "We need to get to the command post five minutes ago."

"Got you covered, sir," Briggs said. He tossed a pocket-sized cellular telephone into the backseat. "I wasn't cleared to peek at General Jarrel's message, but I was cleared to peek at yours. When I read the thing about Space Command, I ordered a direct scrambled call to General Talbot at Falcon Air Force Base. He should be calling back any minute."

True to his word, the phone rang just as Briggs pulled up to the steel and glass headquarters building, so Elliott sat in the car and took the scrambled telephone call from there. A gruff, impatient voice answered, "NORAD, General Talbot," then added with even greater brusqueness, "Make it quick."

"Mike, this is Brad Elliott calling from Ellsworth. How the hell are you?"

"Fine, Brad, just fine. Listen, Brad, can this call wait? I'm up to my ears in 'gators right now."

Brad Elliott knew that was the understatement of the year. Air Force General Michael Talbot had one of the most unusual military jobs in the world: he was a "triple hat," commander of three major military organizations all at the same time. Because the Air Force was the lead agency in space-related matters, Talbot, as commander of the Air Force Space Command, was also commander of the United States Space Command, the new specified military command that directed all military space functions and coordinated all space-related activities for the three services; and because Space Command was the United States' agency in charge of space defense, Talbot was also the current commander of the North American Aerospace Defense Command, which was a joint U.S. and Canadian organization that commanded all long-range radars and air-defense fighter bases for the defense of North America.

As such, Talbot was incredibly busy even during the quiet times—with an air-defense emergency in the works, he was stretched to the limit. Even through the hiss and pop of the secure phone line, Elliott could hear the stress in Talbot's voice. "I know you're busy, Mike, but this is important. I need to talk to you about Jon Masters . . ."

"I got young Doctor Hot-Shot Big-Sky Damn-the-Torpedoes Masters sitting right here, Brad," Talbot said with audible contempt. Talbot's commander of the Air Force Space Command's Second Space Wing (which was in charge of all Defense Department satellites from launch to recovery) had gotten on the phone to Sky Masters' DC-10 the minute the satellite went out. Since the NIRTSat had been launched seventy-one seconds outside of the launch window after disobeying an Air Force request to cancel, Talbot's subordinate, the commander of the Second Space Wing, had ordered up a specifically modified C-130 cargo plane to recover the satellite. Better that, the commander thought, than having a nine-hundred-pound piece of scrap metal in a bad orbit. Masters had no choice but to go along with the Air Force. Either that or face handcuffs at Falcon Air Force Base, where he was now sitting.

"He was just about to let my senior staff in his plant office inspect his records, weren't you, Doctor Masters?"

"That's got to wait," Elliott said. "He just lost a satellite and I've got to get him out to GENESIS right away. It's all connected . . ."

There was a slight pause; then, "Oh . . ."

Few things in this world could knock guys like Talbot back on their heels, but GENESIS, Brad Elliott's classified call sign from Dreamland, was one. Just mentioning the word meant that most of the Pentagon was involved. Which was, Talbot thought, typical of Elliott, who was known to be kicking ass with an array of high-tech toys developed out in his secret labs in Nevada. Rumors had been circulating for months about Elliott's B-2 bombers and other strange planes flying around the desert. God only knows what he needed Masters for. But the fact that Elliott knew all about a classified satellite launch that had gone wrong only twenty minutes before, told Talbot that Elliott was plugged in right at the top.

"Well, you got him, Brad. Now where do you want him?"

"I need him back in his lab in Arkansas soonest. When are you going to be done chewing on him?"

"I'm done. I don't have the time or energy for shit like this anymore," Talbot said in a low voice. "His jet is already fueled. He'll be airborne in thirty minutes and in Arkansas in three hours. Does this have something to do with . . . events this afternoon?"

"It could have *everything* to do with it."

"I was afraid of that. The little prick leads a charmed life. You need his satellite intact as well?"

"Have you deorbited it yet?"

"Just about ready to do it—window opens in about an hour."

"Better leave it, then. The brass hasn't made up their minds what they want."

Talbot knew the "brass" usually included only men who had collected more than fifty million popular votes.

"Whatever you say, Brad. I'll be glad to jettison that little cocksucker anyway. He's a pain in the ass."

"You have that effect on people, my friend."

"Yeah, right. The bastard never stops smiling, too. You notice that? Always with the damned grin on his puss. I don't trust somebody who grins all the time—it usually means they found someone else to put the blame on."

"If he busted one of your rules, Mike, he's gotta pay. When GENESIS is done with him, I'll send him back to you. How's that?"

"Naw. Keep him outta my sight. Just get the bastards who fried my NAVSTAR satellites and we'll call it even."

"Deal, buddy. GENESIS out."

THE WHITE HOUSE SITUATION ROOM

The President had been in the Roosevelt Room listening to a planning meeting for a world economic conference when they told him.

Lloyd Emerson Taylor, forty-third President of the United States and a descendant of the twelfth President, had made a mental note of what he was doing at that moment. It would, after all, be important for the memoirs he was going to write after he left office. And this, Lloyd Emerson Taylor guessed, was going to be one hell of an important chapter in his book.

After his military aide had handed him the Eyes Only message, Taylor had immediately excused himself from the planning meeting and retreated to the Oval Office. From there,
over a secure hot line, he began to get a handle on the situation: he learned that Defense, JCS, and the CIA suspected the
Chinese of setting off the nuke, but no one had been able to
completely verify that. Worse, the President couldn't get word
on how President Mikaso was or what was going on in Manila
because all phone lines were jammed and all satellite and HF
networks had been disrupted. He also learned that even
though the U.S. had been monitoring the situation between
the Chinese and the Philippines since their naval skirmish of
a few months ago, nobody wanted China or the Philippines to
know that the United States had pictures of the explosion.
Apparently the pictures were not taken by a regular satellite
but by a new, highly classified one called PACER SKY, an
experimental system that would allow real-time targeting data
for strategic bombers.

Whatever the hell PACER SKY was, Taylor knew it had just
snapped what might be one of the most famous photographs
in thirty years, thanks to a simple stroke of luck.

Finally, a more formal, albeit hastily arranged, assessment
meeting was scheduled a half-hour later in the Situation Room.

As Taylor, his military aide, his official White House photog-
rapher, his Secret Service bodyguard, and a civilian-clothed
Navy captain who carried his "football," the portable scrambled UHF transceiver that Taylor would use in an emergency
to order his strategic nuclear forces to war, made their way
down the elevator to the Situation Room in the basement of
the White House, the enormity and gravity of the situation
finally began to sink in.

Like his famous great-great-great-great-grandfather, the
President was a bull-nosed, laissez-faire bureaucrat who'd
done well as president because of his quiet, hardworking, rock-
steady style. And like his ancestor, Taylor was an ex-Army
general and judge advocate who had retired to enter politics
at age fifty-one, soon after pinning on his first star. Taylor had,

above everything else, a keen sense of history—and his place in it.

He knew, even as he entered the Situation Room and everyone stood up, that he was the first American president to have to deal with a nuclear weapon crisis since John F. Kennedy.

And he was determined to handle it better than Kennedy did.

He had not been in the Situation Room five minutes when he had his men on the griddle—even as phones rang constantly in the background. His eyes wandered around the table to each and every adviser: Tom Preston, his Secretary of Defense and an experienced politician; General Wilbur Curtis, Chairman of the Joint Chiefs of Staff; Kenneth Wayne, Director of the CIA; and Frank Kellogg, his National Security Advisor.

His eyes settled on General Wilbur Curtis, chief military officer of the United States and Chairman of the Joint Chiefs of Staff. He was the President's principal military adviser but a holdover from the last administration. Unfortunately, he was so well respected on the Hill and at the Pentagon that Taylor knew he couldn't get rid of him even if he wanted to.

"General Curtis, even though you got us in this DEFCON Three posture—and I wish I had been in on that decision from the start and not after your commanders went ahead and did it themselves—the 'bolt from the blue' theory of strategic warfare has been dead for almost a decade."

Curtis could see this was going to be a long, difficult meeting.

"Sir, we were following the OPLAN—the operations plan—established and authorized by you in case of an emergency of this magnitude. DEFCON Three is a very secure posture right now. We're—"

"If there was no apparent attack in progress, then you had time to notify me and let me make the decision," the President interrupted. "That's what I expect. We will need to change the OPLAN after this to rectify it."

"Yes, sir," Curtis acknowledged.

"What else have you got for me, General?"

Curtis cleared his throat. "Our strategic forces are in full readiness, so if this is some sort of prelude to an all-out attack against the United States, we're ready, sir." Curtis glanced at the Navy captain seated near the door, keeping the "football."

The President disliked having the football around—he had once told the press that he likened it to the Grim Reaper, with scythe in hand, following him everywhere he went—but in this he had no choice.

"Well," Taylor grumbled, "I guess the question of whether this is a prelude or not will be answered once we have more information, won't it, General? This PACER SKY thing saw who launched the missile, didn't it?"

"Not exactly, sir," Curtis replied. "The NIRTSat—part of the PACER SKY program—saw the nuclear explosion, but we're trying to keep a lid on that. As you know, we've been monitoring the situation between the Chinese and the Philippines since that original skirmish. But because of our past association with the Philippines, we didn't want it to appear as if we were monitoring anyone—or feeding anyone intelligence information. Still, we do know, thanks to PACER SKY, exactly which ships were in the area. SAC analysts have concluded that only the Chinese could have launched the weapon."

"Well, then, that brings us to the bigger picture, doesn't it?" the President said. "I've been briefed on the shit going down in the Philippines for some time. And you people tell me the Communists are running rampant in the outlying provinces and that if Mikaso kicks the damned bucket we could lose all ties to the Philippines—our stopover and resupply privileges, our radar sites, our listening posts, our practice bombing ranges. I was also briefed on the skirmish a few months ago between the Chinese and the Philippines, but it was characterized as nothing more than a little tiff. When a fucking nuclear bomb goes off, gentlemen, it's not just a little tiff. Now what the hell is going on here? Is it the start of a major war, an illegal test by some country, or an accident?"

Director of Central Intelligence Kenneth Wayne said, "An accident, sir, seems the only plausible explanation. The Chinese Navy could certainly overtake the Philippine Navy without having to resort to nuclear weapons. Also, we've detected only one explosion, which tells us there was no nuclear exchange. Of course," the CIA director said, lighting a pipe, "it also could have been a military response by the Chinese, but a response by . . . say, a lone wolf, and not necessarily the Chinese government itself."

"Lone wolf?" the President asked, raising his eyebrows. "You mean some nutjob in command of a ship?"

The CIA director shrugged his shoulders. "Entirely possible. Not a nutjob, per se, but simply a commander who panicked. But I'd put my money on it being a simple accident."

"JCS doesn't agree with the DCI's estimation, sir," Curtis said. The look the President, as well as Wayne, gave him could have chilled a polar bear. "We don't discount the DCI's theory, but we have evidence of another possibility that I feel it would be more prudent to act upon." The President had a very slight—but very noticeable—exasperated frown—he didn't like being told that he was wrong. He rolled his hand as if to say, "Get on with it." Curtis said, "My staff feels that this attack may be a prelude to an all-out attack and invasion of the Philippines by China . . ."

Everyone in the room sat up. Voices started coming at Curtis and at President Taylor all at once.

"Ridiculous . . ."

"Totally off the mark . . ."

"They'd never try it . . ."

Curtis pressed on. "All I have is speculation, sir, but we're forgetting China has long historical claims to many of the Philippine Islands and the fact that ethnic Chinese make up a great majority of the Philippine population. Couple that with someone like Daniel Teguina, who has strong Communist ties, and you've got the makings of a real land-grab."

Voices of dissent were heard from the CIA director, the Secretary of Defense, the National Security Advisor. The President cleared his throat—loudly. All heads turned to him. "Look, we can speculate all we want, but without any information, speculation's not going to do us a damned bit of good." He turned to the DCI. "No word from Manila yet? Or Mikaso?"

"All lines are still jammed, sir. Satellite and HF networks are still down."

This got a grunt from the President. "And what about China? Have we heard what they think about all this?"

DCI Kenneth Wayne said, "We've got calls in to everyone, sir, including Premier Cheung."

The President turned to Tom Preston, his Secretary of Defense. Preston had been silent so far. "Thomas, what do you think?"

"Well, this is an extremely vulnerable region, sir. And we've lost a lot of influence there since . . . leaving. So I think we've got to do at least an on-site military inspection. A task force sent from Hawaii or Japan would be sufficient and," in partial acknowledgment to Curtis, he added, "would deter any possible aggression, if that were going to happen."

"Uh-huh." The President nodded. "We do have ships patrolling the area all the time, right? So we send a few in, check it out, keep them on station for a while, and get the CIA in as well. Meanwhile I can sell everyone—for the time being—on this being an accident."

"Excuse me, sir, but there are several standard OPLAN responses that should be implemented, and the Joint Chiefs of Staff have a few plans we'd like to offer as suggested responses," Curtis interjected.

"You don't think just a few ships—say, sending one carrier group—are enough?" the President asked. "Why am I not surprised?"

"Sir, the nuclear blast itself is cause enough for concern. But a single twenty-kilometer nuclear device detonated in the middle of one carrier battle group would destroy everyone and everything within five miles, including an aircraft carrier.

"This is why the standard OPLAN calls for the deployment of at least three carrier battle groups to the region, along with a Marine Expeditionary Force, the Twenty-fifth Infantry Division of the Army Western Command, and the Air Force First Air Battle Wing. They would deploy afloat or from Okinawa or Andersen Air Force Base on Guam, as appropriate. It is especially important these days since we have no . . . military forces in the Philippines. Even if we don't use three, at least two carrier battle groups would be more appropriate.

"The only two carrier battle groups available are two fossil-fueled carriers, *Independence* and *Ranger. Ranger* still does not have Hornet fighter-bombers because of her accelerated decommissioning schedule, but *Independence* is fully combat-ready. Two nuclear carriers, *Nimitz* and *Abraham Lincoln,* are both in the Indian Ocean at the present time, but that's several days' steaming time to get back to the South China Sea. We recommend that the Marines' landing-support carrier *Belleau Wood* and her support ships be deployed with the task force; they can carry about two thousand Marines and about thirty helicopters. They can split between the two carrier groups as necessary." Curtis saw the President's eyes when he mentioned the Marines, and he added quickly, "It's routine to send a Marine Expeditionary Unit with such a task force, and if we're dealing with the Philippines it might be necessary."

The President still had that pained look in his eyes, but Curtis continued nonetheless:

"Because the two carrier groups have fewer air-to-ground attack planes, it was suggested to augment the task force by forming the First Air Battle Wing at Andersen Air Force Base on Guam to—"

"The First—what? What the hell is that?" the President asked with irritation.

"The First Air Battle Wing is the new Rapid Deployment Force air combat group, sir," Curtis explained. "According to the current strategic force operations plan under DEFCON Three, the First Air Battle Wing is formed upon alert notification and deployed to one of three locations—Loring Air Force Base in Maine, Diego Garcia in the Indian Ocean, or Andersen on Guam. From these three operating locations, the Air Battle Force can strike at any spot on the globe within twelve hours."

"Who's in this Air Battle Wing?"

"The wing is a collection of strike aircraft, mostly heavy bombers—B-52s, B-1Bs, F-111G, and F-15E bombers—plus tankers, fighters, and cargo planes," Curtis replied. "The Air Battle Force has its own fighter escorts, its own reconnaissance and intelligence aircraft, and its own defense-suppression aircraft—it's a single self-contained combat unit that can operate from remote areas over long distances on very short notice. It—"

"Let me get this straight," the President said, an exasperated edge in his voice. "You want to send in two aircraft carrier battle groups—that's over twelve thousand men if I'm not mistaken—plus two thousand Marines, *plus* all these B-52s and other combat aircraft?" He said the words "B-fifty-two" as if he were uttering a curse. "Do you know something about this operation I don't?"

"Sir, the Joint Chiefs feel it's vital to act quickly, decisively, and with enough firepower into the area very quickly. The carriers can't get into the area for several days—"

"Enough, General," the President said. "I am *not* going to send all those men and all that firepower into that area without first knowing what I might get myself into. You can understand that, right?" He did not wait for a response. "You said it would take a couple of days to get a couple of naval units into the area? Fine. I'll buy that.

"I'll authorize *two* carrier battle groups—not three—to head toward the area where the explosion was detected. They are to take no military action unless I specifically authorize it. Those ships are authorized to protect themselves to the fullest extent. I'll also authorize a small patrol to investigate—no more than three surface ships. Deploy radar aircraft as you see fit. But I don't want any massive armada steaming off the Philippine coast—they'll think it's a damned invasion.

"As for the Air Battle thing, that's out of the question," the President continued. "I know the Air Force has been trying to downplay the nuclear role of the B-52 and show the world that the mere presence of the thing doesn't constitute the end of the world—I believe they call it 'desensitization'—but we're not going to provoke the goddamned Chinese into a full-scale conflict. God only knows where it would lead. . . ."

"Yes, sir, I understand," Curtis replied.

"And another thing," the President added. "I'm allowing you to deploy these two groups against my better judgment. Frankly I'd prefer only one group."

"One last request," Curtis added quickly.

"Yes?" The President sighed.

"I realize you don't want the Air Battle Force involved yet, but I would like permission to deploy the STRATFOR—"

"The what?"

Curtis knew that the President knew what he was talking about. "The Strategic Force. The advance team for the Air Battle Force. I'd like to deploy them for reconnaissance operations in the area."

"And what would you do with the STRATFOR if you got it?" the President asked warily.

"We'd conduct long-range reconnaissance and probe missions from Guam, using E-3C radar planes, RC-135 reconnaissance planes, and EC-135 communications planes—General Tyler of SAC has a team standing by ready to go. The STRATFOR also takes officers and engineers from the Air Battle Force to help set up support facilities—this is especially important now that we have aircraft like the B-2 bomber in inventory."

The President mulled this over. "Uh huh. And then what? What'd be next?"

Curtis pressed on. "Then, if the situation warranted, and you, of course, felt the time was appropriate, we'd deploy the First Air Battle Wing. This is important because they'd be an integrated force of bombers, fighters, and support aircraft to protect the naval forces and clear a path for further operations."

The President looked indecisive and exasperated. He turned to Defense Secretary Tom Preston. "What is it exactly that you want to do, Thomas?"

"Just what General Curtis is recommending: send in the STRATFOR to Guam. SAC will back it up with the Pacific Tanker Task Force, which will provide air refueling support for the deployment."

"Uh huh." The President nodded, still not entirely convinced, but leaning toward a yes.

"Oh . . . and, Mr. President?" General Curtis said. "CINC-SAC is recommending, and I agree, for Major General Richard Stone to be the STRATFOR commander—he's an ex–SAC division commander and was the former base commander at Clark. He knows the Philippines like the back of his hand. General Stone will make his recommendations to Pacific Air Forces and Pacific Command on the type of response necessary and they make recommendations to you. Once approval is granted from you through Pacific Command, the STRAT-FOR will form the Air Battle Force."

The President paused for a few moments, then nodded his head. "All right, General—I have my doubts, but let's do it. Send in the two carrier groups only, put the Marines on standby, and send out the STRATFOR to Guam to help check things out. We'll wait on whether to send your Air Battle Force until we find out what in hell the Chinese are up to. Got all that?"

"Yes, sir, I understand," Curtis replied, and quickly added, "There are a few more items—"

President Lloyd Taylor had had enough, but he said, "Yes, General, make it quick . . ."

"CINCPAC has requested an increased 'safe zone' around his fleet assets in the region . . ."

"Sink—*who?*"

"Sorry, sir . . . Admiral Stoval. Commander in Chief, Pacific Forces. He'll be in overall charge of operations in the South China Sea; he is asking permission to order the fleet that is sent down there to engage unidentified or hostile vessels or aircraft out to a range of two hundred miles instead of the usual one hundred miles."

"Why does he need that?" President Taylor grumbled.

"Sir, if it was a Fei Lung-9 missile that was launched from a Chinese ship, the missile has a range in excess of one hundred miles and is supersonic, which makes the task of shooting it down very difficult. With a nuclear warhead, the kill radius of the missile is that much greater. The commanders in the area will want to keep all unidentified aircraft as far away as possible from their ships and to provide air cover for the reconnaissance planes," Curtis said. "They all operate no closer than two hundred miles from Philippine waters . . ."

"Air cover? I said *no* air operations!" the President snapped.

"This would be for the STRATFOR reconnaissance jets, sir," Curtis explained. "Those jets—the AWACS, the EC-135, and the RC-135 are unarmed recon planes. We have to provide air cover for them if they're operating so close to the Chinese forces . . ."

"I thought you said this would be a *simple* operation, General . . ."

"Sir, for safety's sake, each STRATFOR aircraft should have a minimum of eight fighters with it at all times . . ."

"Eight fighters!" the President exploded. "And how many aircraft will you send from the STRATFOR?"

"Four, sir," Curtis replied.

"You want *thirty-six* aircraft involved in a 'simple' reconnaissance mission? That's out of the question. If I saw that many planes near my ships, I know *I'd* be angry. Good God, man, don't you get it? I'm trying to *avoid* a fucking war! We're sending in all this force and we don't even know what the hell is going on!"

"Our aircraft need that kind of protection . . ."

"Do it with *less*," the President ordered. "If you can't protect the reconnaissance aircraft with *two* fighters each, you can't send them in—we'll rely on satellite data to gather intelligence information instead."

Curtis paused for a moment, then said, "I'll confer with General Falmouth . . ."

"Yes, yes, fine," the President said, waving his hand as if dismissing a bothersome insect. "Do what you want, just make sure you cover those planes with *two* jets each. I don't care how you do it."

"Of course, sir."

"And, Curtis?" the President added, pointing his index finger at the General. "If this thing blows up in our face . . . if this puts my ass in a sling? Guess what? *Your* ass is going to be in a sling."

And with that, Curtis was dismissed. Other aides and staffers were already being buzzed into the Situation Room before Curtis reached the door. Curtis' aide, Colonel Andrew Wyatt, met the Chairman of the Joint Chiefs of Staff in the corridor next to the Marines guard desk. He fell in beside Curtis as they headed for the elevator.

"Well, how'd it go?"

"Don't ask," Curtis said as Wyatt punched the elevator call button.

"That bad?" Wyatt asked.

Curtis said nothing. Instead he was too busy thinking about what was going on halfway around the world. . . .

BUENAVISTA HOSPITAL, ULUGAN BAY, PALAWAN PROVINCE
THE PHILIPPINES
MONDAY, 26 SEPTEMBER 1994, 2109 HOURS LOCAL

Admiral Yin Po L'un awoke to find himself lying on a very soft bed under clean white sheets. Through blurred eyes, he saw several nurses—Filipino nurses, he soon realized—surrounding his bed. One of them, after realizing that he was awake, ran off out of sight.

"Who . . . who are you?" Yin asked in Chinese. The nurses looked at each other, then turned back toward him and shook their heads, replying something in English that obviously meant they did not understand him. But a nurse bent forward to wipe sweat and mucus from his face and eyes, and he was able to see—

—several Filipino soldiers marching into the room, with M-16 rifles slung on their shoulders. So. He was a prisoner of the wretched Philippine Army, or worse, the damned Americans. Even though he saw no American-looking faces, he assumed he would be turned over to them soon.

Presently, a physician in a white lab coat appeared before him, along with, to his great surprise, the senior ship's doctor from the *Hong Lung,* a Vietnamese immigrant named Commander Tran Phu Ko. Finally, a man who appeared to be an officer stood at the foot of the bed, bowing slightly at the neck when he noticed Yin looking at him.

Commander Tran bowed to Admiral Yin. "Thank the gods you are well, Comrade Admiral."

Yin struggled to rise to a sitting position, and Tran helped him. "Report, Doctor. Who are these men? What is the status of the ship? What of the crew?"

"The men are well, Admiral," Tran replied. "Many casualties, but we can speak of that later. The ship is damaged but safe. It is secured in Ulugan Bay, not far from here. Several other ships of our task force are there as well."

Ulugan Bay. Palawan Province, the Philippines. So they *were* prisoners. . . .

Tran motioned toward the officer at the foot of the bed. "This is General Robert Munoz di Silva, commander of the provincial defense force," he said. "He is our . . . host. He speaks no Chinese. I know English, sir; I can interpret for you."

"Ask him then if we are his prisoners," Yin said, "and what sort of treatment my crew and myself can expect from them."

Tran looked puzzled, then relieved. "No, sir, you do not understand . . ."

"Ask him," Yin ordered.

Tran was about to speak once again, but, at a stern glance from Yin, bowed and relayed the question in broken, hesitant English. But obviously General di Silva understood, because the pig-faced bastard threw back his head and laughed out loud, right in Admiral Yin's face!

Then, to Yin's complete surprise, the Philippine General walked over to Yin and kissed him on both cheeks! Yin stared at the man, flabbergasted, while General di Silva babbled on enthusiastically about something or other.

Yin shook his head warily. They must have given him morphine. Or worse. Something was wrong here.

Dr. Tran read his thoughts: "You do not understand, Comrade Admiral. We are not prisoners of General di Silva—we are their liberators and allies."

"What?" Yin asked, sitting up straight. "What are you saying? Their liberators? But—"

"According to General di Silva, he no longer considers his force to be part of the Philippine military," Tran said. "He and his men have been secretly opposed to the capitalist pro-American government in Manila for over forty years. They've been waiting for such an opportunity to strike out at the puppet of the Americans. He is asking for our help in supporting his movement and assisting him and his fellow Communists in severing ties with the rest of the Philippines and establishing a pro-Communist state here on Palawan."

With that, they watched in complete surprise as di Silva stripped off his blue and gold epaulets of the Philippine Integrated National Police and tossed them over his shoulder. A few of the nurses and doctors who had filled the room looked ashen at the demonstration, but most of the others were smiling broadly, some even applauding.

But Admiral Yin couldn't believe his eyes. Although he knew a potential enemy would go to extreme lengths to confuse a prisoner into cooperating or giving up information, this di Silva seemed sincere. Could they have drugged him? Was this all some kind of grand hoax . . . ? "Doctor, ask him what is happening. Ask him if we have been drugged. Tell him I wish to be released immediately and reunited with my crew."

Commander Tran had to raise his voice a bit over the impromptu celebration there in the room, but eventually he communicated the Admiral's question and received a reply: "Sir, he says he is empowered to release all of us and our vessels if we so desire," the physician translated, "but he wishes to say that the revolution has begun and that you are the catalyst for constructive change in Palawan, and perhaps all the Philippines, for all true Communists. He is prepared to offer us protection until we are well enough to function, then he pledges that his loyal forces will rally behind us to free Palawan and create a powerful, respected Communist nation." Di Silva spoke again, and Tran added, "General di Silva is putting you in command of his provincial defense force, sir. You may order him and his men to do as you please. But he asks that you accept the challenge. It would be a dishonor for you and the Republic of China not to . . ."

Admiral Yin Po L'un's head was reeling in confusion. This . . . this was too strange. It had to be a trick of some kind. But what? This charade was different than any other kind of interrogation or con scheme he'd ever heard of—it didn't make sense. At least to him. A foreign militia commander laying down his weapons before a prisoner, then asking the prisoner to take over? It was absurd.

Yin sat back in the bed, trying to absorb it all. Maybe they had given him drugs and weren't admitting to it. But what would be the purpose of this . . . acting?

For a moment everyone in the room simply stared at him. As if waiting for his word . . .

He wanted to shake his head, to think clearly. And yet he *was* thinking clearly. And this proposition was bizarre. He took a deep breath. His head hurt, but otherwise he seemed fine. Maybe a bruise or two, but nothing seemed seriously out of joint or injured.

So if he was okay . . .

Then was this real?

What if it was?

This di Silva character didn't look insane—perhaps he was who he said he was, and he really meant what he said. If so . . . what an opportunity! To occupy a strategic province of the Philippines without firing a shot—the horrible effects of the nuclear detonation notwithstanding—was the decades-long goal of the People's Republic of China. It was even better if the Chinese were *invited* to occupy the islands! It would forever end the domination of the United States in the Pacific; China would have complete strategic control of the South China Sea and most of the eastern Pacific. The Russians, the Japanese, the Indonesians, the Vietnamese, even the Americans—they would all have to step aside . . .

And Admiral Yin Po L'un would be a hero.

But it was crazy. Absolutely crazy. This popinjay who called himself a general had to be insane—wasn't the entire country filled with so-called revolutionaries, peasants who would carry the revolution's flag long enough to get a better-looking woman or a few extra dollars before heading off into the jungle? It would be an insult to throw in with this character.

"Tell him I wish to have my officers taken to the *Hong Lung* immediately," Admiral Yin ordered at Tran. "I request that the men be returned to their ships as soon as possible. Tell him we fully support his revolution, but my first responsibility is to the members of my flotilla. Humor him. Tell him anything as long as we are freed and helped back to the ship."

Tran nodded and began to speak with di Silva, slowly at first, but soon he was rambling on and on, his speech becoming less formal and more flowery—he really seemed to be laying it on thicker and thicker, and di Silva was eating it up. A few moments later, with di Silva wearing a firm but rather dejected expression, the two men were bowing deeply and smiling to each other.

"General di Silva says he admires your sense of duty," Tran reported with a sense of relief. "He has agreed to help us back to the ship and organize the surviving officers."

Yin put on his best smile and extended a hand, and di Silva accepted as if Yin had just offered him the Crown Jewels. "Tell him he should be held up as a shining example of the great leaders of Communism—and any other drivel you think he will be impressed by," Yin said impatiently. "Then ask him to bring the senior officers in here immediately so that I can organize—"

There was a sudden flurry of voices coming from the hallway, and a wave of people pushed their way into Yin's room. Several of them had small automatic weapons and wore earpieces—Secret Service agents, most likely, or Presidential Guards, Yin thought. Well, the Chinese Admiral thought, he was right all along; his room was bugged, and as soon as the Philippine intelligence agents realized that he was not going to cooperate and try to enlist the aid of the Philippine General in trying to escape or overthrow the country, he was going to be captured like any other enemy of the state and hauled away to prison. . . .

The wall of onlookers and guards parted suddenly, revealing a tall, young, handsome man with fair features, a thin dark mustache, and carefully coiffured dark hair. Doctors and nurses were staring at him as if they were looking at a god from Heaven, while the security guards were now gently pushing them away. General di Silva spoke at length to the man, who seemed to be very good friends with him.

The man then stepped up to Yin's bed, his hands crossed before him, smiled pleasantly at Commander Tran, then said in rather good Chinese, "Welcome, Admiral."

Yin was clearly impressed. "Thank you, sir. Whom do I have the pleasure of addressing?"

"I am First Vice President of the Republic of the Philippines, Daniel Francisco Teguina. Admiral Yin Po L'un, I welcome you to Palawan."

The First Vice President! Yin exclaimed to himself. Well, things were getting very interesting—if he was who he claimed. "So. Am I to be your prisoner, Comrade Vice President?"

"No," Teguina replied, struggling through Yin's sentence and struggling to compose a reply. "You are my guest and are to be welcomed."

"As a conquering hero?"

Teguina made a sideways glance at the receding wall of people around the bed—none were within hearing range, and probably did not understand Chinese in any case—then at di Silva, and then back at Yin. "If you have the strength, Admiral, we will speak of it," Teguina replied.

"I will speak of nothing until I am reunited with my officers and receive report from them on the status of the men under my command," Yin said. His words were obviously too much for Teguina, who shook his head, and Yin motioned for Tran to translate.

"You will have what you wish, Admiral Yin," Teguina said. He smiled evenly. "Then, we will speak of the future of the Philippines—and of *our* future."

SIX

General Wilbur Curtis and the other Joint Chiefs of Staff were seated around the triangular table in their Pentagon conference room, the Tank, listening to Navy Captain Rebecca Rodgers give her morning briefing.

Since the nuclear device had been detonated, things had still not cleared up. If anything, save for the fact that no *other* devices had gone off, the situation was worse.

"The Chinese government continues to deny any knowledge or claim any responsibility for the nuclear blast," Rodgers told the assembly. "The official announcement from Beijing stated that People's Liberation Army Navy Forces came under sustained and unprovoked attack by Philippine naval and air forces, and that an F-4E attacked their flagship in the vicinity of ground zero before the blast. They claim that the attack was a retaliation by President Mikaso for the patrol action against the so-called illegal oil-drilling platform in the Spratly Island neutral zone. The Premier denies that Chinese warships carry nuclear devices, but they do point to the presence of nuclear weapons at several former American bases in the Philippines . . ."

"That's bull," General Falmouth of the Air Force retorted. "We took all special weapons out of the Philippines years ago."

"I know, Bill, I know," Curtis said. "We've got inspection records from the United Nations and from the Soviet START Treaty inspection teams to verify it—the President will authorize disclosure of those inspection reports soon. Let Captain Rodgers finish."

Captain Rodgers continued. "ASEAN, the Association of South East Asian Nations—the Philippines, Brunei, Thailand, Indonesia, Singapore, Malaysia, and most recently Vietnam, who are, in effect, a counter-Chinese economic and military coalition—have not made a comment on the disaster. But they are meeting tomorrow in Singapore in emergency session to discuss the issue."

While the Joint Chiefs weren't surprised at China's denial of launching the warhead, they were surprised how readily others in power, namely the President and his advisers, were willing—for the time being—to accept it.

Whatever was going on, and whoever was behind it, one thing Curtis knew without a doubt was that the situation was going to escalate. In fact, it seemed to have already . . .

Captain Rodgers, standing at the end of the triangle behind the podium, kept going. She informed the Joint Chiefs that in accordance with the 1991 START Treaty, the Soviet Union had activated six mobile ICBM battalions in Central Asia, a response to the United States' DEFCON Three status. Along the Chinese and Mongolia borders, the Soviet Union had activated four missile battalions, equaling forty missiles, and were generating nuclear-capable forces at four bomber bases in south-central Russia. Although eleven hundred other known main, reserve, dispersal, rail-mobile ICBM, and cross-country road-mobile ICBM sites were under manual or satellite surveillance, it didn't appear that the USSR was gearing up for a major counteroffensive—at least with long-range nuclear forces.

Rodgers switched to an enlarged chart of the mainland of China. "The source of continuing tensions in the past forty-eight hours continues to be the buildup of Chinese tactical

forces in deployments along the Mongolian and Soviet border," Rodgers said. "This is being done, according to the Chinese, as a response to the Soviet buildup."

General Curtis and the others listened as Captain Rodgers
rattled off the Chinese deployment numbers: nineteen total
active divisions, four reserve divisions, four hundred thousand
troops along a two-thousand-mile front in the north and north-
central provinces. The units included twenty-one infantry
divisions, seven mechanized divisions, one heavy missile division, four air defense divisions . . .

There was an uneasy rustle among the Joint Chiefs. Captain
Rodgers was talking about a force that was almost as large as
America's and the Soviet Union's combined.

General Curtis was shaking his head. Thirty-three divisions—over one-half of China's ground forces and one-third of
their total military, and what had the President of the United
States given him?

Two aircraft carrier groups and the STRATFOR.

Worse, the President later cut Curtis and the Joint Chiefs out
of the loop by insisting that Admiral Stoval, the Commander
in Chief of Pacific Command, who was responsible for the
carrier task force moving to the South China Sea, report to
Thomas Preston, the Defense Secretary, through the National
Security Council. That left Curtis not only seething, but in a
rather embarrassing position with the other Joint Chiefs, who
knew what the President had done.

Rodgers switched her electronic screen to a zoomed-in view
of the South China Sea region. Specifically, the Spratly Island
chain.

"The Chinese are moving half their fleet into the area,"
Curtis observed with some alarm. The other Joint Chiefs murmured in agreement. "Captain, I want to know what ships
they're moving in there and why. I also want a letter from
State spelling out precisely what the Philippine government
has authorized the Chinese Army Navy to do. This makes me
pretty damned uneasy."

"Well, it should," Chief of Naval Operations Randolph Cunningham grumbled. "We don't have diddly in the area and the
damn Chinese know it. They set off a nuke, then rush in and

claim it's a major threat to their sovereignty. They're taking over the South China Sea faster than you can blink—and we're just sitting here. This is bullshit."

It certainly was, but what could Curtis do?

He answered his own question thirty minutes later, after the briefing, when he got back to his office. His aide, Colonel Wyatt, entered and said, "Sir, you have a scrambled phone call from CINCSAC—General Tyler. He says it's a conference call."

"Conference call? With who?"

"General Brad Elliott and a Doctor Jon Masters . . ."

Elliott? A smile came across Curtis' face. He took a sip of the coffee Wyatt had just brought in. He hadn't seen Elliott in months, even though he was one of his favorites. Elliott had had some up and down times—first as Deputy Commander of SAC, then as Director of HAWC, then as head of the government's Border Security, only to be fired and bounced back to HAWC, again.

And Masters? . . . Of Sky Masters, Inc.? The NIRTSats?

Curtis took the phone call. After pleasantries were exchanged all around, Elliott and Tyler got right to the point: "General Curtis, we need clearance on something we think we're going to need down in the Philippines."

Curtis' ears picked up. "Go on . . ."

"We want to deploy the NIRTSat recon system that Doctor Masters has built, with a few of my Megafortress escort bombers that are out at the Strategic Warfare Center. We also want some on a few of the RC-135s that'll be deployed for STRATFOR. We need your blessing, though."

Curtis thought about the briefing he'd just come out of. Two carriers in the face of a possible Chinese land-grab. The President had authorized STRATFOR into position on Guam. They'd have to be ready. "Doctor Masters," Curtis said, "you can really put that reconnaissance system on tactical aircraft?"

"You bet I can, General," Masters said over the pop of the scrambled line. "We can make the Megafortress the most high-tech flying machine this side of *Star Trek.*"

"Plus I've got a B-2 Black Knight bomber equipped the same way, except with even more surprises," Elliott said. "They've all been tearing up the Air Battle Force in exercises out at Jarrel's SWC, and if we have to go out against the Chinese in the Philippines, I think you'll want them out there."

Curtis smiled. "Do it, you old warhorse. You just made my day."

THE PRESIDENT'S RESIDENCE, MANILA, THE PHILIPPINES
THURSDAY, 29 SEPTEMBER 1994, 2212 HOURS LOCAL
(28 SEPTEMBER, 0912 WASHINGTON TIME)

Daniel Teguina was ushered into President Mikaso's residence by a Philippine Presidential Guard, then left alone in front of the door to Mikaso's office. Teguina straightened his tie and his shoulders, cleared his throat quietly, then knocked on the door. After receiving a curt "Come," he entered.

Teguina paced before the small desk in the center of the room and stood impatiently as Mikaso continued to work on something. Everything in this room was small, understated, almost peasantlike—Mikaso kept this office spartan, with only a few native wall hangings, simple wood furnishings, and book-cases crammed with every type of book, written in several languages. It was here that Mikaso did his best work, as produc-tive as a monk in solitude.

Look at him, Teguina thought. An old man trying to act as if he is in control. Teguina wanted to laugh out loud at the absurdity of the scene. Since the nuclear explosion in the Pala-wan Strait there had been a panic throughout the islands. Here in Manila rioting had broken out, troops were in the streets trying to restore order, and the presidential palace had been besieged by protests from thousands of citizens and rebel troops—troops, he smiled inwardly, who were loyal to him. No, things were definitely not in control, no matter what this old man wanted to believe, and if Daniel Teguina had anything to do with it, they would continue to spin into chaos.

"What is your report, Daniel?" Mikaso finally said.

Teguina squinted at Mikaso, feeling anger flush into his tem-ples. Mikaso was dressed in a brown suit, with a miniature Philippine Badge of Honor pinned to his lapel. Teguina knew that the sight of that badge on television made many Filipinos proud—it was the highest honor the military could pay to a civilian. Teguina had never even been considered for such an award. "I have nothing to report," he said lamely.

"You have spent two days in Palawan, with almost no communication with my staff the entire time," Mikaso said. "Yet I see editorials and articles in the newspaper, condemning the United States and the military for releasing the nuclear weapon and praising the Republic of China's navy for its relief efforts. I have been told nothing officially—communications are still disrupted in and out of Palawan. Do you have a report for me?"

"I was not aware that I was required to—"

"I have learned that you have ordered New Armed Forces personnel in Puerto Princesa to surrender to the provincial police, and the airfields there and at Buenavista to be shut down," Mikaso interrupted. "I hear reports that say that Chinese patrol boats were seen in ports throughout Palawan, including Puerto Princesa, Buenavista, Teneguiban, and Araceli, and that Chinese vessels patrol the Cuyo West Pass and even the Mindoro Strait. I hear the screams in the streets outside, saying that you accuse me of being a traitor to our country. Are these reports true?"

"The Philippine Navy is severely crippled, sir," Teguina replied. "The Chinese patrol boats were graciously loaned to provincial police officers in an effort to restore order to the province—"

"Is the Army assisting the provincial police in restoring order?"

"No, Mr. President," Teguina sniffed. "According to my research and the reports I received, it was an American B43 bomb that exploded off the coast of Palawan; the experts I consulted said that the weapon was old and thankfully did not produce a full yield." Teguina knew enough about nuclear bombs to know that it takes a smaller nuclear explosion to trigger the main explosion; this obscure factoid made the lie even easier. "The Chinese vessels were attacked without provocation by a Philippine Air Force F-4 fighter-bomber carrying this American nuclear weapon. The jet fighter crew, who was working for the American Central Intelligence Agency, destroyed a Chinese ship, along with several Philippine ships, during the attack.

"Because I am not sure as yet exactly who is responsible for the unprovoked attack on those Chinese vessels, I thought it best to turn all local police and military functions over to the provincial police and to curtail all military operations until an investigation is completed."

"General di Silva is in command of the Palawan defense forces?" Mikaso asked. He registered surprise for a moment, then relaxed and studied Teguina. "I see," the aged President finally said. "So. Did you encounter resistance when you decided to occupy the Air Force base with provincial police officers and Chinese troops?"

Teguina's eyes widened in surprise when Mikaso mentioned using Chinese troops in his operation; then he realized his mistake in registering such a surprise. Mikaso had suspected all along—whether or not he got the information first hand or simply guessed, it was obvious he knew now.

"The traitors put up a brief battle, but, as all cowards will, they turned and ran when confronted by legitimate forces," Teguina replied. "The Chinese troops supplied transportation to Puerto Princesa, that's all, and they were forced to protect themselves as well as graciously protecting the provincial police units as well. We thanked God the rebels did not drop another nuclear bomb on us."

"I have a simple question, Mr. Vice President," Mikaso said, a gleam of humor now shining in his eyes and a hint of a smile tugging at the corners of his lips. "Do you honestly expect the Philippine people to believe this fairy tale? That the Chinese were victims of Filipino aggression . . . the Chinese graciously offered the *use* of their warships . . . the Chinese *only* protected themselves when you overran Puerto Princesa? Do you honestly expect the world to believe that the Chinese suddenly became our staunch ally simply to fight off the evil, corrupt New Armed Force troops and install your own Communist puppet into power?"

"They will believe it, Mikaso," Teguina said slowly, "because . . . you will tell them."

"Me? You expect me to betray my country, my homeland, just because of your threats and a Chinese rifle pointed at my head? Certainly you are joking," Mikaso scoffed.

"This is the end of the American puppet regime in the Philippines, Mikaso . . ."

"No, it is not. I know you, Daniel. I am not the tottering old fool, the white-haired, senile figurehead you always believed I was. I chose you to become my vice president because your flowery speeches and socialist ranting and raving has awakened the political fire in a lot of people that never cared much for national politics."

"You would not have been elected if it were not for me!" Teguina snarled.

"That's right, Daniel, that's right," Mikaso admitted. "And you will not succeed without *me*. I understand the importance of a coalition government, and I understand that there are factions in this country that desire change. I was willing to accept the opposition party in order to carry our nation forward into the future after the departure of the Americans. You can do the same. If you want change, Teguina, then have your National Democratic Front form its own coalition and defeat UNIDO. Have your party enact laws to give more funds to the people and less toward defense, if that's what you propose. You are the Vice President. You carry considerable political power, more than your confused brain realizes.

"But . . . if you enlist outsiders' help to overthrow the legitimate government and close down the parliament, people all over the world will fear you, and your own people will condemn you. And if you continue to rob the treasury, install yourself in luxury in the presidential palace, and turn our nation into a battleground, you will eventually feel defeat. There is always someone around the corner with a bigger gun and a bigger army—"

Teguina reached over, grabbed Mikaso by the lapels of his jacket, and said in a low, burning voice, "I don't want your prostituted government anymore, old man." He then pushed the President back into his seat and yelled, "Admiral! Enter!"

Mikaso stared as a contingent of about fifty Chinese troops

rushed into his office. Several Presidential Guard soldiers were led in, some carrying the dead bodies of other policemen or soldiers.

Behind them all was a Chinese naval officer, about sixty years old, in white uniform slacks, dark helmet, a dark-blue jacket that appeared thick enough to be a bulletproof vest, and a sidearm. Beside the military officer, to Mikaso's complete surprise, was the ambassador from the People's Republic of China, Dong Sen Kim, who averted his eyes and would not look at Mikaso directly. Along with the Chinese troops came several of Mikaso's Cabinet officials, most of whom were National Democratic Front members—but they also included Eduardo Friscino, the Minister of Interior.

"This is the new governor of the People's Republic of the Sulu Islands, Eduardo Friscino," Teguina said to Mikaso. "He has seen your frail attempts to restore American dictatorship to the Philippines and has agreed to join with me to form a better nation, separate but equal, different yet fused together for the good of all."

Mikaso stared in disbelief at Friscino. "Eduardo—"

Eduardo looked like a whipped dog. Standing in front of all those armed soldiers, he already seemed on the verge of collapse; now, under Mikaso's incredulous glare, he seemed to practically wilt into the floorboards, but said nothing.

"Because of the political and cultural separation that exists between the southern islands and the northern island," Teguina continued, "I have decided to create a new state, a federation of provinces that will be independent yet closely allied to the north. Luzon and the Sibuyan islands will be known as the Democratic Federation of Aguinaldo. It will be under my control, protected by loyal military forces as well as New People's Army groups formed into provincial militias.

"Palawan, Mindanao, and the Sulu Archipelago will be known collectively as the People's Federation of the Sulu Islands," Teguina went on. "Once joined officially, Aguinaldo and the Sulu Federation will once again become the Democratic Republic of Aguinaldo."

"Daniel, you cannot do this," Mikaso said earnestly. "Samar and Mindanao will not join your revolution—they will fight your annexation, resist your attempt to overthrow them, and split themselves off from the rest of the Philippines alto-gether—"

"Yes. Vice President Samar is proving to be difficult," Teguina admitted. José Trujillo Samar, Second Vice President of the Philippines, was the governor of the state of Mindanao. "But once the city of Davao falls, Mindanao will be ours as well."

Mikaso sat back in the chair behind his desk, trying to absorb everything Teguina was saying. This was insane. Teguina had taken the nuclear detonation and allowed the Philippines to be raped by it. His entire country—the nation he loved and served—was evaporating before his eyes. Even its very form of government. He had to stop this, had to buy himself some time . . .

. . . had to stop Teguina.

But he needed time. Moments, if nothing else.

"Daniel," Mikaso said, "what about these Chinese troops here? How do they fit into your master plan?"

"Glad you asked, Mikaso," Teguina said smugly. He mo-tioned to the officer in the helmet and blue bulletproof jacket. "This is Admiral Yin Po L'un, commander of the Spratly Island flotilla, the fleet that your traitorous soldiers bombed and strafed three nights ago. As a fellow Communist, he has agreed—with the full support of the People's Republic of China, communicated to us from Beijing by Ambassador Dong—to assist in establishing my new regime. In exchange I have granted the Chinese Navy complete ownership of illegiti-mate Philippine holdings in the Spratly Islands. I have also authorized them access to our ports on Palawan and, once the rebel military forces have been eliminated, the naval base at Zamboanga and the airfields at Cebu and Davao. They will also have access to the former American military bases at Subic Bay and Angeles . . ."

"You're giving the Chinese *four* military bases?" Mikaso gasped incredulously. "You're insane, Teguina! The people will never allow it—the *world* will never allow such a domi-nation!"

"It is already being done, Mikaso," Teguina said.

"Not if I can help it," Mikaso said, reaching into his desk drawer to pull out a pistol he'd kept there for years.

But it was too late.

Several Type 56 automatic rifles, variants of the Soviet AK-47 assault rifle, swung in his direction and someone fired. Mikaso jerked from the impact of the shot and slumped over the desk before finally collapsing on the floor.

Teguina stood staring at the assassinated President, his mouth slightly agape. He had never meant to kill Mikaso, simply arrest him and have him confined. He continued to stare at the body and realized his breathing was labored. He felt a tap on the shoulder.

"Comrade President . . ." Admiral Yin said, a slight smile on his face.

Teguina had never heard those words before. The reality was dawning on him. Within a few seconds he had become the new President of the Republic of the Philippines—no, the President of the New Democratic Federation of Aguinaldo. He liked the sound of that—President of the Democratic Federation of Aguinaldo. It was a name that recalled the glory days, the days of fervent revolutionaries like Emilio Aguinaldo, a peasant farmer who rose to become the leader of a nation over two world superpowers, Spain and the United States. No matter that Aguinaldo was finally captured by General Funston, capitulated, and swore allegiance to America—it was his indomitable spirit that survived. It would become the rallying cry for a new nation. The Republic of Aguinaldo. The name sounded perfect.

The body in a brown suit had been hastily covered with a tablecloth and was carried out by Chinese soldiers. "Wait!" Teguina shouted. "I want the badge." He pointed to his lapel, then motioned to the body that had been taken away. A Chinese officer went out, returning a few seconds later with the Philippine Badge of Honor. Teguina's eyes registered dark stains spattered across the officer's fingers, but ignored them as he pinned the Badge of Honor to his own lapel. The doors to the President's office were closed by the Chinese troops, and Daniel Francisco Teguina set about the task of planning the important next steps to consolidating his power.

THE WHITE HOUSE OVAL OFFICE
WEDNESDAY, 28 SEPTEMBER 1994, 1035 HOURS LOCAL

The President was at his desk, staring out of one of the bullet-resistant polycarbonate windows looking into the Rose Garden, when the men were ushered in. He didn't even look up. His mind was on something more personal, more immediate than whatever brought the gentlemen in for this next appointment. Secretary of State Dennis Danahall and the President's Chief of Staff, Paul Cesare, were standing near the President's desk.

The President's secretary ushered General Curtis into the Oval Office. Curtis had been summoned for a meeting with the NSC and the President.

"Sir . . ." General Curtis said, letting the President know he was present after Taylor's secretary had shut the door behind him and disappeared back into the outer reception area.

The President said nothing for a moment—nor did the others—and then, finally, he turned and took a deep breath. "Arturo Mikaso may be dead."

Curtis felt his heart skip a beat. "What? Mikaso dead?"

Danahall said, "It's unconfirmed, but we got a report a few minutes ago from British Intelligence, who had a Filipino clerk working in the palace at the time. The clerk says Mikaso was shot by a Chinese guard about an hour ago when the troops moved in. Some other Cabinet members and most of Mikaso's staff and guards were also shot."

"Mikaso could still be alive." The President sighed. "But I doubt it."

"What about the Chinese? Are they assisting in the coup?" asked Curtis.

"The Chinese have occupied a military base on Palawan—they have in fact occupied the entire island—and have been given authorization by Teguina to occupy four more installations in the south," Secretary of Defense Preston said. "There are Chinese infantry and armor units in the capital already, and they are augmenting rebel troops by the hundreds."

Curtis looked at the President of the United States, understanding the terrible anguish within him. President Taylor and
Mikaso had been friends despite the removal of U.S. troops
from the Philippines, and Taylor had always pledged to protect Mikaso and his island country no matter what the political
situation was. The news of his murder in his own house, by
invading troops, must have been devastating to the President.
"Mr. President, I'm very sorry . . ."

"I haven't even briefed the rest of the NSC or the Cabinet
about it yet," the President replied quietly. "Dammit, I should
have been smarter. I should have realized Arturo was in danger from the beginning . . ." The President swiveled his chair
and faced his advisers. "Well, what the hell do we do now?"

"The Chinese have closed off the airport," Danahall said.
"It's too late to evacuate American citizens in Manila. We
should demand that all American citizens that wish to leave be
allowed to leave."

"Yes, absolutely . . . see to it immediately," the President
said. His mind was moving quickly from item to item, all the
while interrupted with the thought of his friend murdered in
cold blood by a Chinese soldier. "What about the carriers? Are
they in danger from the Chinese now?"

General Curtis said, "I believe the carriers can adequately
protect themselves from any sea-based threats, including Chinese submarines. Their main threat would come from long-
range, land-based strike aircraft or antiship missiles, and we
need to determine the seriousness of that threat before sending any carrier task forces too close to occupied territory. The
main thing is, we've got to get all the data we possibly can on
the composition of the Chinese invaders. But if I may speak
freely, sir—the most important question here is what *you* intend to do about the Chinese in the Philippines," Curtis concluded.

"I want the Chinese out, that's what," the President replied
testily. "I want the democratic government in Manila restored.
We will open negotiations with Premier Cheung immediately,
of course, but I want them out. Unconditionally."

"But if they are invited by the Philippine government? Do
we have any right to go in with military force to try to remove

them?" Secretary of Defense Preston asked. "If they pose no direct threat to free trade and free access to the South Pacific or Southeast Asia, why do we want them out of the Philippines?"

"What do you mean . . . ? Of course we have the *right* to remove them from the Philippines," President Taylor said. "They're a destabilizing force, a military and political threat to the democracies in the area. Aren't we in agreement on this?"

"I don't think there is any question about that," Danahall said. "A three-way balance of power—us, the Soviets, and the Chinese—offers the best stability. Reduce it to one nation and the Cold War heats up all over again."

Curtis said, "But Secretary Preston's point is valid, sir. We might not have any legitimate right to try to bump the Chinese out unless we can prove that the invasion is not in our best interests or unless we are asked to intervene."

"We have every right to make demands on the Chinese," Cesare interjected. "They don't own the South China Sea. No nation can just move in and occupy another country."

"Exactly, Paul," the President said, "Mikaso was our friend and ally. I'm sure he didn't give his life to allow the Chinese to march into his capital and take over his country."

"Curtis and Preston have a point, Mr. President," Danahall said. "If the present government—even Teguina—says he invited China in to quell some sort of national uprising, that forces us into a defensive situation. We have to explain to the world why we want to send troops in."

"We're *always* put in a position to defend our actions," the President scoffed. "What else is new?"

"That's often true, Mr. President," Danahall said. "But we've got to try to work in concert with other countries—the more we try to go it alone, the more we're accused of bullying and imperialism. We should get some interested countries involved and get them to ask for our help."

"Like who?"

"ASEAN, for example," Danahall replied. "Most or all of the ASEAN nations have had territorial arguments with China— ASEAN was developed as a counterweight to Chinese aggression. And then there are things we can do to advance our own

military position without unnecessarily provoking the Chinese
or alienating ASEAN . . ."

"Well, sending in a second carrier battle group and a Marine
Expeditionary Unit seems pretty provocative to me," Cesare
said.

"I think that action can be fully justified in the context of a
nuclear-armed Chinese naval group that has moved into the
South China Sea. I mean it's right in the heart of ASEAN,"
Curtis replied. "So would sending in the Air Battle force for
support—"

"I don't want to send in the damned B-52 bombers," the
President grumbled. "Sending them in would be tantamount
to saying we want a nuclear exchange. Christ, Curtis . . ."

"Sir, the biggest threat facing our carrier battle group in the
South China Sea is not sea-based threats, but land-based
threats," Curtis argued. "Heavy bombers and large antiship
weapons launched from shore could devastate the fleet . . ."

"You said that already."

"The same argument applies to the Chinese, sir. Even a
small squadron of Harpoon-equipped B-52s could devastate a
Chinese surface action group—each bomber could destroy two
to four vessels, with minimal risk to themselves."

The point, however grudgingly, was made on the President.
"So what can the Air Force do?" the President asked after a
brief pause. "We don't have bases in the Philippines . . ."

"We'd operate out of Guam, sir, just like STRATFOR is
doing," Curtis replied. "We'd deploy the First Air Battle Wing
and have the manpower and equipment out there on hand for
both fleet defense, sea interdiction, and ground attack. I'm not
asking for permission to send the entire Air Battle Wing, sir,"
Curtis concluded. "We'll need time to set up—at least five to
six days. But General Elliott of HAWC has devised a special
combat-information exchange system aboard several of his aircraft—including several modified B-52s and a B-2 stealth
bomber—that could be extremely valuable to us if the shooting
starts. I'm requesting permission to send Elliott and one aircraft, the stealth bomber, to Guam—under absolute secrecy—
to help get things set up."

"Elliott?" the President asked, rolling his eyes. "Brad Elliott? He's involved in this . . . *already?*"

Curtis went slowly, calmly, trying not to inflame the President any further. "It was his Center's satellite system—PACER SKY—that got the photos of the Chinese ship launching the nuclear missile at the Philippine Navy. We want to expand that same satellite system on all the Air Battle Force aircraft . . ."

"But why send a B-2?" the President asked.

"The B-2 is a part of the Air Battle Force now, sir," General Curtis explained. "It requires a lot more security and a bit more ground-support pre-planning. In addition, this particular B-2 was General Elliott's prototype with the full PACER SKY satellite system installed. It also has greatly enhanced reconnaissance and surveillance capabilities that we will need immediately if the Air Battle Force is activated."

The President thought about the proposal a bit, then, with a weary and exasperated sigh shook his head. "Listen, Wilbur, I can't decide on any of that now. Continue with current directives and keep me advised. I've got some thinking to do."

"Sir, may I?"

"*Save it,* Wilbur. Thank you."

The meeting was definitely over.

RESIDENCE OF THE PREMIER, BAIYUNGUAN TERRACE
BEIJING, REPUBLIC OF CHINA
THURSDAY, 29 SEPTEMBER 1994, 0602 HOURS LOCAL
(WEDNESDAY, 28 SEPTEMBER, 1702 HOURS WASHINGTON TIME)

The streets were still relatively empty as the small motorcade of dark, unmarked cars raced down Shilibao Avenue westward past Tian'anmen Square, then north past Yuyan Tan People's Park toward the Premier's residence in Baiyunguan Terrace, a complex of residences, green rolling hills, parks, and temples built especially for the Communist government leaders. Outer security at the twisting single-lane entrance was provided by a single unarmed guard who would politely point and describe the complex to tourists and children and even offer to take pictures for visitors; inside the narrow portal, however, was a detail of three thousand heavily armed soldiers, hand-picked by Premier Cheung Yat Sing himself, that guarded the sixty-acre complex.

Once inside the complex, the motorcade sped past willow-lined streets and meticulously tended sidewalks as they curved upward toward the center cluster of buildings, the private residence of Premier Cheung. The motorcade came to a sudden halt underneath a long breezeway, and the limousine's occupants hurried inside the reception hall. If they had paused to look, they could have seen one of the grandest vistas in all Beijing—Yuyan Tan Lake to the west, the expansive Peking Zoo to the north, and the massive brick monuments of the Imperial Palace and Tian'anmen Square to the east, now glowing fiery crimson in the rising sun. But the limousine's occupants were hustled directly inside and to the immediate meeting with the Premier himself in his private office.

Leing Yee Tak, ambassador to China from the Republic of Vietnam, hardly had time to remove his shoes before none other than Premier Cheung himself entered the office, along with members of his Cabinet. This was highly unusual: the Premier never met with lowly ambassadors, only heads of state or occasionally minister- or Cabinet-level officials. Leing waited until the Premier had taken his seat at the center of a long dark granite table, then bowed deeply and approached the table. Cheung immediately offered him a seat with a gesture, and Leing sat. His interpreter aide remained standing behind him.

Cheung was old, incredibly old even for a Chinese politician. The ninety-one-year-old leader of the world's most populous nation still moved fairly well without assistance, although two burly Chinese Marines were on hand to help him in and out of his chair. His hair was dark, obviously dyed at the insistence of his advisers or from some deep-seated vanity, but his face was deeply etched from age and his fingers gnarled from arthritis. But Leing had been taught from his first days in the Vietnamese Socialist Party and the People's Foreign Ministry that the eyes were the giveaway—Cheung's eyes were still gleaming, still quick, still alert.

Despite rumors to the contrary, Cheung still appeared to be in charge . . .

But after quickly scanning the faces of the other Cabinet members, perhaps not. The Chinese Foreign Minister, Party Counsel, and Minister of Commerce were present, but the Ministers of Interior, Finance, Defense, and Industry were all replaced by their military counterparts. This was a military tribunal represented here, not a peacetime government.

And Leing knew well the Supreme Commander of the People's Liberation Army, High General Chin Po Zihong. Chin was young for a Chinese government official—sixty-seven, if Leing remembered correctly—but he appeared to be half that age. He was a short, barrel-chested, dark-haired Mongol that instantly reminded one of how the Mongol hordes of centuries past had struck fear into the hearts of soldiers throughout Europe and Asia. Unlike most other high-ranking military officers, Chin wore few accoutrements on his plain, dark grey uniform. He didn't need ribbons and badges to demonstrate his power and authority to others.

Cheung spoke, and afterward his interpreter said, "The Premier extends his government's greeting to Comrade Leing. The Premier wishes to know if there is anything that would make the ambassador from the Republic of Vietnam more comfortable."

"Nothing, Comrade Premier," Leing replied. "I thank you for your generous offer. I too wish to extend the greetings of the Republic of Vietnam." Cheung bowed slightly at the neck, and the civilian members of the Cabinet did likewise—the military members did not move. Chin appeared as immobile as stone, unblinking and inscrutable.

"The Premier wishes to extend an invitation to the ambassador from Vietnam to attend a briefing on the situation in the Philippines and the South China Sea," the interpreter said. "High General Chin will conduct the briefing. We will outline the actions and events that precipitated the current military actions in that nation and explain our objectives and intentions."

Leing could have fallen over backward in surprise. The Chinese Chief of Staff himself, conducting a briefing on his military actions—for a member of the *Vietnamese* government? The offer was astounding.

China and Vietnam had a long, off-again and on-again relationship over the past fifty years. Both were Communist republics; Vietnam's government was fashioned as a smaller copy of China's. Both were military powers in the Pacific, with Vietnam having the world's fourth-largest army and the world's eighth-largest small-boat navy. But political relations were based on expediency and short-term interests, and those relations were usually stormy at best and warlike at worst.

Currently, relations were at the simmering but nonbelligerent level. The Spratly Islands question, long a point of contention, was at an impasse, with China having the definite edge. Vietnam had countered with its full membership in ASEAN, and with improving its relations with the Soviet Union, the United States, and many other countries. The brief but violent war over the Spratly Islands in the late 1980s was all but forgotten, border skirmishes were rare, and things were tense but bloodless for a few years now. Why would China feel the need to advise Vietnam on its current conflict in the Philippines?

"On behalf of my government, I accept your gracious offer, Comrade Premier," Leing replied warily. "The incidents of the past few days in the Philippines have caused much concern in my country."

"Allow me to assure you, Comrade Ambassador," the interpreter said, "that the People's Republic of China harbors no ill feeling toward Vietnam. Our forces will not threaten any Vietnamese facilities or vessels in the region. You have the word of the Premier."

"I thank you for your assurances, Comrade Premier," Leing said. Leing risked a full glance at General Chin, to perhaps see if Chin, the *real* power where Chinese foreign intrigue was concerned, would give similar assurances; he did not. His return stare was powerful enough to make Leing silent: "Your assurances are important, since Chinese naval vessels patrol the entire Spratly archipelago, within striking distance of Vietnamese-settled islands. My government will be relieved to hear that these warships mean no harm."

It was General Chin's turn to speak now, and he did so without waiting for permission. "I give you my assurance that no Chinese vessel will approach any Vietnamese-claimed islands or interfere with Vietnamese naval operations in any way," he said through the interpreter. Leing's own interpreter gave a slightly different version of Chin's statement—he said that no Chinese vessel will *land* on a Vietnamese-claimed island or interfere with *legitimate* Vietnamese naval operations in any way. Leing nodded. The exact wording was not important: these men were not to be trusted no matter what they said. Actions spoke louder than words, and so far their actions suggested the Chinese Navy was in the Spratly Islands to stay.

"So I am to assume, Comrade General, that Chinese warships will continue to patrol north of the neutral zone, in violation of international treaty?"

"We were invited by the government of the Philippines to assist in national self-defense matters," Chin said. "The request included patrolling their islands for signs of rebel activity. We are protecting their interests as well as yours, since as we have seen the rebel military's actions are a threat to all nations."

Lies, Leing thought, struggling to keep his face as impassive as possible. The whole world knows it was a *Chinese* nuclear warhead that exploded in the Palawan Straits. Do they really expect me to believe this fairy tale? "My government appreciates the truth in your words, Comrade General," Leing said evenly, "but also prefers that international treaties be strictly followed."

"The terms of the treaty between us have been altered by recent events," the Chinese Foreign Minister, Zhou Ti Yanbing, said. "Because of the nuclear explosion, we felt our forces were at substantial risk in the South China Sea and that an escalation of our naval presence was necessary. At the same time, we were invited by the government of the Philippines to assist them in putting down a suspected coup and a violent military attack by well-armed forces. Those are the facts, and we speak the truth." Not the *whole* truth, Leing noted: it was the Chinese who set off the nuclear explosion, the Chinese who posed the greatest risk to neighboring nations. The Philippine coup was just a fortuitous opportunity for the Chinese to complete their long sought-after conquest. . . .

"However, the situation has become even more unstable for us and for all nations involved in this incident," Zhou continued. "We realize that new priorities must be established and new ties formed between the affected nations—especially between China and Vietnam."

"What sort of ties are you referring to, Comrade Foreign Minister?"

There was a pause, an uneasy silence notably between General Chin and Premier Cheung—although no words or glances were exchanged, the two men were on edge. Then Cheung spoke, and the interpreter said, "We wish to issue a ninety-nine-year irrevocable lease to the Republic of Vietnam to occupy, develop, patrol, and regulate affairs in the entire Nansha Island archipelago."

Leing was stunned. "I . . . Please, Comrade Premier, if you would be so good to repeat your last statement . . ."

General Chin made a sudden outburst, and Cheung replied hotly without turning toward him. "The General said, 'This is nonsense,' and the Premier ordered him to keep quiet," Leing's interpreter whispered into the ambassador's ear.

"I believe you heard correctly, Comrade Ambassador," Foreign Minister Zhou said through his interpreter. "We wish to turn over control of the Nansha Islands to Vietnam. We will surrender all interests we currently hold in the islands to you for a period of ninety-nine years, after which time we will agree to enter into negotiations for outright transfer of ownership or an extension of the lease to you." Then Leing's interpreter added, "It appears to me that General Chin is opposed to the plan."

Leing was shocked. China, which patrolled the Nansha Islands—the Chinese term for the Spratly Islands—as if they were a mainland province—had even defended their rights to the islands with atomic weapons. Now they were willing to just give the islands up? And give them up to Vietnam, which was once an ally but was now a clear adversary? As early as 1988, China had come a hairsbreadth away from invading Vietnam over the Spratly Islands. . . .

"This is most unexpected, Comrade Premier," Leing said, finally regaining control over his numbed senses. "It is a most attractive offer. Naturally, I assume there is a condition to this transfer?" Of course there was—and Leing finally realized what it might be. . . .

"You are correct, Comrade Ambassador," the interpreter said for Foreign Minister Zhou. "Although we freely admit that an adjustment to the turbulent situation in the Nansha Island chain meant that this action was far overdue:

"We realize that a vote will be forthcoming when the Association of South East Asian Nations meet in Singapore and the question of our occupation of the Philippines is brought forward. We have tried to assure all countries involved in this situation that our involvement was requested by the Philippine government and that we are acting in strict accordance with international law; however, we realize that outside, non-Communist sympathizers will attempt to undermine our efforts to restore peace to the region. China has not been offered an opportunity to voice our side of the matter, which precludes any sort of fair and equitable resolution of this incident.

"We are therefore asking that when the vote is called, the Vietnamese vote against any ASEAN resolutions to interfere in the Philippines, and that you urge other nations in ASEAN to vote against any resolution as well. Since a unanimous vote is necessary for ASEAN to take military action or impose severe economic embargos, your action would postpone any serious consequences.

"In addition, if you agree to assist us militarily in defending our right to remain in the Philippines, the Republic of China will propose a similar lease agreement to the Republic of Vietnam for the western group of the islands known as the Crescent Group in the Xinsha Islands archipelago."

The offer was astounding. China was in effect offering the Vietnamese a controlling position to the entire South China Sea in exchange for cooperation in its operation in the Philippines. In terms of value and strategic importance, it was not an equitable trade—the Philippines was by far a much brighter gem than the Spratlys or the Paracels—but by establishing offshore bases, Vietnam would once again be able to build a blue-water navy and exert its will in Southeast Asia. It could finally be able to counter the growing democratic-oligarchic influence of the Moslem nations of Indonesia, Malaysia, Singapore, and Brunei by being able to effectively operate naval and merchant fleets far from home ports.

"I do not see how such an action can be construed as anything else than conspiracy and duplicity," Ambassador Leing said. Premier Cheung's face was impassive, but Leing measured the government's reaction in General Chin's face—it was obvious the warlord didn't enjoy taking any lip from a Vietnamese politician. "But the return of our territorial islands of Dao Quan Mueng Bang and Dao Phran-Binh would be of immense pleasure and gratification to my government."

The ploy worked. Instead of calling the contested islands by their Chinese names, Leing used the ancestral Vietnamese names—Dao Quan Mueng Bang for the Spratlys, Dao Phran-Binh for the Paracels—and those names infuriated General Chin, who launched into a furious tirade, first at Leing and then at Premier Cheung.

"He says that this is a crazy idea, that it will never be, that Vietnam cannot be allowed to take . . ." his interpreter quickly responded. "He is now telling me to be silent or he will cut off my . . . my penis, and stuff it in my . . . General Chin is very angry, Comrade Ambassador. Perhaps we should leave . . ."

"No," Leing said in Vietnamese in a low voice. "There is obviously a power struggle going on here. We must be witness to it before we can take this proposal to Hanoi."

"We will take nothing if we are *dead!*"

"Keep your comments to yourself and tell me what they are saying," Leing hissed.

"The Premier is telling Chin to be silent . . . Chin is saying to the Foreign Minister that he will not agree to release the Spratlys to Vietnam . . . the Premier repeats his order for silence." The last order seemed to stick; General Chin stopped his bellowing and was content for the moment to shift his weight impatiently from foot to foot and glare at Leing.

The Premier spoke up. "Please deliver this request to your government with all speed and confidentiality. We await your reply."

SEVEN

"Man—living in Arkansas, I thought I knew what humidity felt like," Jon Masters had said. "Guam has Blytheville beat six ways to none." Those were Masters' first words when he stepped off his converted DC-10 airliner onto the tarmac at Andersen Air Force Base in Guam. Everything he touched felt clammy—the railing on the portable stairs, the concrete parking apron, everything. Breathing became a conscious activity, and things like long pants and underwear became serious personal liabilities.

General Brad Elliott had to agree. Although he had spent some months in Guam during the Vietnam War, flying B-52D and -G bombers from Guam over twenty-five hundred miles one-way on bombing missions, he never got accustomed to the oppressive humidity on the tiny tropical island, which felt like 100 percent every hour of every day. The daily three P.M. thunderstorms did nothing to improve conditions—in fact, it felt even worse, as if one were drowning in oceans one could not see, only feel.

Guam had been the linchpin of American military presence in the Pacific since the Spanish-American War of 1898. The

Japanese invaded Guam on December 7, 1941, at the same time that Pearl Harbor was being bombed, but they were ousted in 1944 after days of heavy American bombing, and the militarization of Guam began.

Of the three B-29, B-36, and B-47 bomber bases built on Guam from 1944 to 1950, the largest, Andersen Air Force Base—first known simply as North Field—remained. Andersen Air Force Base was a vast, stark facility on Guam's northern shore that, although reduced to a small fraction of its recent size and relatively quiet, still echoed with the ghosts of missions past. Dominating the base were Andersen's twin two-mile-long runways.

Surrounding the runways, including the "infield" between the parallel runways, were concrete parking stubs big enough for B-52s. During the height of the Vietnam War, during Operation Bullet Shot in 1972, over one hundred and fifty bombers were parked here. The B-52s participated in the massive Arc Light, Young Tiger, and Linebacker bombing missions between 1965 and 1973.

By 1990 the Air Force had removed all the permanently assigned B-52 bombers and KC-135 tankers from Andersen, and the base transitioned to caretaker status of the 633rd Air Base Wing of the Pacific Air Forces.

But Elliott and Masters knew it would become an important base of operations again.

Masters had already launched two ALARM boosters while still over the United States. The young scientist and engineer couldn't believe his NIRTSats were being used in an actual operation that was part of America's response to a nuclear explosion. What better endorsement could Sky Masters, Inc., ask for than from the U.S. government in a crisis situation?

Unfortunately, his other Sky Masters colleagues had been less than enthusiastic. After General Curtis of the Joint Chiefs of Staff had given the go-ahead, the government presented Masters with a request for six satellites and two boosters ASAP—a contract worth $300 million. It was all on a handshake and letter of intent, and Helen Kaddiri, as a board member, was especially vocal about taking satellites contracted for by other buyers and selling them to the government. Masters had had to do some hard lobbying, but the board—even Kaddiri—finally agreed.

Still, it put the ALARM booster program to its most grueling test, but it was the process that Jon Masters had originally devised the system to accomplish: twelve hours from the go-ahead, two space boosters were launched that inserted two completely different satellite constellations into low Earth orbit—not just single satellites, but multiple, interconnected strings of small, highly sophisticated satellites.

Thankfully, both launches went off perfectly, all the satellites' buses were inserted into the proper orbit, and one by one the skies were "seeded" with tiny Sky Masters, Inc., spacecraft. By the time Masters had landed his DC-10 back at his base in Arkansas, loaded the plane with the equipment he needed for the SAC STRATFOR team, and then flown on to Guam, all of his NIRTSats were in their proper orbits and reporting fully functional. The recon satellites were in nearly circular 415-nautical-mile equatorial orbits; the communications satellites were in lower 200-mile orbits inclined 40 degrees to the equator so they could download their data directly to continental U.S. ground stations as well as to facilities on Guam.

Masters was betting everything on this mission—and he was also betting that while he was away Helen Kaddiri would probably try to position herself for a corporate coup d'état. He'd been expecting it for some time. He shrugged, realizing he'd have to deal with that later.

Masters' DC-10, with its distinctive red, white, and blue SKY MASTERS emblem on the sides, was parked just outside the hangar next to the north apron, which was perched atop the five-hundred-foot cliff on Guam's north shore.

Masters and General Brad Elliott, who'd flown in with Masters on the DC-10, met newly appointed SAC STRATFOR commander Major General Rat Stone, his aide, Colonel Michael Krieg, and Colonel Anthony Fusco, who was the commander of the 633rd Air Base Wing. Elliott was there to observe Masters' gear in action, in person. If they were going to be using it at HAWC, he wanted to see it up close.

Introductions were made all around, and after everyone mentioned the humidity, they were taken by military van—in a sudden downpour no less—to the MAC terminal, where a Guamanian customs officer, assisted by a MAC security guard in full combat rig and carrying an M-16 rifle, checked their customs declaration forms and inspected their hand-carried items.

After that, General Stone turned to Masters. "What I'd like is to get your gear in place as soon as possible," Stone said. "I've got an EC-135 communications plane and the recon planes available, so I can use DSCS to collect reconnaissance data, but I don't like sending those planes so far over water unless we get a better idea on what the situation is over there. The sooner we can get your system working, the better." The Defense Satellite Communications System, or DSCS, was the current global voice and data communications system in operation; the system's drawback was that it could relay signals only from ground station to ground station and could not link aircraft. An EC-135 communications plane could act as a pseudo–ground station and could relay signals from another aircraft via DSCS to a ground station, but that meant orbiting the EC-135 near the first aircraft—which meant sending another important aircraft thousands of miles offshore and exposing it to possible enemy action, which in turn meant assigning additional fighters and tankers to support it.

"That's what I'm here for, General," Jon Masters said. "With the NIRTSats in place, we can talk with your AWACS and reconnaissance planes directly. When my computer complex is set up, we can get their radar pictures and they'll be able to receive our PACER SKY pictures." Jon grinned. "It's gonna be awesome. Once we get the rest of the birds tied in, you'll have dozens of planes tied together and linked to Andersen. You'll hear a guy on some B-52 sneeze three thousand miles away just as clearly as if he were sitting right beside you, and you can say 'gesundheit' a second later—and while he's wiping his nose, you can lay his crosshairs on a target for him. Too much!"

Stone turned and smiled at Elliott, who returned his amused grin. The officers and the young scientist piled into the heavy air-conditioned blue Air Force van, and they headed back out on Perimeter Road.

Jon asked, "I understand your first reconnaissance sortie will take off in a few hours?"

Stone nodded. "It's about four hours' flying time from here to the Philippines for the RC-135 and AWACS planes; about three hours for the EC-135. They arrive on station in the Celebes Sea about midnight. They stay on station for four hours, then head on back. They RTB about eight A.M."

"So my crew can have the plane about nine A.M.?"

"That's right. You said installing your PACER SKY gear will take less than five hours, which is good because maintenance needs to get the aircraft ready to go at four P.M. That gives you a little leeway, but not much."

"It'll be plenty," Masters assured him.

"Great." Stone turned to Fusco and said, "Take a swing past the south apron and let's see what's going on, Tony."

They drove south along the flight line road, past an E-3C AWACS radar plane with its distinctive thirty-foot-rotodome atop its fuselage; another camouflaged Boeing 707 aircraft with no distinctive marking except for two canoe-shaped fairings on the underside of the fuselage behind the nose gear and rows of antennae atop the fuselage; and another Boeing 707 aircraft painted white over gray, with a refueling boom on the tail and a large, complex antenna array on the top of the fuselage. There were also two McDonnell-Douglas DC-10 aircraft modified as aerial refueling tankers in dark green and white camouflage nearby, and another two Boeing 707s also modified as tankers in standard light gray livery. Crates and crew members from Sky Masters, Inc., were already congregating around the planes, talking with Air Force maintenance crews.

"Quite a collection of planes out here," Masters exclaimed. "I recognize the AWACS plane and the KC-10 and KC-135 tankers, but what are the other 707s?"

"The dark gray one is an RC-135X radar reconnaissance plane," Stone explained. "The fairings you see house the multimode radars with the inverse synthetic aperture and pulse-Doppler systems, which we'll use to map out ship and troop locations; it can also slave its radar to radiation-detection sensors to map out locations of search, acquisition, fire control, and missile uplink transmitters, and in an emergency we can arm it with antiradar missiles. I believe you'll be installing a PACER SKY set and your communications complex on him so he can receive your PACER SKY data and transmit his data directly here.

"The other is one of SAC's EC-135L radio relay aircraft. We'll be using him on the first few missions to make sure we get a good feed from the recon planes." He paused for a moment, then said, "This is a good way of conducting strategic reconnaissance. Lots of planes, lots of crew dogs, not much sleep. Frankly . . . I still trust this method. No offense, Doctor Masters."

"None taken," Jon said. "I'm sure the crews will enjoy the tropical weather, because they won't be doing much flying. My NIRTSats'll work just fine."

The commander of the Strategic Air Command STRATFOR gave the young scientist an amused nod. This guy's got confidence, Stone had to admit. He wasn't afraid to place his trust in this high-tech crap, although none of it had ever been tested in fast-changing, demanding combat conditions. Unfortunately, it was cockiness like this that usually got such operations in big trouble.

"What exactly is the plan for these recon flights?" Elliott asked.

"Simple," Stone replied. "We're going to do the southern Philippines first; the Chinese defenses are weaker. RC-135 no less than one hundred miles off the coast, well within radar range but nothing too provocative—I got that word loud and clear from JCS. AWACS close enough to monitor the Philippine coast and all our aircraft. Two hundred miles east, we put the EC-135. Between the AWACS and the carriers, we put a Navy E-2 Hawkeye radar plane to control escort fighters coming from the carriers. The Navy will put up tankers to service their fighters after takeoff; we'll have a KC-10 nearby to service all aircraft involved in the recon operation."

"How many fighter escorts will you have up?"

"Not enough," Stone replied grimly. "JCS asked for eight per aircraft; we're only getting two. Apparently the White House thought eight fighters per looked too much like an invasion force."

"So if there's any trouble . . ." Elliott said.

"We run like hell," Stone answered. "The fighters cover the withdrawal; they don't engage. But we're not expecting any trouble. We'll be far enough offshore that we won't seem like a threat. The Chinese should lay off."

The sight across the road from the south apron commanded instant attention; it was a huge black B-52, with a tall, pointed tail, glistening polished steel skin, and racks of bombs hanging from hardpoints under each wing. Masters asked, "What's that? Some sort of memorial?"

"The Arc Light Memorial," Colonel Fusco replied. "Dedicated to the men who flew the heavy bombing missions over Vietnam. That was one of the B-52s that made the last bomb run over North Vietnam in 1972—'Old 100,' the one-hundredth B-52, built in 1955. We keep her in tiptop shape—in fact, it's still considered an operational aircraft. The memorial was dedicated on the first anniversary of the return of the POWs from Vietnam."

"I've crawled all over a B-2," Masters said, "and I know the avionics system on the Space Shuttle like the back of my hand, but you know, I've never seen a B-52 this close before. Weird, huh? That thing is just plain *huge.*"

The other men nodded. It was a war machine with which they all had had very personal experiences. For all of them who flew it, they recalled times when the B-52, seemingly all at once, had tried to kill them and had saved them—such was the nature of that black monster. It was a killing machine that demanded one hundred percent from every man who touched it. Masters stared at the plane and commented on its size, but it had not taken any part of him yet—these two entities, the young scientist and the metallic black monster, were probably born about the same time. For the others, it had affected their lives forever. The group fell silent as Fusco turned around and headed back to the Sixty-fifth Strategic Squadron building.

On the way back, Stone's aide, Krieg, turned to Elliott and asked, "Did you fly Arc Light, sir?"

"Two years," Elliott replied. "Sixty-one sorties. Took an SA-2 missile in the shorts and bailed out over the South China Sea in 1968. I might've even flown Old 100 a few times. But I wouldn't know. I never really *saw* the machines, you see. Instead, I saw the men—wondering whether the machine was going to let them live . . . or die. God, this brings back memories. None of them pleasant, Elliott added to himself. In his opinion, they had had the power to end the Vietnam War five years earlier. By conducting heavy bombing and harbor-mining missions in 1972, they had forced an end to the war, but by then it was too late. The American people had had enough of it, and "Vietnamization" and "withdrawal with honor"— and, ultimately, defeat—were preferable to nightly news reports of mounting casualties.

There was something to be learned here, Elliott thought, and after a few sobering minutes thinking about the men he knew that had died in the Vietnam War, he was glad Fusco had brought them to the Arc Light Memorial before this new Philippine operation started. America had devastating air power back then, Elliott thought—just as now. They controlled the skies over North Vietnam, they controlled the harbors, they neutralized the NVA Air Force and ultimately defeated the dense antiaircraft defenses—but they still lost the war. They lost the Vietnam War because the decision to employ America's massive air forces was delayed and canceled and "committeed" and "staffed" to death.

Although he did not have a direct role in the Philippine operation, and was not in the operational chain of command, Elliott knew that it was his duty to see that those mistakes did not happen again. They had the power to control the escalation and force their will on the Chinese and anyone else involved in this crisis—they had to take the lead. They had to formulate a clearly defined, obtainable objective in this crisis and do everything in their power to achieve that objective.

And it had to be done quickly.

THE WHITE HOUSE OVAL OFFICE, WASHINGTON, D.C.
28 SEPTEMBER 1994, 0712 HOURS LOCAL
(29 SEPTEMBER, 2012 GUAM TIME)

It was very early in the morning for a White House meeting, but President Lloyd Emerson Taylor had been up for two hours and had been fully briefed on the progress of the military operations in the Philippines. He was receiving his first official visitor of the day: Hao Sun Yougao, Chinese ambassador to the United States. This meeting had been called two days earlier, and there had been several meetings between Hao and Secretary of State Dennis Danahall, but this was Hao's first appearance with the President of the United States since the nuclear explosion.

Almost everyone in Washington liked Hao Sun Yougao. He was young, energetic, and had an infectious smile that instantly put one at ease. But that smile was dim this day, and the tension was palpable as Paul Cesare showed Hao to a seat and the President took his. They were accompanied by Danahall, Secretary of Defense Thomas Preston, and Attorney General Richard Benson, the President's brother-in-law; Hao was accompanied by a young woman who was introduced as his secretary and interpreter, should he require one; he did not give her name.

Tea was poured as the meeting began: "Ambassador Hao, the silence from Beijing has us all concerned," the President said. "Premier Cheung has not contacted me directly, nor has he made any public appearances since the disaster. The nuclear explosion near the Philippines, your rapid mobilization of forces, and your actions in the Philippines are cause for great concern in our country. Do you have a message for this government or an explanation of your government's plans to deal with the natural disaster and the political upheaval in the Pacific?"

Hao seemed to consider the question for a moment, although all of the Americans in the room knew that he was a professional and had probably rehearsed every conceivable question and every possible response a dozen times in the past few days, preparing for this meeting. With slow deliberateness, Hao replied, "Yes, Mr. President. Comrade Cheung wishes to extend his warmest greetings to you. He is saddened and distraught by the disaster that has occurred. He wishes to express his sincere wish that peace be preserved at all costs."

"Very noble sentiments, Mr. Ambassador," the President said noncommittally, "ones that we all share, of course.

But ... you have significant naval forces in the Philippines, you have mobilized strategic forces, including nuclear-capable forces, throughout Asia, and you seem to be on a wartime footing although the rest of the world is not. Forgive me for being so blunt but, Mr. Ambassador, but what the *hell* is going on?"

"Mr. President, I'm sure you realize the complicated, confused situation we find ourselves in," Ambassador Hao said. "The government of China found itself torn between a monstrous event and the resultant threat to our security, and the request for assistance that came because of the incident. Our government had no choice but to act, in the hope that our presence could help restore stability to the area and help calm a destructive political situation."

"So you're saying that you have no desire to occupy portions of the Philippines?" Thomas Preston asked the Chinese diplomat. "You will remove your military forces from the Philippines once calm is restored?"

"I cannot say how our military forces will be deployed, Mr. Secretary, now or in the future," Hao replied sincerely, "simply because I do not know this information."

"Mr. Ambassador, in my opinion the Chinese military presence in the Philippines is destabilizing and unwarranted," the President said. "Trade, immigration, free passage, communications, and political stability were all assured before your country's intervention. Why does your government now feel it so necessary to occupy parts of the Philippines?"

"I assure you, Mr. President, China occupies no part of the Philippines . . ."

"I have information that states Chinese troops have occupied several military bases in and around Manila and on the islands of Palawan and Cebu. Is my information inaccurate?"

"Mr. President, the Philippine government requested our assistance in controlling an uprising by well-armed fanatical rebel troops," Hao replied. "Any action we took was at the *specific request* of the Philippine government, in complete cooperation with that government—"

"With President Mikaso's permission?" the President interrupted.

Hao paused for a moment; the question obviously took him by surprise. "I have received word, Mr. President, that President Mikaso is no longer in power. I do not know any details of this. I am sorry, but I assumed you had that information as well . . ."

"I have information that Mikaso is *dead.*"

Hao's Adam's apple bobbed conspicuously, and his eyes grew wider as he said, "I do not know this, Mr. President. Is it true?"

"My sources inform me that Mikaso was killed by Chinese soldiers, Mr. Ambassador. Do you deny this?"

Hao's face registered true surprise, although it was uncharacteristically understated for the usually animated Chinese liaison. "I cannot confirm nor deny this, Mr. President. I have no wish to doubt your word, but I must be certain of this."

"*I* am certain as I need to be, Ambassador Hao," the President said. "I have a great fear that your government, or your military, is ready to occupy the Philippines for good. Tell me I am mistaken, Mr. Ambassador."

"I may only offer assurances, Mr. President," Hao said immediately. "The Chinese are no threat to the United States, and we do not seek any sort of confrontation whatsoever with any power. We are in the Philippines at the request of the Philippine government, and we have the right to offer aid and assistance in any manner consistent with our own national interests. The Americans had troops in the Philippines for nearly a century, as you well know, and no one dared question your right to be there."

"That's because no foreign power saw our presence there as a threat," Thomas Preston said. "We were a force of regional stability—"

"Against the aggression and dominance of the Soviet Union, yes," Hao said. "But you opposed Chinese trade and national security interests as well, something that hurt our efforts to grow and become part of the global economy."

"I will not debate the effect of history on the development of China, Mr. Ambassador," the President said. "I will simply say the American people are very worried about the actions your government is taking in the Philippines, and they and the

Congress want action." He paused to let the import of his words sink in a bit; then: "I believe I can wait no more than thirty days before taking direct action against China, Mr. Ambassador."

"You already have two aircraft carrier battle groups in the Philippine Sea," Hao said, "and another approaching the Celebes Sea. The Philippines are surrounded by American warships. Are you not already taking substantial action?"

"The American people want to know when the Chinese will be leaving the Philippines, Mr. Ambassador," the President emphasized. "I want to know the same thing. Do you have an answer?"

"My government did not inquire of you when you would be leaving Grenada, or Panama, or Saudi Arabia . . ."

"Listen carefully, Mr. Ambassador . . ." the President said with growing impatience. "I want to know what your government's intentions are in the Philippines, and I haven't heard a straight answer from you yet. Your government's actions have been hostile and furtive, Ambassador, and I don't like it. For the past twenty years, we've had a policy of openness and trust between our countries. We consulted each other on important world matters. Ever since the Tian'anmen Square massacre, your government has cut off most communications with us. That breeds distrust and caution."

"Mr. President, I assure you, my government does not seek to disrupt any ties with the Americans . . ."

"Don't tell me, show me. Nothing but your actions will prove to me what your country's intentions are. But let me tell *you* what I intend to do:

"We will use all our available intelligence resources to discover how many troops you have in the Philippines, and we will begin a program to match, and then *exceed*, that number. We may not succeed, but with cooperation from the Association of South East Asian Nations and other countries we may come close. In addition we will seek to surpass the number of warships you have in the Philippines, and we'll sail those ships freely in international waters, as close to your vessels as international law allows. We expect no interference, but let me assure you that our warships will be authorized to defend themselves to the maximum extent should there be *any* threatening moves made against our forces.

"I want the government of China to make a public announcement clearly outlining your objectives and plans for your actions in the Philippines; but in any case, I want China to reduce the number of troops it has in the Philippines by one-half within thirty days, unless a compelling reason is given why you should remain. I also want Arturo Mikaso to be released from custody or his body turned over to his family and let them as well as his close advisers be released; and if it is found that Mikaso *was* killed by Chinese soldiers, I want those responsible brought to trial. China does not operate in a vacuum, Mr. Ambassador—you are responsible for your actions. You cannot invent arguments for naked acts of aggression and expect the rest of the world to play along."

The rapid-fire flurry of demands put Hao on the defensive. He glanced over at his aide to be sure she was taking notes, then said in a flat voice, "My government will make a full disclosure—"

"I should also advise you that this government views the sharp escalation in offensive strategic forces in China a serious threat to world peace and security; we see it as an unwarranted and belligerent act that is clearly over and above any reasonable response to outside military pressure," the President interrupted. "I want China to reduce the number of offensive strategic forces it has on alert and return to a less threatening, more defensive posture. Otherwise the United States and our allies will be forced to respond by increasing strategic force postures as well. China will then be responsible for a serious military escalation that will ultimately lead to disaster.

"There should be no doubt in your minds that we consider this Chinese military buildup in the Philippines a threat to American national security interests, and we will respond accordingly. You may take that message to your government." The President sat back in his seat, paused for a few moments, then said, "Do you have anything further for me, Mr. Ambassador?"

The Chinese ambassador to the United States remained impassive and stone-faced throughout the President's allocution.

"I will take your message to my government immediately," Hao Sun Yougao replied, "and convey your requests and concerns to Comrade Cheung . . . personally."

"Personally?" Secretary of State Dennis Danahall interjected, exchanging a quick glance with the President and his advisers. "You've been recalled?"

"I regret to inform you that I have, Mr. Secretary," Hao said. "The situation obviously requires careful study and discussion, and it was felt that these discussions should take place directly, in Beijing. With your permission, my deputy chargé will be available to serve you. . . ."

The Americans looked at each other with some surprise; this move was completely unexpected. "Why is your government pulling you out?" the President asked.

"I'm sure you understand how this will appear in the press, Mr. Ambassador," Danahall said. "They'll jump all over this. They'll see it as a prelude to a major conflict, perhaps war."

"No one wants war, Mr. Secretary," Hao said. "We only seek peace, security, and stability for all nations. But China has also been asked for assistance, and in a region of the globe so important to us—and less important to you, I feel—it is vital that we respond. My government feels it is important that interference in our affairs be minimized until the extent of the disruption in the Philippines can be properly assessed."

The President glared at Hao. "I hope your government understands our side of this matter and responds quickly to our requests," he said to Hao. "In the meantime you know what we will be doing."

The President rose to his feet and Hao followed suit. "Joyous wishes to you and to your family, Mr. President," Hao said. The two men shook hands, Hao bowing deeply from the waist, and he exchanged greetings with the rest of the President's Cabinet members and departed, escorted out of the Oval Office by Paul Cesare.

When Hao was gone, the Secretary of State turned to the President. "I can schedule teleconferences with the British Foreign Minister immediately, sir . . ."

"Do it," the President replied. "Get the 'leadership' together for a luncheon meeting if you can; if not, schedule a few hours this afternoon for briefings." Danahall departed, leaving the President with his brother-in-law and Secretary of Defense Preston.

"What do you think, Thomas?" the President asked. "What's Cheung up to?"

"I think it is fairly obvious, Mr. President, that he intends to use this episode to fortify his position in the Philippines and fill the void created by our departure," Preston replied. "He's created a substantial resupply line from China to the Philippines that we might find impossible to break, and he's found a way to get the government to offer him basing facilities and local support. We may never be able to shake him loose if he manages to consolidate all his gains."

"So we have no military options?"

"We have many military options, sir," Preston replied, "but it'll mean a serious escalation of our military commitment. Cheung has both the military power and at least the appearance of legitimacy—that's an unbeatable combination no matter how you look at it. If we want to counteract the advantage he has, we have to risk stepping up to the brink of a superpower war."

"We'll wait to hear what the ASEAN has to say," the President said finally. "If they vote to condemn the Chinese, world opinion will start to turn away from them—we can add our evidence of the Chinese firing that nuclear missile if we can get someone to confirm that Sky Masters data. Cheung won't have any choice but to back down then." To the Defense Secretary the President asked, "But in case they won't back down, Thomas, what can we do then?"

"Mr. President, this may be more of a political decision to make with Dennis Danahall and the Congressional leadership, but I see the Chinese as a serious military threat to our national interests in the region," Preston replied. "If they take the Philippines, they can militarily and economically threaten every other Pacific Rim nation. We'll have no choice but to build up our own military forces in the region to counterbalance them. We *must* act."

"So what do we do?" the President asked. "Are you considering sending in the Marines or this Air Battle Force thing?"

Preston considered the question for a moment, then replied. "Yes, sir—in limited numbers and in total secrecy. General Curtis mentioned the equipment installed on Brad Elliott's experimental planes—that may be a good place to start. Sending the entire Air Battle Force would be difficult to keep secret, but sending three or four aircraft would be a simple matter. I recommend approving the STRATFOR's plan to deploy the PACER SKY–equipped combat aircraft as soon as possible."

The President's eyes glanced over to his brother-in-law, Benson, who was enthusiastically nodding his agreement; Secretary of State Danahall looked grim and undecided, but eventually gave a slight nod.

"Approved, Thomas," the President said. "Keep it quiet. I want those planes kept under wrap until I decide to tell the world they're there." He paused, rubbing his eyes wearily, then added, "And I hope to hell we get some good news from Ambassador O'Day in Singapore."

ASEAN HEADQUARTERS CONFERENCE HALL, SINGAPORE
FRIDAY, 30 SEPTEMBER 1994, 0821 HOURS LOCAL
(29 SEPTEMBER, 2121 WASHINGTON TIME)

The emergency meeting of the Association of South East Asian Nations began shortly after the first of five daily prayers for its Moslem members; the crier's call to prayer was played over the building's public-address system, and a shining silver and crystal chandelier on the right-hand wall of the conference center indicated the direction of Mecca. Deborah O'Day, the United Nations ambassador from the United States, had been reminded to stay in the ladies' room until prayers were over— women, even foreign nonbelieving women, were not encouraged to be nearby during prayers.

O'Day was familiar with most aspects of Moslem life; she was especially versed on its feudalistic treatment of women. In many ways ASEAN, where four of the seven member nations were predominantly Islamic, was little more than an exclusive all-male country club, their play interrupted occasionally by short periods of more or less serious work and debate. Women performed the usual secretarial duties and little more—except, of course, for the courtesans who could be seen wandering the halls of the adjacent hotel where most of the delegates and foreign ministers stayed.

It was important for these delegates to not look upon her as a woman, but a representative of the United States government. She even went as far as wearing a very male-cut outfit, with a double-breasted jacket, a long ankle-length skirt that resembled a Muslim robe, and had even cut her hair very short for this meeting. Anything to blend in was fair game.

The meeting got under way with the last series of short speeches concerning the Chinese presence in the Philippines, and one by one the delegates voiced their opposition to China sending so many troops and so many warships to those islands.

As expected, the delegation from the Philippines urged restraint, patience, and understanding through these troubled times. O'Day had not met the new ambassador from the Philippines, knew nothing about him, and had not been granted an appointment with him. The ASEAN executive council had immediately credentialed him, however, so he had full authority to vote and debate during the meeting:

"The Philippines are in the process of enacting the first meaningful, productive change in our nation's history," the Philippine ambassador said. "Our nation has been dominated by foreigners almost since our inception . . ."

O'Day cocked an eyebrow. She got the drift—the ambassador was obviously somebody's parrot. Well, she sure as hell wasn't buying it. "Mr. Ambassador, let's cut to the chase, shall we? Where is President Mikaso? Has he been assassinated? Taken captive?"

"Silence, Ambassador O'Day," the chairman of the executive council, the ambassador from Indonesia, said. "You are not permitted to speak in this forum . . ."

She ignored him. "I would like proof that it was an American weapon that detonated off your shores, as you claim. This council has been given substantial evidence that it was a *Chinese* warhead—"

"Lies," Ambassador Perez spat. "I demand that this woman

be removed from our presence and that her government apologize for her insulting behavior . . ."

"Sit up and take it like a man, Ambassador," O'Day said evenly. "After all, I'm *only* a woman . . ."

That was too much for the ASEAN delegates; even the Brunei Crown Prince, who could not keep his lascivious eyes off her and had nodded approval when she first spoke up, shook his head.

"Ambassador O'Day, you have been granted observer status only," the chairman said. "You are not permitted to speak. You will not be warned again. Ambassador Perez, continue with your statement."

"Thank you. My country has been bled by the former regime's failed economic policies and by American imperialism. The Chinese were victims of rebel aggression as well. When they offered humanitarian aid after the nuclear attack—a gesture that was not made by any other nation until days later, including many nations represented here—we also requested assistance in quelling the well-armed and bloodthirsty rebels . . ."

"You ought to write techno-thrillers, Mr. Perez," the Crown Prince from Brunei said with a laugh. "They are very popular in my country. Unfortunately, your lies are not."

Perez pressed on. "I urge my fellow delegates to vote to disapprove sanctions against my country and to follow continued relief and police efforts by the Chinese government. My people beg for your help and understanding. Thank you." He turned and gave O'Day a murderous glare, then stared straight ahead, waiting for the Council's decision.

"The resolution before the council would approve full economic sanctions against the Republic of China and the Philippines," the chairman summarized, "and would restrict all trade and commerce with China, and would authorize the Association to implement all policies and invoke all measures to urge China to withdraw its military forces from all members' territorial or disputed waters. We vote by open-voice ballot. Five votes are required to pass the resolution. If all discussion is concluded, please record your vote."

One by one, they voted.

Indonesia.

Malaysia.

Singapore.

The Kingdom of Brunei.

All in favor of the resolution.

The Philippines voted against it.

As did Thailand, who along with Vietnam—the last two ASEAN countries to vote—had waived any closing arguments to the resolution. That had O'Day worried. She had tried to talk to each ambassador before the meeting, but had no luck. Both were critical countries; both had borders with China, and their huge neighbor was always a major presence in any political and military situation.

But both were members of ASEAN to counter China's influence, and so far it was working. They finally had the political clout to stand up to their powerful neighbor.

"The kingdom of Thailand," its ambassador said, "is convinced that such a resolution, made in the heat of passion and without extensive study and debate, would be counterproductive. As much as Thailand seeks an end to violence and fear, we cannot support such a resolution without further study. Thailand abstains."

O'Day couldn't believe it. Of all countries, Thailand stood to lose the most if China were allowed to exert a greater influence in the region; she had never expected them to abstain . . .

That left Vietnam as the deciding vote. They would *have* to vote yes, O'Day thought. After all, Vietnam and China were all but enemies. True, Vietnam was the only Communist country in ASEAN, and true, Vietnam and China had once been uneasy allies, but . . .

"Republic of Vietnam."

"Vietnam abstains."

Deborah O'Day shot to her feet in absolute shock. *"What!"* she shouted. "You're abstaining? Why?"

The chairman was pounding his gavel over the sudden flurry of excited voices. "Ambassador O'Day, your outbursts will not be tolerated! You are ordered to leave. I will have order in this chamber . . ."

"I want an explanation!" O'Day shouted. Security guards

were quickly rushing to her side. "Don't you understand? You're handing over the keys to your cities to the Chinese if you don't stop them now!"

O'Day was still shouting as she was unceremoniously pulled to her feet and half-dragged, half-escorted to the rear of the conference room and outside. Her aide was deposited beside her a few moments later.

"I don't believe this," O'Day told her aide as they made their way to the entrance. "What the hell is going on? Vietnam should certainly be opposed to Chinese aggression. . . . Something is very odd . . ."

"We've got to notify Washington about this immediately," her aide said as they made their way to the limousine. "We'll have to brief the President . . ."

The Marine Corps driver from the embassy staff, in full dress blues—spotless white gloves, white belt with .45-caliber sidearm, spit-shined boots, and round hat with the brim pulled down so low it almost obscured his racing-style sunglasses— quickly stepped around from the driver's side to the curbside rear door, opened it, and stood at attention as O'Day and her aide entered the car. "How's the traffic on Bukit Timah Road, Corporal?" she asked her driver distractedly. He grunted a perfunctory, "Poor, ma'am," in reply and quickly closed the door.

"Go ahead and take the central avenue to Government House, then," O'Day's aide said as the driver re-entered the limousine. "Call ahead and ask Communications to get a line open for us." The driver pulled out into the traffic and, with usual Marine flair and urgency, roared down the wide central city avenue toward Singapore's Embassy Row.

"China's just been given the green light to occupy the Philippines and make a grab for the rest of the Pacific," O'Day's aide said. "The President won't have any choice but to respond militarily."

"But he won't like it," O'Day said. "He wants the endorsement of some Pacific Rim government or organization before he commits troops, and he just lost the most important one. God, is he going to be pissed."

"This will be one phone call I don't envy you," her aide said.

He turned to the Marine Corps driver. "Corporal, you didn't call the embassy communications office like the ambassador asked. Now please do it."

His order was answered with a *clunk!* as the locks on all the doors engaged.

O'Day immediately scanned all the windows, looking for pursuing cars or any sign of a threat; there were none. Her aide immediately reached down below the seat to the hidden compartment where a Uzi submachine gun was stored. "Corporal, why'd you lock the doors?" O'Day asked. "What's going on?"

"The Uzi's gone," her aide said. He fingered the door unlock buttons and power window switches—none were operable. "What the hell is going on?" He reached for the cellular phone in the backseat, but the "Ready" lights were all out—the phone too was dead.

A .45-caliber Colt semiautomatic pistol appeared in the hand of the driver; he showed it to O'Day and her aide but then immediately lowered it, out of view. "Please sit still and do not try anything foolish," the driver said. "You will not be harmed unless you try to resist."

It was not until O'Day looked at the man through the rear-view mirror that she realized he was wearing sunglasses—their Marine driver had not been wearing them before because of the early hour and overcast skies. "Where's our driver?"

"Safely asleep in the trunk, Ambassador O'Day," the man replied. "He put up quite a struggle before we could subdue him. He will awaken in a few minutes." The driver eased off the main avenue toward a hotel parking lot where the car could be partially obscured, but not appear too conspicuously isolated. He parked the car and immediately began removing the uniform.

"What are you going to do with us?"

"Nothing," the driver said. Underneath the blue uniform, he wore a T-shirt with palm trees on it, khaki shorts, and white tennis socks; he replaced the spit-shined shoes with tennis shoes. He looked like a tourist from any number of Asian or European countries. Gripping the .45 in his right hand, he glanced nervously at his watch, leaned through the dividing window between the compartments, and said, "I know your embassy tracks all its vehicles by microtransmitter, so I will not stay any longer. I have a message from Second Vice President General Samar . . ."

"Samar!" O'Day exclaimed. "Is he still alive? Is he in hiding . . .?" Samar had disappeared the day Mikaso had been killed. It had been assumed Samar was dead, too.

"Silence," the man said; then, realizing he might have sounded too demanding, added, "Please." Then, "General Samar requests help from your government to relieve Davao on the island of Mindanao. He is resisting the Chinese invaders but cannot hold on for much longer—Puerto Princesa and Zamboanga have fallen, and Cotabato and Davao will be next . . ."

"If Samar wants help," O'Day told the man, "he had better stop playing hide-and-seek and take control of the government. The non-Communist citizens will follow him, but everyone thinks he's dead . . ."

"He may be dead if you do not help," the agent said.

"We need more than just . . ."

"Silence. I have stayed too long already. Listen carefully. General Samar says that the *Ranger* carrier battle group will be attacked by Chinese air forces from Zamboanga if they attempt to enter the Celebes Sea."

"*What?* How in hell do you know that . . . ?"

"General Samar is on Mindanao, organizing his people and his resistance forces. He is carefully monitoring the Chinese military's movements and communications, and he concludes that on the first of October—Revolution Day—Admiral Yin Po L'un's forces will attack any foreign military forces that attempt to pass near Mindanao."

"But that's crazy," O'Day's aide said. "The Chinese wouldn't be stupid enough to attack an American carrier . . ."

"I will not debate you. The General has risked his life to bring this information to you—in exchange, he officially requests military and humanitarian aid from the United States. Please help. Contact him at this number immediately. Do not alert your embassy by radio or telephone; there are spies everywhere." The man reached down and hit the button to unlock the trunk. "Your guard will awaken in ten to fifteen minutes; he will release you then. Do not attempt to follow me. Please help my people."

The man raised the dividing glass screen, stepped out of the car, and ran as fast as he could away from the hotel; they saw him throw the gun into a ditch before he ran out of sight.

EIGHT

They had kept the landing lights off until seconds before touchdown. The only lights on around the entire base were the runway-end identifier lights and blue taxiway lights—all "ball park" lights on the parking ramps, exterior lights, and streetlights near the runway were out. Looking from the cockpit, the entire northern part of the island of Guam appeared as dark and as deserted as the thousands of miles of ocean they had just crossed.

The aircraft, as black as the tropical night sky from which it descended, used the runway closest to the parking area and did not touch down until nearly halfway down the two-mile-long runway at Andersen Air Force Base so it would spend as little time as possible exposed to view while taxiing. At the end of the runway, it taxied rapidly across the wide north ramp to a row of large hangars and pulled straight into the first one. The hangar doors were closed behind it seconds later as the engines were shut down. Security patrols began an immediate sweep of the area, using dogs and light-intensifying night-vision equipment to search for intruders.

The interior of the huge hangar brightly illuminated the

sleek, bat-shaped outline of the B-2 Black Knight stealth bomber. Maintenance crews checked the aircraft and immediately began opening inspection and access panels. A few moments later the belly hatch swung open and three men climbed down the access ladder.

As Major Henry Cobb, Lieutenant Colonel Patrick McLanahan, and Brigadier General John Ormack emerged from the huge black bomber, General Elliott, General Stone, Jon Masters, and Colonel Fusco were there to greet them. "Good to see you guys," Elliott said, shaking each of their hands and handing each of them a beer.

"We're damned glad to be here," Cobb exclaimed. "My butt is wondering if my legs have been cut off." All three aviators looked completely exhausted and thoroughly rumpled, but their smiles were genuine as Elliott made introductions all around.

The formalities of every military flight still had to be accomplished, so Elliott and the others waited patiently as Cobb and McLanahan completed their postflight walkaround inspection of the bomber and sat down with several aircraft-maintenance technicians to explain the few glitches found during flight. Afterward they were taken to a conference room at the command post, where sandwiches, more beer, and several other members of Stone's staff were waiting to greet them.

"I must say, this is a pretty impressive showing," Rat Stone said after the three crew members were settled down. "Deploying a B-2 from South Dakota to Guam with only three hours' notice, then flying nonstop all the way. So what's it like to spend nearly seventeen hours straight in a stealth bomber?"

"The first ten aren't too bad, sir," Ormack replied with a tired grin. "Henry made the takeoff and the first two refuelings, but I was too wired to sleep. We switched just past Hawaii. When we got out of radio range of Hawaii, it was absolute murder to stay awake until the next refueling—near Wake Island, as it so happens. The last four hours were the worst—too keyed up to sleep, too tired to concentrate, having to make those timing orbits so we wouldn't land too early and get our pictures taken by the Chinese spy satellites. I'm too old for these butt-busting missions."

"Well, you did good," Elliott said. "You landed right on time—the Chinese bird should be passing overhead right about now. Unless there's a sub out there we haven't found yet, we may have pulled this off—deploying a stealth bomber seven thousand miles in total secrecy. How's the bomber look?"

"Everything's in the green," McLanahan said. "We brought spares for most of the critical components, and we have the computerized blueprints on the PACER SKY mod installation." He turned to Jon Masters and said, "The system was working like a charm, Doctor Masters. We were able to monitor some of the *Ranger* battle group clear as day. The NIRT-Sats found a few Chinese ships operating in the Celebes, but I don't think there's going to be a problem with them as long as we stay clear of them."

"That's exactly what we intend to do," Stone said. "We got a cryptic but urgent report from the State Department that the Chinese Navy might try something against the fleet if we move into the Celebes Sea, so except for the RC-135 overflight—and he's been instructed to stay at extreme sensor range from any Chinese vessels—we're staying well away."

"Well, the RC was still a few hours from on-station, but he should have the Chinese ships' position from the NIRTSat—he shouldn't have any problem staying out of the way. I recorded the NIRTSat transmissions, and we can download it from the memory banks right away." McLanahan stifled a big yawn, finished the rest of his beer, then added, "Rather, *you* can. I've got to get some sleep."

ABOARD THE RC-135X RADAR RECONNAISSANCE PLANE
OVER THE CELEBES SEA, SOUTHERN PHILIPPINES
SATURDAY, 1 OCTOBER 1994, 0121 HOURS LOCAL
(30 SEPTEMBER, 1221 EASTERN TIME)

From thirty thousand feet, the radar aboard the RC-135X radar reconnaissance aircraft could pick out the dense clusters of islands, atolls, and coral reefs of the Sulu Archipelago. At the very tip of the peninsula was the area that most of the ten radar operators on the RC-135 reconnaissance aircraft were concentrating on.

In the center of the converted Boeing 707 airliner was the command station, where Colonel Rachel Blanchard and her deputy, Captain Samuel Fruntz, sat poring over a stack of four-color charts. "Look at this," Fruntz remarked, pointing at the tip of the Zamboanga peninsula. "Not very subtle, are they? A whole line of vessels stretching from the North Balabac Strait to Zamboanga." He compared the image to another chart. "Checks right on with that NIRTSat printout we received from Andersen. That PACER SKY satellite is far out."

Blanchard looked at her younger deputy and rolled her eyes. Fruntz, Blanchard thought, was another "techie" who believed that, whatever the newest technology was, it had to be better than any of the "older" technology, even if the older technology was only a few years old. Blanchard had been in the reconnaissance business for twelve years, mostly as pilot or copilot flying EC- and RC-135 aircraft for the Strategic Air Command—this was only her second tour as recce section commander—and she had been dismayed at the new emphasis on space-based reconnaissance systems, or "gadgets" as she called them. Even the latest high-tech satellites had serious limitations that only well-equipped planes like the RC-135 or the newer EC-18s could overcome.

Blanchard had flown or seen just about every one of the sixty different iterations of the C-135 special mission/reconnaissance/intelligence–gathering aircraft. The RC-135X, nicknamed "Rivet Joint," was the latest and best of the older RC-series aircraft; the newer series was designated EC-18 and was a hundred times more cosmic than even the RC- models. Rivet Joint had been designed to map out precise locations of coastal enemy air-defense sites for targeting by Short-Range Attack Missiles or cruise missiles that armored long-range bomber aircraft. By combining sensitive radiation sensors with powerful radar and infrared images, one Rivet Joint aircraft could update three thousand miles of coastal air-defense sites in one day. Blanchard used to fly reconnaissance missions in conjunction with SR-71 Blackbird spy planes—the SR-71 would fly toward the Russian coastline until Soviet air-defense missile-site radars activated, and then the RC-135 would plot out all the locations of those missile sites. It was a deadly game of cat-and-mouse that, thankfully, she had never lost.

"Hey, Sam," Blanchard told her younger partner. "Does that gadget's data tell you what *kind* of ships those are?"

"No, but it—"

"Didn't think so. Our radar can *identify* those ships—PACER SKY's printout just gives a position and velocity read-out," Blanchard said. "Without ISAR identification data, we could only report those ships as a *possible* hostile, and that's only based on their formation, not their type." She referred to a sheaf of computer printouts he had received from the RC-135's intensive-signal processors. "Here it is: the largest ship in that string is a probable Hegu-class fast attack missile craft. What good is satellite intelligence that only gives you half the story?"

"Because we wouldn't have to truck three thousand miles to find out the Chinese are moving a big convoy into Zamboanga," Fruntz said.

Blanchard remained unimpressed.

Fruntz continued: "Look at this: PACER SKY is telling us there might be defensive missile batteries set up on the eastern shore of Jolo Island or Pata Island, in the middle of the Sulu Archipelago. See that? That's the kind of info we need before we drive into the area."

"Well, I guess it doesn't make that much difference, because we're *still* going to drive into that area," Blanchard said. "If there's a SAM site or radar on those islands, they're not going to turn 'em on until we get closer."

"It beats getting surprised," Fruntz insisted. "I'd rather be ready for a radar to come up than have the bejeezus scared out of us."

"I like surprises," Blanchard said, but then added quickly, "Sam, you go into these sorties expecting the shit to hit the fan at any time. Too much information, and you start getting complacent. You gotta be ready for *anything*. Expect the unexpected . . ."

"Radar four reports surface contact," one of the radar operators suddenly called out. "Slow velocity . . . now showing ten knots, heading westbound."

"There's something that NIRTSat thing didn't find," Blanchard snickered. "No matter how gee-whiz that satellite is, thirty-minute-old data is still thirty-minute-old data—and it's garbage to us." She turned to the radar operator and said, "I need a designation on that last contact, Radar. Get on it."

"Signal two shows primary search radar on that surface contact," another operator called out. "Showing C-band, three-seventy PRF . . . calling it a Rice Screen air-search radar . . ."

"Radar four has an ISAR probable on that return, calling it a EF4-class destroyer . . . now picking up escorts, probably as many as four, within ten miles of EF4." The ISAR, or Inverse Synthetic Aperture Radar, mounted in the two prominent fairings on the underside of the RC-135's fuselage, could paint a nearly three-dimensional picture of a ship and, by combining it with a computer data base of thousands of such radar images, could usually match the radar image with a ship in its computer memory. The larger the ship, the more accurate the match, and a destroyer-class vessel was a very large radar return.

"Jeez, they got some pretty fancy firepower out here," Blanchard said. "A destroyer-class boat this far south." She turned to the forward part of the aircraft. "Comm, code and send immediately to Andersen and Offutt on separate channels the position of that last contact. It's the biggest gun the Chinese have this far south—I want to make sure everybody knows about it." To the radar operator, she asked, "What's our range to that EF4?"

"Range, four-seven nautical miles," the operator reported.

"That's close enough," Blanchard said to Fruntz. Fruntz was already leafing through pages of computerized text on the EF4 class of Chinese destroyers. "What's the scouting report on those things?"

"Antiship and antisubmarine missile destroyers," Fruntz read. "About ten in the Chinese inventory, possibly with five more in ready reserve and five more overseas. Helicopter pad, big-time antiship launchers . . . holy shit, listen to this gun fit: four 130-millimeter dual purpose, eight 57-millimeter or 37-millimeter antiaircraft guns, and four 25-millimeter antiaircraft guns. Rice Screen three-D long-range air-defense radar system—they call it a 'mini-Aegis' system—X-band ERF-1 or X-band Rice Lamp fire-control radar for the guns. Some fitted with Phalanx self-defense guns, Ku-band radar."

"Anything about antiair missiles?"

"Yes . . . helicopter pad removed from some vessels and replaced with various stern-mounted missile systems," Fruntz replied. "Some fitted possibly with HQ-61 missiles, one twin mount, Fog Lamp H- or I-band fire control, max range of missile, six nautical miles—pretty small missile. Others possibly with French naval Crotale, max range eight nautical miles, X-band fire control. Some with HQ-91 French Masurca dual-rail mount . . . shit, max range thirty nautical miles, S-band pulse-Doppler tracker."

"As far as we're concerned, we'll assume the worst case," Blanchard said. "Forty miles out from that EF4 is perfect for now." She paused for a moment, then added, "But that Rice Screen radar has me worried. That's a no-shit early warning and fighter intercept radar system. Why have a boat with that kind of radar on board way out here unless—"

"Flashlight, Flashlight, Flashlight, this is Basket," the radio report interrupted. Basket was the call sign of the E-3C Sentry Airborne Warning and Control System radar plane that had accompanied the RC-135 on this mission. The AWACS plane could scan for hundreds of miles in all directions, locating aircraft at all altitudes and vector friendly fighters in to intercept. Emergency reports from an AWACS controller were always prefaced by calling out a sortie's call sign three times—the RC-135 was under attack. "Bandits at your twelve o'clock, Blue plus five-five, flight level zero-niner-zero, speed five hundred."

Range calls were always given in color codes in case the enemy fighters somehow were able to eavesdrop on the encrypted radio messages between aircraft; Blue meant fifty miles, Yellow meant twenty miles, Red meant zero miles, and Green meant subtract twenty miles. When a dogfight started, the controller would drop the color codes and issue warnings as fast as he could. All radar targets were being called "bandits," or hostile targets, in this area with Chinese troops nearby—of course, anytime a target began flying over five hundred knots, it was automatically considered an enemy fighter until proven otherwise.

"Showing four targets now, Blue plus forty, speed passing five-zero-zero. Bullet flight, take spacing and stand by."

The AWACS plane not only issued warnings to Flashlight, the RC-135X plane, but also to Shamu Three-One, the KC-10 aerial refueling tanker that was supporting both the Navy and Air Force planes on this mission; two KA-6 Navy tankers to use as tactical spare refueling aircraft; and four Navy F-14A Tomcat fighters of VF-2 Bullets from the USS *Ranger,* which was steaming about one hundred miles east of Talaud Island just outside Indonesian waters. The Tomcats were armed with four medium-range Sparrow radar-guided missiles and four shorter-range Sidewinder heat-seeking missiles; since they were along only as escorts and, according to the Rules of Engagement, not authorized to attack from long range, none of the escorts carried the long-range AIM-54 Phoenix missile.

Two of the F-14s, Bullet Four and Five, were with the RC-135 acting as primary escorts, and the other two, Bullet Two and Three, were shuttling to the KC-10 tanker for refueling. Four more F-14 fighters were ready aboard *Ranger,* loaded with long-range Phoenix missiles as well as Sparrows and Sidewinders, to assist the Air Force recon planes and defend the battle group in case of trouble . . .

. . . And it sounded like there was going to be trouble. With unknown aircraft heading their way, this was no place to be for one of the U.S. Air Force's most sophisticated spy planes. The data was important, but not important enough to risk the manpower or the hardware. "Time to leave, Grasshopper. We're calling it a night," Blanchard said. Being flippant about a possible fighter attack usually wasn't her style, but she had found after pushing a crew for so long that the initial wave of excitement that hit a crewman who suddenly found himself or herself under attack sometimes caused costly mistakes; if you could relax a person during that initial fear-heavy period, he performed better.

"Pilot, this is Recce One, execute egress now," Blanchard continued. "Crew, this is Recce One, terminate all emissions, secure your stations and queue your data for transmission. Report by station when complete." She watched her status board light up with coded intelligence-data packets waiting for transmission; Blanchard and Fruntz could pick out the most important ones for immediate transmission, or send them in all in one quick burst, or send them one by one in ordered, error-checked bundles. They preferred the last method until the bandits got closer and posed a more serious threat. Then Blanchard and Fruntz would use the faster 57,000-kilobit-per second routines, shoveling the data out as fast as the RC-135's computers could handle it.

"Flashlight, turn left heading one-four-zero," the AWACS controller called out. "Manado airfield will be at your twelve o'clock position, two-five-zero miles." Manado, a good-sized city on the Minahasa Peninsula of northern Indonesia, was the first emergency landing site; on a southeast heading, they were also flying away from the Philippines and toward their tanker and the USS *Ranger,* which was stationed in the northern Molucca Sea about five hundred miles farther east.

"Flashlight copies," Blanchard's pilot replied. He unconsciously pushed the throttles up to near military power, trying to claw every bit of distance between himself and the unknowns.

It took only a few moments for Blanchard and Fruntz to finish their primary job—safely transmit the reams of radar and sensor data collected on this short trip. They began yet another error-checking routine after all the data was transmitted, where the receiving station on Guam would compute check sums from each line of data from their transmission, then compare the sums with Blanchard's information. If it matched, Blanchard would erase the verified data and repeat the process with another data file. The verification process was the most time-consuming—satellite transmissions even at the best of times were relatively slow and prone to interruptions—

but it was the safest way of ensuring that the information had been transmitted and received without errors before they would risk erasing it . . . and the information would all be erased before the enemy fighters got within striking distance.

ABOARD THE NAVY F-14A TOMCAT FIGHTER BULLET FOUR

This shit was happening too fast, Lieutenant Greg "Hitman" Povik thought.

Night carrier operations were the absolute worst. Flying combat sorties was bad enough, but a night cat shot was sheer terror. Strapped into a sixty-thousand-pound machine, blasted out into the darkness from zero to one hundred and fifty knots in two seconds. Hard enough to flatten eyeballs. Hard enough that the brain thinks you're in a steep nose-high climb, so your tendency is to push the nose down to the water—that will kill you in one second if you succumb to the feeling. You have no outside reference, no sign of up or down or sideways, no natural cues. The ultimate in sensory deprivation, even though you're surrounded by instruments.

So you keep full afterburner and back pressure on the stick until after the shot, after you've cleared the deck and established a positive rate of climb. Believe the instruments, because your brain will kill you if you let it. Positive rate of climb, positive altitude increase—gear up. Passing one-eighty, flaps and slats up. Passing two-fifty, wings moving back, turn out and listen up for your wingman.

Everything is still dark, so you stay on the instruments. You hear radio calls coming from everywhere, from planes hundreds of miles away and from planes just a few miles away. Slowly, the real poop starts to filter in: wingman's up, wingman's got you locked on his radar so he can catch up without the carrier's radar or the E-2 Hawkeye's radar operators vectoring in. Vector to the tanker—an F-14 sucks a lot of gas for takeoff, and the good guys are three hundred miles and a quarter-tank of gas away still. Check the cockpit, get a check from your RIO—Radar Intercept Officer, Lieutenant JG Bob

"Bear" Blevin—check oxygen and pressurization, check weapons, check everything.

Soon the sounds of the hostile area filtered in. An Air Force reconnaissance plane is less than a hundred miles from the Philippines, within pissing distance of Chinese warships. Intelligence says Chinese patrol planes, with fighter escorts, might be up. They say the Chinese ships might have antiair missiles and guns and might just shoot first and ask questions later. Great. With nothing but black surrounding you, you feel more alone than you've ever felt before—there's nothing but miles of ocean between you and dry land or deck.

Things happen too quickly, even though the Air Force plane is hundreds of miles away. Blevin makes radio contact with the KA-6 tanker, and they maneuver to intercept. The small KA-6 will transfer only a few thousand pounds of fuel, but it's better to fly overwater with full tanks as much as possible in case of trouble.

Night aerial refueling ranks right up there with night catapult shots in the anxiety department. Povik has to drive up behind the KA-6 tanker, find a tiny four-foot-diameter lighted basket, and stick a three-inch nozzle inside it by maneuvering his forty-five-ton air machine around it. Meanwhile, the KA-6 is turning in a racetrack pattern so it won't fly too far from the carrier, which makes the hookup even more difficult. With gentle coaching from Blevin, Povik made the hookup on the second try, and he managed to stay hooked up and made the transfer all at once. He maintained visual contact on the tanker while his wingman made contact and got his gas, and then they got a vector from their E-2C Hawkeye radar plane controller to the west.

No sooner had they finished refueling, and they were transferred to the Air Force E-3 AWACS radar plane's controller, who was providing air coverage for all the planes operating near the Philippines. The Navy guys had trained a few times with Air Force controllers, but they still used different terminology and never seemed to shut up—they seemed determined to read off every number on their radar screens and let the fighter crews work their own navigation solutions. But after filtering out the chatter—obviously those AWACS guys were nervous too—Povik and his wingman in Bullet Five were vectored in to visual range of an Air Force RC-135 reconnaissance plane. It looked like a KC-135 tanker, but without the refueling boom and with lots of odd bumps and antennas all over it.

All that, from cat shot to now, took less than an hour. Now they had unidentified aircraft bearing down on them. Povik didn't even have time to get himself comfortably situated, get his heads-up display set up just right, and tighten his straps—the fight was starting right *now*.

"Bullet flight, take spacing and check your lights," Povik radioed to his wingman. He turned to check that his wingman was configured properly—no missing missiles, lights off, nothing funny-looking out there—before he disappeared into the darkness. Now they were relying on the Air Force AWACS controller to keep them separated, yet working as a team as they prosecuted these bandits.

"Bullet flight, this is Basket. Four bandits twelve o'clock, Blue plus twenty, flight lev—er, angels fifteen. Possible second flight of two bandits, angels ten." The AWACS controller was trying hard to use Navy terminology for this intercept, such as "angels" for "thousands of feet" or "port" and "starboard" for "left" and "right," but the more excited he got the more he was stumbling over his tongue. "Starboard ten for intercept."

"Bullet flight copies." Povik's backseater could just as easily lock onto the incoming Chinese fighters with his AWG-9 radar, but the radar emissions could be detected at incredible distances and the longer he kept his radar off the more they kept the element of surprise.

Just then they heard on the international Guard radio channel: "Unidentified aircraft at ten thousand meters altitude—this is fighter unit seven." The accent was heavily Oriental, not Spanish or Filipino—but Chinese. "You have violated restricted airspace. You will reverse course and drop your landing gear immediately."

"Bullet flight, additional bandits departing Zamboanga area," the AWACS controller radioed on the air frequency. "Number unknown at this time."

"Range from the bandits to Flashlight?" Povik said.

"Range Blue plus zero," the controller replied.

Fifty miles. The fight was going to happen in a matter of seconds. Obviously the Chinese fighters weren't going to be content with chasing the American planes away—they wanted to intercept and capture them.

"Unknown aircraft, you have violated restricted airspace," the warning came again, more insistently this time. "You are not responding as ordered. Decrease velocity, lower your landing gear, and follow us or you will be attacked. This is your final warning!"

Povik considered shutting off the Guard channel, but he might need it later. This guy was getting on his nerves, but he would shut up very soon once the furball started. "Where's Bullet Two Flight?" Povik radioed to the AWACS controller.

"Departing Shamu at this time, range to you Blue plus ten." Sixty miles. It would take them too long to get in on the fight here—they would be in a position to engage just as the Chinese fighters caught up with the RC-135. That was far, far too late.

Povik had a decision to make right now, but it really wasn't much of a chore to make it. Their primary mission was to protect the Air Force recon planes. They had plenty of firepower—all they needed was time. They needed to get those Chinese fighters turned away from the Air Force heavies.

"Bullet Four's coming left forty-five. Bullet Five, stay with me."

"Two."

"Go ahead and lock 'em up, Bear," Povik said. They wanted the Chinese fighters to follow them—it was okay to hit them with the radar now. Povik executed a hard left turn to a westerly heading and pushed his throttles up to full military power. "C'mon, you peckerheads," Povik cursed to himself at the Chinese fighter pilots. "Do it, *do* it!"

"Bullet flight, four bandits turning to intercept, now at your two o'clock position, forty miles. Second flight of bandits confirmed at angels ten, trailing bandits maintaining heading one-four-zero." The tactic worked—sort of. Every degree the Chinese fighters turned, and every five seconds they interrupted their pursuit, meant another two miles of safety for the

RC-135 recon plane. They were obviously going after the more glamorous prize—downing an RC-135 was too easy. Downing a fighter was more macho. But the two extra bandits weren't going to be distracted—they were heading straight for the RC-135.

"Bullet flight, two bandits peeling off from pursuit, returning to heading one-five-zero to intercept on Flashlight."

"Dammit!" Povik berated himself. After a few seconds of obvious confusion, the Chinese fighters decided to break into two groups and go after the RC-135. Well, at least they got the odds more in their favor—two-vee-two heading away from their heavies, and two-vee-four still closing. Another advantage: the farther the Chinese pilots flew away from their radar ship, the harder their job would be. "Bullet Two flight, can you get the four inbounds?"

"Affirmative, Hitman," the pilot of Bullet Two replied, using Povik's call sign. "Bullet Two flight has a contact on the four southeast-bound bandits."

"Bullet flight, be advised, Bullet Six flight of two airborne, ETE ten minutes," the AWACS controller reported. Two more Tomcats were on the way. Well, Povik thought grimly, everybody was paired up and the dancing was going to begin.

"Check the gas gauges, Hitman," Povik's RIO said. "We got about ten minutes before we gotta start heading back."

"Thanks, Bear," Povik replied. "Ten minutes max, then we split."

"Bullet Two flight, push Eagle for your controller." Povik switched to the new pre-planned frequency—as a security precaution, actual frequencies were never read over the air, no matter how secure the radios were—checked in his wingman, and checked in with the new AWACS controller; now the Air Force controller could stop saying "Bullet Two flight" to differentiate them between the other two Tomcats. "Bullet, bandits at your three o'clock, thirty miles. Say your bingo."

"Bullet Two bingos in eight mike," Povik replied. Povik's wingman reported the same—Povik knew he would do so unless his fuel state was worse than his own. The gauges actually said ten minutes, but always subtract two minutes for the wife and kids, he thought. The AWACS controller, if he was worth a shit, would subtract another two minutes and start vectoring the Tomcats toward the carrier after six or seven minutes.

If past experience were any indication, the fight would be over in less than two minutes . . . one way or another.

STRATFOR COMMAND POST, ANDERSEN AFB, GUAM

"Message from Basket, sir," an operator reported. "They report six enemy fighters, probable Chinese origin, engaging the F-14 escorts, three hundred miles northwest of Mandao. Flashlight is southeast-bound, withdrawing from the area."

General Stone was on his feet and beside the radio operator in a heartbeat; Elliott was behind him, listening intently. "Tell Flashlight to dump their data buffers and get the hell out of there. Shamu should stay available for emergency refueling, and Basket should stay to control the intercepts—but I want them as far away from the Philippines as possible."

"All units withdrawing from the area at best speed . . . Basket reports more fighters airborne from Zamboanga. No visual contact made, but Basket reports the enemy fighters made a warning-message broadcast ordering the aircraft to reverse course and follow them. Operators report the pilots spoke English and sounded Oriental." The operator flipped a switch and spoke briefly, then reported, "Communications center confirms a good secure data download via DSCS from Flashlight and Basket." Stone nodded with a silent sigh of relief. The lives of his crew members were vitally important, but it was also important to preserve any data they might have collected up to this point.

"Carrier *Ranger* is launching two more fighters to assist," the operator reported. "Reports of more fighters launching from Zamboanga area. *Ranger* is declaring an air-defense emergency with a two-hundred-mile exclusion zone."

"Verify that all aircraft are in international airspace," Elliott told Stone. "If any of the aircraft are attacked, we've got a case for retaliation."

Stone nodded. To the radio operator, he said, "Order Basket

to download a radar map of the entire area and then verbally read off INS and GPS latitude and longitude, then range and bearing from radio and radar checkpoints to verify position accuracy. Tell them to repeat the report every sixty seconds until they are clear of the attackers." As the radio operator relayed the orders, Stone said to Elliott, "The Chinese not only have attacked Zamboanga, it looks like they've fortified it and brought fighters in to seal the area. That was a major defense installation."

Elliott referred to a chart of the Philippines that had been set up in the command post. "From there they can control access to the southern Philippines."

A Navy captain, who was acting as the Navy liaison to the STRATFOR, said, "That EF4-class destroyer is definitely the key, sir. Flashlight reported a Rice Screen radar system in operation—it's the most sophisticated radar system in the Chinese fleet, and it's almost as good as an Aegis system but without the weapon systems. He can control almost the entire Celebes Sea from that one platform. With shore-based aircraft, he can control antiair and antisurface forces for hundreds of miles."

"What we need," Stone said half aloud, as if daring himself to say the words, "is permission to launch an attack from *Ranger* on that EF4-class boat." Elliott and the others in the command post looked at the Air Force three-star general wordlessly; surprised at his reaction but silently wishing the same thing.

"Unfortunately, that's pretty unlikely," Elliott said. "We're lucky Washington authorized this mission—I would think there's no way they'd approve a preemptive strike on a Chinese naval vessel." He paused, then added grimly, "Unless, of course, one of our recon planes gets shot down. . . ."

ABOARD BULLET FOUR

One of the hardest tasks for a fighter pilot, and the most important skill that every good pilot possessed, was situational awareness—the ability to instantaneously paint a picture of the

world around him in his mind without the help of radar planes,
fancy electronic displays, or even backseaters. Luckily Povik
had that knack—he had been honing it during his twelve years
as a naval aviator, all of them in carrier-based fighters.

Bullet Two and Three, plus the extra Tomcats launched
from *Ranger* a few minutes ago, would have to take care of the
four Chinese fighters chasing the reconnaissance plane. That
left Bullet Four and Five to deal with the two bozos that broke
off to chase them. Bullet Five had closed back with Povik, but
he was not right on his wing. They were in a combat-spread
position that allowed either Tomcat to assist the other if they
came under attack. It was a purely defensive position, but it
could be quickly switched to an offensive one if necessary.

Unfortunately, a more advantageous offensive stance was
not authorized. Under the ROE, the Rules of Engagement
which were carefully briefed to each pilot by the Carrier Air
Group commander, the Tomcat pilots could not attack unless
they were attacked first or unless a hostile aircraft was within
one hundred miles of *Ranger.* The ROE then allowed them to
use their weapons only to break up an engagement and allow
all friendly fighters to disengage—although few commanders
expected their naval aviators to deliberately miss or back away
from a fight.

"Five minutes to bingo," Povik's RIO said. "Time to get out
of here." Povik was continuing to maneuver on a more or less
westerly heading, still trying to put as much distance between
the two Chinese fighters and the RC-135 as he could until the
two extra Bullet fighters arrived.

"Few more turns and then we'll bug out," Povik said. "I
need to make sure those bozos on us can't go after that recon
plane."

The Chinese fighters were laying off for now—they were still
about nine miles somewhere behind them, closing only when
Povik tried a large turn but backing off again when he returned to straight and level. Povik's ALR-45 threat-warning
receiver was showing the Chinese fighter's position as an "S"
with a diamond around it on his rear hemisphere—that was
the fighter's search radar, reported to be a Type 225 Skyranger
range-only radar. That meant the Chinese probably didn't

have radar-guided missiles, which in turn meant they wouldn't attack unless they were within about five to six miles. According to Intelligence, these were supposed to be J-7 fighters, copies of the Soviet Union's MiG-21 fighter. The Chinese had another fighter, called the J-8 "Finback," with an L-band multi-mode radar, but that would show on the threat warning receiver as an inverted V "bat-wing" symbol, not an "S." The Finback was supposed to be deployed only to protect cities and, the spooks said, would probably not be encountered way out here.

"Bullet, Bullet Two flight of two is engaging the other two bandits," the AWACS controller reported. "I show you two minutes to bingo. You've got two, possibly four more bandits northwest of your position at Blue plus forty, closing at six hundred knots."

That was all Povik was waiting for. "Copy, Basket. I'm not getting any radar warning signals from these guys—they just might be sitting on us." Povik's older, less capable ALR-45 threat warning receiver was little more than a glorified fuzz-buster that could tell him that there was a threat out there but not reliably tell where or what. "We're bugging out of here. Bullet Five, I'm coming left first. I'll take anybody who tries to get behind you."

"Two," came the usual wingman's reply.

Povik had just started his hard left turn when he heard his wingman scream, "Missile launch! Hitman, missile on you!"

"Shit," Povik cursed at himself, not one squawk from his threat-warning receivers—sometimes they were useless pieces of garbage. "Gimme chaff and flares, Bear. Find the missile!"

"I can't see it!" Blevin shouted. His oxygen mask was flattened against the right side of the canopy as Povik tightened up his left turn and the G-forces increased. "I can't see it!" He continued to hit the chaff-and-flare buttons; he could see each flare cartridge flying into the darkness, burning as bright as a welder's torch, but not the enemy missile. His F-14 was equipped with one ALE-29 pod loaded with thirty infrared missile-decoy flares and one ALE-39 box loaded with sixty chaff cartridges to decoy radar-guided missiles. The pods were supposed to be slaved to the AAR-47 IR warning sensor and the ALR-45 radar threat-warning receiver so cartridges would eject automatically, but the system had so many false alarms that the decoy dispensers were left on manual all the time.

"Hitman!" his wingman shouted. "On your left! Missile turning inside you! Hit your burners!" Blevin fought the G-forces and stared out the left side. He saw the missile immediately—a tiny yellow phosphorescent dot, growing larger as it spiraled in on them.

Povik didn't hesitate—he jammed both throttles to max afterburner and felt the satisfying kick as eight gallons of raw fuel a second were dumped into the burner cans, creating a flame a hundred feet long behind the Tomcat. It was a last-ditch move to defeat a heat-seeking missile that was locked onto your aircraft instead of on a decoy flare—light the afterburners and hope the long flame steered the missile away in time . . .

Blevin cried out, "Jesus, oh Jesus . . ." But just as he expected the missile to hit, he could see it veer to the right and pass behind them. "It's turning away! Burners off, increase left break!" Blevin was thrown against his shoulder straps as Povik yanked the throttles out of afterburner and into 80-percent power, and he continued to hit the flare eject button until the Chinese missile was lost from sight. Thankfully, the missile did not explode after sensing it had missed—it had passed close enough that its warhead would have done considerable damage. "God *damn!* It's past us . . . I can't see any more." He searched both sides of his Tomcat to make sure it wasn't circling to re-attack.

"That damn thing was locked onto *us,* not just our tailpipe," Povik said. When he spoke, he noticed his chest heaving as strongly as though he'd finished a wind sprint. So *this* is what real combat felt like. . . . He remembered their intel briefings, which told them that the Chinese did not yet have infrared guided missiles with a sensitive enough seeker to lock onto an aircraft fuselage. The Tomcat's AIM-9R Sidewinder missiles were advanced enough to seek a fighter's hot wing leading edges, but the Chinese PL-2 and PL-7 Pen Lung missiles were supposed to be only capable of locking onto a hot exhaust dot. Bullshit. "We got some *bad* intel, I think . . ."

"Bullet Four, bandits turning right away from you, range eleven miles," the AWACS controller reported. "Bullet Five, bandit moving across your nose at six miles . . . Four is well clear at your five o'clock position low."

"Bullet Five, fox two," Povik's wingman cried out. He looked up just as an eerie streak of light flashed out above them. A second streak lashed out—Povik's wingman was going for the jugular, not just to scare anyone off. The heat-seeking AIM-9R Sidewinder missiles curled to the right and dipped lower, chasing the fighters. Seconds later there were two explosions; the second explosion was much larger and more sustained as the damaged Chinese fighter began to cartwheel to the ocean. They caught the Chinese fighter in a perfect pincer maneuver, with the bandit so intent on killing the guy in front of him that he forgot about the second Tomcat slashing in from above. Luckily, the second Chinese bandit didn't try his own pincer move—it might have worked, because Povik's wingman was definitely tunnel-visioned in on his own quarry, and Povik's Tomcat was on the wrong side of the energy curve and probably didn't have the speed to defend.

"Bullet Five, splash one," the AWACS controller reported. "Second bandit at your two o'clock position, high, looks like he might be extending. Heading zero-two-five to intercept. Additional bandits now at your eleven o'clock position, high, Blue plus thirty miles. Be advised, bandit number two heading northwest now, decelerating and descending rapidly, looks like he might be CAPing for his buddy." The second Chinese fighter was apparently going to set up an orbit over his damaged wingman to help out in a search and rescue effort—he was out of the fight for now. "Will advise if he tries to reengage. Bullet flight, say bingo."

That reminded Povik to check his own fuel state, and it was worse than he figured—even those few seconds in afterburner sucked up a lot of precious fuel. He was two thousand pounds below his bingo fuel level—he would be in emergency fuel levels in just a few minutes. They were in big trouble even without four more bad guys on their tail. "Bullet Four is bingo, give me a vector to home plate."

"Bullet Five is three minutes to bingo," Povik's wingman

added. "I can take a vector to Bullet Two flight if they need help."

"Don't think that'll be necessary, Bullet Five," the AWACS controller said. "Bullet Two flight is engaging, Bullet Six flight is airborne, and Bullet Eight flight is reporting ready. Home plate wants you to RTB. Heading one-three-two, stand by for your approach controller."

"Copy, Basket," Povik replied. That was perfectly fine with him, Povik thought. There was a time to fight and a time to run, and there was nothing ignoble about running now.

ABOARD BULLET TWO

"Take the shot, Banger!" Lieutenant Commander Carl Roberts shouted. "Take the damned shot!"

Chasing down the four Chinese fighters—they still did not know what kind of fighters they were dealing with—was getting deadly serious. While continuing warning messages on the Guard channel, the four Chinese fighters continued barreling straight for the RC-135, not bothering to perform any diversionary jinks or heading changes. Although the four aircraft had split into two groups, with one group going high and the others a few thousand feet lower, they were just barreling in on the four Tomcats, not trying to maneuver or jink around at all. They were simply going balls to the wall—the higher group nearly at five hundred and fifty knots, the lower jets about five hundred knots.

The threat to the Air Force plane was obvious to Carl Roberts, the radar intercept officer on Bullet Two. He had locked up the bandits on radar immediately, hoping that the squeal of the AWG-9 radar on the Chinese fighter's threat warning receivers might make them turn away. No such luck. The Chinese fighters kept coming. "You got no choice, Banger," Roberts shouted again to his pilot, Lieutenant James Douglas. "These guys will blow past us unless we slow 'em down, and a missile launch is the only way."

Douglas was only on his second cruise as an F-14 aviator after spending several years in "mud pounders" like A-7s and

A-6 bombers. Air-to-mud guys, Roberts thought, were much different than fighter pilots. Bomb runs took discipline, timing, strict adherence to the plan—qualities that were probably big minuses in fighter pilots. Real fighter jocks used the ROE as a guideline, but relied on their wits to defeat an enemy—you never went into a fight with the whole thing worked out in your mind ahead of time. Unfortunately, Douglas always did. "The ROE says . . ."

"Screw the ROE, Banger," Roberts said. "You gotta attack. *Ranger*'s declared an air-defense emergency, and the bubble's out to two hundred miles now. These guys are too close already. Take the shot . . ."

"Bullet, bandit at twelve o'clock, twenty miles," the AWACS controller reported. "Range to Flashlight, forty miles. Range to home plate, Blue plus seventy . . ." The controller kept on rattling off an endless stream of numbers at Douglas; the young pilot turned the litany out of his mind. They had the intercept, that's all that mattered now . . .

"A head-on shot will miss. It's low percentage . . ."

"So what? If he jinks away from the Sparrow, we mix it up with him. Take the shot . . ."

"Gimme a few seconds to get an angle on 'em . . ."

"We don't have time for that, Banger—those bozos might even hit each other. Either way, we keep them from driving right into the recon plane. Take the damned shot . . ."

"A nose-to-nose Sparrow shot won't do shit," Douglas said— Roberts knew he was really confused when his young pilot used first names instead of his call sign. "We gotta try something else." On interplane frequency, Douglas said, "Lead's going vertical. Take spacing and watch my tail."

"Two."

"Hang on," he said to Roberts. "I'll try a vertical jink; maybe these guys will break off and go for me." Roberts was going to protest, but Douglas wasn't ready to listen: he pulled his F-14 Tomcat up into a 45-degree climb, a radical move but well within the 65-degree maximum-depression angle for the AWG-9 radar—losing a lock-on with the Chinese fighters would be disastrous right now—waited a few seconds for about a hundred knots of airspeed to bleed off, then began to level off. The radar remained locked on with the range now closing to fifteen miles.

"Shit. Nothing's happening . . ."

"You gotta take a shot, Banger. These guys won't stop."

"Lead, this is Two. No dice. The Chinks aren't moving. I'm well clear." Douglas' wingman was prompting him to take a missile shot as well.

Just then they heard on their AWACS controller's frequency, "Bullet flight, home plate sends code Zulu-Red-Seven, repeat, Zulu-Red-Seven, proceed immediately. Acknowledge."

"Jesus, Banger, get the sonofabitch . . ." Roberts knew they had screwed up. While Douglas was trying to decide whether or not to shoot, the Chinese fighters were about to blast within the one-hundred-mile "bubble" surrounding *Ranger* and her escorts, which were demarcated by the Indonesian island of Talaud. Now the fighters were a clear threat not only to the Air Force reconnaissance planes but to the carrier itself, and the role of the Tomcats changed as well; now their job was to protect the five thousand men on *Ranger* and the other ships in its battle group. *Ranger* was ordering the Tomcats to engage and defend the carrier at all costs. The RC-135 and the EC might have to be sacrificed. . . .

"Bullet Six has a judy," the third flight of Tomcats reported. "Clear Poppa." The third and probably the fourth flights of Tomcats were armed with AIM-54 Phoenix missiles, which were designed to kill enemy aircraft from ranges of over eighty nautical miles—as soon as the RIO locked onto a target, a Phoenix missile could probably hit it. But a Phoenix usually shot into a "basket," a section of airspace near the enemy fighter, and then the missile homed in on illumination signals from the launch aircraft—that made it very dangerous for any nearby fighters who might be in or near the missile's basket. Bullet Six could not engage as long as Bullet Two was in the area.

"Bullet Two is engaging," Douglas cried out on the interplane frequency. He snapped his Tomcat into a steep left rolling dive, pulling on the stick to keep the fast-moving Chinese attackers on his radarscope. "Bullet Three, release, clear, and cover to the right."

"Bullet Three's clearing right." Douglas' wingman made a hard climbing right turn, quickly moving up and away from the kill zone and accelerating back toward the fleet. If Douglas missed and the Phoenix missiles from Bullet Six and Seven missed, Bullet Three could make one last shot at the fighters with his Sparrow radar-guided missiles; it was up to *Ranger*'s escorts to get the bandits.

Roberts coached his frontseater in as they completed the turn above and behind the Chinese attackers: "Range twenty miles . . . seventeen miles . . . holding at seventeen miles . . . good tone, clear to shoot . . ."

"Fox one, fox one," Douglas called out as he pressed the button to launch a Sparrow missile.

He was preparing to arm a second one for immediate launch when he saw a dim flash of light ahead of them, then another, then several more brilliant long tongues of flame slash across the darkness. Even at their extreme range, there was no mistaking it—eight huge missiles, with exhaust plumes the size of space-shuttle boosters, were being launched by the Chinese fighters! "Missile launch! Bandits launching missiles . . . six . . . seven . . . eight of 'em, big ones!"

The plumes reared back and down as the missiles climbed skyward. Douglas thought he could hear the rumble and even feel the power of those huge missiles as they climbed nearly out of sight. "Can you pick 'em up on radar, Zippo?" Douglas screamed. "Can you see those fuckin' missiles?"

"I'm tryin'! Shit! Get your nose up! I'll try for a lock-on!" Roberts cried out. Douglas hauled back on the stick and hit the afterburners as Roberts put the AWG-9 radar into range-while-search mode for maximum range capability against the big, fast-moving missiles. "Contact! Got 'em! Got one at thirty miles! Locked on!"

"Fox one, fox one, Bullet Two," Douglas called out on the interplane frequency. The big Sparrow missile slid off the rails and immediately went straight up, using its powerful first-stage motor to gain maximum altitude.

"It's not gonna make it," Roberts said. He could feel an uncontrollable shiver coursing up and down his back. The Sparrow was launched near its extreme maximum range and it climbed too high, too fast, and he could see that the missile's motor had already burned out. His AWG-9 radar showed the Chinese missiles already accelerating to six hundred knots, but the Sparrow was closing at only eight hundred knots because it had to climb so high to sustain its unpowered glide. "Shit, shit, it's not gonna make it . . ."

"Bullet Three has a judy on the missiles," Douglas' wingman suddenly shouted on the radios. "I got a lock-on! I'm going after them!"

"Bullet Two is clearing off the missiles," Douglas radioed to the inbound Tomcat fighters as he pulled into a steep left climb and turned away from the Chinese fighters. "Bullet Two is clear." The incoming Tomcat pilots immediately let loose with a four-missile barrage of Phoenix missiles—some designated for the Chinese fighters, others for the missiles that were now headed for the *Ranger* and her escorts.

With their heavy missile loads gone, however, the Chinese fighters really began to move. Seconds after the missiles were in the sky, the AWACS reported the Chinese going nearly supersonic and making a sweeping left turn back to the northeast. "Bullet flight, be advised, Basket's got music," the AWACS radar plane reported—they were picking up jamming signals from the enemy fighter-bombers. "Bullet Two, bandits at your ten o'clock position, twenty miles. Bullet Three, bandits at your six o'clock, ten miles." Suddenly a huge explosion, followed by a ripple of orange and yellow fireballs, erupted in the sky ahead of Douglas as one of the Phoenix missiles found its target.

"Splash one bandit, splash one! Bullet Two's got the other one," Roberts cried out. The last remaining Chinese fighter had pulled directly into his line of fire as he made his postattack turn, and even at his present speed the tight turn bled off all his energy, which made the shot even easier. The steady warbling tone in Douglas' headset was replaced by a high-pitched tone as the AWG-9 radar switched from range-while-search mode to pulse-Doppler-single-target-track mode for missile lock-on, and Douglas squeezed the trigger and let fly his third Sparrow missile.

But the jamming from the Chinese attackers was too great—the missile tracked well for only a few seconds before veering right and beginning a death-spiral to the dark waters below. There was still one enemy fighter out there.

Douglas found himself in a near-panic. He had only one Sparrow remaining—his Sidewinders were useless against a target so far away—and no fuel to continue the chase. He was helpless. If he jammed in the afterburners to chase down the last fighter, he would run out of fuel long before reaching *Ranger.*

The decision was made for him moments later: "Bullet Two, disengage," the AWACS controller called. "Bullet Six flight is at your six o'clock, thirty miles. Clear up and starboard and RTB; I show you four past your bingo." Douglas checked their fuel, and it was worse than that—they were just a few minutes from emergency fuel—they needed an AK-6 tanker immediately. Douglas and Roberts could do nothing else but head back to *Ranger* and hope they still had a deck to land on as they listened to the chase unfold. . . .

ABOARD BULLET THREE

"Bullet Three, contact home plate immediately," the AWACS controller reported. Lieutenant Commander John "Horn" Kelly flicked his radios as fast as his shaking fingers could work the buttons.

"Bullet Three, go."

"Bullet Three, take a shot and clear," the controller aboard *Ranger* said. "Five-two is ready to engage in sixty seconds." "Five-two" was CG-52, the USS *Bunker Hill,* an Aegis-class guided-missile cruiser-escort that could detect targets out to 175 miles and track and engage sea-skimming targets out to 40 miles; it carried SM-2 Aegis vertical-launch surface-to-air missiles. In addition, a special system called BGAAWC, or Battle

Group Anti-Aircraft Warfare Coordination, allowed the *Bunker Hill* to remotely control the SM-2 Standard antiaircraft missiles aboard the cruiser *Sterett* and the Sea Sparrow missiles aboard the destroyers *Hewitt* and *Fife,* which were the *Ranger*'s other three escorts.

Kelly's RIO, Lieutenant "Faker" Markey, sang out immediately, "Got a judy on the missiles, Horn . . . I got 'em locked up. Shoot away."

"Good work, Faker." On the *Ranger*'s tactical frequency, Kelly radioed, "Bullet Three, copy, fox . . ."

Suddenly, on the emergency Guard frequency, they heard, "Missiles! Bandits firing missiles! Horn, check six . . . !"

The AAR-47 infrared warning receiver beeped just then, and several flare cartridges shot off into the night sky as Markey's left index finger began to madly jab the "Flare" button—the supercoded electronic "eye" of the infrared warning seeker had detected the motor-ignition flash of a missile less than eight miles behind them. Kelly pulled the throttles to near idle power, rolled inverted, and pulled the nose to the ocean, trying to get his hot tail vertical and away from the missile's seeker. "Find that missile!" Kelly shouted.

Markey's response was almost immediate: "I see it! I see it! High above us . . . it's passing over us . . ."

A flash of light caught Kelly's attention—to his horror, he noticed the flash was one of his own decoy flares. The hot phosphorus blob seemed to float just a few yards alongside the American fighter. It was bright enough to attract the enemy missile. "Stop ejecting flares!" Kelly screamed. "It'll follow us down . . . !"

But it was too late.

In his panic, Markey kept on ejecting decoy flares as the Tomcat continued its break and dive, and the trail of flares caused the Chinese Pen Lung-9 heat-seeking missile to snap down in the wake of the Tomcat, where it reacquired the F-14's hot exhaust and finished its deadly voyage. The PL-9's twenty-two-pound high-explosive warhead detonated on contact, shredding both engines instantly and destroying the Tomcat long before the crew had a chance to eject.

ABOARD THE TICONDEROGA-CLASS CRUISER USS *BUNKER HILL*

The Combat Information Center in an Aegis-class guided missile cruiser was like sitting in a giant big-screen video arcade. Four operators—the embarked group commander of the *Ranger* battle group and his assistant plus the TAO, or tactical action officer, and his assistant—each sat in front of two 42-inch-square, four-color computer screens that showed the entire *Ranger* battle group, using computer-generated symbology and digitized coastal maps, creating a "big picture" of the entire battle area and highlighting friendly and enemy vessels and aircraft in relation to the fleet and any nearby political boundaries. The incredible MK-7 Aegis weapon system could track and process over one hundred different targets beyond five hundred miles in range by integrating radar information from other surface, land, or airborne search radars; the SPY-1 phased-array radar on the *Bunker Hill* itself had a range of almost two hundred miles and could spot a sea-skimming missile on the horizon at a range of over forty miles. Aegis was designed to defend a large carrier battle group from dense and complicated enemy air and sea assault by integrating the entire group's air-defense network into a single display and control area, and then providing long-range, high-speed decision-making and automatic-weapon employment for not only the Aegis cruiser's weapon itself, but for all the ships of the battle group—*Bunker Hill*'s Aegis system could control the weapons of all the *Ranger*'s battle group.

It all sounded complicated, very high-tech, and foolproof—but at that moment, staring down the barrel of a gun, it did not seem very foolproof.

The Aegis air-defense system was designed to have the battle group commander and the ship's commanding officer direct fleet defense from the Tactical Flag Command Center, but with an aircraft carrier in the group and a rather tightly packed deployment of ships, the *Ranger* battle group commander, Rear Admiral Conner Walheim, was aboard *Ranger* consulting directly with the carrier's officers, so his deputy for antiaircraft warfare, Captain Richard Feinemann, was on the Aegis console. And because the *Bunker Hill*'s skipper preferred to stay on the bridge during such operations, the ship's Tactical Action Officer was representing him on the Aegis console.

Lieutenant Commander Paul Hart was the *Bunker Hill*'s TAC, and the Aegis system was his pride and joy—while the captain preferred to stay on the bridge during these engagements and monitor them on his ASTAB automated status board monitors, Hart was in his element in the dark, rather claustrophobic confines on the CIC. Feinemann was a lot like Hart's skipper—he was a boat driver who had little patience for the dazzling and sometimes confusing array of electronic gadgets deep within the heart of a warship. He was an ex–destroyer skipper and antisubmarine-warfare action group commander who had spent a length of time on shore studying newer antiair radar integration systems such as Aegis, but had little actual experience of it. Although Hart was the Aegis expert, Feinemann was still in overall command of antiair fleet defense and would command all antiair assets in the group from *Bunker Hill*.

The big LSDs, or large-screen displays, were a bit intimidating for Feinemann, so he had his data-input technician give him a constant verbal readout of significant events on the screen while he tried to keep up. The data-input officer made a comment to Feinemann, prefaced with a short expletive, and the group AAW officer scanned the screen in momentary confusion—both because he couldn't spot the event and because no one in *Bunker Hill*'s CIC seemed very excited. "We've lost contact with one of our fighters?" Feinemann asked incredulously.

"Yes, sir," Hart responded. "That B-6 must've got him before Bullet Three could take a shot. It was a long-range crossing snapshot, too—he must've been carrying PL-9 missiles."

Feinemann stared at Hart in complete surprise, wondering what in hell the young officer was babbling about.

Hart continued. "Those C601 missiles got past both the Tomcats and the Phoenix missiles." He turned to the tactical-

alert intercom and radioed, "Bridge, CIC, I show four inbounds, altitude seven hundred feet, speed five hundred fifty
knots, bearing two-niner-seven, range forty-two miles and
closing, Charlie-601 antiship missiles. One bandit turning out-
bound, range now six-seven miles." To his communications
officer he said, "I need all Bullet aircraft to stay clear. Have
Basket take them northwest for their refueling and to counter
the new inbound bandits, but tell Basket to keep them away
from my engagement lane. If *Ranger* launches the ready-alert
birds, make sure Hawkeye or Basket takes them well north."

"How do you know those are C601 missiles, and how do you
know those were Chinese B-6 bombers, son?" Feinemann
snapped. "You're making reports to your bridge on enemy
aircraft that, as far as I can see, you have absolutely no information to make. You're also chasing away three air-defense fighters from possible engagements without knowing all the facts."

"The flight profiles, sir," Hart explained patiently. "They
launched two missiles each from over a hundred miles'
range—that's too far for a C801. Those missiles climbed first,
but now they're descending to about a hundred feet, and
they're cruising at about six hundred knots—typical profile of
a C601 missile . . ."

"It's also the profile of an Exocet, a Harpoon, or a Soviet AS-5
missile, or any number of antiship missiles," Feinemann
pointed out, his eyes narrowing on Hart.

"If we were facing off against the French or the Soviets, I'd
agree, sir," Hart replied. "The reports from the recon plane
say that a Chinese EF4-class ship was in the area and that
Chinese troops invaded Mindanao; I'd assume that the fighters
and these missiles are Chinese. My guess is still a C601, and
that's what I'll assume when we begin responding.

"As far as the carrier aircraft—each plane was carrying two
missiles plus air-to-air weapons, and it was doing some heavy
active jamming, not just uplink trackbreaking. That's too much
payload for a J-7, B-7, or Q-5 fighter—it has to be a B-6 Badger
bomber.

"And as far as the Tomcats are concerned, I want them out
of the way. Aegis can prosecute sea-skimming targets better
than a Tomcat, and I'm not worried about enemy fighters right

now—I'm worried about those missiles. In sixty seconds I'll start worrying about the inbound fighters." Hart was expecting a reply; when he got none, he added, "Sir, I need clearance to release batteries and engage when those missiles cross the horizon."

"Your captain might be impressed with your amateur intelligence analysis, Commander Hart," Feinemann said irritably, "but the Admiral needs *concrete* data before he can commit any forces under his command. He can't operate on guesses."

"Then you can tell him, *sir*, that we've got four subsonic inbounds that broke the group's bubble a minute ago," Hart said, trying to control his temper. He couldn't believe he was having an *argument* over target identification with this man, with four deadly—and possibly nuclear—missiles heading straight for them. "I make estimates on the threat based on my observations, but the bottom line is that I want weapons online to stop these things from hitting the carrier. In thirty seconds I start acting on my own authority; I'm requesting permission to commit *now*."

"You commit when the Admiral *tells* you to!"

Hart had had enough. He hit the intercom button. "Bridge, CIC, emergency, request permission to release the batteries fore and aft and engage."

The *Bunker Hill*'s skipper did not hear the argument between his TAO and the group commander's AAW deputy, and he certainly knew the procedures with an embarked group commander, but with a threat this big heading in, he didn't hesitate. "Bridge to CIC, batteries released fore and aft, clear to engage."

"Understand clear to engage. Clear forward and aft missile decks, clear forward and aft missile decks." From that point on, Hart ignored Feinemann—everything else was inconsequential except his radar, his console, and his weapon system. If the man had anything to say, it would have to wait until after he dealt with the inbounds.

The *Bunker Hill* was the first Aegis cruiser to use the Mk 41 vertical-launch system, where missiles were loaded into individual canisters and then fired vertically—the system was far less complex, more redundant, faster, and required fewer guided-missile mates to operate the launchers than the older Mk 26, Mk 22, or Mk 13 "merry-go-round" launchers. *Bunker Hill* had two VLS launchers, one fore and one aft, each with sixty-one missiles—combinations of SM-2 Aegis antiaircraft missiles, Tomahawk ship-and-land-attack cruise missiles— some with low-yield nuclear warheads—and ASROC antisubmarine rocket torpedoes.

Hart had been extensively briefed on exactly what options were open to him as tactical action officer—he knew that the only weapon in his arsenal right now was the SM-2 Aegis missile, and his only job was to protect *Ranger* and its escorts. Even though this was probably the exact situation that the Chinese People's Liberation Army Navy was in when they launched their nuclear antiship missile at the tiny Philippine fleet near Palawan, Hart knew he would never be authorized to let fly with one of his nuclear-tipped Tomahawks, even in retaliation.

Hart checked to be sure the Aegis system was in AAW COMMIT mode and used a trackball on his console to move a circle cursor to the data blocks representing the inbound antiship missiles. The ASTAB monitors instantly gave him performance data on the inbounds, displayed IFF radio-identification information—there was none—and classified them as hostile. If they *were* friendlies—unlikely but possible—they were flying without radios, without exchanging coded identification signals, and flying well off the established fleet approach procedures—and they were going to die. "Give me trial engage," he told his data-entry technician.

"Trial engage," the tech replied. Instantly the data block began to blink and a readout on the ASTAB monitor gave a list of the missiles that Aegis would select. On the LSD, a yellow line showed the computer's best guess as to the Aegis missile's track, the intercept points with the incoming missiles, and the positions of all the ships and aircraft in the battle group once the engagement was made. "Aegis wants to commit ten missiles," the data-entry tech reported. "We got Bullet Two within twenty miles on impact."

The number was significant because if there were nuclear-tipped C601 antiship missiles, the Tomcats would fry in the blast. But if Hart waited any longer, *Bunker Hill* would be doing the frying. It was also significant because the Mk 41 launcher could rapid-fire only seven missiles at one time. He selected sixty-four nautical miles range on his LSD to keep careful watch on the intercept, then said, "Understood. We'll do six from the forward launcher and the rest from the aft launcher. Clear trial engage, sound the horn, engage weapon commit."

"Trial engage clear." A muted horn sounded throughout the ship, followed by, "Attention all hands, missile alert actual, missile alert actual, stand by for missile launch." The tech then reported, "Launchers in the green and reporting clear. CDS enable. Weapon commit in three, two, one, now." The ASTAB monitors cleared, and they began to show the Mk 41 launcher status and the status of the missiles in the forward launcher that were being chosen by the Aegis system for the first ripple. A button marked "Hold Fire" was blinking rapidly in the lower-left corner of the communications panel, where both Hart and his data-entry tech could reach it—Feinemann had a blinking Hold Fire button as well, and he had full authority to use it.

Aegis selected ten missiles and began a pre-programmed ten-second warmup and target-data transfer cycle. "Missile counting down, ten missiles in the green . . . missile one forward in five . . . four . . . three . . . two . . . one . . . launch! Missiles away."

Up on the forward deck of the *Bunker Hill*, a twenty-five-square-inch white door popped open atop the Mk 41 VLS launcher, and a cloud of white smoke engulfed the entire forward portion of the cruiser. Once every two seconds, an Aegis SM-2 missile lifted free of the *Bunker Hill*, climbed to ten thousand feet in just a few seconds, then arched over and began its intercept. The missiles' autopilots steered them into an intercept "basket," an area in which the incoming targets were predicted to fly. When the Aegis SPY-1 radar detected the SM-2 missiles approaching the "basket," the SPY-1 would activate an SPG-62 X-band target illuminator which would "paint" the incoming Chinese missiles, and the SM-2 Aegis missiles would home in on the radar energy reflected off the enemy missiles.

"Six missiles away forward," the tech reported. "Forward launcher secure and reporting clear, plenum status normal, refire status normal. Counting down on aft launcher . . . in three . . . two . . . one . . . mark."

The canister door on the aft launcher flipped open and the first SM-2 fired . . .

But something happened.

Instead of shooting skyward, the SM-2 rose about twenty feet above the launcher, the solid-propellant motor stopped running, and the missile slipped backwards, crashed to the deck, and exploded.

The concussion threw half of the Aegis crew members to the deck. Feinemann was the only one able to react—he hit the Hold Fire button to ensure that no other missiles from the aft launcher tried to launch. "Status report!" he cried out. "Get me a status report!"

The damage-control alarm was ringing throughout the *Bunker Hill,* and there were a few seconds of momentary panic as the CIC lights went out, the emergency lights finally clicked on, and a few purple wisps of smoke issued from the ventilators, "Status report, dammit!"

Hart's ears were ringing hard—from the blast, the confusion, or the sudden disorientation of having the normally steady deck heaving beneath him, he couldn't tell which—but he managed to straighten himself in his seat and help his tech up. Several ASTAB monitors had gone down, and Feinemann's LSDs were blank. "Mark 7 system is faulted . . . both launchers shut down . . . SPY-1 is still on-line," he reported. On the intercom, he shouted, "Bridge, CIC, Mark 7 system fault, recommend immediate AAW command transfer."

"CIC, bridge, copy, command transfer to *Sterett.*" With SPY-1 still operating, the cruiser *Sterett* could act as pseudo-Aegis cruiser by receiving Aegis data via the Battle Group Anti Aircraft Warfare Coordination system on its Mk 76 weapons-control consoles.

The transfer was made, but far too late.

Three C601 antiship missiles, air-launched versions of the huge Silkworm missile, survived the Aegis counterattack made by *Bunker Hill* and the Sea Sparrow antimissile barrage by *Sterett.* One missile was destroyed by combined Sea Sparrow missile hits by *Sterett* and Phalanx Close-In-Weapon System gunfire seconds before it reached *Bunker Hill,* and a second missile was destroyed by a last-second burst of gunfire from the *Ranger*'s portside Phalanx gun just a few hundred yards before striking the carrier . . .

The last missile hit the carrier *Ranger* just aft of the port bow.

The missile's titanium nosecap pierced the outer hull of the carrier before the eleven-hundred-pound high-explosive warhead detonated, ensuring that most of the missile's deadly force was directed inside the vessel.

ABOARD BULLET SIX

"Bullet Six flight, say your bingo status," the controller aboard the Air Force E-3C AWACS plane radioed.

"Bullet Six is seven minutes to bingo," Lieutenant Jason "Razor" Penrose reported.

"Ditto for Bullet Seven."

"Copy. Stand by . . . Bullet flight, code is 'slippery,' repeat, 'slippery.'"

Razor Penrose couldn't believe what he just heard. The code word "slippery" meant that their carrier *Ranger* was damaged, extent unknown, and no one would either launch or land. Dammit all to hell. They missed and it had cost them! Because they couldn't get the fighters or the big missiles, *Ranger* was hit.

Fortunately, there were other code words for more serious damage, so there was a possibility that they wouldn't have to divert—it could be something as noncritical as a damaged aircraft on the deck or foul arresting gear. There were a few nearby divert runways available, and dozens more as long as the K-10 tanker was still available. The closest landing facility was a small runway on the island of Sangihe, one hundred and thirty miles to the southeast. With a KC-10, however, they could reach and rearm on Guam, fourteen hundred miles to the northeast. They still had lots of options. . . .

But Penrose had no plans on diverting right now. As long as he had gas and guns, he was going to stay aloft. Their primary job now was to protect their damaged carrier.

"Three bandits at twelve o'clock, forty miles, high, north-west-bound at high speed, they appear to be withdrawing," the AWACS controller continued as calmly as if he were reporting the weather. The three surviving first-wave fighters had done their job—deliver the big antiship missiles—so they were bugging out. "Four additional bandits, one o'clock, Blue plus twenty miles, southeast bound, looks like they want to engage."

"Basket, give me a SITREP. Who do we get up?"

"Bullet Two, Four and Five are emergency fuel and are rendezvousing with Shamu," the AWACS controller reported. "They report nine AIM-7s and five AIM-9s between them. They will stay with Shamu and Basket after refueling." No report on Bullet Three, Penrose noted—the Chink bastards got Kelly, damn them. "Bullet Eight and Nine are airborne, ETE ten minutes; they are staying within a hundred miles from home plate for inner defense. They are max loaded with four AIM-54s, two AIM-7s, and two AIM-9s apiece. You've got two KA-6s up but they'll have to tank with Shamu before you can use them. One Hawkeye up, range one-niner-zero miles east. Flashlight is at your three o'clock, eight miles, low, southeast bound at vee-max." The big spy plane was on the deck, trying to lose itself in the radar clutter of the sea. "Basket is southeast of your position, one-one-zero miles. Say your load and fuel."

"Bullet Six flight of two, two -7s, two -9s, seven minutes to bingo."

"Copy, Bullet Six flight. Vector to join on Flashlight, starboard to heading one-one-zero, take angels eight."

"Negative. Bullet Six flight wants a vector to the inbounds." Penrose had had enough of screwing with trying to protect the Air Force's radar plane—his job was to protect the fleet and keep any more Chinks from lobbing missiles at his home.

"Your OPORD says to escort the RC, Bullet flight . . ."

"Fuck the ops orders, Basket. I want a vector to the inbounds." On interphone, he told his RIO, Lieutenant Commander John Watson, "Lion Tamer, lock those inbounds up if this bozo doesn't give us a vector . . ."

That was usually not very good practice—they would keep the element of surprise if Penrose's RIO kept his radar off—but if he had to, they would go it alone. . . .

There was a brief pause from the AWACS controller, but he was obviously not in the mood or not authorized to argue. "Roger . . . Bullet Six flight, four bandits at one o'clock, fifty miles, take angels three-five, that'll put you ten thousand above them."

"Six flight." Penrose held his heading and started his climb. "Bogey-dope."

"Bandits at your one o'clock, level, fifty miles, closure rate eleven hundred. Be advised, Bullet flight, Flashlight reported naval radar and possible naval antiair at your twelve o'clock, two hundred miles. You may be coming within detection range."

"Six copies." Well, if that happened, they'd be about even— it was a two-vee-four, but there was not yet any sign that they'd been detected. Penrose wasn't going to turn on his radar until absolutely necessary.

"Two."

"One o'clock, moving to one-thirty, forty miles . . . thirty miles, two o'clock, low . . ."

They weren't going in completely blind. Penrose's RIO was adjusting his IRSTS, or Infrared Search and Track System, a long-range heat-seeking imager that could detect and display hot targets at medium to short range; his was one of the few older F-14A models with both an IRSTS sensor as well as the typical TCS telescopic camera system, in side-by-side chin pods. IRSTS allowed the crew to launch missiles against targets at long range and activate their AWG-9 radar only a few seconds before the missiles impacted—that was precisely what they were trying to do now.

"Two-thirty position, thirty miles . . ." Penrose corrected his course to keep the bandits within the 30-degree limit of the

IRSTS seeker. "Cowboy, can you get an IR track on these guys?"

"We got 'em all the way," Penrose's wingman, Lieutenant Commander Paul "Cowboy" Bowman, replied. "Ready when you are."

"Stand by." On interphone Penrose asked, "Got 'em yet, Lion Tamer?"

"Hold on . . . tally-ho, finally got 'em . . . IR track. Compiling data . . . got a good data feed. Wish we had a laser ranger right now—their guys would be dog meat. Be advised, Razor, my radar's coming on three seconds after missile launch. We won't be invisible no more . . . okay. I got a firing solution. Clear to launch."

"Good. Lock up the rest as soon as the radar's on." On the interplane frequency, he called out, "Seven, give it to 'em. Bullet Six, fox one."

"Seven, fox one."

Penrose squeezed the launch button on his radar, and the light-gray outline of his Tomcat fighter lit up again as the big Sparrow missile leaped into the dark sky. He could see a missile from his wingman slash through the sky just a few hundred feet away—the two missiles appeared to be flying in formation as they streaked toward their targets. The missiles seemed to track perfectly . . .

But suddenly Penrose's missile seemed to diverge away faster and faster—his wingman's missile curved to the right, tracking all the way, but Penrose's Sparrow was going off in the weeds. "Lion Tamer, what's going on . . . ?"

"Damn! Radar's not coming up!" Watson shouted. "Shit, it cooled down too much!" A status light to the right of the RIO's tactical information display read ENV STBY, meaning that the system would stay in nonradiating mode until the electronics fully warmed up.

"Two! Take the lead! Six is gadget-bent!"

"Seven's taking the lead." Penrose began searching to his right, hoping he could see his wingman, but he made it easy for him: Bullet Seven had his left engine in min afterburner, both to help Penrose find him and start closing in on the Chinese fighters faster.

"Cowboy, got a tally on you, kill your burner," Penrose said. The burner flicked off. They continued their right turn to put themselves right on the four Chinese fighters' tails.

Lion Tamer's APR-45 radar threat scope suddenly came to life. It showed first a friendly search radar directly ahead— Bullet Seven—and, seconds later, several bat-wing symbols appeared off to the right as the Chinese fighters, after detecting the Tomcat's radars, activated their own search radars to find their ambushers. All four bat-wings were superimposed, with a diamond around the closest one.

As Penrose searched out his canopy bubble to see if he could see any of the enemy fighters, he saw a tiny puff of fire in the distance—Bullet Seven's Sparrow missile had exploded.

One of the bat-wings promptly disappeared.

"Bullet flight, splash one bandit," the AWACS controller reported. "Dead bandit descending rapidly, turning right, decelerating. Two bandits breaking left, same altitude, nine miles. One bandit looks like he's descending, heading straight ahead . . . lone bandit is thirty miles from Flashlight, appears to be closing on him."

"Six, go after the solo. I'll take these two."

"Negative. I'm bent. I'm staying with you."

"I can take these two. Use your IR and the AWACS. Get the solo."

"Dammit, Cowboy, if those two are bugging out, let 'em. Don't get sucked into a one-vee-two. Let's go get the solo together."

"We got these two locked up, no sweat. Take the solo. I'll be back in a flash." He punctuated his sentence by banking hard left in pursuit. Penrose and Watson were suddenly right between two enemy cells.

"You gotta protect the recon plane, Razor," Watson told him.

"Fuck the recon plane. My wingman might be in trouble . . ."

"So what happens when that bandit smokes that RC-135? There's eighteen guys on that thing."

He was right—he had no choice. "Shit. We're going after the solo. Basket, Bullet Six, vector to the solo inbound."

"Bullet Six, bandit at your twelve to one o'clock, eleven miles, five thousand below you, airspeed six hundred thirty." Penrose shoved his throttles to full military power, anxious to get within missile-firing range but not enough to risk using afterburners and getting himself in a low-fuel situation—he fully intended to go back and see to Cowboy after dealing with the lone bandit. "Lion Tamer, what's with the radar? Can't you get it going?"

"Keeps resetting. I'm recycling it . . ."

This is going from bad to worse, Penrose thought. On interplane, he asked, "Cowboy, how goes it?"

"We got one in the kill zone," Penrose and Watson heard on the interplane frequency. "Looks like the other guy's bugging out—he's out of it. Thirty seconds and I'm back with you."

"Don't get cocky," Penrose said. "Shoot and clear. Basket, dammit, keep an eye out for Seven's trailer."

"Basket copies. Second bandit on Bullet Seven is two o'clock, eleven miles, accelerating, descending. Bullet Six, your bandit is twelve o'clock, ten miles. Your bandit is twenty-five miles from Flashlight and closing . . ."

Watson manually slewed the IRSTS along the bearing given by the AWACS controller and finally found the Chinese fighter, a tiny green dot on his screen. He hit the "Lock" button, and a big square superimposed itself on the dot; a second later as the IRSTS refined its aiming and stabilized its gyro platform, the square compressed to slightly larger than the dot, and a stream of tracking figures appeared on the screen. Watson slaved one AIM-9R Sidewinder missile to the IRSTS boresight, and Penrose heard a low, menacing growl as the missile's seeker head locked on. "Got the Chink on IR, Razor," Watson said. "Select a Sidewinder and nail this bugger."

"Bullet Seven, second bandit climbing through your altitude, two o'clock, twelve miles . . ."

"Bullet Six, fox two . . ." Penrose shot one Sidewinder, decided against selecting his last one—Cowboy might need the extra missile.

The tiny missile raced ahead, obliterating the IR sensor in the sudden glare, but the missile tracked straight and true this time and they were rewarded by a huge ball of fire far ahead of them.

"Bullet Six, splash two."

"Good shooting, Razor," Penrose heard Bowman reply in between deep grunts—Bowman was performing his anti–G force grunts called M-maneuvers. He was obviously right in the middle of a hard-turning battle, but the cocky sonofabitch still found time to chatter on the radios. "Bullet Seven, fox one . . . die, sucker, die!"

"Bullet Seven, warning, second bandit four o'clock, high, eight miles, descending behind you . . ."

"Cowboy, dammit, get out of there!" Penrose shouted. "Cowboy, extend, extend!"

"Bullet Seven, starboard turn to evade . . . Bullet Seven, extend . . . Bullet Seven heading zero-nine-zero, thirty degrees starboard to extend . . . Bullet Seven, check altitude . . . Bullet Seven, if you are in a spin, release your controls . . . Bullet Seven, if you are in a spin, release your controls and lower your landing gear . . . Bullet Seven, Bullet Seven, altitude warning . . . Bullet Seven only, Bullet Seven only, eject, eject, eject . . ." No use.

Penrose never got another transmission from Bowman.

"Basket, this is Six, vector to Bullet Seven's last position."

Penrose could hear the panic, the gut-wrenching anxiety, in the controller's voice. "Er . . . Bullet Six, lone bandit at your nine o'clock, forty miles, he's northwest-bound at six hundred knots, altitude ten thousand and descending. Appears to be withdrawing. No other bandits detected. Say your bingo."

"I said, I want a vector to Seven's last known position, dammit . . ."

"No ELT, no transmissions . . . Six, say your *fuel.*"

Penrose finally curbed his anger long enough to check his fuel—he was well past bingo, and with a damaged carrier and his tankers more than a hundred miles away, he was in emergency fuel conditions now. "Basket, Six requests you vector a KA-6 over here, because I'm not *moving* from this spot until I make sure there's no ELT or distress calls. You better call

Sterett or *Fife* or somebody over here to investigate, because I'm staying right here until we find Cowboy."

"Bullet Six . . . Six, all group vessels involved at this time." The controller sounded as if he were trying to think of some detached, official-sounding terminology to tell Penrose that no one was likely to come and search for wreckage or survivors. Penrose suddenly remembered the *Ranger* and knew they weren't going to send any big ships anywhere near this area for a long time—the Chinese held it too tightly. "Shamu rendezvousing with Basket and Flashlight for recovery. Orders from home plate, return and prepare for divert recovery. Acknowledge."

The battle was over. The Chinese lost four plus damaged a carrier, the Americans lost two. Penrose felt as if he had been beaten up by an entire street gang.

Who won this one?

Who the *hell* won this one?

NINE

The National Military Command Center, located three stories beneath the inner ring of the Pentagon, was a large, sophisticated command post where members of the Joint Chiefs of Staff, their senior staff officers, and members of the National Command Authority and National Security Council could monitor crisis developments anywhere in the world, receive real-time satellite imagery, and speak directly with anyone from foreign leaders to theater commanders to individual crew members via secure, high-tech worldwide communications gear. The place was much like the Strategic Air Command's underground command center, with ultratight electronic and physical security, several huge wall-size, full-color monitors, banks of telephones, a secure code room, and a huge support staff—except this was where national military strategy and command decisions were made and disseminated, not received and executed. A gallery above the main floor allowed high-ranking visitors to view the proceedings; a few persons were up there now.

Most of the J-Staff and several other members of the Joint

Chiefs were already present in the NMCC when General Wilbur Curtis trotted in and took his place in the front row center seat. Beside him, sitting in the seat reserved for the highest-ranking civilian present—usually Frank Kellogg, the President's National Security Advisor, or even Thomas Preston, the Secretary of Defense himself—was Paul Cesare, the President's Chief of Staff. Curtis gave him a brief nod but ignored him as he clicked on the microphone at his seat. He didn't care for Cesare. Never had. Shortly after Curtis had been dismissed from the last Situation Room meeting on this crisis, he'd phoned Cesare, trying to get in to see the President alone, to privately make the case for more fighters to accompany the carriers as well as deploying the Air Battle Force. He'd gotten nothing from Cesare but a chilly "The issue is closed." He was Machiavellian and ruthless. He'd play either side of the fence as long as it was the side the President was on, and mow down anyone who got in his way. Curtis more than disliked him, he couldn't stand him. "Curtis here. Situation report, please."

Navy Captain Rebecca Rodgers' voice came over the NMCC's loudspeaker: "Good afternoon, sir, Captain Rodgers here. This briefing is classified Top Secret, no foreign nationals, sensitive intelligence sources and methods involved. The command center is secure, with the gallery sound-isolated. Briefing contents describe a priority-two incident." She paused for a moment in case Curtis wanted to configure the NMCC any differently. He did not, and she went on.

Damn, Curtis thought, here it comes . . .

"About fifteen minutes ago the aircraft carrier *Ranger,* her escorts, several Navy fighters, and an Air Force reconnaissance plane were attacked by Chinese land-based fighters and bombers south of the Philippines."

There was considerable murmuring among the assembled. Several of the Joint Chiefs shifted in their seats, bracing themselves for more. Paul Cesare sat there shaking his head, not believing what he'd just heard.

Well, Wilbur Curtis thought, the shit's hitting the fan a lot faster than anyone expected. And with the President's Chief of Staff sitting right here, the news was going to travel faster than Curtis could respond. He needed to have a list of options prepared for the National Command Authority literally *before* the President knew about the crisis. Without a plan of action, the entire JCS might seem like a bunch of bumbling idiots. If things got out of control now, Curtis would be lucky to remain JCS chairman for the rest of the day. "Wait one, Captain." Curtis turned to Cesare. "Mr. Cesare, what exactly are you doing here?"

Curtis expected an argument out of the President's big aide—Cesare certainly had the security clearance and the "need to know" for everything that went on in the NMCC— but to his surprise, Cesare was acting rather stunned, and not just from the news he had just heard. "Um . . . I was notified that a group of senators was going to meet with the Secretary of Defense at one o'clock," he replied. "Something to do with the Philippine crises and the Chinese . . . our military options, something like that. These senators want to keep the President from committing any troops at all to Southeast Asia—they're afraid we might be starting another Vietnam conflict, or World War Three. They're pressing Secretary Preston—which means the President—into withdrawing all forces from the Philippines. Preston's trying to walk a balancing act, but he thought the meeting here was at least a little further away from . . . the public eye and the press . . . than on the Hill or at Defense."

Curtis couldn't believe it. Once again the White House was pulling the Pentagon into a political mudfight. It was typical. God, how he hated politics. He turned to Cesare. "That's all well and fine, Mr. Cesare, but that doesn't explain what you're doing here."

"Uh . . . well, gathering information. So that, um, the President can make an informed response when the senators press him."

Admiral Cunningham, the Chief of Naval Operations, discreetly cleared his throat behind him. Curtis could feel the gaze of his JCS colleagues and staffers on him, silently urging him to deal with the emergency at hand—Cesare would have to wait. "I'll provide you with whatever you need later, Mr. Cesare, but for this situation, your place is up in the gallery."

"I'd really prefer to sit here and—"

"Mr. Cesare—"

"General—"

Curtis motioned to the NMCC's senior security policeman, Army Command Sergeant Major Jefferson, who stepped over immediately in front of Cesare. "Jake, please see that Mr. Cesare finds his way upstairs to the gallery with the other visitors, and double-check everyone's credentials up there."

Cesare rose to his feet. "The President will expect a full report . . ."

"He'll get more than that," Curtis said. He turned to his communications officer beside him. "Get the President on the line, priority two." Priority codes issued from the Pentagon were in numbers of non-nuclear threats and colors for nuclear ones; "one" was the highest conventional code, associated with major military or terrorist actions against the continental United States, its bases or territories. "Two" was reserved for major attacks against American overseas bases, embassies, deployed vessels, or nonembassy citizens; and so on. Priority "red" was reserved for an all-out nuclear attack on the United States and was never used in simulations or exercises.

Curtis then turned back to Cesare with a hint of a smile. This was Curtis' game now. "Have a nice day, Mr. Cesare. Sergeant Jefferson will show you upstairs." Curtis motioned to the door with his head, and the guard motioned to the door and escorted Cesare out.

The Chairman of the Joint Chiefs of Staff turned his attention back to the big screens and computer monitors before him, but the information Cesare had parted with lingered. The surveillance operation in the Philippines blows up right when there's a major congressional push to pull out. What the hell else could go wrong?

When Cesare was safely gone, Curtis double-checked to be sure the intercom was shut off in the gallery—the ranking person in the command center could restrict all information dissemination, no matter what the other person's security clearance—and said, "Continue, Captain Rodgers. Casualty and damage report, start with *Ranger.*"

"Current casualty report: forty-seven dead, two hundred injured." A ripple of anger and dismay spread throughout the room. Curtis felt sick. "*Ranger* is still afloat, heading to the port city of Manado in Indonesia at minimum speed, escorted by destroyers *Hewitt* and *Fife* and cruiser *Bunker Hill.* Wounded have been airlifted to Manado as well."

A chart of the area was put up immediately on one of the large computer monitors when a foreign city or nation was mentioned, so Curtis and his staff could get a look at the area in question. Curtis found his mouth going dry, his pulse quickening. *Forty-seven* dead . . .

"Aegis cruiser *Bunker Hill* damaged during action," Rodgers continued, "but sustained no casualties and only minor injuries. It is fully combat-capable and is assisting *Ranger.*"

"Action approved," Curtis said. Dammit, the *Bunker Hill* too. Two major warships damaged, with more casualties in one day than practically the entire 1991 Persian Gulf crisis. "Wait one. Wasn't there another ship with *Ranger?* Another cruiser?"

"Yes, sir. USS *Sterett* is en route to the Celebes Sea to attempt to recover two F-14 fighters downed in action with Chinese fighter-bombers. The Tomcat crews are listed as missing in action."

Two fighters? Jesus, four aviators. How many more were going to be lost? "Goddammit, Captain, give us the casualties all at once. Are there any more?"

"No, sir. American casualties only on *Ranger* and two Tomcats."

"Thank you," Curtis said, taking a deep breath. "Hold on that last action by *Sterett.* Can *Ranger* provide any air support for *Sterett?*"

"Not at this time, sir," Rodgers replied. *"Ranger* unable to launch or recover aircraft. Admiral Walheim advised that he does not suggest sending any heavy Air Force aircraft within six hundred miles of Zamboanga on Mindanao due to heavy Chinese fighter and antiair naval activity. He is trying to organize a fighter patrol using carrier-based tankers that were stranded from *Ranger . . ."*

"How can he rearm his fighters if they can't use *Ranger?*"

"His fighters received permission to land in Indonesia along with the medical helicopters," Rodgers replied. "Admiral Walheim has organized land-based rearming for the fighters by transferring stores from *Ranger* by helicopter to Ratulangi Airport near Manado, Indonesia, but he has not yet received permission from the Indonesian government to allow those helicopters to land or to conduct offensive operations from Indonesia. In addition, the Indonesian government has requested that the armed aircraft not depart Ratulangi until their status has been confirmed."

Pretty fast thinking, Curtis thought—Walheim, another youngster commanding his first carrier battle group, was already devising ways to continue the fight even without a carrier deck. An X marked the spot on the chart where the fighters went down—about three to four hundred miles from Manado.

Admiral Cunningham asked, "How many fighters are stranded off *Ranger,* Captain?"

"Six F-14 Tomcats, two KA-6 tankers, one E-2C Hawkeye," Rodgers replied. "Weapons include total of four Phoenix missiles, fifteen Sparrow missiles, ten Sidewinder missiles, and full ammunition loads."

Cunningham nodded thoughtfully and said to Curtis, "Depending on fuel availability, Walheim can mount a credible air-defense operation from Ratulangi for a rescue operation if they could get full cooperation from the Indonesian government."

"It's unlikely, considering all the shit that's going on," Curtis said, "but we've got to find out." To Rodgers, Curtis said, "I want to talk with the State Department ASAP. Danahall himself if he's available, otherwise his Pacific deputy."

"Admiral Walheim suggested going ahead with search and rescue efforts anyway; a lone vessel broadcasting that it is part of a rescue effort might be allowed to proceed."

"The STRATFOR can organize a cover counter-air operation from Andersen," General Falmouth, the Air Force Chief of Staff, suggested. "PACAF has a number of fighters on Guam we can use . . ."

"Action denied," Curtis replied. "I want *Sterett* to stay out of the Celebes and outside six hundred miles from Zamboanga until I talk directly with State and Admiral Walheim. No vessels enter the Celebes without support." He thought of the four Tomcat naval aviators that were down, but he also knew the result of a damaged plane slamming into the sea from thousands of feet in the sky—unless someone saw parachutes, there were probably no survivors, and certainly there was no reason to risk hundreds of lives on *Sterett* to save four men. As much as Curtis hated to admit it, a rescue operation now was out of the question. "Continue. Status of the Air Force aircraft?"

"Minor injuries sustained during escape maneuvers when the crew thought they were under attack," Rodgers said. "The RC-135 refueled inflight and safely recovered at Andersen Air Force Base on Guam. The E-3C AWACS plane and the KC-10 are still on station in the southern Philippine Sea north of Manado between the Philippines and Indonesia; the AWACS plane is keeping an eye on Chinese fighter activity and attempting to locate the two downed aircraft. They have four of the six Tomcat fighters with them for air cover; the other two Tomcats landed in Indonesia with the medevac helicopters. They estimate they can stay on station until daybreak, then they must withdraw for aircraft servicing."

Curtis checked the row of world clocks below the NMCC's "big board"—it was almost two-thirty in the morning Guam time. "I want the AWACS plane back on Guam by sunrise," Curtis said. "Have them stay long enough to cover any naval flight operations in progress, but I don't want any heavy American military aircraft airborne during daylight hours, with or without escorts." He then thought of Dr. Jon Masters' satellite system—what the hell did he call them, NIRTSats?—and said, "I want to talk with General Stone on Guam immediately."

"Yes, sir."

Curtis turned to Cunningham. "We got a satellite system up there that can find a Chevy in a parking lot full of Fords, on a cloudy night, from four hundred miles in space—now's the time to use it."

"Amen to that," Cunningham said. "Sir, the *Independence* carrier group should be notified of the incident and briefed on their actions. I'd like to set up the two-hundred-mile exclusion zone and put fire-first provisions in the ROEs."

"Two-hundred-mile exclusion zone approved," Curtis said.

"Fire-first provisions only for aircraft on antiship cruise-missile profiles. Any other actions have to come through the NCA.

"Get a full report from Admiral Walheim on *Ranger,* then brief me ASAP on what we need to send to Manado to assist our troops in Indonesia; I need a laundry list for the State Department. Find out what ships are available to replace *Ranger*—including submarines. I want to be able to take control of those waters as quickly as I can." Cunningham turned to his communications console to begin issuing his orders.

The orange light on his console illuminated, and Curtis donned a headset and plugged it into the phone jack. "Curtis here."

"Hold for the President, please." A moment later: "Yes, Wilbur, what's going on?"

"Mr. President, we have an incident near the Philippines. The aircraft carrier *Ranger* was hit by a Chinese air-launched cruise missile and damaged with loss of life. Two Navy fighter planes were shot down as well."

"Oh, no . . ." the President murmured, obviously not wishing his feelings to be heard by others with him. He was speaking on a scrambled cellular phone, but from the background noise Curtis heard, it sounded as if he were at a luncheon and were still right at the table. "I'll be out of here in ten minutes. Ask 'laddie' to come up and see me when he can." The line went dead.

Curtis could not help but smile at the casual, almost backwoods code words the President liked to use during conversations like this: "laddie" was this month's code word for the National Security Council, whom he wanted assembled in the White House Situation Room immediately. To his communications officer, Curtis said, "Call the White House communication office and get the NSC in the Situation Room ASAP."

The phone line began to come alive at that moment, and Curtis motioned for someone to get him a glass of water as he settled in. Two or three calls to get a better picture of the situation, then formulate a plan of action during the car ride to the White House. It was as it always was: he was cut out of the loop for most of the really important policy decisions, but when the shit hit the fan, he was expected to have all the answers. Well, he told himself, he was going to *have* all the answers when the National Security Council met.

The next call came from Guam: "General Stone here, sir."

"Rat, got a report for me?"

"The *Ranger* got jumped by B-6 bombers and Q-5 or B-7 fighters, sir," Stone replied. The exhaustion in his voice was obvious, even over the scrambled satellite link. "We didn't see them coming until about a hundred and fifty miles out. We had the radar planes bug out, and we thought the Navy fighters turned them away, but they weren't after the radar planes— they were going after ships right away. Only two of the first flight of six were armed for air defense; the other four were carrying two each C601 missiles as well as heat-seeking air-to-airs . . ."

"Are you sure they were 601s?"

"Pretty sure, judging by the flight profile and the damage they caused. They were a hell of a lot bigger than C801s or Exocets."

"No evidence of . . . special warheads?" It was possible that the C601 missiles were carrying nuclear warheads but they simply failed to go off.

Curtis could hear a genuine sigh of relief even through the static-charged transmission: "No, thank God." The alternative, as Curtis well knew, could have been much worse. In 1946, during secret tests code-named OPERATION CROSSROADS, the Navy wanted to see the effects of a twenty-kiloton nuclear blast on an aircraft carrier. CV-3 USS *Saratoga* was towed out to Bikini Atoll and the device set off five hundred yards away. The blast of that one warhead threw the forty-thousand-ton aircraft carrier nearly fifty feet out of the water, pushed it sideways nearly a half-mile, crushed its seventeen-inch armor plating and caved in the flight deck, then sank it in seven hours. *Ranger* would have suffered much the same fate.

"We got pictures of the aircraft on the ground in Zamboanga after the attack—they were B-6 bombers all right," Stone continued, shaking Curtis out of his reverie. "The Chinese put their top-of-the-line maritime-attack plane in Zamboanga. Each one had two C601 missiles and two PL-7 or PL-9 missiles. No definite ID on the fighters—only the B-7, F-8, or the A-5 with air refueling have the legs these guys had to go after *Ranger* from that distance. We also got pictures of Y-8 reconnaissance planes and PS-5 antisubmarine-warfare planes out there."

The Chinese were moving a major naval air force into the south Philippines, Curtis decided. With this force they could seal off the entire area and conduct bombing raids on the government bases on Mindanao. Curtis asked, "Do they own the Celebes Sea, Rat Killer?"

"I'm afraid so, sir," Stone replied. "Air, land, sea, everything. We gotta go in hard if we want to have access."

Curtis knew what that meant—no more fucking soft probes, no more RC-135s no matter how many escorts they had. Sending *Sterett* into the Celebes Sea now would be a big mistake. "I copy. Looks like Doctor Masters' gadgets are going to be the only intel we get for a while."

"He's giving us some great poop, sir," Stone said. "His gadgets are working just fine. I've already transmitted some pictures to you via Offutt; they should be in your hands very soon. You should have some more detailed shots of the Chinese positions in Zamboanga within a couple hours."

"Good. I meet with the boss in thirty minutes; he's going to want to see them. What else have you got for me?"

"With Masters' gear set up here, General Harbaugh from Third Air Division, General Houston from Fifteenth Air Force, and I have already played out a couple strike scenarios for the south Philippines," Stone replied. "We're definitely going to need the Air Battle Force—and then some—to dislodge our Oriental buddies."

"What kind of scenarios have you come up with?" Curtis asked. "Can you send me some of your data?"

"I sent the scenarios to you along with the photos," Stone said. "It'll make interesting reading for you. Masters practically duplicated the entire Air War College and Naval Postgraduate School war-gaming computer models right here in my command post, complete with up-to-the-minute intelligence data, and we've built and revised data tapes for the B-52's Offensive Avionics System suite and for the B-1's AP-

1750 strike computers for the Air Battle Force aircraft. We've fought the battle of Mindanao three times already."

Curtis remembered the old saying, "Don't ask the question if you can't stand the answer," but he asked anyway: "Who won?"

"It depends, sir," Stone replied. "Exactly how bad do we want the Chinese out of the Philippines?"

"What I want is to send a ship into the Celebes to search for the downed crews from the Tomcats we lost. I also want to get the Navy back in there just to tell the Chinese they can't lock us out. I need some air cover. The Navy planes are grounded for now."

"Sorry, sir. Don't think we can help," Stone said. "We've only got seven F-15 fighters on station—we'd need at least twenty to cover a rescue operation. None are modified for air-to-surface ops."

Curtis swore to himself. With *Ranger* out of the fight, they were really stuck for both offensive and defensive punch. It would take time to send in another carrier group, and that would allow the Chinese to fortify their own sea and land forces.

What they needed was *real* offensive and defensive power. They needed the Air Battle Force in there—right *now.*

THE WHITE HOUSE SITUATION ROOM
THIRTY MINUTES LATER

"You told me the carrier battle groups could protect themselves, General," the President began. "One hit, and now we've got sixty dead and hundreds more injured."

All eyes of the members of the National Security Council swung toward him.

. . . All but Thomas Preston. The Secretary of Defense believed that this confrontation was inevitable, but he obviously saw it not as the beginning of the end of tensions in the Philippines, but the beginning of dangerous hostilities. Like looking down the barrel of a nuclear-loaded gun. Curtis rarely agreed with him, but this time he very well may be right. . . .

"Sir, there was a malfunction of one SM-2 Aegis missile during the cruiser *Bunker Hill*'s response," Curtis explained. Thirteen more men had died of their injuries in the past thirty minutes alone; thirty more were given no better than a fifty-fifty chance of survival. It was hard for Curtis to formulate an objective, detached analysis of why and how so many men had died. He was numb, but pressed on: "*Bunker Hill* had positive control of the situation until the time of the mishap. Admiral Walheim's antiair-warfare deputy, who was in command of the engagement from *Bunker Hill*'s CIC, terminated all the rest of the missile launches that, in all probability, would have destroyed the last incoming missiles. Control of antiair functions transferred to the cruiser *Sterett,* and the switch was made smoothly, but *Sterett* couldn't put enough firepower in the air to stop all the missiles."

"What about inner defenses? Didn't *Ranger* have any guns to protect itself?"

"*Ranger*'s fighters shot down one of the aircraft carrying the antiship missiles and took shots at the missiles themselves, but F-14 Tomcats are not really designed for chasing down cruise missiles, especially with enemy fighters in the area. *Ranger* itself had two operational short-range RAM launchers—heat-seeking missiles mounted on a steerable box launcher—plus two Phalanx automatic Gatling-gun defense systems, but although both systems were functioning neither could hit the incoming missiles. We're investigating."

"We also lost two fighters. Why?"

Curtis bristled at the notion that *he* was responsible for explaining the vagaries of aerial combat, but he explained. "Sir, the fighters faced multiple enemy aircraft at all times—at no time did we have better than a one-on-two match-up. The fighters were responsible not only for protecting themselves and their ship, but the Air Force aircraft as well . . ."

"But why did we have such poor odds?" the Vice President, Kevin Martindale, asked. "Why did we have only eight fighters airborne? We should have had sixteen or twenty . . ."

There was a hushed tension in the room; Martindale followed the furtive glances of those around him to the President. "We authorized only two escorts per aircraft," Taylor explained to the Vice President. Everyone could tell that the President's admission was a stab wound for him. "They were talking about thirty-plus fighter escorts up there . . ."

"Sir, our objective from the beginning was not to get into a big furball with dozens of aircraft in this area," Curtis explained. "If we had huge waves of fighters up there, it might've looked like an invasion force. Besides, we had no way of knowing the Chinese would not only send fighters to chase down our recon planes, but launch antiship missiles as well . . ."

"I should have known." The President sighed. "I should have erred on the side of protecting our troops . . ."

"Perhaps it would have been better to have more fighters up initially," Curtis allowed, "but our aircraft were in international airspace and outside the established Philippine air-defense zone at all times. Our reconnaissance plane came no closer than forty miles to a Chinese vessel that was fifty miles offshore—well within the law. Our aircraft broadcast identification signals, they were in constant contact with international overwater flight-following agencies, and they used no type of jammers whatsoever. The *Ranger* was over three hundred miles away and never entered the Celebes Sea. We behaved as nonthreatening as we possibly could . . ."

"It seems that we underestimated the Chinese, then," Thomas Preston said. "This is no mere foray they're involved in—this is a major military operation. They are prepared to defend their positions with everything they have and do whatever it takes—including attacking a United States aircraft carrier."

"And that should not be tolerated," General Curtis added. "They're professing their innocence and at the same time blasting away at our reconnaissance aircraft and carriers—"

"Hold on, hold on, Wilbur," the President interrupted. "I understand your anger—believe me, I share it. I need to hear some more options first before I consider a military response." He turned to Secretary of State Danahall. "Dennis, you said you had something for us on the ASEAN meeting?"

"Yes, sir," Danahall replied. "The Association of South East

Asian Nations concluded its emergency session in Singapore yesterday. We've got Deborah O'Day over there as our observer." Curtis glanced quickly at Thomas Preston and detected a slight edge in his expression. O'Day was once Preston's Assistant Secretary of Defense for the Pacific—one of a multitude of positions she held in two White House administrations—and had been fired from that post for her outspoken advocacy of expanded involvement in Pacific affairs in general and specifically her opposition to the U.S. pullout of the Philippines. Curtis could imagine the reception O'Day got from the predominantly Moslem and generally anti-female men.

"Miss O'Day reports," Danahall continued, "that the vote to bring sanctions against China was defeated in the ASEAN assembly."

"What?" the President asked, alarmed. "But they can't . . . The Chinese are tearing up the Philippines and ASEAN isn't going to do anything about it . . . ?"

"That's not all, sir," Danahall said. "After the meeting, O'Day was briefly kidnapped . . ."

The room crackled with tension.

"Kidnapped!" The President found himself sitting straight up. "Jesus, is she all right? What happened . . . ?"

"She's all right, sir. Not a scratch. Her assailant says he was sent by Second Vice President Samar to officially request military assistance from the United States—and O'Day reports that Samar had delivered a warning not to enter the Celebes Sea region because the Chinese Fleet Admiral was ready to attack." He held up a sheet of paper. "Here's her communiqué from the embassy in Singapore, dated sixteen hours before the attack began."

The President scanned the communiqué quickly, then returned to his chair stiff with shock. He turned to Preston, then to Curtis. "Did you know about this?"

"Yes, sir," Preston replied. "I immediately issued a message to Admiral Walheim about the warning, but we gave this warning little credence at the time."

"Why?"

"Because the *Ranger* group was never scheduled to enter the Celebes Sea in the first place, per your orders," Preston explained. "I decided to go ahead with the aerial surveillance, since the risk was far less and because we needed the 'eyes' up there to see what the Chinese were doing. We never expected the Chinese to attack our reconnaissance aircraft, let alone the *Ranger* carrier group." Preston looked decidedly uncomfortable, then added, "Miss O'Day has had a . . . uh, reputation for sensationalizing a situation, sir. I'm afraid I have to admit I gave her warning little credibility. It sounded like a fanatical tirade by a Filipino guerrilla soldier . . ."

"We did everything we could do to protect the fleet, sir," Curtis said. "The proper warnings were issued, the commanders in the field knew the situation . . ."

"I take full responsibility, sir," Preston said uneasily. "I should have brought the matter to your attention immediately."

The President stared at Preston but his eyes seemed dead. After a moment he shook his head and waved a hand at Preston. "It's not your fault, Thomas. If you had told me that the Chinese were ready to attack the fleet, I would've said you were crazy and told you to continue as planned." He paused, then said, "All right. We've got several dozen dead sailors, a damaged aircraft carrier, and apparently a live Filipino vice president asking for our assistance. What do we do about it?"

"JCS has devised an operation that we think can send a clear message to China, sir . . ."

The President was obviously still hesitating. That single nuclear explosion, a relatively small burst that occurred ten thousand miles away, was hamstringing this President, casting doubts that only served to increase his anger and frustration— like Reagan's inner torment about the American hostages held in Lebanon, the nuclear explosion and the fear of an escalating conflict between the United States and China was plunging the President into indecision.

"Sir, I've got to reiterate this point: every day we hesitate in sending offensive forces into Guam and put them into a position to act, the worse our situation will be. We will reach a point where we will be unable to respond at all to stop China. It's even more important to send the Air Battle Force in right now," Curtis continued, "because they now become the only offensive weapon we have against the Chinese in the Philippines, except submarines and long-range cruise missiles." He referred to a wall map of the area as he spoke: "We won't risk sending any more warships into the Celebes Sea, and the South China Sea region and the seas within the Philippines are too dangerous or shallow. China controls the south, west, and north sides of the Philippines, and they control the South China Sea itself.

"However, they do not control the east side of the Philippines, and that's their weakness. Air strikes from either carrier-based or land-based bombers can come in from the east and strike at Chinese positions . . .

"Using Doctor Masters' computer systems on Guam as well as the reconnaissance data from both the RC-135 flight and his lightweight satellites, the STRATFOR has developed several strike options designed to achieve an entire range of results. The plans require using the Air Battle Force. Without *Ranger* or another carrier group available, we simply don't have the counter-air defensive capability on Guam right now. The Air Battle Force is the only unit we can send on short notice that has the firepower we need.

"In short, I think Masters has developed a workable plan for dealing with the Chinese in the south Philippines. We see a pretty good chance of success, even with anticipated Chinese reinforcements in the Celebes. The primary plan is relatively small, controlled, and does not directly involve any carrier battle groups or any Marine Expeditionary Units. Masters' war-game computer calls the plan Operation WINTER HAMMER . . ."

"Winter?" Vice President Martindale retorted. "You're going to wait until winter to do something?" The Vice President was not known for being too swift.

"The name was simply a random combination of words made by his war-gaming computer, and its use is strictly internal. We can pick a different name for media purposes if you wish . . ."

"Just let me know what you're proposing to send over there," the President said irritably. "How much equipment, how many men."

"The first Air Battle Wing, which is the only one currently organized," Curtis replied, "consists of eighteen B-52 bombers, ten F-111G bombers, twenty F-15B, C, and E–model fighters, twelve F-4 fighters, three KC-10 tankers, six KC-135 tankers, one E-3C AWACS plane, one RC-135 radar plane, one EC-135 airborne command post, three C-5 cargo planes, and ten C-141 cargo planes. It totals about two thousand men and women. The current force includes three B-2 stealth bombers as well, which have been training for use with the Air Battle Force. We also have the use of the destroyers *Hewitt* and *Fife* and the cruiser *Sterett,* which were part of the *Ranger* battle group; the two destroyers carry Tomahawk cruise missiles that can go in ahead of the bombers and take out seaborne radars and large vessels. The Second Air Battle Wing has about twice as many troops and equipment, but can't be assembled for another thirty to sixty days.

"According to our intelligence figures, the Chinese have approximately ten thousand troops in Zamboanga itself, plus another five thousand afloat in the Celebes," Curtis continued, "including a full Marine regiment on Mindanao and another afloat.

"They have the equivalent of three surface action groups in the Celebes, which is twelve capital warships including submarines in *each* group. We have mapped out at least twenty different possible surface-to-air missile sites surrounding the Celebes. They have closed off or actively patrol all sea-lanes and all air routes around the southern Philippines for a radius of a thousand miles from Zamboanga.

"In addition, they have another twenty thousand troops, thirty more ships, and at least a hundred more aircraft in Puerto Princesa, only five hundred miles away. And this is only a quarter of what they have sent to Luzon: Clark Air Base and Subic Bay Naval Base both have as many Chinese troops and machines there as the United States once had there at the height of the Vietnam War—"

"Wait a minute," the President said in complete surprise. "You want to take on fifteen thousand Chinese troops with only two thousand men? That's *it?*"

"Sir, numbers don't make the difference here," Curtis explained. "The Air Battle Force has the striking power of two, perhaps three aircraft-carrier battle groups, and they have speed and flexibility that the carriers themselves don't. We have the air power to force the Chinese out of Zamboanga and perhaps out of the south Philippines altogether. We need to activate this unit as soon as possible. I recommend to you that we activate the Air Battle Force and deploy them to Guam. Once they're there, we can present a more detailed plan to you."

"I object to General Curtis characterizing this group as the ultimate solution to this problem," Preston said. "I am very much in support of the Air Battle Force concept, but General Curtis is fantasizing, sir." To Curtis he said, "I'm on your side, Wilbur. I believe in the work you've done. The Air Battle Force concept is great, and you've implemented it superbly. No one is questioning it or you. But we have to be more realistic or optimistic—we have to be ultraconservative. We've been surprised so many times in this conflict that we have to increase our requirements that much more to compose a credible picture." To the President he said, "We can build a fighting force to take the Philippines, sir, but do you want to pay the price to do it?"

"The Air Battle Force doesn't fight alone, Thomas," Curtis said. "WINTER HAMMER includes the *Wisconsin* battle group. Six ships, led by the battleship *Wisconsin,* are at Pearl Harbor ready to go. This group has trained with the Air Battle Force in maritime operations, so when you do decide to send the ABF, they'll operate well together. In the meantime they can act as an escort for the *Ranger* when they're ready to pull out of Indonesia, and they can monitor ship and submarine activity in the Celebes from long range. They also carry Tomahawk cruise missiles, which will be important if we do start hostilities with the Chinese.

"The task force also includes the Second Marine Pre-positioning Force based on Mariana Island near Guam. One amphibious assault carrier, one tank landing ship, two escorts, two support ships, twenty helicopters, thirty armored vehicles, five thousand Marines and naval personnel. Half of the force is there now—the other half deployed by air from Hawaii, pick up their ships on Mariana, then embark to their standby positions in the Philippine Sea. It will take at least five days for this group to arrive on station. We send a flight of P-3 Orion sub hunters from Japan or Guam with them until they get some air support from shore or from a carrier group."

"An invasion force," the President said. "You're recommending a full-scale invasion . . ."

A telephone in front of the President buzzed; Cesare picked it up and listened, then replaced it on its cradle. "Press release from the Chinese government, coming in from the wire services," he told the President. "Communications is sending down a copy."

A few moments later a Secret Service agent on duty arrived and passed a computer printout to Cesare, who remained standing as he read it to the National Security Council:

" 'The Chinese government is claiming that an American military strike force was detected and intercepted over the Celebes Sea,' " Cesare read. " 'The strike force, composed they say of several large subsonic bombers believed to be B-52 bombers from the island of Guam, was escorted by fighters from an aircraft carrier. They claim the Philippine government requested that the Chinese People's Liberation Army Air Force, some of whom were stationed at military bases in the southern Philippines at the request of the Philippine government, help defend them.'

" 'The Chinese claim they launched a small defense force of fighters, which managed to drive the bombers away. They claim four Chinese fighters were downed and two American fighters were shot down . . .' " Cesare read ahead, then added, " 'No mention of the strike against the *Ranger,* except that American warships also threatened several Filipino coastal towns with bombers and rocket attacks, and that an unarmed Chinese supply ship carrying medicine and food to Filipino refugees in western Mindanao came under attack by an American bomber. They go on to charge that the United States is trying to retake the Philippines by force and blames us again for the nuclear-weapon detonation near Palawan and for threatening the world with thermonuclear chaos.' "

"Those bastards," the President grumbled angrily. Then,

almost as an afterthought, he turned to Curtis: "We did *not* have any B-52s involved in this mission over the Celebes Sea, did we, General?"

"Absolutely not, sir. We have no bombers of any size stationed in Diego Garcia, Australia, Japan, or anywhere west of Guam . . ."

"Could it have been someone else? The Australians? Brunei? Vietnam? Australia has F-111 bombers, right . . .?"

"Unlikely, sir. Our AWACS radar plane picked up no other aircraft in the area . . ."

"What about ground forces? It wasn't a Marine or special operations attack? Anything like that?"

"Nothing authorized by me or any of my staff, sir," Curtis said. His mind began running through a multitude of other possibilities—mercenaries, a rogue combat unit, perhaps even the downed Tomcat crews blowing things up to mask their escape—but he quickly discarded each one. "Sir, it's an obvious propaganda story. When the CIA investigates the story, they'll discover it wasn't a bomber attack—they'll probably find there was no attack at all. The Chinese released the story because of its propaganda value—they want to be the first to complain, because it shifts blame on the other party."

The President had also discarded all other possibilities, for his face became darker and angrier by the second. "Those bastards," he muttered. "They attack our unarmed reconnaissance aircraft and an aircraft carrier, then claim *we're* trying to start a war. And even if we admit that the *Ranger* was attacked by Chinese antiship missiles, it makes us look even worse—we're going to get blamed for trying to start a war, then criticized for not doing a good job of it. Bastards . . ."

The President fell silent, as did the rest of the Council. This was the turning point, Curtis thought grimly: this was the point at which all presidents facing a conflict had to decide whether to explore more peaceful, less hazardous options, or go ahead with preparing for battle. Like his famous relative, this President wanted to avoid a conflict—he would do almost anything to avoid going to war, or even doing something that might threaten war. It was simply not in his nature.

But he had sixty dead sailors and two damaged warships to

think about as well. When the American people learned about this incident, which was bound to happen at any minute, what would they say? Would they expect a military response? Would they understand if the President of the United States still tried to pursue a peaceful solution?

"Mr. President, I'm ready to brief you at any time on WIN-TER HAMMER . . ."

"General, I can't consider sending in more bombers and fighters *now*," the President said angrily. "I'm supposed to stand up in front of the American people and deny that we sent bombers to attack the Philippines—and *then* the press learns of all those bombers sitting over there on Guam? I look bad enough as it is."

"We can disprove each and every accusation by the Chinese," Curtis said. "We can prove we had unarmed reconnaissance planes up there, not bombers, and that the Chinese fighters attacked first. We can also prove that the *Ranger* was hundreds of miles from the Philippines and no threat to any coastal towns or Chinese positions, and that their antiship missile attack on the fleet was unprovoked." But the President seemed distant, worried, unreachable. "You don't have to submit to this blackmail, sir. We've got dozens of options . . ."

"I know, I know . . ." He paused, his gaze scanning his advisers arranged around him, although it was obvious he didn't notice any of them—it was his way of making tough decisions. He made another glance at Thomas Preston, who was grim-faced but remained silent. The President was alone with his decision:

"I know I'm being too cautious, Wilbur, but you've got to understand," he said, "I need cooperation with the other countries in the region before I commit American troops to fight the Chinese. The world is touchier than a warm bottle of nitroglycerin right now. If I send your bombers and fighters into the Philippines to square off against the Chinese, I need to make sure that the American people realize we've exhausted every possible option first . . ."

"We've got the authorization you need, sir," Curtis said. "Second Vice President Samar."

"Samar? What does he have to do with this . . . ?" President Taylor asked.

"Samar is a legitimate head of the government, sir," Curtis said. "He is also the governor of the Commonwealth of Mindanao, which is virtually a republic of its own. His designated representative has formally requested assistance from the United States. That's the legal spark we need to move."

Danahall sniffed aloud and shook his head. "That's not even close to the truth, General . . ."

"It doesn't have to be the absolute truth, Dennis," Curtis pointed out. "We're not talking about a court case here—we're looking for justification to act, and we have it . . ."

"Unless Samar is dead," the Vice President said, "in which case Teguina retains control of the government and becomes de facto governor of Mindanao . . ."

"Then we go in and rescue Samar," Curtis said. "Ambassador O'Day was given information on how to contact Samar—we'll arrange for a special-operations group to go in and get him out so he can make an announcement to the world that he is resisting the Chinese."

"But we need to be in a better position to react when we get Samar out, sir," Curtis said to the President. "Sir, you have to order the Air Battle Force into Guam and the Marines to deploy into the Philippine Sea, and have them prepare for action. If we wait too long, Samar's militia will collapse and Mindanao will fall—and then nothing short of a nuclear war *will* dislodge the Chinese from the Philippines."

The President thought about this, scanning the faces around him; then, to General Curtis: "Okay, Wilbur, you got the green light. Get the Air Battle Force moving to Andersen as quickly as possible. You're also authorized to deploy the Army and Marine Pre-positioned Forces as you outlined earlier, and the destroyers and cruiser you mentioned before can go on standby with their Tomahawk cruise missiles. I want no offensive operations to begin without my specific approval. I want a full briefing on WINTER HAMMER within the hour, here . . . Paul, get the 'leadership' together for the briefing, and try to get as many of the allies notified as possible."

"And the B-2 bombers that are part of the Air Battle Force . . . ?"

The President scowled his displeasure at the question, but replied, "That's up to you and your people. It's bad enough I'm ordering bombers and cruise missiles into the area—I might as well get all the protests packed into one order. If the crews have been training with your Air Battle Force and if they know their shit, you're authorized to send them."

PUJADA PENINSULA, SOUTHEASTERN MINDANAO
THE PHILIPPINES
SUNDAY, 2 OCTOBER 1994, 0430 HOURS LOCAL

The only warmth United States Navy Lieutenant Commander Paul "Cowboy" Bowman had felt in two days came from a tiny burning white fuel tablet about the size of a quarter. He had lit the tablet with a match from a waterproof container, placed the fuel tablet in a small palm-sized aluminum cookstove from his survival kit, then folded a sheet of an old Tagalog-language magazine cover into the shallow pan—he had lost the original metal cup long ago during their mad races through the Mindanao jungles—filled it with brackish water, and set it on the stove.

To Second Vice President José Trujillo Samar's surprise, the paper pan did not burn. "Why does the paper not burn, Bowman?" Samar asked.

"Dunno," Bowman replied. "Too cool, I guess." He dumped a packet of soup mix into the water and began stirring it with a twig. This whole trip was actually too cool, Bowman thought. The escort mission for the Air Force, the dogfights with the Chinks, getting his ass shot down, splashing down in some unheard-of sea thousands of miles from home and hundreds of miles from his carrier—at night, no less—being chased through the swamps and jungles of the Philippines, running from Chinese infantry patrols, losing his RIO.

And to top everything off, here he was with the Second Vice President of the Philippines, a man who was legally the President of the country, but was, in reality, on the run from his First Vice President.

Bowman had been pulled out of the Celebes by a fishing boat and delivered to Samar's militia. His flight suit was crusted with dried saltwater and mud and he was dog-tired. He'd been unable to sleep before his patrol and had been awake nearly eighteen hours *before* his sortie, so he was going on almost three days of no sleep, not to mention that his left elbow was probably broken when it hit the cockpit sill on ejection. But that wasn't the worst part of this excruciating evasion. The worst part of the trip was lying in the sewn-up canvas bag a few feet away from him—the body of Bowman's RIO, Lieutenant Kenny "Cookin" Miller. Miller's parachute had apparently not fully opened, and by the time Bowman somehow found him in the dark, warm water, he had either drowned or had died instantly after hitting the water. He had dragged Miller's battered body into his one-man life raft with him, ignoring the horribly shattered neck and twisted limbs.

Bowman and Miller had been together for three cruises, and the two bachelors had lots of shore-leave experiences. They were more than shipmates or fellow crew dogs—they were friends. Bowman was determined not to leave his friend alone, to be eaten by sharks in the Celebes Sea. As long as it was humanly possible, Bowman was going to carry, drag, or push Miller's body with him.

Since being retrieved from the water, Bowman and his grisly companion had been on the move. They had been transferred to two more fishing boats, then between several groups, once being taken to shore. Their ID cards were taken immediately, he was kept tied up and blindfolded, and he was warned that if he disobeyed any order or did anything to arouse suspicion, he would be disposed of without remorse or hesitation. They had traveled uphill for two days, moving only at night or in bad weather; then they moved quickly downhill to the eastern shoreline—the sun was coming up somewhere over Samar's shoulder right now, in the direction of the sea. They were kept hidden in mud pits, the hollowed-out insides of huge tropical trees, or in rotting grass huts. Food was usually a muddy green banana or some other undigestible piece of fruit, and rainwater.

Samar himself had shown up only last night. His militiamen treated him like Caesar. He held several military councils, speaking Tagalog in low whispers.

Bowman thought General José Samar had to be the most mysterious, enigmatic, unfathomable man he had ever encountered. Here he was, President of the Philippines, the leader of the Commonwealth of Mindanao, a powerful state in its own right, a wealthy plantation owner and industrialist. And what was he doing? Hiding out in the middle of nowhere, wearing filthy fatigues, within minutes or mere yards of getting his head blown off, and leading a group of rebel soldiers around deadly Chinese air and naval patrols.

Samar was a born leader, and he looked the part. Tall for a Filipino, light-skinned, broad-shouldered and powerful like a farmer, which he was on his family's Jolo Island estate before he entered politics. He was an Army Academy graduate and a former armored cavalry officer, advancing in grade to captain before joining Ferdinand Marcos' secret intelligence organization. He rose to the rank of general in very short order, commanding the ex-Philippine President's Mindanao intelligence organization. He had reportedly executed and imprisoned thousands of Moslem rebels in the prison at Puerto Princesa in his five years as chief of intelligence . . .

. . . until he got religion. Somehow, sometime, the teachings of Islam had penetrated that handsome head. Perhaps it was the tortured cries of his victims or their families; perhaps it was his Sulu heritage, which had been influenced for centuries by sailors and traders from the Middle East; perhaps it was Allah or the Prophet speaking to him in his dreams—whatever it was, General Samar became an avowed Moslem warrior. Bowman had heard his Islamic name, but had forgotten it—his men called him "General" or occasionally "Jabal," which meant "mountain."

Samar had tried several rebellions against the Marcos regime—all had been put down violently and efficiently, and a huge price had been placed on his head. He learned to live off the land, fleeing from one isolated jungle village to another, always one or two steps ahead of his ex-colleagues in the secret police. His exploits as a hunted criminal and guerrilla soldier against Marcos had earned him a widespread heroic reputation on Mindanao, and many villagers regarded him as a modern-day Robin Hood, if not a god. He was very successful in rallying the Moslem faithful to his side and demonstrating to all Filipinos the cruelty and opprobrium imposed on the Filipino people by the Marcos regime.

Samar was more than ready to continue the battle with Aquino and Mikaso of the new ruling UNIDO party, and he did stage several raids against army barracks in Cagayan de Oro and Davao, but times were changing. The Philippines were immersed in abject poverty, the Communists were veering out of control, and foreign investment was slipping away. To keep the republic from destroying itself from within, Corazon Aquino had held out her hand in peace to the two main warring factions, and Samar eagerly accepted it. In return for peace, and to prevent Mindanao from splitting off from the rest of the Philippines, Samar, once considered no greater than a dirty rodent in the wild jungles of Mindanao, became the Second Vice President of the Philippines, constitutionally third in line of succession for the presidency. Five provinces in central and eastern Mindanao—Cotabato, Davao, Bukidnon, Agusan, and Surigao—became one free state, with its own legislature and militia, and Samar became its first governor.

Now this man was suddenly on the run again. He was as surprised as everyone by the Chinese invasion, and by the time he rallied his forces it was too late to save Zamboanga and Cotabato. But Davao had to be saved.

The water in the paper pan began to boil—the paper *would* burn if he let it boil too long. Bowman took a sip. It was terribly salty, with a pungent, slimy aftertaste that stuck to the back of his mouth and tongue like grease, but the warm liquid in his belly made the naval aviator feel a million times better. "Try some, General?" he asked Samar.

The rebel leader shook his head. "I have tasted your American emergency rations—I lived on it for several months once.

I have had my fill." Even though the man was smiling, the tone of voice described a very unpleasant experience.

It was Samar who had ordered Bowman to be untied and for him to be allowed to use the items in his survival kit.

"What are you going to do with me . . . us?" Bowman asked Samar.

"I do not know," Samar said. "It may not matter in any case. We may all be captured at sunrise. The Chinese are all around us."

"Then why don't you run?" Bowman said. "Head back for the hills and the jungle. I know we're near the coast—I can hide out until help arrives."

"Help does not appear to be at hand," Samar said. "We took an awful chance coming here, and we have failed." He turned to Bowman and said, "You must leave your crewman here."

"No way . . ."

"He will slow us down. The jungle will be too thick . . ."

"I'm *not* leaving him."

Samar shoved a raised hand in his face to silence him, then stomped on Bowman's aluminum cookstove to extinguish the fire. Bowman heard nothing, but after six years of flying F-14s off aircraft carriers, he wouldn't be surprised if his hearing had deteriorated. He moved to his feet and went over to hoist Miller onto his back, but two of Samar's troops restrained him and snapped handcuffs on his wrists, binding his hands in front of his body. "You can't do this, Samar . . ."

"Be silent." He raised his rifle, scanning the skies to the east . . . then stopped. Bowman followed his gaze. Far off on the horizon, toward the northeast, three specks, arranged in a tight diamond formation, were highlighted against the dawning sky. "Chinese patrol helicopters. Pray they haven't found us . . ."

The diamond formation was heading south, about a mile offshore, but the specs suddenly began to wheel right toward the coastline.

"Damn. They must have triangulated our radio transmissions . . ."

"Radio transmissions . . . ?"

"Silence. Stay here." Samar hurried off into the thicket toward his perimeter guards. He returned ten seconds later. "Three men are running north to create a diversion. The rest say they will fight. I wanted you to know that. There's an inlet about three hundred meters away; we must reach it before the helicopters arrive. Run for your life." Samar wheeled and dashed into the thicket, keeping as many trees as possible between him and the oncoming helicopters. Bowman followed close behind but was immediately passed by four of Samar's soldiers. Soon Bowman lost sight of the five men and could do nothing else but trust his hearing to tell which direction they were heading.

It seemed they had been running only for a few seconds when suddenly a ripple of explosions behind him threw Bowman to the slimy jungle floor. Two of the helicopters were shredding the forests with rocket fire; the third was hovering offshore, scanning the trees for the rebel soldiers. Bowman heard animal-like screams from the jungle as the Chinese rockets found their targets—the three rebel soldiers that were acting as decoys.

Bowman struggled to his feet. He was about to run when a dark figure body-tackled him to the ground. "Stay down!" Samar cried. He pressed something into Bowman's hands—it was his PRC-23D survival radio from his survival kit. "Use this when the time comes—"

"Wait! What are you—"

"Start crawling toward the heavy jungle. Stay as hidden as you can—they are using infrared scanners to find us." The third helicopter had started toward shore, bearing down on them—it was less than a half-mile away . . .

A burst of rifle fire opened up to their right. "No!" Samar screamed in Tagalog. "Don't shoot!" But it was too late. Samar's soldiers had started to fire their rifles at the third helicopter, which was exactly what its pilots were waiting for. The chopper banked hard left, and a pod-mounted machine gun chattered to life, spitting a long tongue of flame at each one-second burst.

"Our only hope is to get back into the heavy forest," Samar said in English. "Run away from the sunrise. When you hear the rotors, find a mud pit or wet thicket and hide in it. When the sound goes away, run again. The chopper's fuel must be getting low, so we may have enough time." He was suddenly on his feet, dragging Bowman with him. "Now! Run!"

Bowman had taken one step when he heard rotors. He found a patch of mud and dived onto it, but it was not deep enough to cover him. Samar was nowhere to be seen. He rolled to his back just in time to see one helicopter fly overhead and one hover nearby, less than a hundred yards away—the first two choppers had returned. It was close enough for Bowman to see the chopper's infrared scanner ball under the nose and an outrigger on each side holding a torpedo-shaped weapon pod.

It had him . . .

There was nowhere to run anymore . . .

There was a scream from somewhere off to Bowman's left, some sort of battle cry, and a long staccato ripple of automatic rifle fire. Several sparks flew off the nose of the chopper, and it suddenly nose-dived almost straight down into the jungle not fifty yards away. Bowman needed no more encouragement— he turned around and raced as hard as he could away from the stricken chopper.

But he could not escape. Bowman heard a short *pwoooosh*, and a split second later a terrific explosion erupted in the first level of jungle canopy only twenty feet overhead and a few yards ahead. The dimly lit jungle suddenly turned bright yellow, his head felt as if it had exploded, and he felt himself cartwheel several feet away from the concussion.

He opened his eyes. The chopper was just a few dozen yards away, nose aimed right at him. Its rotors were whipping the foliage around as if they were in a hurricane, but Bowman could not hear or feel anything. The chopper was translating, lining up the blunt muzzle of the weapon pods directly on him. When he tried to move his arms or legs, nothing worked. His vision was blurring, growing dimmer, everything was going dark. . . .

With the target flitting over the jungle, it would have made a difficult shot—not impossible, but very difficult—but the chopper suddenly stopped, obviously lining up for the kill, and now it made an easy target. Marine Corps Captain Fred Collins swung the nose of his MV-22A Sea Hammer tilt-rotor aircraft a bit farther left to line up the aiming "donut" of his Stinger missile system on the infrared image of the Chinese patrol helicopter, then waited until he heard the familiar "growl" in his headset, indicating that one of his heat-seeking missiles had locked on. He lifted the protective cover off the safety release, pressed the release with his right thumb, got a "Ready Shoot" indication on his integrated helmet display system, then pulled the trigger with his right index finger. "Fox two, Able Zero-Seven."

From less than a half-mile away, the kill was quick and spectacular. The Stinger missile flew directly into the unbaffled, unprotected engine exhaust of the Chinese Zhishengji-9 combat patrol helicopter, turning both engines and its fuel tanks into balloons of fire. The orange and yellow balloons seemed to hold the helicopter in midair for several seconds, but soon it dropped straight down and crashed into the jungle.

"Splash one chopper," Collins radioed. "Where's the other two?"

"Lost contact with bandit two," replied the controller aboard an Air Force E-3A Sentry radar plane from Andersen Air Force Base. "Bandit three is at your nine o'clock position, same altitude, range six miles, airspeed niner-zero and accelerating, turning south. He appears to be extending."

"I'm coming up on bingo fuel, Basket," Collins said. "I either chase him or continue with the pickup. I can't do both. Where's he now?"

"Bandit three now heading southwest, your ten o'clock position, eight miles, airspeed one-zero-zero knots, altitude three thousand. Appears to be buggin' out."

Collins knew that the guys could turn and re-attack quickly, but he had no choice—he was too far away to pursue. "All right, Basket, I'm staying. Give me a heads-up if he comes back. Switching to Guard channel." To his copilot in the Sea Hammer's left seat, Collins said, "You got the aircraft." The copilot shook the control stick to acknowledge the order, and Collins released the controls. "Start an orbit over the area. I'll see if I can find him on the FLIR."

Collins' copilot climbed to five hundred feet, stabilized, then began a slow orbit over the area. Collins activated the AN/AAQ-16 FLIR, or Forward Looking Infrared, sensor ball, which presented a thermal image of the forest below in his helmet-mounted sights. At the same time he keyed the microphone button: "Bullet, this is Able Zero-Seven on Guard. Bullet, if you read me, give me a tone on Rescue one. Over."

A few seconds later, Collins heard, "Able Zero-Seven, this is Bullet on Guard. I read you loud and clear." The DF direction-finder read southwest. The accent was strange, the voice clipped and precise—too precise. There was also a lot of background noise. It could be his own rotors . . . or it could be someone else.

Collins said, "Bullet, go to Rescue One and hold down for ten. Over."

"Able Zero-Seven, I cannot. Land on shoreline. I can see you. Land on shoreline."

"Bullet, go to Rescue One. Over."

"Able Zero-Seven, I am injured. I cannot work my radio. Land on the shoreline. I am just a few meters inland. Hurry. Over."

The DF readout still read southwest—but that could mean a hundred yards southwest or ten miles southwest. The Navy pilot was not following orders because he was panicking—or because it wasn't a Navy pilot talking. The term "meters" worried Collins, but more military guys were using metric measurements like meters and "klicks," so that wasn't a definite giveaway. On the Guard emergency channel, Collins said, "Stand by, Bullet." To his copilot, Collins said, "Swing west a few miles. Let's see if we can triangulate this DF steer." The MV-22 swung west away from the coastline, keeping as close to the treetops as possible.

"Able Zero-Seven, this is Bullet, come in. Come in, Able."

Bowman was groggy but awake. He had a pounding headache and completely washed-out vision. He felt paralyzed, and when he tried to move, a red-hot wave of pain rolled up and down his back. Same for his left arm—it wasn't just his elbow anymore, the entire arm felt broken. His wrists were still hand-cuffed together and the survival radio was gone . . .

No, not gone. He could hear faint voices coming from somewhere. Fighting through the pain in his back and arm, he scratched his fingers across the mud and foliage toward the sound. Just as he thought he was going to pass out from the pain, his fingers brushed the thick rubber of the short antenna. A spark of hope shot through his pain-tortured brain, and he was able to grab the radio and drag it to his body.

"Stand by, Bullet," Bowman heard. "Bullet, switch to Rescue One, if able. Over."

"Unable to switch. Help me. Land on the shoreline. I will find you."

Able . . . that was the call sign of the Navy rescue choppers on *Ranger* on the day that Bowman was shot down. The PJs finally found him! But who was he talking to? There was another Bullet crew member out here? Who was he talking to? Miller? Was Cookin' alive? He couldn't believe it—Miller had really made it!

But he suddenly realized that wasn't right. Miller was dead. The voice on the radio didn't sound American—it sounded too smooth, too practiced. It had to be Chinese! The Chinese were trying to coax the Navy rescue bird into landing. No downed aircrewman would ever do that—a downed aircrewman's responsibility was to first get himself located, then follow instructions from the rescue bird. He was not supposed to issue orders.

Bowman's radio was set to the Guard channel. On the PRC-23D radio, there was a four-position rotary dial: full clockwise, toward the side with the antenna, was Guard, one click counterclockwise was Off, one more click was Rescue One, and one more was Rescue Two. With trembling fingers, Bowman depressed the rotary dial and twisted the knob once to the Off position; then, with a tremendous effort, twisted the dial to Rescue One and depressed a rubber switch on the side of the unit. . . .

* * *

The DF readout on radio number one was moving slightly south. "Few more miles," Collins said to his copilot, "and we can plot out his position . . ."

Suddenly, radio number two came alive with a distinctive *Piiinng! Piiinng! Piiinng! Piiinng!* tone. The DF readout on the second channel pointed directly east. "I got a tone on Rescue One!" Collins shouted. "Coming from the area we just left!"

"That guy on Guard must be an eavesdropper," the copilot said.

"I almost fell for it, too. Follow the DF steer from Rescue One." Collins switched from Guard channel to Rescue One. "Bullet on Rescue One, I copy your tone. Give me a tone when we fly overhead."

They were about sixty seconds on the new heading toward the east when Collins said, "I think I have something down there. PJs, stand by." In the rear of the MV-22 tilt-rotor aircraft were four pararescue jumpers, or PJs, two sitting on the port and starboard cargo doors, wearing rappelling gear.

Collins tracked the warm spot below him with the FLIR. Just before the object was directly beneath them, they heard another series of tones on Rescue One. The copilot flew past the spot, but Collins continued to track the warm spot and hit a button on the AN/AYK-14 mission computer, which would store the latitude and longitude of the spot they flew over.

"Bullet, this is Able Zero-Seven, authenticate Victor-Kilo. Victor-Kilo." No response. "Bullet, this is Able, I say again, authenticate Victor-Kilo. Over."

"We're coming up on bingo fuel," the copilot said, "and the Chinese are bound to bring reinforcements. We can't stay . . ."

"Once more, then we're outta here," Collins said. On Rescue One, he said, "Bullet, I say again . . ."

"Bullet . . . authenticates . . . Poppa Zero . . . Poppa-Zero . . ."

"He didn't give the whole response," the copilot said.

"Close enough for me," Collins said.

"But you don't know . . ."

"I'm taking the chance. I've got the aircraft." Collins took the controls, gave them a shake to verify transfer of control, then banked sharply to the left and lined up on the object he was tracking on the FLIR. When he was pointing at it, he moved a switch on the power quadrant, which rotated the twin rotor nacelles on the wingtips of the MV-22 vertically and transformed the Sea Hammer aircraft from an airplane to a helicopter. He maneuvered the big cargo-plane-turned-helicopter into a hover, then translated slightly sideways until he found a clearing beneath the airplane. On interphone, he said, "PJs, our boy's off the nose, about thirty yards. No complete ID, but I don't see a weapon and he's alone. Out."

Using their rappelling gear, the PJs edged off the Sea Hammer and slid to the ground. Unslinging their rifles, they took a bearing from the MV-22 and proceeded toward the subject. A few cautious minutes later, they found Bowman.

"Able, this is PJ One, I got him. Looks like one of our boys." The rescue technician quickly searched Bowman for hidden explosives or booby traps as the second PJ stood a safe distance away, guarding the area. "Move in position." Collins edged the Sea Hammer aircraft forward, and the crewmen in the cargo hold lowered a rescue hoist with a forest-penetrator device down to the men on the ground. He unfolded the petal-like seats on the forest penetrator, lifted Bowman up, and secured him into the seat. Bowman had enough strength to wrap his arms around the rescue device and do as he was told.

"Samar . . . Samar. Don't forget Samar . . ." Bowman told the PJ. It was hard to hear over the roar of the MV-22 overhead, but the first PJ caught a snippet of Bowman's words.

"He seems to be saying Sammy something," the PJ said on a helmet radio to Collins. "There might be someone else nearby."

"We don't have time to search for anybody else," Collins' copilot said. "We're past bingo already."

Collins was using the FLIR scanner to search the area around the rescue site. Suddenly he stopped. "I got someone else," he said. "Thirty yards to the right. He's not moving. Check it out. Hoist Robby on board." The first PJ on the ground climbed onto another seat on the forest penetrator, strapped himself on, then pushed Bowman's head down and wrapped his arms around him as the cargo hold crew hoisted them up through the foliage. The second PJ began moving toward the second object, taking directions from Collins, using the gradually brightening morning skies to find cover until he was close enough.

The crew in the cargo hold of the MV-22 dragged Bowman inside and wrapped him in a blanket. One PJ shined a flashlight in his face, then compared the face to a sheet of ID-card photographs of downed crewmen from the *Saratoga.* "He matches," the PJ shouted on interphone. "Bowman. Bullet Seven's pilot."

Collins let out a sigh of relief. "Dammit, I don't believe it. We got one. The other guy might be his RIO."

The second PJ on the ground reached the body. "He looks like a Filipino . . . wait. He's wearing general's stars. No name tag, but he's got two stars on his collar."

Collins maneuvered closer to his ground crewman. "General's stars . . . a general? Named Sammy? Sammy . . . *Samar?* Holy shit, that might be General Samar, the fucking Vice President! Get him on board! Hurry!"

ABOARD THE USS *RANGER*, IN THE PHILIPPINE SEA
MONDAY, 3 OCTOBER 1994, 0600 HOURS MANILA TIME

The Philippine national anthem played in the background. The television transmission showed a sign written in English, Tagalog, and Chinese, telling the viewer to stand by for an important message from the Philippine government. After two minutes, the scene dissolved, to be replaced by the grim face of Second Vice President General José Trujillo Samar. Most of his hair was burned off, and one eye was swollen shut— he had refused to wear any bandages, however, because he was afraid his countrymen might not recognize him, and because he wanted all the world to see what the Chinese military had done to him. He was wearing his uniform, freshly cleaned and starched, which hid a tightly wrapped separated shoulder and burns across most of his upper torso.

"My fellow Filipinos and all others who can hear my voice.

I am José Samar, Second Vice President of the Republic of the Philippines. I am speaking to you from a control room aboard the American aircraft carrier USS *Ranger,* which is en route to Guam after being viciously attacked by Chinese warplanes three days ago. This message is being broadcast to you at six o'clock A.M. on the third of October, Manila time, via Philippine TV channels two and three, on the Voice of America, the British Broadcasting Channel shortwave channel seventeen, and on other international radio and television channels.

"As you can see, I am injured but alive. I was rescued on the second of October from the island of Mindanao by American Marines shortly after being attacked and nearly killed by patrols from the People's Republic of China. The Chinese patrols killed several of my militiamen while we were engaged in rescue operations, trying to save the life of an American Navy pilot shot down by Chinese fighter planes several days ago.

"I am speaking to you today to tell you that, as the governor of the Commonwealth of Mindanao and Second Vice President of the Republic of the Philippines, that the People's Republic of China is engaged in a full-scale military invasion of my country. Do not be deceived by stories of cooperation with the Philippine government. The Chinese are believed to have murdered President Arturo Mikaso. Chinese warships have taken the Commonwealth cities of Puerto Princesa, Zamboanga, Cotabato, and Cagayan de Oro, and they are preparing to launch an all-out assault on the Commonwealth of Mindanao capital city of Davao. The Chinese are not liberators, nor are they assisting any legitimate Philippine government officials. They are *invaders.* They are moving large-scale military forces into my country with the intent of permanently occupying and annexing the Philippines. The Chinese invaders have attacked and killed Philippine citizens and have also attacked unarmed American reconnaissance planes.

"I am hereby urging all nations to impose economic and political sanctions on the People's Republic of China for their illegal invasion, and to do everything in their power to help remove all Chinese military forces from my country. As Second Vice President and the only legitimate government leader of the Philippines, I hereby proclaim all incursions into the Philippines by the People's Republic of China to be illegal, and I formally order the People's Republic of China to remove all personnel, warships, and aircraft from our territories immediately.

"My authority may be challenged by the Communist government in Manila, led by the murderer Daniel Teguina. Teguina has called me a traitor and a rebel, but it was he who conspired to assassinate President Mikaso, allow the Chinese Army to invade the country, and take power for himself behind the brutal arm of the Red Chinese. His allegations are unfounded, but only the Supreme Court and the Parliament of the Republic of the Philippines can decide our guilt or innocence.

"But in the Commonwealth of Mindanao my authority is absolute, and I am still in command despite my injuries. My militia forces have denied the Chinese complete access to Cotabato Airport, we have continually routed them from the Cabagan, Davao, and Pulangi river valleys, and we have prepared a strong defense and a few surprises for them in Davao if they try to invade us there. This will be the greatest battle in Philippine history since World War Two. But we cannot hold off the Chinese hordes alone.

"I am therefore formally requesting military and economic assistance from the government of the United States in helping me to repel the Chinese invaders. I hereby authorize the American government full overflight, landing rights, and sailing rights into all Philippine and Commonwealth territories, and hereby grant full authority to conduct military, security, safety, and other operations in my country. I also authorize the President of the United States and his designated representatives, civil and military, to act with full presidential authority in the Commonwealth of Mindanao, including full authority for all defense matters, and I order my state militia to obey all orders of the President of the United States or his theater commanders as if those orders were my own. If I die of my injuries or am killed by hostile forces, my orders here stated will remain in force until my state is returned to peace, with all foreign powers removed.

"I hope that all loyal Filipinos hear my words. These are my standing orders to all loyal Filipinos:

"All active, reserve, national guard, inactive reserve, and former militia members under the age of sixty are ordered to active duty immediately. Report only to a district or city militia commander; do not report to a federal, National People's Party, or New People's Army official, or to anyone you do not know personally. If it is not possible to contact a militia commander, attempt to travel to Davao and report to a militia outpost.

"To all other citizens of Mindanao: Do not report for work. Do not surrender your weapons to anyone under any circumstances; keep them hidden. Report movements of Chinese or New People's Army troops, or anyone you suspect of aiding or informing to the Chinese or NPA, to a militia member known to you. My militiamen will attempt to contact all residents of Davao, Samal, Panabo, Santo Tomas, and other towns on the Davao Gulf and take your women and children out of any known battle areas.

"If your town is under attack or is threatened, move toward the coast as quickly as you can. Do not move toward Davao, as you might move into the middle of a battle area, trapped between opposing forces. Avoid Chinese or NPA troops; travel on secondary or back roads, at night if possible. If you can travel by boat, do so only at night, stay hidden near the coastline, and avoid all large coastal towns. Do not assist any Chinese or federal government representatives or military personnel. If you are forced to assist them, do so to save your own life, but escape when it is safe to do so and resist to the best of your ability. Provide aid and comfort to any of my militia members known to you.

"Above all, pray for the strength and courage we will need to resist the Chinese invaders. As long as I live, I will do everything in my powers to remove the foreign invaders from our homeland. May God give me, and you, my loyal brothers and sisters, the strength to continue fighting until our country is once again free.

"This transmission will be recorded and repeated several times daily. Do not give up the fight. *Allah akbar.* God is great.

Good luck." The opening sign reappeared, along with the national anthem, and then Samar began to repeat the message, this time in Tagalog, the native language of the Philippines.

"What do you mean, it's down?" Brad Elliott asked. He kicked off the sheets, and his one good foot was hitting the floor milliseconds later as he readjusted the phone.

"Sorry, General, but that's what it looks like," Jon Masters said over the phone. "Carter-Seven didn't download its last sensor pass over Mindanao. We're checking on it right now, but I think our ground equipment is malfunctioning. I can't poll the satellites."

"I'll be right there."

Five minutes later, Major General Stone and Lieutenant General Elliott were racing for the command post. They found half of the back panels off the control consoles, the large-screen high-definition computer monitor was blank, and technicians scrambling everywhere. In the midst of it all was Jon Masters, wearing cut-off jeans and a flowered Hawaiian shirt, with his ever-present squeeze bottle of Pepsi in hand.

"Doctor Masters, what's happening . . . ?"

"We're finishing our checks, Brad," Masters replied. "It's no problem. We'll have the birds back on-line in no time."

"You mean we lost *both* of them . . . ?"

"It's only temporary . . ."

"Can you launch another one?" Stone asked. "Do you have a backup?"

Masters wore an uncomfortably pained expression. "Ahhh . . . I might have a problem there, Dick," Masters said. "I have the launch aircraft here, but I didn't bring a spare booster or payload. They're all back in Arkansas."

"Big deal. Fly back to Arkansas and launch another one," Stone snapped. "The EB-52s from HAWC will be here in less than fourteen hours, and the First Air Battle Wing will be here in less than eighteen . . ."

"You see, I got a problem back home," Masters said. "My

board of directors voted not to approve any more launches until our other contractual obligations are—"

"Doctor Masters, you have a contract with the United States Fucking Government!" Stone exploded. "I don't want excuses, I want your butt back on that plane of yours so we can get another satellite up there. Now you either get me one or I'll fry your ass."

"That's not necessary, General," Masters said, totally unperturbed. "I can have the satellite back up shortly. Not one NIRTSat has ever failed, and this will not be the first, I promise you. Now let me get back to work." He did not wait for a reply, but turned and left Stone with a drop-dead apoplectic look on his face.

Brigadier General Thomas Harbaugh, commander of the Strategic Air Command's Third Air Division, the headquarters responsible for all SAC's air operations in the Pacific, and the senior member of the Strategic Air Command's STRATFOR team for Pacific operations, had joined Stone in the command post. To Harbaugh, Stone said, "Tom, we just lost the NIRTSat system. Masters doesn't know when it'll be back up. I need some current intel of Mindanao, and I need it *now.*"

"I can call DIA and Space Command and get a KH-11 or LACROSSE satellite overflight," Harbaugh said, "and you should get the photos by the time your birds start arriving here."

"Hop on it," Stone said. "But I want to discuss aircraft overflights as well. Unless we get Masters' system on-line again, getting satellite imagery from Washington out here is too long for a naval battle. Besides, I want a few probes of the Chinese defenses. Let's go over the Air Battle Force plans for 'ferret' flights; I want several packages put together to hand to General Jarrel when his birds start arriving."

ELLSWORTH AIR FORCE BASE, SOUTH DAKOTA
TWO HOURS LATER

The officers in charge of each weapon squadron of the First Air Battle Wing were assembled in the Strategic Warfare Center briefing auditorium; the room was secured, the building closed down, and the doors guarded as the meeting began.

"Orders are as follows, ladies and gentlemen," General Jarrel began. "By order of the President, all elements of the First Air Battle Wing have been directed to deploy immediately to Andersen Air Force Base, Guam, and prepare for air operations under the direction of Pacific Air Forces and Pacific Command. Commander, First Air Battle Wing, will be myself, who will report to Major General Richard Stone, Chief, Strategic Forces deployed, Andersen Air Force Base, Guam, immediately upon arrival. Major General Stone becomes the overall Joint Task Force Commander effective immediately. First Air Battle Wing commander is dual-hatted as Joint Task Force Air Commander. The orders outline a few Marine Corps air units involved in the operation, along with naval air operations commanders. Rear Admiral Conner Walheim becomes Joint Naval Forces Commander. Joint Task Force Ground Forces Commander is Army Brigadier General Joseph Towle." Jarrel folded the message form and stuck it in a flight-suit pocket. "No other details were given in the message, but that's all we need to get going.

"I have distributed copies of the list of today's nonflying crews and airframes; it composes about half of the force located here at Ellsworth, including eight B-52s, four B-1s, ten KC-135s, two KC-10s, all twelve of our F-4Ds and Fs, ten F-15s, and six C-141s. That's about all Andersen can handle at one time anyway.

"Crew rest is hereby waived for these crew members. They will pick up pre-planned mission packages, brief, and prepare for departure within six hours." There was a rustle of surprise throughout the audience—they had planned and discussed a rapid deployment of a large number of aircraft such as this, but it had never been done before. "The bombers, KC-135 tankers, and some of the cargo aircraft will deploy nonstop to Andersen; the fighters and KC-10s will get crew rest at Hickam before proceeding.

"All bomber aircraft will be fully loaded in ferry configuration; you have the list of stores they will carry. Deploying to

Guam with weapons on board is always tricky because of the high fuel load needed for divert reserves, but we'll have lots of tankers to support us, so we will load the bombers to get as close to max landing weight as possible with normal IFR fuel reserves . . ."

"Why was this decided, sir?" one of the squadron commanders asked. "Andersen has weapons—why not load up on gas and supplies and upload the weapons once they arrive on Guam?"

"I want those bombers ready to fight the minute they arrive at Andersen," Jarrel replied. "My orders state that we are on combat alert as of right now, and the less time we spend getting ready for a mission after arriving on Guam, the more flexibility we'll have. We could be tasked for strike operations while the Wing is en route, so I want to be ready—our crews better be ready to get a few hours' sleep, mission plan, brief, pull the pins on the weapons, and go. If necessary, they will land, get their mission packets, pull the pins, do a hot refueling, and take off immediately.

"The remaining aircraft at Ellsworth will deploy after six hours' crew rest under the same system—bombers go direct with weapons in ferry configuration, fighters RON at Hickam. Our OPLAN specifies eighty percent of the First Air Battle Wing on the ramp at Andersen within twenty-four hours. I think we can do better: I think we can have eighty percent of the Wing flying in combat in twenty-four hours. That is my goal. I know this is our first actual combat deployment, and we're bound to be inventing procedures as we go along, but this staff has practiced these procedures now for several months, so I think we can do it. Questions?" No reply. "Next meeting in one hour; that should be our last meeting before we start launching planes. I expect the first group to be ready to go by then. Let's get to it, ladies and gentlemen—move!"

Jarrel watched as the members of the First Air Battle Wing rapidly filed out of the auditorium. He knew the danger these men and women were facing, and he didn't envy them. His own father had been killed in action in Korea in 1953, and he had flown over five hundred combat sorties as an F-5 and A-7 pilot during two tours in Vietnam. He'd seen a lot of battle, a lot of death.

No, he didn't envy them at all. But they had a job to do, just as he did. He turned and headed back to his office. "God be with them," he said to no one but himself.

TEN

There was no mistaking its identity or its purpose—few aircraft in the world could fly like this. "Identity confirmed, sir," the Combat Information Center officer on the Chinese People's Liberation Army Navy destroyer *Feylin* reported. "American subsonic spy plane, bearing zero-six-five, altitude two-three-thousand meters, range ninety-two kilometers and closing. Probably a U-2 or TR-1."

The commander of the *Feylin* shook his head in amazement. "Say speed and altitude again?"

"Speed six-five-zero kilometers per hour, altitude . . . altitude now twenty-three thousand meters."

The destroyer captain could do nothing but smile in astonishment. Twenty-three thousand meters—that was almost twice the altitude that any Chinese fighter could safely go, and very close to the upper-altitude limit of the Hong Qian-61 surface-to-air missile system on the Chinese frigates stationed in the Philippine Sea. "No response to our warning broadcasts, I assume," the captain said.

"None, sir. Continuing west as before, on course for Davao."

"Then we will make good on our promise," the captain said eagerly. "Have *Zhangyhum* and *Kaifeng* moved into position?"

"Yes, sir. Destroyer *Zunyi* ready as well."

"Very well. Let us see if we can get ourselves an American spy plane. Range to target?"

"Eighty-three kilometers and closing."

"Begin engagement procedures at seventy-five kilometers." The frigates had only the shorter-range HQ-61 SAM system, but four of the five destroyers in the Philippine Sea and eastern Celebes Sea area had the Hong Qian-91 surface-to-air missile, with four times the range of the HQ-61—and the U-2 was coming within range of *Feylin*'s system right now. Undoubtedly the U-2 would be able to evade the first missile, but two more destroyers, *Zhangyhum* to the north and *Kaifeng* to the south, were surrounding the U-2, so that no matter which way it turned, it would be within range of someone's missile system.

The U-2 was being tracked by another destroyer, *Zunyi*. This destroyer carried only surface-to-surface missiles, but it had the Sea Eagle radar system, which could direct missile attacks launched from other ships without using the telltale DRBR-51 missile-tracking radars. They would not have to activate target-tracking radars until a few seconds from impact, so the U-2 would have no chance to react.

They were going to make their first kill since October first, which, ironically, was Revolution Day. This would serve as a warning to all other American aircraft: stay away from the Philippines.

"Bomb doors coming open, stand by . . . bomb doors open."

This had to be the first time in Patrick McLanahan's recent memory that he was going to open the bomb doors on his B-2 Black Knight stealth bomber—and not attack something. He and Major Henry Cobb had already flown their B-2 nearly two thousand miles, right into the heart of what seemed like half the Chinese Navy, all to carry two bulbous objects that would not go "boom."

They were flying at two thousand feet over the dark waters of the Philippine Sea, threading the needle through what appeared to be two long lines of Chinese warships arranged north and south to protect the east coast of Mindanao. Twice now they had opened the dual side-by-side bomb-bay doors and deployed the two pods on their hydraulically operated arms, left them in the slipstream for a few minutes, then retracted them again. And they knew that with each passing minute, every time they lowered those pods they were exposing themselves to incredible danger that would only increase the closer they flew toward Mindanao.

The two pods were not weapons, but reconnaissance systems housed in aerodynamic pods that resembled a fighter's standard 330-gallon external fuel tanks. In the right bomb bay they had an ATARS pod, which stood for Advanced Tactical Air Reconnaissance System. It housed two electronic charge–coupled device reconnaissance cameras and an infrared line scanner to photograph large sections of the sea in all directions in just a few minutes. In another pod in the left bomb bay, on a longer hydraulic arm that would project it eighteen inches lower than the ATARS pod, was a UPD-9 synthetic aperture radar pod that would take high-resolution radar images for fifty miles in all directions. All of the images were digitized, then transmitted via NIRTSat back to Andersen for analysis. They also had their usual complement of radar warning receivers and countermeasures systems, but on this flight they used high-speed digital data links to transmit the threat information they received back to Andersen.

Although the pods were incredibly effective and relatively small, they had one major drawback—they had a radar signature thousands of times larger than the B-2 carrying them. Every time they were lowered out of the bomb bay, Cobb and McLanahan lost all their stealth capabilities—and it was time to do it again. "Stand by for pod deploy . . ."

Suddenly, a huge yellow dome appeared on McLanahan's Super Multi Function Display, not very far to the north of them—the dome nearly touched the B-2 icon, meaning they were very close to being within detection range of the radar. "Charlie-band radar . . . Sea Eagle air-search radar, either on a frigate or destroyer," McLanahan reported. "We may be inside detection range now—if we lower the pods, we'll definitely be in range."

"Then let's get it over with," Cobb said. It was one of the few words he had said throughout the entire flight—obviously he wished he were someplace else right now.

"Rog. Pods coming down . . ."

True to his word, the second the two pods were deployed, the computer re-evaluated their new radar cross-section, remeasured the Sea Eagle radar's output power, and redrew the radar's effective detection range "dome"—this time placing it squarely over the B-2 icon at the lower center part of the SMFD. The radar cross-section of the two pods was so large that Patrick estimated they'd have to fly at least forty miles to get out of enemy radar coverage. "Air-search radar got us, three o'clock, range . . . range forty miles."

As the UPD-9 pod finished its first circular sweep, more details of the area surrounding them appeared—including one very unwelcome one. "Surface target, nine o'clock, ten miles, no radar emissions, looks like a patrol boat . . . shit, we got another patrol boat at twelve miles, two o'clock position. Jesus, we're surrounded by Chinese patrol boats . . ." McLanahan commanded the pods to retract immediately before any one of them got a lock on the B-2.

"Air target warning! Bearing one-eight-eight degrees, range seventy-four kilometers . . . no speed or altitude reading available . . . search radar active . . ."

"What? Are you sure? Get a track on that last contact!" the skipper of the *Feylin* shouted.

"Negative track . . . target disappeared, sir. Lost contact."

The new radar contact puzzled the destroyer commander, but it was obviously an anomaly or a very small target, like a flock of birds. The real quarry was still driving closer. "Status of the U-2."

"Range approaching seventy-five kilometers . . . now."

"Very well. Combat, bridge, commit forward HQ-91 system, stand by on DRBR-51 missile-guidance radar . . . now. Order *Kaifeng* and *Zhangyhum* to prepare to engage."

At that order, two HQ-91 missiles were fired from the forward twin launchers of the destroyer *Feylin* at the U-2 spy plane, lighting up the deck with brilliant flashes of light and a long tongue of flame as the missiles shot skyward. The big supersonic missiles reached full speed in seconds, exceeding twenty-five kilometers per minute in the blink of an eye.

There was no other radar that came up, but even at a range of forty miles the sudden glare of the HQ-91 missile's rocket motor streaking off into space could clearly be seen. The Chinese patrols were going after the U-2 spy plane. The forty-year-old U-2 used a new aerial camera, the CA-990, which could take high-resolution pictures from long standoff distances, but to get pictures of Davao, the U-2 had to fly as close as possible to the Mindanao coast—very close to the Chinese warships.

McLanahan risked it: he deployed the reconnaissance pods again to get more photographs—and perhaps to divert the Chinese warship's attention away from the vulnerable U-2, although he realized that was a real long shot—and at the same time hit the "Transmit" switch on his scrambled command radio: "Kelly, this is Shadow, Giant Zero, Giant Zero. Out." "Giant Zero" was a standard code name to warn an aircraft of a missile launch without an associated missile-guidance radar appearing first. McLanahan let the pods out for two spherical radar scans, about fifteen seconds, then quickly retracted them once again . . .

But even as he did, the yellow dome surrounding them turned briefly to red, with riblike lines through it. "Sea Eagle radar switching to target acquisition mode . . . they may have found us. Pods retracted, bomb doors closed . . ."

Suddenly, more radar domes appeared north and south of the B-2. "Air-search radars from those patrol boats!" McLanahan shouted. He looked on in horror as the southernmost radar dome engulfed them, then changed from yellow to red. "Target-acquisition radar got us, bearing one-six-three, range eleven miles. No missile-tracking radars yet, but he might be radioing our position to his big sister out there. Henry, take us down to two hundred feet, and let's hope these bozos can't lock onto us. . . ."

"New radar contact aircraft, bearing from destroyer *Zunyi,* two-zero-zero, range seventy-four kilometers, speed nine-three-zero kilometers per hour, altitude six hundred meters."

Curse it! the skipper of the destroyer *Feylin* thought furiously. An aircraft somehow managed to sneak past their gauntlets. "Order all patrol boats to begin air search immediately . . ."

"Sir, target number one turning north, appears to be disengaging . . . altitude of target one increasing to twenty-four thousand meters, speed increasing to eight hundred."

"Activate DRBR-51 missile-tracking radars. Do not let the U-2 get away."

"Sir, patrol boat 124 reports radar contact on air target." The technicians at the vertical-plot board on the bridge of the destroyer *Feylin* drew in the location of the contact—it was between two patrol boats, heading northwest, near the Indonesian archipelago called Nenusa.

"Sir! Destroyer *Zhangyhum* reports radar contact north of his position, intermittent contact, low altitude. He suspects an American stealth aircraft."

That was it! Stealth aircraft, probably stealth bombers launched from Guam. Obviously they were on reconnaissance runs, because if they were carrying antiship missiles they would have sunk a half-dozen vessels by now. So . . . a U-2 *and* a stealth bomber . . .

"Alert all task force vessels, inbound stealth bombers, suspect at least two inbound toward Davao Gulf. No weapons fired at outer gauntlet vessels, but suspect an attack against inner defenses. Warn all patrol aircraft to search the area north and northwest of Nenusa Archipelago for low-altitude bombers."

"Sir! Destroyer *Zhangyhum* reports engaging with HQ-91 missiles . . . they may have hit the U-2. Dispatching a frigate and patrol boat to investigate."

"One down," the destroyer commander said with a quiet smile—"two more to go. . . ."

"Mayday, Mayday, Kelly is hit, heading east, no—" The radio transmission from the U-2 went dead.

"Fuck," was all Cobb could say. "Patrick, let's get out of here."

"Few more seconds and we should get all the ships near Davao Gulf," McLanahan replied. They had flown over a hundred miles farther west than they had planned, within thirty miles of the mouth of Davao Gulf itself. The closer they got to Mindanao, the more ships they saw—ranging in size from huge destroyers, frigates, and amphibious assault craft, to small liaison and patrol craft—even a return that the UPD-9 pod classified as a submarine periscope could be seen.

One more radar sweep, two minutes, and they had all the data they needed. As Cobb began a turn south to head toward the relative safety of the radar clutter around the Nenusa and Talaud islands, the Super Multi Function Display seemed to light up like an old-style switchboard, with radar domes popping up everywhere. It was as if every vessel with a transmitter had flipped it on. "Christ almighty . . . Charlie-band search radar at our twelve o'clock . . . another one at our two o'clock . . . now I've got X-band fire-control radars at our ten o'clock position. You're going to have to take us right over Talaud Island, Henry. We're surrounded."

"Fuck," Cobb muttered. On this trip, that seemed to be the veteran pilot's favorite reply.

"Fifty miles to Talaud," McLanahan said. With the reconnaissance pods stowed, the radar dome belonging to the vessel to the northeast no longer reached them, but they could still watch it as it changed modes. It had changed from target acquisition mode, to air search, and now back to rapid-scan air search, which was displayed as a yellow-striped dome now. "Fast PRF scan on that Charlie-band radar," McLanahan reported. "They might be vectoring a fighter in."

"Fuck . . ."

The miles seemed to crawl by. More ships had their search radars on to the west, well inside Indonesian waters but still broadcasting Chinese radar signals. A few vessels even activated fire-control radars—Patrick guessed they might have been mistakenly fired on by their own fighter! "Twenty miles. Nenusa Archipelago is on the left, Talaud is right of—"

Suddenly a yellow radar dome appeared right in front of the B-2 icon on the SMFD. The dome instantly turned red, and the two crewmen could see gunfire popping on the horizon directly in front of them. "Break right!" Patrick shouted as he hammered the "Chaff" button for the left ejector racks; the electronic countermeasures jammers activated automatically. "Descend!" Cobb threw the big bomber into a 45-degree bank turn, letting the sudden loss of lift over the wings pull the nose down. He rolled wings-level at one hundred feet above the sea—just one wingspan above the dark waters below. Patrick could see tracers lashing out into the darkness, firing at the chaff blob that he had just released. "Where the hell did *he* come from?"

"Fuck . . ."

The terrain-following computer began to command a climb to clear the tall, spirelike mountains ahead, and the two crewmen could start to see the island on the forward-looking infrared scanner. The largest island in the Talaud archipelago, Karakelong Island, was a lush green island with gently rolling hills through the middle, but the central hills were studded with two tall rock spires, one that towered seven hundred feet above the forest and the other that rose an incredible twelve hundred feet above the ridge.

The tracers swung farther to the west as the chaff blob cleared and the Chinese patrol boat reacquired the B-2. "Can't go too much farther west," Patrick said. "There's another group of ships just forty miles west of this island."

"They were waiting for someone to try to sneak in over these hills," Cobb said. "They knew we'd try it, even though these islands are in Indonesia. That means—"

"Shit. That means we don't want to fly over these islands . . . !"

As if someone on Karakelong Island heard him, just then on the infrared scanner they could see a sharp flare of light, and a missile arced skyward, then heeled over and headed straight for them. "I see it!" Cobb cried out. "Stand by on flares right!" They had a little room to try a hard break, so Cobb began pushing and pulling the control stick, beginning a fifty-to-one-hundred-foot vertical oscillation. The closer the missile got, the more they could see it mimicking that oscillation.

As soon as the motor on the missile winked out, Cobb yelled, *"Now!"* then threw the B-2 into a hard turn to the left. Simultaneously, Patrick pumped out flares from the right ejector, keeping his finger on the button.

The missile passed directly over the cockpit, missing the Black Knight by just a few scant yards. Luckily, there was no explosion—either the missile failed to fuze or was still locked on the flare decoys.

"Altitude!" Patrick shouted. "Climb!" The bomber had entered initial buffet to a stall in the steep turn and had lost precious altitude—the radar altimeter, which measured exact distance below the bomber's belly, was faulted because the distance was less than fifty feet. Cobb rolled wings-level, let the airspeed build up, then gently pulled back on the sidestick controller, careful not to throw the bomber into a full stall by pulling back too fast.

"Screw this," Cobb muttered. As soon as he had his airspeed back, he pulled back on the controller, starting a steep climb. "I'm getting out of here."

The Super Multi Function Display was alive with radar domes—one was right ahead of them, a Sea Eagle search radar was highlighting them from the right, and far to the north another Sea Eagle radar was about to envelop them. "Descend, Henry, we've got radars all around us . . ."

"Let 'em try to get us," Cobb said.

Tracers lit up the sky ahead of them as they drove through the red-colored radar dome ahead of them. Cobb kept the bomber climbing at full military power—the nose was higher than Patrick could ever remember it as Cobb traded every knot of available airspeed for altitude. He made a few hard turns, no more than 20 degrees at a time. Antiaircraft artillery shells began exploding all around them, and several were close enough to pummel the B-2. "Airspeed, Henry!" Patrick shouted. "Watch the stall . . . !"

But Cobb held the nose up, kept the airspeed right on the edge of initial buffet to stall, and kept the climb going. Moments later, Patrick noticed that the shells were exploding well below them. As he looked down, he could see a blanket of fireworks below them as tracers and exploding shells lit up the night sky. Cobb began to decrease his climb rate at twenty thousand feet, but he kept the throttle in full military power and kept climbing at five thousand feet per minute until they passed forty thousand feet. The destroyer to the south of them tried one missile launch on them, but the B-2's jammers and laser countermeasures system reported that the missile never approached within lethal range. As they climbed, the red radar dome shrunk until it was a tiny inverted teacup well behind them.

Patrick looked over at his aircraft commander. Cobb had returned to his typical flying position—oxygen mask on, hands on stick and throttles, staring straight ahead, unmoving as a rock. Patrick turned the cockpit lights up a bit so he could do a careful cockpit check to investigate for damage—except for a few popped circuit breakers, he found nothing.

As he swept his tiny red-lens flashlight across his partner, he could see that the only evidence there was that Henry Cobb had just saved their butts from crashing in a huge fireball in the Philippine Sea was a tiny trickle of sweat dripping from the edge of his oxygen mask. But save them he did.

"Cabin check complete," Patrick reported. Then: "Thanks, Henry." The only acknowledgment he got was two clicks on the interphone button.

OFFICE OF THE NATIONAL SECURITY ADVISOR,
THE WHITE HOUSE
FRIDAY, 7 OCTOBER 1994, 1005 HOURS LOCAL

"We had better start talking about a peaceful settlement to all this, Mr. Ambassador," Secretary of State Dennis Danahall said, "or things will surely go out of control."

The Deputy Chargé d'affaires of the People's Republic of China's embassy, Tang Shou Dian, serenely folded his hands on his lap as he regarded the three American government officials before him: Secretary of State Danahall, National Security Advisor Kellogg, and the President's Chief of Staff, Paul Cesare, along with interpreters and confidential secretaries. The ambassador had brought an assistant and interpreter as well; because the ambassador's "assistant" was a known Chinese intelligence operative, Secret Service agents were posted outside the office and in the anteroom to Kellogg's office.

"I would be pleased to promptly report any requests or proposals to my government, Mr. Danahall," Tang said without his interpreter. The interpreter would bend forward and speak in Tang's assistant's ear as if she were translating for him, but everyone knew he spoke and understood English very well.

"These are not proposals or requests, Mr. Ambassador," Frank Kellogg said. "These are statements of policy. The United States will regard any further aggressive acts on the island of Mindanao as hostile acts against the United States, and we will respond accordingly to counter the threat, including the use of military force. That is the message we want to convey to your government."

"That message was made very clear by your President's television announcement yesterday," Tang said. "As we indicated in our response, the Teguina government has stated that José Samar has no authority to conduct foreign policy or dictate military terms anywhere in the Philippines, including Mindanao or the separate southern state. Therefore, Samar's words have no meaning and your position is illegal and completely without merit."

"The Philippine constitution granted Samar's state the right of self-defense," Danahall pointed out. "Samar is completely within his powers to delegate that responsibility."

"That is a matter for the United Nations to decide," Tang said. "They should be allowed to deliberate the matter."

"We agree," Danahall said. "But the survival of the autonomous government of José Samar is in the best interest of the United States, and the position and strength of Chinese forces threaten their survival. Will the Chinese military agree to cease all hostile actions and pull its forces back until the matter of Mindanao sovereignty is decided?"

"I think that would be an important consideration," Tang said, "except for José Samar's rebel forces. President Teguina maintains, and my government agrees, that a cease-fire will only allow the rebels to consolidate their position and stage more and deadlier attacks on innocent citizens. We have tried to negotiate with Samar, with no success—we have even sent envoys to Guam to attempt to talk with Samar there. He will not speak with us. He ties our hands . . ."

"Your military forces are much more powerful than his," Kellogg observed. "You have nearly a hundred warships in the south Philippines alone; your forces outnumber his ten to one. It's reasonable to assume he's afraid of being crushed to death by the sheer size of your forces."

"A cease-fire has to be made in the spirit of cooperation and fairness," Tang said. "We will hold our present positions and stop all new troop additions if Samar agrees to withdraw his forces and come to the bargaining table."

"You must withdraw your forces from the Philippines first . . ."

"We are in the Philippines by *invitation* of the legitimate President," Tang said calmly. "We need not deal with rebel leaders such as Samar, or for that matter with the American government . . ."

"Samar is also a member of the Philippine government," Danahall said pointedly.

"I understand Samar has been brought up on charges of treason and corruption by the government," Tang said. "He has been stripped of his authority until his trial—*if* he ever surrenders himself to justice . . ."

"The United States does not recognize the Teguina government, because we have no evidence that President Arturo Mikaso is dead," Cesare said. Tang shifted his interlaced hands slightly, as if gesturing that, yes, Mikaso was really dead. "Can you confirm Mikaso's present situation? Is he dead?"

"I cannot confirm that, sir . . ."

"If you cannot confirm it, we will not recognize Teguina's

presidency," Danahall said. "In which case the constitution is still valid and Samar has equal power and authority as Te-guina . . ."

"Samar appears to be fleeing from justice—he is acting like a common criminal," Tang said. "He is hiding in the jungles, he refuses to speak with his own government, he is inciting the people to revolt. Stories I have heard say that he has the backing of several Islamic terrorist organizations to help him win the presidency by violence. How can the United States back such a man?"

Those rumors about the terrorist groups, unfortunately, were true—several Moslem terrorist groups had pledged themselves to Samar to help him overthrow the Chinese, the Americans, and the Manila government. It was a major source of embarrassment for President Taylor right now. But Dana-hall replied, "Samar is understandably in fear for his life, especially with Chinese troops in Manila. He is not in hiding; he is en route to Guam under the protection of the U.S. government until this matter can be resolved.

"I think the best option right now is for all foreign troops to get out of the Philippines and leave that government to itself. If we can have reasonable assurances that the will of the people is being done and that peace is being restored, then we will not object to any further Chinese incursions. But the United States regards the current level of Chinese military involvement as an invasion, and we are now in a position to stop it. Will the Chinese pull out of the Philippines?"

Tang made a few notes in a small notebook. "I will deliver your query to my government," the ambassador said, "along with your earlier statements and concerns." Tang then closed his notebook, as if signaling an end to their meeting; it had lasted only a few minutes.

"Have you any messages from your government, Mr. Ambassador?" Secretary Danahall asked. "Does your government simply request that the world allow you to occupy the Philippines with large military forces? Or do you want nothing more than to be a willing mercenary for Daniel Teguina's first coup?"

"We are not seeking conquest, only stability for my country," Tang said. "We see the unrest in the Philippines as extremely injurious to Chinese trade, foreign relations, and social and political stability in our own country. As you know, gentlemen, the Philippines has many ethnic Chinese in its population, as well as loyal supporters of the world socialist movement, all of whom have suffered in past years. If we fail to support Communist leaders overseas and allow those with common beliefs and heritage to be slain and dominated by others, how would my government appear in the eyes of its own people?"

Danahall, Cesare, and Kellogg refrained from replying or voicing their outrage at Tang's flamboyant, rhetorical remarks. Finally, after all these weeks of waiting, all these days of threats of military conflict, the Chinese were going to get around to their demands—it would not be useful at this point to interrupt, no matter how offbeat or disagreeable his words were.

"We are also very concerned about other problems in the South China Sea region, namely the dispute over the Spratly Islands and Palawan. China has claimed possession of those islands for hundreds of years; we feel we have the right to develop those islands, *all* of those islands, as we see fit. The current inequitable division of the Spratly Islands will no doubt cause much bloodshed in the future.

"The Philippine island of Palawan also once belonged to China, as evidenced by the large number of ethnic Chinese living there." Tang paused knowingly, making eye contact with the Americans before him, and said, "If Chinese claims to the Spratly Islands and Palawan could be resolved in a way favorable to all concerned, perhaps a way might be found to avert disaster and bloodshed."

So that was it, Danahall thought: China wanted the Spratly Islands and Palawan.

Danahall and his staff had had to do some serious cramming in recent days to reacquaint themselves with those two island chains that China seemed ready to go to war over. And, historically, Tang was right—several hundred years ago, before European explorers ventured to the Orient in large numbers, Chinese merchantmen, fishermen, and refugees did populate most of the islands in the South China Sea, including the Spratlys and most of the Philippines. Like the Spratlys, Palawan had been occupied and claimed by many Asian, Polynesian, and European nations over the centuries. At least a dozen countries had claims for these rugged, dangerous islands.

But all that was rather ancient history. China might have a fairly solid claim to the Spratly Islands—which they had already reportedly traded to Vietnam, at least for the time being—but whether they had any modern claim to Palawan was another thing entirely. What possible use China had for Palawan was a mystery to Danahall. The island was mountainous, sparsely populated, and useless as a shipping or trading port because of its proximity to the "Dangerous Ground," the shallow waters of the South China Sea, so hazardous to commercial freighters. It might make a strategic air-base location from which to threaten islands and waters belonging to other ASEAN countries, but even that was doubtful. Was this some sort of new manifest destiny for China—or a cover for something else . . . ?

"I think negotiations over these two areas of concern are important and can be implemented immediately, Mr. Ambassador," Secretary Danahall said. "Of course, other affected nations will have to participate—and an immediate cessation of all hostilities must be declared . . ."

"If that can include Samar and his Moslem rebel militia, I agree wholeheartedly, Mr. Secretary," Tang replied.

"I think we can be helpful in securing Vice President Samar's cooperation," Frank Kellogg said, "but it would be a waste of time to try to begin negotiations without first calling for an immediate cease-fire and a pullback of all forces . . ."

"If we can receive assurances that your naval and air forces will not try to fortify or assist the Samar rebels, and promise not to attack any Chinese forces at any time, a cease-fire might be possible. But it would be supercilious for us to abandon our agreement with President Teguina and simply leave him alone and unprotected without first guaranteeing that his government will remain intact during our negotiations. Now, if Samar's rebel forces would give up their hold on the city of

Davao and the Samar International Airport, perhaps my government would be more amenable to encouraging a dialogue with the Philippine government."

This time all the Americans paused. They were afraid this might happen. Promising not to attack Chinese forces was no problem—the President didn't want to do it in any case—but they knew that Davao was the last pin keeping the Philippines from falling apart. If Samar's people abandoned the city, the Philippines would fall forever—if not to the Chinese, then to Teguina's Communists. Samar might be a Moslem, but he also believed in a unified Philippines. It was obvious that Teguina believed in nothing but himself and his power. Tang was asking assistance from the U.S. government to destroy the last obstruction to total domination by the Communists.

"I think that discussion can wait for more detailed negotiations between our representatives," Danahall said—he didn't want to encourage him with even a veiled "maybe," but he didn't want to indicate that it was out of the question, either. "We're getting ahead of ourselves here. Let's get our respective governments to agree on an immediate cease-fire first . . ."

But Tang recognized Danahall's hesitation and had obviously concluded that the Americans would agree to nothing here. "Why do you support this Moslem Samar?" Tang asked. "He is nothing but a rabble-rouser. He is a definite hindrance to peace, Mr. Secretary. He is not deserving of your country's support."

"We support a peaceful solution to this crisis, Mr. Ambassador . . ."

"I truly hope so, Mr. Secretary," Tang said. "It appears to my government, however, that the United States wishes to regain its lost military dominance in the Philippines. You are aligning yourself with a traitor and criminal, blinding your citizens to Samar's violent and revolutionary past, in an obvious attempt to gain some sort of legitimacy for a military invasion of your own. That is not the way to solve this crisis, sir."

"There are those who feel that China is trying to exert its influence in the region by the use of force," Kellogg said, "and that you will stop at nothing to achieve it. They fear China may use *another* nuclear weapon to obliterate Samar's militia . . ."

Tang bristled at the mention of the word "nuclear," and the Americans knew that the meeting was at an end. He rose to his feet, his hands still folded before him; his face was just as impassive and expressionless as ever. "I believe we have discussed all pertinent topics. With your permission, we will deliver your messages to my government with all speed."

"Include this message, Mr. Ambassador," Danahall said coldly. "If the United States detects *any* further activity in the Davao Gulf or on Mindanao to suggest that Chinese troops are moving to take the city of Davao, its airport, or the towns around the northern part of the Davao Gulf or delta, the United States will consider that a hostile act against an ally and will respond appropriately." Danahall and the others rose. "Good day, Mr. Ambassador." Danahall kept his fingertips on the table, without extending a hand. Tang gave a short bow, as did his interpreter and assistant, and they departed.

"God, I must be getting old," Danahall said. He dropped into a chair, letting Kellogg take his desk back. "I can't sell it like I used to."

Kellogg's outer office phone buzzed. "Yes?"

"Staff meeting in five minutes, sir," his secretary said. Kellogg acknowledged the call and hung up. The message was a simple code to let them all know that the Secret Service wanted to come in to sweep the office, hallways, and anterooms for newly planted listening devices before the men began talking about anything of substance.

"I wanted to avoid giving the man a damned ultimatum, and that's exactly what I ended up giving him," Danahall said. "Dumb . . ."

"I'm sorry I mentioned the 'N' word," Kellogg said. "I guess I'll never make much of a diplomat."

"We're all thinking about it, and he knew it. It had to come out sooner or later." Danahall paused, then said, "But I think he did leave us a few cracks we can explore—not very big cracks, but at least it's something to work on."

"I hope something happens in the next twenty-four hours," Kellogg said grimly as they stood to allow the Secret Service to begin their work, "because otherwise I think the diplomatic side has just run its course."

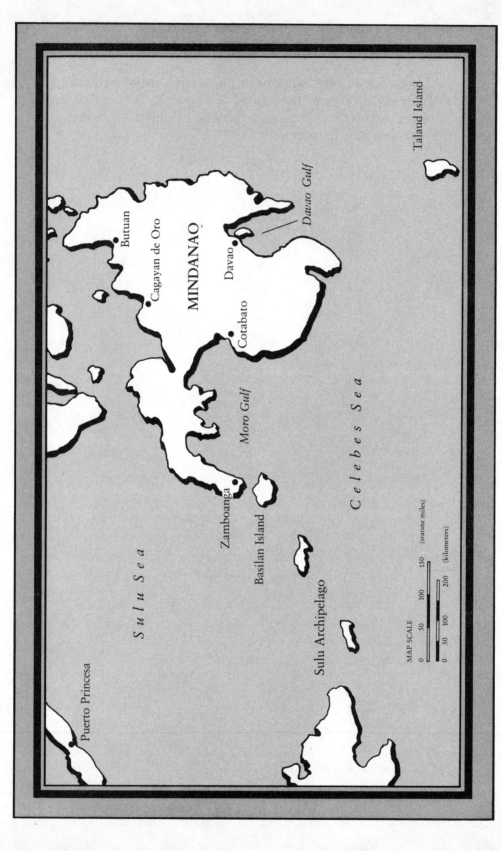

ELEVEN

Duty aboard the Chinese Liberation Army Navy destroyer *Hong Lung* for the day watch and flag staff began at five A.M. with reveille shortly before sunrise, prayers for those who were so inclined (Admiral Yin Po L'un, and therefore most of his flag staff, were not), a thirty-minute exercise period, cleanup, and breakfast, which usually consisted of chicken or fish soup, rice, tea, and hard candy or caramel squares for the enlisted men. Morning inspection began at six-fifteen, and the reports from each section aboard ship were received by the captain by ten minutes to seven. By seven A.M. the executive officers of each ship of the fleet escorting the *Hong Lung* reported to the Admiral's chief of operations, as did the group commanders from the three other naval battle groups in the southern Philippines; Yin's chief of operations then compiled the morning report for the Admiral for presentation precisely at seven-fifteen.

The Admiral first received a synopsis of incoming-message-traffic from Beijing or South China Sea fleet headquarters in Zhanjiang (important messages would of course have received his immediate attention), then a theater situation briefing and intelligence briefing. Yin's chief of operations, Captain Sun Ji Guoming, bowed deeply as he began: "Sir, I am pleased to provide you with the following theater briefing summary at this time, updated as of five A.M. local time:

"The primary threat to People's Liberation Army Navy's forces involved in the Philippines conflict currently is the United States Navy's aircraft carrier *Independence* battle group from Japan operating in the Luzon Strait, the U.S. Army Twenty-fifth Infantry Division deployed to Guam, elements of the U.S. Marine Corps Third Marine Amphibious Force mobilized on Okinawa and deployed with the *Independence* carrier battle group, and the deployment of the Air Force First Air Battle Wing to Andersen Air Force Base on Guam. It is important to point out that these all represent partial deployments of each unit, with approximately thirty to forty percent held in reserve at their home bases.

"Major elements of the U.S. Army's Twenty-fifth Infantry Division were recently relocated to Andersen Air Force Base from Hawaii, with approximately eight thousand troops. It is designed to be a light, quickly deployable force. Our intelligence estimates state, however, that insufficient air or sealift capability exists to move this force from Guam to the Philippines with any speed. However, if they did move this force, we would oppose them with twice the number of infantry troops already in place on Mindanao and four times the number on Luzon and other areas of the Philippines. Elements of the Second Infantry Division in South Korea and Japan have also been mobilized, but we estimate they are still several days from being called into action and at least a week after that to see action in the Philippines.

"The Third Marine Division and elements of the First Marine Aircraft Wing have been deployed with the *Independence* carrier battle group, which is now stationed offshore approximately sixty kilometers northeast of Y'ami Island in the Luzon Strait; this is approximately three hundred and fifty kilometers north of the Philippines. In our estimation, the carrier battle group is not in position to strike into Luzon at this time, although they can be in position to strike with their aircraft within twenty-four hours and in position to begin ground operations on Luzon within forty-eight to seventy-two hours; this is what is currently driving our threat condition status throughout the People's Liberation Army. The total American naval force includes approximately sixteen warships, ten support ships, four to six submarines—perhaps more, the exact number is uncertain—twenty fighter aircraft, and fifty fixed-wing strike aircraft.

"The Fifth Marine Pre-positioning Force from Hawaii has been activated and is deployed in the Philippine Sea with approximately five thousand Marines and forty helicopters, including the MV-22 tilt-rotor transport aircraft that was apparently used in the rescue of Samar and the American pilot on Mindanao. This force can strike in the central Philippines within twenty-four to forty-eight hours' notice as well. This force includes two landing-ship carriers, four tank-landing carriers, and four support vessels.

"The greatest naval threat to our forces in the southern Philippines was the *Ranger* carrier battle group," Sun continued. "The carrier itself is still heavily damaged and considered out of commission; it is being towed to Pearl Harbor, Hawaii, and except for vertical takeoff and landing aircraft is unable to conduct any flight operations."

A rustle of approving voices filled the conference room.

"However, the latest report has shown that a destroyer and a guided-missile cruiser from the *Ranger* group are en route to the Celebes from Indonesia and will be within missile range of some of our ships within the next four to five hours. They are being joined by a six-ship surface action group led by the battleship *Wisconsin,* en route from Hawaii, which our estimates say will be in position to attack in three to five days; these groups carry land-attack Tomahawk cruise missiles. Our embassy has received word that the *Ranger*'s support ships intend to conduct search and rescue operations for their downed crew members lost in the air battle last week—"

"They will not be permitted to enter the Celebes Sea," Admiral Yin said solemnly. "That I can promise. When Davao has been taken, Group One and Group Two will form to oppose these task forces until additional forces arrive from the mainland."

"Yes, sir," Sun continued. "This leaves the greatest threat to the southern Philippines task force, in the estimation of our intelligence section: the American Air Force. The First Air Battle Wing currently deployed on Guam reportedly has two dozen B-52 heavy bombers, perhaps eight long-range supersonic B-1 and F-111 bombers, nearly a dozen medium-range F-15 supersonic bombers, two dozen F-15 and F-16 fighter escorts, and various support aircraft, including reconnaissance, early warning, intelligence, and aerial refueling aircraft. Unverified reports from our patrols in the Philippine Sea say that the Americans might have sent B-2s as well.

"This force can strike within three hours with enough stand-off weaponry to devastate large sections of our deployed battle groups. They have been flying reconnaissance flights as far west as Talaud Island, within radar range of our warships outside Davao Gulf. One U-2 spy plane was shot down last night by the destroyer *Zhangyhum:* we estimate the U-2 was able to get pictures of our vessels in Davao Gulf itself."

"It does not sound like much of a threat to me, Captain," Admiral Yin said. "Only thirty-two long-range strike aircraft, most of which are over forty years old? I see no substantial threat."

"Their medium-range bombers and fighters are also a threat because of their aerial-refueling capability, sir," Captain Sun replied. "And we should not underestimate the payload capability of the B-52. Fully armed, they can carry twenty-four Harpoon antiship missiles, which can strike from as far as one hundred and fifty kilometers—"

"Yes, the heavy bombers are a threat, Captain," Admiral Yin said, "but once we secure Davao Airport, we can launch *twenty* fighters for every *one* of their bombers. The odds are clearly in our favor. The closest American air base on Okinawa is almost sixteen hundred kilometers from Manila, and the American air base on Guam is over two thousand kilometers from Davao. Even if the Americans were granted permission to use the British air base at Bandar Seri Begawan in Brunei, that is still eight hundred kilometers to Zamboanga and twelve hundred kilometers to Davao—plenty of time to organize our air, ground, and surface defenses. Once reliable radar early-warning networks are established around the Philippines, no American planes would be able to approach any Chinese positions without being detected. . . .

"The key, however, is our impending attack on Davao. What is the status of our forces and the status of our operation against Davao?" Yin asked.

"The Admiral's headquarters fleet afloat reports fully operational," Captain Sun replied. "All vessels report fully manned, ready, and combat-capable, with no operational defects.

"The schedule briefed yesterday is still valid, sir," Captain Sun continued. "At two A.M. tomorrow morning, Marine paratroopers will land on the coast outside the city of Davao and secure the Subasta and Sibuyan highways. Other Marine units will take Talikud Island and seal off the coastal towns of Samal and Bangoy on Samal Island. This will allow the minesweepers to enter Dadaotan Bay ahead of the destroyers and landing craft transports, without fear of attack in the narrow channel."

That was the same objective during the invasion of Zamboanga, when the heavily populated Santa Cruz Channel had to be sanitized before Yin's fleet could take up positions, except then they had more air power flying from Puerto Princesa and the element of surprise. That was gone now—unlike Zamboanga, Davao was ready for a siege.

Many things were different between Davao and the relatively easy siege of Zamboanga. Davao was the heart of the Samar government and the capital of the autonomous pro-Islamic government on Mindanao. Few officials and residents here were from Luzon—although Davao had as much natural beauty as Zamboanga and was the largest city on Mindanao, with a population of over seventy-five thousand, it was considered an isolated, remote, untamed frontier town and never gained the popularity of its more contemporary sister city to the west. Davao had no large military base, so there was no large-scale government facility from which to stage a "popular revolt." Nevertheless, Yin was determined to see Davao fall.

"By five A.M. the destroyers should be in place, and the LSTs will begin deploying landing craft," Sun continued. "The Air Force will move in to soften the beach area, and the destroyers with their escorts and shallow-draft patrol craft will secure the bay and harbors and provide gun support for the landing craft. The landing should begin at six A.M. and should be complete by eleven. Sometime tomorrow afternoon, perhaps earlier, Samar International Airport will be ours.

"The Air Force will continue to patrol the area, especially the six private airstrips within fifty kilometers of Samar International—these are known marshaling areas and resupply points for the Samar militia. Army troops should have these areas secured by day after tomorrow, along with the Cadeco River valley. General Yuhan's forces should have also secured the radar site on Mount Apo and the Cagayan Highway to the north. With the Mount Apo radar site, we can scan the region for almost five hundred kilometers in all directions—we can detect a flock of birds or a group of whales approaching the Philippines.

"Once this is accomplished, Group One can begin patrols of the east Celebes Sea and provide escorts for supply vessels entering Davao Gulf. Group Three can begin resupply sorties to Davao via sealift until the Davao-Cotaban Highway is secure or until the area around Samar International Airport is secure and we can begin airlifting in supplies. We have no firm timetable on this as of yet, however. Our best option is to secure the sea-lanes for resupply until substantial numbers of troops are in place on Mindanao—it may take as long as a month.

"We can reasonably expect the fall of Davao to split the rebel forces into at least three separate groups, located roughly on the east coast, the southern coast, and the north-central parts of Mindanao," Sun concluded. "This will reduce their ability to fight and dramatically disrupt their own resupply chain. We will force them into more and more austere conditions and reduce their ability to fight."

Yin nodded thoughtfully. He was impressed with Sun's briefing. If Sun had started briefing tactics and weapons, Yin would have been upset and concerned. Tactics and weapons did not win invasion campaigns—logistics won invasions. Everything his fleet and ground troops did ultimately had to open and secure supply lines or the invasion was doomed to failure. They were going to pour thousands of men and millions of tons of warships into Davao just to be able to land a few cargo aircraft at the airport or dock a supply ship in the harbor. Sun's briefing emphasized resupply—that was the way it should be. If the supply lines were cut, he was doomed.

"Excellent, Captain Sun," Admiral Yin said, bowing from the neck. "I congratulate you and your staff for a well-organized plan, and I wish us all success. Now tell me about areas in which we are weakest."

"I see two areas of concern for this operation, sir," Captain Sun replied. "Both relate to the remote possibility of counter-attack from American or ASEAN forces.

"First, our close air support and fighter aircraft must launch from Zamboanga Airport—Cotabato Airport is still not secure enough for aircraft operations because of rebel activity. This means our fighters must fly four hundred kilometers one-way to reach Davao Gulf, and almost six hundred kilometers to intercept bombers carrying antiship missiles capable of hitting our warships in Davao Gulf. With the return trip and combat reserves, this leaves almost no loiter time for all our aircraft."

"Why was a plan not developed to secure the airport at Cotabato?" Yin asked angrily. "It was a major part of our invasion operation. You had several days and plenty of support, Captain—why am I now being told it is not safe to use this airport?"

"Sir, as I mentioned before to you, we depleted the reserve forces of Group Two to dangerous levels during the assault on Cotabato," Sun replied. "As you know, we had to abandon our patrols of most of the Sulu Archipelago and create the hundred-kilometer safe zone around Zamboanga to form the invasion fleet for the Cotabato operation. It was barely enough for the job. We have taken the airport at Cotabato, but the staff and I agree that it is not wise to count on using it for the Davao operation. It is suitable as a landing base, and our aircraft recovering there can be refueled, but . . ."

"Can we not rearm our fighters and attack planes there as well?"

Sun shook his head reluctantly. "We deemed it too dangerous to ship massive amounts of rockets, bombs, and missiles to Cotabato, sir," he replied. "Fuel trucks and bladders make poor targets for guerrillas with mortars or RPGs, but bomb dumps or parked cargo aircraft make convenient and inviting targets. Guerrilla attacks are too frequent . . ."

"Curse you, I should have been advised of all this sooner!" Yin exploded. He waved his hand irritably at Sun. "Continue, Captain. What other difficulties do you envision?"

Sun swallowed hard before continuing: he had previously briefed Admiral Yin on the problems with air cover if Cotabato was not secured, and now he was being blamed for not telling him; he had also briefed Yin on the next topic, and it appeared likely that Yin was going to forget about being advised of this as well.

"Sir, with the destroyers moving to the north Davao Gulf and their escorts taking their positions to support the landing, we have decreased our air coverage of the eastern Celebes Sea to a dangerous level," Sun said.

"What air attacks are you concerned about, Captain?" Yin asked. "The American aircraft carrier is out of position, it cannot launch its strike aircraft, and no other carriers are within range . . ."

"The land-based bombers are our biggest threat, sir," Sun replied. "The American Air Battle Force has been on the island of Guam ready to strike . . ."

"The Americans will not use the heavy bombers against us," Yin said. "Our intelligence reports stated that the American President did not even want those bombers there. Besides, you reported that the Americans had only a handful of bombers there, less than thirty—is that not so . . . ?"

"The count is accurate, sir," Sun acknowledged, "but each can carry a number of Harpoon antiship missiles and bombs . . ."

"They have to get close enough to use them first," Yin snapped. "Even one of our small patrol boats can destroy a Harpoon missile in flight. And the closer those bombers come to Davao during the invasion, the more effective our antiaircraft guns become."

Sun paused momentarily. Yin seemed to have an answer for

everything. Sun did not dispute his commander's thoughts, but he was being extraordinarily confident of his own fleet's power and recklessly unconcerned about the American Air Force's power. "I agree with you, sir," Sun said slowly, "but I think it would be wise to augment our air-defense preparations by moving the *Hong Lung* and some of its antiair-equipped escorts to the eastern Celebes Sea area. That would give us four ships with surface-to-air missiles and four more ships with large-caliber radar-guided antiaircraft guns. Zamboanga is secure—our presence is not needed here."

Yin thought about the suggestion, and he liked it—Sun would make a fine fleet commander one day. The *Hong Lung* was one of the most powerful ships in the world, well suited for both antiair as well as antiship operations. It was also a very potent weapon for simple show-of-force, but since Yin liked to keep his warships mostly out of sight of the local population, it wasn't doing much good as a weapon of intimidation in Zamboanga. His shore setups here were in place and operating well—it was time the *Hong Lung,* the Red Dragon, got back into the fight.

"An excellent suggestion, Captain," Yin said. "I want one vessel to remain here, positioned so residents of the city can see it clearly; the rest of the Fleet Master will accompany the *Hong Lung* to the battle area. Choose your escorts and alert the fleet: we sail immediately for the eastern Celebes Sea."

Sun looked much more pleased—it was obvious he disagreed with Yin's estimation of the American air threat—and he bowed to acknowledge the order. "If there is nothing else, publish the orders and proceed." His flag staff stood, bowed, and exited the office.

Yin was alone in his office for several minutes when his executive officer knocked. "Sir, you have a visitor: Philippine President Daniel Teguina. He is requesting a short meeting with you in private."

Yin had to struggle to maintain his composure. What in hell does Teguina want with *me . . . ?* Since the coup, Teguina had dealt exclusively with the People's Liberation Army Supreme Commander, High General Chin Po Zihong, on any military matters; otherwise he dealt with Dong Sen Kim, the ambassador to the Philippines, or to the Foreign Minister directly. Just a few weeks earlier, Teguina would have gladly kissed Yin's feet if he had helped him with his coup—now that the coup was completed, Teguina was actually starting to believe the myth about China just assisting Teguina to defeat the "rebels" and save his country.

"Tell him I'm too . . . never mind. I'll meet him. Have this room cleaned and coffee and pastries served . . . and put his flags back, too, his stupid Aguinaldo flag and the Sulu flag. And make sure our conversation is recorded and the video cameras are activated—I want a complete record of this entire meeting."

The executive officer nodded and hurried off to issue the orders.

It was just like that pompous ass Teguina, Yin thought, to make up new flags for his two new "countries" before consolidating power—the flags only become a butt of jokes and an object of derision if the coup fails.

Accompanied by a heavily armed Marine guard, Admiral Yin made his way to the quarterdeck and onto the receiving area. He was kept waiting as several escort vessels made their way toward the Chinese destroyer, under the careful scrutiny of deck-gun crews. An honor guard was quickly assembled, and several crewmen were positioned on the port rail, standing at parade rest, as Teguina's liaison craft approached. Teguina's boat was stopped several times and inspected before being allowed to dock at the *Hong Lung*'s boarding platform, and the new Philippine President started up the stairs. The honor guard snapped to attention, and a broadcast was made on the public address system announcing the arrival of the Philippine President.

Yin forced himself to raise a hand to the brim of his cap in salute. Teguina ignored the Chinese colors and Yin's salute. "I must speak with you immediately, Admiral," Teguina said without preamble.

"By all means, Mr. President," Yin's interpreter replied. He quickly translated both Teguina's words and his own hasty reply for the Admiral, and Yin scowled darkly as he followed

Teguina through the quarterdeck doors. A few moments later they were in Yin's flag briefing room.

"The Admiral wishes to extend his warmest greeting to the President of the Democratic Federation of Aguinaldo," Yin's interpreter said in English. "The Admiral considers it a great honor that you have come for a visit and wishes to offer you . . ."

Teguina started talking, a long, completely unintelligible diatribe. The interpreter tried to tell Yin what the man was saying but was stopped by a sudden outburst of anger as Teguina angrily spit out his words. "He said he wants an explanation of why the Chinese government has made an alliance with Vietnam for the Spratly Islands," the interpreter finally said. "He is angry that his country has lost all rights to the Spratly Islands to the Vietnamese."

"What is he talking about?" Yin asked angrily. "We did not make a deal with Vietnam for anything!"

"Mr. Teguina says that Vietnam abstained in a recent vote of the Association of South East Asian Nations," the interpreter said, "and the rumor that was passed to the Aguinaldo government was that the Chinese government made a deal with Vietnam to give them rights to the Spratly Islands in exchange for blocking a key vote."

Yin was about to rebuff the accusation, but the words died in his throat. That *had* to be the reason why he had heard the tremendous outcry from the ASEAN nations concerning the Chinese invasion, yet nothing had been done—because two nations, Thailand and Vietnam, abstained. High General Chin Po Zihong must have lost a key argument in Beijing if he allowed the Nansha Dao—what the world called the Spratly Islands—to fall back into Vietnam's hands . . . Chin would *never* have allowed that to happen unless his voice was firmly stilled by Premier Cheung.

"I assure you," Yin calmly told Teguina, "that our alliance is firm and there is no duplicity involved. The vote to censure us was defeated in ASEAN because the members believe in what we're doing, not because of any back-room deals, especially with the reprehensible Vietnamese government . . ."

But Teguina didn't seem to be waiting for the interpreter to finish; he began lashing out more accusations. "He is saying that his alliance is ruined, that the Chinese are out to get him, that he can trust no one . . ."

"Calm yourself, Mr. President," Yin said via the interpreter. "We will brief you on our preparations for assisting your forces to retake Davao, and we will give you a tour of our flagship. You may even speak to our officers. They will all tell you that they fully support your government in this struggle." That seemed to mollify Teguina a little, and he allowed himself to be escorted out of Yin's office to the Battle staff briefing area.

But as they were leaving, with Teguina well out of earshot, Yin grabbed Captain Sun and hissed, "Get headquarters' political section on the line immediately. I want to find out about the ASEAN vote and the status of Nansha Dao. Do it immediately."

THE WHITE HOUSE OVAL OFFICE
SATURDAY, 8 OCTOBER 1994, 0627 HOURS LOCAL

The President of the United States had extended his hand to greet United Nations ambassador Deborah O'Day as she walked into the Oval Office, but by some sort of sudden urge he found himself giving her a cordial hug. "Welcome back home, Deborah," the President said, guiding her to a chair. Secretary of State Danahall, Secretary of Defense Preston, Joint Chiefs of Staff Chairman Curtis, and several members of the House and Senate armed services committees stayed on their feet until O'Day was seated, then took their place around her. "You've had a hell of an ordeal, haven't you?"

"Dealing with the ASEAN representatives and the Chinese delegation has been tougher than getting kidnapped by Samar's rebels," O'Day admitted. She extended a hand, and her aide placed a leather-jacketed folder into it. "Mr. President, I've been given a communiqué by the Chinese government, a reply to your last message requesting withdrawal from the Philippines."

"I take it by your tone that it's not good news."

"I haven't read the letter itself, sir, but the Chinese ambassador was not cordial. I think it's bad news." The President took the folder, broke the seal, initialed the original Chinese-language version of the letter and placed it aside, then read the United Nations and State Department translations.

"Just as we thought," Taylor said wearily. "China rejects our demands for an immediate withdrawal. They say they are in the Philippines with the permission and full sanction of the Philippine government, and the American involvement there is illegal meddling in the internal affairs of another government. They say they do not know the whereabouts of Arturo Mikaso and said we should make inquiries with the Filipino government as to his status, but as far as they are concerned Daniel Teguina is in charge and José Trujillo Samar has no authority in the government.

"They regret the attacks on our aircraft and warships, but in the current unstable world climate such interference should have been anticipated and therefore we should carry as much of the blame for the loss as they . . ."

"Bullshit," Curtis murmured.

"They further regard the deployment of heavy bombers and carrier battle groups around the Philippines as an extremely hostile act and they will use any and all means at their disposal to protect their citizens and property." The President tossed the communiqué aside and regarded the advisers around him. "Well? Thoughts?"

"Samar's rebels come under attack in less than five hours, sir," O'Day said. She glanced at Wilbur Curtis. "Is that right, General?"

"Yes, it is," Curtis said. He referred to the pile of mounted satellite photos on the coffee table before him—the photos taken from the B-2 and U-2 reconnaissance flights. "It may have begun already. Chinese warships were in position to bombard Davao by sundown. When their landing craft get into position, they'll start the invasion."

"Five hours? So you're saying it's too late . . . ?"

"No, sir, I'm not," Curtis said. "As we discussed in the tactics briefing, the Chinese troops are most vulnerable while they're still in their troop transports. They've already begun unloading

troops along the Buoyan peninsula east of Mount Apo to secure
the coastal towns, but the main force still hasn't landed in
Davao yet—Samar's rebels are mining the straits and inlets,
trying to slow the convoys up. We still have time to stop them."

The President nodded to Curtis. "Thank you, General." To
Secretary of Defense Preston, he asked, "Thomas? What do
you have for me?"

"Only my wish that we wait and bring the *Lincoln* and
Nimitz carrier battle groups, and the *Wisconsin* surface action
group, forward into position first," Preston replied. "But I
know if we still desire to support Samar and his Islamic rebels
that we must act quickly."

The President seemed to consider his words for a moment.
"Thank you." He continued around the room, getting last
thoughts from Danahall and the congressional leadership. A
few voiced hesitation, but all seemed to want to act.

From the front of his desk, the President withdrew a red-
covered folder and opened it. Below large dark letters that
read Top Secret were the words *Executive Order 94-21, Air
Operations, Strike, Island of Mindanao, Republic of the Philippines*. Without any further hesitation, the President signed
the order and several copies, then replaced it in the folder and
resealed it.

Wilbur Curtis was on the phone thirty seconds later to the
National Military Command Center.

ANDERSEN AFB, GUAM
SUNDAY, 9 OCTOBER 1994, 1915 HOURS LOCAL
(SATURDAY, 8 OCTOBER, 0815 WASHINGTON TIME)

Patrick McLanahan awoke thirty minutes before his alarm
rang. Two hours before the first daily standby situation briefing—he needed rest, but he knew his mind was not going to
let him have any more.

His bedroom was a maintenance office on the top floor of
hangar building number 509, on Andersen's expansive north
parking ramp, which he shared with his aircraft commander,
Major Henry Cobb. Down below them in the huge hangar

were two very unusual machines—Patrick's B-2A Black Knight stealth bomber and an EB-52C Megafortress strategic escort aircraft—the same Megafortress that had "saved" their tails from the F-23 Wildcat fighters during General Jarrel's training sorties three weeks ago in Powder River Run. The hangar also housed all the other flight, maintenance, and support crews for the HAWC aircraft, as well as a full squadron of heavily armed security police.

Careful not to disturb his aircraft commander, Patrick pulled on his flight suit, picked up his socks and boots from their place under his canvas folding cot, and tried to tiptoe out.

"Up already, Colonel?" Cobb said from his cot.

"Yep. Sorry to wake you."

"You didn't. I never went to sleep." Cobb threw off the sheet covering him and swung his feet onto the floor. "Never slept in a hangar before. Don't think I want to again after this."

"Amen," Patrick said. "The smell really gets you after a while. I started to have . . . bad dreams." He wasn't going to say what those dreams were like or what mission he was flying in his dreams. He got the same dreams every time he was exposed to kerosene-like fumes—a morning long ago and far away . . . a tiny snow-covered fighter base at Anadyr, Siberia, in the Soviet Union, when he pumped thousands of gallons of kerosene into a B-52 by hand in subzero weather so they could take off again before the Soviet Army found them. David Luger had sacrificed himself to make sure they could escape, driving a fuel truck into a machine gun emplacement—and Patrick relived that horrible moment every night after smelling jet-fuel fumes. He would probably do so for the rest of his life.

Henry Cobb hadn't heard all the stories about the Old Dog mission—he had of course met all the survivors of that mission, most of whom worked—some called it "exiled"—at the HAWC, and he had seen the first Megafortress itself after Ormack and McLanahan flew it from Alaska back to Dreamland—but he could guess that it was some event in that mission that starred in McLanahan's bad dreams.

Both men quickly washed up in the lavatory down the hall, then returned to their rooms to dress. Despite the warm, muggy afternoon, they donned thin, fire-resistant long underwear and thick padded socks under their flight suits. Under the long underwear were regular cotton briefs and T-shirts.

They wore metal military dog tags next to their skin so they wouldn't rattle or fly loose during ejection. Many crew members laced dog tags into their boots as well, because many times lower body parts survived aerial combat better than upper body parts. They both carried survival knives in ankle sheaths, lightweight composite-bladed knives with both straight and serrated edges, a built-in magnetic compass in the butt cap, and a watertight compartment in the handle that carried waterproof matches, fishing line, sunscreen, a small signal mirror, and a tiny first-aid and survival booklet. In thigh pockets they carried another knife, this one attached to their flight suits by a six-foot-long cord—this knife was a legal switchblade knife with a hook blade for cutting parachute risers. The thigh pocket also contained a vial with earplugs, which were often mistaken by curious nonflyers for suicide pills.

They carried no wallets, at least not the same ones they carried normally. Into a specially prepared nylon "sortie" wallet they placed their military identification cards, some cash, credit cards, and traveler's checks—these were many times more valuable than the "blood chits" used to buy assistance during earlier wars. During the intelligence briefing before a mission, they would receive "pointee-talkee" native language cards and small escape-and-evasion maps of the area, which both went into the sortie wallet.

Just about every pocket in a flight suit contained something, usually personal survival items devised after years of experience. In his ankle pockets, Patrick carried fireproof Nomex flying gloves, extra pencils, and a large plastic Ziplok bag containing a hip flask filled with water and a small vial with water purification tablets. Cobb took a small Bible, a flask of some unidentifiable liquid, and included an unusual multipurpose tool that fit neatly inside his sortie wallet. They packed up their charts, flight manuals, and other documents in a Nomex flying bag, picked up a lightweight nylon flying jacket—which had its own assortment of survival articles in its pockets—and departed.

While they were up on the upper-floor "catwalk" in the hangar, they had a good opportunity to look at the EB-52C escort bomber that was in the hangar with their B-2. Unlike the B-2, where there was little activity, the technicians and munitions maintenance crews were swarming around the Megafortress like worker bees in a hive.

It had to be the weirdest plane—and the most deadly looking plane—either of them had ever seen. The long, sleek, pointed nose was canted down in taxi position, with the aerodynamically raked windscreens looking Oriental and menacing. The dorsal SAR synthetic aperture radar radome, which ran from just aft of the crew compartment and ended in a neat fairing that blended back into the fuselage and the diagonal stabilators near the aft end, made the Megafortress seem broad-shouldered and evil, like some warlock's hunchbacked assistant. The pointed aerodynamic tip tanks, two on each wingtip, looked like twin stilettos challenging all comers, like lowered lances held by charging knights on horseback. Short low-drag pylons mounted between the inboard engine nacelles and the ebony fuselage on each side held six AIM-120 Scorpion air-to-air missiles, their red ground-safety streamers still visible.

Faired under the wings were sensor pods that contained laser target designators, infrared scanners, telescopic cameras for long-range air-target identification, and millimeter-wave radars to scan for large metallic objects hidden by trees or fog that normally could not be picked up by other sensors, such as tanks and armored vehicles. This was one of the older Megafortress escort bombers—it still had the older, conventional metal wings that drooped so far down that the wingtips were only a few feet above the ground and had to be supported by "pogo" wheels. The new Megafortress wings were made of composite materials and wouldn't sag one inch, even fully loaded with fuel and weapons.

Other weapons were just being uploaded, and Henry Cobb, who had had little experience with the Megafortress project, could only shake his head in amazement. The forward section of the bomb bay contained two four-round clip-in racks that held AGM-136 TACIT RAINBOW antiradar cruise missiles.

The aft bomb bay contained a Common Strategy Rotary Launcher filled with smooth, oblong-bodied missiles—eight TV-guided AGM-84E SLAMs, or Standoff Land Attack Missiles.

"Looks like the Megafortresses are getting loaded for bear," Cobb remarked. They could also see the loading procedures for the Stinger airmine rockets in the tail launcher.

Watching this Megafortress getting ready for combat made McLanahan feel strange—a crashing wave of *déjà vu* was descending on him. The hangar in a remote location, the weapons loaded and ready, the plane fueled and ready to go—it was horribly like the last time he had taken a B-52 into combat all those years ago.

But that wasn't his bird now. He had a new one, a bigger, darker, more lethal one—the B-2 Black Knight, modified like the EB-52 to be a strategic escort bomber. All of the B-2's weapons were internal, and the sophisticated sensors were buried within the wing leading edges or in the sensor bay in the nose under the crew compartment. The reconnaissance pods were gone, to be replaced by rotary launchers that would carry much more lethal warloads than cameras and radars.

The B-2's ground crew had just arrived for the pre-takeoff inspection, and since the two crewmen were awake at least an hour before they intended, they had time to look over their Black Knight before reporting to the briefing room. They found little changed. The maintenance crews were going through a normal pre-flight as if the plane were going on another training sortie—they were less than four hours from takeoff and no weapons had been uploaded yet. "Where are the missiles?" Cobb asked McLanahan. "I thought we were loading up on Harpoons or SLAMs for this run."

"Won't know what we'll be doing for at least another two hours yet," Patrick replied. "We don't know yet if we're going after ships, or radars, or ground targets—it could be anything. Once the Joint Battle Staff decides, it'll take them just a few minutes to snap those launchers and bomb racks in and do a ground check. They can probably do it while other planes are launching."

They completed a casual walkaround inspection, chatting

with the maintenance crews along the way. It was apparent that each and every one of them was just as apprehensive, just as nervous, just as concerned for what was happening on Andersen Air Force Base and in the rest of the Pacific as Cobb and McLanahan.

One of the munitions maintenance men stopped inspecting a SLAM missile seeker head when McLanahan greeted him. "Think we'll be flying tonight, sir?" the man asked. The "we" was not just a demonstrative—ground crews were just as emotionally and professionally tied to their aircraft as the flight crews. When McLanahan's B-2 rolled down the runway, a hundred other minds and hearts were right in there with him.

"Wish I could tell you, Paul," Patrick said. "They tell us to be ready, that's all."

The man stepped closer to McLanahan, as if afraid to ask the question that had obviously been nagging at his consciousness: "Are you scared, sir?" he asked in a low voice.

Patrick looked back at the man with a touch of astonishment at the question. Before he could reply, however, some other technician had pulled the man away. "That's McLanahan, you butthead. He's the best there is," Patrick heard the second tech tell him. "He's too good to get scared." None of the other crew chiefs dared to speak with the two aviators.

Cobb and McLanahan finished their inspection, checked in with the security guard, who inspected their bags before allowing them to leave, and then the two B-2 crew members stepped out of the hangar into the twilight.

Unlike the controlled, calm tension inside hangar 509, outside it was sheer bedlam. The ramp space in front of the hangars was the only clear space as far as either man could see—the rest of the base was filled with aircraft of every possible description, and the access roads and taxiways were clogged with maintenance and support vehicles.

The north ramp to their far right was choked full of cargo aircraft—C-141 Starlifters, C-5 Galaxys, and C-130 Hercules planes, all surrounded by cargo-handling equipment offloading their precious pallets of spare parts, personnel, weapons, and other supplies. Like a line of ants along a crack in a sidewalk, there was a steady stream of forklift trucks, tractor-trailers, flatbed trucks, and "mules" carrying supplies from the aircraft to the inspection and distribution warehouses. Every few minutes, another cargo plane would arrive on one of the Andersen AFB's twin parallel runways, taxi off to a waiting area, then be met by a "Follow-Me" truck which would direct it to another parking spot. Empty cargo planes that had crews with duty day hours remaining went to a refueling pit on the south side of the base and were immediately marshaled to the end of the runway for takeoff; planes that were not due to take off until later were directed to waiting areas along the northeast side of the base, at the edge of the steep cliffs of Pati Point.

West of the north ramp, near the north end of the east runway, were the parking spots for the aerial refueling tankers. These were perhaps the most important aircraft on Guam. The KC-135 Stratotanker, KC-10 Extender, and KC-130 Hercules tankers provided the only means for most of the Air Battle Force's aircraft to conduct strike operations from Guam—indeed, most of the aircraft there could not have arrived without the tankers supplying them fuel. Tankers were airborne almost continually in support of flight operations, and several tankers were on "strip alert" status to respond to emergency requests of fuel. The tankers also acted as cargo aircraft themselves—one KC-10 tanker could deploy all of the support personnel, equipment, and spare parts for six F-16 fighters from Hawaii to Guam, *and* refuel those six planes, all on the same trip.

Directly ahead of the hangars were the parking spots for the air-defense fighters. Only half of the Air Battle Force's twenty F-15s and fifteen F-16s were parked there, because the rest were either flying escort missions with the "ferret" bombers or were on air-defense alert on the south parking apron. Four F-15s and six F-16s were fueled, armed, and ready to respond should the Chinese attempt an air raid on Andersen Air Force Base itself. The complement included four F-23 Advance Tactical Fighters, deployed for the first time out of the fifty states. A few of the F-14s stranded from the stricken aircraft carrier USS *Ranger* were also parked there.

Each fighter carried relatively few weapons, only two radar-

guided and two heat-seeking missiles total: the most prominent store on each fighter was the huge seven-hundred-gallon
centerline fuel tank. When flying from Guam, where alternate
landing bases were hundreds of miles apart, fuel was a very
precious commodity. The incredible offensive power of these
fighters was severely limited by fuel availability—if one aerial
refueling tanker failed to launch or could not transfer fuel, it
could take dozens of fighters out of the battle.

Cobb and McLanahan waited near a group of soldiers until
a civilian contractor–hired "Guam Bomb" jeepney bus, its
body rusting and its broken leaf springs squeaking with every
movement, trundled by, then stepped on board—the bus was
so full it looked as if the fat native Chamorro driver had to sit
sideways to let riders on. The sea of men and machines on
Guam was simply amazing—it seemed every patch of sandy
lawn, every square foot of concrete or asphalt, every empty
space was occupied by a vehicle or aircraft. Lines were everywhere—lines to the chow hall, lines to maintenance or radio
trucks, lines in front of water trucks. Traffic crisscrossed the
streets and access roads, ignoring security-police whistles and
traffic guards—being a pedestrian on the flight line was a definite health risk. The cloying, stupefying smells of burning jet
fuel, hydraulic fluid, sweat, mildew—and, yes, fear—were everywhere. The noise was deafening and inescapable—even
with earplugs or ear protectors, the screams of jet engines,
auxiliary power carts, honking horns, yelling men and women,
and public address speakers could not be reduced. The bus had
no windows, so those without ear protectors stuck fingers in
their ears to blot out the din of the parking ramp.

McLanahan had never felt so insignificant. He had participated in lots of aircraft generation exercises, when his unit's
fleet of bombers and tankers was fueled and armed in preparation for a strategic war, but this was at least twenty times
greater in magnitude than he had ever seen before. Even
during Air Battle Force generation exercises at Ellsworth Air
Force Base—which, even in these few days since arriving on
Guam, seemed a billion miles away and years ago—things
seemed to go in a smooth, orderly fashion: here, it was like

some kind of controlled riot, or like the world's largest exhibition hall with thousands of participants milling around from building to aircraft and back again.

Parked south of the air-defense fighters and on the other side of base operations were the support aircraft. They had one E-3C Sentry Airborne Warning and Control System radar plane, one EC-135L radio relay plane, and one RC-135X reconnaissance plane parked there; an E-3 and another EC-135 were already airborne, participating in intelligence and "ferret" flights near the Philippines—obviously Masters' NIRTSats were still down. There were also three EF-111A Raven electronic countermeasure aircraft, two Navy EA-6 electronic warfare aircraft, another U-2R spy plane like the one that was shot down near the Philippines, and a Navy E-2 Hawkeye radar plane from the *Ranger.* A few small "liaison" jets and supply helicopters were parked in front of base operations—these were fast transport jets that flitted all across the Mariana Islands, carrying urgent supplies or staff officers from base to base. On the other side of the support planes was the "Christmas tree" parking area for the alert fighters and tankers, situated so they could quickly and easily take off in case of emergency.

Barely visible across and in between the runways were the parking areas for the strike aircraft, surrounded by twelve-foot-high corrugated steel revetments to protect each other from damage should a bomb go off on one parking area. The smaller fighter-bombers—the F-15E Strike Eagles, the F-4 Phantoms, and the F-111G bombers, along with a few Navy A-6 Intruder bombers, were in the infield parking spots between the parallel runways, while the "heavies"—the B-52, B-1, and B-2 bombers—were on the west parking areas.

Construction crews had built huge shelters for the three B-2 Black Knights to protect them as much as possible, not only from the elements—with their nonmetallic composite construction, the B-2s were more resilient to the harsh tropical climate and corroding effects of salt air than the other planes— but from the prying eyes of spy satellites and newsmen.

Although the B-2 had been operational for some years and was no longer the oddity it first was when it was unveiled in

1989, it still attracted a lot of undue attention. Just beyond the aircraft parking areas to the west, McLanahan could just barely make out the Patriot air-defense-missile canisters poking just above the treeline, already erected and ready to fire in case of an air attack.

Air defense of Andersen, as well as the Seventh Fleet combat groups, Okinawa, and the other island bases supporting the Philippines operation, was a very important consideration. The primary concern was attack from submarine-launched weapons. The Chinese Navy operated six Wuhan-class cruise-missile submarines that fired antiship missiles with ranges varying from twenty to one hundred nautical miles; these missiles were thought to have a secondary land-attack role by programming the missile's autopilot to impact a selected set of geographical coordinates. Navy and Air Force radar planes were used to scan the skies around Andersen for any low-flying aircraft, while Navy ships and antisubmarine aircraft patrolled for signs of submarines. The Patriot missile was somewhat effective against low-flying cruise missiles, and even the F-16 fighters with their AIM-120C Scorpion missiles were fairly effective at chasing down subsonic cruise missiles.

China also possessed four sea-launched ballistic nuclear missile submarines, all of which had been deployed into the Pacific and were thought to be a threat to all American forces. These submarines were being located and shadowed as best as could be expected—the diesel-powered submarines were hundreds of times quieter submerged than their nuclear-powered counterparts—but the feeling was that if the fight escalated to a nuclear exchange, the weapons being used in this battle would be quickly supplanted by the full strategic nuclear might of the United States anyway.

The two B-2 crew members edged their way through the crush of bodies off the jeepney at the headquarters building and stepped inside, feeling the uncomfortable chill as the building's heavy-duty air conditioning instantly turned the thin layer of sweat over their bodies to ice. McLanahan went immediately to the command post, waiting patiently as his ID was checked by the security guards and a metal detector was swept over his body—he had to unstrap his survival knife and keep it with the guards. He went and checked in at the room where the PACER SKY satellite system had been installed.

"Patrick?" a surprised General Brad Elliott asked as the young navigator-bombardier walked in. Elliott checked his watch. "You're early—about an hour and a half early." The veteran aviator looked at McLanahan's hardened, concerned, somewhat distracted eyes. "Couldn't sleep, eh?"

Patrick shook his head. "Henry either."

"It always happens that way, I think," Elliott said. "The time you need sleep the most is when you can't do it." He regarded his younger colleague with an inquisitive expression; McLanahan seemed to pick up on the pause right away.

"We got the order, didn't we?" Patrick asked.

"Couple hours ago," Elliott said. "They wanted to be sure the three Navy ships in the Philippine Sea could get into position; we just got the word that they reported ready. They may wait one more day to see if we get the NIRTSats back on-line, but the recon photos you got last night are pretty good quality so we might do it tonight."

Strangely, Patrick felt no fear, no apprehension, not even a trace of nervousness—his churning stomach and restless mind had kept him from sleep all afternoon, but now his body was quiet. It was as if he had already been told they were going to fly, that Elliott had somehow given him secondhand information. He nodded wordlessly to Elliott; then his eyes sought out the large high-definition monitor on which the NIRTSat reconnaissance data was usually displayed. "I can't believe these are still down . . ."

"Yeah, well, *nothing* is ever guaranteed, as you know. Even the best stuff."

Patrick stepped over to a large chart on which was drawn the positions of the known Chinese warships that he, Cobb, and the dead U-2 pilot had photographed a few nights earlier. A second board had the intelligence section's best guess as to how the ships were going to be deployed when the strike aircraft were set to go over the target.

Elliott was amazed by the flyers he encountered in all his years of flying, but Patrick McLanahan had to be the most . . . admirable. His expression, his demeanor, his attitude were constant—distant, unshakable, almost detached. It was the same whether he was meeting the President of the United States or when getting promoted—unflappable coolness. Was it an act or was it real? Was McLanahan really such a cool character or was he destined for some huge heart attack or ulcer down the road for keeping all those emotions locked inside? He didn't want to guess. He was just glad McLanahan was on *their* team.

Elliott noticed Patrick's eyes on the briefing board behind him. "Can't wait to see what you're up against either, eh? We have one more NIRTSat pass before the mass briefing, so this won't be the final picture—and hopefully PACER SKY will be working by then—but the pictures you got us are spectacular and very useful."

They stepped toward the screen. "The Chinese are not only continuing on with their invasion plans, but they've set up a pretty sophisticated naval defense network around eastern Mindanao. It's all being controlled from the radar installation here . . ."

"Don't tell me," McLanahan said wearily. "The Chinese got Mount Apo."

"Took it yesterday and set up shop immediately. They've got big-picture coverage of all Mindanao now—almost unlimited fighter-intercept coverage, early-warning, maritime, even ground and fire control. Samar's boys held out for days against a huge Chinese task force—the word is, it took five thousand Chinese and New People's Army troops to take Samar's two-hundred-man garrison. Samar's men were wiped out completely."

McLanahan felt his throat go instantly dry.

"Here's the easternmost ship—it's a destroyer, extensive air-search radar, early-warning capability, long-range HQ-91 SAM coverage," Elliott continued. "There's a line of six frigates two hundred miles offshore, giving them four-hundred-mile early warning—a good thirty- to forty-five-minute warning at least. Nothing sophisticated but still effective.

"One hundred and twenty miles offshore is the real gauntlet—three destroyers, six frigates, twelve patrol boats, in a three-hundred-mile-wide band around eastern Mindanao. The destroyers are spaced so that their anti air-missile lethal ranges don't quite overlap, but they put a frigate with massed triple-A guns on it in the gaps. That's how the U-2 was hit—they used one destroyer with an air-search radar to herd the U-2 into missile range of another destroyer that wasn't transmitting. A few of these southern ships are in Indonesian waters, but there's not a darn thing Indonesia can do about it. Between the missiles and guns, it's overlapping, layered antiair coverage over all altitudes.

"Inside that first band is another layer of frigates and patrol boats—no destroyers, thank God, but the frigates are bad enough. They stay in basically a semicircular band around the mouth of Davao Gulf. There's one destroyer and six escorts sitting in the Sangihe Strait in the south Celebes Sea to oppose the two Navy cruisers we got moving up from Indonesia.

"The main body is already in Davao Gulf itself, and it's a real mess—the Chinese have one major warship for every ten square miles. That means they can theoretically shoot a shell or launch a missile and hit every part of Davao Gulf and every spot three miles above it." Despite the ominous information, Patrick had to smile—it was very much like Elliott to describe such firepower, even the enemy's, in such weird terms.

"We've counted twelve minesweepers, ten frigates, two destroyers, about thirty fast guided-missile patrol boats, twenty amphibious-assault ships, tank-landing ships, dock ships, amphibious-landing craft everywhere—over a hundred vessels," Elliott continued. "To make matters worse, a battalion-sized airborne unit may have landed at one of the small airfields north of Davao and are making their way south. We don't think the airfield is big enough to land fighters or transports, but if they can air-drop armor and artillery pieces there, Davao has had it.

"To cap it all off, they also may be sending another destroyer surface-action group from Zamboanga to reinforce this armada—the *Hong Lung* battle group this time. It's their most powerful warship. It's escorted by three frigates and six patrol boats. *Hong Lung* was also the vessel that reportedly fired the nuclear-tipped antiship missile near Palawan, and of course the staff feels the Chinese task force commander might just do it again.

"Their fighter coverage is pretty good," Elliott continued, "good enough that the Joint Task Force commander, General Stone, has decided not to risk sending the AWACS or tankers within two hundred miles of Mindanao . . ."

"That means no combat air patrol for the strike packages?" McLanahan asked.

"So far it looks unlikely, Patrick," Elliott replied. "We may be able to send up a few F-15s to cover the withdrawal, but we can't send a tanker close enough to cover the strikers going into the target area. The Megafortresses will have to take on the fighters."

Patrick felt his throat go dry—the Megafortresses were well equipped for air-to-air combat, but not against massed numbers of fighters. They would have to contend with the naval threats, too.

The odds were looking worse every minute . . .

"The Chinese have at least a hundred fighters in the area, half of which have the endurance for long overwater patrols," Elliott continued. "The Chinese can effectively layer their defenses—warships, fighters, warships, fighters, then warships, in the target area. If they take Samar International Airport near Davao and start using it as a forward staging base, it *definitely* means no AWACS or tankers—and it may mean no Air Battle Force over Mindanao."

"You got any good news on that screen, General?" McLanahan asked wryly.

"Sort of. The New People's Army and the Chinese lost a big battle for the city of Cotabato, here on Moro Gulf. We think the Chinese wanted to use the airport there to stage fighters to support their upcoming assault on Davao. Samar's guerrillas held out—for a while. But it was long enough, because they demolished the airfield before they were driven out by Chinese air raids. Pretty clever how they did it, too—instead of just cratering the runway, which would have made it easy for Chinese engineers to repair, they stripped out sections of runway, buried stolen bombs in it, then cemented trucks over the bombs. It's going to take the Chinese two or three days to repair the runway and another few days to make it a usable staging base."

"So what do we do, then?" McLanahan asked. "This is what might be called a target-rich environment. What's first?"

"General Stone and the Joint Task Force still haven't decided," Elliott replied. "They have a general outline to work with, but they'll wait for the latest satellite data from Washington before going ahead with a frag order. If Jon Masters' setup was working, we'd be done by now—it only takes a few minutes to build a frag order from PACER SKY data. We get flight plans, data cartridges, computer tapes, charts, briefing boards, even slides from his system here. Now we have to program all this stuff by hand."

McLanahan saw Masters on the master console. "Masters, how are you doing?"

"Cool, Mac, my man, real cool," Masters said. Masters was dressed in white shorts, a flowered Hawaiian shirt, and sneakers with no socks—it looked as if he had just returned from Tarague Beach, Andersen Air Force Base's recreation area. "Brad, we got ten more minutes until the data comes in . . ."

"Is it back on-line, Doctor Masters?"

"Not quite," Masters admitted. "But, hey, you gotta think positive. Everything looks good so far. Say, Mac, you ready to kick some Chinese butt out there tonight?"

Patrick stared, not believing what he had just heard. "Excuse me, Doctor?"

"Yeah, man, you're gonna clean up," Masters enthused. "We got spectacular photos and data, and we've got ingress and egress routes scoped out so well that the Chinks won't even know you've just kicked their sloped asses . . ."

"I don't think we better—"

"Hey, loosen up," Masters said, taking a big swallow from his ever-present squeeze bottle of Pepsi. "Just sit back in that big B-2 cockpit of yours, put on some tunes, turn on the BNS, and send Uncle Cheung's squids to the bottom of the Celebes Sea. You can come back and we'll check out the Japanese babes out on Tumon Beach . . ."

Patrick noticed General Elliott take a step toward Masters,

but Patrick was already moving by then. Without another word, Patrick had taken Masters' skinny left arm in his big left hand and had pulled the young scientist up out of his chair and out of the battle staff area.

"Hey, Mac, I can't leave the board quite yet . . ."

The adjacent office near the Command Post was unoccupied and unlocked, so McLanahan took Masters right inside, closed the door behind him, and deposited him unceremoniously onto the worn Naugahyde sofa. "Let's get something straight, Doctor. First, the name is Lieutenant Colonel Patrick *McLanahan*. Second, you've got a big mouth."

Masters stared at the looming, six-foot blond pilot. He looked a lot bigger standing over him than he had a moment ago. "Look, Colonel, I know you're a little nervous about—"

"You don't know jack-shit, including when to keep your mouth shut about classified material and when to conduct yourself in an appropriate manner—"

Masters smiled weakly. "Hey, who are you, Dirty Harry?" He tried to rise, but McLanahan pushed him back down.

"Get this straight, Doctor. While you're in this command post, you'll not wear shorts or sneakers, you'll address the senior officer in the room as 'sir' or by their rank, not their first name, and you'll keep your bigoted comments to yourself. You're supposed to be a professional, so start acting like one." McLanahan looked at his watch. "You've got about ten minutes before your satellite data comes in—that's plenty of time for you to go back to your barracks and change."

"Hey, man, you're not my father," Masters complained. "Get off your Clint Eastwood act and off my case . . ."

McLanahan leaned over the couch, putting his face within an inch of Masters' own. They were but eight years apart in age, but worlds apart in experience. McLanahan looked directly into Masters' eyes. "I shouldn't have to be on your case, Doctor. But if you'd open your eyes, you might learn a thing or two about what's going on here."

Masters cleared his throat and tried to look away from McLanahan, but couldn't. "Hey," he said calmly, "I *know* what's going on. I know the weapons you're going to use, the routes you'll fly. I wrote the friggin' scenarios, for Godssake."

"You may have," McLanahan said, moving back a bit from Masters, "but you don't know anything about combat. About what it's like to be in a war machine facing your own mortality. Have General Elliott or Ormack or Cobb tell you sometime about combat, about life in the cockpit . . ."

"Yeah, yeah, I've heard that before—your secret society, your brotherhood of aviators. Brad—General Elliott—and his B-52s during Vietnam, out at that Arc Light Memorial, he tried to get into it, but he couldn't explain it. He says, 'You gotta be there.' Stone, Jarrel, and all the others, even *you*—you've *all* been in combat before. But you treat it like a game, so why shouldn't I?"

McLanahan bristled. He pulled out his dog tags from under his flight suit. "A game? What are these, Doctor? Tell me."

Masters rolled his eyes. This was boring. "Dog tags. Next."

"You're partially right. Out here, Doctor, we have them for more than ornaments on a key ring. See how one is on the neck chain and one's a small chain all by itself? There's a reason for that. One they bring back to headquarters to prove you were killed in action—*if* they find your body, that is. The other they keep on the body, usually clamped shut in your mouth."

He pulled out his water bottle from his left leg pocket. "You see this? Emergency water supply in case I lose my survival kit after ejection—this could be the only fresh water for a thousand miles if I have to punch out over the Philippine Sea." He ripped off his unit patches and name tag from their Velcro strips on his flight suit. "Patches Velcroed on and removed before we take off in case we get shot down and captured—so the enemy won't know what unit we're from. Some chaplain will come around and collect them before we go out to our planes. They'll check if we made out a will, check to see if they know who our next of kin are.

"Take a look at that data you're generating sometime, Masters. Those ships your satellites are locating represent hundreds of sailors whose job it is to find and destroy me. There are thousands of sailors out there waiting for us—"

"But we know where they are . . . we know *who* they are . . ."

"We know where they are because men risked their lives to

get that data," McLanahan said. "A man *died* getting us those pictures . . ."

"Well, once the NIRTSat comes back on-line, that won't happen again . . ."

"It doesn't matter, my friend. Combat isn't a series of pre-programmed parameters on a computer monitor—it's men and women who are scared, and brave, and angry, and who feel hopeless. It's not a clear-cut engagement. *Anything* can happen. You gotta realize that the people around you don't think in absolutes, because they know that anything can happen . . ."

"Maybe in wars past that was true," Masters offered. "When the enemy was a mystery, when you couldn't see over the horizon or through the fog or under the ocean, maybe it wasn't so clear-cut. But things are different now. Hell, you know more than anyone else how different it is—you fly the most advanced warplane in the friggin' universe! We know *exactly* where the bad guys are. Once the NIRTSats are working again, I can steer your weapons, I can warn you of danger, I can tell you exactly how many weapons you need to win, and I can tell you how long it will take you to achieve any objective . . ."

"Then tell me this, Doctor Masters," McLanahan said, affixing his steel-blue eyes on the scientist and letting his glare bore into him: "Tell me who's going to die out there."

Masters opened his mouth as if to speak, then closed it suddenly, thought a moment, then replied, "I estimate your losses at less than five percent for the duration of this conflict . . ."

"No, I didn't ask you how many. I asked *who.*"

"Well, how the fuck am I supposed to know *who?* If you follow the plan and put your weapons on target, no one should die . . ."

"You said *should* die, Doctor. That means that even if everything turns out perfectly, someone may still die. Right?"

Masters shrugged. "Well, it's very unlikely, but—anything can happen."

"You're damned right it can. Now tell me how to deal with that. Tell me how a highly trained professional pilot or navigator can climb into a bomber or fighter and fly into the teeth of the enemy and know that even if everything goes *perfectly,* he may still end up at the bottom of the sea, and I'll let you act like a cocky little punk peacock all you want in my command post. Until then you will give this campaign and the people who fight it—*all* the people who fight it, the combatants on *both* sides—the proper respect."

Masters was finally silent. McLanahan backed away from Masters, allowing him to get up, but Masters stayed where he was.

"So what you're saying is—you're scared," Masters said after a few long moments. He looked at McLanahan, and when the officer didn't reply for several seconds, Masters' eyes opened wide in surprise. "You're *scared? You?* But you're the—"

"Yeah, yeah, I know," Patrick said. "I'm supposed to be the best. But it's bullshit. I know my shit, and I'm lucky. That doesn't make me invincible, and it doesn't give you or anyone the right to think this is going to be easy—for any of us. Nothing is cut and dried. Nothing is certain. We know our equipment, know our procedures, but when you go into combat we learn not to trust it. We trust *ourselves.* We look to ourselves to find the strength to get through the mission."

Masters rose and stood before McLanahan, afraid to look into the Air Force officer's face but respectful enough to want to be able to do it. "I never realized that, Patrick. Really. I always thought, 'Well, the gear's in place, everything's running, so everything's going to be okay.' I guess . . . well, I don't work with people that much. I'm really so used to dealing with computers and machines . . ."

McLanahan shrugged. "Hell, listen to me. A few years ago I never gave a shit much about people either. I wasn't exactly what you'd call a team player. I did my job and went home. I hate to say it, but we were a lot alike back then."

Masters smiled at that. "Oh yeah? Dirty Harry was laid-back and mellow? You drank beer and chased girls and got stupid?"

It was McLanahan's turn to smile this time. He remembered the B-52 crew parties back in California, the weekends rafting down the American River—one big twelve-person raft for crew dogs, wives, and girlfriends; another slightly smaller raft for the numerous ice chests full of six-packs—the bar-hopping in Old Sacramento till two in the morning, the ski trips to Lake

Tahoe when they'd get back to base just minutes before show time for a training mission. "All the damned time, Jon."

"What happened to you?"

McLanahan's smile vanished, and all his fond recollections of life back home exploded in a bright yellow fireball called reality. He put his dog tags back under his shirt and put his water flask back in its pocket. The pungent odor of jet exhaust and the roar of a plane on its takeoff run invaded the office, and the horrors of another impossible mission thousands of miles away flooded back into his consciousness once again.

"Combat," was all he said, and he turned and walked away.

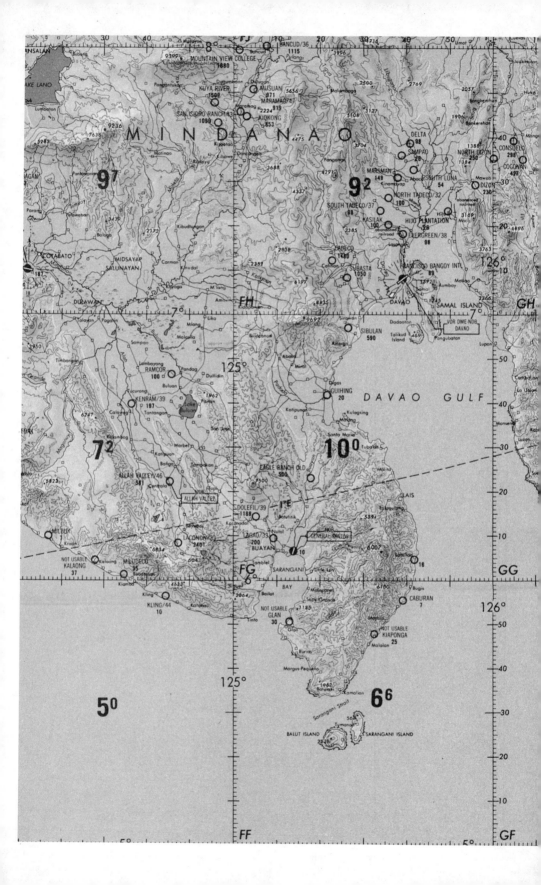

TWELVE

It had been hanging around for so long now, big, slow, and galumphing, that they had humorously dubbed it *Syensheng Tz*, Old Gas. They could see the thing easily, almost a hundred miles away and at high altitude—a single, unescorted, vulnerable B-52 bomber. It was cruising westward at a leisurely four hundred and twenty nautical miles per hour. Although it was definitely getting closer, on its present course it would pass well out of HQ-91 missile range of the Chinese People's Liberation Army Navy missile destroyer *Kaifeng*. It was obviously giving the Chinese ships a wide berth.

Even so, if the aircraft carried antiship missiles, it was still a substantial threat: it was within Harpoon missile range of the destroyer, yet outside the range of the destroyer's missiles, and there were no fighters nearby that could reach it. The commander of the destroyer *Kaifeng*, a Luda-class destroyer with over three hundred men on board, wanted very close tabs kept on this intruder. "CIC, bridge, status of that B-52," the commander of the *Kaifeng* requested.

"Bridge, CIC, air target one still at seventy-eight-nautical-miles range, altitude ten thousand meters, speed four-two-zero knots, offset range six-zero nautical miles. No detectable radar transmissions from aircraft. It is within Harpoon missile range at this time."

"Copy." The commander was carefully trying not to let his frustration and impatience show. American B-52s had been flying these "ferret" missions for many days now, passing just inside missile range of the destroyer's missiles, then hightailing it out when missile-guidance signals were aimed at it. It was always one bomber, always at thirty thousand feet, always challenging in this same location. It stayed high and relatively slow—very nonthreatening despite being within extreme range of Harpoon antiship missiles it might be carrying. It was obviously collecting intelligence information—it was probably crammed with sensors and recorders, hoping to intercept radio messages or analyze missile fire control radar signals . . .

. . . or it was crammed with antiship missiles, ready to strike. "Comm, bridge, any response from that plane about our air-defense warnings?"

"None, sir," the communications officer replied. *Kaifeng,* as well as other ships in the South Philippines Task Force commanded by Admiral Yin Po L'un, had been warning all aircraft to stay away from this area for days now. The area over the Celebes Sea had been a very well used airway for travelers heading to Brunei, Malaysia, Indonesia, and Singapore through Samar International Airport, but the People's Liberation Army Air Force had refused all access to the region, and air traffic to and from Manila was tightly controlled. All air traffic was forced to fly farther south through the sparsely populated islands of northern Indonesia. Philippines supply routes in the South China Sea were virtually isolated. But with the nuclear explosion near Palawan and the extreme danger of radiation poisoning and contamination, these areas were being studiously avoided anyhow.

The American Air Battle Force, however, was obviously ignoring all warnings.

"CIC, bridge, position of our fighter coverage."

"Sir, Liang-Two flight of eight J-7 fighters are over Nenusa Archipelago, one hundred eleven kilometers northwest of the B-52. They are less than ten minutes from bingo fuel and have already received permission to return to Zamboanga for refueling. Sichuan-One-Zero flight of four Q-5 fighters are three hundred kilometers northwest of the B-52, headed southeast to take over for Liang-Two flight."

Damned sparse fighter coverage, *Kaifeng*'s commander thought to himself. Because that bomber was a "ferret," running away at the first sign of trouble, they were not giving it as much fighter attention as they should. Well, that was going to stop right here and *now*.

"CIC, bridge, chase that damned plane out of here," *Kaifeng*'s commander ordered. At this point chasing "Old Gas" out of antiship-missile range was more important than revealing radar frequencies. "Hit them with the fire-control radar." That was usually plenty to make the B-52 turn and run.

"Yes, sir," the combat information officer responded. "Shall I recall Liang-Two flight to provide air cover?"

"Get a fuel state from them. If they have not reached bingo fuel yet, have them engage. If they have reached bingo, engage with the HQ-91 system. Then vector in Sichuan-Ten flight and have them chase that B-52 out past two hundred kilometers."

The warning tone over the interphone system for a missile acquisition radar was different from a search radar—in general, the more serious a threat, the faster and more insistent the tone. The appearance of a "Search" radar gave a rather leisurely *"Deeedle . . . Deeedle . . . Deeedle."* When the Chinese Golf–band air-search radar changed to an India-band missile acquisition radar, the tone was a fast, loud *"Deeedledeeedledeeedledeeedle!"* At the same time, "Missile Warning" lights illuminated at every station of the EB-52C Megafortress bomber orbiting at thirty thousand feet over the Philippine Sea.

"Missile warning, twelve o'clock," the electronic warfare officer, First Lieutenant Robert Atkins, announced. "India-band radar . . . 'Fog Lamp' SAM director for an HQ-91 missile.

This'll change to missile launch at any second." Atkins' voice became squeakier with every passing moment—he was an engineer, not a crew dog, and he never thought he'd be taking these behemoth modified B-52s into battle.

"Don't sweat it," Major Kelvin Carter, the Megafortress's pilot, said, trying to project the most confident voice he could. "They're just trying to scare us out. Easy on the jammers until the shit starts rollin'."

Carter's words did little to calm young Atkins down, so he turned back to the peace and security he usually got from the one thing that he *knew* he could trust in this screwed-up world—his equipment. Designed at the High Technology Aerospace Weapons Center several years ago by a near-mythical engineer named Wendy Tork, Atkins had improved on Tork's groundbreaking designs and produced what was probably the best electronic warfare suite ever to leave the ground.

Atkins was sitting before a complex of multi-function displays on the Megafortress Plus's upper deck, scanning the skies for enemy radars and programming the bomber's array of jammers against each one. His ECM system automatically processed the electronic signals, analyzed them, identified them, pointed out their range and bearing from the Megafortress, and selected the appropriate jamming packages to use against them. It could do the same with a hundred other signals from very long ranges. The system would also automatically dispense decoys against radar or heat-seeking missiles to protect them from missile attacks.

A B-52G or -H Stratofortress bomber had performed all the other "ferret" flights from Guam in the past few days, but tonight it was an EB-52 Megafortress pulling the unenviable task of drawing the attention of the Chinese Navy and assessing the threats present around eastern Mindanao—a regular B-52 was hardly qualified to take such a risk.

All in all, the system relegated Atkins to a "verbal squawk box" role—what the others called "crew coordination" was still a foreign concept to him, since everything on the Megafortress was so automated—as it should be, of course. Why risk an extra human life on board, when a computer could do the job faster, better, and cheaper anyway?

His directed defensive weapons were designed to operate automatically as well. The Megafortress had eight AGM-136A TACIT RAINBOW antiradar cruise missiles in clip-in racks in the forward part of the bomb bay, plus a rotary launcher with eight AGM-88B HARM High-Speed Anti-Radar Missiles in the aft bomb bay. The electronic countermeasures system would automatically program both the HARM and TACIT RAINBOW missiles for a particular enemy radar system they encountered. In case that particular radar was shut down during a TACIT RAINBOW attack, the missile would stay aloft for several minutes, search for just that radar, home in on it, and destroy it after reactivation. If another ship tried to shoot down the subsonic TACIT RAINBOW cruise missile with radar-controlled guns, Atkins could launch supersonic HARM missiles at the radar and destroy it.

The bottom line: he had designed all this to be totally automatic, and it was obvious that he didn't fit in with this crew. Why in hell then was he here?

Seated beside Atkins was the Megafortress's "gunner," Master Sergeant Kory Karbayjal. Karbayjal and the other noncommissioned officers flying that position still liked the name "gunner" or "bulldog," although the term was an anachronism—the old .50-caliber machine guns or 20-millimeter Gatling gun of other, more conventional BUFFs were gone, replaced by the EB-52's array of defensive missiles. The Megafortress carried twelve AIM-120C AMRAAM missiles on wing pylons, and it carried fifty small Stinger rear-firing heat-seeking antiaircraft missiles in the tail launcher.

That was another job that could be done by computers, too, although Karbayjal obviously enjoyed his work. Karbayjal, a twenty-six-year veteran of the B-52, had flown the old D-model BUFFs, the ones where the gunner sat in the tail in a tiny compartment with his machine guns and used only his eyes to spot enemy fighters. He took it upon himself to look after young Atkins just as much as he looked for enemy fighters, something that Atkins resented as well.

The navigators, Captains Paul Scott and Alicia Kellerman, were downstairs keeping track of their position and preparing for fighter combat—the four Megafortress strategic escort bombers on this mission carried no ground-attack weapons because they were all designed to blast through enemy defenses and give the other strike aircraft a better chance of reaching their targets. Scott could use his attack radar to designate and track targets for their AIM-120 air-to-air missiles, while Alicia Kellerman controlled the dorsal ISAR radar and kept track of all other aircraft and enemy ships in the area. The pilots, Major Kelvin Carter and Lieutenant Nancy Cheshire, were very quiet—they were obviously steeling themselves for the battle that was about to begin.

Using the large dorsal side-looking radar in ISAR (inverse-synthetic aperture radar) mode, Kellerman had already identified the largest ship ahead as a Luda-class destroyer even before its weapons radars came up, so Atkins had already anticipated what kind of radars and weapons the vessel had and how to deal with each one. The Megafortress's ISAR system had also mapped out the locations and movements of the other vessels in the south and west groups of Chinese ships and had passed that information to other aircraft.

The "Missile Warning" light was still on, and they were driving closer and closer to the Chinese destroyer. Atkins still had no jammers on the missile acquisition radar—jamming the signal too early would surely elicit a very angry response from the Chinese. "We gotta shit or get off the pot here, kids . . . a few more miles and we'll be under attack. . . ."

"Sixty seconds," the crew navigator, Captain Alicia Kellerman, announced. Like most of the crews from the High Technology Aerospace Weapons Center, Kellerman was an ex–crew member—formerly on KC-135 tankers—who put their engineering degrees to good use at the Dreamland research facility. Although flying was part of their job descriptions, flying into combat was completely unexpected—but Kellerman loved it. "Start countermeasures in forty seconds, release configuration checks completed . . . thirty seconds."

Suddenly Atkins got an inverted "V" bat-wing signal on his radar threat-warning scope. The computer monitor hesitated momentarily, then issued a stream of identification data. "I've got a fighter, twelve o'clock, range . . . range is undetermined yet, but he's outside forty miles. Stand by, Paul." Paul Scott was ready to use the EB-52's attack radar to lock onto the fighter and provide fire control instructions for their AIM-120 air-to-air missiles, but it might not yet be necessary. "I've got a range-only radar. Skyranger type 226, probably a J-7 fighter, Chinese copy of a MiG-21F. Max range of the radar is only twenty miles, and he's well outside that . . . fighter radar's down." The Skyranger radar was useless for searching for targets because it supplied only range information to the fighter's computers—this J-7 fighter needed ground-controlled intercept radar to attack targets. It was still deadly, but it was not very sophisticated—Atkins' tiny AIM-120C missiles had a better radar than the J-7 fighter. "There could be more than one out there."

Great, Carter thought. Here's where the shit hits the fan. "Paul, get a range and a firing solution on them," Carter said. "We can't stay radar-silent forever."

"Copy," Scott said. He slaved his attack radar antenna to Atkins' threat-warning receiver bearing and switched it to "Radiate." "Got 'em," Scott called out, switching off the radar immediately. "I counted at least four fighters, forty-five nautical miles, slightly above us. Could be four groups of two."

LIANG-2 FIGHT, CHINESE PLA NAVY J-7 FIGHTER GROUP

Aboard the lead JS-7 fighter of Liang-2 air-defense group, the threat radar suddenly lit up with a fighter-style threat symbol—but it was from one of his own fighters. "Liang flight, lead, keep your damned radars off." The radar indication quickly disappeared. He was leading a group of rather young, inexperienced pilots on their sixth overwater air-defense mission, and they were constantly flipping switches in their cockpits to keep from getting too bored.

The JS-7 fighter was one of the newest and best fighters in the People's Liberation Army Air Force. Originally offered only for export as the Super-7, but later purchased in small numbers by the Chinese government itself, it was a major upgrade of the J-7 fighter, incorporating a lot of imported technology to bring it up-to-date with the rest of the world's best fighters—a French-made multimode attack radar and heads-up display similar to the American F-16 Fighting Falcon, West German/British/Italian–built high-performance Turbo-Union RB199 engines, additional weapons racks to carry ECM pods, and greater fuel capacity. Because there were so few, and because they were so far advanced over their older J-7 cousins, they were used only as flight leads for fighter patrols, where they could vector other J-7 fighters in on targets while attacking targets of their own.

Another radar threat indication flashed on his Thomson-CSF BF screen. He was about to chastise his charges once again . . . before realizing it was from in front of him instead of beside him this time! There was *another* fighter out there! An American fighter—out *here?*

"Fayling, this is Liang flight," the lead J-7 pilot radioed, using the universal call-sign for all Chinese seaborne radar controllers instead of broadcasting the destroyer's name. "Fighter warning. Twelve o'clock, type unknown. What are you tracking?"

The Sea Eagle radar operator aboard *Kaifeng* replied, "Liang flight, we have been tracking a B-52 bomber at your twelve o'clock position, not a fighter. Over."

"I have a fighter-type radar, not a bomber." Curse it, the destroyer had been tracking this intruder all this time thinking it was a *bomber.* How could he be so stupid . . . ? "Request permission to close and identify. Over."

"Liang flight and Sichuan flight, you are clear to close and identify. Liang flight, say your bingo."

"Liang flight is two minutes to bingo," the flight leader reported. "Request permission to send all but myself and one wingman back to base. We will identify the aircraft and engage until Sichuan-Ten flight is in position. Over."

After a short wait, the radar controller aboard *Kaifeng* replied, "Request approved. Homebound Liang elements, climb clear to twelve thousand meters on heading two-nine-zero, vector clear of inbound Sichuan-Ten flight. Liang-Two flight of two, your target is at twelve o'clock, seventy kilometers, altitude ten thousand meters, climb to twelve thousand meters to intercept. Sichuan-Ten flight maintain heading one-five-three. Low patrol, descend to five thousand meters and go to frequency yellow. High patrol, descend to nine thousand five hundred and meet your controller on frequency yellow-5. Target is four-four-zero bullseye. Good hunting."

The lead pilot aboard the JS-7 fighter quickly determined the target's range by the bullseye call—the distance from Davao Airport, a common navigation point for all Chinese fighters—and found that he was within radar range. The JS-7 fighter used an upgraded French radar system called Cyrano-IV, which was very close in capability to the amazing American F-16 fighter radar—it could lock onto multiple targets at fantastic ranges and could attack several targets at once with missiles or guns. "Liang flight, take combat spacing and stand by to engage. . . ."

Up in the cockpit, Major Kelvin Carter took a firm grip on the Megafortress's sidestick controller. This was not going to be an easy run. A million things were zipping through his head: G-limits on the composite fibersteel structures, angle-of-attack limits, airspeed warnings, pitch-angle versus airspeed . . .

"Fighter!" Atkins suddenly screamed out. "Twelve o'clock . . . Jesus, very close, X-band pulse Doppler . . . calling it a Chinese JS-7 fighter. Man, he's right on top of us . . . !"

"Lock him up and engage," Carter cried out. He double-checked the rows of consent switches on his left panel. "Stand by for descent, crew."

Scott reacted first, hitting the "Transmit" button on his attack radar and letting the radar lock onto the fighters ahead. "Two targets, twelve o'clock, closure rate eleven hundred . . . additional targets, climbing and going away, looks like they're disengaging . . . I've got a lock on the two heading for us . . ."

Atkins reacted next, activating his forward jammers to shut down the X-band fire-control radar. He readied other jammers to get the Skyranger radar when it came up as well . . .

Karbayjal activated his weapons computers and watched as each AIM-120 Scorpion missile completed its split-second built-in checks. "BIT checks completed, data transfer . . . missiles away." Two bright streaks of light flashed past the cockpit as two radar-guided missiles sped into the darkness.

Just then Kellerman noticed several low-flying objects on her ISAR side-locking radar display, overtaking them from the left. They formed a slowly dispersing trail of subsonic missiles, all traveling northwestbound. "Tomahawks away, Tomahawks away!" she cried out.

"Missiles tracking . . . active seekers on . . . bad track on one Scorpion, looks like a tracking fault," Karbayjal called out. Carter could see the missile plume from the right pylon wobble a bit, seconds before exploding. "Lost track on one missile."

"Descending, crew," Carter called out. "Nancy, watch my redlines. Here we go . . ." Carter pulled the Megafortress's eight throttles to 70-percent power, waited for fifty knots of airspeed to bleed off, raised the airbrakes, then tipped the Megafortress into a steep 70-degree right bank, keeping forward pressure on the control stick but keeping the long, pointed SST-style nose on the horizon. With no more lift being developed by the huge wings, the four-hundred-thousand-pound bomber descended like Lucifer cast into Hell. . . .

The radar target on his Cyrano-IV fire-control radar had suddenly started descending, so fast the radar could hardly keep up with it—it looked like it was crashing, and no one had shot a missile yet . . .

Just then his radar threat-receiver flashed a "Missile Launch" indication. "Liang flight, break!" he shouted on the radio. In a pre-determined sequence, the J-7 fighter climbed and turned right, and the JS-7 fighter, because it was more powerful and could climb faster to re-attack, descended and turned left. The JS-7 fighter also carried radar-jamming and chaff and flare pods, and the pilot made sure all were activated as he brought his weapons on-line and prepared to attack. "Fayling, Fayling, Liang-Two flight under missile attack!" He dumped chaff and flare bundles, rolled right, went to military power, and raised the nose to re-acquire the bomber . . . or whatever it was.

Just as he did, he saw a flash of light above and a bit behind him, then a growing trail of fire, and he knew his wingman was hit. "Fayling, Liang-507 is hit. 507, 507 can you hear me? You are on fire. Repeat you are on fire. Eject! Eject! Eject!" No response. The trail of fire began to grow as the J-7 fighter spiraled to the sea and disappeared.

CHINESE DESTROYER *KAIFENG*

The radar blips first appeared as helicopters and were classified as such by the destroyer's Sea Eagle three-dimensional search radar, but it was quickly obvious that the air target was climbing and accelerating much too quickly for a rotary-wing machine. The radar operator aboard the destroyer *Kaifeng* immediately rang his superior officer in the ship's Combat Information Center.

"Sir, rapidly moving air target launched from a vessel in the *Sterett* surface-action group, bearing one-four-eight, speed . . . speed approaching four hundred knots and accelerating, altitude decreasing to below one hundred meters, range five-zero nautical miles." There was no aircraft carrier out there, so it could only be one thing—"Suspected Tomahawk cruise missiles in flight . . ."

The officer in CIC reacted immediately: he hit the alarm button and rang the line direct to the bridge: "Bridge, CIC, missile alert, missile alert, we have suspected American cruise missiles being launched from the *Sterett* surface action group."

"Bridge copies," came the reply. "Give us a count and stand by to engage."

"CIC copies."

"Sir! Aircraft warning, attack warning, Liang-Two fighter group reports they are under fighter attack . . ."

"Fighter attack!" the commander shouted. *"What fighters?* You said there was only one bomber up there!"

"Liang-Two reports a missile attack, sir. He reports his wingman has been hit by a missile. Sir, the B-52 bomber aircraft rapidly decelerating, range closing to sixty nautical miles, airspeed six-one-zero and accelerating, altitude now seven thousand meters . . . six thousand meters . . . five thousand . . . sir, heavy jamming on my scope . . . attempting frequency jumping . . . heavy jamming persisting on all search frequencies. I cannot hop away to clear frequency!"

CHINESE DESTROYER *JINAN*, IN THE CELEBES SEA, NEAR DAVAO GULF

"Sir, destroyer *Kaifeng* reports incoming Tomahawk cruise missiles from the southeast and has issued an air-defense warning for all vessels. He also reports a suspected B-52 bomber in a rapid descent heading northwest, and heavy radar jamming on all frequencies. There was also a report about a fighter attack, number and type unknown."

Captain Jhijun Lin of the People's Liberation Army Navy destroyer *Jinan* nodded resolutely. "Sound general quarters, alert the task force, begin intermittent radar search pattern. We can expect our own air threats any—"

"Sir! Frigate *Yingtan* reports radar contact, aircraft, bearing two-zero-five, range forty-seven nautical miles, altitude . . . altitude three hundred meters, sir, speed four hundred seventy knots. No IFF codes observed. They report possible multiple inbounds on this bearing."

"Understood," Captain Jhijun acknowledged. As the combat-readiness alarm sounded throughout the ship, the manual track operator on the bridge of the EF4-class destroyer *Jinan* drew in the position of the radar contact on a large grease board. "I want a positive identification immediately."

It was finally beginning, Captain Jhijun told himself. Although the intruder aircraft were detected very late—sea-skimming targets should be detectable at twenty miles by the frigate *Yingtan*'s Sea Eagle radar, but targets at three hundred meters should be seen easily at fifty miles—he wished it were starting a bit more dramatically.

After learning what the American Air Battle Force had in their arsenal on the island of Guam, he would have expected an attack by B-1 or FB-111 bombers, flying supersonic at sea-skimming altitudes. From these radar contact's flight profiles, these appeared to be nothing more than B-52 bombers lumbering in. And they were coming in from the south, which was totally expected as well—the two layers of destroyers, frigates, and patrol boats in the Philippine Sea east of Mindanao were designed to herd the American bombers in the only "safe" flight path they could take—fly in from the south right into the mouth of Davao Gulf.

"Sir, missile warning. *Yingtan*'s escorts report missiles inbound, no count, all sea-skimmers. Patrol boats maneuvering to intercept. Good radar track on all inbounds, intercept confidence is high. Identity now confirmed by flight profile as B-52 bombers."

So it was confirmed—not B-1s, only B-52 bombers. An easy kill.

The B-52s were flying right into a trap. Four frigates, one destroyer, and sixteen antiaircraft escort patrol boats were waiting for anyone stupid enough to allow themselves to be steered around by surface threats. Two of the frigates, *Yingtan* stationed on the southern perimeter and *Xiamen* on the northern side, were armed with short-range Hong Qian-61 surface-to-air missiles—deadly within their limited range—but his destroyer *Jinan,* in the center of the two-hundred-kilometer-long gauntlet, had the HQ-91 surface-to-air missile system, a licensed copy of the French Masurca medium-range SAM system. The HQ-91 was deadly out to forty-five kilometers even to low-flying supersonic aircraft—this B-52 would be an easy kill. *Jinan* had already seen action—it was that ship that had successfully guided the fighters in on the arrogant American Navy fighters over the Celebes Sea not too long ago. The little patrol boats were deadly as well—their guns could knock down any antiship missile in the American inventory and throw up a cloud of lead in front of any aircraft stupid enough to stray within a few kilometers of them.

But even the B-52s could carry a big punch. "Radio to all attack-group ships and to Task Force Master, we are under attack, request air support against incoming B-52 bombers," Jhijun said.

Obviously Harpoon antiship missiles, he thought. They were

lucky—they did not start their attack until they had a radar fix on *Yingtan*. That meant the Americans had no other radar aircraft in the area spotting targets for the B-52s. Jhijun checked the plot board. The B-52s will be coming within range of *Jinan*'s radars in a few minutes—if they survived that long—and the longer-range HQ-91 missiles would not miss. But Jhijun fully expected the B-52s to turn tail and run after all their Harpoon missiles were expended.

"Patrol boat 682 engaging antiship missiles . . . patrol boat 688 engaging missiles . . . *Yingtan* now reporting six incoming aircraft, all from the south, range to closest aircraft twenty nautical miles. Same flight profile, reported as B-52 bombers on low-level antiship attack." The reports began coming in as one by one the Harpoon missiles were destroyed. "First B-52 turning west, appears to be disengaging."

"Lost contact with patrol boat 642, sir," the combat information center officer on *Jinan* reported. "Patrol boat 688 reports two vessels afire, suspect the other as patrol boat 651. Frigate *Yingtan* reports minor damage from antiship missile, but is still under way and combat capable." With six B-52s on the loose, each with the capacity to carry twelve Harpoon missiles, they had to expect some attrition. "Second B-52 disengaging . . ."

So the B-52s were going to be content with launching a few Harpoon missiles and fleeing. The fighters would be able to mop them up then, Jhijun thought—they still had to contend with the Harpoon missiles and Tomahawk cruise missiles, though. . . .

This was incredible, the Chinese pilot of the JS-7 fighter thought—one moment he was leading an eight-ship attack group on a routine night patrol, the next moment he was alone and under attack by an unseen, unidentified foe.

"Fayling, Fayling," the pilot radioed to the destroyer *Kaifeng*, which was controlling the intercept in this sector, "where is the target? I need a vector."

"Liang flight, target is in a rapid descent at your eight o'clock position, thirty kilometers, altitude four thousand meters," the radar controller reported—apparently he was too excited to remember that the other J-7 fighter had been destroyed. "Turn left heading two-niner-five and descend to three thousand meters to intercept."

Four thousand meters? Less than sixty seconds ago he was at ten thousand meters! The JS-7 pilot threw his fighter into a steep left turn and pushed the nose down, using his airbrakes judiciously to avoid ripping his PL-7 and PL-2 missiles from their pylons.

"Liang, your target is at your eleven to twelve o'clock, twenty-seven kilometers."

He was getting heavy jamming, but his French-made radar was sophisticated enough to frequency-hop and avoid most of it. "Intermittent contact," the JS-7 pilot reported. The lock-on was good enough for a radar range and firing solution, so he quickly selected a PL-7 radar-guided missile. "Liang shooting radar one . . ." He waited a few seconds, then fired his second one. "Shooting radar two . . ."

Atkins was so sure the fighter back there was going to take a shot that he found himself staring at the threat-indicator light. As soon as it illuminated, he shouted, "Missile launch! Level off!" He found himself crushed into his seat by G-forces as Carter pulled the B-52 out of its high-banked dive, the fuselage and wings creaking so loudly from the stress that it seemed they would shatter like a crystal champagne glass. "Break left!" Atkins shouted on interphone as he ejected chaff out the right ejector racks. Carter heeled the EB-52 Megafortress hard left, so hard that Atkins' helmet banged against his left instrument panel—but he kept his finger on the chaff button long enough to create a good-sized cloud. Carter shoved the Megafortress's nose down below the horizon to regain his airspeed, and the negative-Gs he created caused dirt, loose checklists and papers, and all sorts of unrecognizable garbage to float around the cabin as if they were suddenly weightless in orbit. Atkins felt his stomach go up with the floating junk, and he ripped off his oxygen mask to keep from filling it up with vomit.

"You OK, E-dub?" Karbayjal said. Atkins turned and saw his gunner with a worried expression on his face and one hand on his shoulder. The plane was in a gut-wrenching turn, they were under attack by a Chinese fighter—but Karbayjal was worried about *him*.

"Sure . . . sure . . ." Atkins moaned.

"Good," Karbayjal said. He settled himself back into his seat as calmly and as easily as could be, as if being tossed around and squished by four times Earth's gravity were a normal occurrence for him. "You're doing good, E-dub," Karbayjal added. "Keep it up and let's get that sucker. Set up your jammers and take care of the uplink."

Atkins struggled to refocus his eyes on his threat display. His automatic jamming system picked out the best frequency range and applied it to the correct antennae for the threat—in this case, an X3-band uplink signal driven to the tail antennae—and it would pump out chaff as well, but it would not tell the pilot when or in what direction to turn to avoid the missile. Tracked on the tail radar, the Chinese missile appeared to be wavering from the chaff to the EB-52, not entirely fooled. This close-in, the missile might lock onto the Megafortress if they made another turn. "Pilot, roll out!" Atkins called out. "Guns, stand by with Stingers!"

Karbayjal smiled at Atkins—he was finally taking charge of this intercept. "Roger, E-dub." Karbayjal already had a good lock on the incoming Chinese missiles and was waiting for them to close in. It was a risky move—hoping that the Megafortress's low radar cross-section would defeat the missiles more than maneuvering would. They needed to build up a new speed reserve as well, since even the Megafortress bled off a lot of airspeed in tight turns.

But the jammers weren't completely shutting down the Chinese fighter's uplink—the missiles were still tracking. "Missiles still coming!" Atkins shouted on the interphone.

"I'm ready with Stingers," Karbayjal told him, "but you gotta do it. My Stingers are strictly last resort . . ."

Atkins took another calculated risk—as he began pumping out chaff once more from the left ejectors, he overrode the automatic jammers and reduced the transmitter power in half, letting a strong fighter fire control lock on the bleedthrough, then shouted, "Pilot, break right!"

The missiles continued to bore in. . . .

Now there were *three* radar targets out there, the Chinese JS-7 pilot cursed. The first was obviously a chaff cloud—it had begun to dissipate very quickly, and his PL-7 missiles weren't fooled. His radar seemed to get a firm lock-on just then on the real target, but it turned out it was a firm lock on another chaff cloud. The target was scooting right at nearly a thousand kilometers an hour, while the big, bright, original target was dead ahead—at zero kilometers per hour. Obviously a chaff cloud—and his missiles were both going for it. A clean miss.

"Fayling, Liang, where is Sichuan-Ten flight? I have no radar missiles left."

"Liang, Sichuan-Ten flight has been separated into two flights of two, high patrol diverting north to intercept air targets under control by destroyer *Zunyi.* Your helpers will be designated Sichuan-31 flight of two, now at ten thousand meters, range two-one-five bullseye."

"What about the rest of my Liang-Two flight?"

"Liang-Two homebound are still at twelve thousand meters, northwest-bound."

"Are you crazy?" the JS-7 pilot shouted. "Turn those bastards around! Liang-Two flight of six, reverse course, descend to three thousand meters, prepare to engage!"

There was a scratchy reply on the radio—they heard him, although they probably wished they did not. If they turned around, there was no chance they'd land back at Zamboanga—but ditching in the Celebes Sea or landing at Cotabato was better than allowing this B-52 or whatever it was to head in toward the fleet unopposed.

He had one more chance before he had to return to base—throttles to max afterburner, close in fast, two PL-2 heat-seeking missile shots, a gun pass with his 23-millimeter cannon, then abort. The JS-7 pilot pushed his throttle to max afterburner, watched the range quickly decrease to less than fifteen kilometers, got a seeker lock-on from his two remaining PL-2 missiles, then launched them both at once. . . .

• • •

"Bandit at six o'clock, crew, descending behind us," Karbay-jal called out, carefully watching the Chinese fighter on his tail radar. The Chinese fighter was sending out jamming signals, but at this range even the Megafortress's smaller tail radar burned through it easily. "Bandit's accelerating . . . Jesus, stand by for missile attack . . . E-dub, stand by for flares on the right . . ."

The infrared tail warning receiver's "Missile Warning" light in all crew stations, which detected the heat of a fighter in the rear quadrant and locked onto it, was immediately replaced by a high-pitched tone in everyone's headset and a "Missile Launch" warning light. "IR missile attack!" Atkins shouted. "Break left!" Atkins immediately released four bundles of flares simultaneously from the right ejector.

But Karbayjal had seen the missile launch and was ready. Careful not to aim the Stinger airmine rockets at the flares, he waited until the missiles tracked, then ejected the flares and re-acquired the Megafortress's hot engine exhausts, then opened fire with a stream of missiles. He launched six Stingers, then watched for any sign of pursuit. When he saw at least one Chinese missile survive, he shouted on interphone, "Reverse! Climb if possible!"

When Karbayjal made his call, Atkins had switched ejector racks, selecting the left ejector, and pumped out four more flares. Simultaneously, Carter immediately threw the Megafortress into a screaming right bank and held it until the stall-warning horn came on. "Can't climb, guns!" Carter shouted.

"Disregard," the gunner said as the last missile disappeared from his radarscope. "Fighter's coming in, four miles . . . three miles . . . Stingers firing . . ." The Megafortress crew could hear the heavy *Crack! Crack! Crack! Crack!* and a rumble through-out the bomber as Karbayjal fired four more missiles at the fighter closing in. . . .

It had to be a fighter, the JS-7 pilot thought, since only a fighter could possibly move that *fast.* The flares that the target was ejecting seemed as bright as the sun in the complete dark-ness of the Celebes Sea. His PL-2 missiles obviously thought so, because they tracked and destroyed the flares with ease. He was now weaponless except for his twin-barreled 23-millimeter cannon.

But the stream of flares pointed to the target's location, even if it wasn't apparent on radar, so the pilot kept his throttle at min afterburner and closed in to cannon range . . .

Suddenly four bright bursts of light erupted right in front of his fighter, stretching from his left wingtip all the way across the nose. His JS-7 fighter began to shudder, as if shivering with fear, and the shudder continued right into a full-blown stall.

"Fayling, Fayling, Liang-Two, Mayday, Mayday, Mayday, I'm hit, I'm hit . . ." He saw the "Engine Overspeed" and "Hydraulic Press" lights illuminate and pulled his ejection handle seconds before his controls locked and his fighter began a death spiral to the sea.

DESTROYER *JINAN*

"Sir! Destroyer *Zunyi* reports he is under attack by antiship missiles from the east," another report suddenly came in. *"Zunyi* is engaging. Sichuan-Ten flight of two Q-5 fighters are engaging suspected B-52 bombers at low altitude."

"Where's *Zunyi?*" Jhijun shouted. The answer came a few moments later—only one hundred nautical miles east of *Jinan*. *Zunyi* was an older Luda-class destroyer, part of the Philippine Sea cordon; it carried no surface-to-air missile system because it was designed to engage surface ships and submarines, not aircraft. "Get a feed from *Zunyi*'s CIC and integrate their plots on our—"

"Sir! Incoming missiles! Bearing two-six-five, high altitude, range twenty nautical miles, speed subsonic, multiple inbounds, intercept course!"

"*What?*" Jhijun resisted the urge to swivel around in his seat and look at the west—it was pitch black outside, with a light overcast sky, and he knew he wouldn't see a thing. "How the hell could missiles get that close? Radar, get your heads out of your asses or I will have you on deck when those missiles hit! Report on fire-control status—immediately!"

"Fire control reports fully operational, good track on all inbounds, intercept confidence is high." Jhijun wished he could be more confident himself—first contact at twenty miles was far, far too close.

"Targets maneuvering slightly," the CIC officer reported. "Range to air targets, mark, fifteen nautical miles, bearing two-six-five, speed five hundred . . ."

The targets weren't maneuvering . . . offset range was decreasing . . . bearing was constant . . . "Antiradar missiles!" Jhijun suddenly shouted. He knew all about the Americans' radar-homing missiles, especially the loitering cruise missiles— this was probably a flight of them coming in now. But how in hell did those missiles get so close before being detected . . . ?

Pushing the big Megafortress bomber to descend at over twelve thousand feet per minute, it took less than three minutes to descend to two hundred feet—yet with Chinese warships all around them, it felt like an eternity.

"Golf-band search radar at eleven o'clock . . ." Atkins shouted on interphone; "India-band gun fire control radar now at one to two o'clock position . . . Christ, Golf-band radar changing to Charlie-band missile director . . . another India-band fire control radar at two-thirty . . . dammit, are we in range of that destroyer yet? We're going to get nailed . . . ! I've got a possible fighter GCI signal from that destroyer now, he might be vectoring in more fighters."

"Ready in range with the first TACIT RAINBOW missile," Kellerman called out after checking the information on the side-looking radar display once again and updating her map of all the ships in the area. "Right turn thirty degrees to escape, next target will be off the nose at twenty miles."

Atkins rechecked the weapon indications one more time— missile engine, guidance, autopilot, data link, warhead continuity all reporting ready. "Doors coming open . . . missile one away . . . missile two away . . ."

As the Megafortress banked away to the right, the AGM-136A TACIT RAINBOW missiles sped off to the left and descended to less than one hundred feet above the sea, then continued their left turn until they were aiming directly at the Chinese destroyer. At the same time, Atkins programmed another missile on the next target, what ISAR reported as a Huangfeng-class guided-missile patrol boat transmitting with an India-band gun fire control radar. "Missile three reporting ready."

"Left turn ten degrees to escape," Kellerman called out. "I'll take us within ten miles of that patrol boat unless a missile radar comes up." In which case, Kellerman thought, Atkins better hold it together long enough to warn the crew. She knew it was a big mistake to send that scrawny little BB-stacker on this mission—Atkins might have an IQ larger than the national debt and could modify a wristwatch to jam half of Cleveland, and he seemed to do OK with Karbayjal holding his hand, but he simply wasn't cut out for combat.

"Pilots copy," Carter acknowledged.

"Missile three counting down . . . missile three away . . . doors closed, clear left turn."

DESTROYER *JINAN*

"Sir, destroyer *Kaifeng* reports their patrol boats are engaging inbound cruise missiles. Admiral Feng is recommending frigate *Yingtan* move east to help cover the southeast approaches."

"Negative," Captain Jhijun shot back. "My vessels are under attack by antiradar missiles—they are right on top of us. *Yingtan* will remain where it is until—"

And then he realized that if antiradar missiles were appearing out of nowhere—it had to be a stealth bomber attack. The stealth bomber itself would not show on radar right away, but the antiradar missiles would show once they were launched—the missiles would have a smaller radar cross-section than the bombers that launched them. . . . "Radio to all task force vessels, suspect stealth bomber attack, number unknown," Captain Jhijun cried. "CIC, directed search for carrier aircraft by visual and infrared scanners. Find that damned bomber! Find it!"

"Sir, *Kaifeng* reports B-52 bomber is launching subsonic

missiles . . . no successful hit on any Tomahawk missiles because of heavy radar jamming. B-52 bomber closing to within thirty miles of *Kaifeng* . . ."

"Sir, destroyer *Kaifeng* reports one hit by a Tomahawk cruise missile."

No one spoke on the combat bridge. They couldn't believe it. What was going on? *"Kaifeng* radioing for assistance. Task force group commander dispatching frigate *Yingtan* to assist . . . *Kaifeng* reports additional hits by antiradar missiles from the B-52, sir! Destroyer *Zunyi* now reports under attack by sea-skimming antiship missiles . . . patrol boat 6114 hit by Harpoon antiship missile, extensive damage . . . lost contact with patrol boat . . . *Zunyi* reports contact with B-52 bombers east of their position, number unknown . . ."

Damn them! With *Yingtan* moving out of position and *Kaifeng* damaged, *Jinan* was now the southernmost warship guarding Davao Gulf. Ships as large as destroyers needed a frigate for heavy close-in air support, and Jhijun was losing his! Well, he was not going to suffer the same fate as *Kaifeng*. "Emitters in standby!" the commander of the destroyer *Jinan* shouted. "Turn the radars off! Use all available personnel with infrared and electro-optical spotters, but *find those bombers!"*

The nightmare was back.

Only two days since first stirring up the hornet's nest with their reconnaissance overflight, McLanahan and Cobb were back at it again in their B-2 Black Knight stealth bomber—only this time they not only had to examine and count the hornets coming out of the hive, they had to swat at them. To make things worse, there appeared to be more hornets than ever out here, and they seemed mad as hell and ready to inflict some serious stings.

"Radar down on that destroyer . . . fire-control radars going down on all area vessels," Patrick McLanahan reported to Henry Cobb. "Fourteen miles before impact—they figured it out pretty fast. Most operators won't figure out their radars are under attack until the first few hit." He expanded the God's-eye view on the Super Multi Function Display before him, inundating his screen with NIRTSat satellite data received only a few minutes earlier. "I've got a few fire-control radars still up from those patrol boats, but most don't have anything but surface-search radars." Cobb clicked his mike in reply, still seated in his usual frozen position—hands on stick and throttles, eyes straight ahead, unmoving.

How the hell could Cobb stay so calm? McLanahan wondered to himself. He sees everything that goes on, he studies the Super Multi Function Display, he sees the threat warnings, yet he sits as calmly as ever, staring straight ahead. He looks the same on training flights as he does in combat.

"TACIT RAINBOW missiles are entering their holding pattern until the radar comes up," McLanahan added. "Go to five-twenty on the airspeed and let's get out of here before the radars come back up." Cobb clicked again and pushed power up to full military thrust—the faster the B-2 could get past these ships, the better.

McLanahan's B-2 Black Knight had a few stings itself this time around—no more reconnaissance pods, now that the NIRTSats appeared to be working again. The B-2 carried four AGM-136A TACIT RAINBOW antiradar cruise missiles and four AGM-88C HARM antiradar missiles in clip-in racks in its left bomb bay, plus a Common Strategic Rotary Launcher with six AGM-84E SLAM TV-guided missiles in the right bomb bay. The TACIT RAINBOW antiradar missiles homed in on radar transmissions, and they had turbojet engines, wings, and autopilots that allowed them to stay aloft and, if an enemy radar was turned off, orbit a suspected target area to wait for the radar to be reactivated. The four TACIT RAINBOW missiles that McLanahan had launched from thirty miles away would remain in their orbits for another ten minutes within a few miles of the last-known position of the radars—this would give all the strike aircraft the chance to get past the Chinese warships and move into the target area.

FRIGATE *YINGTAN,* **FORTY MILES SOUTH OF DESTROYER** *JINAN*

Several minutes had passed, and no hits reported by any ships since *Kaifeng.* If the carrier aircraft were the same speed or a bit faster than the antiradar missiles, the carrier aircraft would be very close by now. They had sailors with night-vision goggles and infrared scanners looking for the missiles, but unless they heard it or got lucky there was almost no chance of their finding a tiny loitering cruise missile up there without radar. A few of the larger patrol boats had low-light TV cameras and infrared fire-control sensors on their 57- and 37-millimeter guns, but their field of view was very small, and getting a lock on a fast-moving target was difficult.

The intercom clicked on: "Bridge, CIC, request permission to activate search radar for two sweeps."

There was a slight pause; then: "Acknowledged." To the radar operator, he said, "Two sweeps. Shut down immediately if there's a target within five miles. Call out bearings to contacts for gun control."

"Acknowledged. Radar coming on in three, two, one . . . now."

One sweep, twelve seconds, and they knew the awful truth: "Bridge, CIC, multiple small targets within five miles, all bearings. Additional air targets, two large targets in trail formation, bearing two-seven-eight, range to closest target ten nautical miles. Radar down."

The commander of the frigate *Yingtan* was on the all-stations call intercom immediately. "CIC, all thirty-seven gun stations, all thirty-seven gun stations, fire defensive pattern, multiple inbound missiles, all quadrants. Attempt visual acquisition. Release radar decoys. Shut down all radars and verify."

Almost immediately the frigate's four twin 37-millimeter antiaircraft guns began firing, sweeping the sky with shells in predetermined patterns that would cover all but the ship's centerline area—fortunately the patrol boats were dispersed at least six kilometers away to avoid being hit by the frigate's barrage.

"Helm, forty degrees starboard. CIC, ship turning starboard, shoot portside chaff rockets."

From the sky, the barrage of gunfire might have looked like a fireworks-show finale, with winks of muzzle flashes and tracers shooting out in all directions. The frigate meanwhile began a series of sharp turns and accelerations designed to get as far away as possible from the last spot where the radar was turned on—they knew that was where the loitering missile was headed. *Yingtan* also had mortars that fired radar-decoying chaff rockets into the air, launching them on the side opposite the ship's turn—they would act as decoys if the missiles carried active radar seekers.

Yingtan's gunners were rewarded with several spectacular flashes as the guns found targets, and missiles could be seen splashing down in their wake—a few dangerously close, less than a dozen meters away—but none hit. Two missiles went after the tiny radar-emitting decoy buoys dropped overboard by the frigate, and the bridge crew was treated to a good-sized explosion just a hundred meters aft as the missile impacted. In just a few seconds, all of the antiradar missiles were defeated by the frigate *Yingtan*.

But all that gunfire only saved them from the small antiradar missiles—the aircraft that launched all those missiles were getting away. "CIC, concentrate one hundred-millimeter guns at the last position of that bomber. Maybe we will get lucky. Prepare to engage with HQ-61 missiles. Comm, radio to all patrol boats and to Fleet Master, suspected heavy stealth bomber aircraft inbound to Davao Gulf, number unknown."

The sudden flurry of gunfire into the night sky was spectacular and frightening at the same time. It looked like a dome of sparklers had formed over the frigate in the distance, like some unearthly glittering spaceship half-submerged in the ocean—except they both knew that those pretty sparklers meant death to any aircraft that strayed too close. Cobb instinctively banked farther west to avoid the area where most of the gunfire was being concentrated, even though McLanahan estimated they were at least ten miles abeam the closest ship. "Jesus Christ," McLanahan muttered. "Look at that . . ."

Cobb said nothing.

"And we're only seeing about one every twelve tracer rounds . . ."

"It's not the guns I'm worried about," Cobb said. "I'm waiting for the SAMs from that frigate."

"He hit us with a radar sweep powerful enough to paint us," McLanahan said. "He must know we're out here." McLanahan used the tracer rounds to find the frigate with his forward-looking infrared scanner, and the imaging heat-seeking telescope locked on easily to the huge vessel. "I got a lock on the big mother ship. That must be the frigate. Laser rangefinder on . . . laser firing . . ." Immediately the laser rangefinder computed the precise distance to the target, completed the firing solution for the B-2's complement of weapons. McLanahan touched the right-bomb-bay icon on the bottom of his Super Multi Function Display, and the weapons computer picked a SLAM TV-guided missile, automatically reducing the SMFD screen in half and using the right side of the big screen to display SLAM seeker video transmission. "The shit's going to hit the fan as soon as this puppy goes," McLanahan reminded Cobb, then he moved the Bombing System Switch from "Manual" to "Auto." "Missile Counting down . . . missile one away . . ."

The right bomb-bay doors slid open, and the single CSRL launcher ejected a SLAM guided missile into the slipstream. The missile fell about fifty feet as its gyroscope stabilization system steadied the fifteen-hundred-pound missile; then, when the air data probes detected the proper airflow and deceleration parameters indicating a clean release from the Black Knight bomber, the powerful turbojet engine kicked in. Following the initial heading from the B-2's master computer, it descended to less than one hundred feet in the blink of an eye and steered immediately on course for the frigate, taking it on an "over-the-shoulder" trajectory as the B-2 sped away. Seven seconds later, the launcher had rotated and ejected a second missile.

The radar operator on *Yingtan* had just reactivated the Sea Eagle air-search radar at that precise moment—and what he saw caused stars to shoot through his head. "Two aircraft, bearing two-eight-one, altitude two hundred meters, speed . . . *incoming missiles, incoming missiles,* bearing two-eight-one, range fifteen miles, speed six hundred twenty knots, altitude twenty meters!"

And then he made a fateful mistake—he shut down his radar a second time, thinking they were under attack by antiradar missiles again.

The CIC officer in charge realized the Sea Eagle radar was down again, but hesitated a few seconds before ordering it reactivated so the antiaircraft guns could train on the supersonic targets. There were other supersonic antiradar missiles in the American arsenal, such as the HARM missile—this could be one of them. "Deploy decoys. Bridge, CIC, incoming missiles, evasive action, radar down." He waited a few seconds for the antiradar-missile decoys to be ejected, then ordered the Sea Eagle radar reactivated and the antiaircraft guns brought on-line.

But at almost Mach one, it took only sixty seconds for the first SLAM missile to reach its target. With less than thirty seconds left in the first missile's flight, they had just enough time to acquire the missile and let the Sea Eagle search radar slave the I-band "Rice Lamp" fire-control radars on the incoming missiles. The 37-millimeter guns on the *Yingtan* were just as accurate as on the TACIT RAINBOW missiles, but only the two starboard mounts were committed this time. . . .

The left half of the Super Multi Function Display was displaying video transmitted from the imaging infrared camera on the first SLAM missile, and even Henry Cobb, who normally sat with eyes caged straight ahead on his instrument panel, couldn't help but take a few glances at the picture as the missile bore into its target. The image was incredible— the sea, seen as shimmering green streaks along the bottom of the picture, whizzed past like some sort of early sci-fi warp drive; and, in the center, the hot dot slowly enlarged and took the shape of a huge warship. The missile was right on course.

Suddenly, several flashes of light could be seen popping from the warship. "They got a lock on the SLAM," McLanahan said. On the right side of the SMFD, he touched the spinning circular cursor on the 3-D image of the destroyer, spoke "Change target," then slid his finger to the left. The SLAM missile veered left in response. Just as the video image of the destroyer was about to disappear off the screen, McLanahan slid the cursor to the right, and the missile followed. A few seconds later, McLanahan replaced the cursor on the destroyer. "Thirty seconds to impact," he told Cobb. "C'mon, baby, you can do it . . ."

But his efforts were useless. As soon as the missile settled back on course to the destroyer, another large flash erupted, and the video went dark. "Dammit! Lost the first SLAM." The words SLAM 1 NO CONTACT flashed three times on the left half of the SMFD, then the video from the second missile filled the screen.

"You're not getting this one," Patrick said. Using the touchscreen, he pre-programmed a zigzag course for the second SLAM. "Hit *that,* you peckerheads . . ."

The ship's defensive guns successfully hit the first SLAM seconds before it hit them, but the second missile was impossible to hit—it was all over the sky, skimming just a few meters above the water, and the guns could not keep up with it. The missile finally plowed into the starboard gunwale just below the number six 37-millimeter gun turret.

The penetrating warhead cap, propelled by the missile's powerful rocket motor, drove the missile through the number-twelve lifeboat on its davits and barely managed to pierce the heavy armor of the number-six gun turret before detonating the five-hundred-pound high-explosive. The blast ripped a gaping hole in the side of the frigate, killing the gun turret's ten-man crew and instantly knocking the gun out of commission.

"Good hit!" Patrick McLanahan cried out. "One impact . . . only minor secondaries, good hit but no kill." The Super Multi Function Display automatically switched back to full integrated "God's-eye" view, and Patrick scanned the area. "Search radars down . . . cancel that, search radars back up. Everybody's transmitting . . . I've got air-search radars at five o'clock and a new one at two o'clock. India-band missile radar's still up at five o'clock. Damn . . . we didn't knock out that frigate yet. So he can still launch missiles . . ."

Just then a "Missile Warning" light began to blink on both the Super Multi Function Display and the pilot's center CRT monitor.

Patrick said, "Now I've got another Charlie-band missile director radar at one to two o'clock—that must be from the center destroyer." He was about to touch the electronic coun-termeasures icon on the bottom of the SMFD, but the computer had already brought the ECM status panel forward on the screen—and what he saw caused his throat to go instantly dry. "Charlie-band missile director . . . compu-ter's calling it a DRBC-51 radar directing an HQ-91 SAM system . . ."

"A -91?" Cobb asked. "Shit, we're well inside that mother's range!"

"I know, I know," McLanahan moaned. He had spent too long screwing with the SLAM missiles and lost track of all the other warships around them. "All trackbreakers active, missile warning system and HAVE GLANCE jammers ready, chaff and flares ready, HARM missile programming against that radar . . . shit, shit! Charlie-band tracker changing to Charlie-three command . . ."

The "Missile Warning" indication changed to a "Missile Lock" warning. "Missile radar locked on!" McLanahan shouted. "Trackbreakers on . . . descend and accelerate if possi-ble . . ."

They were already as low as they could safely go at night—the huge B-2 was less than one hundred feet above the Celebes Sea, with Cobb hand-flying the Black Knight, since the terrain-following computer would not fly the bomber overwater below two hundred feet. "C'mon, you guys, where the *hell* are you . . . ?"

McLanahan was rewarded a second later with precise range and bearing information from his B-2 to the destroyer dis-played on his SMFD. He knew he was not using radars or lasers to get that data—that meant that his wingman, the second B-2 stealth bomber in his attack formation, was ranging on the destroyer and data-sharing the information with him. The question was, who was going to get there first?

CHINESE DESTROYER *JINAN*

"Locked onto first air target," the operator of *Jinan*'s aft HQ-91 missile fire control radar reported. "Slight jamming on lower bands, switching to frequency-agile mode . . . Temporarily clear of jamming, ready with missile detector, sir."

"Understood," the chief of the *Jinan*'s Combat Information Center replied. "Aft launcher, report."

In the large aft missile magazine, a large eighteen-missile rotating drum dropped an HQ-91 onto a rail and fed it forward to an open station, where four missileers snapped large triangular fins on the nose and tail sections of the missile body. Two other technicians made a fast check of the finning process, and the missile was sent forward, erected, and rammed upwards onto the launcher rails. A second magazine crew had done the same with a second missile for the twin-rail launcher. As the missiles clicked into place on the launcher, a continuity check was automatically performed and an electronic report received from each missile—if the "report" was missing or erroneous, the launcher would immediately swivel over and down and spit the bad missile down an armored safety chute for examination or disposal.

Thirty seconds after the alert was sounded, the aft launcher was loaded and ready, with two more missiles belowdecks finned and ready. "Aft launcher reports ready, sir," the aft launch operator reported.

"Deck clear, stand by to launch on three, two, one, *launch . . .*" The HQ-91 missiles operator checked his readouts, gripped the launch handle, squeezed the safety grip, pulled the trigger, and hit the launch button with his thumb. "Missile one away . . . missile two . . . !"

"Incoming missiles!" one of the Sea Eagle radar operators suddenly shouted. "High-speed, bearing two-four-one degrees . . ." Two AGM-84E SLAM missiles from the *second*

B-2 Black Knight in McLanahan's attack formation had detected the HQ-91 missile fire-control radar and homed in on it just after missile launch.

But like the TACIT RAINBOW missiles, the SLAMS were big, subsonic targets, and easy for the destroyer to lock on radar. The vessel's guns began firing, and with full radar tracking and fire control, they could not miss—both SLAMS were destroyed well before they reached *Jinan.*

But that left them vulnerable to two HARM missiles fired from McLanahan's B-2. Like TACIT RAINBOW, the High-Speed Anti-Radar Missiles homed in on enemy radar transmission, but instead of cruising to their targets over long distances and being very inviting targets for enemy gunfire, HARM flew at speeds over Mach three and were often untouched or even undetectable. The longer *Jinan* kept radars on to track the incoming SLAM missiles, the easier it was for the HARMS to find their targets. The missiles homed in precisely on the fore and aft radar dishes of the "Fog Lamp" fire-control radars, hit, and exploded.

Although the HARMs only hit the emitters on the tall fore-and-aft antenna masts on the destroyer *Jinan,* and the two HARMs' warheads were a scant fifty pounds, the results in the Combat Information Center belowdecks were as disruptive as a nuclear bomb blast. All the cabin and console lights in CIC flicked off immediately, replaced by emergency lights for the cabin only—most of the weapons control systems were dead or in rest. "Hold your positions!" the CIC officer shouted to his console and weapons technicians. "Put your sets in reset and stand by!" The CIC officer picked up the emergency battery-powered telephone. "Bridge, CIC, weapons systems and sensors in full reset. I say again, weapon systems in full reset. Over."

"Bridge copies," a reply came. "Missile impact on both main and aft mast."

The CIC officer felt his jaw drop. Both masts—that meant both HQ-91 missile directors were down. The Sea Eagle search radar, which was still operational, could be used for fire control, but it was highly inaccurate. They could still direct attacks by the other patrol boats, however, but in just a split second

a four-thousand-ton warship was rendered virtually impotent . . .

. . . But not entirely impotent. When the lights came back
on a few moments later, most of the CIC's equipment was still
in working order. "There's a second bomber out there somewhere, and I want it," he shouted at his Combat Information
Center crew. "Get a report from up on deck, make sure all our
weapons are clear to fire—the forward 100 and the aft HQ-91
launcher should both be clear. I want infrared and low-light
sensor manned, and I want Sea Eagle slaved to the one-hun-
dred-millimeter cannon and HQ-91. Bridge, CIC, I show the
aft HQ-91 system still operational. Clear me to engage the
second stealth bomber."

"C-3 band uplink shut down . . . search radar only," McLanahan reported. "I think I got the missile director. Damn, I wish
I could say thank you to those guys in the other B-2. I think
they saved our bacon with those SLAM launches." His eyes
were glued to the SMFD, checking the rear hemisphere tail
warning radar for any sign of tracking Masurca missiles. But
after two minutes, nothing appeared. Patrick took a deep
breath, as if it were the first time all day he'd been able to
breathe, and Cobb rustled uneasily in his seat as the threat
from the destroyer passed—for Cobb, that was akin to a wild
shout of relief.

McLanahan said, "Still got two India-band control radars at
two o'clock. Give me thirty degrees left, let's give these guys
a wide berth." He opened the left bomb bay and readied two
more HARM missiles of his own to engage the patrol boats.
"Search radar only, six o'clock . . . that destroyer must still have
its air-search radar on . . ." Patrick considered turning back to
get within range of one more HARM missile launch at the
destroyer's big search radar, or perhaps even a SLAM missile
launch at the destroyer itself, but the patrol boat's gun-control
radars ahead were a bigger threat now. With the destroyer's
big threat, the HQ-91 surface-to-air missile, gone, the B-52s
could take care of the destroyer now. . . .

•　　•　　•

"Tracking air target at bearing three-four-two, range eleven miles and increasing, altitude less than eighty meters . . ." The radar operator quickly checked the track history of that target; it had none. It had literally appeared out of nowhere, right in the middle of the Chinese fleet, and it was about to disappear once again . . .

So this is what a stealth bomber looked like on radar!

"Commit aft HQ-91 missiles," the CIC officer aboard *Jinan* ordered.

"Yes, sir . . . aft HQ-91 missiles showing faulted, track error."

"Bypass it. Slave to the Sea Eagle system for command guidance."

"Copy . . . fault log cleared, HQ-91 slaved to air-search radar only, no target illuminations, beam-riding mode only . . . launcher crew reports ready."

"Four-missile salvo . . . shoot."

It was the definition of a long shot all the way—a faint radar return from the suspected stealth bomber, no solid lock-on, heavy jamming, no target illumination for the HQ-91 to follow, no lead-computing mathematics or sophisticated intercept trigonometry, no proximity detonation—the missiles were going to either miss or hit the target square-on.

The second B-2 had the unfortunate luck to make a slight turn to line up on a Chinese patrol boat that had locked onto it with a fire-control radar. The first HQ-91 streaked by just to the left of the bomber, but the second of the four-missile salvo hit the Black Knight on the left wing, exploding and turning the entire left side of the high-tech bomber into a huge yellow fireball in seconds.

The bomber hit the warm waters of the Celebes Sea with the force of a car crusher, killing the crew instantly. The boomerang-shaped aircraft cartwheeled edge-on across the water for several thousand yards before plunging into the waters and disappearing from sight forever.

"Target hit! Good hit on number-two aircraft!" A cheer went up in *Jinan*'s Combat Information Center . . .

. . . but it was very short-lived. "Warning! Incoming missiles, multiple contacts, bearing . . . opposite side, one-four-three, range thirty miles, altitude . . . altitude less than fifty meters, speed six hundred knots!"

It had to be the Tomahawk missiles, the ones that had survived *Kaifeng*'s counterattack. "Radio to all vessels, missile warning, direct defensive fire on . . ."

"B-52 bombers launching missiles, bearing two-zero-five, range fifty-one nautical miles . . . encountering heavy jamming now, all frequencies . . ."

Missiles coming from two sides now . . . one, maybe more B-2s roaming around . . . a B-52 that everyone has lost track of . . . things were not going well all of a sudden. At less than thirty miles' range, the Tomahawk missiles were his first priority. Captain Jhijun screamed so loud into the intercom that it probably didn't need an amplifier: *"CIC, bridge, I need an intercept estimate. Can you get the Tomahawk missiles?"*

"Jamming is heavy, but I think we can manually maintain a lock. Intercept confidence is good. But the number of inbounds is unknown . . ."

"Engage as many as you can," Jhijun said. "Our close-in weapons should get the rest." Along with its 130-millimeter, and 25-millimeter antiaircraft guns, the destroyer *Jinan* carried two American-made Mk 15 Phalanx cannons, one on each side, which were automatic radar–guided Gatling guns designed to destroy incoming missiles at close range. Ironic that they would be used to engage American missiles . . .

"Sir! Three B-52 bombers that were reported turning west and disengaging—they are now turning northbound and appear to be re-engaging. They are at forty-three nautical miles, at extreme HQ-91 range."

Damn them! Jhijun cursed to himself. There were just too many of them. Well, the bombers were out of range—at least he still had a chance to get the cruise missiles before they started attacking the landing ships. "Message to all units: at least three, perhaps as many as six B-52s and at least one B-2 inbound from the south of Davao Gulf. Destroyer *Jinan* is unable to engage because of Tomahawk cruise missiles coming in from the southeast. Request fighter and surface support."

He received a reply moments later: "Sir, destroyer *Hong Lung* will provide support. Admiral Yin sends his compliments and advises you that the Tomahawk missiles are your priority . . . your *personal* priority."

Captain Jhijun swallowed hard when he heard the name *Hong Lung,* but when he got the message from Yin himself, his skin turned to ice. Every cruise missile he allowed to pass him, he knew, would mean a year in prison or a full reduction in grade. His career—more precisely, his *life*—rested on his performance now.

DESTROYER *HONG LUNG,*
SIXTY MILES WEST OF DESTROYER *JINAN*

Aboard the flag bridge of the flagship of the South Philippines Task Force, three large grease boards were kept constantly updated on the deployment of warships in this operation. It was beginning to resemble a child's crayon-drawn rendering of a beehive—Mindanao—with swarms of angry bees surrounding it. And the bees were getting closer and closer to the hive every minute. . . .

Admiral Yin Po L'un could easily see the American tactic now: strike at the Chinese fleet from simultaneous, multiple axes of attack. Along with the reported B-2s and B-52s coming in from the south and the Tomahawk cruise missiles from the southeast, he had also received word of more B-52s from the east and B-1s from the northeast, followed by more B-52s and faster bombers, possibly F-111s, accompanying them. Jamming was heavy in all areas, so obviously a few of the aircraft were not strikers but electronic-countermeasure planes.

Captain Sun Ji Guoming, Yin's chief of staff, said, "A rough estimate so far is twenty-six B-52 bombers, six B-1 bombers, four B-2 bombers—one reportedly shot down already by *Jinan*—possibly two EF-111 electronic-countermeasure planes, and perhaps four to six F-111 fighter-bombers involved in this raid. If this is so, the First Air Battle Wing has committed at least three-fourths and possibly as much as four-fifths of its force on this one escapade." Sun smiled knowingly. "We can crush the American Air Force in one night's work."

"Is that so, Captain?" Yin asked in a low voice. "You say we have shot down only one plane so far, yet they have sunk one destroyer and one frigate, damaged two other frigates, and sunk or damaged nearly two dozen patrol boats. In less than thirty minutes they can be over Davao Gulf itself. I see no evidence of anyone being crushed so far."

"They have suffered a great loss well before striking the target area or even coming within range of concentrated fire-power," Sun explained. "They will suffer tremendous losses when they come within range of the destroyers *Yinchuan* and *Dalian* near Davao itself. The American forces are undisci-plined—they are launching antiradar and other guided weap-ons at every small patrol boat they encounter, without bothering to save their weapons for the frigates, destroyers, or landing-craft carriers. It was sheer luck that they sunk *Huang-shi* and *Kaifeng*, and *Yingtan* is still operational . . ."

"You failed to adequately take into account the possibility of a Tomahawk cruise missile attack," Admiral Yin said angrily. "They were able to overwhelm our outer defenses too easily. And why was I never advised of the presence of B-2 stealth bombers on Guam . . . ?"

"Sir, the fleet intelligence center reported that the *Ranger*'s battle group was still in Manado and that Indonesia had not given permission for offensive operations," Sun explained. "If those cruisers launched their missiles from Indonesian waters, that is an illegal act . . ."

Yin glared at Sun, not satisfied with *that* explanation at all.

"Admiral, *Hong Lung* is engaging B-52 bombers at extreme range," the communications officer reported. They could feel the distant rumble of the destroyer's two big combination die-sel-turbine engines spooling up to maximum speed, and the ship made a hard turn to starboard briefly before settling down. "Antiship missiles launched . . . jamming ineffective at this range, good radar contact, intercept confidence is high on all tracks."

Yin looked away from Captain Sun, finding it hard to fault Sun too much—had he not suggested that *Hong Lung* travel east to assist in the invasion defense, all these aged American bombers might well be attacking his Marines by now. "Report on the invasion force," Yin ordered. "Are they ready to land?"

"All vessels in position," Captain Sun reported. "The bombardment was to commence in two hours, and the invasion was to begin in three . . ."

"It can no longer wait," Yin said. "Order the landing craft to head ashore immediately."

"But sir, we have not had time to prepare the beachhead for our forces," Sun argued. "There could be anything waiting for them. We should proceed with the bombardment first and shell the beachhead for at least an hour before—"

"We may not have an hour before those bombers and cruise missiles are on top of them," Yin said. "Issue the orders and get those Marines on the beach."

"There is no need for haste, sir," Sun tried one last time. "We should wait to see if any of the American bombers go overhead—perhaps the American bombers will even bomb the beach for us. In any case, our forces should not be on the beach when the bombers come in . . ."

"Neither should they be in the landing craft on Davao Gulf," Yin said, his voice louder and sharper this time. Sun knew enough to hold his tongue then. The uncomfortable silence in the flag staff was broken by the combat-alert horn as the destroyer began prosecuting its attack on the B-52s swarming around them. . . .

FORTY MILES EAST OF THE CHINESE DESTROYER *HONG LUNG*

The six B-52 G-model Stratofortress bombers in the southern strike group were threading the needle here in the worst possible sense—trapped between two Chinese destroyers, with no place to hide except for an electronic curtain of jammers. Their only hope: throttles to military power, altitude pegged at one hundred feet, and hope to make landfall at Balut Island or Sarangani Island, twenty miles ahead, before the crush of Chinese antiair missiles found them. Although they were not receiving any missile fire-control signals from the eastern destroyer, it had still somehow shot down the B-2 with a missile— they were going to give both destroyers as much space as possible.

"Trick Zero-Two, this is One," the lead B-52 pilot called out on the tactical frequency. "We've got a radar fix on those ships to the west. I've got four Harpoons left. We're going for it." As soon as the navigators plotted the position of the ships, they commanded a climb to three hundred feet and launched their last four AGM-84 Harpoon missiles at the ships.

The first two Harpoons were the original air-launched model, which flew directly toward the ships at five hundred and fifty miles per hour; the second two missiles were the advanced AGM-84E SLAM missile, which was far more flexible in selecting an evasive course and attacking from multiple directions and altitudes.

While the first two Harpoons sped directly for *Hong Lung,* the second two split north and south of the destroyer, so in effect the *Hong Lung* was attacked from three sides simultaneously.

The engagement worked—the southerly missile, being steered by the first B-52's radar navigator, impacted just above the waterline on the starboard side of the escort frigate *Change De,* putting it out of action immediately, and one minesweeper/patrol boat riding point for the *Hong Lung* was hit by a Harpoon missile. The other Harpoon and SLAM missiles were destroyed by gunfire from *Hong Lung* and its surviving escorts.

But the counterattack by *Hong Lung* was devastating—the sky filled with antiair missiles as soon as the B-52 attacked. Releasing all four of its remaining Harpoon missiles on the *Hong Lung* battle group created a big, bright "arrow" to point the way for the Chinese fire-control operators, and *Hong Lung* released four HQ-91 air-to-air missiles at the B-52 within a few seconds, followed by a volley of four more.

"Time to get the hell out of here," the pilot of the first B-52 shouted—for his own benefit more than for his copilot or the rest of the crew. "Get rid of those mines and let's split!"

The last of the conventional B-52's weapons were four Mk 60 CAPTOR torpedoes on clip racks in the forward part of the bomb bay. CAPTOR, which stood for Encapsulated Torpedo, was a large canister containing an Mk 46 torpedo and complex sensor gear. As the B-52 began a tight right turn away from the western destroyer, it began sowing the CAPTOR mines in the eastern Celebes Sea. After activation, the canisters would lie on the seabed or hang suspended in the water until a warship passed by. When the sound, pressure, and magnetic parameters matched its pre-programmed settings, the mine would track the target and launch the torpedo. The torpedo had a range of six miles, and one CAPTOR by itself could sink all but the largest class of Chinese surface ships or submarines.

In two minutes, all four CAPTOR mines were released, and the airspeed of the B-52 increased dramatically. Now weaponless, it dropped a cloud of radar-decoying chaff and continued its right turn to a safe southerly heading. But at its high speed the tightest turn the bomber could make was still twenty-five miles—directly in the path of two of the stricken destroyer *Jinan*'s patrol-boat escorts.

Guided by *Jinan*'s one remaining air-search radar and using infrared sights, the patrol boats opened fire on the bomber with 57-millimeter, 37-millimeter, and 25-millimeter gunfire, rattling every inch of the big jet with shells. The B-52's cockpit windows shattered, decapitating the two pilots and sending the stricken aircraft crashing into the sea.

The crash of the B-52 not more than three kilometers away was the most incredible sight any of the seventy-man crew of the Haijui-class patrol boat *Yingkou* had ever seen. The mushroom cloud of fire had to be a kilometer high, and flames were so big and so hot that the captain could swear he felt the heat from inside the bridge. The fireball skipped across the water, rolling and rushing along like a huge orange-and-red tidal wave. It was utterly spectacular. After a few minutes of awe, the bridge crew broke out into wild cheers as the flames began to die away—and then the crew ran for cover as bits of flying metal and thick clouds of smoke rolled across the water.

"Radar contact, second and third B-52 bombers," came the report from his fire-control officer. "I have a good track on both planes—they should be turning this way just like the first. Five minutes before the next one passes close enough."

This was going to be incredible, the captain thought—he might easily kill a second, and perhaps even a third B-52 with his 57-millimeter gun tonight. He would certainly get his own frigate after tonight . . . "Move farther west," he ordered his helmsman. "I want to be as close as possible to these last two bombers." The helmsman went to flank speed in order to get a few meters closer to the bomber's track—every hundred meters closer was another dozen rounds on target.

"Second bomber turning east, range decreasing . . . he's coming this way, sir . . . I'm getting jamming on my fire-control radar . . . forward 57 switching to electro-optical sights with data link from *Jinan* . . . target reacquired, forward 57- and port 30-millimeter report ready."

This was perfect, really perfect. The other patrol boat escorting the destroyer *Jinan* had no data link with the destroyer's air-search radar, so all he could do was follow *Yingkou*'s tracers. He would never be credited with a kill . . .

"Thirty seconds . . . twenty seconds . . . all gun mounts report ready . . . fifteen seconds . . . all guns stand . . ."

He never finished the sentence. The first CAPTOR torpedo mine had armed immediately upon hitting the water and, despite the incredible sounds of destruction from the B-52 crash, had locked onto the engine sounds of the Haijui-class patrol boat as soon as he gunned his engine, and ejected its deadly torpedo. The torpedo switched on its active sonar, acquired and locked onto the patrol boat, accelerated to nearly fifty miles per hour, and hit the patrol boat near the engine compartment one foot below the waterline. A shaped charge rammed a titanium nosecap through the patrol boat's hull, and the torpedo actually swam three feet inside the port engine room before its eight-hundred-pound warhead exploded. With most of its stern blown apart, *Yingkou* slipped under the surface in less than two minutes—about as long as it took the last of the burning debris of Trick Zero-One to hit the water.

The other two B-52s in the first south attack group avenged their leader's death with a flurry of Harpoon missile launches, and within minutes three more of *Jinan*'s patrol boats had been destroyed. *Jinan* itself, overwhelmed by Harpoon missiles from the south as well as the flight of Tomahawk cruise missiles from the southeast, was hit by both a Tomahawk and a Harpoon and was put out of action.

ABOARD THE EB-52C MEGAFORTRESS DIAMOND ONE-ONE

It was a surprise for Major Kelvin Carter to see the COLA (Computer Generated Lowest Altitude) computer command a climb after so many hours at one relatively stable altitude, but as the Megafortress approached the tall, rocky peaks of the Nenusa Archipelago islands, the EB-52 wanted to climb six hundred feet to clear the tallest peak. Carter edged his Megafortress slightly south of the tiny radar dots, and, after the computer realized it would safely clear all the terrain, the Megafortress sank back to one hundred feet above the eastern Celebes Sea.

Alicia Kellerman was busily plotting the positions of the other planes in the strike team as she heard position reports come over the radio. "All right!" she said. "All six BUFFS in the number-two east group and Diamond One-Two made it through. They're two minutes ahead of us."

"What about the others?" Carter asked.

"The south group got hit real bad," Kellerman summarized. "One of the B-2s and a B-52 from Castle got shot down . . ."

"Our B-2? Cobb and McLanahan?"

"Cobb and McLanahan made it through OK. It was a Whiteman bird. One other 509th Black Knight from the north group aborted when they lost an engine; all the other planes from the north group made it.

"The other five B-52s from the south group look like they took out that destroyer to their east and a few patrol boats, so they might make it through. There's another destroyer battle group coming in from the west—that might be a problem when the strike package egresses to the south. No other reports: everyone else appears to be heading in on schedule. Kane on the EB-52 escorting the east number-two strike group got two Chinese fighters."

"Search radar at eleven o'clock," Atkins reported. "Golf-band search . . . Sea Eagle 3-D air-search radar, Luda-class destroyer. GCI signals, possibly more fighters coming in from the northwest."

"That destroyer's at forty miles, and he's got five escorts with him," Kellerman added, checking her updated ISAR radar display. "We'll be going in about sixty seconds ahead of the south B-52s. We're within TACIT RAINBOW range, EW. Line 'em up and let's get those suckers."

**BANGOY STRAIT, NEAR DAVAO, MINDANAO, THE PHILIPPINES
SAME TIME**

It was the largest assembly of Chinese warships since the Korean Conflict, all concentrated within ten miles of the city of Davao—and they were ready to begin their assault.

The assault group was split into two groups, each led by a People's Liberation Army Navy destroyer. North of Samar International Airport in Bangoy Bay was the destroyer *Dalian,* with six patrol boats as escorts, in overall command of five ex–United States LST-1-class tank-landing ships, each with two hundred and fifty People's Liberation Army Marines, ten light tanks, and twenty armored personnel carriers; and four *Yukan-*class landing ships, each with over four hundred Marines and one thousand tons of cargo and equipment. Each amphibious assault ship had several smaller landing craft that would each drop thirty Marine engineers ashore to clear wires or traps and soften up beach defenses; then the landing ships themselves would drive to shore, beach themselves, and disgorge their fighting men in massive waves. Helicopters from the Yukan-class ships would then begin to drop Marines and artillery pieces nearby, and the whole company would fan out across the countryside, secure the coastal inlands north of the airport, then drive south.

The main attack force was four miles south of Davao, in Davao Gulf itself. Led by the destroyer *Yinchuan,* its amphibious assault force had ten LST-1–class tank-landing ships and eight Yukan-class landing ships, plus numerous smaller landing craft, minesweepers, and support ships. This group had the responsibility of securing the highlands west of Davao, encircling the city itself, and then linking up with the northern group to help secure the airport.

By 0135 hours, two hours ahead of schedule, the two Luda-class destroyers had moved to within eight miles of the landing area and opened up with their 130-millimeter cannons, peppering the beach and treelines near the intended landing zones with one round every second per vessel. The rounds were of all different types—most were standard shells weighing fifty pounds and carrying eight pounds of high-explosives, but some were shells that carried infrared sensors that homed in on heat sources such as vehicles or machine gun nests, incendiary warheads that spattered napalm to set buildings or heavy brush afire, or bomblets that spread out over a wide area to increase the destruction of each shell. Helicopters with infrared spotting scopes were used to spot targets for some of the guns, but mostly the Chinese were content to bombard the area without regard to specific targets. The destroyer *Yinchuan* turned a few of its rounds on the area surrounding Samar International Airport, hoping to scatter some of the defenders that were certainly waiting for the Chinese to come ashore.

After twenty minutes of continuous bombardment, the Chinese assault ships began launching wave after wave of small landing craft with Marine engineers and security guards to clear a way for the assault ships to beach themselves. The gunfire from the destroyers became much more selective, targeting and hitting a few large-caliber shore-gun emplacements to provide covering fire for the landing craft. While raking the shore with 37- and 25-millimeter gunfire, the landing craft dropped some frogmen overboard to search for water traps or mines, while the others went ashore to begin hunting for minefields and to suppress heavy gun emplacements on shore. Except for a few widely scattered mines, they encountered almost no resistance. It took the first waves of landing craft less than ten minutes to reach the beach.

After twenty-five minutes of bombardment, each 130-millimeter gun on the destroyers had expended one-third of the rated life for its barrels, so the heavy shelling ceased and the search began for attacks against the landing craft. They found a few snipers and encountered light resistance from hit-and-run grenade attacks, but the Chinese Marines sustained only a few casualties.

"Sir, report from Rear Admiral Yanlai," Captain Sun Ji Guoming, the chief of staff for Admiral Yin Po L'un's flag staff, said. "The amphibious assault has gone better than he expected. The first landing craft are ashore with few casualties; the second wave will land in a few minutes. No heavy resistance is being encountered from Samar's forces."

A tremendous weight seemed to be lifted from Admiral Yin's shoulders. Ever since Captain Sun and a few of his other advisers had recommended against Marine landing until the American Air Battle Force was dealt with, he had been worried that his decision to proceed with the assault was a bad one—now it seemed to be remarkably prescient. "Does Admiral Yanlai have any suggestions?"

"No, sir," Sun replied. "He is proceeding with the planned operation."

"The plan supposed Samar's usual stiff guerrilla resistance to the landing forces," Yin said. "Samar has obviously fled. It is time to step up the attack—with the American force nearby, it is essential. Order Admiral Yanlai to land the LSTs and troop-landing ships after the second wave of Marines ashore."

The flag staff turned toward Yin in complete shock, and Captain Sun could not help but blink at his commanding officer in surprise. "But . . . sir, in only two landing-craft waves, we have less than three hundred troops ashore, and most of those are lightly armed engineers and Marines. They don't have the equipment or strength to conduct a thorough search and destroy operation. In daylight hours they can hardly proceed faster than a half-mile inland—at night they may be on the beach for hours, easily until daylight. They have not even begun to probe the area for resistance. It would be madn— I beg your pardon, sir, in my opinion it would be *unwise* to send in the large landing ships until we can be sure the area is free of resistance."

Captain Sun sustained Yin's furious glare with uneasy fear. He had come very close to total insubordination by calling Yin's order "madness," and only Sun's long-standing relationship with Yin, as well as the fact that they were in the middle of a war, prevented him from being dismissed right then and there.

"As you were, Captain," Yin growled. "Our plans and normal operating procedures are based on the level of resistance and the greatest threat facing our forces. The resistance so far is low, and the threat from American bombers is very high. Those ships are vulnerable. The more men we can get off those ships and safely on land, the better. Order the landing ships ashore *immediately.*"

By using a Mode Two interrogator, which broadcast a short, coded signal to other American aircraft in the area commanding the other aircraft's beacons to emit a short identification signal in reply, Patrick McLanahan could discover where other aircraft in the strike force were located and display it on the God's-eye view on his Super Multi Function Display—in turn, this would be transmitted to the EB-52C escorts in the other strike packages so they could update their situational displays. The data would also be transmitted via NIRTSat communications satellites to the Joint Task Force commander on Guam and to the National Military Command Center at the Pentagon.

The Mode Two told a horrifying story—they had already lost one B-52 and one B-2, and they were still hundreds of miles from the Chinese amphibious assault force. McLanahan found his throat dry and his forehead hot and moist, and he found he could not control the slight trembling in his fingers—the trembling of real fear. He felt alone up here, and he felt as if every enemy vessel on that SMFD could see him and was waiting to kill him.

After spending weeks with these men at the Strategic Warfare Center—swapping stories, techniques, and complaints; mission planning and debriefing until late at night at the O-Club or at the Black Hills Saloon until being tossed out; and learning how to fight as a unit instead of as lone penetrators—it was as if a bit of his own soul had disappeared with each missing icon on that screen. They were dead, quickly and suddenly—and the toughest part of the mission was still ahead.

The faces of the crew dogs that manned the missing bombers floated unbidden before his eyes, and burning drips of sweat that rolled into his eyes couldn't blur those horrible images.

Patrick had seen combat, had seen men close to him die, but this was harder than he ever imagined. All those faces, all those names—this morning they were all together, and now they were never coming back. Just like that . . .

"What do you got, Patrick?"

McLanahan shook himself out of reverie and focused his eyes past the ghostly faces he saw in the SMFD and concentrated again on the situation. The faces did not haunt him— they seemed to help him, seemed to encourage him to continue . . .

"Patrick . . . ?"

Patrick looked over at Cobb and nodded. "I'm all right, Henry . . ." Cobb had glanced at his partner briefly, waiting to see if he would get back into the fight, before resuming his usual stone-still stance. The faces had moved away from the SMFD—they felt as if they were looking over his shoulder now, marveling at the technology McLanahan commanded and waiting for him to continue the fight—and that made him feel much better.

"We are twenty miles from the coastline near Kiaponga," Patrick said. "The B-52s behind us are joining up with Carter's EB-52. There's a destroyer battle group in the mouth of the Davao Gulf, and I think Carter and his B-52s from the south group are going after it. The number-two east strike group will follow—they're all intact with all six B-52s."

"Where are the Tomahawks?" Cobb asked.

McLanahan touched an icon on his SMFD, and several blinking objects and a short data list appeared on the God's-eye view. The Tomahawk cruise missiles could be interrogated just like a manned aircraft. "About ten miles ahead of the B-52s and not far behind us. We'll go feet-dry, turn west, and let the Tomahawks go past us as they head inland; when they get ahead of us, we'll head north and proceed to our targets." McLanahan studied the display for a moment, then ceased his Mode-2 interrogations—even though the Mode-2 signals were encoded and transmitted in very short bursts, the enemy could still track an aircraft from them. "Looks like about half the Tomahawks are still with us."

"Good," Cobb said. "I'd just as soon let those puppies beat the bushes for us."

The grease-board plotting technician drew a line from a frigate icon near the mouth of Davao Gulf to near the tiny village of Kiaponga. Out of all the other dots, circles, icons, and lines on the board, that one line commanded Admiral Yin's attention. "What is that?" he asked.

"Sir, frigate *Xiamen* reports a weak UHF signal along this bearing," the situation officer replied. "Several microburst transmissions. Computer projection calling it a possible aircraft, airspeed eight hundred kilometers per hour, heading northwest."

Yin seemed to be transfixed by this line. "Any primary radar target? Altitude readout?"

"No, sir."

"Do they have an analysis of the signal itself?"

"Not yet, sir."

Captain Sun was completely perplexed—a destroyer and a frigate were coming under attack, but Yin was wondering about a microburst radio transmission. "Sir, *Jinan* is under attack by antiship missiles again—he cannot hold out much longer. We must assist him. I recommend ordering him to withdraw to the west so we can provide surface-to-air missile coverage for him. And we should head farther to the northeast to provide similar coverage for *Xiamen*—he is tracking numerous Tomahawk cruise missiles heading in his direction as well as the B-52 bombers . . ."

"I want to know what that signal was, Captain."

"Very well, sir," Sun replied. "And as for *Jinan* and *Xiamen* . . . ?"

"Steer *Hong Lung* northeast to cover Davao Gulf as much as possible, but *Jinan* will hold its position," Yin said with a hint of exasperation in his voice. "They have almost as much firepower as we do, and they have more escorts. I will not allow my ship commanders to start running all over the Celebes Sea at the first sign of trouble. I also want a report on our fighter coverage—I have not seen one fighter on that board since the first group of J-7s and Q-5s were engaged."

A few moments later a new manual plotting technician took over on the vertical-plot greaseboard, and he began filling in icons for a group of fighters just west of Mount Apo. "Sir, fighter groups fourteen, with six total Jianjiji-7 fighters, and composite fighter-attack group two, with three Qiangjiji-5 fighters and three A-5K fighter-bombers, are thirty-seven kilometers west of Mount Apo," Captain Sun reported. "They will be on station over Davao Gulf in three minutes."

Yin slammed a fist down on the table before him and hissed, "That is not *good* enough! We're supposed to have a hundred fighters available to us on this operation, and there are only *twelve?* I had better see two more groups airborne immediately. I want all available J-7 and Q-5 fighters airborne immediately to attack the inbound bombers . . ."

"It will be done immediately, sir . . . but I must remind you that it leaves no Q-5 fighters available for close air support for our Marines," Sun said. "The Q-5 and the A-5 are the only planes we have that can aerial refuel. Also, few of these aircraft are equipped for night combat . . ."

"We will have no Marines to provide close air support *for* if we do not stop these bombers!" Yin shouted. "Launch all available fighters now! And I want two fighters dispatched to search along the projected trackline of that microburst transmission. I want *nothing* to get past our defenses and strike our Marines . . . *nothing!*"

The updated NIRTSat data feed came in just as Cobb and McLanahan's B-2 crossed the coastline south of Kiaponga. Cobb had reactivated the terrain-comparison COLA computer, and they were snaking just two hundred feet above the lush coastal hills and valleys of the Sarangani Peninsula of southern Mindanao. On his Super Multi Function Display, McLanahan could see the updated positions of three Tomahawk cruise missiles that were to go in ahead of his B-2 Black

Knight bomber; the computer used the missile's last reported heading and speed, along with a knowledge of the missile's pre-programmed flight plan, to estimate the missile's position. "We'll be ready for a turn in about sixty seconds," McLanahan told Cobb. The aircraft commander clicked his mike in response.

The terrain sloped up steeply from the eastern cliffs facing the Celebes Sea in the Glan River Valley; the valley was at least six miles wide and did not rise as steeply on the west side. "Stay on the west slope of the coastal hills, on the 'military crest,'" McLanahan said. "It's not the best place to be, but it's better than getting trapped down in the valley. The hills should shield us from the warships off the coast as well." Another double click in response as Cobb banked the B-2 gently right and began flying north-northeast along the western side of the coastal hills, not flying too high but not diving too deeply into the valley.

McLanahan expanded his SMFD out to sixty miles' range. At the top of the north-up display was their primary target, the radar site on Mount Apo. A yellow-colored dome surrounded the point, representing the range of the Chinese radar site operating there—that was their target. The edge of the yellow dome did not quite touch the B-2 icon—not because they were out of the radar's range, but because the energy levels being recorded from the radar were less than those required to get a radar return off the stealth bomber. From that radar site the Chinese could vector in fighters against every American bomber in the strike package.

McLanahan immediately designated the top of the mountain as the target for two SLAM missiles, programming in evasive turnpoints and data-link activation points and checking the Global Position System satellite signal for good navigational data feed to the missiles. He had to program in a terminal "pop-up" maneuver for the missiles in order to hit the radar domes from above rather than from the side.

The one deficiency with the SLAM missile system over land was that the aircraft that was to steer the missile onto its target needed to have a clear line-of-sight radio signal between the two—that meant climbing away from the radar-clutter sanctuary of the terrain, which could expose the launch aircraft to enemy radar. The navigation-missile control computer interface would advise Cobb and McLanahan when it was time to climb, based on the bomber's altitude and the signal strength—usually it commanded a climb in time to establish a clear signal sixty seconds before missile impact. Fortunately the B-2's low radar cross-section made it less vulnerable to enemy radar than other SLAM-capable launch aircraft. "Missile programmed, Henry, ready for launch . . ."

Just as he said those words, two red-colored triangles appeared at the top of the display, with yellow arcs extending from the apex of the triangles out toward the B-2's icon at the bottom of the scope—again, the arcs did not quite touch the icon, probably because of the B-2's stealth characteristics. "Fighters at ten o'clock, forty miles," McLanahan said. "Two . . . now showing six, at *least* six, heading this way . . . I don't think they see us yet. . . ."

"Fighter group fourteen, your targets are at thirty nautical miles, twelve o'clock, airspeed four-fifty, altitude less than one hundred meters," the radar controller on Mount Apo reported. "Suspected cruise missiles heading northwest. Recommend right break and spacing for single intercept. Composite group two, your bandits are at eleven o'clock, twenty-seven miles. Groups fourteen and two, your flight leaders are directed to depart your formations for special patrol, designated Group Delta. Delta, come right to heading one-six-eight, take one-thousand-meters altitude and switch to controller frequency gold. Acknowledge."

Two fighters broke out of the pack of fighter-bombers and headed southeast: a JS-7 fighter and an A-5K fighter-bomber. The A-5K was the upgraded version of the Q-5 good-weather attack plane, with sophisticated Aeritalia-made avionics that gave it an all-weather bombing capability, including a low-light TV camera and laser rangefinder.

"Group Delta, unidentified bogey possible at low altitude, estimated position at your twelve o'clock position, forty nautical miles. Report identification and pursue. Over."

· · ·

The two enemy aircraft triangles did not appear right away, and when they did appear their radar arcs immediately swept across the B-2 icon. "Two fighters separated from the rest of the pack," McLanahan shouted. "Twelve o'clock. X-band search radars. They might have spotted us."

The B-2 had just left the protective cover of the coastal hills of the Sarangani Peninsula and was now racing across the Buayan River valley, a flat, fertile area about forty miles southwest of Davao. The lone peak of Mount Apo was the only significant terrain around for fifty miles—it was the worst moment to be caught by fighters. To the east, ten miles southwest of Davao, the icons of several warships were just visible.

"We've got a little rolling terrain about twenty miles to the west, and nothing but Davao Gulf and another destroyer off to the east," McLanahan said. "Otherwise it's flat, flat, flat. The fighters are at our twelve o'clock . . . getting a range estimate now of twenty-two miles. They'll be in missile range soon."

"We go west then," Cobb said. He banked his B-2 hard to the left, scurrying across the wide valley for the relative safety of a hilly ridge.

"Fifteen minutes until we reach that ridge . . . about two minutes," McLanahan reported. "Bandits one o'clock, fifteen minutes . . ." At that moment one of the yellow arcs representing the enemy's radar swept across the B-2 icon, and the yellow instantly turned to red as the radar locked on. "Shit, shit, *shit,* they got us. . . ."

The heads-up display on the Chinese JS-7 first locked onto the air target briefly, and the attack radar quickly computed the target's altitude, heading, airspeed, and closure rate—but it was the A-5K's low-light TV sensor that first caught a glimpse of the enemy. The sensor's contrast-tracking function immediately locked onto the warm object and began to track it . . .

And, as the target made a slight turn to the west, there was no mistaking its identity—the pilot of the A-5K saw the distinctive boomerang profile of an American B-2 bomber. "A stealth bomber! Stealth bomber!" the A-5 pilot shouted excitedly on the command radio. "Very low, heading west . . ." He was so excited that he forgot to give a proper report . . .

. . . And he also forgot he was in formation with another airplane. The two Chinese planes almost collided as the A-5 pilot turned westward to try to keep the fast-flying bomber within his low-light TV's field of view. *"Kong Yun One-Seven, hold your position!"* the JS-7 pilot shouted. "Formation coming right to intercept. Control, this is Delta, we have an American B-2 stealth bomber on radar, turning to intercept at this time . . ."

But as they did, extremely heavy jamming from the B-2 continually broke radar-lock—the massive energy even put the Cyrano-IV radar in "Reset" twice. *"Kong Yun* One-Seven," the JS-7 pilot asked of the A-5K pilot, "do you still have him on your TV sensor?"

"Affirmative, *Jian,* Zero-Niner."

"I'm receiving heavy jamming and I can't maintain a radar lock. Close us within PL-2 missile range. You have the lead."

"I have the lead." The JS-7 pilot could feel the tension grow in his arms and shoulders as he made the dangerous transition from following his radar cues and searching out the windscreen for terrain to picking up the A-5K's dim formation-lights. He used a few notches of airbrakes to slide back and ease into a comfortable position on the A-5's right wing, but he immediately edged away from the fighter-bomber in a momentary panic when he thought he was getting sucked in too close. It took several moments of adjusting before he could inch back in to proper wingman position.

At night, only a few meters away from another fighter loaded with weapons, traveling over sixteen kilometers per minute close to the ground, chasing down a heavily armed and dangerous intruder—it was some of the most dangerous flying around.

The two crew members of the B-2 Black Knight stealth bomber only seventeen miles ahead of the Chinese pilots might have disagreed.

Cobb had the power up to full military thrust, trying desperately to make it to the cover of the hills to the west. "Fighter's crossing behind us," McLanahan told him. "They found us . . . fighter radar's down now. They might be engaging visually or by IR." He set the B-2's MAWS system from "Passive" to "Active." MAWS, or Missile Approach Warning System, used small passive infrared sensors to search for nearby aircraft that might be a threat. Once a threat was located, it would lock onto it and continue to track it. If MAWS detected a second flash of light from that same target—indicating the ignition of a missile's rocket motor—it would activate the bomber's ALQ-199A Doppler radar missile tracking system to track the missiles and begin active countermeasures.

"I'm launching the SLAM missiles—at least we'll take out the radar before these bozos get us." McLanahan touched the weapon icons at the bottom of the Super Multi Function Display, overrode the mission timing schedule of the computer that deconflicted weapon releases for the entire strike package, then commanded the two Standoff Land Attack Missiles to launch. Cobb had to allow the bomber to climb an excruciatingly high one hundred extra feet before the missiles would start their countdown: "Altitude hold off . . . missile one counting down . . . doors open . . . missile one away . . . launcher rotating . . . missile two away . . . doors closed . . . altitude hold back on, descend back to one hundred feet TFR."

Although they still had two SLAMs and two HARM antiradar missiles remaining, their primary mission was completed—as the old bomber pilot's saying goes, once the bombs are gone, you're not flying for Uncle Sam anymore; you're flying for yourself.

Cobb and McLanahan started flying for their lives. . . .

"Missiles! Bomber launching missiles!" the A-5K pilot screamed. On his TV sensor he could clearly see the two missiles slowly speed away from the bomber's belly . . . and the sight filled him with an almost overwhelming red-hot rage. He selected a PL-2 heat-seeking missile and hit the "Launch" button when the bomber was directly in front of him. He realized after launching the missile that he was still too far out and did not give the missile enough time to lock on, but at this range, he could not miss. . . .

• • •

"We're not going to find anyplace to hide in these hills here," McLanahan said, checking the computer-generated terrain depiction on the Super Multi Function Display. Without one squeak of radar energy being transmitted, the computer drew all the terrain, rivers, valleys, and cities on the SMFD, updating their position with every turn—but right now it was not giving them any good news. Unless they flew their B-2 below one hundred feet, those hills would not provide enough cover to shake off their pursuers. "We should—"

He was interrupted with a flashing "Missile Launch" indication and the computer-generated words, *"Infrared Missile Launch . . . Break . . . Infrared Missile Launch . . . Break"* in the interphone. "Break right!" McLanahan shouted. At the same time, he checked to make sure that the electronic-countermeasures computer had launched decoy flares and had activated their HAVE GLANCE infrared jammers, a device that would use laser beams guided by the ALQ-199 missile warning radar to blind and distort the enemy missile's seeker heads and make it difficult for a heat-seeking missile to lock onto the B-2's engine exhausts.

It was the first time Patrick had ever observed a missile launch on the Super Multi Function Display, and it was weirdly fascinating—like watching an arrow speeding to its target in slow motion, except this arrow was speeding at *them!* The MAWS sensors had tracked the fighters to the rear quadrant, and when the heat-seeking sensors detected the missile launch, it automatically activated the ALQ-199 tracking radars and laser jammers. The fighters were depicted as red triangles with squares around them, highlighting them as the major threat against the B-2, and when the missiles were picked up by the ALQ-199 they appeared as blinking red circles. The SMFD redrew the scene, zooming in on the B-2 icon, the terrain immediately surrounding the bomber, and the pursuing fighters.

The dots initially swerved left to follow the decoy flares as they ejected from the left ejector racks, but they immediately realigned themselves on the B-2. A tiny data block showed time since launch and estimated time to impact—the "time-to-die meter." It had initially started at twelve seconds, but as the Chinese PL-2 missile accelerated to its top speed of Mach three, the time to impact wound down to five seconds and counted down swiftly.

But the missile had to make a hard left turn to follow the decoy flare, and when it reacquired the bomber's hot exhausts it began a hard right turn. The missile was "stressed," losing energy and skidding all over the sky—it was ready to be aced.

"Break left!" McLanahan shouted, and he ejected two flares from the right ejectors.

At the same time, the HAVE GLANCE laser jammer, which had begun tracking the missile via the ALQ-199 warning radar, had locked onto the PL-2 and began bombarding it with high-energy laser light. As the missile swung back to the left to reacquire the bomber, the laser beam shined directly on the seeker head, instantly burning out its sensitive gallium-arsenide "eye" and rendering the missile useless.

But McLanahan couldn't celebrate yet—the Chinese fighter had launched a second missile, this time from even closer range—McLanahan noticed a 00:04:39 in the time-to-die meter almost immediately. There was no time to turn, no time for a break maneuver. "Climb!" McLanahan shouted, and he began pumping out flares as fast as he could.

The tactic worked. The second missile, the A-5K's last heat-seeker, lost the hot engine exhausts for a split second. Although the missile started a climb in pursuit, the lock-on was lost, and the PL-2's twenty-eight-pound warhead automatically detonated—but only thirty feet away from the B-2's left engine nacelle.

The explosion sawed off twenty feet of the left inboard elevon, the flaplike control surface on the wing's trailing edge, completely separating it from the bomber. It sliced into hydraulic lines, cut open the left trailing edge fuel tank, and blew out two of the left main gear tires, which ripped open the left fuel tank completely. Raw fuel began streaming out of the bomber; the self-sealing foam fuel tanks kept the fuel from spreading to the engine compartment, but within seconds the left trailing edge fuel tank was empty and the number-one primary hydraulic system was dead.

Inside the cockpit, the explosion, the shock, the concussion, and the vibration were as severe as if they had hit the ground. The airspeed dropped one hundred knots as the huge bomber uncontrollably heaved and rocked across the sky—the Black Knight seemed to spin violently to the left, toward the dead number-one engine. The controls shook violently, then turned mushy and completely unresponsive, then seemed to freeze. The left wing dipped lower and lower, and there seemed nothing Cobb could do to stop it.

"We're hit!" Cobb screamed. He hauled on the sidestick controller with all the strength of his right arm. "Get on the controls!" he shouted to McLanahan. "Get the left wing up!"

McLanahan unstowed his sidestick controller, which was normally stowed underneath the right instrument panel glare shield. He moved the grip but nothing happened. "It's not active!"

The interphone died as the number-one generator popped off-line. Cobb ripped off his oxygen mask and screamed, "Then get out, Patrick! Get out!" Despite the emergency, Cobb still wasn't going to yell "Eject!"—that would elicit an immediate response from any well-trained crew dog.

"Get the wing up, Henry!" McLanahan yelled. Cobb took his left hand off the throttles and pushed on his control stick. Slowly, almost imperceptibly, the left wing seemed to rise— and McLanahan decided right then and there that he wasn't going to eject. The bomber could be milliseconds from hitting the ground, there could be a fire spreading through the bomb bays—but unless Cobb ordered him to eject he was going to stay. There was enough of a hint of aircraft control left to convince him they still had a chance . . .

Several loud bangs rattled the three-hundred-thousand-pound bomber as if a giant hand were throwing them against a mountainside, picking them up, then hurling them again.

McLanahan turned away from his pilot and scanned the engine and flight instruments. "Airspeed one-eighty . . . RPMs on number-one engine fifty percent, TIT and EGT on redline . . . number-one engine compressor stall, shut down number one. Number-one throttle." McLanahan put his left hand on the center console throttle quadrant, guarding the three good engines to make sure Cobb didn't shut off a good engine. The leftmost throttle snapped back to idle, then to "Cutoff." A compressor stall was a common but potentially dangerous engine malfunction in which the airflow through the engine is disrupted and the engine stops producing thrust—but fuel continues to flow through the engine and ignite in terrific shuddering explosions, one after the other, causing a huge fire inside the combustion chamber.

"Off!" Cobb yelled back.

"Turbine inlet temperature and exhaust temps," McLanahan said. He checked the right-side multi-function display, but it had gone dead when the number-one engine generator popped off-line, so he went to the rows of tiny standby gauges. "RPMs on number-one forty percent, TIT and EGT still redline. All the others are OK. Gotta shut number one down." Since the MFDs had shut off, they couldn't tell if the computer had already initiated the shutdown procedures, so they assumed it had not. "Fuel cutoff T-handle, number-one engine, pull."

"You get it!" Cobb yelled—he dared not take a hand off the control stick. McLanahan released the inertial reel lock on his shoulder harness and reached across the forward instrument panel to a row of yellow-and-black-striped handles labeled "Emergency Fuel Cutoff Pull." He laid his left hand on the first handle, stopped, double-checked that he had the right one— again, to avoid shutting down a good engine and killing them for sure—then pulled the handle.

"Number one T-handle, pull. Fire lights." McLanahan checked the row of engine fire lights near each T-handle—all four were out. He hit the "Press to Test" button to double-check that the bulbs were still good—they were. "Fire lights out. Engine instruments." The pilot's right multi-function display was black, so McLanahan ran his fingers across the standby engine instrument gauges at the bottom center of the forward instrument panel. "TIT and EGT high but coming down . . . EGT below redline. I think we got it. Number-one primary hydraulic system is out. Electric system is reset—turn the number-one generator off when you can."

"I can't."

McLanahan was going to continue reciting the rest of the emergency checklist, but all of the critical "bold print" items were done—the rest of the items were double-checks. The Black Knight bomber apeared to be wings-level, and finally Cobb was able to take his left hand off the control stick. He spent a few moments shutting off equipment that ran off the number-one engine, then slowly resumed his usual stony position—one hand on the throttle, one hand on the sidestick controller, eyes caged straight ahead, although this time with a few more noticeable glances around the cockpit.

It was hard to believe, but it had taken only ten seconds from the missile explosion to wings-level—to McLanahan, it seemed like a slow-motion eternity. He had once again experienced Death creeping toward him, and it was even more horrifying the second time. The feeling of utter helplessness was so overwhelming that it often threatened to shut crews down. Only their long hours of drill, training, and simulator sessions pulled them through it in time.

"Bring us right if you can," McLanahan said. He put his SMFD in reset, then reactivated it and found to his surprise that the navigation system was still running. "Mount Apo is at our two o'clock position, eight miles. It's our last hope. Heading zero-three-five."

The single bright flash of light was followed by a long tongue of flame that lasted for several seconds, and part of that flame seemed to shoot out forwards as well as backwards. "Good hit! Good hit!" the A-5K pilot cried out. "Strike . . . !"

But in his exuberance, the pilot again forgot he was in formation. When the trail of fire began to arc to the right he immediately banked right in response, directly into the path of the JS-7 fighter.

With the excitement of the missile launch, the blood pounding in his head, and the adrenaline rushing through his brain, the JS-7 pilot immediately broke right and climbed away. *"Jian* Zero-Nine, lost wingman," he cried over the command radio. Suddenly realizing that he didn't know where he was—except that he was at three hundred meters altitude, flying near a 3,200-meter-high mountain—he immediately began a climb to his area minimum safe altitude, which in this sector was 3,300 meters. "Zero-Nine climbing to min safe altitude."

"Get back here!" the pilot of the A-5K shouted furiously on the radio. "I have no more heat-seekers. You have to engage!"

"Zero-Nine is lost-wingman, no contact with the terrain," the JS-7 shouted. "*I* do not have a TV camera to watch for terrain. I will re-acquire. Stand by. . . ."

"EGT is back below redline," McLanahan said. "Try a restart." Cobb pushed the fuel cutoff T-handle back in to reopen the fuel lines, selected the "Engine Status" menu on his left MFD, selected "Restart," and advanced the number-one throttle when directed by the computer.

It was a mistake. As soon as the engine began spooling up, the bright-red "Fire" light came on. The computer immediately began shutdown procedures, and this time Cobb manually activated the fuel cutoff T-handle himself and hit the number-one engine's fire extinguisher system to make sure the fire was out. The "Fire" light extinguished immediately, and all other systems remained normal.

"Must be hydraulic fuel leaking into the engine or a serious fuel leak," Cobb said. "Looks like we finish this mission on three engines." He put the B-2's infrared scanner image on his right MFD and resumed his usual position, staring straight ahead, unmoving. "Where are those fighters?"

"One still on our tail; he's dropped back to eight miles, and he hasn't taken another shot yet," McLanahan said. "The other guy broke off to our five o'clock position and went high—he might be setting up for a high gun pass or a home-on-jam missile shot if they got a missile that'll do it. All trackbreakers are still active." He quickly switched to the data-link channel for the SLAM missiles, but the screen on the left side of his SMFD was blank. "Shit, looks like we lost contact with the missiles when the power dropped out. I'll try to reacquire it . . ."

"What do we do when we reach Mount Apo?"

"Fly around it . . . and pray," McLanahan said. "It's our only hope of losing these jokers." McLanahan expanded his SMFD display back to its normal God's-eye display—and then he saw them. "Henry!" he called over to Cobb. "Turn right to one-two-zero and climb to nine thousand seven hundred feet. Fly right over the peak of Mount Apo."

"Nine thousand feet!" Cobb said. "We'll be exposed! Half the Chinese fleet will be able to see us!"

"But we'll have some help if we make it on time," McLanahan said. "Do it." Cobb pulled back on the control stick and maintained as steep a climb as the stricken bomber could manage. The Black Knight barely held two hundred and fifty knots as Cobb put the nose right on the infrared image of the radar dome atop Mount Apo and headed straight for it. . . .

The B-2 momentarily disappeared from the narrow field-of-view image on the low-light TV screen, and the pilot of the Chinese A-5K fighter-bomber hurriedly expanded his screen and searched frantically for the intruder. He was surprised to see it climbing, not descending—in fact, it had passed two thousand meters already and was still climbing. He was also heading right for the radar site on Mount Apo. What was he trying to do? Kamikaze himself onto the radar site? Launch another missile? Eject? Nothing made sense. But one thing was certain—high and slow, it was an easy kill now. He pushed up his throttles to min afterburner—he was getting low on fuel, but that certainly didn't matter now—and began to close to cannon range.

At about ten kilometers' range, he activated his laser range-finder. Immediately his fire-control computer began computing lead angles and aimpoints for his two 23-millimeter cannons in each wing root; unfortunately he had only one hundred rounds in each gun, so he had time for only two one-second bursts. But that would be all that was needed here. The B-2 was trailing black smoke from its leftmost engine, and the crew was obviously trying to trade airspeed for altitude in preparation for ejection or self-destruction. They were not going to get the chance.

The huge B-2 made a sudden right turn at a very steep angle—possibly a last-ditch effort to evade destruction. The A-5 pilot simply pulled his nose around tighter, leading the bomber's turn, and put his aiming reticle back on the target.

The TV camera clearly showed the Mount Apo radar site not twenty meters below the B-2—he had turned a fraction of a second before plowing into the radar dome. The pilot was indeed skillful, but that was not going to save him. He closed to within one kilometer, squeezed his gun trigger, and let the first one-second burst rake the B-2s ungainly fuselage . . .

And at that moment it seemed as if the entire universe erupted into flames. Two Tomahawk cruise missiles had actually flown *over* the two aircraft and had hit the captured Mount Apo radar site, just a few hundred feet away from the Chinese fighter. The explosion tossed the Chinese fighter-bomber nearly a half-mile sideways in the air, blinding the pilot and sending him crashing into the lush green valley below.

The explosion on the Mount Apo radar site rattled the B-2, but compared to the pounding they had taken when the Chinese PL-2 missile hit, it was minor. Cobb lowered the big bomber's nose once again, trying to build up his waning airspeed and regain full control . . .

And at that instant a horrifying sight filled his forward-looking infrared scanner scene on his right MFD—the sight of a large Chinese vessel, only miles ahead of them. They had turned east too far, and now they were exposed to the entire southern Chinese invasion fleet. "Holy shit, we gotta get out of here!" Cobb shouted.

"As long as we're here, let's start the party," McLanahan said dryly. As Cobb continued his tight right descending turn, McLanahan quickly programmed his last two SLAM missiles on the fleet ahead of them, ran through the release checklist, and launched the missiles at the Chinese warships.

"Missile one *away* . . ." launcher rotating . . ." At that moment, warning lights illuminated on the forward instrument panel. "Damn, we just lost the primary hydraulic system—but I think the launcher still moved to launch position . . . missile two *away*. Closing bomb doors electrically."

Cobb was busily running through emergency-procedure menu items on his MFDs. "I switched to the auxiliary hydraulic system," he told McLanahan. "Autopilot's off, flight-control computers switched to secondary mode. No more automatic terrain following or jinking for us—a full-scale flight-control deflection will kill our entire hydraulic system. We've got fuel leaks on the left wing as well, and I think we're losing cabin pressurization. He shot us up pretty bad." But at least they were still flying, Cobb thought, and they were still fighting . . .

. . . and they were still under attack. "Bandit at our four o'clock position, range ten miles, turning right and coming around behind us," McLanahan shouted. "Descend as low as you can . . ."

"I'm going, I'm going . . . hell, if we descend too much we won't be able to climb back up." Cobb was straining on the control stick, since the auxiliary hydraulic system provided only 70 percent of the primary system's power, and the flight-control system was no longer assisting. "I'm having trouble controlling, Patrick. If that bozo attacks, we've had it. I can't maneuver . . . I can barely hold it as it is. Tighten your shoulder straps again. Get ready to jump out if he attacks . . ."

"He's got to find us first, Henry," Patrick said as he pulled his shoulder straps as tight as he could stand it. "Range seven miles . . . turning on our six . . . keep descending, Henry. We're still jamming . . . maybe he won't be able to see us . . . five miles and closing . . ."

The Black Knight bomber began to rumble, and the nose began to oscillate as Cobb fought to hold it steady. "Get ready to go, Patrick. It's still flying, but I don't know how . . ."

"Just hang in there, Henry—" But McLanahan watched the SMFD as the fighter icon closed mercilessly—the Chinese fighter was coming in for the kill, and there was nothing they could do to stop it. . . .

The JS-7 pilot was more experienced in air-to-air engagements than his former leader—A-5 pilots did more ground-attack training than dogfighting—and he knew, judging by the B-2's slow airspeed and erratic flight path, that he was in danger of crashing at any moment anyway. The A-5 pilot—he did not even know the man's name—rushed his shots, not closing in enough for the inherently poor PL-2 missiles to get a solid lock-on. A boresight missile launch was the best way to go—the PL-2 missile was especially prone to decoys, so if the seeker head was bypassed it was more deadly. He switched the attack system to "Boresight" and kept his power high, closing the distance rapidly. A boresight launch made the missile nothing more than a big, powerful bullet—far more deadly than his 23-millimeter cannon, but with the same effective range. It had to be led on target just like a gun, but that was easy in this case, since the B-2 wasn't maneuvering and seemed virtually incapable of doing so.

He had no laser rangefinder, no TV camera, and no usable radar to judge distance, but when he could see the ghostly shape of the American B-2 highlighted against the faint glow of the sky, he knew he was close enough . . .

His radar warning receiver suddenly screamed to life. There were no warning beeps, no search radar, no hint of the approach of any fighter—just an enemy fighter symbol superimposed on the center circle of his threat scope, meaning that it was already within lethal range. He was distracted away from the B-2 for only a split second after deciding he was going to attack instead of taking evasive action, but that split second was all that was needed—the B-2 made a gentle 30-degree bank turn to the west, and it took several seconds of frantic searching to reacquire it again in the darkness of the forests of Mindanao below. The boresight launch was spoiled.

With a fighter somewhere on him, there was no time to line up another boresight launch. The JS-7 immediately switched to seeker guidance and received a lock-on indication with a few seconds . . .

. . . but he never got to fire the missile. Two AIM-130 Scorpion missiles from Major Kelvin Carter's Megafortress bomber ripped into the Chinese fighter, slicing it into three pieces and flinging it across the Padada River valley below.

"Keep it coming to the right, Horse," Major Kelvin Carter told Cobb and McLanahan. "We'll take it over central Mindanao and try to escape to the northeast. Is this Horse One-Six?"

"Affirm, Diamond One-Three," Cobb replied on the scrambled tactical frequency, recognizing Carter's voice. "Thanks for clearing our tail."

"No problem. We got you on the FLIR, and you're trailing smoke from your number one. What's your situation?"

"Lost number one, lost our primary hydraulics, lost part of our left flight controls, losing fuel out the left wing," Cobb replied. "We're going to need a tanker in about thirty minutes."

"If you're still hooked up to the network, they'll be alerted and someone will be waiting for you," Carter reminded him. The Dreamland aircraft that could receive and transmit NIRTSat data were constantly being monitored by the Air Battle Force officers back on Guam—the computers would automatically upload a status report to a NIRTSat as it passed overhead every fifteen minutes, and the satellite would relay the aircraft reports to General Stone on Guam. "We'll stay with you— we're out of air-to-surface stuff anyway."

"What's the status of the strike package?" McLanahan asked.

"We lost two BUFFs and one Black Knight going in, not counting you guys," Carter said, "and that was before we dropped one damned weapon on the assault force invading Davao. The real fight should be starting . . . right about now."

THIRTEEN

President Lloyd Emerson Taylor sat with hands folded under his chin, staring at a spot atop his desk. He was still wearing his brown leather Air Force–issue flight jacket over casual slacks and a red flannel shirt, the same things he had put on the day before. He had taken Marine Corps One to Camp David yesterday at six P.M., arriving just before sunset. After his arrival, he wordlessly kissed his wife, Jean, good-bye, then proceeded directly to the Emergency Conference Room, seated himself at that desk and, almost literally, had not moved since. Members of the National Security Council and key members of Congress had been filing in and out of the Emergency Conference Room all day—he all but ignored them.

Military communications technicians were manning phones and headsets nearby, but the President had only two phones on his desk: one direct to the National Military Command Center at the Pentagon, where General Curtis and Secretary of Defense Preston had been since the President had signed the executive order authorizing the mission against the Chinese; the other was direct to the White House Communications Center, where calls from overseas could be immediately transferred to him. There was also a series of reports transmitted to him via secure teletype from General Curtis—including some casualty reports. Those he dreaded most of all.

The news crushed him, especially the word that a B-2 had been lost. He resisted the urge to wad up the teletype paper instead laying it flat on top of the growing stack of urgent reports from Curtis, then returned to his stoic position at the desk. But the more he thought about the reports that had just come in, the more he realized it was the loss of the B-2 that bothered him the most. Yes, it was horrible that they'd lost six B-52 crew members, and the F-14 Tomcat aviators, and the sailors from the USS *Ranger.* But he'd always thought of the B-2 as . . . almost invincible. For the kind of money and research that had gone into those planes, they should have been. And yet, as he more than anyone knew, nothing was ever certain in life.

Nothing.

Paul Cesare had been keeping the President's coffee mug filled and hot all this time, even though the President had only taken two or three sips in nearly twenty-four hours; now, he replaced the thick, white Navy galley mug of coffee with a mug of chicken soup. "Eat something, Mr. President," Cesare said. "Get up and stretch . . ."

Taylor considered it, but the ringing of the White House phone glued him to the desk. Cesare picked it up, listened, then handed it right to the President. "Sir, it's the Chinese Foreign Minister on the line from Beijing."

Taylor would have loved to tell Zhou to piss off backwards, or tell him that, yes, we won't bomb your ships anymore—hell, he wasn't sure what he would tell Zhou. Instead, he motioned to Secretary of State Danahall to take the phone. They had already discussed in great detail exactly what was going to be said—now was the moment to start the drama.

The President turned to a separate no-voice phone to listen in while Danahall cleared his throat and said, "Secretary Danahall speaking."

"Mr. Secretary, this is Zhou Ti Yanbing," the Chinese Foreign Minister announced himself. "I thank you for taking my call, sir."

"Do you have a message for us?"

"Yes, Mr. Secretary," Zhou said. "Premier Cheung wishes to officially protest the unwarranted and brutal attack on the People's Republic of China's fleet in the southern Philippines. Premier Cheung demands to know if a state of war has been declared and whether Article Four of the Brussels Conference is hereby implemented." Article Four dealt with the formal declaration of hostilities between nations, setting in motion all the legal and diplomatic formalities of war.

Taylor couldn't believe it. He listened with a growing sense of fury and frustration. God, how he'd love to tell Zhou and Cheung to go to hell. Better yet, to bomb them back into the Stone Age. With that one nuclear explosion they had set off the most maddening and aggravating chain of events in his administration. And now the fuckers were demanding that the United States follow the letter of the law. The audacity . . .

He shook his head and took a deep breath. Even going on twenty-four hours without sleep, he knew, as much as he'd rather not, that rules had to be obeyed, protocol observed, words exchanged. He nodded for Secretary Danahall to continue . . .

Danahall took a deep breath and said calmly, "Please advise Premier Cheung that the government of the United States desires no direct communication with the government of the People's Republic of China except to receive an offer of an immediate cease-fire and guaranteed promise to halt all military operations in the Philippines. Any official notification this government has with your government will be through the United Nations."

"I understand the formal notification procedures, Mr. Secretary, and we will of course abide by them as well," Zhou said in his polished, fluent English-Oriental accent. "My government has already delivered an official letter of protest to the Secretary General, and I trust Ambassador O'Day will contact you in short order. But any nation that embraces peace, freedom, and human rights would surely desire to begin negotiations to end all hostilities as soon as possible. You do not wish to fight a war, do you, Mr. Secretary? Will you simply make demands of us without opening any sort of dialogue?"

"We have no message or statements for your government, Mr. Foreign Secretary," Danahall said resolutely, "except that we expect your guaranteed promise to withdraw all military forces from the Philippines immediately. Do you have a message for my government?"

There was a slight pause; then: "Mr. Secretary, please convey . . ."

And then the line went dead.

THE PRESIDENTIAL RESIDENCE, BEIJING
PEOPLE'S REPUBLIC OF CHINA
MONDAY, 10 OCTOBER 1994, 0231 HRS. LOCAL

"You will *not* capitulate to the Americans!" Chinese High General Chin Po Zihong said as he grabbed the phone from the Foreign Minister's hand. Several other members of Premier Cheung Yat Sing's Cabinet shot to their feet in absolute shock. Premier Cheung himself remained impassive, his hands folded on his desk, watching the spectacle with a stone-cold, expressionless visage.

"How dare you disrupt a call to a foreign ministry like that!" Zhou shouted. "Explain yourself, Comrade General. You are violating a direct order from the Comrade Premier himself . . ."

"I am in charge of this military operation, Comrade Zhou," General Chin said. "Any communications that involve it must go through myself. I have full authority—"

"You are out of line, General," Zhou said angrily. "You were insane to begin this foolish military incursion, you were insane to place that criminal Admiral Yin in charge of an invasion force on Mindanao, and you are a fool to refuse to open a dialogue with the Americans."

He turned and motioned to a stack of reports piled on a granite conference table nearby. "You have read these reports. Four destroyers have been sunk out there! *Four destroy-*

ers! That is *half* of the destroyers assigned to Admiral Yin, and one-fourth of all the destroyers in the entire People's Liberation Army Navy fleet! At first report, ten frigates and nearly thirty patrol boats were sunk or put out of commission as well. There is no report of casualties yet, but they must number in the *thousands!* This operation must be terminated immediately!"

"Impossible!" Chin shouted. "Out of the question. We are hours away from final victory, Zhou Ti Yanbing. The invasion has already begun, and the early indications are that there is no resistance . . ."

"No resistance? Four destroyers on the bottom of the Celebes Sea, and you say no resistance? You cannot hope to ever claim a *victory* in this debacle!"

"I was referring to rebel resistance in Davao," General Chin said. "We expected heavy losses from the very beginning . . ."

"You told this government that we could expect twenty to thirty percent losses maximum throughout the duration of this conflict," Zhou argued. "You did not say we would sustain thirty percent losses *in three hours . . . !"*

"The objective of the operation was to seize Samar International Airport and secure the island of Mindanao," General Chin said. "This government authorized that operation—you authorized it as well, Comrade Zhou, with your affirmative vote. That objective is still within my reach. Loss figures have not been verified, and all my reports indicate that the objective can still be achieved in less than six hours. So far only the American Air Battle Force has been involved in this operation. They have sustained heavy losses as well, and even if they complete their raids we can still achieve total victory. Once Samar International Airport falls, not one single American aircraft will be able to approach within five hundred kilometers of the Philippines again . . ."

"It appears obvious to me, General, that even if you do take Samar International Airport, you have gained nothing," Zhou said. "The losses we are experiencing are staggering. We must withdraw immediately or we will not have an army to land on Davao Airport when you finally take it—or should I add, *if* you take it." Zhou turned to Premier Cheung, who had not said a word during the entire argument. "Comrade, I request, with all due respect, that General Chin's operation be terminated and that we return—"

"You cannot do this," General Chin shouted. "You cannot abandon a military operation simply because of unverified reports of heavy losses in the first few hours of a battle." To Premier Cheung, he said, "Comrade Premier, we know the Americans cannot mount a follow-on attack with the Air Battle Force—Admiral Yin estimates they are using two-thirds of their strength on this raid alone and are sustaining heavy losses. This is nothing more than a warning—the Americans want us to know that they are serious about the status of the Philippines.

"But if we back out now, we have no claim to make for Palawan, Mindanao, or the Spratly Islands whatsoever. If we take Davao and secure Mindanao, we can negotiate for favorable terms. The Americans might even be forced to disengage if their losses are heavy enough and if both world and popular opinion turns against them, and then we begin our consolidation of the Philippines under Chinese stewardship." He lowered his voice, stared the Premier straight in the eyes, and said, "I can guarantee you a victory, Comrade Premier. If I am stopped, I can guarantee you only embarrassment and defeat."

After several long moments, the aged Cheung rose, assisted by two bodyguards. In a low, creaking voice, he said, "You can guarantee nothing, General Chin, but death and destruction. However, for your sake, I hope you can inflict more on the enemy than he does on us. I will require updates every thirty minutes."

"Yes, Comrade Premier," Chin said, bowing. "Be assured, we will see victory today."

Cheung ignored Chin's boasting. To his Foreign Minister, Cheung said, "Comrade Zhou, I will speak with you for a moment." Chin was not invited in on the brief discussion. Cheung said a few words to Zhou, who bowed deeply and hurried off. Chin was left alone with his thoughts.

The Americans were doing incredible damage to his fleet in the south Philippines, Chin thought grimly. There was a very real possibility that he could lose this conflict—if the American bombers managed to sweep across to the landing ships, every last one of the Marines landing near Davao could be wiped out. He would be completely disgraced. He could not allow a defeat in Davao . . .

Zhou criticized him for putting Admiral Yin Po L'un in charge of the invasion, but suddenly a fearsome thought occurred to General Chin that Admiral Yin might provide a way out of this mess. The question was: was Admiral Yin really insane enough to do it?

He stepped quickly out of the Premier's office suites and directly to the palace communications center to put through an urgent call to Admiral Yin on the destroyer *Hong Lung*. The answer to his question: yes, Yin was that crazy.

ANDERSEN AIR FORCE BASE, GUAM

"General, we got the satellite picture back!" Jon Masters said.

Generals Stone, Elliott, Harbaugh, and the rest of the Joint Task Force staff crowded around the reactivated high-definition computer screen. It showed the entire Davao Gulf area in extraordinary detail, with IFF data blocks on every American aircraft, and computer-generated data blocks on the Chinese vessels.

"Great, Jon, just great," Stone said. The staff studied the board for several moments. "We're going to have to divide the screen up between the staff and prepare a summary of the Chinese ships that are still out there. We'll have to make a decision about the second wave pretty soon." After checking that the individual consoles were working out properly, Stone assigned each staff member a section of the Davao, Celebes Sea, and Philippine Sea areas to search for Chinese ships.

"Looks like the southern packages are coming off the target, the eastern packages are over the target, and the northern packages are two minutes out," Calvin Jarrell summarized. "The southern group got hit pretty hard . . . the eastern group looks almost intact . . . God, the northern planes are taking a beating from that one ship right there near the airport."

"It'll take awhile to see which ships have been hit or not," Masters said, "but several are showing zero velocity—we can probably assume those were struck. Luckily we've still got memorized satellite data, so we can retrace a ship's movements along with our aircraft and determine whether or not someone hit it."

Elliott called Stone over to his console after only a few minutes. "I think you better see this, Rat Killer," he said. There were two large vessels and three smaller escort vessels in a small group, farther west than the main battle group. "Obviously reinforcements," Elliott said. "But the ISAR radar report that Cobb and McLanahan got for us said something about this group . . ."

As Stone watched, Elliott zoomed in on the group of five vessels, zoomed in on the largest one in the group, then switched to an ISAR view of the ship. Using ISAR, or inverse synthetic aperture radar, mode, the motion of the ship itself as well as the motion of the satellite created a very high-definition three-dimensional view of the vessel, which when run through a computer's stored catalog of ships could yield the identity of the ship itself . . .

And when they found out, Stone muttered a curse to himself. *"Hong Lung,"* he said. "They're sailing *Hong Lung* itself back into battle . . ."

"General Stone," one of the battle staff communications officers said. "Sir . . . the base operator received an urgent phone call—from the embassy in Manila." The officers turned to face the communications officer—they could tell from the man's voice that something was happening.

"What is it?"

"Sir . . . the embassy got a call from an officer who identified himself as a member of the Fleet Admiral's Staff of the Chinese People's Liberation Army Navy South Philippines Task Force. He advises us that Admiral Yin Po L'un, the Fleet Admiral, has ordered that the city of Davao be attacked and destroyed with nuclear weapons if the American bombers do not withdraw immediately."

"What?" Everyone in the command post was on their feet.

"That was the ship . . . the guy . . . that launched the antiship nuclear missile . . . wasn't it?" Masters asked Stone. No one replied, but the answer was clear.

"It's a bluff," Cal Jarrel said resolutely.

"The message origin was verified, sir," the communications officer reported. "Came directly from the Premier's offices themselves through military channels. The State Department is notifying the White House now."

"Back up that call with one of our own," Stone ordered. "Get the President on the line for me immediately."

"Can he do it?" Elliott asked. "Can his missiles attack ground targets?"

"Easily, and with pretty good precision," Stone replied. "The Fei Lung-9 has a range of almost two hundred kilometers—that's over a hundred nautical miles. It was originally a mobile land-based missile, modified for shipboard use."

"You can't take this seriously," Jarrel protested. "We were expecting something like this. The next call that comes in will say that the Chinese will launch a sea-launched ballistic missile on Guam or Hong Kong or Okinawa if we don't withdraw." But faces were still grave—they were taking the threat very seriously. Jarrel said, "There's nothing we can do anyway—the planes are over their targets now. In three minutes the B-1s will go over the target."

"We can withdraw them," Harbaugh said.

"That's crazy, Tom . . ."

"Look at the board, Cal," Harbaugh said. "Your boys have done enough damage already. What's the big deal if we abort the northern strike group?"

"The big deal is, the Chinese Marines will make it on the beach," Jarrel argued. "We would have used all the other bombers for nothing . . . we will have lost all those other crews for nothing."

"We can't take the chance that he'll do it," Harbaugh said.

"He'll wipe out a bunch of his own guys, won't he?" Masters asked.

"If they're already wiped out by the Air Battle Force, he might not care."

"Order a strike by the Tomahawk cruise missiles again," Elliott said. "What's the range from the *Wisconsin* group to the *Hong Lung?*" But the measurement was quickly made and verified—it was over six hundred miles. The Tomahawk cruise missile crews would need at least thirty minutes to program a new strike, and then the missiles would take at least an hour to fly that distance.

"We can order one of the bombers to attack the *Hong Lung,*" Harbaugh said. "They can withhold a couple weapons, head south, and attack. We can use a couple of the B-1s in the northern strike group—they only have mines and fuel-air explosives left by now, but that should do the job." He pointed at the high-definition monitor. *"Hong Lung* will need to move farther north, right to the mouth of Davao Gulf, before firing. That means we have about twenty minutes to get someone in position . . ."

"There isn't time to send retargeting data to the B-1s, Tom," Jarrel said. "We've got two orders we can give the bombers now—attack or withhold. If we order two planes to withhold, they abort right in the middle of all that air defense. They have to traverse a hundred and twenty miles of stiff defenses, find the right ship, and attack. It's crazy. I say send the B-1s in and finish the job. This is an obvious bluff, and we're falling for it . . ."

"But if it's not a bluff . . ."

"I have a suggestion, sir," Masters said. "I think I have a way we can strike that Chinese destroyer in time."

And Jon Masters began to outline his plan to his audience. . . .

MINDANAO, THE PHILIPPINES

The frigate *Xiamen* had been hit by no less than six Harpoon missiles and was burning as fiercely as a volcano in the mouth of Davao Gulf—its patrol boat escorts could not get within five kilometers of it because of burning fuel oil on the water, the intense heat, and the occasional explosions in her weapon magazines. Three of *Xiamen*'s six patrol boat escorts had been hit by Harpoon missiles, which left Davao Gulf wide open for the strike package to enter. Two B-52s took heavy-caliber gun-

fire hits from patrol boats and were forced to jettison their
ordnance armed before penetrating into the target area, and
one was shot down as it withdrew from the area; all of the
crewmen safely ejected and were taken prisoner.

The destroyer *Yinchuan,* which had few antiair weapons in
its arsenal, was the next to fall. Ten B-52s from the three
southern strike packages descended on it and her escorts, filling the air with forty Harpoon missiles designated just for one
vessel. Most of the missiles struck other vessels or were intercepted by *Yinchuan*'s escorts, but ten Harpoon missiles found
the heavy destroyer. It sank in less than twenty minutes.

The destroyer *Dalian,* which was equipped with the Hong
Qian-91 surface-to-air missile system, and its antiair-equipped
escorts wreaked havoc on the six B-52s that were fragged to
attack it. Two B-52s sustained heavy damage and were forced
to withdraw; one crashed over land to the east of Bangoy Bay,
while the other was attacked by fighters and destroyed as it
tried to escape the target area. But *Dalian* had expended most
of its weapons defending the amphibious assault force against
Tomahawk cruise missiles, and it soon found that it could not
defend itself against an onslaught of twelve Harpoon antiship
missiles launched against it. Battered and listing to starboard,
the destroyer's captain finally decided to beach his vessel near
Matiao rather than have it sink in Bangoy Bay.

The vertical-plot greaseboard in the flag bridge of the destroyer *Hong Lung* was physically painful to look at. Destroyed vessels were in red, damaged and out-of-commission
vessels were in black, damaged but operational vessels were in
green-and-black stripes, and fully operational vessels were in
green—and there were damned few of those. Fortunately,
most of the green vessels were amphibious assault ships—the
attackers still had not reached the Marines on the beach.

"Flag, bridge, we have visual sighting on destroyer *Xiamen,*" the skipper of the *Hong Lung* radioed to Admiral Yin.
"He is signaling a request for assistance. Shall we come alongside?"

Captain Sun looked at Yin, who silently shook his head. Sun
considered asking the Admiral to reconsider, thought better of

it, then radioed, "Bridge from flag. Tactical recovery only, longboats and stage-three damage-control parties. Maintain course and speed to establish patrol position. Flag out." Sun shut off the intercom before the captain could argue as well.

"*Dalian* reports he is safely aground, sir," a radioman reported. "Captain Yeng reports he can repair his fire-control system, estimated time to completion, thirty minutes." Another silent nod from Yin.

"Tell Captain Yeng to continue antiair coverage with electro-optical and visual means until his radar fire-control system is repaired," Sun said. "Add that the Admiral commends him for saving his vessel and for his confirmed kills, but that he is still the primary antiair warship for the invasion force." Captain Sun stepped over to the vertical plot, studied it for a moment, then said, "We should have the transports evade north into Bangoy Bay—it will hide them better from any bombers that are still in the area. When the all-clear sounds, they can travel at flank speed south with their escorts to recover."

"What escorts?" Yin muttered. "What escorts are left?"

"You see, sir, we have at least six patrol boats . . . and the *Hong Lung* group will be in position to cover their withdrawal, of course. Once past us, our air coverage will protect them until they dock at Zamboanga to load reinforcements."

"Six . . . patrol . . . boats . . ." Yin said in a low, wavering voice. "Six . . . I began this operation with eight destroyers, twenty frigates, and nearly sixty patrol boats. There are *no* capital ships left that can escort the amphibious assault ships back to port? None?"

"Sir, most of our frigates and patrol boats are still operational and still on patrol in the Philippine Sea," Sun said. "We have recalled a few of them, along with the destroyer *Zhangzhou*, to bolster our inner defenses." Sun stepped toward Yin, straightened his back, and said, "Sir, you deployed your forces like a true master tactician. You fought a superb battle against the best the Americans could throw at us. Your objective, the Marine invasion and the occupation of Davao and Samar International Airport, is almost complete. You have won, sir. You have—"

"Sir! Enemy aircraft inbound from the northeast and east of Davao," the radioman reported. The vertical plot technician began drawing in the aircraft reported inbound, and the number seemed to grow to alarming size every second.

The northeast aircraft were farther behind the eastern group, but were moving in rapidly. "What kind of aircraft are they?" Sun ordered. "The Admiral needs type of aircraft. Get it!"

"Aircraft in eastern group reported as B-52 aircraft only," the radioman replied after several inquiries. "No identification yet on northeast aircraft." But judging by the speed at which the vertical plot technician was updating their position, Sun could easily guess—B-52 bombers, followed by B-1 and F-111 bombers. The three southern groups were just the first wave— the second package, not as large as the first but even more powerful, were going after the Marines themselves.

"Issue an air-defense alert to all vessels and all forces; enemy bombers inbound from the east and northeast," Sun ordered. "Have all forces take cover on the beach. Disperse landing craft and assault vessels as much as possible."

Admiral Yin looked as if he had been deflated with a knife. He could only stare at the vertical plot, muttering something to himself that Sun could not hear. "Sir? Do you have further orders?" Sun asked. The Chinese Fleet Admiral could only mutter something unintelligible, stare at a slip of paper he had been given by the communications section, and stare at the board in absolute horror.

"Attention! Attention! Air-defense warning! Gunners man your batteries and stand by."

Colonel of Marines Yang Yi Shuxin glanced nervously at the loudspeakers on the "island" superstructure above him, then at the turrets where the ship's numerous 37-millimeter antiair-craft guns were mounted, but he quickly turned his attention back to the men on his landing craft. No one said a word, but Yang raised his voice easily above the amplified voice and said, "Be silent, all of you. The gunners have their job and you have yours. Stand by."

Yang was leading a troop of forty heavily armed Chinese

Marines in the invasion of Davao. They were aboard the air-cushion landing craft *Dagu,* a monstrous sixty-ton vessel that skimmed above the surface of the water on a cushion of air created by six gas-turbine-powered propellers on the bottom of the craft; two turboprop propellers above pushed the craft to over seventy kilometers per hour over land or sea. *Dagu* carried two small armored personnel carriers, each with 30-millimeter machine guns on board; the landing craft itself was armed with two 14.5-millimeter guns manned by four very young-looking soldiers. Unlike other landing craft, *Dagu* would take her Marines right up onto dry ground instead of into chest-deep water.

The amphibious landing ship they were on carried two such air-cushion landing craft, plus four conventional landing craft, along with twenty armored troop-carriers on the tank deck and thirty "deuce-and-a-half" utility trucks on the main deck, plus a total of four hundred Marines. Other amphibious assault tank-landing ships carried air-cushion landing craft, but they always called on Colonel Yang to lead any assault. Yang's men would be the first Chinese soldiers to occupy Samar International Airport and lay siege to the city of Davao itself.

Other smaller Yuchai or Yunnan-class landing craft had gone ahead to try to draw fire, spot targets for the destroyer's guns, or dismantle beach defenses. *Dagu* would lead the main Marine assault on the beach itself. After Yang's Marines and APCs captured the beach, they would bring the amphibious assault ship into shallow water, deploy the pontoon bridge sections carried on the hull sides, and start rolling the trucks off the forward ramp. Once on the road, the trucks would rush forward and take Samar Airport—and victory.

The LST's two big twin 76.2-millimeter guns began pounding away on the beach as the amphibious assault ship made a slight turn to bring both guns to bear. "Ready!" Yang shouted, and his men gave an animal-like growl in response. *Dagu*'s helmsman started the engines, and the air-cushion vehicle's four-meter-tall armor-covered skirt quickly inflated. A horn blared on the aft deck, the stern ramp lowered, and *Dagu*'s helmsman gunned the twin turbojet propellers. The air-cushion craft leaped out into the darkness, hit the water, and sped toward the beach.

What Yang saw when they cleared the amphibious assault ship looked like something out of a child's nightmare.

Ships were on fire everywhere. At least two other tank- and troop-landing ships were burning fiercely, with smoke billowing out of two more. Antiaircraft guns were sweeping the skies in seemingly random patterns. The water that Yang could see was littered with bodies, capsized landing craft, and debris. As he watched, another explosion ripped across the water, the shock wave strong enough to stagger him.

He had to remind himself that he could not show fear in front of his men, most of whom he knew were watching him. One of the toughest things for a Marine to do was step off a fast, safe landing craft and hit the beach, and for most of them only the sight of a brave leader would make them do it.

They had been dropped into the water over two kilometers offshore, but the air-cushion vehicle ate up the distance quickly—less than thirty seconds to go, and they would be on dry land. The helmsman was taking a zigzag course into shore—he was probably only dodging other destroyed landing craft or pools of burning fuel, but Yang always told his troops that they did that to confound the enemy gunners. *Dagu*'s gunners opened fire several times on the beach, but Yang heard no mortars, bazookas, or heavy gunfire coming from there.

"No resistance from the beach!" he yelled to his men. The Marines around him growled happily in reply. "Drive and conquer! Split into threes, divide, and run for cover! Watch for engineers ahead of you." Minesweeping engineers who had gone ahead of them had fluorescent orange tapes on their arms and backs to distinguish them from . . .

A huge explosion erupted behind them, lighting up the horizon so brightly that Yang could easily see the treeline. "Eyes front!" Yang shouted as his men ducked, then began to try to turn around in the close confines to see what had been hit. "Get ready!" Yang did not look either, although judging by the secondary explosions, their amphibious assault ship had been hit. He could faintly hear the roar of heavy jet planes overhead, and *Dagu*'s gunners even swung their puny machine guns futilely in the sky after the engine sounds. That did nothing but highlight their positions. "Guns front! Reload! Cover the landing!" Yang shouted. The gunners and their loaders were too scared to listen—they were either watching the destruction of their mother ship or scanning the dark skies above for enemy bombers. "APCs, start engines!" The heavy diesel engines on the armored personnel carriers roared to life, and gunners in the top turrets chambered rounds.

Seconds later, the air-cushion landing craft hit the shore, the turbojet engines surged to full power, the craft raced up onto the beach, and the forward part of the air-cushion skirt began to deflate for offloading. The gunners finally began to rake the treeline with gunfire. "Ready!" Yang shouted, and the adrenaline-pumped men growled once again. The forward lip of the air-cushion vehicle hit the ground and the ramp swung down. Yang leaped up onto the ramp, ran down it onto the beach, then waved at his men, pointing toward the treeline not thirty meters away. *"Marines! Go! Go!* G—"

His last word was drowned out by a massive cloud of fire and a head-pounding explosion—Yang felt as if all the air had been sucked out of his lungs and replaced by sheets of pure fire. Several Marines scampering down the ramp were blown off their feet and onto the beach as a shock wave larger than any Yang could ever recall rolled over them. His night vision was completely wiped out by a blinding burst of light, and his eardrums felt as if they had burst—no, his whole *head* felt as if it had burst . . .

Four F-111G fighter-bombers screamed into the area nearly at supersonic speed, right into the midst of the lines of landing craft trying to land their forces on the beaches south of Davao. They did not carry Harpoon missiles or bombs. Instead, each carried four 2,000-pound BLU-96 HADES FAE, or fuel-air explosives, canisters. Each HADES canister contained three hundred gallons of explosive fuel-oil, and the canisters were toss-released about a thousand feet over a group of eight landing craft. About eight hundred feet above the water, the canisters popped open, and the fuel oil began to disperse in large white clouds of vapor. Seconds later, when the vapor cloud was about five hundred feet above the landing craft and had expanded to one hundred feet in diameter, tiny sodium detonators in the vapor clouds fired off.

The resulting explosion was greater than the force of a twenty-thousand-pound high-explosive bomb, creating a mushroom cloud of fire that stretched across the water for nearly half a mile and a shock wave that churned the water into a boiling froth for two miles in all directions, deafening or knocking soldiers unconscious and setting the landing craft underneath the explosions immediately afire. Two of the HADES canisters sailed over the beach, amidst several platoons of Chinese Marine engineers, and the incredible force of the explosion was just as devastating on land.

The closest HADES canister went off three miles away, but to Yang and his Marines it felt as if they were in the middle of an erupting volcano. Yang found himself dazed but unhurt, flat on his stomach, his rifle thrown several meters away. He low-crawled to his rifle, picked it up, then rose cautiously to his knees. "Marines! Forward! APCs! Move out!" Thankfully, the first APC began to lumber off the air-cushion landing craft; the second showed no signs of moving. "Get those APCs off the landing craft! *Move it! Move it!*" Slowly, his men got to their feet, stumbling toward the APCs to take cover behind them as they got their senses back.

As Yang urged his men to get off the landing craft, he was able to scan out toward the straits toward his amphibious landing ship—and what he saw horrified him. The entire interior of the ship seemed to be on fire. Pieces of the pontoon bridges were hanging off the sides, all afire, and in the glare of the fires he could see men flinging themselves overboard into the burning-oil-covered gulf. A spectacular explosion sent a column of flames a hundred meters into the night sky as the fires finally found the twenty-five million decaliters of diesel fuel still in the LST's storage tanks.

A few of his men stopped to look at the dying ship, and Yang grabbed them and shoved them forward. "Move it! Secure that treeline! Search that house! Move it . . . !"

The gunners aboard *Dagu* began firing into the sky again,

and Yang could hear the sounds of fast and heavy jets getting closer. "Get off the landing craft!" he yelled. "Run toward the trees! *Run!*"

But it was too late.

Two minutes after the F-111s delivered their canisters of fire, the next strike package began its ingress from the northeast: four B-52s that had survived the battle with the destroyer *Dalian* continued their attacks with Harpoon missiles and CAPTOR mines; their escort EB-52C Megafortress had been shot down by a JS-7 fighter over Mindanao as it tried to turn away from the target area. The four B-52s claimed kills on two amphibious assault ships and seeded the straits with over a dozen CAPTOR mines that began to seek out and destroy the surviving vessels that tried to escape across the straits to Samal Island.

Then, sixty seconds after the last B-52 came off the target, the last and the heaviest-armed warplanes in the entire battle began their assault; six B-1B bombers swooped in from the north at treetop level. They were never detected until it was far, far too late.

Colonel Yang could see the bright globes of red and orange walk down the beach toward him, stitching a path of destruction fifty meters wide and hundreds of meters long. There was no place to run—the bomblets from the aerial-mine canisters covered the entire beach. He could only raise his rifle and fire at the hissing sound as the sleek American bomber, highlighted for a brief moment against the glare of the burning tank-landing ship, streaked overhead. Yang turned his back to the approaching chemical meat-grinder of bomblets and continued to fire at the bomber until he was cut down by the devastating explosions and clouds of shrapnel.

Never had Major Pete Fletcher, the B-1B's OSO (Offensive Systems Officer), taken such an incredible array of weapons into battle before—in fact, never had he even *heard* of so many different kinds of weapons carried into battle. His B-1B Excalibur bomber, Blade Two-Five, had carried eight SLAM missiles on the external hardpoints—those had already been expended on the larger Chinese vessels in the Philippine Sea that survived the B-52s' initial onslaught; eight Mk 65 QUICK-STRIKE mines in the aft bomb bay, which were shallow-water high-explosive antiship mines that were to be dropped in Dadaotan Straits and Bangoy Harbor itself; twenty-four GATOR mines in the middle bomb bay, which were to be released on the beach—each bomb would disperse hundreds of small softball-sized mines along a wide area that could destroy small vehicles or kill large numbers of troops who tried to move through the area after the raid; and finally they carried eight BLU-96 HADES FAE canisters in the forward bomb bay, which were designated against the landing craft and Marines ashore north of Samar International Airport.

All of the remaining weapons were to be dropped within a distance of only twenty miles, on three separate two-mile-long tracks—and while flying at treetop level at nearly six miles per minute, it left almost no time to think about procedures. He had taken a fix in between fighter attacks while going coast-in, and the navigation system was tight and ready to go. If he had time, Fletcher would try to take another radar fix going into the target area, but he doubted that would happen. The bombing computer would have to take care of everything.

"Coming up on initial point . . . ready, ready, now," Fletcher called out. "Heading is good. Thirty seconds to release. Multiple GATOR release on heading one-eight-one, then right turn to heading two-one-six for a multiple QUICKSTRIKE mine release, then right turn to heading two-six-eight for a multiple HADES release. Stand by . . . fifteen seconds."

The fires that were already burning in Dadaotan Straits and Bangoy Harbor were spectacular—there had to be at least a dozen large troopships burning, with spots of fires dotting the entire bay. "My God, it looks like the end of the fucking world," the copilot muttered on interphone.

"Five seconds . . . stand by to turn . . ."

But the huge fires that made it so easy for the B-1 crew to see the target area also made it easy for the Chinese troops to see the incoming bomber. A row of tracers from a few of the surviving amphibious assault ships arced into the sky, the undulating lines of shells sweeping the sky in seemingly random patterns—and suddenly several of those lines swept across the nose of the B-1 bomber.

The impact of the 57-millimeter shells from one of the tank-landing ships felt like hammer blows from Thor himself. The cabin pressure immediately dumped, replaced a millisecond later with a thunderous roar of the windblast hammering in through the cockpit windows. Airspeed seemed to drop to zero, and the crew experienced a feeling of weightlessness as the B-1 started to drift and fall across the sky.

Fletcher reacted instantly. While struggling to keep himself upright in his seat as much as possible, he selected all remaining stores stations, opened the bomb doors, and hit the "Emergency Armed Release" button once again. "All weapons away! Weapons away!" he shouted. "Right turn to escape, Doug!" He called to the pilot, Captain Doug Wendt. "Right turn! Head west!"

All of the mines and BLU-96 canisters made a normal release—except one. One of the racks in the forward bomb bay was hit by gunfire, the rack jammed, then released, and the canister was flung against the aft bomb-bay bulkhead and detonated. Fire and debris from the bomb and the damaged bomb bay flew into the right engine intakes, shelling the starboard engines and causing another terrific explosion.

There was a sound like a raging waterfall filling the entire crew compartment, and smoke began to fill the cabin. The B-1 seemed to be hanging upside down, twisting left and right and fishtailing around the sky. "Doug? Answer up!" No reply. "George?" Again no reply. Without thinking of what he was doing, Fletcher pulled the parachute release mechanism on his ejection seat, which unclipped him from his seat but kept his parachute on his back. He dropped to the deck and began crawling on his hands and feet toward the clipboard.

"Pete!" Lieutenant Colonel Terry Rowenki, the DSO (Defensive Systems Operator), yelled behind him. "What the hell are you doing? Get back here!"

Fletcher ignored him. Flat on his stomach, he made his way through the howling windblast to the cockpit. Through the glare of flares outside, he could see that all of the windshields were blown in, and both Wendt and Lleck were slumped over in their seats, unconscious. The autopilot was not on, but the B-1 was light and trimmed enough to maintain wings-level even without hands on the control stick.

"Terry! Get out! Eject!" Fletcher screamed, but he could not be heard over the windblast. Crawling forward another few feet, he pulled himself up onto the center console, keeping as far below the murderous wind coming through the shattered windows as he could, reached across, and lifted the right-side ejection handle on Doug Wendt's seat. The large red "Eject" light snapped on in every section of the cabin—it came on automatically whenever the pilot's ejection handles were raised. Fighting the force of the wind hammering on his entire body, he reached up and hit the ejection trigger with his left hand.

The inertial reel thankfully yanked Doug Wendt's body up-right in his seat a fraction of a second before the overhead escape hatch blew off and the seat roared off into space. But the ejection seat's rocket motor flared right in Fletcher's face, and he screamed again as his vision was replaced by angry stars of pure pain. He was on the verge of unconsciousness, and only another explosion from somewhere inside the bomber brought him back to his senses. Struggling through the pain to regain his vision, he finally gave up trying to open his eyes, groped around for Lleck's ejection handle, found it, and pulled. This time the white-hot fire from the motor seared his chest and stomach, and he slumped to the deck.

"Pete! Pete, dammit, wake up!"

Someone was calling his name . . . someone . . . Fletcher raised his head.

"Pete! This way! Crawl this way! Hurry!"

It was Terry Rowenki—the idiot hadn't ejected yet. Fletcher's head hit the deck with a dull thud. That was his problem, he thought blissfully as he drifted off toward uncon-sciousness—the man had a perfectly good ejection seat, now was the time to use it.

But sleep wouldn't come. He soon felt someone pulling his legs. "Pete, dammit, crawl this way . . . you motherfucker, wake up, dammit, wake up . . ."

To humor him, Fletcher pushed against the center cockpit console toward the systems compartment. The odd pitch angles of the deck seemed to help him—the Excalibur's nose was high in the air, as if they were in a steep climb—and Rowenki's grasp was extraordinarily strong. He heard another loud sound, more windblast sounds the farther back he moved—until he realized that it was the big entry hatch. Rowenki had jettisoned the hatch and the entry ladder and was trying to pull Fletcher out!

Somehow Rowenki managed to get Fletcher pulled to the hatch and over onto his stomach, head toward the open hatch. "What the fuck did you think you were doing up there?" Rowenki yelled as he continued to wrestle with Fletcher's ragdoll-like body. "Being a damned hero? You get me killed up here, Fletcher, and I'll fucking haunt you for a hundred years."

Attaching the emergency rescue rope to the D-ring on Fletcher's parachute harness, Rowenki used his feet and shoved Fletcher headfirst out the entry hatch. The escape rope yanked taut, spinning Fletcher's body around but pulling the ripcord D-ring and opening the parachute. One of Fletcher's legs got tangled in the parachute risers, but it whipped free and the chute safely opened. Rowenki was right behind him, leaping out of the hatch as if he were going to do a cannonball from a high-diving board. He broke his left foot when it hit the aft edge of the hatch, but the pain only served to remind him to pull the D-ring as he sailed toward the lush tropical forests below.

The stricken B-1 continued to sail in a nose-high climbing right turn for several minutes, almost executing a full 180-degree turn, until it finally ran out of airspeed, stalled, and crashed to earth near the town of Cadeco. The last aircraft of the first raid of the Air Battle Force had completed its journey.

"Sir, report from a J-7 fighter over Samar International Airport," the radioman announced.

Admiral Yin was on his feet. "Speak!" he shouted, loud enough to startle just about everyone in the room. "Is the airport taken?"

The radioman listened for a several moments, his face looking more ashen and disbelieving every second. He glanced at Yin, then at Sun, then back toward his equipment. "Well? Speak!"

"Sir . . . sir, the pilot reports numerous vessels afire in Dadaotan Straits and Bangoy Harbor," the radioman said. "No contact from any ground units on any tactical channel. Several explosions . . . secondary explosions . . . indications of some troop movement on the ground, but none that will answer on any frequency."

Admiral Yin was absolutely thunderstruck. "No . . . contact . . . no contact from any of my Marines?"

"Sir, it does not mean anything," Captain Sun Ji Guoming said. "The Marines most assuredly went into deep cover when the American air strike came in. They must be safe." But his words did nothing to assuage Yin's feelings of utter despair and hopelessness. Eight thousand Marines . . . six thousand sailors . . . no contact with any of them . . .

"Status of the American bombers," Captain Sun ordered. Action was the best therapy now—they had an invasion force to run. Just because contact was lost did not mean that the battle was lost. "Have they withdrawn?"

"Yes, sir," the radioman reported. "All aircraft have disengaged. One B-1 destroyed during the last raid."

"Very good," Sun said. "Excellent. Sir, did you hear that report?"

Finally, an incredible sense of relief seemed to wash over every man on the *Hong Lung*'s flag bridge, and especially over Admiral Yin Po L'un. They knew that the American Air Battle Force had sent most of their aircraft on this one raid, and that they had sustained rather heavy losses. There would not be another air raid for several days, if at all—still plenty of time to take Samar Airport and win this battle.

"Order that J-7 pilot to investigate at Samar International Airport," Yin ordered. "See if any of our troops have managed to take the airfield. It is impossible for only a handful of bombers to completely stop thousands of Marines."

Several minutes passed. Then: "Sir, message from Jian Four-Four. He has made contact with a Marine company commander, who wishes to relay a status report to you."

"Excellent! I knew our forces were still on the move! Open the channel."

After a few anxious moments, they heard, *"Hong Lung,* this is Tiger. *Hong Lung,* this is Tiger. How do you read?"

"It is Colonel Liyujiang," Captain Sun said excitedly. "I recognize his voice. He is the commander of the northern assault force."

Yin himself picked up the microphone. "We read you, Tiger. What is your location? What is your status?"

The voice seemed weary, but the man spoke in a clear voice. "Tiger reports from inside the northeast gate of Samar International Airport," Liyujiang said.

"Inside the airport! We have made it!" one of the flag staff members shouted. "The Marines are going to capture the airport!"

"Status as follows . . ." There was a short pause, as if Liyujiang had to refer to a chart.

Then, to Yin's horror, he heard a voice in English. "This is Colonel Renaldo Carigata, Admiral Yin, acting deputy commander, Commonwealth of Mindanao Defense Force. Colonel Liyujiang will not be giving any reports for quite some time, so allow me to proceed. Status as follows: General Samar's forces still hold the airport and the city. My snipers are going out to greet what is left of your invasion force right now. *Allah akbar.* Good day, Admiral Yin." And the line went dead.

Yin stepped back from the radioman, horrified. The members of his flag staff looked on in absolute shock. Captain Sun led the crushed Fleet Admiral back to his seat.

"Don't worry, Admiral," Captain Sun said. "Wait for the complete status report. Do not lose faith in your men. The air raids are over now—we can reassemble our forces and finish this battle. We can—"

"Sir!" the intercom from the *Hong Lung*'s Combat Information Center blared out. "Missile warning! Patrol boat reports possible inbound Tomahawk cruise missiles from the southeast. Multiple inbounds, heading northwest . . . sir! Possible sighting of aircraft from patrol boat 403, two hundred and twenty kilometers east of our position . . . sir, first estimate of missiles inbound from the southeast number twenty . . . sir, do you copy . . . ?"

Yin was numb. He had lost. The Americans had not only decimated his spearhead forces, but had quickly assembled another attack force and were pressing the engagement.

There was only one thing to do.

Slowly, the look of shock still frozen on his face, Yin withdrew a silver key on a chain about his neck. Every member of his flag staff shot to their feet in horror . . . it was the execution key for the Fei Lung-9 nuclear missiles. But despite their horror no one tried to stop Yin—they realized that it was his only option. Good or bad, Yin would ultimately win this battle and do what he set out to accomplish—destroy the city of Davao, crush the rebel opposition, and occupy Mindanao.

Yin inserted the key into the execution order box and pressed a button inside the recessed chamber. The alarm began to ring through the ship. No one on the flag staff moved. Crewmen scurried about, handing out protective gear and running to their Fei Lung-9 battle stations. Yin picked up the telephone.

"Battle Cry. Battle Cry," the Admiral said. His face was ghostly, muffled, almost strangled—he could have had his protective facemask on, but he did not.

"Initial code verified," the voice of the Fei Lung-9 weapon systems officer on the other end of the line asked. "Targets, sir?"

Yin paused, his eyes trying to fix on something in the darkness beyond the slanted windows of the flag bridge. He then said, "Davao."

"Understood, sir. Execution automatic. Awaiting authentication code." Yin seemed to be frozen. "Comrade Admiral? Authentication code?"

"Red . . . Moon . . ."

"Understood, sir. Authentication verified. Full connectivity checked . . . received. Execution in three minutes . . . mark. System automatic engaged, extreme range of system but coming within range, attack profile confidence is good. Countdown hold in two minutes. Combat out."

The two-minutes-to-automatic-countdown hold passed very, very quickly. The phone to Yin's panel rang and he raised it to his lips. "Final countdown hold, sir. Target now within range. Orders?"

"Orders . . . Dragon Sword. Dragon Sword," Yin replied.

"Understood, sir. Final code verified." The sixty-second-launch warning to all decks blared . . .

And then there was another sound, except it was not a horn—it was a high-pitched scream, rising in intensity to almost painful proportions. Just as the scream became almost physically unbearable, the destroyer was rocked by a spectacular explosion that dimmed the lights throughout the ship and sent most of the flag staff sprawling.

Jon Masters had commanded the second NIRTSat reconnaissance satellite to deorbit while it was still thirty thousand miles away. The satellite had retracted its charge-coupled device scanners and sensitive radar antennae within its protective housing, then powerful thrusters began to slow the satellite at a precise moment. As the satellite slowed from its orbital speed of seventeen thousand miles per hour, it began to descend through the atmosphere. The thrusters kept the satellite's protective tiles facing its direction of travel as it re-entered the atmosphere, burning off bits of the ablative armor as it careened through space like an asteroid.

But unlike an asteroid, the NIRTSat was still under control from a console on Guam. Once the satellite had safely decelerated, Masters ordered the on-board sensors activated. The satellite was right on course, right on the same track it had been following since its launch—right over the Celebes Sea near Davao Gulf. Masters had simply locked the synthetic aperture radar and infrared scanner on the fleet of five ships; then, as it got closer and closer, he positively identified the large destroyer and steered it directly onto the aft deck of the *Hong Lung.*

The satellite was of course not carrying a warhead, but falling at over five times the speed of sound, the destructive power of the titanium-armored four-hundred-pound satellite was akin to a large torpedo. The force of the impact drove the *Hong Lung*'s stern down several meters; then the satellite crashed through the engine compartment belowdecks and literally pushed one of the diesel-turbine engines down ten feet through the keel. The engine compartment began to flood, and the ship had already begun to heavily list to one side and by the stern before enough watertight doors could be closed to contain the damage . . .

. . . and, most importantly, the impact and the momentary power interruption had automatically canceled the Fei Lung-9 launch.

Yin's last attempt at revenge and victory had been stopped.

Captain Sun stepped over to Admiral Yin, bowed, and said, "Comrade Admiral, the flooding is nearly out of control. The frigate *Jiujiang* is alongside. Will you transfer your flag, sir?"

There was no reply.

Admiral Yin was staring blankly ahead, his thoughts a confused jumble of his past, the present—and the dismal future. Returning to China and facing the general staff would be devastating, utterly devastating. His honor would be ripped apart in full view of the entire world. His court-martial and execution would be public and brutal. He would be totally, utterly humiliated.

Yin turned to Captain Sun, and he saw that the man's demeanor, far from being the attentive chief of staff, now appeared to be more like a second at a duel, making sure that Yin realized and fulfilled his obligation.

His obligation . . . to lead his forces into victory, or die.

Sun understood the humiliation that awaited the Admiral upon his return, and he silently reminded him that he need not subject himself to it.

Captain Sun and the Admiral's flag staff watched with awe and, yes, a bit of admiration and respect, as Admiral Yin Po L'un stepped toward the small personal shrine installed in one corner of the Admiral's flag bridge, knelt before it, withdrew his Type 54 7.62-millimeter sidearm from his holster, placed the muzzle to his right temple, and calmly blew his brains out across his flag bridge.

EPILOGUE

Escorted by two aides and two soldiers, High General Chin Po Zihong marched through the halls to the offices of the Premier of the People's Republic of China. He was quickly escorted by the Premier's protocol staff to the main conference room and asked to enter immediately.

At least two hundred heads swung toward him as he entered: it was as if the entire Communist Party of China were assembled in that room. Cheung was alone at the head of the conference table; the seat normally reserved for him at Cheung's left was taken by Cheung's Home Minister. There was no way Chin could reach his usual seat—and, after decades of studying and developing military tactics, it was obvious that it was precisely what Cheung had in mind. He stepped quickly over to the end of the long conference table directly opposite Cheung, and the bureaucrats and politicians of the Party closed in around the table.

General Chin bowed deeply from the waist. "Comrade Premier, I am reporting as ordered."

"Do you have a status report for me, General?" Cheung asked in a surprisingly strong, loud voice.

"Yes, Comrade Premier . . ." He stopped, realizing Cheung

couldn't hear him, and raised his voice: "Yes, Comrade Premier. But I would prefer the briefing to be given . . . privately."

"Please give your report now, Comrade General," Cheung said.

"But sir, some of these men are not cleared for—"

"They are authorized, General. Please give your report."

This was not a military briefing, Chin realized coldly—this was an inquisition. Obviously word of the battle of Davao had already reached the Premier—there was no use in trying to withhold any information now.

"Comrade Premier. First, I regret to inform you that the honorable commander of the People's Liberation Army Navy South Philippines Task Force, Admiral Yin Po L'un, is no longer in command of the people's forces near Mindanao. Until a suitable replacement has been designated, I have placed Admiral Lower Class Sun Ji Guoming, the Admiral's Chief of Staff, in charge of all forces in the south Philippines. Admiral Yin . . . died an honorable death while engaging enemy forces in the course of his duties to the people."

"Very tragic," Cheung said. "He will be remembered as a loyal servant to the people of the republic."

That of course was the proper response—in China, as in Japan and other Asian cultures, death by suicide was as acceptable a form of death as any other cause, even in this so-called enlightened society run by the Communists. Cheung, however, did not seem too upset by the news, although by his facial and body expressions Chin deduced that the Premier did not know about Yin's sudden departure.

"The operation to capture Davao and the airport there is progressing; however, the American bomber attacks on our naval and Marine forces have been severe. Along with air-launched antiship missiles and long-range cruise missiles, the Americans reportedly used fuel-air explosives against Marine landing craft and soldiers entrenched on the beach—these weapons are many times more powerful than conventional explosives and create a devastating shock wave and fireball, very much like a nuclear explosion." His words did not have the effect he desired—he was hoping the words "nuclear explosion" would inflame this audience a bit. They did not. "A second wave of attacks is now under way. Admiral Lower Class Sun reports that he is organizing antiaircraft defenses and can soon mount a defense of the people's warships.

"I have a plan of action to counter the American bomber attacks that I would like to submit—to the Premier's Cabinet and senior Party members—for your approval."

"General Chin," the Foreign Minister, Zhou Ti Yanbing, chimed in, "would it be possible for your forces to safely disengage and withdraw to . . . Puerto Princesa, on the island of Palawan, or perhaps even to Nansha Dao?"

"Disengage? Withdraw?" General Chin gasped. "Why would we withdraw? We—"

"—still have the advantage? Will capture Davao and Samar Airport without further serious loss of life? Will have a cursed navy after this conflict is over?" Zhou asked.

"We have weapons that we have not yet brought to bear," Chin said. "We sought to control this conflict, to use ground forces and conventional weapons only. The Americans escalated the conflict by employing B-1 and B-2 bombers, Tomahawk cruise missiles fired from battleships and submarines, and with such terror weapons as fuel-air explosives. We should step up our efforts as well. I have outlined a plan where we may—"

"The conquest of Mindanao and our support for a puppet like Teguina is not worth a war with America or the loss of another capital warship," Zhou said angrily. "I ask you again, General—can our forces safely withdraw to Puerto Princesa or Nansha Dao?"

"Do not speak to me of withdrawal!" Chin shouted. "You politicians can organize a retreat far better than I." And Chin did something he thought he would never do to a living premier—he turned his back and left.

"If you leave now, General Chin, you leave as the *former* commander of the People's Liberation Army," Foreign Minister Zhou said. "The Politburo has already decided to open a dialogue with the Americans for an orderly withdrawal. You can be part of the process—or you can retire from your post and be done with it."

Chin froze, then turned back to face the assembly before

him. In a loud, clear voice, he said, "I command the most powerful army in the universe. I will lead them into battle—I will not lead them in capitulation."

"You have already led them to defeat, General, you and Admiral Yin," Premier Cheung said. "Will you not lead them in reconstruction and retraining as well? You can leave here known in history as the man who had a fleet destroyed in the Philippines—or you can be known as the man who led the People's Liberation Army into the twenty-first century. The choice is yours."

He knew that he should not accept this, Chin told himself. The honorable thing would be to leave this place and do as Yin did—put a gun to his head or a knife to his stomach and kill himself . . .

But he did not leave; instead, he stepped toward the conference table and seated himself.

No one was more surprised than he when the assembled politicians applauded.

If these idiots ever found out, Chin thought grimly to himself, that I ordered Yin to use nuclear weapons to destroy Davao, they would certainly not be applauding—they would be calling for my execution. Sun and the rest of Yin's surviving flag staff would have to be bribed, exiled, or killed to ensure their silence, but that was an easy matter. General Chin Po Zihong's power, his authority, were still safe . . . and with the blissfully ignorant best wishes of the government raining down upon him, Chin began to plot his revenge on José Trujillo Samar and on the Americans who had razed his forces so badly.

Yes, revenge . . .

ANDERSEN AIR FORCE BASE, GUAM

It was daylight by the time Patrick McLanahan and Henry Cobb crawled out of their damaged B-2 stealth bomber into the already warm, humid tropical air. It seemed ten times stickier than usual—but to the two crew members, it felt like heaven.

The flight back from the Philippines was quiet, despite the

damage they had sustained. The autopilot, electronic flight-control computers, and electronic stability systems were use-less, and the mission commander's side controls were inoperable, so the two crewmen took turns in the pilot's seat—McClanahan flew the straight and level portions while Cobb napped, and Cobb flew the air-refueling hookups that they received every thirty minutes because of fuel leakage and the long overwater legs. The crew then spent another hour orbit-ing Guam while two-seat F-16 fighters with engineers and maintenance crews on board examined the damage to the flight controls and landing gear. Exhausted but riding yet an-other adrenaline rush, Cobb overrode all suggestions to eject and attempts to get more opinions from Stateside, and he made a picture-perfect landing at Andersen's left runway. Somehow the damaged left landing gear held, and the Black Knight bomber was shut down at the north end of the runway, surrounded by fire crews.

Although McLanahan and Cobb climbed out of the plane on their own power, because of the observed damage to the Black Knight they were settled into gurneys and transported to a massive green tent set up near the flight line that acted as a triage center for returning crews. Doctors found Henry Cobb's pulse and blood pressure sky-high, so he was ordered into a separate tent where crews that were well enough could be debriefed by intelligence officers while under a doctor's care; that was when General Elliott found him and McLanahan shortly after he was taken there.

"Henry, Patrick, damn your hide, good to have you back," Elliott said, giving his officers a hearty handshake and a pat on the shoulder. "Terrific landing, Henry. How do you two feel? You look okay. Henry, how do *you* feel?"

"I'm fine, General, just fine," Cobb replied. "I'm in adrena-line withdrawal, that's all. I'm too old for this shit, sir."

"I think half the base is on an adrenaline high, watching you bring that B-2 in," Elliott said. "I think the cheer that went up could be heard in China." He looked at McLanahan and smiled a knowing smile. "You brought back another bent bird, Pa-trick. This time the commendation will be public—nothing red-jacketed this time. For both of you."

"I'd be happy if we could just finish this thing and go home," the navigator said. "So what kind of losses are we looking at?"

"We've taken some serious hits," Elliott admitted. "Sorry to tell you this, but we lost John Cochran's Megafortress. A BUFF saw them go down. They couldn't see chutes in the darkness, although they heard plenty of emergency locator beacons. The crew is still listed as missing." Along with Major Kelvin Carter, Lieutenant Colonel John Cochran was one of the High Technology Aerospace Weapons Center's pioneers in the application of the strategic battleship escort concept; they had all worked very closely together for many months. "His was the only HAWC crew to go down. His crew got six confirmed kills, though. Every Megafortress got at least three—an incredibly awesome display."

"I hope they find him," Patrick said. "How about the rest?"

Elliott took a deep breath. "Five B-52s, one B-1, one B-2," he said in a quiet voice, his face hard and somber. "No confirmed KIAs, though."

"And how goes the war?"

Elliott's face brightened a bit as he replied, "Preliminary post-strike data is hard to believe—I mean, really hard to believe. It's too early to tell for sure, but we might have sunk or damaged as many as one-third of the damned Chinese navy's destroyers. We've counted as many as fifteen frigates sunk or severely damaged, and we lost count of all the patrol boats we nailed. Even better, we've got reports of several amphibious-assault ships damaged or destroyed in Davao Gulf, and we're still receiving shortwave radio messages from Samar's troops broadcasting from the airport. The broadcasts talk about thousands of Chinese Marines dead, a couple hundred captured, and the entire Bangoy Harbor burning from all the dead ships." He tried not to sound too happy over apparent high Chinese casualties, but from the warrior's point of view, the first night of battle had gone well for the Air Battle Force.

McLanahan felt a tingle over his entire body when he heard the news—no matter how horrible war was, if there had to be a war, then news of success on the battlefield was always welcome. "So when do we go back out?"

"We may be called in for air operations over Zamboanga and

Puerto Princesa," Elliott replied, "but with only two or three destroyers left for Chinese air defense and fighter control, the bombers should have free rein over Mindanao. We should be able to bring tankers closer to Mindanao, so we can set up real fighter combat air patrols for the bombers and Navy ships—and if that's true, they won't need Megafortress escort bombers anymore. I'm sure they won't use B-2s either, now that most of their big warships and the Mount Apo radar site have been destroyed. HAWC might be out of the battle, I think.

"The Army's Twenty-fifth Infantry Division might try an invasion to Davao in order to keep the Chinese ground troops from massing on Mindanao," Elliott added. "But the Chinese Navy got a pretty good thrashing last night, and they know we can do it again—the second round of Tomahawk and bomber attacks began shortly after the first strike package withdrew, and initial indications look like they encountered virtually no resistance even in daylight hours. I hope the politicians in Washington and Beijing get their acts together and call a halt to this thing right *now.*"

That, Patrick McLanahan agreed, was every warrior's silent prayer—go and get ready to fight, but hope like hell they don't have to.

MALACANANG PRESIDENTIAL PALACE, MANILA
REPUBLIC OF THE PHILIPPINES

The door to the rooftop helicopter landing pad burst open, and First Vice President Daniel Teguina, surrounded by no fewer than ten bodyguards, rushed through the doorway. While six soldiers spread out to cover each side of the pad, the other four kept Teguina hidden from view, M16 rifles at the ready.

Despite his formidable protection, Teguina looked like the animal being hunted—which in effect he was. He carried with him a suitcase filled with American currency, Filipino bearer bonds, gold bullion, and other various treasures he could find in Arturo Mikaso's vaults and in government museums—that would help establish him in some Southeast Asia country loyal to China—or perhaps Pakistan, Madagascar, or Sri Lanka—and it would ensure his safety for several years until he thought it safe to return to the Philippines.

A few moments later, a low-flying helicopter could be heard in the distance, swooping out from the south and approaching the palace fast. Teguina was about to rise to his feet in the doorway when automatic gunfire rang out. Teguina cried out, clutching the suitcase, as a bodyguard leaped on top of him to cover him from the assassin's bullets—or at least that was what Teguina thought, until he heard the bodyguard's animal-like cry of pain and felt warm blood seep over his neck and chest.

The gunfire abruptly stopped, and someone lifted the bodyguard's bleeding body free of the ex-President of the Philippines. Teguina turned and was going to rush back down the stairs, but collided into a soldier wearing the dark-green jungle fatigues favored by José Samar's Commonwealth Defense Forces.

"But your helicopter is just arriving, Mr. President," he heard a voice say. He turned and found General José Trujillo Samar himself standing before him. His face and shoulders were still heavily bandaged, and the hair had not started to grow back on his eyebrows or eyelids yet, giving him a horrifying specterlike appearance. He wore jungle fatigues and carried an American-made .45-caliber automatic pistol in his holster, but it was not drawn. Teguina could see all but two of his bodyguards dead on the roof; the rest were on their knees with their hands on top of their heads.

Teguina let the suitcase fall, both as a show of defiance, because he felt guilty by having it in his possession, and because he suddenly did not have the strength to hold it. He placed his hands casually behind his back where Samar would not see them shake, and sneered, "I see your time with your American friends has not helped to improve your looks, Samar."

"Nor has your time with your Chinese friends improved your integrity," Samar said. "Where are they, by the way? We saw very few in the city today."

"I no longer need the Chinese to help me secure my country," Teguina said. "Your revolution has failed, your followers have been destroyed, your troops have been slaughtered. The people know that I am their President—"

"The people now know that you are a liar, a thief, and a traitor," Samar said casually. He motioned to a man standing behind him, who was photographing the whole scene with a professional-quality videotape camera. A soldier carried the suitcase over to him and opened it so they could photograph its contents; then the cameraman swung it back and took pictures of Teguina's shocked, disbelieving expression. "You will be taken into custody and tried by the Parliament and the Supreme Court. I hope they vote to execute you."

"And do you expect to preside over the trial yourself?" Teguina asked mockingly. "You are hated in this country. The people blame you for all that has happened. You as President of the Philippines will ensure civil unrest and political hatred for the next generation—you will tear this country apart far worse than I ever could. If I am sentenced to die on the gallows of Marikina Cathedral, I will certainly see you there beside me."

"I will let the people and the Parliament decide that," Samar said. "And I will not preside over your trial—the President will."

Teguina's smile vanished, and he looked at Samar's face in complete confusion. "The . . . President? But if you will not preside—"

Samar turned to watch as the helicopter that had been safely orbiting the rooftop now began its descent. When it landed, the left side opened . . .

. . . and out stepped Arturo Mikaso.

Teguina could not believe his eyes. His jaw dropped open in complete surprise as Mikaso stepped toward him. "Hello, Daniel," the Philippine President said. "Thank you for allowing us the use of your getaway helicopter."

Teguina also noticed that a Chinese Army officer and two American military officers also stepped out of the same helicopter. "What . . . what kind of conspiracy is this?" he stammered.

"No conspiracy, Daniel," Mikaso said. "The Chinese military has always said that they are in the Philippines to support the legitimate government against rebels who wish to seize power. Well, I am the legitimate government, and you are a traitor. They now support my government, along with the American military. Now that the Filipino military is firmly behind me once more, their services are no longer required, and they have advised us that they are departing immediately—as are the Americans."

"But . . . but I thought you were dead!"

"You mean, you thought I had been executed," Mikaso corrected him. "I have learned that the Chinese dislike the stain of honor that goes with executing a head of state. They shot me all right—but it was only a superficial wound. Then they put me in protective custody—a prison in any sense of the word, but I think a far better fate than one that you had in store for me." He nodded to the Commonwealth Defense Force guards. "Take the First Vice President into custody. I have already advised the Speaker of the Parliament of this action; he will meet you at Government House with a copy of my warrant sworn out against Teguina."

After Teguina was led away, Mikaso and Samar stood and faced each other. Samar wore an expressionless visage; Mikaso a slight smile. "So, General Samar. Are you happy to see me as well?"

"Why did you stay in custody so long?" Samar asked bitterly. "The country has suffered much because of your silence."

"I had little choice in the matter, José," Mikaso explained. "While I was recuperating, the Chinese were trying to decide which way the wind was blowing before really killing me. If they had not seen what kind of fool Teguina was, I would be six feet under a dungheap in Manchuria by now." He sighed, looking across to the surrounding skyscrapers and tropical trees of Manila, then added, "The country needed to experience a little suffering, José," Mikaso said. "There will always be those who think that armed struggle and revolution will accomplish more than democracy. I think the people had a taste of what happens when democracy is not allowed to work. If democracy fails, the will of whoever has the biggest or the best guns prevails. That means death and destruction on a massive scale."

Mikaso's smile did not dim one bit as he continued. "You were once a proponent of such a struggle not too long ago, General—in fact, I believe the Chinese would have gladly followed *you* if you decided to lead the nation in revolt. Could it be that the fearsome jungle fighter José Trujillo Samar believes in democracy after all?"

Samar shrugged, his features still hard-looking and dark despite his hairless face. "Times change, politics change, politics change . . . but I do not."

"We shall see," Mikaso said. "We . . . shall . . . see." He turned to face the two American and the Chinese military officers. "So. Should we now expel all foreign military forces from our country, José?"

"Part of the problem in this country was that we excluded some but invited others," Samar said. "Our country is still too poor to hope we can survive by isolating ourselves from all contact with the outside world—perhaps we should try opening our ports to all foreign military vessels. If the Americans have use of port facilities for their military fleets, why not the Chinese, or the Vietnamese, or the Russians? Is one society more or less corrupting than another?"

"Interesting idea," Mikaso said. "Interesting . . ."

"I know, I know—you did not expect it of me," Samar said. "I am just a poor dumb soldier, forced to dress like a politician."

"Is that how you see yourself?"

"If I could control what others thought of me, it would be different," Samar said. There was a rather long and comfortable pause between the two men; then: "What will you do with Teguina? Will you push for the gallows?"

"Good question, José. What would you do?"

Samar adopted a faraway glance. "I've seen enough death in this country," he said. "Frankly, I do not think that fool Teguina had a chance in hell of succeeding—he is too greedy and self-serving to lead a country in revolution . . ."

"Are *you*?"

Samar gave Mikaso an irritated glance. "You speak like some kind of amateur psychiatrist, Mr. President, answering questions with questions." He ignored Mikaso's question and concluded, "I don't think such blind idiocy deserves the gallows. The prison at Puerto Princesa would be an appropriate home for him for the rest of his life."

"Good answer," Mikaso said. He took a deep breath, expelled it, and said, "I have decided to advise the Parliament tomorrow morning that I will step down as President and that you serve out the remainder of my term. What do you think of that, José?"

Without eyebrows, it was hard to tell if Samar reacted at all to the announcement with anything that might be considered surprise. With characteristic calm, he nodded at Mikaso and said with just a hint of a smile, "I approve of your decision, Mr. President."

THE WHITE HOUSE ROSE GARDEN
WEDNESDAY, 2 NOVEMBER 1994, 1007 HOURS ET

"Attention to orders," Colonel Michael Krieg, General Richard "Rat Killer" Stone's aide, began. "Citation to accompany the award of the Air Force Distinguished Flying Cross to Patrick S. McLanahan."

General Stone stood in front of Patrick McLanahan in the Rose Garden of the White House. Just a few steps away was the President of the United States, the Vice President, and just about every other Cabinet member, important Congressmen, and a host of other dignitaries. Aligned along the front steps of the White House were twelve crew members—one B-52 crew from Fairchild AFB in Washington state, one B-1 crew from Dyess AFB in Texas, and Cobb and McLanahan—selected to receive the prestigious DFC in a White House ceremony. All members of the Air Battle Force had received Joint Service Commendation Medals, and many had received Bronze Stars for their roles in the Philippine conflict.

"Lieutenant Colonel Patrick S. McLanahan distinguished himself by meritorious service as Mission Commander, B-2A, from 1 October 1994 to 2 November 1994. During this period, the outstanding professional skill, exceptional leadership, and selfless efforts of Lieutenant Colonel McLanahan aided significantly in the successful battle against invading People's Republic of China forces in the Republic of the Philippines."

Anyone who knew about individual citations, as Patrick did, would know that the unit designation had been purposely omitted from his award citation—even though this award was unclassified (he had received the Air Force Cross, the highest Air Force award except for the Medal of Honor, after the Old Dog mission, but was prohibited from wearing the ribbon), the citation still had to be doctored to keep secret the fact that Patrick worked at a secret flight-test facility.

"Lieutenant Colonel McLanahan flew in two combat sorties during the Philippine campaign: the first, while unarmed and carrying only reconnaissance equipment, Lieutenant Colonel McLanahan flew his B-2 bomber over heavily defended airspace close to enemy warships to gather intelligence data vital to the successful execution of the campaign. The second mission, flown only twenty-four hours later, Lieutenant Colonel McLanahan destroyed several enemy warships and a key air-defense radar site in enemy-held territory, was hit by enemy fire several times, yet helped his aircraft commander to bring their crippled aircraft back and landed safely. The distinctive accomplishments of Lieutenant Colonel McLanahan reflect great credit upon himself and the United States Air Force."

General Stone pinned the medal onto Patrick's uniform, stepped back, and saluted; Patrick returned the salute, then shook hands. "Thank you, sir," Patrick said.

"I think it's time for you to get out of Dreamland, Patrick," Stone said. "There's a job at SAC headquarters waiting for you. Just say the word."

"I appreciate that," Patrick replied, "but as long as General Elliott is at HAWC, that's where I want to be."

Stone smiled knowingly and gave a short laugh. "Yep, he does have that effect on people. Good luck, Patrick."

A short reception was held in the West Wing afterward, and it was then that Patrick noticed that Jon Masters had disappeared. After inquiring with one of Paul Cesare's secretaries, he was escorted by a Secret Service agent downstairs to the White House Situation Room, where he found Jon Masters and Brad Elliott watching a newly installed PACER SKY satellite terminal from the Situation Room conference table.

Patrick was not surprised to see that the screen was focused on the south Philippines near Zamboanga. "What's going on?" he asked. "Something happening out there . . . ?"

"No, it's going along pretty smoothly," Elliott replied. "Looks like PACAF air patrols are flying out of Zamboanga already. We've got the *Wisconsin* battle group in the Sulu Sea, too."

"It was pretty hairy out there," Patrick admitted. "I'm glad the thing defused so quickly. But why are you guys down here?"

"Jon wanted to take a look . . ."

"At your satellite terminal?"

"No," Masters said. "At the Philippines; at the planes." He paused for a few moments, then added: "You know something, Patrick: I'll never look at this stuff the same way again."

"What do you mean?"

"Well, I always used to see icons . . . pictures . . . nothing but computer-processed data on those screens," Jon said. "I worried more about the quality of the image, how long it's been since the data was updated, the readability—and the profits. You know, the usual . . .

"But now . . . I see the pilots, crew chiefs, sailors, husbands and fathers out there. I think of how far they are from home. I wonder if they've got enough water, or if they've been up for a long time, or if they've been able to call home or gotten a letter from home—and I worry. I don't think I've worried about *anything* or *anybody* in ten years. I think about how dangerous it is to be flying at night—hell, I never used to know, or care, about what time of day it was out there. I never used to think about those icons, never realized that each symbol represented so many Americans fighting and dying in a strange land."

He looked at the screen, then at McLanahan and Elliott with a faint smile and said, "It's like what you said back at the Arc Light Memorial on Guam, General, looking at that old B-52: I only saw the machine out there, but you saw the men. I didn't understand you then, but I think I understand now."

"I think you do too, Jon," Brad Elliott said. "And you know what? I don't think you'll ever be the same."

Masters nodded, knowing Elliott was right.

McLanahan knew it, too. . . .

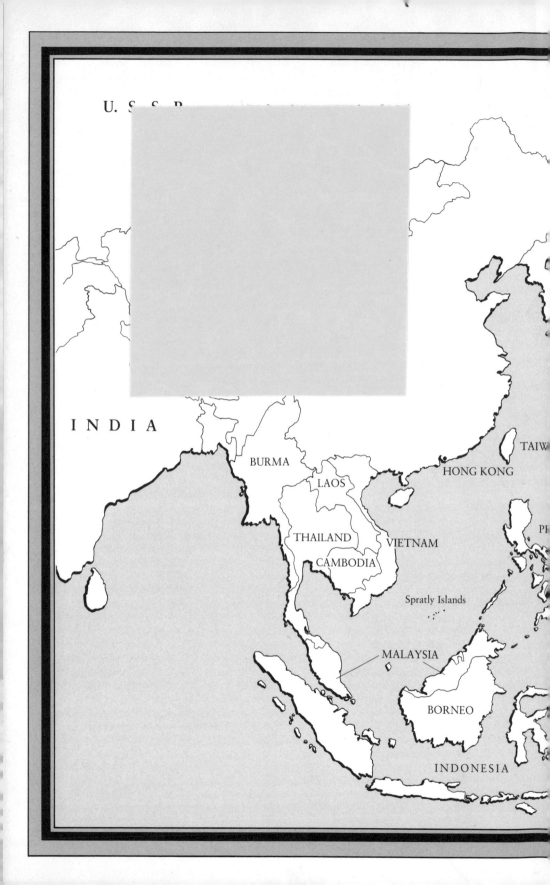